I0695229

Notebook Mysteries

Notebook Mysteries

Books
4 - 5 - 6

KIMBERLY
MULLINS

NOTEBOOK MYSTERIES ~ Books 4-5-6

Notebook Mysteries Series

Copyright © JKJ books, LLC 2023

First edition: October 2023

Mailing address for JKJ books, LLC; 17350 State Highway 249, STE 220 #3515 Houston, Texas 77064

Library of Congress Control Number: 2023917819

ISBN: 979-8-9886080-6-6 (paperback)

ISBN: 979-8-9886080-7-3 (ebook)

This is a work of fiction. It is based on historical events within Chicago during the time period of the 1880s.

Edited by Kaitlyn Johnson, Strictly Textual

Cover Art by Miblart

So many books written now—and so many supportive people in my life- Jonathan for Alpha reading everything I write, Joshua for finding the final errors and Claudia for unending support.

To my Readers—I have included Haunted Christmas here as a bonus. I hope you enjoy it!!

NOTEBOOK MYSTERIES ~ UNEXPECTED OUTCOMES (BOOK 4)

Notebook Mysteries

KIMBERLY MULLINS

CHAPTER 1

1887 AT THE BOSTONIAN BRIDGE

*E*mma woke suddenly, feeling like she was falling. She reached out for Jeremy, and then everything went black.

What's on me? she thought shifting her legs, trying to shift the weight off of her. She forced an eye open. *Where am I? Train! Jeremy!* Panicking, she sat up quickly and immediately regretted that decision. Boom! Boom! sounded within her head. She put her hands up to brace it and waited for the nausea to pass. When the pain finally subsided, she realized her hands were wet. Slowly she brought them down and held them in front of her. *Blood?* Her mind couldn't process what she was seeing and her gaze swept the area around them. The car wasn't just in disarray it was upside down!

The floor seemed very close to her head; she reached up and touched it. There was some room to move but the height of the car had been decreased by at least half and most of the room seemed on top of her. "Jeremy," she said loudly, "where are you?" Continuing to stay still she was unsure how stable their situation was; she remembered falling but nothing after that.

Jeremy, where was he? The weight she felt was their luggage, it had been dislodged when they turned over. She moved slowly, sitting up higher to see if it was safe to move about. Through the broken windows, she could see the rail cars scattered down the hill by the bridge. The sun was high in the east; they must have been knocked out for hours. It had been early morning and still dark when they crashed.

The car stayed still as she tentatively moved. They appeared to be stable, but she would have to get more data before confirming that fact. She moved the debris off her body to determine if she was okay. *I am good,* she thought moving her arms and legs. *Except for the eye and head.*

She started to remove the rest of the luggage and found Jeremy. "Dear-one, wake up," she said as she stroked his face. He stirred and slowly opened one eye; the other one was black.

"Emma," he said slowly, trying to orientate himself.

"Jeremy, are you okay?"

He moved his right arm and grimaced. "Ouch, I don't know. I think it's strained."

"Are you sure it isn't broken?" she asked.

He twisted it slowly and flexed his fingers. "Definitely not broken, probably just deep bruises and strain."

"You'll still need to see a doctor. What about your legs, can you move them?" she asked, concerned about further damage.

He helped Emma move the debris off of his legs, both visibly relieved as he stretched them. There seemed to be no visible damage. "What happened?" he asked, still a bit hazy from the pain in his arm and eye.

"From what I can tell, we were in a train accident," she stated.

"You think so?" he asked wryly, looking around.

She eyed her nightgown. "For now, let me make you a sling. Can you sit up?"

He sat up slowly in the limited space. "We seem to have matching eyes," he said, trying to find humor in the situation. He noticed her head and said with some panic, "Emma, you're bleeding."

"Oh, still bleeding," she said, reaching up again to touch it. *Enough of that*, she thought. Reaching down she tore two strips off the bottom of her nightgown. She used one to make him a sling and wrapped the other around her head.

"Can you see anything? Are we in any danger in here?" he asked, not able to sit as high as her.

She looked out of the window again and said, "I think we're stable, but I wouldn't move around much until I can climb out and take a look."

"We're somewhat wedged in here," he observed; the wood had splintered inward along with the broken windows.

"Yes, but I think I can get out of that one," she said, pointing to the window next to her; it was compressed but looked big enough for her to exit through.

"Be careful. There's glass everywhere and you're in your night-dress," he cautioned.

She looked down and said, "You know, I just didn't consider that." She saw Jeremy's pants were within reach, grabbed them, and laid on her back to pull them on.

"Hey!" he protested. She was going to leave him without pants.

She paused, gave him a long look, and said, "I need to look around out there and a dress is just not practical. You have your pajama bottoms." She looked around and saw their books strewn about. She grabbed one, using it to knock out the rest of the glass in the small window. It should be just big enough for her to climb out. She located her boots and slipped them on, pulling the laces tight. Turning toward him, she kissed him softly on the lips. "I'll see if I can get some help to get you out."

As she turned to crawl toward the window, he said, "Hey, Emma, I found something." He tossed her hat at her. She grabbed it and found it more than a little crumpled. She pulled out the long knife to check for any damage; when she didn't find any, she slipped it back into its slot.

As she smoothed out the hat, she studied the window and

thought, *I can either go face or feet first*. She nodded and said aloud, "Feet."

"Makes sense." He watched as she tossed her hat out the window and edged over to the casing to start through. If not for the wreck, he would have enjoyed the view.

She made her way out slowly, putting her legs through first and felt for ground, easing the rest of her body out, arms last. As she gained purchase, she straightened slowly, her head pounding with the movement. The view made her world tilt; the train was in pieces around her. She stumbled and almost fell before she stabilized herself against the car.

"Are you okay, Emma? Should you sit down?" Jeremy asked, suddenly concerned she may have a more serious injury than they first thought.

"No. I'm okay. I just lost my balance for a moment," she said, taking a deep breath as she took in the massive destruction. She walked further away from the car and looked up toward the bridge. The engine coal cars were upright and still on the rails; other cars were scattered down the incline. The cars made marks on the ground, she followed it and saw one of the sleeper cars appear to have been dragged sideways for about 200 feet and plunged more than 50 feet down a steep embankment before entering the river. Three additional passenger cars were pulled down the precipice by that car, one of those their own.

Emma called an update to Jeremy. "From the placement of the sun, I'd say we were out for a long while."

"Why is that an issue?" he called back.

She walked back to the car, her face strained. "The timing is important because it looks like we went off a bridge. The engine is still on the tracks, and we were pulled by the last cars. That last car has been in the water for a few hours."

"Can you get to them?" asked Jeremy, concerned. He tried to sit up higher.

She shook her head and said regretfully, "I don't think so. The embankment's very steep, and the car fell to its side as it went in. It appears to be fully submerged, and the river looks like it has a strong current. I'm going to look around and see if I can determine anything."

Slowly making her way down she had to be sure that she stayed on even ground. As she got further from her car, she noticed a group of men down by the water. She paused when she realized they were trying to get close enough to see if anyone could be saved. They were lined up, interlocking their arms, forming a human chain. The water proved strong, and she watched them struggling to stay upright. They persevered and reached the submerged car. The first man got to the window; he looked back at the group supporting him and shook his head. She could tell from where she was that the news was bad. *Those poor people,* she thought, wiping her eyes.

She pulled herself together and made her way up the hill to the suspended car. It was better supported than she thought, and. It also appeared to have people in it. Hearing crying, she called to them, "Try not to move! You appear to be safe. I'll go for help."

There's nothing I can do here; we need strong men to help these people from their cars. We also need medical help.

She glanced around and noticed a ragtag bunch of other survivors had made it out. Most wore their nightclothes, three men and two women; they appeared to have cuts and bruises, but no broken bones. They were discussing what to do next when she walked up. Emma listened for a moment before saying, "Hello, I'm glad you're okay."

"You, too," one of the men answered. He nodded to the group around him. "We were talking about how to get people out of the rest of the cars."

A woman in the group spoke up. "We can start by finding out who's mobile and can get out through the windows." Introductions were not necessary.

"As long as it's safe," cautioned Emma. "I told people in that suspended car to stay as still as possible. I wouldn't try to move them until we can get some additional supports to stabilize it."

"I agree. There are other cars we can work on first," the same man answered.

"I think I can go for help. I know the town is about two miles that way," she said, pointing to the east. "We need medical help and equipment to get people out."

They agreed. One of the other men asked, "Do you need someone to go with you?"

"No, I'll make good time on my own."

"Okay, we'll continue to work on getting people out."

She nodded and hurriedly returned to Jeremy's car.

"How is it?" he asked leaning toward her through the window.

"Not great. Jeremy, you mentioned last night that we're about two miles outside of town. I have to go there to get help."

He grimaced when he tried to shrug his shoulders. "I think you're right. Stay with the rails and be careful. Are you dizzy at all?"

She tentatively touched her head as she replied, "I have a headache. but no dizziness."

"Okay, on your way," he said lightly, but concern darkened his eyes.

Throwing him a kiss, she turned to make her way slowly around the wreckage. Several more people had climbed out of the cars and sat looking dazed. She directed them to the group she'd conferred with earlier and told them she was going for help.

Making her way up the hill to where the engine sat, she decided to check on the engineers, hoping they'd survived. With that hope in mind, she grabbed the side rails and pulled herself into the engine room. What she saw caused her to grow dizzy again. Shaking herself out of it, she tried not to let emotion take her over.

The impact had driven both men into the front of the train; neither survived. She shook her head regretfully and turned around to climb back down. Before she started down the rail, toward town, she gave the wreckage one last long look, trying to commit the placement of cars to memory.

She started her walk into town. It would take longer since she was sticking to the raised terrain, it was uneven and her step had to be precise. When she thought she couldn't walk anymore, the town came into view. Her head had started to pound again but she pushed herself forward. Hopefully, they were big enough to have a train stop; some of the smaller towns were just pass-through locations.

The sun was still high, indicating it was still morning and, with luck, someone would be at the station. She headed straight there, thinking, *They should be able to put out a call for help and respond to the wreck.*

She barely noticed the odd looks she received in her night-shirt, pants, and crumpled hat. She trudged those last steps and made her way to the ticket booth, sparing a minute to lay her head down on the counter. The man was turned away from her but startled when he heard, "Sir I've been in a train wreck some two miles from here. Many people have died and others are injured. We need lots of men and tools to get people out."

He jerked himself around. "Oh no," he said hoarsely. He exited the door beside her, where there was a bell and he pulled the rope firmly. They listened to it clang out the notification. When he stopped, he said, "We have this in place in case of emergency." With that, he stood watching and waiting. It took a few minutes before wagons started arriving. The entire town appeared to have shown up to help.

A tall blond man, apparently a leader in the town, jumped down from his wagon and said, "Terrance, what happened?"

"Train wreck," he said, nodding at Emma to give more details.

"We'll need rope to support one car that is still on the embank-ment. There are additional cars turned upside down or fallen on their sides. We need hatchets and other items to cut into the cars.

Some people can't get out of the windows. We need a doctor and the undertaker at the bridge, just two miles from here."

"That's Bostian's bridge; it's located over a creek. Did any cars go into the water?" one of the men in the crowd asked.

"Yes," she said regretfully. "I think one is a loss. We wrecked last night; they've been submerged for hours."

The tall blond man took over directing the group. "You men, go get as much rope as you can find. Harrold, get the store opened. We will need as many hatchets as we can find. Hester, get blankets; bring the doctor and the undertaker."

Terrance said loudly, "We'll also need food and water. I'll get them to open the restaurant to bring baskets to the site."

The tall blond man nodded and, as the group headed out, he said, "Meet back here and bring anyone else you think could help." He turned to Emma and said, "Little lady, I'm Preacher. What's your name? Do we need to get you to the doctor?"

"Emma," she said. "And no, I just want to get back to the site."

"Would you like to ride back with me?" he asked in a kindly manner.

"Yes," she said gratefully. He helped her onto his wagon and waited for everyone to return. The groups made good time, appearing with wagons full of supplies. Word had gotten out and even more people showed up, wanting to help.

They headed to the wreck site; Emma and Preacher arrived first. She climbed down without waiting to be helped and rushed over to the incline. As she hurried down, she could see there were significantly more people standing around than when she had left. She spotted Jeremy and started to run to him. "Jeremy!!" He moved toward her at the same pace. "You're out," she said, relieved.

He bent and kissed her softly. He looked around her and up the hill, saying, "You weren't able to get help?" He was concerned about the people still stuck in the wreckage.

They couldn't see the people she had brought. She looked up

the embankment and smiled slightly. "Oh, I brought people." At that moment, men started overflowing the incline, carrying ropes and tools.

Jeremy just watched them descend like a wave. "Wow."

Her eyes shined with tears. "Yes, they came as soon as I asked."

As soon as everyone made it down the hill, Preacher called for the groups to come together. "My name is Preacher, and we'll need to work together to stabilize the one car and get the people off." He looked to the survivors and requested, "If you're able-bodied, please join us." Several of the men left their group to help those in the suspended car.

As they gathered around it, looking a bit lost as to where to start, Jeremy eyed Emma. "You should go help them." He knew she was talented in structural engineering and could assist them in how to respond safely.

"Will you be okay here?" she asked, concerned about leaving him again.

"Yes, go," he said, waving her on.

Emma went to Preacher and said, "I can help with where to place the ropes, to offer stability, while we get the people out." She went on to explain, "I have an engineering background that could be beneficial."

He thought about that and asked, "What do you have in mind?"

"Let me walk around." She noticed the base of the train car was pushed deep into the ground. She returned the front and called, "Preacher, we could use some rather large logs to help wedge the wheels." He nodded and sent off a group of men to cut down some thick trees.

"What next?" he asked expectantly.

"The rope should anchor from the top." She guided him to the locations where the ropes could be safely anchored. "Wrap them around the heavy structural parts," she directed.

He agreed and waited for the men to bring the logs to the rail car. They had cut wedges into the ends to allow them to be put into the ground and offer some support behind each set of wheels. Next, he took her advice and called out instructions to stabilize the car. The ropes were placed with six men at each anchor point. Once they confirmed they were stable, Preacher and Emma went to the front of the car. "Any more advice?" he asked before they climbed up.

"Yes, have them empty the car, starting with the people in the back first. They need to exit one at a time and slowly."

He nodded, agreeing with the plan.

Once they climbed into the car, Preacher said in a firm, clear voice, "Okay, ladies and gentlemen, we're going to take this slow. We'll start in the back and each person will come up one at a time."

Emma saw people hugging their bags and said clearly, "You'll need to leave your bags in the car. We don't want to do anything that might upset the balance."

"But we need our bags," protested several people.

Emma said, "No, what you need is to get out of here safely. If we can get to the bags later, then we'll get them to you. Please don't jeopardize the people around you for things." That final statement seemed to get through, and bags were put down. They started exiting from the back to the front. The train car groaned but remained steady. There were small children in the car and they were taken out quietly. When the last person had climbed out, Preacher motioned to the men to loosen the ropes. The car started to slip but abruptly stopped a few feet down. The evacuated people screamed in response.

Preacher warned the group, "We don't want anyone near that car at this time. Once we deem it safe, we'll retrieve your belongings and get them to you." He continued, "Those of you who are able, I'll need you to come with us and help with evacuations of the other cars. We need to find other people who are trapped."

With that, they separated, with women and children helping the doctor and the men breaking into groups of five each. Each group was given hatchets and other tools. Working together, they cleared a car at a time, three more in total.

The doctor had set up a triage area on a flat spot near the river. He was setting broken bones and treating other ailments as best he could with the supplies, he had available.

Sometime later, the food arrived. The wives of the men from the town brought enough for everyone. They ate together in silence and rested. After lunch, people who were mobile moved to wagons to be transported to town. The injured followed more slowly, assisted as necessary, or were carried up as needed.

The caretaker had also arrived for the grim task of body recovery. Emma and Jeremy stayed behind, watching the body removal, feeling they should be there. They witnessed the event silently as bodies were lined up on the grass. The number would be higher once the car in the river was retrieved.

Emma and Jeremy approached a tired-looking Preacher, looking at the rows of bodies. "So many deaths," he said, bending his head in prayer. Jeremy and Emma did the same, crossing themselves as they finished.

"We'll need to gather personal belongings and descriptions of each one for identification," stated Jeremy as Preacher finished his prayers.

"Agreed," said Emma. "We also need to look at the rails and see if we can determine why we wrecked."

"Do you both feel well enough to help?" asked Preacher.

Jeremy looked at Emma, who nodded. "I'm good. I'll start with the descriptions. I need..." She looked around.

"Your notebook?" Jeremy teased. "I might have something." He pulled several notebooks and pens out of his pocket. "I found them when I was waiting to be rescued."

She smiled as she took them. "My hero." She moved to the first body. "Let's do this one at a time."

Preacher, Emma, and Jeremy went to each person, with Emma writing descriptions and adding a number to each for identification. Jeremy searched their clothes for something that would help identify them later, and Emma added the items to her description. Preacher went last, praying over each one.

Jeremy looked at the items they were collecting, some were valuable. "We shouldn't leave these with the bodies, they might be taken." He spotted a bag nearby, picked it up, and opened it. It had some clothes but nothing else. "Let's use this." He and Preacher started adding the items to the bag.

The job was arduous but, working together, they completed the survey of the forty people. Preacher took custody of the bag and list. "You should both head to town before it gets too late." They agreed and followed him up the incline. The sun was lower and the day was beginning to turn into evening.

As they reached the rails and looked down at the wreckage, they saw the men had started a fire and set out bedrolls. They looked questioningly at Preacher, and he explained. "We'll stay until the railroad men arrive."

"Good idea. Before we go, I would like to examine the rails where the cars went off," she commented.

One of the men at the fire called to Preacher. "I'll be just a moment," he said and headed down.

Jeremy and Emma continued to walk down the tracks. "How fast do you think the train was moving?" she asked.

"I would expect about twenty to thirty miles an hour," Jeremy said as he walked ahead. He saw something and bent down. "Come here, I think this might be it."

Emma knelt next to him. She reached down and saw that the tie crumbled at their touch. "Rotten ties. The engine was lucky to make it across. It failed on that last car and pulled us down."

Jeremy looked at the late afternoon sky and said, "Emma, we should head into town. We need to send telegrams and let the family know we're okay."

"Yes, you're right," she said, looking around. Preacher had

finished his business and was waiting for them. "Though, before we go, I need to talk to Preacher about our case."

Jeremy nodded. "I'll wait here." He was starting to feel his energy wane.

"I'll be right back." She called to Preacher, "Can I get a moment with you before we head to town?"

He waved her over to him. She walked up to him and said in a low voice, "Preacher, we need to make a request. Could you let us know the location of the bags when they are brought to town, prior to their distribution?"

"Can you tell me why?" he asked before answering.

Emma explained in a low voice. He nodded and said, "I'll keep an eye out."

"Ready to go?" called Jeremy from his position further down the tracks.

"Yes," she called back. She looked to Preacher and said, "Thank you for all of your help today."

He nodded and watched her thoughtfully as she walked away with Jeremy. She was unlike anyone he had met before. He shook his head and descended back down the hill to check the luggage.

Emma and Jeremy made their way to town. The walk wasn't bad but he was still in pain and would need some rest. The best thing she could think of was to head to the rail station for a recommendation on housing.

"Over there," she said, pointing to the rail station building. "The manager was very helpful this morning. Hopefully, he can lead us to some housing."

"Yes," said Jeremy, so tired and in pain, he could only provide short answers.

She looked at him, concerned he needed to get some rest.

They made their way to the office. When the manager saw her, he said with a smile, "So, little girl, you're back?"

Emma asked, "Do you know of a hotel where we could rest?"

He shook his head. "We're full up. Local people have taken in the passengers until we can get another train in here to get them home."

Emma bit her lip, pensive in her worry for Jeremy.

The manager saw her worry and hastened to assure her, "My Martha has prepared a room for you at our house."

Emma let the relief show and said, "Thank you so much for that. I'm Emma and this is Jeremy." She didn't mention their last names, she didn't want to be separated from him at this time.

"It's nice to meet you. I'm Dennis Connor," he said.

"May we go there now?" she asked as she continued to watch Jeremy. He was slumped against the wall, his eyes closed.

"Well, I can't go at this time; I've got to wait for the railroad people. Local stations will be sending men to help clear the tracks and make any necessary repairs."

Emma said, "You might want to mention to them that we think it was rotten ties that led to the derailment."

"I'll do so, thank you. Randy!" he called suddenly.

Feet came running and a boy of about ten said, "Yes, Pa."

"These people…" he started, looking at them.

"Emma and Jeremy," she reminded him.

"Yes," he said with a smile. "Emma and Jeremy need to be taken to your ma for some rest, food, and from the looks of it, a bath."

She returned the smile gratefully.

Randy said, "We live near here. Are you okay with walking?"

Emma looked at Jeremy and asked, "Can you make it?"

"I can make it," he said confidently, hoping he was right. Emma lifted his unharmed arm and placed it over her shoulder for support. They made their way to a small house colorfully painted in yellow and white, with a well-tended yard and a white picket fence. The front door opened before they could reach it. A pretty woman in her late thirties stood in the doorway.

She said, "Come in, we've been expecting you. I'm Martha. Now, don't say anything, we're going to get you to your room.

Randy, bring that water from the kitchen. We have a wash basin you two can use."

Emma guided Jeremy into the room Martha had indicated. She eased him on the bed, careful not to jostle his arm. He was asleep before he hit the pillow. She pulled a cover over him, sat down next to him, and brushed the hair off of his face.

She heard something behind her and turned around as Martha entered with the water pitcher. "For you," she said in a low voice.

"Thank you," Emma replied quietly.

Martha nodded and set it down on the dresser. "I thought you might want this also." She pulled a hairbrush out of her pocket and reached out to give it to her. Emma looked at the brush questioningly but accepted it. Martha waved her hand at Randy to exit the room. They pulled the door closed behind them.

Emma looked at the brush, shrugged, and laid it down. Turning toward the bed, she happened to glance at the mirror above the dresser and saw her hair. *What a mess.* She laughed, finding the humor in the situation. *It looks like a blonde bird's nest.* She slowly unwrapped the bandage from around her head; it was still sore but the bleeding seemed to have stopped. Leaning forward, she touched her eye lightly with her fingers. It was still pounding and could use some cool water. She took off her top and started washing. When she finished, she felt immeasurably better. The clothes lay in a dirty heap at her feet. She hated wearing the dirty top again but saw no other way. Slipping it on, she sat on the bed, brushing her knotted hair slowly.

When it was smooth, she reached for a wet cloth and placed it on Jeremy's eye. Moving as little as possible, she climbed into the bed and settled in. She didn't remember her head hitting the pillow, yet she slept heavy and long. When she awoke, the room was dark. She lay there for a moment, trying to remember where they were.

"Are you doing okay?" asked Jeremy.

"Yes," she said. She turned toward him slowly so as not to jostle him too much and asked, "When did you wake up?"

"Not long ago," he admitted.

"How's the arm?" she asked, concerned it may have gotten worse.

"Sore, but sleep helped. You?" he responded.

"Me, too. Though I'm feeling my bruises," she said, stretching her arms over her head.

"Can you see about getting me some water to wash with?" he grimaced when he looked down at himself.

"I'll go check the kitchen," she said and rose to grab the basin and pitcher. As she carried it out, she saw the family in the sitting room. *It must not be as late as I thought.*

Martha noticed her and put down her sewing. "We were hoping you would wake up in time for us to get you something to eat." She noticed the basin and pitcher and said, "Randy, take that for her."

He immediately stood and said, "Sure, Ma." He went over to take the items.

"Could we have some fresh water?" Emma asked tentatively.

Martha smiled at her. "Yes, of course. Randy, go ahead and get that for her. We also have your bags. They said you marked them before you left the site."

"Yes, Jeremy did that when he was waiting to be removed from the car," Emma said. "Where was all of the other luggage taken to?"

Dennis folded his newspaper. "Oh, Preacher is managing that. He has it at the church and will work on distributing them to the people. He said to let you know they're doing it tonight."

Emma nodded. "That sounds like a good plan."

Randy returned with clean water and Martha said, "Please take that to their room." She looked back to Emma and asked, "Would you like something to eat?"

Emma's stomach growled, answering for her. They all laughed and Martha stood. "Are sandwiches all right?"

"That sounds wonderful," she said gratefully.

"Why don't you go to your room? I'll get your food organized and bring it to you," Martha suggested.

Emma passed Randy in the hallway on his way back. She smiled and thanked him.

"Any time," he said, breezing by her.

She went into the room and found Jeremy sitting up. "You should have waited for help," she scolded him.

"Randy helped me sit up and said he would help me to the water closet," he explained.

Randy reappeared behind her and said, "I went to get your bags." He set them down and walked over to the bed. "Ready?"

"Ready," said Jeremy and grimaced as Randy helped him stand. When he was steady on his feet, they made their way down the hall.

Emma watched to make sure they didn't need additional support. When the door to the lavatory closed, she went back into the room. Going to their bags, she opened them and pulled out clean clothes for them to change into. When they came back, Jeremy looked steadier. He said, "Thanks for the help, Randy."

"No problem," Randy said and headed out.

Jeremy sat back on the bed as Emma wetted a cloth to help him clean up. His shirt had been ripped off his arm to allow the doctor to check it. She removed the remnants and saw many bruises. She looked into his eyes, saying, "You're sure nothing else is hurt?"

He moved his unhurt arm and said, "I think I just got stiff when I laid down."

She helped him wash and retrieved a white undershirt and a pair of pants. He was dressed when they heard a knock at the door. Emma answered it and found Martha there with a tray of food.

"Thank you so much," Emma said as she took the tray and moved it to the dresser.

Martha said, "We wanted to let you know that we have a telegraph office in town in case you need to send a message. He's staying open late tonight to get all of the messages out about the train wreck."

Jeremy thanked Martha and looked at Emma. "We do need to send several telegrams."

"Let us know when you're ready to leave and we'll give you directions. It's just up the road."

"We'll be ready soon," said Emma. She thought of something and asked, "Martha, where were the wounded taken?"

"A large number of mostly healthy or mobile people were taken in by families in town and by Preacher at the church. The more severe ones are in the school, with the doctor onsite monitoring them."

She shut the door to give them some privacy to let them finish dressing.

Sitting on the bed, they ate their sandwiches and drank their milk. "This case certainly went off the rails," Jeremy said wryly.

"Yes," she agreed with a laugh. She suddenly grew serious and said, "I'm glad we're both okay."

"Come here," he said. He folded her to him, and she leaned in carefully to avoid his hurt arm.

"We need to get those telegrams out," Emma murmured into his chest.

"Yes," said Jeremy, "it'll be nice to walk a bit." He kissed her on the neck and said, "Let's finish getting dressed so we can leave."

She sat up, removing her nightshirt and Jeremy's pants. "I'll miss the pants."

"I like you better in skirts," he commented as he slipped on his jacket.

She smiled and continued to dress, donning her white blouse and dark skirt and adding her slightly crumpled hat.

"Were you able to find out the location of the bags?" he asked in a low voice.

"Yes," she said in a low voice. "Let's head out and I'll tell you on the way."

They finished getting dressed and took their dinner tray to the kitchen. They made their way back to the living room and got directions from the family to the telegraph office and church.

As they exited the house, Emma said, "Preacher agreed to check the bags before they were distributed."

"If he finds anything?" he asked expectantly.

Emma replied, "Then he'll remove the items and place them in a secure location."

Jeremy was thinking of ways this might be found out and asked, "What about the weight difference?"

"Preacher said he would find a substitute. He said that, unless the railroad representatives had issues, they were going to distribute the bags tonight."

"Telegraph office first," he said and Emma nodded in agreement. Neither wanted their families to worry.

They approached the well-lit office and saw there was no one waiting. "We must have missed the rush," she said as they entered the building and found the telegraph clerk alone at his desk.

As they walked in, he looked up and asked, "Are you from the train wreck?"

"Yes, we need to send telegraphs to our families," stated Emma.

"Yes, of course," he said and hurriedly walked over to the counter, handing them paper and pencils.

Jeremy took them and handed one to Emma. She started: *Dora, our train crashed early this morning near Statesville. We are fine, just minor injuries. We will be staying here until alternate transportation can be arranged. Love to everyone.*

Jeremy looked over at hers and copied the first few lines: *Pops, our train crashed early this morning near Statesville. We are fine, just minor injuries. We will be staying here until alternate transportation can be arranged. We are retrieving the luggage soon.*

Cole knew the code "luggage" meant they had the silver stolen from the bank and would need him to send agents to pick it up. He took his and Emma's information and handed it to the telegraph operator.

Jeremy started to pull out his wallet to pay, but the telegraph operator stopped him. "The railroad will cover the cost."

Emma and Jeremy were surprised but thanked him. The clerk confirmed they would be sent immediately.

"Can you point us in the direction of the church?" asked Emma.

He walked them to the door, opened it, and pointed straight ahead. "It's hard to miss. It's that large white building."

They thanked him again and headed there. It was a short walk and they reached the wooden stairs leading to the main doors. They opened the doors to the large room, the sanctuary was located at the far end. Numerous people sat on the floor on one side and Preacher stood on the opposite side.

He was working on the bag dispersal plan. When he saw them, he nodded and indicated they could take a seat with the others. He waited until they were settled before he started talking. "Okay, everyone. I'd like to start this meeting with a prayer." Everyone bowed their head. "God, we pray for those who were lost and those who are injured and are thankful for the people who are here with us. Amen."

The group responded with an, "Amen."

He looked to the two men in suits on his left and motioned to them to join him. "Okay, folks. Let's get down to business. This is Joe Locke and Mike Carter with the railroad. They're here to make some announcements about the bag distribution."

One man stepped forward and said, "As Preacher indicated, I'm Joe Locke, the Railroad representative. We have a system that makes sure your bags get to you. I'll call on you to describe the bag, then we'll retrieve it from the other room and bring it to you."

A lady raised her hand and said, "What if two are similar?"

Joe went on to explain, "Then we open the bag and you'll identify what it contains."

As they waited for the bag dispersal to start, Emma sat there thinking about how they had gotten here.

Chicago, Pinkerton offices—about a week before

Emma and Jeremy entered Cole's office. Jeremy asked, "What's up, Pops?"

He looked distracted as he waved them to the seats in front of his desk. "Please, sit. I have a case to review with both of you."

Emma nodded and pulled out her notebook, ready to take down the details as Cole started. "We have information, from a confidential informant, about the two men who robbed the Chambers Bank in Denver, Colorado. They'll be on the train on its way through South Carolina. We know the dates and I would like you and Jeremy on that train."

Jeremy frowned and asked the obvious question. "Why the train, if we know who they are, can't we wait and get them at one of the stops?"

Cole frowned and responded, "Well, we don't actually know who they are. The informant didn't give us that information, just that the two men who robbed the bank will be on the train."

"Who is this informant?" asked Emma.

Cole shook his head. "We do not know that either. A telegraph was delivered from Denver and addressed to this office."

"Can't we find who sent it?" Jeremy asked.

"I notified the telegraph office, but the clerk didn't have a record of the sender."

"What makes you think it's credible?" asked Emma curiously.

"They provided details that were withheld from the public," Cole explained.

"Such as?" inquired Jeremy.

"Such as that it wasn't gold that was taken, but silver," said Cole.

Jeremy asked, "Why take the silver and not the gold? It seems like it would be easier to turn into cash."

"Silver mining's more profitable and popular right now. The Bland-Allison Act, passed in 1878, opened up a new market for silver to be used for minting dollars. I'm sure they assume it will be one big score," replied Cole.

Jeremy saw the glint of mischief in Emma's eyes and asked, "How about a trip, Emma?"

"I would love to," she replied.

Their tickets were secured, and they moved quickly to catch the train leaving that night. They would have to switch trains several times but should be able to make the date mentioned by the informant.

On the first leg of their trip, Emma asked, "What's the plan?"

"We use our observation skills to rule people out," indicated Jeremy.

~

Back to church, after the accident

As the bag dispersal began, Emma and Jeremy watched the process closely. The individuals were called upon to describe their bag; the bag was brought out and confirmed to be the right one. Since they were looking for two men, families were discounted. They had their eye on two passengers who seemed to be together. She had first seen them in the rail car that had to be stabilized. Both were clutching their bags when asked to leave them behind.

The first of these two was called up and described his bag as a brown leather carrying case.

Preacher cleared his throat and said, "Of course this way." Emma caught his eye and his slight nod. The man asking for the luggage did not notice the signal. He looked relieved when his bag was brought out. The man carrying the bag commented, "Heavy."

"Just books," he assured him as he took it and went to sit down next to his friend.

The friend was next and went up to describe his bag, similar to the other man's, but it had a black ribbon tied on the handle. It was brought out and the same heavy comment was made. The man explained, "We're booksellers." He moved back to his previous location.

The rest of the bags were dispersed and most of the people opened them to check their belongings. Emma and Jeremy watched the two men, noting they did not open theirs. *That will work in our favor*, Emma thought.

Preacher went to each person, checking on them to see if anything might be needed. When he reached Jeremy and Emma, he ask, "How are you both doing?"

Emma leaned forward and asked in a low voice, "Were you able to remove the item?"

"Yes. I have it put away," he answered in a similar tone. "What happens now?"

"We notified the proper officials and they are on the way to pick them up," Jeremy responded.

A young woman, assisting Preacher, came over to him and said, "We have the water ready."

"Thank you, Eve. I'll let everyone know."

He went to the front of the group and said, "Water is being heated in the bath so you may get washed up; you may go in one at a time. We'll change the water out as each of you finishes, so you can get refreshed."

The people looked relieved and started going in and out of the bathing area. One of their targets took his turn in the bathing chamber. He didn't make a move toward his bag. Instead, he nodded toward his friend and headed in. He returned a little while later, dressed in the same clothes but looking relaxed. His friend left his bag and also returned in the same clothes. It took about two hours for everyone to get cleaned up.

"They aren't opening the bags," Emma murmured to Jeremy.

"Yes," he said in the same low voice. "It gives us more time. We've got the word out and help should be here soon."

Just after everyone finished and was settling down, Mike Carter came back in and said, "We've gotten word that the repairs will be started tomorrow morning. We hope to have you moving in the next two days."

One of the two men they were watching spoke up, saying, "Is there alternative transportation out of this town? We have to get somewhere." There were a few nods from other people.

Mike answered, keeping his tone polite. "This town is not easily accessible to other towns. I also know the animals that have been used to transport you from the crash site will need rest and feed for at least a day. It's best that you let us do our job and get you on your way."

One of the two men looked like they still might argue, but the other tapped him and shook his head.

Jeremy leaned over and said to Emma, "We should be able to get some Pinkertons here before those repairs are completed."

"So, we wait and hope they don't open the bags?" she inquired.

"We wait," he confirmed.

They settled into their pallets provided by Preacher. He agreed to let them relocate to the church, which allowed a family with a baby to move into their room at the house.

From their pallets, they had a view of the two men. They watched them closely but saw they made no further effort to leave. They seemed content to wait for the railroad to provide transportation.

The two days went by quietly. Jeremy grew nervous that the detectives would not arrive in time to take them into custody. They were hesitant to confront them for fear of hurting the families staying in the church, so they continued to watch and wait.

That third morning, Joe Locke announced to the group, "There's an update for you. The rail has been repaired." A cheer went up. "There is a slight delay because the train is being outfitted to move the injured people who need to lie down and another car for the deceased." Everyone got very quiet at those words. "It will be here in another day." They understood the arrangements and settled in for another day.

Jeremy came to a decision and said close to her ear, "Emma, I'm going to check if there are any telegrams for us."

"I'll stay here and read." She had her book out and covertly watched the whispering men. They looked quite confident in their plans.

Jeremy seemed troubled when he returned. He handed her the telegram and said in a low voice, "They may not make it in time. We'll have to come up with a plan."

Emma mulled that over. "We don't want them to board the train. We will have to stop them ourselves."

"Agreed," murmured Jeremy.

She drummed her fingers on her lips. "It's funny," she said. "I thought we had such luck that they stayed around so we could keep an eye on them. Now, as I see it, they are using the victims as protection."

Jeremy nodded. "We need to find a way to separate them from the group."

As they thought about that, Emma said, "I have a plan. Let's keep it simple." She explained it in detail and Jeremy offered suggestions.

The next day, the newly outfitted train arrived. Everyone lined up to go outside to be transported to the rail station. Emma and Jeremy did not join then and were talking quietly in the corner.

Their targets were last in the line. She closed her carpet bag and moved to the first man and asked if she could go ahead of him. He nodded and waved his hand, allowing her in. Jeremy moved to the end of the line behind the second man.

As they started to move, Emma delayed stepping forward and let some distance open up between her and the family in front of her. To further the distance, she dropped her coat and turned to apologize for the delay. She picked it up and then again delayed them by stopping abruptly, causing the men to run into her. These delays caused a significant gap in the line. She continued to walk so slowly that the rest people had exited the room, leaving them behind. The men behind her were starting to grumble about how slow she was but were not yet being pushy.

As they neared the door, it slammed shut. Emma had prearranged that with Preacher and was ready for the move. She turned, her knife pulled and a smile on her face. "Gentlemen, I think we need to talk."

"She's just a girl. You can take her," the second man said with false bravado. They had forgotten Jeremy was behind them. The first man went after her and Jeremy knocked out the second man before he could turn around. He was tying him up while Emma fought the first man.

Emma pointed her knife at him and said, "I think you need to realize you're caught."

He wasn't listening. Instead, he swung his heavy bag to hit her, trying to dislodge the knife. The bag was unwieldy and did nothing other than twirl him around. She jumped back, taunting him. "Ready to give up yet?"

"No!" he tried to hit her again and finally noticed his friend was tied up on the floor. He stopped abruptly and asked, "Zach, are you okay?" He forgot about Emma and bent down to check on his partner. Emma took the moment to jump on his back and push him down to the floor with her knee. Jeremy handed her some rope to secure him.

Jeremy tapped the person he had tied up, saying, "Wake up." He stirred and realized he and his partner were caught.

"You can have it," he said through gritted teeth.

"Have what?" Jeremy asked innocently.

Emma bent over and opened one of their bags. "Look here, Jeremy."

He went over and said with a frown, "All of this for pig iron?"

The two men looked confused.

She opened the other bag and found the same thing.

"Where did it go?" the second man asked.

They heard a knock and saw the knob turn on the door. Preacher stuck his head in and said, "Can I come in now?"

"Yes, Preacher, please join us," indicated Emma.

"I have some company with me." He came in carrying two bags, followed by two men in black suits.

Jeremy raised his eyebrows at the two Pinkerton men. "A bit late, aren't you?"

One of the men looked around the room and took in the two tied up on the floor. "Yeah, but looks like you didn't need much help."

Emma smiled broadly and said, "We had it under control."

"But where's the silver?" one of the men on the floor whined.

"Oh, we have it here," said Preacher as he handed the two bags he was carrying to the Pinkerton men.

"We'll take custody of these two and get the silver back to its owners," one of the Pinkerton men stated.

Jeremy stood and said, "Can I see your credentials?"

"Of course. I'm Edward James and this is Mason Baker. We're from the South Carolina branch of Pinkerton." He pulled out his paperwork and handed it to him.

Jeremy reviewed it thoroughly and handed it back before saying, "This confirms what I was sent from the Pinkerton office in Chicago. Where will you go from here?"

"We'll take them with us and be with you on the train for the next two stops. We'll process them locally and transport the silver back to the bank after their court case," he explained.

Preacher said, "Not to rush you, but they're holding the train for you and they're eager to get going."

The Pinkerton men took custody of the bank robbers and escorted them out. Emma and Jeremy picked up their bags and followed.

Just before exiting the church, Emma looked over at Preacher and said sincerely, "Thank you so much for everything. We couldn't have done it without you."

"You're very welcome. Please come back and visit us," he said warmly.

"We will," promised Jeremy.

They were finally on the train and sitting with the other passengers in third class. The first and second classes were taken up with the injured or dead. Emma pulled out her and Jeremy's books so they had something to occupy their time during the journey. Jeremy opened his immediately and started to read. Emma found herself distracted by a crying baby. She missed her time with her niece Charlotte. She was a little over a year old now and the night she was born brought a few surprises.

The thunderstorm had been blowing through loudly with lightning strikes booming, but the loudest sound in the house was not the thunder—it was Dora. She was lying in the bed, trying to bring her baby into the world. She'd gone into labor hours earlier; the midwife had been called and the long wait had begun.

The midwife was checking Dora and said, "I think this is it." Tim looked faint but stayed next to her. The midwife gave him more directions. "Get behind her and give her some support." He helped Dora to sit up.

Emma was there, holding Dora's hand, and watched as the

baby came into the world. She had never wanted a baby or this experience for herself, but the birth affected her. She felt an immediate love for that red wrinkly mess. The midwife clean her up and gave her to a crying Dora. Tim's face was shining and he didn't seem to be able to stop smiling.

Emma watched the baby with curious eyes. She held out her finger to her, rubbing her little hand. The baby grabbed on and Emma laughed. "She's strong," said Tim, in awe of his new daughter.

"She is," said Dora, touching her face lightly. The baby followed her hand and started rubbing against it.

The midwife had completed cleaning up Dora and covered her back up, saying, "The baby's hungry. You'll need to put her to your breast."

"I'll step out," said Emma, hoping to give them some privacy.

"Thanks, Aunt Emma," said Dora in a soft voice.

Emma smiled and leaned down to kiss her on the cheek. She headed toward the door and turned back. "What's her name?"

Dora looked at Tim and he supplied it. "Charlotte Emma."

Emma's eyes overflowed with tears and she ran over to hug them both. She exited the room to head downstairs to share the news.

Patrick had stayed up to wait for the baby to be born. Dora and Tim had adopted him when his parents were murdered in a child abduction scheme. He danced around the room in the excitement of the impending birth. He spotted Emma and shouted, "Is the baby here?"

Papa put his hands on Patrick's shoulders and said quietly, "Let her tell us."

Patrick was still excited but he waited. Papa prompted, "Emma?"

"A beautiful baby girl," Emma said in a rush.

"Wonderful!" said Papa. "How is Dora?"

"She's also wonderful, tired but wonderful," said Emma with a long sigh.

Jeremy came up behind her, pulling her to him, and said, "You need to rest." He guided her to the settee.

Cole was there as well and Emma sat next to him, saying, "Cole, were you here waiting all night?"

"I was," he murmured. "I couldn't miss out on seeing the newest member of our family."

"Yes, we are family," she said, reaching out to touch his hand.

Tim came downstairs, grinning widely, and inquired, "Would you like to see the baby?"

"I do! I do!" shouted Patrick, running up to him.

Tim swung him up in a big hug and looked around. "Where's Jake?"

Papa said, "Jake said it was time for bed, so we told him we would tell him about the baby in the morning."

Tim frowned but knew Jake had his schedule. He would make sure he felt included in the morning. Lifting Patrick onto his shoulder, he led everyone upstairs to see the baby. He knocked lightly on the door. Inside, Dora sat up, holding a sleeping baby. "Come in," she said to the group, "and meet Charlotte Emma."

Tim took Patrick off his shoulders and walked him to the bed. He had grown quiet as Tim took him closer. "Patrick, this is your new baby sister," he said.

"My sister?" he asked, fascinated.

"Yes, your sister, your family," Dora confirmed.

"Can I touch her?" he asked, looking at the small creature in his mom's arms.

"Lightly," she cautioned.

He put out two fingers and gently touched Charlotte's arm. "She's so soft."

Dora looked up at Tim and said, "He needs to go to bed."

Tim leaned down and kissed her on the forehead. "I'll take him. Bedtime big guy."

Patrick yawned broadly and said, "Okay, night, Charlotte. Night, Mom. I love you,"

"I love you, too, Patrick," she said and wiped her eyes, watching them leave the room.

The rest family moved toward the bed to see the baby.

They received word that the storms had brought more than Charlotte. Claire and Thomas had a surprise that night as well. Their baby Mary Elizabeth had also been born that same night.

❧

Back to the train

Jeremy asked, "Did you want to stop somewhere and rest?"

"No," she said. "I'd like to go home."

"Then, that's where we shall go," he said as he pulled her closer.

It would be more than a week of train travel and communications to get them there. The train finally pulled into the Chicago station in the early morning and they exited to make their way home. Suddenly, their names were being yelled across the platform. "Emma! Jeremy!"

They looked toward the voices and saw their family. *Yes,* she thought, *all of our family is here. Papa, Cole, Dora, Tim.* As they started hugging her, Emma said, "You all came."

"Of course, we did. We're family," said Cole, kissing her on the cheek.

Cole saw Jeremy was in pain and said, "Let's get them to the boarding house so they can eat and rest."

Jeremy nodded, grateful they were there for them.

Dora linked arms with Emma and said, "I'm glad you weren't hurt worse than you were. Though that eye is still looking bad."

She gently probed it and said, "Yes, it's probably colorful. I'm so glad to be home." She changed the subject after they climbed into the waiting carriages. "How is Charlotte?"

"She's sleeping, finally. The colic is better." Charlotte had suffered a bout of colic that kept everyone awake.

"Was Jake able to move back into the boarding house?" Jake had been forced to relocate to Cole and Ellis' house for a while. The crying had upset him and disrupted his schedule.

Dora nodded. "It was better for him to be away while Charlotte was loud, but he is back now. We missed him." She hugged her close and said, "I missed you, too."

"I can't wait to see her," Emma said as she laid her head on Dora's shoulder until they arrived home.

CHAPTER 2

PINKERTON OFFICE

The next morning, Cole sat at his desk, reviewing the information from the silver case. He looked at Emma and Jeremy and said, "Thank you both for coming in to discuss this. I know you are fatigued from your travels."

"No, we don't mind getting out some. We need the exercise," said Jeremy. Emma nodded in agreement.

"Okay, then I will get on with it. Good job getting the silver back and arresting the two people involved. As I understand it, the Pinkertons who arrived in Statesville didn't have to do much."

Jeremy and Emma laughed. "It was an interesting couple of days."

Emma looked at Cole and asked, "Did you find out who gave us the information that led to the arrest?"

"Family," said Cole simply. "We did some checking into the telegraph operator once we had the bank robber's information. One of the robbers was named Michael Cannon. It turns out his sister Martha is married to Jerry Stanton, the clerk who sent the note."

Emma asked unexpectantly, "Cole, where does Martha work?"

"Why do you ask?" Cole asked, curious what she was thinking.

"The bank robbers didn't seem intelligent enough to pull this off on their own," Emma commented.

"That's worth looking into," Cole acknowledged. "I'll have the Colorado office check into it."

A few days later, Cole sent over a note that said, *An accounting of the silver showed it wasn't all recovered. Martha did work at the bank and was involved; she and the husband are missing. They're now persons of interest in the case.*

Emma had answered the door and was walking back into the sitting room while she read the note. She sat next to Jeremy, who noticed it and asked, "Who sent it?"

"Cole," she said, absently handing it to him. As he read it, she said, thinking out loud, "Jeremy, I think there's a chance to catch them. We know they're on their way to Washington D.C. since that's where the buyers are located. I'll bet that train crash also delayed their arrival." Train schedules had to be changed after the wreck.

"There may still be time to intercept them," he said, following her line of thought. "But why turn the brother and friend in?"

"I'm assuming to give them time to escape. We went after Michael and Nick, not knowing the others were part of the plan. They would have made it without being detected."

"Except for the train wreck," he said thoughtfully. They couldn't have known they would have a significant delay in their schedule. "I'll head over to the Pinkerton office now and let Cole know what we're thinking. Do you want to come with me?"

"No," she said. "I have to help with the baking. We have the meeting tonight for the charity."

"Okay." He grabbed his hat and carefully put on his jacket. He walked over and gave her a quick kiss. "See you soon," he promised.

"Count on it. Watch that arm," she reminded him.

"I will."

"Emma," called Dora from the kitchen.

"On my way," she called back. She looked around and saw a flash of pink run behind the chair next to her. She called out teasingly, "Lottie, where are you? We're going to do some baking in the kitchen."

She heard a squeal and one-year-old Lottie wobbled out from behind a chair.

Emma caught her up and tickled her as they moved to the kitchen. As they entered, they saw Dora gathering the ingredients. "What are we making?" asked Emma.

"Chocolate Lebkuchen," said Dora. She looked at Lottie and asked, "And you, little lady, will you be helping today?" Instead of responding, Lottie giggled and buried her head in Emma's shoulder.

CHAPTER 3

They sat around the large table, waiting for the board meeting to begin. They were snacking on the Chocolate Lebkuchen that Emma and Dora had brought. Papa looked at the shape of the pastry and asked Dora, "Are these different types of lebkuchen?"

"No," she said with a laugh. "Emma thought it would be fun to have Lottie help with the shapes."

"Oh," he said with a smile. "It doesn't seem to affect the flavor."

Emma and Jeremy sat near Cole, talking quietly about the bank robbery while they waited for Clair to start the meeting.

"Any word yet on the sister and husband? Have they been seen in D.C.?" asked Jeremy.

Cole answered in a low voice, "Pinkerton has the train station monitored with agents and others are assigned to watch for the black-market contact. They already had an idea of who the contact might be. We should know something in the next few days."

"We can't discount alternative transportation given the disruption in rail," suggested Emma

"Yes, that's why they have agents watching the most likely persons to be involved in the case," indicated Cole.

Clair entered the room with Thomas. They took their seats and the room quieted. "The first order of business," said Clair, "is to settle on a new name for the charity. We have been calling it "the charity" for long enough."

Emma looked at her with interest and asked, "What do you suggest?"

"I was thinking of naming it after our benefactor," Clair said.

"You're right, we should have done this earlier," agreed Emma.

"I'm calling for a vote," stated Clair in a businesslike manner. "Those voting yes," she looked around the table and documented all hands were raised. "The yesses have it. The charity will now be called the Carlyle Foundation. I'll submit the paperwork to our lawyer tomorrow."

Clair read down her list, looked up, and said, "The second item on the agenda. I would like to start organizing a gala to raise money."

"Why?" asked Emma. They had always kept the charity based solely on investments of Mr. Carlyle's money.

Clair laid her list down and said, "I've been discussing this with our lawyer and our accountant." She nodded at Tim and received a nod back. "We need to fundraise to make us more visible. With more money, we could help more people."

Cole asked concern etched on his face, "Are we having money problems? Have we had a business loss?"

"No." She laughed. "Since we got rid of Sam, the accounts have been perfect and they are making money." Sam had been Clair's assistant when the charity first opened. The money disappeared from accounts and he was caught, admitting it had been part of a private vendetta.

"Who would we invite?" asked Emma, unsure how to proceed. They didn't occupy the same circles as people who could donate large sums of money.

"The elite of society, the people who have money to spend and to donate. I have a list of prospective donors for us to review," said Claire firmly.

"Where did you get the list?" Emma asked curiously. "We don't have a social register in Chicago."

"I made a list similar to that one in New York. I used the paper's society section to build it."

"There's also the University club," stated Cole. "I believe their goals and the Carlyle Foundation's goals match up. Their focus is around the values of a common educational experience."

"We do put a lot of money into education," stated Clair. "Can you inquire if they would be willing to attend?"

"I can. I'm also a member."

"The others on your list, would they come?" inquired Emma.

"I think that, if we list the groups of people we've helped in the past and show the ones we hope to have in the future, then yes," said Clair, positive about her idea. "I planned to put together a package and send it out with the invitations."

Tim looked contemplative and said, "We have several previous clients I believe would attend and encourage friends. I'll get you their names."

"Thanks, Tim. Any other ideas?" asked Clair expectantly.

"My client roster would also be a good start," said Ellis. He rattled off a few well-known names. "Aaron Montgomery—founder of Montgomery Ward; Potted Palmer and Marshal Fields—major department store leaders; George Pullman—Pullman manufacturing, rail cars." He had worked with each to rebuild after the '71 fire.

Clair nodded. "That's an amazing start. Once we approach the first people and get an acceptance, that should open up the door for more donors."

"Clair, have you chosen a venue?" asked Tony, thinking how he could help.

"I've looked around," she admitted. "But I haven't found the right place yet."

Tony said, "The museum would make an excellent location for this event."

Clair looked hopeful and asked, "Do you think Philip would mind?" He was the curator at the local museum and Tony worked as his assistant.

"I'll speak with him. Have you picked some dates?" he asked, knowing Philip wanted to expand the usage of the museum.

Clair pulled out her calendar. "I was thinking of three months from now."

Tony wrote the date down and promised to get back to her.

Dora had been attentive and asked, "What about food?"

"I think we would serve a full dinner," said Clair.

"And desserts," supplied Dora.

"Yes, and desserts." Clair laughed. "We will have tables full of desserts."

"We should cater the dinner and use the bakery to provide the desserts," suggested Dora. "I can also assist in picking them out and setting up the menu." She had some extra time because she had added a cook to their boarding house as her pregnancy progressed, After the baby was born, she kept the new staff on full time. She continued to manage Patrick, the baby, and both boarding houses.

"Are you sure? It'll be a lot of work?" asked Clair.

"I'm sure," confirmed Dora firmly.

"And I'll help her," said Tim, covering her hand with his. She smiled over at him, still so happy he was in her life.

Dora looked over at Jake and said, "Clair, Jake could provide photographs for us also."

Clair said, "That would be excellent. Jake, can you do that for us?"

Dora tapped his book to get his attention. He usually brought one to their meetings. "Can you take pictures at the event?"

"They're not my normal pictures," he stated without answering the question. His pictures were usually murder scenes for the police department. Jake tended to be very literal and sometimes required extra explanation for the easiest things.

Dora explained that it was a part of his role as a board member. Once he understood it was a rule, he agreed.

Clair handed out the assignments:

Tony: to confirm the venue and how many people could be invited.

Emma, Cole, and Tim: to build a guest list.

Dora and Clair: food.

Jake: to take the pictures.

Jeremy and Cole: to review the security setup and provide Pinkerton agents as security guards.

The team worked to organize the event. It was arranged for three months from that day. Philip graciously provided the museum as the venue, and an orchestra was arranged as entertainment. Clair and her assistant secured tables and chairs for the evening, while Claire then met with Philip and Tony to design the setup.

The invitations went out and everything was in place for the big night.

CHAPTER 4

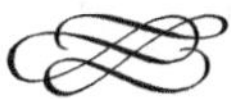

THE NIGHT OF THE GALA

The event came together quickly. Ellis had met with each of his clients and explained what the Carlyle foundation was working on. With that and the information Clair provided, each agreed to be there to support the charity.

Clair was right. Once the news was circulated that Pullman and Fields would be there, they had trouble keeping people out. The list had to be reviewed and trimmed several times. Security at the event would be tight.

The museum was the perfect atmosphere for the occasion. Gas lights offered a glow on the room, the orchestra played throughout the night. The main area floor had been cleared and round tables surrounded the dance floor for people to observe. The dinner had been served with Clair and several guest speakers discussing the projects the foundation was supporting. As that wound down, the dancing had begun.

Ellis and Cole spent much of the evening together. They stood off to the side of the dance floor, watching the dancers twirl by. Ellis listened absently as Cole talked about the follow-up to the silver case. He was saying, "They were able to pick up both the robbers and the buyers."

"That's nice," Ellis said, not hearing him. He noticed Emma and Jeremy dancing. She was lovely in a brilliant red ball gown with black lace trim and Jeremy wore a black tuxedo.

He watched them twirl by, and Emma sent him a small wave. As he waved back, he noticed Tony out of the corner of his eye. He was lounging against the wall, watching Emma and Jeremy dance with a dark expression on his face.

A triangle, he thought. *Emma, Jeremy, and Tony*. He could understand Tony's hurt feelings. That particular triangle reminded him of the past where he and Cole had also pined for one woman. *Funny*, he thought. *I haven't thought about Abbey in years.* Suddenly, the memories flooded his mind, recalling their first meeting.

~

He and Cole were about fifteen at that time and had been living on the streets for a few years. They lived in a structure they had constructed out of wood from various delivery drivers. *Some had been gotten honestly, some weren't,* he thought with a smile. They had been in the shelter that night; the rain pounded down on them as they sat talking. It was at that moment their small door rattled and flew open. At first, they thought it was the wind, but then they saw someone crawling into their space.

"Hey!" Cole said loudly, angry the wind had almost blown out their light. "You weren't invited in here."

The boy closed the door and looked around, saying, "Pretty nice place."

Cole continued to frown. "You're not wanted here."

Ellis saw something Cole didn't and smiled to himself. His thoughts were confirmed when "the boy" whipped off her hat to reveal auburn curls.

Cole finally saw what Ellis saw and said, "Oh!"

"I'm Abbey," she said, introducing herself.

Ellis spoke up and said, "I'm Ellis and this is Cole."

"How did you know we were here?" Cole questioned softly. They were pretty well hidden in the back of the alley.

"I've been following you," she said simply.

"What! Why?" Cole asked, puzzled. What could this girl want?

"You're both pretty good pickpockets," she said. "I was working a few of the same places and watched your technique."

"Yeah, we've been doing it for a while," Ellis answered for them.

"You never thought to move into other things?" she asked innocently.

"What types of things?" asked Ellis cautiously.

"Well, let's just say you could be doing better than this," she said, looking around.

Cole was resolute. "No, we don't want to be involved in something like that. We're getting along fine now."

Ellis had been thinking the same thing; he didn't want to get further into criminal activities.

"Suit yourself," she said and shrugged off the negative reply. "I just thought you might want to make more money."

They sat quietly after that, waiting for the rain to abate. As it let up, she said." I have plans. I'll check back in with you both at a later date."

They nodded and watched her leave. They both knew they had made the right decision.

Over the next few weeks, they were conscious of her being in the neighborhood. She continued to dress as a boy and seemed to know everyone in the area. That day, Ellis was at the fruit stand when Abbey strolled up. She ignored him and started a conversation with the owner of the stand. The owner's back was to Ellis and she kept him talking. *Cover.* he thought and grabbed three apples and put them in his pockets. Starting to move away, he hesitated, wanting to hear what they were talking about.

The vendor asked, "Is your mom getting out soon?"

Getting out, thought Ellis. *Prison?*

Abbey answered in a lighthearted voice, "Sure, Mom will be out at the end of the week."

He realized they were wrapping up, so he strolled in the opposite direction.

Later that night, Ellis mentioned to Cole that Abbey's mom was in prison. "What about her dad?"

"Not sure."

Hmm, thought Cole, *there are layers to this girl.*

They continued to see her throughout the week.

The next Monday, they were in their shelter when once again the door opened and Abbey entered.

"Becoming a habit?" asked Cole wryly.

"Perhaps," she said. "My mom is back and I thought you might like to have a warm place to sleep tonight."

Cole looked at Ellis and he shrugged. "Why not?" They gathered their things, books, and blankets to head out.

Abbey saw what they were carrying and asked, "Books?"

"Yes, we both like to read. We get them from the library," explained Ellis.

She raised an eyebrow at that. "Do you check them out?" She knew they couldn't get a library card without an address.

Cole responded, "We return them when we've finished reading."

They continued to follow her to a small apartment a few blocks away. Abbey opened the door with her key and said, "Mom, I've brought them back with me."

Her mom stepped out. She had similar hair to her daughter, though grayer throughout. She was a striking woman; wiry intelligence shined in her eyes. "Hello, boys," she said. "Tell me your names."

"Cole."

"Ellis."

"Mine is Marjorie. You may call me Miss Marjorie."

"Thank you," both boys answered.

"You can stay with us as long as you want. Though," she said looking around, "it could be better."

"It's fine, Mom." Abbey knew what she was thinking; better meant a job. A job meant a risk of going back to prison and she would like her to stick around longer this time.

Miss Marjorie pretended not to hear her and said, "All right, boys, the evening dinner is a simple event. Cooking's not my forte."

"Anything would be fine," said Ellis, thinking that a warm meal, whatever it was, would be nice. Cole nodded in agreement.

Miss Marjorie wasn't shy about why she went to prison and talked about it at dinner. "I picked the wrong people for that last bank robbery." The boys were fascinated; Abbey appeared to be less so.

Abbey remarked as she finished, "You got careless about the amount of money you were spending, that's why you got picked up."

Miss Marjorie sent her a look and said, "Listen, girl, when I want advice on how to do my job, I'll ask for it."

"I could do better and do it by myself," she muttered.

Miss Marjorie stood and got out the bread. She pulled a knife from seemingly thin air and slammed it into the loaf. "You need to refine your skills more. I need you to be ready to start doing jobs with me."

Abbey said in a low voice, "There's nothing wrong with my skills. I just prefer to work alone."

Miss Marjorie didn't respond to that statement, but she narrowed her eyes as she watched her.

Cole and Ellis sat silently, eating the meal and eyeing them both, not sure what to say.

After a while, a truce seemed to be called and they moved into the small living room.

"You boys can sleep here as long as you want. We have plenty of food and, once I get my next score, we'll move to a bigger place."

"However temporary that will be," Abbey said.

Miss Marjorie glared but chose not to enter into another argument.

The next morning, they woke up and saw that Abbey was already gone. Miss Marjorie was working on lock sets in the small dining room. "Boys," she said. "There's pastry and fruit in the kitchen."

"Thanks," said Cole as he headed that way.

"What's that you're working on?" Ellis asked, interested. He hesitated by the table, watching what she was doing.

Miss Marjorie didn't look up when she said, "Lock sets."

Ellis sat down and continued to watch her.

Miss Marjorie picked one up, handed it to him, and explained, "These are examples of the lock sets used in most homes and businesses at this time. When I plan to enter a building, I like to practice picking ones that are of different ages; they can become trickier to open with time."

He turned it slowly in his hands, examining it, and said, "This slot looks like a flat key."

"Yes, that is the new Yale design," she commented.

"Would a business use only one type of lock?" he asked, thinking of the types of keys used in homes.

"Yes, most have moved to the lock sets that use a pin and tumbler design. Interestingly, the design was an improvement on the simple wooden tumbler lock created by the Egyptians." She looked at him with a gleam in her eye and asked, "Would you like to learn to pick locks?"

Ellis had an interest in how things worked and said, "Yes, please."

They worked together quite happily, taking apart the various locks and putting them back together. Cole called out from the kitchen, "Ellis, you should eat breakfast."

He called absently back, looking at the lock set in his hand intently, "I'll be there in a moment."

Cole knew that tone and said, "I'll bring it to you."

Ellis sat there for the next three days, working diligently on each one. He took them apart to learn how they operated and then worked on the techniques used to pick them. Miss Marjorie stayed with him, working out the details and the questions.

At the end of the week, Miss Marjorie said, "I think you're ready."

"Ready?" he asked absently.

"Yes, ready to help me with the locks on a job I'm planning."

Cole, who was sitting in the room with them, said, "Wow, I don't think he should be doing that." He was always protective of Ellis.

Ellis looked contemplative and said, "I'd like to see if stress in the field affects my performance."

"Seriously, you aren't considering it?" Cole asked, frustrated at this turn of events.

"I am," he said.

"Well, you can't."

"Can't? Cole, you're not my parent," he said simply.

"No, you're right," he conceded. "But we haven't gotten caught yet and doing something like this could get you sent to the work-house or prison." Cole was always thinking ahead to the possible consequences.

"I know, but I would like to do this."

"I don't support your involvement."

Miss Marjorie looked over at Cole and said in a sarcastic tone, "I don't think you were asked."

Abbey, who was sitting nearby, giggled.

"What are you laughing at?" asked Cole belligerently.

"You. You're a thief. Why try to stop him from basically doing the same thing?" Abbey asked.

"It's not though, is it? This moves him into areas that could have serious consequences," said Cole.

"I think he can make decisions for himself," she said, looking at Ellis consideringly.

"Abbey, will you be going?" Cole demanded.

"I work on my own," she said evasively.

Cole watched her closely, wondering what her game was.

She laughed, noticing his gaze, and said, "Don't try to figure me out."

"Hmm, you know if I had more data, I might be able to work it out. Would you like to go to the park with me for a walk?" Cole said smoothly.

She smiled softly and said, "Only if it's the three of us."

He frowned. He would rather be with her on his own but decided that some time with her was better than none. "Okay, how about the three of us go out this evening?" he suggested.

She said, "Now, that we can do."

They started to go out together, the three of them. They spent all of their time together, walking, talking, and generally enjoying each other's company. It was also the first time in a while that Cole and Ellis could relax, knowing they had a warm place to sleep and food to eat.

As the week progressed, Ellis continued to work with Miss Marjorie. They had the job scheduled for that Friday night, a robbery of a known gangster location. The safe was located inside a large multiroom building. Ellis would manage the door locks and Miss Marjorie would work on the safe.

Cole and Abbey had monitored the location and noted there were external guards day and night, with a shift change at 9pm. They were also able to confirm that no one entered or exited the building after that time. Miss Marjorie used this information to set her schedule for the heist. She went the night before to test the time and to loosen a spot in the roof to drop into the area where the safe was located.

Friday night, Ellis and Miss Marjorie left for the job. Cole and Abbey waited for them to return. They were dozing on the chairs in the sitting room when they heard a banging at the door. Abbey ran to the door to let them in; Ellis was supporting Miss Marjorie and moved her to the couch.

"What happened!" Abbey demanded as she followed them.

Ellis was looking at Miss Marjorie, concerned. "I'm fine. She saved my life. She stepped in front of me and took the bullet. I was standing like a statue, not moving. She tried to get me to move but I just froze." He looked over at Cole and said, "Looks like you were right. I shouldn't have gone."

Cole nodded but didn't say anything more. He knew Ellis already felt terrible about the situation.

Abbey saw the blood and tore Miss Marjorie's sleeve off. She looked at it carefully and said in a relieved voice, "She's fine. It's just a scratch. I'll clean it and bandage it."

"Thank goodness," said Cole.

"Ellis, come here," Miss Marjorie called to him as Abbey worked on her arm. He bent down next to her. She said quietly, "None of this is your fault. You were amazing tonight; you got into every door faster than I could have. Without you, we wouldn't have made it inside."

"Without you, we wouldn't have made it out," he said quietly, feeling guilty he hadn't responded better in the high-pressure situation.

"Enough of that. Bed for you both," Abbey told them firmly.

"Yes, I could use some rest," said Miss Marjorie, fatigue making her look older than her years.

Cole called, "What do you want me to do with this?" They looked toward him and saw he was holding bundles of money he had pulled from the bag.

"Wow," said Abbey, rushing over. "That's a good haul."

"Yeah, it'll get us a nicer place," said Miss Marjorie in a tired voice.

Abbey frowned. It was always a nicer place, but only temporarily. She tried to reason with her. "Mom, we could stay here and save money. Not blow it."

"Little girl, that's my money and a cut of it belongs to Ellis. You have no stake in this."

"And no say in where we end up," she said bitterly.

Miss Marjorie frowned at her, not answering.

Ellis stepped in before they could argue further. "You need some rest. Let's get you to bed."

"Thank you, *Ellis*," Miss Marjorie said, looking pointedly at Abbey.

Ellis and Cole watched the interaction between Miss Marjorie and Abbey over the next week. Abbey had voiced her opinion about how the money should be spent and didn't bring it up again. Miss Marjorie made all of the arrangements and announced the date of the move.

After they moved to a larger place, Abbey grew moodier with every week. "Hey, what's wrong?" asked Ellis.

"This," she said, waving her hand, indicating the stylish, fully furnished room around them. "It's just temporary. She gets a score and spends it immediately."

"She likes to live this way," he said in a calm voice.

"Well, I don't," she said and stomped off.

Miss Marjorie started planning another job. The nicer apartment was a priority for her. She looked over at Ellis; he was good in the field but had said a definite no when she tried to get him involved. Backup would be needed. Her eyes found Abbey and she said in a firm voice, "Abbey, I need you on this job."

"I thought you said my skills weren't good enough," she answered in the same tone.

"Well, it's time to test you in the field," Miss Marjorie commented.

"I prefer to work alone," she said forcefully.

"If you want to stay here, you need to work with me. I need help. I need someone I can trust."

Abbey felt forced and she didn't like it, but she had nowhere else to go and finally said reluctantly, "All right."

The job was located at a local department store. The safe was a large one in the manager's office. They also had onsite security staff. Miss Marjorie set up the job so they would enter a weak point in the roof structure. She had weakened it herself over the past two weeks. She had Cole and Ellis case the location at night to check for security schedules.

The final plans were set for that Thursday at 1am. Miss Marjorie and Abbey set off, dressed in black. Cole and Ellis would wait up for them.

The evening wore on slowly for Cole and Ellis, each watching the clock.

When it got past the hour they should have returned, they decided to go to the job. At that moment, Miss Marjorie crashed opened the door, and said, "Abbey's caught." She threw her bag down and sat.

The boys looked at one another, their worst fears coming true. "What happened?" asked Cole. "Who got her? Was it the security guards?"

"Yes," she muttered, not explaining further.

Ellis insisted, "We need to try to get her out."

"No," she said. "We lay low. They'll know someone else is involved and arrest whoever shows up."

"We can't just leave her there!" said Cole forcefully. Ellis agreed.

Miss Marjorie had gone quiet.

They sat there, watching her for the next hour, whispering back and forth, trying to work out how to get Abbey home.

A loud knock was heard from the door. Miss Marjorie reacted violently and almost fell out of her chair. "Hide! I have to hide!" she said as she ran into the bedroom.

The knocking grew louder.

Ellis looked at the door and asked in a low voice, "Should I get it?"

Cole replied in the same tone, "Yes."

Ellis got up to answer it. It was Abbey. "How did you get away?" he asked.

She didn't answer. Instead, she narrowed her eyes and asked, "Where is she?"

Miss Marjorie stood in the doorway of her bedroom and said with false bravado, "See, I knew you'd make it out. How did you get away?"

Abbey looked in disgust at her mother. "Did she tell you what she did? Did she tell you she left me behind?"

The boys looked at her in disbelief. Miss Marjorie had saved Ellis' life and helped them so much, but had left her daughter behind at a job?

"You're like a cat, always landing on your feet. I knew I didn't have to worry about you. You got back here, didn't you?" Miss Marjorie said defensively.

"What happened?" asked Ellis, taking Abbey's hands in his.

Abbey swallowed the lump in her throat and started. "We had emptied the safe and were making our way back out, through the roof. I thought we had time before the next security rounds, but we got spotted. I lost my footing on the roof and slid down the shingles. When I called for help from this one," indicating her mom with her head, "she just left me."

"What happened next?" asked Cole, caught up in the story.

"The guards rescued me and took me into custody. They put me in cuffs and placed me in a room until the police were noti-fied. I got out of the cuffs and crawled through the window," she explained.

"Well, you're home now and safe. You'll just need to keep a low profile for a while, maybe change your appearance," Miss Marjorie said consideringly.

Abbey looked at her incredulously and said in a loud voice, so no one could mistake her meaning, "I'm done! Done with you and done with this life!" Her mom was not as careful as she used to be, and she would get caught sooner or later. Abbey didn't want to go down with her.

"If you're done, then I think you should plan on living elsewhere," said Miss Marjorie in a voice ringing with anger.

"I plan to. I want my cut from tonight's heist," Abbey insisted.

Miss Marjorie pulled out a bundle of bills and tossed it at her.

Abbey counted it quickly and said, "Hey, there was much more than just this."

"Think about it as a finder's fee. I have expenses," muttered Miss Marjorie.

Abbey stomped off to her room. Cole and Ellis followed and watched her pack.

"Where are you going?" asked Cole.

"As far from her as possible. I can't stay here; they'll be looking for me. I'm heading to New York City, then to Europe."

Both boys frowned at that statement.

"Would you like to come with me?" she asked, not looking up.

"Who are you talking to?" asked Ellis.

"Both of you."

"You can't have both of us," said Cole and looked at Ellis. "Right?" Ellis nodded in agreement; he didn't want to share either. All three of them were so young, trying to make a decision like this. Cole wanted her all for himself and Abbey had always shared her time between them.

"I don't see why there should be a decision. Can't we just continue as we are?" she said, looking at them. She was happy with things as they were.

"No," said Cole resolutely. He wanted this worked out.

Ellis spoke up and said in a kind voice, "Abbey, it isn't fair to any of us. The one you don't choose can still be your friend."

With tears in her eyes, she looked directly at him and asked, "What if I said Cole, instead of you?"

"Then I would have two best friends," he said resolutely, not willing to lose either of them. They were his family and he would do anything for them.

Abbey looked at him and said in a low voice, "Ellis, can't you fight for me? Show some emotion?"

Even at that time, Ellis was more removed and not as emotional as his peers. He lived a lot of his life in his head. His response to her was just to shake his head.

She stomped her food and said, "I won't do it. I won't choose."

They went down to the train station with her, keeping a lookout for any persons who might be following them. "Abbey."

"Yes, Ellis?"

"I have something for you." He handed her a large portion of the money from the heist he had been involved in.

"Oh," she said with tears in her eyes. "I can't take all of your money."

"It isn't all of it," he assured her, but it was most of it. "Take it and be safe."

"I will." She kissed both boys' cheeks and boarded the train for New York.

That was the last time Ellis had seen her.

He continued to watch the dancers, absently trying to place Abbey's head on each of the women. He seemed to have achieved this and saw her dancing by him. He shook his head to clear the memory, but when he looked again, he could have sworn that was her. *My imagination is getting away from me.*

"What was that?" asked Cole.

Ellis started when he realized Cole was still beside him, that he'd muttered his thought out loud. "Nothing," he said absently. "I just thought I saw someone." He continued to watch the dancers intently to see if he would see her again. They twirled past and the music came to a stop. The woman he was watching turned toward him and strode deliberately over to where he and Cole stood. Cole was not facing the dance floor and had not noticed her walking up to them.

"Abbey," said Ellis in a faint voice, "is it really you?"

"It is," she said as he moved to hug her. She returned it warmly. He stepped back but kept her hand in his. She looked happy to let her hand stay where it was.

Cole had turned to speak with an associate, but immediately turned back when he heard her voice. He watched as Ellis stepped back after hugging her.

His voice was hard when he said, "Abigail, why are you here?"

Ellis turned and gave him a long look. He hadn't seen Abbey since that day she refused to choose between them. He narrowed his eyes at Cole, wondering if *he* had seen Abbey since then.

Before she could answer, Jeremy and Emma strolled up. "Hey, Pops," said Jeremy as he put his arm around Cole's shoulders. "Are you having a nice time?"

"Yes, you need to dance," he said in a firm voice to Jeremy.

"I believe my card is open if you would like to dance with me," suggested Emma in a teasing voice.

"I'm not sure I want to let you go," Jeremy teased her.

Emma laughed, but no one else in their small group did. Emma noticed they were very quiet and nudged Jeremy, nodding toward them.

Jeremy looked curiously at the woman standing with Cole and Ellis. She had not turned toward them. He noticed Cole and Ellis were also preoccupied.

Cole looked over at Jeremy and said with a smile, "Why don't you take the next one with Emma and save one later for me?"

Jeremy raised a brow at him, but took the hint and said to Emma, "Shall we?"

"We shall," she said with a smile, but concern lit her eyes. They went to the dance floor and, as Jeremy twirled her into his arms, she asked, "Should we be concerned?"

He looked over her shoulder toward their two fathers and finally said, "No, I don't think so. I'll check with them later."

Cole looked harder at Abigail and asked again, "Why are you here?"

She smiled innocently. "What, I can't attend a charity dance? I paid for my ticket."

He looked around for a place where he could speak to her privately. "This way." He turned away from them and strode out of the room, expecting them to follow.

Ellis shrugged and offered his elbow to her; she took it moving at a slower pace behind him. As they entered, Cole's calm demeanor vanished as he slammed the door behind them. He turned to her and said, "What are your plans?"

"I plan to meet my son," she said simply.

"Here? Tonight?" he asked loudly.

"Yes, I don't want to waste a moment," she said, using the same loud voice.

"No!" Cole shouted.

Ellis stepped in, "I feel like I have started to read a book in the middle. I assume the two of you were…"

"Married," supplied Abbey.

"When?" Ellis asked, confused that his two closest friends had been married… meaning Abbey was Jeremy's mother.

Cole sat on the long leather couch, leaned his head back, and closed his eyes. "It was after you and Mary had married, and Dora was on the way."

Abbey sat slowly and said, "I was in New York and I was headed to see you both here in Chicago."

"Why didn't I see you?" Ellis asked.

"I never made it there. I ran into Cole in New York," she said quietly. She didn't say that she had told Cole she had finally made her decision about who she wanted, and she was on her way to Chicago to tell Ellis she loved him.

New York 1865

Cole watched as the rain fell. It was hard and cold on his face that early morning, but at least the gale-force winds and fog had abated. He was on a whaleboat that belonged to the U.S. Revenue Cutter Richard Rush. They were chasing a steamer; they had information that indicated it was carrying a large amount of opium.

Cole stood on the side of the whaleboat with his men, waiting for the steamer to give up the chase. It tried to outrun them but it was no use; the winds were with them.

They had caught up and boarded the mostly empty ship steamer. One of his men called from down in the hold, "Opium!"

"How much?" Cole shouted back.

"More than 500lbs of opium packed in 1/2lb tins."

Drug use had increased in the U.S. with large amounts of Chinese-made opium being smuggled in on ships. The U.S. Treasury had hired the Pinkertons to help out with the case. Cole was already a lead investigator, making a name for himself within the agency.

The drug smugglers were taken into custody and moved to the whaleboat. They left several sailors from the whaleboat to bring in the steamer. The smugglers were escorted off and given into the custody of the U.S. Treasury Department.

As Cole and his men started to exit the boat, the Treasury representative thanked him for their assistance in taking down the steamer and recovering the opium. They shook hands and he departed with the smugglers and drugs. Cole stood on the boardwalk and watched as they moved the carriages and wagons away.

"Always involved in something, aren't you?" asked a female voice.

Cole stilled immediately when he recognized that voice. He said without looking back, "Abigail."

"Yes. Did you get bored waiting for me?" she teased him.

He turned slowly; it had been so long since he had seen her. She was the same girl he remembered, but now she had a polished look. "I didn't know you were back in the country."

"I just got back," she said lightly. "I'm on my way to Chicago."

"You are?" he teased back. "On the way to see me?"

"Why don't you give me a ride to my hotel, maybe dinner tonight? I can explain things then," she said quietly.

"I can do that," he said, looking at her for answers he wasn't sure he wanted to hear.

The trip to her hotel was full of conversation. They had been friends a long time and they had plenty to catch up on. They were laughing about a story involving Ellis, Cole, and Abigail as they pulled up to the hotel. "I'll pick you up at 7 for dinner?" he suggested.

"That would be lovely," she said. The stories brought her back in time when they were all friends. When they tried to get her to decide between them, she had opted not to make one and left. Now she was older, she felt she could make that choice. They said goodbye and agreed to meet in the lobby later that evening. She rested in her room and then picked out an outfit to see an old friend.

She felt a bit nervous as she walked down the stairs to the lobby. The decision she was planning to share might hurt Cole. Pausing, she looked around and saw him sitting on one of the settees. He was taking in the whole room, observing everything. *He hasn't changed through the years*, she thought.

He turned, as though he had felt her gaze. She could feel the heat across the room. *Wow*, she thought, *this will be harder than I thought.*

He stood and walked over to greet her. "Abigail," he said and leaned down to kiss her on the cheek.

"Cole," she replied.

He offered her his elbow, which she accepted, and they departed for the restaurant. The carriage ride was silent and once they reached the restaurant, it continued. Cole reached across the table and took her hand in his. "Abigail, is there something you want to tell me?"

She took a deep breath and said, "You could always see to the heart of things. I'm here because I wanted to see you and Ellis."

"And," he prompted.

"I finally made a decision," she said decisively.

He didn't have to inquire what she was talking about; he knew. He looked at her for a long time and said, "You didn't choose me."

"No," she said softly. "I chose Ellis."

He shook his head and said with a twisted smile, "It would have been better if you had chosen me."

She frowned and said, "I don't understand."

"Abigail, you waited too long," he started.

"Why has he forgotten about me?" she asked coyly.

That made him laugh; no one could forget Abigail. "No, he never forgot you."

"Then why did you say I waited too long?" She was feeling bewildered by the turn of the conversation.

His face went solemn. "He's married."

She felt her stomach drop and asked in a casual voice, "Do you think it will last?"

"I do," he said. "He's very happy and they have a baby on the way."

"Happy and a baby. I guess there's nowhere to go from there," she said, feeling down. *All that way and to not even see him.*

"Aren't I a good substitute?" he asked, trying to lighten up the atmosphere.

"Yes," she said, letting him lighten her mood. "I don't know why I thought he would wait for me."

Cole didn't tell her that Ellis did wait, far longer than he should have. He looked at her and knew he wanted the opportunity to win her himself. "Let's enjoy our dinner."

"Yes," she said, picking up her fork.

"And a stroll after," he tempted her.

"That would be lovely," she commented.

The next few weeks were a whirlwind. Cole applied himself to entertaining her. As they got to know each other again, she remembered why the choice had been so hard. Cole was wonderful company and they got along so well. She watched him as much as he watched her. Studying him, she came to a conclusion and it was Cole. They had similar backgrounds and wanted similar things.

So, when he stopped her on their stroll a few weeks later to ask her to marry him, she said, "Yes."

∼

Back to present-day Chicago

"We decided to get married. Jeremy came about a year after that," Abigail explained to Ellis, without mentioning she thought she would end up married to him and not Cole.

"Why have I never heard about this?" asked Ellis, feeling hurt that his two closest friends had kept something so vital from him.

"We weren't exactly close during that time," Cole muttered.

"That's true," admitted Ellis, acknowledging that he'd had a part in their separation. He asked the obvious question, "So, why aren't you together now?"

Instead of answering, Cole stared at Abigail. She stood, agitated. "Fine, I admit it. I screwed up."

And when she didn't continue, Cole said quietly, "She was on the run when we married."

She walked toward the fireplace and turned back to them, saying, "I was in prison in France. I took a necklace. I didn't think it would be missed."

"Not missed! It had an emerald and was surrounded by diamonds," Cole said in disbelief.

"I returned it," she said defensively.

"Yes, after you were caught," he said, still bitter about the event that destroyed their family.

"Yes," she said, not adding more.

Cole looked at Ellis and said, "She escaped prison in Europe and went on the run. When the men showed up to take her, I had to stay to look after Jeremy. He was just a little guy and he needed me."

"And left me to fend for myself," she said, bitterness now coloring her voice. "Just like *she* did."

That statement almost broke Cole's heart. He wanted to defend his actions but didn't think he could. He sighed and said, "I'll talk to Jeremy tomorrow." He looked at Ellis. "I'll include Emma, also. Jeremy will need the support."

"Emma?" asked Abbey, clearly bewildered at this person's name being introduced into a private family matter.

"Yes," said Ellis. "She's my daughter. She and Jeremy have been together for a while."

"Are they married?" she asked, curious about her son's life.

"No, but fully committed to one another," said Cole.

"Whose idea was it to not get married?" asked Abigail, studying Ellis.

"I believe it was a joint decision," Cole answered smoothly. He knew it was Emma's request, but Jeremy supported her.

She let that go, for now, knowing she would want to hear more about this commitment. "You'll make sure that I see him tomorrow?" she asked Cole.

"If I can work it out, plan on dinner at our house," he said, looking at Ellis.

She looked at both and laughed out loud. "You're living together?"

"We are. The kids have Ellis' house for their business ventures. We get along well together," said Cole. He decided that was enough for one night and stood. "I would prefer that you left now."

"Now, Cole," she chided him, "I would like to dance with Ellis. After all, I paid for my ticket."

He leaned forward, placing his hands on his thighs, and said, "As long as you don't approach Jeremy and no funny business."

"You mean like this?" she asked as she pulled his watch from her bosom.

"That's my watch," said Cole. She handed it to him with a coy smile. Cole took it from her and shook his head, thinking, *She's the same person she has always been, a charming thief.*

"Don't worry, I'll be on my best behavior," she assured them.

Cole quickly checked his pocket and Abigail noticed, saying in a wry voice, "Don't worry, Cole. Your wallet is safe." She watched as he slowly dropped his hands. She turned away from him and asked Ellis, "Shall we?" He happily obliged and offered her his elbow.

As they were walking back, Ellis noticed she had to wipe her eyes. "That scene affected you more than you let on," he said quietly.

"Yes, I just didn't want him to see," she said. "He always thinks the worst of me."

Ellis changed the subject and asked, "How about that dance?"

She smiled gratefully and said, "I would love that, dear Ellis." He showed a debonair side to his personality by twirling her onto the dance floor. They danced three more dances together.

Ellis was captivated. Outside of Mary, Abbey was the only

other woman he had loved. He murmured in her ear, "You didn't come back to see me like you did Cole."

She shivered as she felt his hot breath on her neck and said, "I had planned to see you, but Cole intercepted me in New York City." That made him stop abruptly on the dance floor as he looked down at her.

Abigail didn't like to call attention to herself and said, "Ellis, we should keep moving."

He stood there a bit longer, then pulled her back to him and started moving again. "You were going to choose me?" he asked hoarsely.

"Yes," she said, softly laying her head on his shoulder. They danced closer, enjoying their time together.

CHAPTER 5

*E*mma looked around as they danced and asked curiously, "Did you see who Papa is dancing with?"

"Hmm, not really," murmured Jeremy, his face in her neck. "I only have eyes for you."

"Really?" she asked with a low laugh, letting her attention be pulled back to her escort.

"Yes," he replied, "and I believe there's a lovely, warm bed at home."

"I'd like that," she said and took his hand to exit the dance floor. Just as they walked past the first table, someone grabbed her arm. She looked back to find Tony standing before her. "Hi, Tony," she said with a smile, one that faded quickly when she realized he'd been drinking.

"You promised me a dance," he reminded her rather forcefully.

"Yes, I did," she said as she turned to Jeremy. She asked lightly, her eyes silently pleading with him to understand, "Jeremy, would you mind?" She didn't want to bring attention to Tony's drinking in his place of work. There were a lot of people there who knew and respected him.

Jeremy nodded, understanding. "I'll be over there." He went to where Dora and Tim were seated and joined them.

"Where's Emma?" asked Dora curiously.

"Tony wanted a dance," he said and his voice betrayed his displeasure.

Dora heard the tone and watched him closely before she commented, "I understand Peggy has been away visiting family. He's probably lonely."

Jeremy nodded but thought to himself, *No, it's just his drinking has shown that he wants Emma back.* He continued to watch them closely.

On the dance floor, Tony tried to pull her in close; Emma placed her elbows between them. "Tony, not so close. Let's enjoy our dance."

"Yes," he said, "let's do that." They continued to dance quietly. He finally burst out in a desperate tone, "Emma, why him and not me?"

"Tony, you know why. We were growing up and apart. It was time," she said in a calming voice.

He seemed to sober abruptly and asked, "What if I want to get back together?"

She answered him in a quiet tone, looking him in the eye. "We aren't going to get back together. We're better friends than anything else. Can't you be okay with that?"

"I'm trying," he muttered.

"Where's Peggy?" she asked, knowing he had real feelings for her.

"She went to visit family," he said shortly.

Emma studied him and asked searchingly, "Was there a reason she left town?"

He turned a bit red and admitted, "She wants to get married."

"And what do you want, Tony?" she asked bluntly.

"I had thought the answer was you. I just wanted to go back to when it was simpler," he said lamely.

"Tony, we've all grown up and moved into our lives. Don't use me as an excuse to delay your future."

He didn't want to talk anymore and requested, "Can we just dance?"

"Yes," she murmured and moved to the music.

When the dance was done, she had him escort her to where Jeremy stood with Tim and Dora. She looked over at Tim and said firmly, "Tim, I think Tony wants to head home."

He glanced from Emma to Tony and said, "Yes, I see that he does." He slapped him on the back, saying cheerfully, "Tony, old man, let's go." He looked over at Dora and asked, "Are you ready?"

She got the message and said quickly, "Yes, I'm tired also. Amy's probably ready to go home, too." She had stayed at the boarding house to babysit the kids. They gathered up their things and, with Tony firmly in hand, headed out. Emma watched them leave and took the chair next to Jeremy.

He was quiet, thinking about Tony. He looked contemplative as he asked, "Anything I need to worry about?"

"No," she said, shaking her head. "I don't think so. I think he just had too much to drink and is missing Peggy."

Jeremy nodded, not voicing his doubts.

Cole walked over to them and said, "Looks like things are breaking up."

Jeremy glanced around and said, "Yes, seems to be a successful night for the Carlyle Foundation."

Emma nodded as she looked around; she wanted to check in and see if they needed to help clean up. "Have you seen Clair?" she inquired.

Cole indicated by nodding his head. "She's just over there."

Emma looked where he gestured and saw Clair speaking intently to a tall man in a suit. *I wonder what that's about,* she thought. Clair didn't seem upset. She continued watching as Thomas approached them; Clair gave him a sweet smile. *He must be a benefactor*, she concluded. Clair and Thomas excused themselves and made their way to Emma's table.

"Did everyone have a nice evening?" Clair asked their small group.

Emma responded with a smile. "The event has been lovely. It also appears to have been successful."

"We were able to fill all of the tables and meet our goals for new projects."

"Wonderful," said Cole, and Jeremy nodded in agreement.

Jeremy asked, "Do you need anything? Would you like us to stay and help clean up?"

"No, no," she assured them, "we have a crew coming in."

Cole said, "Our detectives are in place and will be here through the night. "

Clair said, "I'll get with them and confirm the next steps. Lily will also oversee the closeout." Lilly Edwards had been involved peripherally in another case that the group had solved. She had been caught with stolen merchandise and served some jail time. It was limited because she turned in her boyfriend as the main person behind the thefts. She was truly repentant of her mistakes. After she served her time, she returned and was sent to business school by the foundation. When Clair saw how talented she was, she made Lily her assistant.

At that moment, Lily walked up, wearing a black dress with a white collar. "Clair, we're just about ready to start taking things down."

"Wonderful. Do you think you can handle this cleanup?"

"Yes," she said competently. "I can handle it."

Clair looked at the group and said, "Thank you so much for your support. I'll organize a meeting to review the contributions and suggestions for new projects." She looked back at Lily and said, "Let's move to the office and confirm the details." Lilly nodded and followed her.

Jeremy noticed Cole looked like something was bothering

him. "Pops, are you okay?"

"Yes," he said and took a deep breath to steady himself. "Jeremy, can you and Emma stop by tomorrow? I need to discuss something with you."

Jeremy frowned as he watched him, growing more concerned by the minute. "Pops, do you want to talk to us tonight? We can come by the house."

Cole shook his head. "No, it can wait until tomorrow." *It has waited this long*, he thought. *One night won't make a difference.*

"We will come by the house in the morning," confirmed Jeremy.

"I will see you then."

Emma stood up decisively and said, "I'm ready to head home. What about you?"

Jeremy stood up as well and said, "I am. Pops, would you like to ride with us?"

"Yes," he said laconically, knowing his ride had left without him.

Their hired carriage was waiting outside to take them home. They dropped off Cole on their way. Once they arrived home, Jeremy helped Emma down and they walked into the house, talking softly.

Voices sounded from the sitting room as they took off their coats in the foyer. Dora called out, "Emma, Jeremy, come in, sit down."

They joined the other couple, winding down for the evening. Emma looked at Tim and asked, "Did Tony get home okay?"

Tim grimaced, and said, "Yeah, I think he'll be nursing his head tomorrow morning."

Dora couldn't wait any longer and said, "Emma, did you get a chance to see who was dancing with Papa?"

"What?" Emma asked, distracted.

Dora continued, "The lady dancing with Papa. I saw them together, then they were gone."

Emma frowned at that. "He didn't tell you he was leaving?"

"No," Dora said.

"That is odd," she murmured.

"Yes, he was gone, and I noticed that woman with him was also gone."

"Are we already calling her 'that woman'?" Emma teased.

Dora frowned, thinking Emma wasn't taking this seriously enough.

Emma yawned and said, "We can ask him tomorrow. Cole wants us to stop by in the morning."

Jeremy said, looking at his watch, "I hope we can get some sleep before that."

Emma leaned over and murmured suggestively in his ear, "Maybe."

He laughed in a low voice and said to Tim and Dora, "We'll see you in the morning." Tim's laugh followed them up to their rooms.

Jeremy and Emma had an enjoyable interlude and slept in the next day. "We need to get up," Jeremy said softly into her hair.

Emma moaned and said into his chest, without looking up, "I guess we have to. Why did we make a morning date with your father?"

"He needs us, and I think it might be important," he reminded her.

"You're right," she said as she turned over and stretched. "Up we go." They both rose, with Jeremy exiting through the secret entrance to his room to prepare for the day. Emma finished getting ready and tucked her white tailored shirt into her green skirt. She put a red tie around her collar. Rather than her bowler, she picked up a straw hat with a matching green ribbon. Strapping her clutch knife to her leg, she heard Jeremy call through the door, "Ready?"

She went and opened it, seeing him. "Let me grab my bag and notebook."

"Thinking of investigating something today?" he teased.

"No, just habit," she commented absently as she placed it in her pocket.

He took her hand as they made their way downstairs. It was about 9am on Sunday; everyone was free to get breakfast for themselves, so the family could usually attend church. As they reached the bottom of the steps, Emma heard the sound of children laughing. She turned toward it and saw Dora, Tim, and the children. They had mentioned they'd decided to skip church and spend the morning with the kids. Tim was chasing Patrick around the room.

Emma watched Patrick with Tim and thought, *He's so much a part of our family.* Dora was enjoying their antics, holding baby Lottie and laughing. She was such a beautiful baby girl, with strawberry blond hair, a mix of colors from Dora and Tim.

Lottie was struggling to get down; she wanted to join in on the fun with the boys. Dora finally gave in but said, "Careful, she wants to play also." Patrick and Tim slowed a bit to include her in their chase.

Dora noticed them in the hallway and called out, "There's some pastry and fruit in the kitchen if you're hungry."

"I am," said Emma. "We have to eat quickly; we're on our way to see Cole."

"Hmm. While you are there, could you see if you can figure out who Papa was dancing with last night?" she asked nonchalantly.

Emma grinned wickedly. "I can do that."

"Food?" asked Jeremy, wanting to get their day started.

"Yes," she said and walked with him to the kitchen. Once there, they put together a quick breakfast. Emma noticed Jeremy was quieter than normal and inquired, "Are you okay?"

"Yes. I'm just worried about Pops. He seemed troubled last night," he explained.

They finished their breakfast and passed the sitting room to let Dora and Tim know they were heading out. "Let us know if he needs anything," Dora said over the noise of Lottie's happy screams as Tim tossed her into the air.

Jeremy said, "We will." He looked at Emma and asked, "Carriage or trolly?"

"Let's take the trolly, get some wind in our faces," she suggested.

"Sounds like a plan," he said as they headed to catch it.

They got off the trolly and walked the two blocks to Cole and Papa's house. Jeremy opened the door and called out for Cole.

They heard him say, "I'm in here, my boy." They walked through the foyer and saw him standing in the sitting room, holding a coffee cup. "Come in. come in. Would you like something to drink? Eat?"

"No, but thank you," Jeremy answered for them. "We ate before we came over."

"Good. Well, sit," he said.

As they sat, they looked at Cole expectantly.

He placed his coffee cup on the side table and sat on the chair opposite them. He appeared at a loss for words as he stared at Jeremy.

Jeremy burst out, "Pops, you're scaring me. Out with it. What's wrong?"

Cole thought the best way was to say it straight out. He leaned toward Jeremy and said, "Your mother is back."

That took Jeremy a moment to process, and he closed his eyes. He felt Emma's hand squeeze his. When he didn't say anything, Emma inquired softly, "How long has it been since you have seen her?"

"I'm not sure," commented Jeremy in a hoarse voice, opening his eyes.

"I am," commented Cole in a bitter tone. "She went away when he was about two."

Jeremy could barely take it in and asked, "Pops, where's she been all this time?"

Cole exhaled deeply. "I'm afraid she'll have to answer that. I only know why she left initially but not why she stayed away."

"Pops, you never told me why she left. You just said she had to go," Jeremy said.

Cole didn't answer. Instead, he asked him a question. "Did I ever tell you how we met?"

"No, I don't think so."

"It was back when we were homeless and making money by pickpocketing and doing odd jobs. Kids tended to stay in groups to survive. You know how close Ellis and I were?" Cole asked, lost in his thoughts.

They nodded for him to go on.

He continued, "We were about fifteen when we met Abigail. She had been on the streets longer than us and had graduated from pickpocketing to actual theft. She was excellent at stealing things and not getting caught. When we were taken in by the Giblers, she had already left for Europe."

"What happened then? How did you get together?" asked Jeremy, eager to hear more about her.

There was no reason to disclose that he and Ellis had asked her to choose between them before she left. "All three of us made our way forward, Ellis here, me in New York, and Abigail in Europe."

"When did you see her again?"

"I was in New York working for Pinkerton and I was waiting at the ship dock. I had a case that was wrapping up. Then I heard her voice. She looked so elegant," he reminisced. "We started to see each other and decided to marry and settle down. That's when we had you."

"Were you happy?" asked Jeremy, curious about their life together.

"Yes, very much so. We were together for about a year before we knew you were on the way. We were still in New York at that time. I was working for Pinkerton and Abbey was setting up the house for us. It was a busy time,"

They sounded happy. How did things get so bad that they separated? Jeremy wondered. He asked, "Pops, what happened? Why did she leave?"

"I told you she did well in Europe, and she was heading home to settle down?" They nodded as he continued. "What she did well, what she was good at, was being a thief. She was very good at it and could get in and out of a building with no one noticing."

"Thief!" exclaimed Jeremy.

Something occurred to Emma. She had come across the name of a lady thief in Europe. "Was she called Mistress K?"

"She was," he acknowledged with a twist of his mouth. "She liked the romance of it."

Jeremy had heard of her also. "She's famous, or rather, infamous."

Cole nodded.

"So, what happened?" Emma asked. Abbey had managed to have a very adventurous life.

"She got caught and went to a Paris prison. She escaped and managed to get enough money to get a boat to New York," he continued.

So, maybe I shouldn't model my life after her, Emma thought with a wry smile.

"Did you have any idea?" asked Jeremy, wondering if Pops had shielded her from the police.

"None. It wasn't until you were about two that there was a knock on our door. It was a Saturday. We were home, relaxing, playing with you. I got up to answer the door and it was the local authorities standing there. They asked for Abigail and said they were working with the Paris police. I remember she just stood there, looking poleaxed, holding you so tightly." Cole seemed lost in his memories.

"How did they know she was there?" asked Emma, gently trying to pull him into the present.

"There had been a local jewel robbery that matched her modus operandi. They tracked her there; she had been selling small loose jewels in local pawn shops," he explained.

"Was she arrested?" asked Jeremy, bewildered.

Emma watched Jeremy's reaction and realized this wasn't an exciting story about a stranger, but a story of why Jeremy's mom had chosen that life over him.

"Yes, they took her immediately," Cole said.

"Did you ask her if she did it?" Jeremy asked, still hoping she was not guilty.

"They found a necklace when they searched the house," Cole said, shaking his head. "I confronted her and she admitted it. I asked her why she did it, and why she jeopardized everything we had. All she said was she enjoyed it."

"Enjoyed?" Jeremy echoed.

"Yes, the thrill, the chase," Cole said and stopped talking for a moment. "I thought, when she settled with us, that she had changed. I was wrong. She had not."

"Did you help her?" Jeremy asked, unsure what to say, not wanting to take sides in the family drama that had happened so long ago.

"I did."

Cole paced around the small interrogation room.

"It won't do any good to wear yourself out. You might as well sit down," Abbey commented.

"Sit! How can I sit? They're sending you to Paris," he said.

She cuddled the baby to her chest, not wanting to let him go. She brushed the curls off of his head and kissed him. He was content to lay with his mom.

Cole watched and thought, *She is so good with him.* He sat down and placed his head in his hands, mumbling, "What are we going to do?"

"It looks like I'm going back to Paris. I'm not sure how long I'll be there," she teased.

"You escaped once before. Do you plan to do it again?"

"Cole, we can get through this—" she started to say.

He interrupted her. "Why didn't you tell me you were on the run? We could have tried to work it out."

"Really?" she said incredulously. "So, had I stepped off the boat and said, *By the way, I'm on the run*, would you have married me?"

Cole just looked at her, not speaking.

"You really went all the way to the other side, didn't you? You never asked me why I took the necklace here or why I was in prison in Paris. All you have cared about is that I was in the wrong."

"No, that's not true," he protested, knowing he was losing something special.

She heard the doubt in his voice. She continued to hug Jeremy close as an officer came to the door and said, "It's time."

She stood slowly and looked at the now sleeping baby. *How can I leave him?* she thought as she carried him with her to the door.

"You'll need to come alone," said the officer kindly.

"Yes." She kept her tear-filled eyes directed away from Cole as she handed him the baby. She said in a low voice, "Take care of him."

Cole took Jeremy and held him close, watching her leave.

"I got her a lawyer and even traveled to Paris to make sure she was okay. But it was no use. She was guilty," he said quietly. "I went to find out if she stayed with us as a cover or if it was genuine."

"What did she say?" Jeremy asked, wanting to know the answer.

"She said she loved us," he admitted.

"Did you just leave her there?" asked Jeremy, not wanting to believe he would do that.

"No! No," he said rather loudly. "I did not. I went to see her in Paris, but Jeremy, I had to get back to you. I left you in New York with friends. I also had responsibilities with my job. I saw her that last time at the prison and told her that I would write, and we would wait for her to get out."

~

The trip to Paris was long and difficult. When Cole finally made it there, they had already pronounced Abigail guilty of a jailbreak and added more time to her sentence. He was able to get the French police to let him see her.

There was no big reunion. He entered the room and saw her, wearing a gray cotton dress, standing near a table. She didn't rush over to him. He got the message and stayed away.

She asked, without looking at him, "You didn't bring Jeremy?"

"No," he said as he frowned. "It wasn't possible."

"Who is he with?"

"I have him with the Martins. They'll take care of him until I return."

"You return," she said slowly.

"Yes, I can't stay here. My life and Jeremy's are there," he said bluntly.

"What about me, Cole? Am I just to be left behind as a bad mistake?"

"I don't know what else to do. I have an attorney for you. I'd like you to meet him and see if he can get your sentence reduced."

"I'll see him, not for you, but Jeremy."

"I'll…" he started.

"No," she said shortly, "you'll not do anything. I don't want you to see me again."

"Why?" he asked, bewildered.

"I never should have chosen you, Cole. It wasn't right for us when we were teenagers, and it isn't right now."

"What about Jeremy?"

"I don't know. I hope to come back and be with him someday."

"Did you leave her there?" Jeremy asked, somewhat accusingly.

"You think I would leave your mother alone in a foreign country?" he asked, wondering if his son thought so little of him.

"I don't know what to think."

"I sent letters letting her know about you. I went over several times, but she refused to see me. When I heard she was finally getting out, I made my way back to Paris to pick her up, but she was already gone. That was the last time I heard from her."

Emma spoke up. "This is your first contact since then?" Something occurred to her and she asked, "Are you still married?"

Jeremy had wondered that as well.

"No," said Cole. "I waited the mandatory time and filed for a divorce. You don't need the other spouse present if you wait."

"Do you think she's still stealing things?" asked Jeremy.

"I don't know," he said honestly, "but her fingers are nimble as ever." He told them about the watch.

Emma burst out laughing. "Got you, did she?"

"Yes, it looks like it's my lot in life to be bested by intelligent women." He smiled for the first time that morning.

That made Jeremy smile, too. "It must be hereditary." Emma nudged him playfully.

"You'll have to ask her when you see her," Cole said. He closed his eyes and took a deep breath. "Would you like me to set up a meeting?"

"Could we do it today?" Jeremy looked over at Emma. "I don't think I can stand the wait."

Cole looked serious as he said, "I'll arrange it for you, Emma and Abbey. Is this afternoon at 4pm, all right?" At Emma's nod, he continued. "She's staying at the Palmer Hotel."

Jeremy and Emma stood to go. Cole looked hesitant when he walked over, looking him directly in the eye. "My boy, I never meant to keep her from you."

"I know, Pops." He reached over to hug him tight.

Cole returned the hug in full measure. When he pulled away, he had to wipe his eyes. Jeremy's were also shining bright.

"Let me know how things go if you want to come by after. I'll be home all evening," he stated gruffly, patting Jeremy's arms.

Jeremy could tell that was important to him. "Yes, Pops, I'll come by after."

Emma hugged Cole, and they exited the building. Jeremy took her hand in his as they descended. He paused at the bottom and faced her. "I didn't expect that would be the topic."

"No, that was a surprise. Do you remember her at all?" she asked.

"Just vague memories. A song, a voice," he said musingly.

"Nothing else?" she inquired.

"No."

"Did he tell you anything about her over the years?"

"He told me she was lovely."

"Did he say why she left?"

"I don't think I ever asked."

"Weren't you curious?"

"No, I don't think so. It was always just Pops and me. We were —are—happy. There didn't seem to be a gap needing to be filled."

"Yes, I can see that." She knew how close they were in their personal and professional lives.

"Let's head home." They turned and continued holding hands as they walked. Taking their time, each lost in their thoughts.

They reached the house and entered through the kitchen. It was just about time for lunch. Amy and Ethyl didn't work on Sunday and Dora liked to put together a later lunch for the family.

They found her working efficiently. She called over to them, saying, "Great timing, could you grab the trays and move them to the table?"

"Of course. Sorry, we weren't here sooner," Emma said, moving to the table to help.

"That's okay, I understand family stuff," said Dora as she put together the bread tray.

They grabbed the roast chicken and assorted vegetables to move to the table. "Patrick, Tim, bring Lottie in," called Dora. Jake was already at the table.

Emma asked, "Is Savannah going to be on the road for a while?"

"Yes, that show she's working will be out for another six weeks," said Dora.

Tim came into the dining room carrying Lottie under one arm and Patrick under his other. He asked, "Were you looking for two packages?" They were giggling as he put them in their seats. Patrick sat by Jake; Emma and Jeremy sat down near Tim and Dora.

Dora had baby Lottie in a chair that placed her higher at the table. Papa had built guards around it so she couldn't fall. Dora started to cut the chicken and mushed the veggies up a small mound and placed them in front of Lottie.

Once the family said prayers and started eating, Dora asked, "Well, what was up with Cole this morning?"

Emma looked at Jeremy, leaving the answer up to him.

Jeremy looked around, realizing this was his family and he could tell them. "My mother has come back," he said simply.

Dora dropped her fork in surprise. She knew he hadn't had contact with her in a long while. "Have you seen her?" she asked.

"No, not until this afternoon. Pops is sending over a confirmation as soon as he speaks to her," he explained.

"Emma, are you going to accompany him?" Tim asked curiously, buttering his bread.

"She is," Jeremy stated firmly, taking her hand in his. She squeezed it in response.

Dora said sincerely, "Jeremy, I know everything's going to be okay."

"Thanks, Dora. I hope so," he replied, still feeling out of sorts about the situation.

Dinner continued and conversation flowed around them. Jeremy ate quietly, lost in his thoughts. They helped clear the table and cleaned up. Jake headed to his lab, and the rest of the family moved to the sitting room. Emma asked Jeremy quietly, "Do you want to talk?"

"No, no, I just want to sit here and try not to think about it."

Emma got a book from the side table and started to read. After a while, they heard a knock on the door. She looked around and said, "I'll get it. You stay here."

She went to the door to retrieve the note from the courier and carried it unsealed to Jeremy. He opened it. "It says she would like us to go to the hotel at 4pm."

"We can do that," said Emma.

"I'll arrange a carriage," said Tim and excused himself. Patrick had gotten his toys and was playing on the floor, while Dora continued to entertain Lottie.

Emma picked up a book to distract her mind until it was time to leave.

Tim returned and said, "The carriage is arranged for 3:30."

"Thanks," said Jeremy gratefully.

"No problem," he said and settled down on the floor to play cards with Patrick.

The time came around quickly and they heard a knock on the door. Emma glanced at Jeremy and asked, "Ready?"

He took a deep breath. "Yes." He stood and offered her his hand, saying to Tim and Dora, "We'll be on our way."

Dora grabbed his hand as he moved by her. "Jeremy, we're here for you if you need anything."

"Thanks, Dora," he said sincerely, leaning down to kiss her cheek.

In the foyer, they put on their jackets, opened the door, and found the carriage driver there waiting. "I have a pickup?" the driver said.

Jeremy nodded and indicated, "That's us. We need to go to the Palmer Hotel. On second thought, drop us two blocks from there." He looked over at Emma and she nodded in agreement.

"Yes, sir," the driver said and waited for them to climb into the carriage. Emma stood on the box and Jeremy swung her in, entering behind her. He left them off as instructed; they paid him and walked the last two blocks to the hotel.

They arrived there and took a moment outside. He couldn't make himself go in. Emma asked tentatively, "Jeremy?" When he didn't reply, she said, "Jeremy, we don't have to go in. We can leave a note."

"No," he said. "I need to see her." He took her hand and they went in, making their way through the dramatic lobby, with glittering chandeliers and a painted ceiling. Emma had not been in this hotel before and was looking everywhere as she walked. Jeremy didn't see the interior; he was focused on the task at hand.

They approached the front desk and Jeremy said, "We're looking for Abigail Lancaster. She should be expecting us."

The man at the desk was dressed smartly in a blue suit with a blue tie and a white shirt. He nodded and checked his cards. He looked up at Jeremy and asked, "Your name?"

"Jeremy Tilden."

He smiled and said, "Yes, sir, Ms. Lancaster left word that she would like you to join her in her room. It's room 4987." He clicked to the bellman to show them the way. They followed him up the stairs and made their way to her door.

The bellman knocked on the door briskly and a woman answered. She smiled at him and said, "Thank you." He left and went back downstairs.

All three stood very still until Emma realized where she had seen her. "It was you last night! You were dancing with Papa." She looked closer. "The hair, Jeremy has your hair!"

Abbey patted it and said with a nervous laugh, "Yes, with some highlights." Emma noticed the gray threaded through it. She also noticed her eyes, the same shape, and color as Jeremey's.

"Won't you both come in?" Abigail watched them enter and thought, *I don't get time alone with my son. I also have to have the girlfriend.*

Emma looked around; Abigail had a lovely large room with wood floors, plus a sitting room with couches and side chairs. "Sit, please," Abigail said. "I've ordered some tea and pastries for us."

They sat and removed their hats. Jeremy placed them in a side chair next to him. They sat there for a few moments in silence before Abigail said, "Well, I guess I'll start. What did Cole tell you about me?"

Jeremy straightened. "Pops didn't say much. He just said you were lovely and a great mom."

"He did?" She thought about that statement before she sat up abruptly and said, "He said nothing about my profession?"

"No, not until this morning," said Jeremy, not sure what more to say.

The conversation was making her visibly uncomfortable. She changed the topic and asked, "Can we move to some pleasanter things. I'd like to hear about you."

"I'm twenty-two now, and I'm with Emma," he answered.

"How long have you been together?"

"Four years," he stated, reaching for her hand. Emma placed hers in his and squeezed. Abigail watched that movement.

"Where do you work? What's your profession?"

"I work with Pops at Pinkerton as an investigator."

"Law enforcement, that's nice. Must run in the family. You live on your own?"

"We both live in Emma's family boarding house," he said,

looking over at Emma.

"Hmm," Abbey said.

Emma spoke up then. "We'd like to have you over for dinner sometime while you're in town."

"That would be nice," she said noncommittally. She still wasn't sure about this young lady. She did notice Emma had looked around the room carefully as they sat down. Almost like she would if she were casing the place. *That can't be right. I must be mistaken.*

"Mom, may I call you that?" he asked tentatively.

His question brought all of her interest back to him. Her eyes welled up. "I would love that."

"Mom, how long are you back for?" he asked with hope in his voice.

"I'd figured to be here at least six months. I have something I'm working on that will take some time," she said.

That verbiage made Emma uneasy and she frowned, clearing her face before Abbey could see it.

Jeremey asked a hard question. "Mom, I have to ask. Are you on the run from something or someone? We can help."

"No, that won't be necessary. I'm okay. I won't need any help," she answered. Again, the way she said it gave Emma pause.

Turning her eyes to Emma, she asked, "What do you do?" Implying that she didn't do much.

There isn't anything friendly here for me, she thought.

Jeremy started to talk, but Emma stopped him by giving his hand a slight squeeze. "Really, nothing much. I design lace patterns and work at the family bakery occasionally, things like that." She didn't want to share that she was also an investigator, especially at that moment. Her current case involved the diamond merchants and improving their security measures.

Jeremy got the message and said, "My favorite is her strudel."

"Oh, I have that here," Abigail indicated as she uncovered the pastry tray. She was happy she had gotten him something he liked.

Jeremy and Emma smiled, recognizing the pastry. Emma said, "You got that from my family bakery."

"How do you know that?" she asked, puzzled.

Emma explained, "The design is specific to us, how the pastry is folded."

"Oh, that's interesting." She didn't think it was. The silly girl with no other ambitions, they were not going to get together at all. She must be like her mother, not like Ellis.

They each took a piece of pastry to eat. Jeremy finished his, took a sip of tea, and said, "I'd like to hear more about where you were during our time apart."

She smiled graciously. "I think we'll have time for that later. And I would like to be alone with you to discuss that."

Emma smiled genuinely and said, "I think that's a wonderful idea. I'll be busy for a while; that will give you both some time alone."

Abbey looked at her in surprise and said without thinking, "An important lace appointment perhaps or pastry emergency?"

Emma heard the tone and understood it as being protective of Jeremy. She laughed and said, "Something like that."

Abigail gave her a considering look. She had thought Emma would be pushy and intrusive into her time with her son. Instead, she volunteered to be absent and allowed them time together. She looked at Jeremy and said, "Lunch in a few days?"

"How about dinner instead?" he suggested.

She countered with, "How about dinner out and then back here to talk."

Jeremy nodded his agreement.

Emma watched them talk, glad they were making plans to meet again. He looked over at her and said, "Ready to go?"

She nodded and they stood. Jeremy said, "Mom, I'll see you in a few days. Would you like me to pick you up?"

"Please, I'll meet you in the lobby."

"I'll be here at seven."

CHAPTER 6

They were quiet and contemplative as they left the room and exited down the stairs. "Jeremy?" asked Emma.

"After we leave the building," he requested. She nodded and walked with him through the lobby and outside. They walked down the block when he stopped and turned her to him. "Emma, what did you think of her?"

She reached over and brushed his hair off of his forehead. "Well, I did love her hair and her eyes," she teased.

"No, really, what did you think?" He wanted to hear her honest impression.

She looked into his eyes for a long moment before saying, with a sigh, "I don't know her."

"But you saw something." He could see it in her eyes.

"I saw what you saw, a woman trying to reconnect with her son." She hesitated before saying, "Though I do feel she's keeping something back about why she's here."

"Emma, you did see something. Is that why you didn't let me tell her you're an investigator?"

"I don't know exactly. Part of it was playing into the role she assumed for me."

"And what role was that?" asked Jeremy, not seeing what she had.

Emma laughed. "She thinks I'm after you for nefarious reasons."

He chuckled and said suggestively, "But you are, aren't you?" He grew serious and asked, "Why the subterfuge?"

"I do have a case right now that's private. It just seemed easier, if she wasn't going to be around very long, to have her think I'm just a bit of light fluff."

He nodded. "You're right. If she stays, things will unfold naturally. Are you sure you don't want to come with me when I meet with her?"

"I would like to be there and hear more about her life. But I realize she wants to do this in private." She touched his face before warning him softly, "Just be cautious, Jeremy. We don't know her and what she's involved in."

"Yes, I'll take that to heart. We promised to go by Pop's place. Would you like to head over there?" he asked. She nodded and he lowered his head to kiss her slowly. After a long moment, he said, "Let's go." He stepped back and held out his hand; she took it and they headed off together.

CHAPTER 7

They didn't see Ellis pull up in a carriage just as they were leaving. He did see them and told the driver to hold a moment. He noticed they seemed to be wrapped up in an intense conversation. They kissed and walked off in the opposite direction of his carriage.

He paid his driver and climbed down. Straightening his jacket, he looked down at the clothes he had chosen carefully for this meeting. Taking a deep breath, he headed into the hotel. *It's hard,* he thought, *to see someone you haven't seen since you were young.* He was conscious of the gray in his hair and the wrinkles he hadn't noticed until this morning. He hadn't felt like this since Mary. A twinge of guilt spiked at the thought of her; they had something special and two amazing daughters. But Mary had been gone a long time. He shook off any feeling of betrayal and focused his thoughts on Abbey.

He had no delusions about her. They had known each other for a long time. They had slept in the streets and lifted wallets to get food. That last day still haunted him, pushing her to decide between them. But last night, she said she had made a decision all those years ago and was on her way to see him. *I was her choice,* he thought. *What if she had come to Chicago?* He knew what would have happened; he would have stayed with his lovely Mary and his almost born baby. He shook his head, thinking, *It's best it happened this way.*

Ellis thought about that as he walked up to Abbey's room. Cole had kept Jeremy's mother a secret from him all of these years. *But did he or did I just choose not to ask? In all of our time together, rebuilding a friendship, and living together, I never brought it up. Had I seen her in Jeremy, but ignored it?*

He headed up the stairs, knowing he was expected. He strolled to the door and knocked briskly. She opened it immediately. "Ellis," she said warmly. "Please, come in."

He looked at her a long time and thought, *I knew who his mother was all along.* He went in and closed the door quietly behind him.

CHAPTER 8

$\mathcal{E}$mma and Jeremy walked up the steps to Cole and Ellis' house. They entered and called out, "Pops!"

"In here." They followed his voice into the study. He was sitting at the desk going through several files and looked up as they entered. "Come in, have a seat. You weren't there long," he observed.

"No, it was more of just an initial meeting," explained Jeremy.

"I don't think she liked me there," commented Emma, sitting down in one of the dark leather chairs. She took off her hat and tossed it onto the desk.

"Really?" said Cole, eyeing her. He swung his gaze to Jeremy. "Did something happen?"

Jeremy sat in the chair opposite Emma's and said, "No, I think she wanted to see me alone. I don't think she felt she could talk openly with Emma there. She kept everything to short answers."

"Will you be seeing her again?" he asked.

"Yes, in a few days," Jeremy confirmed.

He nodded and asked them both, "Do we think she's involved in something here?"

Jeremy answered first, saying, "I hope not. I'd like to get to know her."

"Emma?" asked Cole, clearly valuing her thoughts.

"I have some hesitation about her," she admitted, "but I think Jeremy needs to have his time with her."

"Thanks, Em," said Jeremy, his love for her shining in his eyes.

"Just don't mention our current project," Cole warned her softly.

"I won't. She doesn't know I'm working for you. We told her about my other jobs instead," she said ambiguously.

"I'm just covering us in case she's here for something other than a family reunion. Keep your eyes open and don't get pulled into anything." He frowned at Jeremy. "I prefer to have Emma accompany you on these meetings with your mother and have her give you a rational view."

Jeremy was getting a bit exasperated. "What if," he asked, "she's actually here to see me and doesn't have an ulterior motive?"

Emma and Cole looked at one another and nodded. "We'll give her the benefit of the doubt," Cole said.

"Yes, we will," echoed Emma.

"All right then," he said, gratified at their response. Something occurred to him and he asked, "Just what is this current case you're both involved in?"

"That, we have to keep private," Cole said smoothly. "We'll bring you in when we are further along."

That seemed to satisfy Jeremy and he nodded in understanding. Cases were usually kept to minimal staffing for privacy and he was not involved in all of Emma's assignments.

Cole switched topics and said, "Would you both like to stay for dinner?"

"Will Papa be here," asked Emma.

"No, I believe he has other plans," he said quietly.

Emma frowned but didn't ask any more questions. She looked over to make sure Jeremy was okay with staying. "We would love to," he said. They sent a note over to Dora, letting her know they wouldn't be there for dinner.

They got off the topic of Jeremy's mother and discussed current cases and books. It was a pleasant evening. On their way out, Cole asked, "Emma, could you stop by in the morning to review the case?"

"I'll be there," she confirmed.

As they left, Jeremy said, "Do you think she's here for something nefarious?"

"I'd just caution you to remember she's quite famous in her field. She's also a very clever woman."

Jeremy considered her words. "I'll keep it personal. I may never have another opportunity to get to know her." He put his arm across her shoulders, pulling her in close.

CHAPTER 9

The next morning, Emma accompanied Jeremy to the Pinkerton office. "Are you okay with going on your own?" she asked him, concerned about this new person in their lives.

"To see Mom? Yeah, I'm fine. I think she'll share more if we are alone," he explained.

"Yes," she agreed. She also knew that, if Abbey tried to involve him in something, he could handle it. And if he couldn't, she would be there.

They entered the building and said a quick goodbye as she continued down to Cole's office. She knocked on his door and heard him call her in. As she entered, she saw him at the desk. He looked up with a smile. "Good morning, Emma. Thanks for coming to see me this morning."

She sat down in the chair and pulled out her notebook. "Ready?" he asked.

"I am," she said firmly.

He started his review, "The couriers are on their way with the diamonds." Diamonds were considered a rare item and were associated with the aristocracy in the 19th century. The discovery in the 1870s of diamond deposits in South Africa changed diamonds from a rare gem to one that could be available to all who could afford them.

Emma was curious about something. "Cole, how did Tiffany & Co. get the diamonds from the French Government?"

Cole looked down at the file in front of him and pulled out a newspaper article. "The Crown Jewels were auctioned in France after the fall of Napoleon III in 1871. The Third Republic of France was uncomfortable with what the jewels stood for. Tiffany & Co. was there to bid and managed to buy more than two-thirds of the merchandise and a place in history."

"And all of these are on the way here. Why did they choose Chicago as the beginning of their tour?"

"Philip Johnson, the museum curator, has a fine reputation for protecting works of art. That case you worked with him in Paris?" Emma nodded and he continued. "He came highly recommended as the first stop."

The case Cole referenced involved Philip, Tony, and Emma working in Paris to recover valuable art.

"Why the tour?" she asked, knowing security would be involved.

"The company wants the jewels seen before they're sold off. I believe it's to raise the price of already priceless jewels. There's also the historical aspect; it'll generate a large amount of press for them."

"What will happen to them eventually? Will they be sold?"

"Yes, and probably for a tidy sum."

Cole went on to the details of the pickup. "We have word they'll be on the Friday train. They will want to keep this as low profile as possible. I'd like you to take delivery at a stop before Chicago. I was also thinking, maybe you should take a friend with you," he suggested.

She frowned. "I'm not sure I want someone along with me. They might get in the way."

Cole tried to explain. "We need it to look like a short trip to shop or such thing. You're getting a reputation as a courier and an investigator."

"Hmm, your right. I have someone I could use. How about Savannah?" she suggested.

He considered that and said, "Not a bad idea. With her acting skills, she can blend in."

"I'll arrange it; she got back from her tour earlier than expected." Emma had seen her at the boarding house that morning.

"Fine, fine. I'll send the train tickets to you. You'll need to stay there a day and return. Of course," he teased, "you'll need to bring things back, to prove you shopped."

"Knowing Savannah, I think I can manage that," she said wryly. She documented the details of who she was meeting in her notebook, continuing to use shorthand to code them.

"I'll leave it to you to figure out the best way to carry them back," Cole said.

Emma thought about that and asked, "Do you have a list of the items?"

"Yes," he said. He reached back into the file and handed it to her.

She evaluated the list and said, "I have an idea that might work." She went on to explain it to him.

He nodded. "I like that. No one will suspect it."

"That wraps us up. I'll be working at the lawyer's office the rest of today if you have anything else to communicate on the case," Emma said.

"Very good. Thanks, Emma. I know this will go well with you involved." With that, she gathered up her belongings, said her goodbyes, and exited the room. She stopped by Jeremy's office to confirm she would meet him here before going home that evening.

On her way out, she grabbed her bike and headed to her temporary job at the Law office. She had started there a few months ago, working mornings as a typist and file clerk. As she and Mr. Pennington had gotten to know each other, he started to add to her responsibilities. Currently, she was working with him to put together background data for various clients.

The day should be interesting. She would be sitting in on interviews with a client, typing up notes as they worked on her testimony. This was the first time she had done this task.

She entered the office and stored her bike before approaching the secretary's desk. "Good morning, Ethan."

He didn't look up when he responded, "Conference room. Mr. Pennington is there and the client should be here soon."

"On my way in," she said and took out her notebook before knocking on the door.

Mr. Pennington called her to enter. Emma went in to be briefed about the client they would be interviewing that day.

CHAPTER 10

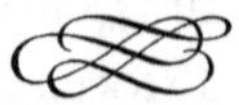

At the end of her day, Emma met Jeremy at the Pinkerton office. When she arrived, he was talking to one of the secretaries. He looked up when he heard the door, smiled, and asked, "Ready to go?"

"I am. Can I leave my bike here?" she asked.

The secretary, Stan Ellington, said, "Emma, I can drop it by on my way home." He lived a few houses down from them.

She smiled at him and said, "I would appreciate that."

"Anything you can share on the new case?" Jeremy asked as they were leaving.

"Not yet, but soon," she promised. They headed home, holding hands and talking quietly, enjoying their evening together. They had planned a dinner out, alone.

It was late when they arrived home, but Dora was waiting up for them, holding a sleeping Lottie. "Hi," she said softly. "I waited up to see how it went with your mom. I didn't get a chance to ask yesterday."

They sat with her in the sitting room and, speaking in the same tone as Dora, he said, "It went okay."

Emma looked at Dora and said, "Dora, she looks like Jeremy."

"How do you mean?" she asked curiously.

Emma explained. "She has his curly auburn hair and his eyes."

"Really?" said Dora, and the description stirred a memory. She looked at Jeremy and asked, "Was she at the gala?"

"I didn't see her, but Pops said she was," he confirmed.

"Emma!" she said, louder than expected. The baby stirred and she lowered her voice. "Emma, that's who Papa was dancing with."

"Pops did say they grew up together." Jeremy yawned the last words. "I'm going up to bed." He looked at Emma and asked, "Coming?"

"I'll be up in a while," she said as he leaned down to kiss her. She returned it warmly.

Emma and Dora watched as he strolled up the stairs. Dora leaned closer to Emma and asked, "Should we worry about Papa?"

She smiled slowly. "I don't think we have to worry about that. Papa knows how to take care of himself. Also, I think he'll tire of the excitement and go back to his basement."

Dora mulled that over before saying, "I'm not so sure about that. I remember how he was when Mama was alive. He wasn't always like he is now."

Emma hadn't expected that answer and responded in a serious tone, "I'll keep an eye on the situation."

CHAPTER 11

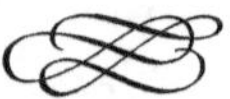

The next morning, Emma and Jeremy were readying for their day. She had just slipped her dress over her head, pulled it down, and asked, "Jeremy, will you help me with this?" She indicated the buttons on the back of her dress.

"Sure," he said, moving over to her.

As he handled the buttons, she asked, "What are you working on today?"

"I'm clearing up some casework and organizing some mug books. We're applying the method you reviewed in Paris: signaletics. We are adding in the measurements for the of head and body, shape formation of the ear, eyebrow, mouth, and eye."

"And that will also include such marking such as tattoos, scars, and personality characteristics?"

"Yes." As he finished the last button, he said, "All done." He gave her a pat on the back.

"Too bad we can't just get everyone's information on file to be able to access."

"Yes, but what file room could handle that?" he asked with a laugh.

She returned his laugh and asked, "Have you approached Jake about taking pictures to add to your books?"

"Yes, he's interested. I'm also thinking we should utilize Dora's skills at drawing when we have a description but a photo isn't available." He looked at his watch and asked, "Where are you today?"

"I'm still working at the lawyer's office—mornings this week and courier stuff in the afternoons. One of the jobs will have me at the museum later today."

"Tell Tony hello for me," he commented, watching her reaction.

"Oops," she said with a grimace, pausing while putting on her jacket. "I forgot about the last time we saw each other."

Jeremy saw her expression and said," I wouldn't worry. He just got a bit too far into his cups. I'm sure he didn't mean the things he said." He hoped he was right.

She straightened her shoulders, pulled her jacket down, and said, "It'll be fine." She put that out of her mind and looked at Jeremy. "Any thought on the questions you might ask your mother tonight?"

"No, not really. I mean, the hard question is: why haven't you come back before this?"

"Will you ask it?"

"I'm not sure. I'm wondering if I should just enjoy the time with her and let the past go."

"Can you do that?" asked Emma, knowing she would have to ask the hard questions.

"I'll see how it plays out," he said noncommittally.

She put her hand on his. "Jeremy, will you let me know if something comes up that you need my help on?"

He frowned and sat down slowly on the bed. "That's the same tone you and Pops had last night. Was there something you saw in her that I didn't?"

She sat next to him, took his hand, and said, "We're naturally cautious and we care deeply for you. Jeremy, I just don't want you to get hurt."

He squeezed her hand and sat mulling over what she'd said. He sighed. "I'll be going into this with my eyes opened."

"Good, that's all we ask."

"I would ask that you also give her a chance if she does turn out to be genuine."

"Deal," she said as she stood. She picked up her blue belt and clipped it around her waist. Her knife was strapped to her thigh and she started to gather her notebook and pens.

He stood to finish dressing and said, "Hey, Em, one more thing before you leave." He pulled her into a long embrace, then pulled back and said, "Off to work."

"Will you be coming home before going to dinner?"

"Yes," he said absently as he got his jacket. He slipped it on and departed to his room through the secret entrance. He called, "See you on the other side." He closed the door and bookshelf.

She waved her hand at him with a smile, then moved to the door and opened it. She saw Jeremy exit his room and said in a singsong voice, "Good morning, Jeremy."

He said in a similar tone, "Good morning, Emma," and held out his hand to her. She took it and walked with him downstairs. They ate breakfast with the family and headed out to their jobs. Emma got her bike out and walked Jeremy to the trolley. She kissed him, saying, "Goodbye. See you this evening."

"Yes," he said softly and rubbed his finger across her furrowed brow. "Don't worry about me."

"I'll try not to." She looked over his shoulder and saw the trolley arrive. "You need to get going."

He looked quickly over his shoulder and said, "I have to go," and grabbed her up for a fast kiss. He pulled back abruptly and grinned before running for the trolley.

She pulled in a shaky breath and watched him jump onto the moving car. Getting on her bike, she headed to the law office. As she arrived, she got off the bike and placed it on her shoulder to climb the stoop to enter the building. The job allowed her to learn more about the law, knowing that a better understanding could be beneficial in her investigations.

Making her way in, she could see Ethan was in place, already reviewing files on his desk. After she stored her bike, she walked up and said, "Ethan, what's on the calendar today?"

Without looking up, he reached for his bound black book. He opened it and said, "Full day. Mr. Pennington is in court all day on the Banks case."

Emma knew that case well. She had written briefs, sat in on interviews, pulled files, and double-checked the background of the witnesses. "What would you like me to work on today?" she asked, knowing she reported to him when Mr. Pennington was not there.

He finally met her eyes and said, "Mr. Pennington thought you might enjoy observing voir dire today." Emma knew from working with them that voir dire is a time prior to the trial when the lawyers can ask questions to determine the competency of a witness or juror.

She knew Ethan didn't like small talk, so she gathered up her materials and bike and headed to the courthouse. She hid the bike behind some bushes and walked in. Following the long hallway, she made her way to the courtrooms. She knew what court Mr. Pennington was assigned to and found the right location, confirming with a glance that he was in the room. He sat with his client at the table to the left of the judge, and she walked swiftly up to him. The client saw her approach and tapped his shoulder. He turned to see who it was.

"Emma," he said. "Thank you for coming up to the court today. We will be doing voir dire, questioning the jury. I would like you to sit behind me and watch how it works."

"Of course," she said. She leaned closer and asked in a low voice, "What if I see something that might help?"

He had seen her observation skills in the office and her background checks contained more than just data, they included an in-depth analysis of character. He wanted to see if she could use that skill to help him with the voir dire. "If you see something, get my attention. Tap your pencil on your notebook, but don't be obvious about it."

"Okay, but what if I don't see any concerns?" she asked, looking forward to observing the process.

"Then I will use my best judgment." He stopped talking as the judge entered and took his place.

Emma thought about the interview she'd sat in on yesterday. It involved the case she was here to observe; the plaintiff was being charged with bigamy. Mr. Pennington had reviewed it with her before meeting the client for the first time.

"Bigamy?" Emma asked Mr. Pennington as they waited for their client to arrive.

Mr. Pennington explained that bigamy was when a person was married to more than one spouse at a time. It was a federal enactment of the United States Congress that was signed into law on July 8, 1862, by President Abraham Lincoln.

"Our client, as you know, is Elle Gilmore/Banks, and her husband, Mr. Banks, contends she knowingly married a second man—Mr. Gilmore—after he went away for business," he explained.

Emma had completed the background check and asked, "Wasn't her husband gone more than fourteen years? Isn't only a year required for her to claim abandonment as grounds for a divorce?"

"Well, it might be," he allowed, "except she didn't wait the mandatory year and she never filed for divorce. He will also try to prove that he sent money in that first year and, when she did remarry, she did so without a divorce."

"Why is the money important?" she asked.

"Unfortunately, it's that one thing, that money in the first year, could meet the provision of necessary support and prove he didn't abandon her."

"He was contending that his sending letters and some money were necessary support? That would be so little. Also, why come back now?" she asked, bewildered by his intent. *What is he trying to accomplish with all of this?*

"That is what we need to find out. We need to know his motivation for coming forward after all this time."

"Is he staying at a local hotel?" asked Emma, thinking ahead.

"We have information from his lawyer that he's at the Smith Tower," he commented, watching her take notes.

"I'll check to see if he has talked to anyone. Can I talk to your client's husband, er... her current husband?" she asked with a slight smile.

He chuckled in return. "Well, yes."

She checked her watch attached to her blouse and said, "I have an appointment this afternoon. I'll follow up."

"We have some time; our court date is set for next month."

Back to the present day in court

Emma sat in the gallery behind Mr. Pennington, evaluating the jury pool as they waited for the judge to enter. The rows had been marked so the public would not accidentally sit with jury members. *Who we want on the jury are people who have an understanding of our client's plight.* She watched as the court officer escorted the first twelve people into the jury box. Emma knew that, once one juror was removed, another from the individuals gathered would replace them.

She wanted to tell Mr. Pennington something before they started, so she dropped her notebook to get his attention. When he leaned over to pick it up for her, she leaned in and said, "We don't want strong personalities. We need ones that understand the woman's role."

The judge looked at Mr. Pennington and said, "You may begin." He nodded, stood up, and approached the jury box to start his questioning.

As he walked up, Emma studied the jurors. *No women,* she thought with a shake of her head. *One day, we'll be better represented.*

He asked a few general questions of the group. "First, how many of you are married?"

An easy question to start, Emma thought as she continued to watch. Hands were raised quickly and most were married.

He continued. "How many of you have been divorced?" A few hands came up slower. He started with those men first. He pointed to one, saying, "You, sir, are you happier since your divorce?"

"Well, yes," he said loudly. Laughter could be heard in the courtroom. The judge sent a warning glance toward them. They quieted down in response.

"Why is that, sir?" asked Mr. Pennington.

"Well, she wasn't nice and she wouldn't fix my dinner," he answered candidly. More laughter from the court.

The judge had enough and lowered his gavel, demanding, "Silence." The court quieted again.

Mr. Pennington looked around the room and didn't see Emma's pencil move. He asked similar questions of the other divorced persons. He kept all three.

He started questioning the married men. "Sir, are you happily married?" The man he was asking squirmed in his chair and avoided eye contact. At this point, it didn't matter what his answer was. Mr. Pennington saw Emma's pencil going. He said, "That is all right, you don't have to answer. We would like to thank this juror and dismiss him." He continued; they had gotten four that might be more willing to listen to the reasons why their client decided to move on with her life without getting a divorce.

Mr. Pennington completed his questions and strolled over to his desk. He murmured so only Emma could hear him. "Any others you want to strike?"

She dropped her notebook and, as she picked it up, murmured, "The preacher and the schoolteacher."

He nodded, pretending to look at his notes before signaling to the judge. "I would like to remove two people." He listed their names.

The judge nodded and dismissed the jurors, thanking them for their time. Two others took their place and Mr. Pennington sat down with no further objections. The State, who was prosecuting the matter, went next. His examination of the jury was more perfunctory. Emma could see he felt confident and didn't make any changes. The judge set the trial date, locked in the jury, and dismissed everyone.

Emma rose with the others and went out ahead of Mr. Pennington. As she exited the court, she looked to her left and saw Mr. Banks, the defendant's first husband, the man who had started this. She was curious about him. The background check she had completed indicated he didn't live in the area but instead lived in Cleveland, Ohio. *Judging by the cut of his clothes, it looks like he is doing quite well.*

She continued watching him and saw him staring down the hall behind her. She turned, following his gaze to Mr. Gilmore, the defendant's second husband. His anger seemed focused on Mr. Gilmore and not on his wife. *Was it because he'd married his wife or was it something else?* Emma pulled out her notebook to refresh her memory on the relationship between the husbands.

Their interview indicated the two men were close friends before the marriage and Mr. Gilmore was the best man at the wedding.

She continued to watch the scene play out. At that moment, Mrs. Gilmore exited the courtroom with Mr. Pennington. She immediately went over to Mr. Gilmore and was drawn into his arms. Emma glanced at Mr. Banks to see his reaction. His face darkened, his expression meaner, and he started toward them. Emma reached into her pocket for her clutch knife, ready to step in if needed. He took two steps toward them and noticed the policeman in the hallway. Turning abruptly, he left the building.

Hmm, she thought, *we may need to schedule some protection for Mr. and Mrs. Gilmore. I'll mention it to Mr. Pennington.* Once the threat was gone, she gave one last glance toward Mr. Pennington and the Gilmores before heading out.

She would meet Mr. Pennington back at the office. As she left, she noticed the sun was up and bright. *It's a lovely day,* she thought. She retrieved her bike from the bushes and rode it back to the office.

As she was storing it in the office, she heard Ethan say, "Back already?"

"Yes, jury selection went fast," she said brightly.

He commented, not looking up, "That's good."

Mr. Pennington heard them as he walked into the building. "It was excellent. Emma, step into my office, please."

Ethan did look up when this request was made and seemed surprised. Most of Emma's instructions came through him. She would like to have stuck her tongue out at him, but thought better of it and followed Mr. Pennington instead.

Emma entered his office and watched as he set his briefcase on the desk. He sat quickly and leaned forward. "Emma, sit down," he said briskly. She sat in a heavy chair in front of the desk. "I was very impressed with your performance at the courthouse today."

"Thank you," she said, waiting for him to continue.

"Emma, I think we can work together more. Would you be interested in helping with future voir dire's?"

She tried to stay calm as she answered, "I'd like to help with that."

"I think we could be a good team."

She liked the idea of further involvement in this and other cases. Something occurred to her, and she said, "I'm thinking we might find something that could, hopefully, get this case closed before the trial date. The background we put together was based on information we have here in town and some telegrams we used to confirm his business address."

"What are you thinking?" he asked expectantly.

"I've been thinking about Hugo Banks and his long absence. We've taken him at his word about his life outside of Chicago. I'd like to go there and look more into his background. Has he been alone all of this time? Why hasn't he come back before now? Why did he stop sending money that first year? I'm thinking it's odd that he married her and left town immediately. He's accusing her of bigamy, but was *he* the perfect husband?"

"You make a good point," he said contemplatively. "Do you have an idea?"

"Yes," she said, pulling out her notebook, "what is the business address?" She took it down and said, "I have another project that will put me in that area in the next few days. I'd like to go to his house and see if there's anything out of the ordinary."

"You might find nothing," he suggested.

"Or I might find something," she countered.

"Let's take a chance and have you go there to investigate. I have something that might help; in speaking to the client, I learned she was dating Mr. Gilmore before her marriage to Mr. Banks."

"Really? Why the switch-up?"

"It happens that Mr. Gilmore and Mrs. Gilmore were quite serious and then something happened to have him leave town abruptly. During the following period, Mr. Banks started spending a large amount of time with her."

"She was lonely," Emma guessed.

"It looks that way, and he took advantage. They were married on the day Mr. Gilmore returned."

Emma frowned. "I'll need to interview the husband when I return."

"I think that would be a good idea."

CHAPTER 12

She was mulling over her ideas for the trip and how to tie both cases together as she rode over to the museum. Once there she stopped her bike and placed it on her shoulder and headed up the marble staircase leading up to the entrance. The pickup would be packages that needed to go to the rail station. Entering the museum; the guards took the bike from her to store it and directed her to Tony's office.

Casual, she thought. She didn't want to add to his worries, but she needed to check in with him. Placing her hand on the door, she raised it and knocked. When his voice called out for her to enter, she opened the door and saw him busy at his desk.

He looked up and said, "Good afternoon, Emma. I appreciate your taking this package to the train station for me."

"It's no problem." He was trying to rush her out without talking, but she wasn't going to let him off the hook that easily. She was always one to ask the hard question. "Tony, do you have a minute?"

He looked resigned. He knew she would want to talk, even if he didn't want to. "Yes."

She shut the door and moved farther into the room. "Tony, are you okay? I was worried about you."

He didn't pretend to misunderstand and said, "I'm fine. Truly. I think you were right; I missed Peggy and drank too much."

"Do you want to talk about it?"

He looked at her, smiled, and said, "I love that you care about me."

"You know I always will."

"I know. I sent Peggy a letter this morning, telling her I'm an idiot and want her to come back."

"That's wonderful, not that you're an idiot." She laughed. "She's a lovely person."

"Yes, and probably too good for me."

"It looks like I don't need to involve myself further."

"No," he agreed.

"I'll take the package and head out."

"See you soon."

"You, too."

CHAPTER 13

That evening after dinner, Emma covered the information with the team on the bigamy case. "Why would anyone want more than one spouse? Isn't one plenty?" asked Tim, wondering about people.

Dora laughed and teased, "I agree, I wouldn't want to have to manage two of you."

"Oh, I don't know," teased Tim. "You could have an army and still manage."

"That is true. When will you leave, Emma?" asked Dora, changing the subject.

"I expect by the weekend."

Savannah was there and spoke up. "I'll be accompanying her. I understand there's some excellent shopping in that area." Emma had reviewed the other case with her and she knew not to mention it to anyone.

Dora didn't change her expression but thought something else was going on. *Emma wouldn't just take someone with her on a case, even Savannah.* Dora knew the rules and wouldn't ask in front of the group.

"It'll be nice to have the company on the trip," Emma said warmly.

Cole asked, "How long do you expect the case to take?"

She knew he was asking when she would be back with the jewels. "Oh," she said casually, "just two-to-three days. It shouldn't be long."

Emma looked at Jake and said, "I will need to borrow your camera."

"Will you take care of it?" he asked seriously.

"Of course," she responded in the same tone.

"I will have it ready and loaded with film."

"Thank you."

As they finished their meeting, Dora mentioned, "We filled another room at the boarding house. A Mr. and Mrs. Miller. He's a war veteran and he and his wife are newlyweds."

"That's nice," commented Emma, "that they found each other."

"They're due here in two or three days."

"I'd like to meet them," Emma said sincerely.

"Emma," said Cole, "can you walk me out?"

"I can." She looked over at Jeremy and said, "I'll join you in the sitting room."

Jeremy said, "Bye, Pops. See you at the office." He watched them leave. *It must involve the other case; I wonder how this connects to the trip Emma is about to take?*

Cole and Emma walked out the front door; he slipped his hand into his pocket and pulled out an envelope. "These are your and Savannah's tickets. Your rooms are also arranged and paid for. You'll be there under your names; it's less trouble that way."

"Agreed," she said as she took the envelope and checked its contents.

"Emma," he said, his voice lowering with his concern, "be careful. The people who want these jewels will be watching closely."

"We'll take every precaution and return safely," she promised.

"Okay then." He kissed her on the cheek and headed down the stoop toward home.

Watching him closely, she acknowledged she had been worried about him as of late. Ellis was spending more and more time with Abbey. She would have to keep an eye on Cole.

CHAPTER 14

The next day, Emma was getting organized for her afternoon meeting. She looked at her list and confirmed she had everything she needed. She grabbed her hat and headed down to get her bike for her appointment at the museum.

A lunch date had been arranged with Tony to confirm the plans for picking up the jewels. She made her way there and placed her bike on her shoulder to enter the museum. The guards took it from her and told her Tony was waiting in his office. She smiled as she took her lunch pail and headed that way. Knocking lightly, Tony's voice called, "Come in."

She entered and saw both Philip and Tony were present. Philip said, "Emma, thank you for making time for us today."

She sent a quick smile to Tony as she handed him her lunch pail and sat down. Philip said, "Business first."

Emma nodded and looked toward Tony, who also nodded. She pulled out her notebook to read the details the Pinkertons had provided. She started with, "We have confirmed that Tiffany & Co. is sending a selection of the French Crown Jewels to the

Museum from New York City. They've already set out to the predetermined location."

"How are they protected?" asked Philip.

"They'll have two guards accompanying the courier. The plan is for me to go by rail and meet them halfway. I'll meet the courier and take it over from there."

"By yourself?" asked Tony.

"No, we've approached Savannah. The cover story is that we're shopping and will be there overnight." She went into detail on how it would work.

CHAPTER 15

Friday morning came quickly; Savannah and Emma would be taking the early train. "I can take you and Savannah to the station," said Jeremy, yawning and sitting up in the bed.

"No, we're good. I've arranged a carriage for us." She closed her bag with a snap and walked over to the bed. She leaned down to kiss him and said, "I appreciate the thought."

When she got close, he pulled her to him and said, "I'll miss you."

"I'll miss you also." She kissed him softly. She leaned into him for a moment and asked, "How is your visit going with your mom?"

He pulled her closer to him and laid his chin on her head. "She's talking but she's used to hiding parts of herself. I think it'll take some time. I just hope I have it."

"Do you expect her to leave soon?"

"No, just a feeling."

She kissed him again and got up to finish getting dressed.

He stayed in bed, watching her close her bag and place her

knives in her hat and on her thigh. "Do you need help with the bag?"

"No, don't get up. It's early. You stay in bed," she said in a low voice. She heard someone going by the door. "Sounds like Savannah's moving downstairs. I have to go," she said, picking up her bag and heading to the door.

Smiling at him, she left the room and headed downstairs. She saw Savannah ready and waiting by the door She asked expectantly, holding her bag and a hand on the door knob, "Ready to go?"

Emma nodded and slipped on her hat, motioning for Savannah to exit ahead of her. Their carriage was waiting on the street for them. They handed the driver their bags and waited for him to help them inside. "Train station, please," indicated Emma.

They were silent as they made their way. The driver helped them down from the carriage, and they paid him before walking toward their train. Emma said, "We should go straight to our car."

They found their sleeper and settled in. Emma asked, "Do you want to go over the plans for both cases?"

"Yes, please. I like to be prepared."

"First, we arrive and check-in at the hotel. From there, we will go to the Cramer Paper Company. I'll be going in alone, dressed as a courier, and you'll wait for me outside."

CHAPTER 16

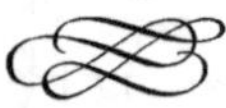

CRAMER PAPER COMPANY

*E*mma entered the office dressed in pants, a loose shirt with a vest, and a slightly worn jacket. Her hair was braided and tucked into her hat, giving her a boyish appearance. Savannah waited for her outside, as Emma directed.

Emma approached the reception desk and indicated the envelope she was carrying. "I have a package for Mr. Hugo Banks."

"I can take that," said the man sitting there.

Emma pulled it back. "No, this has to be given directly to Mr. Banks."

"Well, he isn't in the office just now," he said, sounding exasperated. He tried again to take it.

She kept it from him and countered with, "Do you have a home address? This has to be delivered today."

He gave her a long look, pushed his chair back, and said, "Yes, just a moment." He pulled open the file drawer beside his desk, flipped through the files, and pulled out a card. "That's interesting, I hadn't noticed that before."

Emma waited for him to continue his thoughts.

"There are two addresses. One for here in Cleveland and one for Cleveland Heights—ten minutes away."

Two, Emma thought. *That is interesting.* She pulled out her notebook and asked, "Could you let me see them?" He handed her the cards. She copied the addresses and handed them back, saying, "I'll check both. Thank you so much for your time."

He put the cards back up and returned to work.

She exited the office building and found Savannah. She held up her notebook and said, with a grin, "Got it."

Savannah grinned back and said, "Where to now?"

Emma looked down at her clothes. "First, I think I need to change." She linked arms with Savannah to stroll back to the hotel. "You won't believe what I found out. He has two addresses."

"Two? Why two?" asked Savannah, bewildered.

"I think it might be two different wives."

CHAPTER 17

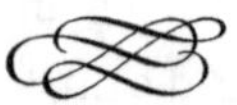

The trip to the hotel was made in silence, with Emma and Savannah lost in their thoughts about what they'd learned When they were alone in their hotel room, Savannah said in amazement, "Two?"

"And the first one is in Chicago," she reminded her.

"Three," said Savannah as she collapsed on the bed, looking very confused.

Emma watched with a slight smile as she changed into a light blue skirt and fitted high neck white lace blouse. "Don't try to make sense of it. People are motivated by things that others wouldn't understand."

"Yes, I guess so," she said, pulling herself into a sitting position. "All right, what's the plan?"

Emma finished packing her camera and other supplies as she explained her plans and Savannah's role in them. After the briefing, they picked up their things and headed to the front of the hotel where carriages stood waiting. They gave the first address to the driver, it was time to meet the second Mrs. Banks.

As they pulled up, they noted the house was a lovely green

Victorian style with white trim and flower boxes in the windows. Emma looked at Savannah, and Savannah commented softly, "Just believe what you're saying."

Emma nodded and climbed down with the help of the driver. After they paid him, they walked up the wide steps to the porch. They saw two girls of about eight and ten sitting on the porch swing. Emma glanced over at them and asked, "Is your mother home?"

The older girl looked up from her drawing pad and said, "Mama's inside. Do you want me to call her?"

"I would appreciate that, thank you," Emma said.

The older girl walked to the door, opened it, and called, "Mama!" She went back to pick up her drawing pad and, before starting her sketch, said, "She should be out momentarily."

"Thank you," said Emma with a smile.

"You're welcome," she replied.

Emma looked at Savannah and mouthed, "Polite."

Savannah nodded.

A lovely woman came to the door. She didn't notice the ladies waiting for her. "Patrice, did you call me?"

"Yes, Mama. These ladies wanted to see you," she said, indicating Savannah and Emma.

As Mrs. Banks turned toward them, Emma watched her closely. She appeared to be in her early thirties, pretty and elegant, with her dark brown hair worn in a chignon. Her clothes also seemed well made.

She looked at the two strangers curiously and said, "I'm Mrs. Banks; can I help you?"

Emma took the lead. "I'm Emma Evans and this is Savannah Woods. We're with a new women's group here in town. We're doing an article for our magazine on important women in the area."

"Really?" she asked. "And I was selected?" Her cheeks flushed and her smile went wider. She believed them, it would make the subterfuge easier to carry off.

"Yes," said Savannah, assuming her role as interviewer and distracting her so Emma could look around. "We have some questions for you and then we would like to take some pictures of you and the house."

"Oh, that is lovely. Would you like to come inside?" she said graciously as she backed up and held the door open for them.

"Thank you," said Savannah. She kept talking while Emma took in her surroundings. She got an idea of the layout of the house. The foyer was lovely; it was a light blue and white trim. A small table and chair sat in the corner. To her right was a large opening revealing a dining room with a large brown table. To her left, there was a sitting room, done in the same white and light blue tones as the foyer. The mantle was visible from the doorway and had pictures on it. Emma nudged Savannah; she got the message and said motioning to the sitting room, "Such a lovely room. Can we start here?"

"Yes, of course."

Emma stepped over to the mantel to see the pictures. It was definitely Mr. Banks. "Can I take some pictures of the room?" Emma asked, holding up the camera she had brought with her.

"For the article?" Mrs. Banks asked, delighted. "That would be wonderful."

Emma pulled out her camera and started taking pictures. She made sure to get more than just the mantle.

Savannah continued with her questions and asked about the mantel. "Is that your husband in that picture?"

"Well, yes!" She laughed. "He's a wonderful man. We've been married for close to fourteen years."

Fourteen years, Emma thought, continuing to take pictures. *That's very close to the number the defendant has been married. So, who is the bigamist here?*

"Can we have one of you?" Emma inquired.

"That would be lovely. How would you like me? By the chair?" she suggested.

"That would be just fine," said Emma. She steadied her camera and took several pictures.

Savannah inquired, "Can we see the rest of the house?"

"Of course." They finished their tour and assured her that the article would be coming out soon. Savannah waited until they had walked about a block away before she asked, "Do you think she knows?"

"About her husband? No, she was too open. Allowing us in the house was not expected."

"What about that second address?" asked Savannah.

She checked her watch and said, "Lunch first?"

"Yes, please." They hailed a carriage and inquired about the next address located in Cleveland Heights.

"It will be about twenty minutes from here," the driver commented.

"Do you know if there are any local restaurants near there?" Emma asked.

"I do. I can take you to one."

They agreed and had a nice carriage ride to the restaurant. As he helped them down, he inquired, "Should I come back for you?"

Emma handed him the money and said, "No, we'll walk there. Thank you." They watched as he drove off.

CHAPTER 18

They finished lunch and strolled to Mr. Banks' second address. "Same as before?" asked Savannah.

"Yes. It worked last time, Let's give it a try," commented Emma.

The house was very similar on the outside to the other house, even the colors—green and white. Kids were playing in the yard, two girls about the same age as the first two from this morning. She and Savannah continued to the door and knocked. As they waited, the sound of heels clicking on the floor reached them. A woman opened the door, perhaps a little older than the other Mrs. Banks. She smiled, though Emma thought her face was more guarded than the first wife. She asked, "May I help you?"

Savannah spoke up and said, "Are you, Mrs. Banks?"

"I am, and you are?" she inquired, her tone pleasant.

"I'm Savannah Woods and this is Emma Evans." She gave the same story as before about the women's organization interviewing important women in town.

This Mrs. Banks gave them a look through narrowed eyes, the pleasant expression fading. "Won't you come in?"

She stepped back and they entered the house. The second house was set up eerily the same as the other one. They went to a similar sitting room, with a similar mantel picture. *Two wives; no, three wives. Why?* Emma was itching to take her pictures but would have to wait for the questions. She glanced at the wife, seeing the distrust in her eyes and the set expression on her face. *This conversation is going to go differently than the last one.*

This Mrs. Banks didn't wait for them to start. She stated, "Caught on to him, have you?"

"I'm sorry, I don't understand," said Savannah, trying to stay on script.

Mrs. Banks looked at both of them. "I know why you're here. You found out about my husband's other wives."

Emma knew their cover had been blown. "May we sit down?"

She nodded and indicated the settee.

They sat and Emma started. "Okay, yes, we are investigating him. He's turning over evidence against another wife."

"The first one? The one in Chicago?" she inquired.

"Yes," Emma confirmed.

"I should have known. He had a thing about her." She stood, went to a box sitting next to the couch, and pulled out a newspaper. It was folded to the one article and she handed it to Emma.

Emma took the paper and read it out loud. "Mr. and Mrs. Gilmore are celebrating their fourteenth wedding anniversary and a great success in their business."

"He fixated on that story; he would pull it out and read it over and over again," Mrs. Banks said with a sigh.

"But he left her. Why do that if he wanted her?" asked Emma with a frown.

"He never really wanted her, you see. He just didn't want Mr. Gilmore to have her."

"This was about Mr. Gilmore, the man she married after him?" Emma asked, wondering if they had found a key puzzle piece.

"Yes, he had everything a little better than Hugo. He had the better grades in school and always got first place in contests. Hugo just felt he couldn't win, but after Mr. Gilmore left town, he pursued Lily, doing whatever he could to get her to agree to marry him."

"But if she loved Mr. Gilmore, why did she say yes to Mr. Banks?" asked Savannah.

"Hugo let slip that, a few years ago, he lied and told her Mr. Gilmore had met someone else on his trip and didn't want her anymore."

"She believed him?" Savannah asked in disbelief.

"She was young and very naïve," she said with a shrug. "He not only lied; he also hid something from her."

"What was that?" Emma asked curiously.

"Mr. Gilmore planned to ask her to marry him as soon as he returned."

"So, all of this was so Mr. Gilmore couldn't have her as his wife," Emma said contemplatively. "But they got together anyway."

"Yes. He thought she wouldn't have done that without trying to divorce him. Too proper, he figured."

"You knew about the other two wives. Why did you stay with him?" Emma asked, curious about the circumstance this Mrs. Banks found herself in.

She got up and went to look at Hugo's picture on the mantel; she turned slowly back to them and explained. "I didn't know initially. I was young when we met and my parents had passed away. I wanted a family and I knew he could take care of me financially. We had been married for over 10 years when I found out. We had the girls and I didn't want to break up the family. He splits his time between the houses."

She looked at them both and asked, "What will you do with this information? Will you turn us in?"

"I won't do anything without giving you fair warning," Emma stated.

She squinted her eyes, not sure she believed her.

"I give you, my word."

She took a moment to consider Emma and said, "Okay, then. I trust you."

"Thank you."

"If you need a place to go… if this situation doesn't work out for you, I have an address for people who can help with the next steps." Emma quickly wrote out the Carlyle Foundation's address and Clair's name. She handed it to Mrs. Banks.

"Thank you," she said graciously, taking the information.

"Would you mind if I take a few pictures for my files?" asked Emma.

"As long as you keep them private," Mrs. Banks cautioned.

"I will," she promised.

Emma took pictures, identical to those of the other house, and Mrs. Banks graciously allowed one of her. They finished and said their goodbyes.

After they left the house and were out of hearing range, Savannah asked, "Will you keep your word?"

She looked at her and said, "Yes. I think this will give us a bargaining position."

Savannah nodded and asked, "Where to now?"

She checked her watch. "I think dress shopping is next."

Savannah grinned. "That sounds like a great idea."

They spotted a carriage and waved for it. It pulled up, and they asked to be taken to their appointment at the dressmakers. They had seen some previous designs they thought would suit them.

CHAPTER 19

At the dress shop, Savannah twirled in her blue jewel-toned suit dress. It had a full bustle in the back. "I haven't had a dress with a bustle before. I always thought they looked a bit ridiculous. But honestly, I kind of like it." Their measurements had been sent over when the plans for the trip were first put together, so only minimal changes had been necessary.

Emma came out a lovely vision in pink, a suit dress similar to Savannah's.

"Oh, lovely," the seamstress said as she saw them together.

"The measurements are perfect," said Emma admiringly.

"Yes. It was short notice, but we were able to get them completed."

"The adjustments we mentioned?"

The seamstress nodded and showed her how to access them.

"Good."

"I have something else for you." She went to the next room and brought out two large boxes, saying, "I have some lovely hats for you to try."

She pulled them out and Emma said, "I like those." Savannah

agreed and they tried on the hats and Emma said, "These are perfect. We'll wear these out."

They thanked her for the clothes and the fast service. Emma gave her the envelope Cole had sent to pay for the dresses. The seamstress' eyes widened at the amount. "Thank you!"

As they exited the shop, Emma said, "I believe we have a bit of time before we are due back to pick up our bags. Would you like to shop some more?"

"That would be nice." They browsed a few more stores and boutiques before returning to the hotel. They entered and went to the desk to confirm their train tickets and their luggage pickup. As they were finishing the details, Emma felt a tap on her arm. She turned toward it and saw a boy of about ten.

"Miss," he inquired. He waved to her to bend down, so he could speak into her ear. "They want to see you over there."

She glanced over and said, "I'll be there," and slipped him some coins. He grinned brightly and left.

Emma looked at Savannah and said casually, "Let's stroll around the hotel a bit before heading out."

Savannah got the silent message and said, "Lovely idea." She took Emma's arm and they walked around the lobby and into the area where the conference rooms were located.

"I heard there's some art this way," indicated Emma.

They headed away from the lobby and entered the conference room on their right. As they did so, Emma shut the door softly behind her and said, "Mr. Morgan, I presume." She studied at the average-looking man with one bodyguard.

"Miss Evans," he said.

She nodded and said, "This is Savannah Woods. She's helping out on this case."

"Miss Woods and Miss Evans, we appreciate your help with this transport." He took his briefcase and placed it on the table. As he opened it up the brilliance of the diamonds took their breath away.

"How will you transport this safely?" he asked.

Emma smiled and looked at Savannah. "Could you turn around?"

The man looked confused at her directions to Savannah. She turned and Emma reached into her bustle and opened a slot. "We have several of these made and lined to house the jewels."

He smiled. "Ingenious." He removed them and handed them to her to place in the hiding place. Emma turned to allow them to do the same to her.

Once the jewels were safely hidden away, Mr. Morgan said in a satisfied voice, "It has been a pleasure doing business with you ladies. You'll be heading to the train directly?"

"Yes. We'll wire you when we have made the delivery to the museum."

"Very good. We'll be staying in the hotel for a few more days."

Emma nodded. "That will help with our cover. We'll head out now. Please wait a while before exiting."

"We will. Thank you, Miss Evans and Miss Woods."

They made their way to the rail station and entered their sleeper car. As they opened the door, they saw the bags were already there. The hotel had arranged for them to be delivered to the train ahead of them.

Emma opened her bag and said, "I've been searched. Check your bag."

Savannah opened her bag and said, "Yes, mine was searched also. So, you think they know why we were here?"

Emma said, "Possibly. They may have checked as a precaution. We only have a two-day trip to get home. We will need to be on guard," As she saw the porter passing, she opened the door and waved him over saying, "We're tired and would like some privacy." She gave him a tip.

He took the money and nodded. "I'll take care of it."

She went back into the room and closed the door. "That should give us our privacy. We should be left alone."

"Good," Savannah said as she fluffed the bustle and sat down.

The train moved forward with a jerk. Once the motion smoothed out, they took off their hats. The day moved slowly into the evening. Emma kept her bag close to her; she had Jake's camera in there and she knew there would be dire consequences if she did not return with it. *Both from Mr. Pennington and Jake*, she thought.

As the evening progressed, she thought, *Maybe this will be a quiet trip.* At that moment, there was a knock on the door.

"Odd, I told him we wanted to be left alone," said Emma.

"It might be the dinner we ordered earlier," suggested Savannah.

"Yes, that's true," said Emma absently.

"I'll get it," said Savannah, standing up to approach the door.

Emma was beginning to unbutton her jacket when she noticed something odd about the porter's shadow. The figure was much taller than the porter she had spoken with earlier, and he appeared to have two other people with him. Savannah was reaching for the door when Emma shouted, "Stop!"

The door swung open before Savannah could reach it. Three men pointed guns at them. "Hands up, please." Emma did not have access to either of her knives. She and Savannah were pressed to the windows in the car.

The smallest of the three spoke, "Let's move out."

"Move?" asked Emma. "Where to?"

"Just follow directions," the little man said, waving his gun at her.

Emma grabbed her bag and left the sleeper at their direction. There was no one in the hallways at this late hour. They pushed them to the end of the car, toward the outer door. One man pried it open while the others watched. They were traveling at a fast clip and would soon be approaching a river.

The man, apparently their leader, said, "The jewels. We know you have them."

Emma frowned. "Who are you?"

He replied his voice harsh, "That's none of your business! Now, give us those jewels!"

She looked at them, knowing arguments wear futile. There

was only one way out and she said to no one in particular, "Jump wide, slide, then barrel roll."

Savannah got the message as Emma reached for her arm with one hand, the other clutching her bag, before pulling them both through the door that had been opened. As Emma planned, there was a grassy incline before they started over water. Both she and Savannah slid, then tumbled down the hill. Gunfire sounded from the train and, as they rolled to a stop, she shouted, "Stay down!"

They stayed crouched for a few moments as the train went by before Savannah inquired, "Is anyone coming after us?"

"I don't think so," said Emma, straightening slowly watching the departing train. "I expect they'll try again in Chicago." They sat for another moment and she asked, "Are you okay? Stand up and let's see if we have any injuries to deal with."

Savannah stood slowly and said, "Yes, I think I'm okay."

"Me, too," Emma said. "Train travel has been exciting lately."

"Well, at least no crash this time," said Savannah wryly.

"Agreed," said Emma. "Turn around, let me check the jewels." They were still in their compartments and appeared to be unharmed.

"I will check yours." Savannah checked Emma, and again, no problems. "So, what now?" she asked.

Emma looked around, recognizing the area. "I think I know someone who lives nearby. We'll head that way." She grabbed her bag and they helped each other up the incline.

As they got onto firmer footing, Savannah asked, "So, who do you know in the area?"

"You know Clair's safe house, the one where we move women who need protection? This is one of those ladies we helped."

"When was the last time you saw her? Will she remember you?"

"I think so. I saw her at her wedding about a year ago. She was very happy."

Savannah gave her a look. "Did you investigate her new husband?"

"I did. It was my wedding present to her," she said with a laugh.

"Was she upset that you looked into his background?"

"No, I think she was relieved. Marriage is such a gamble and so much is taken at someone's word." They walked and walked. "Not much further now," said Emma. A large house appeared ahead and to the right. The area was lush and green. They walked up to the house and Emma knocked on the door.

A few moments later, it opened and a little maid asked, "Yes, how may I help you?"

"I would like to see Mrs. Landry, please."

They heard a woman's voice behind the maid. "Who is it, Betsy?" Emma knew that voice and smiled.

Betsy moved out of the way and they saw Mrs. Landry. "Emma! How wonderful to see you. Betsy, let her in." The maid was still hesitant to let the disheveled women into the door but backed away.

Emma and Savannah entered the large foyer; dark wood gleamed from a recent cleaning. "Alison, this is Savannah Woods."

"It is nice to meet you," commented Savannah.

Alison got a good look at them and said, "Goodness! Were you in an accident? Please follow me into the sitting room. Betsy, please bring us some tea and cakes and some cookies."

"That does sound good," said Savannah with a sigh and she sat down on one of the sofas.

Emma pulled her up before she hit the chair, "Wait a moment."

"Oh, yes," remembered a tired Savannah and turned around with her back to Emma.

She unhooked Savannah's bustle and turned to have Savannah due her own.

"That is an odd thing, a removable bustle. It would make it more comfortable to sit down," Alison said, examining the back of the dresses.

Emma folded up the bustles and put them into her bag.

"Now, tell me what happened."

"Well," Emma started.

Savannah interrupted in an excited voice, "We jumped from a train!"

"Really?" Alison asked, fascinated. "Why on earth would you do that?"

Emma looked at her and smirked. "We didn't plan it."

"So, tell me!" exclaimed Alison.

"Not much to tell. Some men were trying to get something from us." She cut her eyes to Savannah, who got the message.

"And you jumped out of a moving train? What did they want?"

At that moment, Betsy came in pushing a tea table. They waited until she set it up and left.

Savannah had already made her way to the cart and was pouring tea for everyone.

"Oh, it's a case," Alison said knowingly.

Emma leaned forward and said in earnest, "You must not tell anyone."

Alison assured her, "I would never say anything. I owe you my life." They clasped hands for a long moment. Savannah brought over their tea and as they finished Alison said, "We need to get you both into some clean clothes."

Emma said, "We would appreciate that. Also, is there any way we can get some transportation to Chicago?"

Alison looked thoughtful and said," I'll ask my husband. Jim should know what to do."

"When will he be home?"

She checked her watch and said, "Soon. Let's get you both cleaned up."

Emma said, "Just a moment," and opened her notebook, writing quickly. "Could you see that this note is sent by telegram to this address?"

Alison took the note and said, "Of course. Let me step out and get this taken care of."

As she left the room, Emma looked at Savannah and said, "I sent a note to Cole to let him know we're not on the train and to be on the lookout for the three men who tried to rob us."

Alison was back in a few minutes and escorted the ladies upstairs. They went into what must be a guest room. "You both get comfortable and let me get you some clothes to change into." She closed the door quietly behind her, allowing them some privacy.

Savannah looked down at her dress in regret. "It was a lovely dress."

Emma laughed suddenly. "Yes, they were."

Savannah saw the humor in the situation and said, "Well, that just means you owe me another dress."

"That I do." She took off her jacket and held it in front of her. It was shredded down the back. "It was a pretty dress," she said regretfully.

Alison walked in and said, "There's fresh water coming up for you." She laid down the dresses she carried on the bed. "Emma, I think you'll like the dark green and, Savannah, for you I have the dark blue."

"These are lovely. Thank you," said Savannah, touching the dresses.

"Yes, thank you," said Emma. "We'll get these back to you."

"No," she said softly. "Consider them a gift."

"Do you think we'll be able to get transportation to Chicago this evening?" asked Emma.

"I think Jim will provide it," said Alison. "I'll leave you now."

They cleaned up and finished dressing. Emma looked down at her boots and said, "I think it's time for a replacement." The leather was torn, and the heels look beat up.

"Me, too," said Savannah, pulling up her skirt and showing shoes in a similar condition.

"Let's go downstairs and see if Jim has arrived," suggested Emma.

They walked down together and saw a nice-looking man leaning against the molding at the entrance of the sitting room. When he saw Emma, he straightened and came over to them. "Emma! So good to see you again." He was genuinely happy to see her.

Emma felt the same and smiled. She leaned forward and kissed him on his cheek. "It's good to see you also. Jim, this is Savannah. We're traveling together this week, shopping and meeting some people." It was all the truth; when working a case, you needed to keep certain items private. Alison wouldn't disclose what she had learned.

He understood her ambiguity and said, "Alison says you need transportation to Chicago. I have my carriage set up for you. I would just ask that you house and feed the horses for a few days before sending them back."

"I think we can handle that," Emma said.

Savannah nodded in agreement.

Alison walked in carrying boxes and said, "Betsy put together sandwiches and fruit for you. I assume you want to get back as soon as possible."

"Yes," Emma said gratefully, accepting them.

"Well, let's get you on your way." Jim led them down the front steps, then reached over to take the bag from Emma. She immediately pulled it close to her. "No, no, I will keep it with me."

He looked like he wanted to ask a question, but knew it was not the best time. Alison asked him to help with no questions asked and he had agreed. He knew Emma's approval had moved Alison to accept his proposal. He would do anything for her.

Emma hugged Alison and Jim, saying, "Next time, I'll stay longer. I promise."

"Make sure you do," said Jim. He looked over to Savannah and said, "It was very nice to have met you."

"Thank you, and it was nice to meet you also," said Savannah.

He handed both ladies into the carriage. "Be on your way," he told the driver.

The carriage moved forward, and Savannah said with a sigh, "Off we go again."

"Do you want to try to close your eyes for a while?" She could tell Savannah had been fighting sleep.

Savannah yawned widely and said, "Yes, it just hit me."

"This happens when you go through something traumatic. You either get too much energy or too little."

"What do you get? Too much or too little?"

She shrugged and said, "Probably too much. I'll be awake for a little while."

"Wake me in a bit."

"I will."

"Are you concerned about something happening between here and Chicago?" Savannah asked sleepily as she closed her eyes.

"No, we're in a closed carriage and no one is aware of our movements. I told Cole we'd wait for the next train."

"Oh, in case someone in the telegraph office shares that information," she said intuitively.

"In cases like this, it is best to tell as few people as possible."

"Yes," she said as she laid her head back and went to sleep.

As they bumped along, Emma thought about what to do when they reached Chicago. After a while, she let the carriage rock her to sleep. A few hours into the trip, she was jostled awake when they slowed. As they stopped, she stuck her head out of the door and called, "Is everything okay?"

The driver called back, "I need to let the horses rest."

"Of course. We have some sandwiches if you'd like to have one with us," she offered.

"Betsy made me a box," he called back down.

"I'll wake Savannah and we can eat while we are stopped." She pulled herself back into the carriage and nudged Savannah. "We need to eat."

She nodded as she sat up and yawned broadly. Emma handed Savannah her box. She opened it and took out her sandwich and an apple. She bit into the sandwich enthusiastically, saying, "I didn't realize I was so hungry."

"Me either," said Emma, eating at a similar speed.

When they finished eating, they stepped down from the carriage and looked around. "Where's the driver?" asked Savannah.

"He's tending the horses and, once they've rested, we'll be on our way," said Emma. Savannah nodded.

They sat talking quietly and heard the horses being hooked back up.

When they didn't hear anything else, Emma called, "Everything okay?" She looked around for the driver and noticed his box lunch on the ground, unopened. Stepping back against the carriage, she retrieved her clutch knife.

She said in a low voice to Savannah, "Stay with the carriage and stay down." A crunch of branches directed her to the right; she turned and threw her knife toward the sound. The blade made contact and she saw a man stumble into view, the knife sticking out of his shoulder.

"You bitch. Why don't you just give us what we want?" he snapped, holding a gun on her.

We, she thought, looking to her left and then right.

"Oh, it's just me. I was following up on a hunch that you'd survive and, as a bonus, I'd get the jewels."

"Where are your partners?"

"They're on their way to Chicago, waiting for you or me to show up."

"It sounds like you don't plan to meet them."

"Why should I?" he groused. "I'm the one who jumped off a train and got a knife stuck in my shoulder. "

Emma kept him talking to distract him while Savannah swung a very large tree branch against his head, taking him unawares. He fell to his knees, dropping the gun.

"Ow," he said, grabbing his head. He saw who hit him and said, "I didn't figure you as a threat." He also realized he no longer had his gun in his hand.

"Are you looking for this?" said Emma. She had retrieved the gun during the confusion and was pointing it at him.

"You'd never shoot me."

"Oh?" She pulled the trigger, sending a bullet close to his ear.

"Hey, that almost hit me!" he said, outraged.

"Next time, it will," she promised. "Where's the driver?"

He indicated to the right with his head. Emma said, "Savannah, go check on him and see if he's okay. Also, check the seat for rope or something to tie him up."

Savannah nodded and did as ask. She soon returned, supporting the driver. He appeared to have a head injury.

Emma asked, "Are you okay?"

"I'm dizzy, but I think okay. I just need to sit down," the driver responded.

Savannah helped him into the carriage and tossed the rope to Emma.

Emma called back, "Hey, bring me the wine."

Weird time to drink, thought Savannah, but she brought it out of the carriage and over to her.

Emma took it and, surprisingly, handed her the gun and said, "Shoot him if he tries anything."

The man jumped when he heard this direction.

Emma turned around and reached down to rip some of her petticoats off. She took the wine and rope with her and headed toward the man.

"Hey, what are you up to now?" he asked, not trusting her.

She reached up and removed her knife from his shoulder. "I

need to bandage you before we tie you up." He barely heard her answer due to the pain washing over him. She examined the wound and said, "It doesn't appear to be too serious. You need to sit down." When he looked like he might argue, Savannah cocked the gun.

"Okay, where do you want me?"

"Here is fine. Now, can you remove your jacket?"

He was able to get it off and knelt for her so she could dress the wound. He watched her and said, begrudgingly, "Thank you for helping me."

She looked at him out of the corner of her eye and said, "If you had killed the driver, I wouldn't be."

He shut up after that and let her work on his shoulder. She lifted the bottle and poured it on the wound without warning him. "Ahh!" he screamed and raised an arm to hit her.

Savannah said, "I wouldn't do that." She had moved closer and had the gun trained on his head.

He calmed himself and tried to keep still. Emma completed tending to the wound and told him, "Move to the tree and sit down." He did as he was told. Winding the rope around the tree, she tied it securely around him.

"Hey, you're not just going to leave me here?"

"I'll send a telegram and have someone come get you in a few hours."

He didn't say anything in response. Emma thought, *He thinks he can get away.* She shrugged. *That's a chance we have to take.*

She walked toward Savannah and took the gun from her. "Let's get going."

They headed back to the carriage. "The driver can't drive," protested Savannah.

Emma smiled. "I can drive it." She leaned over into the carriage and asked, "How are you feeling?"

"Yes, I'm fine. Are you sure you can handle it?" the driver asked.

"I can," she said firmly. "Savannah, grab my bag." She did so and they secured the door.

The driver leaned out the window to give the last instructions. "Miss, just continue west. We're about two hours out of Chicago."

"Thank you," said Emma.

"Can I ride up with you?" asked Savannah, excited at the idea.

"Of course." They both climbed up and Emma took the reins. She looked over at Savannah and asked, "Ready?"

"Yes!"

Emma clicked at the horses and got them moving.

Savannah sat quietly as they moved along. She finally asked, "Why did you help him?"

Emma was silent for a long moment and said, "I don't know, except that I saw he had spared the driver. I felt I could do the same for him."

Savannah considered that as they road through the evening. The horses were rested, and they made good time to the city. "Where to first?" she asked.

"Hospital," she said firmly. "We need to take the driver to the Sisters; they'll take care of him." They headed there and when they arrived, Emma said, "Wait here. I'll go in and get help."

She hopped down and made her way into the hospital. A few moments later, she returned, accompanied by a Sister and two orderlies. She went to the door of the carriage and opened it. "He's in here."

The Sister climbed in to check his status. She said to the orderlies, "Take him inside. We need to give him a full evaluation."

Emma stood by as she watched them move him. "Sister, I'll stop by to check on him in the morning. I'll also alert his employer of what happened."

The Sister agreed and headed in with her patient.

Savannah leaned over and said, "Where next?"

"Next, we get the horses fed and settled for the night."

They headed to the Cousin's stable and Emma unlocked the

door with her hairpin while Savannah unhooked the horses. The doors were pulled wide and each walked a horse into an empty stall. They got them water and food and brushed them down.

When they finished, Emma said, "We need to get to Cole's house."

"Do you expect to find him there?"

Emma thought about that and said, "You're right. They might be at the rail station. Rather than run all over the city, let's go to Tony's. We need to get the items to a safe location."

They made their way on foot to Tony's apartment. As his career had moved forward at the museum, he began doing well enough to get an apartment of his own. He had been there since their return from Paris. They made their way up to the third floor and Savannah said, "It's late." It was after 10pm and she was worried they would disturb him.

"We'll knock until he wakes up," Emma said simply.

They stood in front of his door and knocked; Emma leaned on the door, hearing more than one voice. She raised her eyebrow at Savannah, who shrugged.

"Who is it?" Tony asked through the door.

Emma called, "Tony, it's Emma and Savannah. We're back and need to speak with you as soon as possible."

Tony opened the door immediately and was shrugging into his jacket.

Emma looked behind him and saw Peggy standing there. She appeared to be trying to fix her hair. What got Emma's attention wasn't her hair; it was the ring on her finger. She made a mental note to ask about that.

"Emma, you were expected back on the train," Tony said.

"We had to find some alternate transportation," she said dryly.

"You could say that," said Savannah in the same tone.

Emma was all business. "Tony, we need to get these items to the museum and contact Cole."

"Cole is at the train station investigating. We will need to contact him."

"Tony," Peggy said quietly. "Should I leave?"

"You might need to," he said regretfully and went over to take her hand. "Would you mind if I tell them?"

She blushed prettily and said, "Yes."

They turned toward Emma and Savannah and said with a wide grin, "We're getting married."

Emma looked closely and thought, *He looks happy*. She smiled back and said sincerely, "Congratulations! That's a lovely ring."

"Congratulations!" said Savannah.

"Thank you. We're so happy," Peggy said.

"I can tell," Emma said. She grew serious. "Tony, you might want to have Peggy accompany us until we get these items safely to the museum."

"Do you think someone followed you?" he asked, concerned for Peggy's safety.

"No, I think we took care of that, but I want to be sure."

He nodded and said, "I agree." He looked over at his fiancé. "Would you mind coming with us?"

She answered quickly, "No, of course not."

Tony and Peggy finished getting organized and all four went downstairs. They made their way on foot to the museum. The group climbed the front stoop and saw the guards outside. Tony spoke to them. "William, I will need you to go get Mr. Johnson."

"Yes, sir. There are three other guards inside. I'll have one replace me here."

Emma had written the note for Philip and handed it to William.

Tony said, "And after you confirm with Mr. Johnson, please also get Mr. Tilden at the rail station. He's needed also."

He nodded and went inside to brief his replacement before leaving.

Emma spoke with the guards outside. "Be vigilant about any

visitors to the museum that were not cleared by Mr. Johnson or Tony. Do not let anyone in."

They agreed and watched as the group entered the doors of the museum.

Cole and Philip arrived in the next half hour. They found the group in Tony's office. Emma had waited to reveal the jewels until they arrived.

Cole immediately went to Emma and Savannah and asked, "Are you both all right?"

"We are," said Emma, speaking for them both. "Though we did leave an injured man tied to a tree about two hours from here by carriage."

Cole smiled wryly and said, "I'll have someone pick him up."

Emma asked, "Were you able to get the other two?" The room went quiet as everyone waited for that answer

Cole looked around and said, "Can I trust you not to let this go outside of this room?"

"Yes," everyone agreed.

Cole looked at each one and nodded. He started, "We knew you were on the 8pm train and three men were involved. I received your wire and we were waiting when it arrived." The room was on the edge of their seat, wondering what happened next. "They weren't there."

"Not there? Did they get mixed up with the other people disembarking?" asked Emma, confused at the information.

"No, we had the train stopped and allowed no one off. They may have jumped before it got to Chicago."

"Really, isn't that dangerous?" asked Emma sarcastically.

Cole smiled slightly and asked her, "Can you give us a description?"

"Yes, I can get with Dora and have her put together some sketches as soon as possible."

"We'll get them," Cole promised.

Philip said, a bit impatiently, "I would like to see the jewels."

Emma looked at him and said, "Yes, I'm sure you do." She opened her bag and pulled out the bustles. Philip gave her an odd look. She explained as she opened each pocket. "I had these made to transport the jewels, in case we were intercepted."

"Clever," he said in approval.

When she started to pull them out, he said, "Wait a minute," and cleared off his desk, laying a cloth liner over it. Emma waited for him to set up and then started removing the jewels. Everyone went quiet as she pulled each one out.

"The queen's jewels," murmured Peggy, recognizing them. Her family had, in part, come from France.

"Yes," commented Philip, admiring them. "We are the first stop to display them to the public. These will show beautifully."

Emma was tired and wanted these items secured. She said, "Where do we store these tonight? And how many men are in place to protect them?"

"For that, I'll need to reduce the number of people in the room. Sorry, ladies," Cole said to Savannah and Peggy.

Tony said, "Let me escort you to the photography exhibit while they work out the security details."

Emma watched the door close, and Philip took over from there. "We'll have normal security, but we'll be adding two men outside and one to the display."

"Will you lock the jewels up each night?"

"Yes, they will be moved to the safe each night."

"Who has the combination to the lock?" asked Emma.

"Just me," said Philip.

"We need to keep it that way," said Cole.

"We will," he said firmly.

They completed their review and Emma said, "If we're good, I'd like to go home. It's been a long day."

Cole said, "I'll take you and Savannah home."

"I would appreciate it," she said, grateful for the transportation.

They watched as Philip relocated the jewels to the wall safe. Tony's office had no windows and was the best location to secure them. Cole waved one of his men to the room and said, "You'll need to stay in here and make sure no one has access to that safe except for this gentleman."

He nodded and sat down at the desk.

Cole asked, "Ready?"

They stepped out of the office and Emma said, "Savannah, let's go home. Goodnight, Peggy, and Tony."

Cole had a carriage waiting and helped the ladies inside. "Savannah, we were able to get your bag. It's in the carriage."

"Good, thank you," Savannah said, relieved.

As they headed home, Cole looked at Emma, stroked his goatee, and said, "We need to talk about what all happened."

"Cole, I agree, but could I please get some sleep first?"

"Okay then. I'll come by in the morning."

"If you could come early, I'd appreciate it. I have to get some information over to Mr. Pennington's office. I also need to check in with Jake on some photos I need to be developed."

He agreed. They made it over to the boarding house and he helped them down. "Do you need any help inside?" he asked as he handed their bags down.

"No, we're fine," Emma said, her voice sounding tired. He nodded and watched until they made it safely inside.

Savannah said quietly as they entered the house, "Well, that was exciting, but I'll need some time before the next one."

"Agreed," said Emma. "Do you need anything to eat?"

"What I need is a bed."

"Me, too. Up we go."

Emma made her way upstairs and into the dark bedroom. She heard a rustling of sheets and Jeremy asked, "Finally home?"

"Yes," she said softly, making her way in the dark. She leaned down and kissed him. "Let me get cleaned up and I'll join you."

"I'll be waiting," he said softly back. He had missed her and wanted to just hold her to him.

She took her robe and nightdress and made her way to the bathroom to wash up and brush her teeth. As she completed her task, she gathered up her items and headed back to her bedroom in the silent house. The door closed behind her with a click and she reached to lock it before laying her clothes on the chair. Jeremy held the covers for her and she walked swiftly over, sliding in beside him. "Mmmm," she said as he folded her into his arms, her back against his chest.

"Welcome back."

"Thank you."

"Would you like to talk or..." He looked down and saw she was already asleep. *I think that means we'll talk in the morning.* He closed his eyes, thankful she was back.

CHAPTER 21

*E*mma slept hard and didn't wake until the next day. When she awoke, the sun was streaming into the room. She turned over and saw Jeremy watching her.

"Good morning."

"Good morning," he said, pulling her to him. They spent some time enjoying each other's company. After the quiet interlude, they both got out of bed to begin their day. He noticed her back as the sheet fell away; it was black and blue with bruises. "Hey, what happened? Are you okay?"

"I'm fine, just sore. I'll put on some compresses today. I'll explain later, I promise," she said.

He took her at her word and said, "Meet you in the hallway?"

"Yes, I need to clean up and get dressed," she commented.

"Me, too," he confirmed and moved to open the bookcase. He looked over his shoulder and called to her softly.

"I'm glad you are back," he said.

Her gaze softened. "Me, too."

"Can we talk this morning?" he asked.

She shook her head regretfully. "I may not have a lot of time."

"Let's grab breakfast and see if we can have some time alone in the kitchen."

The bookcase closed and she moved around, grimacing as she felt every bruise. Her body had tightened up overnight. It would be slow going this morning.

They dressed and met in the hallway to walk downstairs, holding hands. It was early and there were few people up at this hour. "Should you have gotten some more sleep?" He noticed she was moving a bit slower than normal.

"No, too much going on today."

"Do I get to hear about the assignment?"

"Not yet, but soon," she promised. "I can tell you about the other case I was there for. It became interesting quickly."

"Then I want to hear about it."

Emma stopped and said, "Dear-one, I didn't ask. How did the dinner go with your mom?"

"Again, a topic that will take some time," he said softly.

"Tonight? Just the two of us."

"I think that can be worked out." He leaned over to kiss her.

They entered the kitchen and the first person Emma saw was Cole talking to Dora. When he saw her, he set down his coffee cup. "You did say early," he reminded her.

"I did, but can I get some breakfast?"

"Yes, I think we have time."

Dora had given them space to talk before she said to Emma, "I'm glad your back," and hugged her tightly.

"Oh!" Emma moaned in surprise.

"What? Did I hurt you?" she asked, pulling back quickly.

"No, just an event last night that I had to deal with," she assured her. "Let Savannah sleep in this morning. She'll also be a bit tired."

Dora got them some breakfast and Emma ate without talking. She had been very hungry even before going to bed. When she finally looked up from her food, she saw that the group was watching her with a look of awe on their faces. She looked down and realized the quantity of food she had eaten. Smiling ruefully. "Well, I was hungry."

Ethyl came over to take her plate to the sink. She had been hired as a kitchen helper when Amy got promoted to cook. "Thank you." Ethyl smiled and continued with her work.

When Emma finished, Cole said, "Ready to talk?"

"Yes," she said decisively. She kissed Jeremy and smoothed the worry lines on his forehead. She looked over at Tim and asked, "Can we use the study?" He had been using it as an office since Papa moved in with Cole.

"Sure," he said. "I can stay in here and torture Patrick," he teased. He made a lunge for the boy and Patrick ran around the table.

Dora and Lottie were laughing, watching their antics. Emma followed Cole and sat carefully as he shut the door. He joined her on the couch. "Okay, tell me about the pickup."

She pulled out her notebook. "We arrived and worked my other case. We then went to our appointment to get our dresses with hidden pockets. After we went straight to the hotel to meet with the courier; he had one armed guard."

"Was there anything out of the ordinary about him?"

"No, I felt he was honest. We took custody of the jewels and caught the later afternoon train The couriers indicated they would be staying at the hotel for a few days waiting for confirmation that we arrived safely. Could you send a telegraph to the hotel to confirm our safe arrival?"

"I can do that," he said, making a note. He continued, "Did the thieves try immediately?"

"No, but our bags were searched, we noticed that on the train. It was a few hours into the trip when they appeared."

"Why do you think that was?"

"At the time, I didn't think. I just reacted."

"But now?"

"I think they meant to get the jewels and toss us off the bridge."

"But you jumped before they could push you?"

She acknowledged the statement with a nod. "I knew where we were on the trip. I've taken that route many times and knew we were coming up on the bridge. I figured the best way out was to jump where we could slide down the embankment. We slid and then rolled. Oh, and by the way, we owe Savannah a new dress and a pair of boots."

"We'll take care of that," he assured her. "What happened next?"

"I remembered that Alison and Jim Landry live nearby, so we walked and were able to get a carriage from her and her husband to take us to Chicago. "

"The rest I know. We had the man picked up last night."

"Did he give up the two other would-be jewel thieves?" she asked, thinking they might get a notice out to have them picked up.

Cole shook his head. "He was dead."

"Dead? But how can that be? I patched him up and I didn't hit anything vital," she exclaimed.

"It wasn't the knife wound. He was shot."

"Shot? So, he wasn't alone. They must have dropped off the train also."

"They must have been separated somehow, and he found you first."

"I didn't expect that news," she mused.

"Yes, so the identifications of the two other men are more important than we thought."

"I'll work with Dora this morning and get the drawings over to you."

"Great." He stood and waited for her. When she didn't stand, he said, "Is there more to discuss?"

"Cole, please, sit back down," she said, looking serious.

He sat.

"Cole, what about Abbey? Do we have a concern with her showing up in town at this particular time?"

He sat silent for a long moment before saying, "I want to believe she's here for Jeremy, but my experience says she's here for the jewels."

"Is she using him as an excuse?"

He just shook his head. "I don't think so."

"But you are still suspicious of her?"

"How can I not be?"

"Should we talk to Jeremy, come clean about everything?"

"We'll have to tell him soon, before the museum opening this weekend."

"Agreed. Do we mention our concern?"

"That's tricky. We don't have any evidence against Abigail."

"Cole, this is Jeremy. He's a trained investigator. I think we should tell him our concerns."

"Could we get the drawings done first and bring them to the office?"

"Yes, I'll tell Jeremy I'm working."

She followed him out to the hallway and into the dining room. They found Jeremy and Tim talking while Patrick ran around the table, making the baby laugh.

Jeremy held out his hand to Emma, and she went forward to take it. "Have you seen Jake yet this morning?"

"Yes, he's in talking to Ethyl. They get along rather well."

"Let me step in quickly. I need some film developed from my trip."

He nodded and watched her leave. He turned to Cole and asked, "Everything all right?"

"Yes, just wrapping up a case. Jeremy, we'd like to brief you on it today at lunch." Jeremy looked surprised because the case had been kept very quiet.

Jeremy shook his head. "I told Mom that I would meet her for lunch and show her some sites."

"Oh," Cole said casually, "what are you taking her to see?"

He listed some buildings around town and then said, "Oh, and the museum. She wants to see what types of art they have on display there."

Cole didn't know what to say. It seemed awfully coincidental. "I'd like you to be read in on this today. Could you delay?"

Jeremy heard his tone and said, "I'll be there. I'll send a note as soon as we get to the office and ask her to reschedule."

"Thanks."

"Pops?"

"Yes?"

"I appreciate you giving me room to get to know her. I know this can't be easy for you."

He sighed. "I am trying, but know you can come to me no matter what."

"I know, Pops, but I just want to spend time with her while I can."

"Is she planning on leaving soon?" he asked quietly.

"Not yet, but I'm not sure she's here permanently."

"Has she said anything?"

"No." He didn't continue.

"Would you like to go into the office with me?" Cole asked

"Sure, I'll get my jacket and tell Emma we're headed out."

The door swung open from the kitchen and Emma walked out talking to Jake.

"We have to head to the office," Jeremy said. Nodding she accompanied them both out and kissed Jeremy goodbye.

Once they were gone, she went in search of Dora, she had a question for her "Dora," she called.

"We are still in the dining room."

Emma entered and saw her feeding the baby small cut-up bites. "I need a favor after breakfast."

Dora looked up and said, "Sure, anything for you."

"Let me know when you're ready." She sat and watched them finish their meal.

Dora wiped Lottie's face and called to Tim, "Tim, I need you to watch Lottie."

Tim came out of the study and said, "Of course, come to Papa. Would you like to spend time with me?" She giggled as he took her out of the room.

"Where's Patrick?" Emma asked, looking around for him.

"He's in the study with Tim. Papa has started him on a school program, so he's working on his letters and his numbers. Okay, what can I do for you?"

Emma got up and retrieve Dora's sketchpad from the buffet. She handed it to her.

Dora frowned, taking it, and said, "What do you need to be sketched?"

"Three men tried to take the items I was delivering to the museum last night." Dora's face reflected her concern. Emma immediately said, "Not to worry, we were able to evade them. One was picked up last night. I told Cole we'd get him some sketches of the other two this morning."

Dora opened up her pad and held her pencil ready. "Okay, let's get started. Tell me about the first gentleman."

"Kind of a large square face. Smallish eyes." Emma watched her draw and said, "Like that, but a bit further apart. A strong nose, looks like it might have been broken. There is a bump here," she said, pointing to her nose.

She made the adjustment and asked, "Hairline?"

"Not yet receded, full head of brown hair, probably late 30s. Some lines around his eyes."

"Ears?"

"Nothing outstanding."

Dora turned the sketch pad toward Emma, revealing the drawing. "That's him," she confirmed.

Dora turned it back around, flipped to the next page, and said, "You mentioned a second person?"

"He was significantly smaller than the two big guys. Angular face, long nose." Emma looked at her drawings and said, "Narrower in the chin."

Dora made the change. "The eyes?" she asked.

"Larger."

"Like this?"

"No, a bit more."

"Ears?"

"Larger."

"A real looker this one," Dora commented. She turned the finished product toward Emma, who nodded. Dora carefully tore the pages out of the sketchbook and handed them to her. "Is Jake developing some pictures for you?"

Emma was looking at the sketches and said, "Yes, he said they should be ready later today."

"Did he mind helping?"

Emma smiled and said, "He finds the subject matter boring, but he'll get them printed."

CHAPTER 22

LAWYER'S OFFICE

"*E*mma, you're back!" Ethan was so surprised, that he looked up at her.

"I am. Is he in?" she asked.

"He is, and he's with our very worried client."

"Well, I think I have some helpful information."

"Then go right in."

She nodded and headed to the conference room. Knocking lightly on the door, she called, "Mr. Pennington. "

She waited for his response and was surprised when he opened the door and stepped out. "Emma, I hope you have good news for me."

"I do."

He looked contemplative, trying to determine if he should review the information with her first. He came to a decision. "Emma, I'm going to bring you in and let you discuss what you found. I'll let you know if you need to stop."

Emma nodded understanding; this was his business and she needed to follow his direction. "Let's go in." She entered the office and saw Mrs. Gilmore weeping into her handkerchief. Mr. Gilmore was patting her back.

"Mr. and Mrs. Gilmore, you remember my assistant Emma."

Mrs. Gilmore took a deep shuttering breath and said, "Yes, you were in my interview and also in court with us?"

"Yes, I was," Emma confirmed.

"Emma has found out some information that may be beneficial to our case. Emma," he prompted.

She pulled out her notebook and started, "I went to Cleveland where your…" she hesitated a moment and then said, "where Mr. Banks lives. I first went to his business address. You were correct; he has worked there since you were first married. Have you ever been there?" she asked Mrs. Gilmore.

"No, he wouldn't allow it," she said quietly.

Emma nodded. "I went to the personnel office and got his home addresses." She let that sink in for a moment.

Mr. Gilmore caught it first. He frowned and asked, "Addresses, as in plural?"

"Yes," she confirmed. "It was baffling to me also, so I decided to investigate further. I went to the first one and I found a lovely woman there. She's been married to him as long as you've been married to Mr. Gilmore."

All three were shocked and just stared at her. She continued. "I spoke to her for a long period and I got pictures."

Mr. Pennington jumped on that statement. "Where are they?"

"Being developed, so you'll have them tomorrow morning." She looked at her notes and said, "They have two little girls. They seem to be doing well." She looked up and saw the mention of children had made Mrs. Gilmore start crying again.

Her husband explained, "We waited, you see, to make sure we wouldn't harm the child."

Emma nodded understanding that a violation of that partic-ular societal rule could be bad. She waited for the client to calm again. "Then I went to the second address."

"Was it in the same town?" Mr. Pennington asked.

"No, but only about 20 minutes away in Cleveland Heights."

He nodded for her to continue.

"I got to the second address and found a very similar house. So similar that there were even identical pictures on the mantel."

"Was it…" Mrs. Gilmore asked.

"Another wife? Yes," Emma confirmed.

"Children?" Mr. Gilmore asked, not really wanting to hear the answer.

"Two," she confirmed. "And they have been married about the same amount of time."

Mr. Gilmore looked at Mr. Pennington and asked pleadingly, "I hope that, at last, there's a way out of this mess. He has two more wives; can't we use that to help us?"

"We shall see," said the lawyer. "Emma, what else did you find?" He figured there was additional information.

"Yes, the wife in Cleveland Heights is aware of his other marriages."

"She went along with this?" asked Mrs. Gilmore in amazement.

"Yes. She lost her family at a young age and she also seems to have genuine affection for him," she said by way of explanation.

"Then why would he do this to me?" she asked, bewildered, remembering the young man who wanted to marry her so badly, they'd married the day he asked her.

Emma stood with that question and paced a bit, then looked over and said, "I believe it's a long-standing grudge against Mr. Gilmore. As I understand it, the three of you were close growing up."

"Best friends in fact," Mr. Gilmore confirmed. "We were both in love with Elle." She smiled and squeezed his hands. "We were also involved in the same activities and the same classes in school."

"You weren't just in the same activities; you were competitors," Emma guessed.

"Friendly competitors. At least, I thought we were."

His wife touched his arm and said, "You were always first in every competition."

"And he was always second. I guess I just never thought about it before."

"Did the competition extend to Mrs. Gilmore?" asked Emma.

He looked at Elle and said, "Yes, we were always trying to one-up each other."

"How did he end up marrying her, instead of you?" Emma asked curiously.

"Well, I had to leave for a few months; my father needed help at home."

"That was when Hugo started pressuring me," stated Mrs. Gilmore.

"Had you told him something before you left?" Emma asked Mr. Gilmore.

"How did you know?" he asked in amazement, not looking at his wife.

"The second Mrs. Banks mentioned he lied to Mrs. Gilmore."

"What did you tell him?" asked Elle, making him look her in the eyes.

"I had planned to ask you to marry me when I returned," he said quietly.

"And he knew that? When you left?" asked Elle.

"Yes, he took the opportunity and convinced you to marry him instead."

The tears dried up, replaced by anger. "He took advantage and treated us like pieces in his very own chess game."

Mr. Pennington spoke up and tried to diffuse the emotion starting to envelop the room. "Did you marry Mr. Banks while Mr. Gilmore was gone?"

"No. Hugo wanted to wait for Gerald to return. He wanted him there, as our witness," said Elle.

"What happened after the ceremony?" Mr. Pennington asked.

"Hugo seemed so happy about the marriage," said Elle, remembering that day.

"What he looked was satisfied," Mr. Gilmore commented. He was also thinking about that day and the misery he'd felt.

She nodded in agreement. "He left a few days later for his new job and said he would send for me."

"But he didn't," Mr. Pennington confirmed.

"No, there were occasional letters with promises that he would come get me, but I never saw him until now," she said.

"Why didn't you just divorce him? Call it abandonment?" Emma pressed.

"It's hard to prove it because he would send a note a few times a year, acting like we never were apart. Gerald and I decided we would take the chance of being together. We got married in a local town and told people we eloped."

"How did you think this would end?" Emma inquired.

"We didn't know. We just knew we wanted to be together," Mrs. Gilmore said simply.

"So, what are our next steps?" asked Mr. Gilmore.

Mr. Pennington looked at Emma and said, "Once we have the pictures, we'll have a private meeting with Mr. Banks and talk about a nice quiet divorce."

They looked so relieved; Emma nearly smiled.

"I'll set up a meeting with him for tomorrow. Emma, can you have the pictures here in time?" asked Mr. Pennington.

"I'll have them ready," she promised.

"I'll set up the appointment. You two will not have any contact with Mr. Banks." He went as far as shaking his hand at them to make his point.

They understood that they shouldn't let their emotions ruin their plans to resolve the situation. They stood and approached Emma. Mrs. Gilmore said, "Thank you so much for helping us. We didn't think there was a way out of this mess."

"You're welcome," she said sincerely.

Mr. Pennington showed them out and came back into the room. He looked at Emma and said, "Very good work. Did you manage to get a copy of the marriage licenses?"

"You mean these?" she asked as she pulled the papers out of her purse. "They had copies in the file."

He chortled and rubbed his hands together. He reached out for them and said, "Emma, I will be putting you on permanent retainer after this."

Emma blushed; she liked the idea of working for him in a more permanent manner. "Thank you, Mr. Pennington, I would enjoy that." She glanced at her watch and said, "If you don't have anything else for me, I need to type up some letters before lunch."

"That's fine," he said as he sat down, taking notes to prepare for the next day. Emma headed to her office.

Finishing up her letters, she called goodbye to Ethan as she was leaving. She jumped on her bike and headed to the Pinkerton office to talk about the jewels with Cole and Jeremy. Jeremy would be there and they would have to discuss the possibility his mom was in town for the jewels. She and Cole would have to tread carefully.

It was sunny and a bit chilly, but she enjoyed the ride. She stopped at the office and put her bike on her shoulder to walk up the stoop. As she entered, the man at the desk said, "Emma, they're in Cole's office."

"Thanks, Joseph." She handed off her bike to him, adjusted her jacket, and patted her hair before she knocked on the door. Her hand was shaking as she reached for the knob, taking a deep breath, she entered.

Jeremy and Cole sat with a tea service at the small dining table in the office. She walked toward it and leaned down to kiss Jeremy. He smiled and said, "Active morning?"

"Yes, we made significant headway on the case I was research-ing. I still have some follow-up to do in the next few days." He nodded, standing to hold her chair for her to take a seat.

Cole had a file opened in front of him and pulled out pictures. Emma knew what it contained. He started by looking over at them, saying, "Let's get started. Emma was assigned a case to work on a delivery for the museum." Jeremy listened intently but did not understand their apparent tension. "She went to pick up the items and, on the way back, she and Savannah were attacked and had to jump from the train to get away."

"Emma!" Looking at her quickly, he said, "Is this the reason for the bruises? Did you or Savannah break anything?"

"No, we're okay," she assured him. "Though I'm sure Savannah would disagree."

He frowned in question.

"Her dress was ruined when we tumbled out," she explained.

He would have to get more data from her on that jump from the train. "What was so important about the package? I assume it was something you could carry."

"Yes." She nodded at Cole, and he handed out the pictures.

"These are the Crown Jewels from France. Tiffany & Co. has purchased this lot." He laid out the pictures in front of Jeremy.

Emma didn't need to look at them; she had seen the beautiful gems in person.

"Emma and Savannah got alternate transportation to get back here." He left out the henchman who had been executed. "They delivered them to the museum last night."

"I understand the secrecy on something like this. Why do you both appear nervous about reading me in on this case?" Jeremy asked. He had seen Cole's tell; he was tapping his foot. Emma was sitting still, too still.

"We're concerned about the jewels and a theft that may occur at the museum," stated Cole.

"Yes, I would expect so. These are amazing," he said, picking up the pictures, looking at each one. "Did you want my help with the design of the security at the museum?"

"Yes. But we also want to speak with you about your mother," Cole said bluntly.

"My mother?" he said, astonished. "Why bring her into this?"

"Well," Cole said wryly, "she is the queen of crime." A name that had been given to her in France.

Jeremy shot him a glance and said, "That was who she used to be; she's changed. You haven't spent any time with her."

"No," Cole said consideringly, "I haven't. I guess I should change that."

Jeremy didn't know what to say about that statement.

"Jeremy," Emma said gently, placing her hand on his. "We're concerned about the timing of her arrival." She held up her hand when he would have interrupted. "We understand she came directly here from France as the jewels were moved to the States."

"If that's true, why didn't she just steal them in transit? It would have been easier," commented Jeremy, still angry at their assumptions.

"I don't know," she said honestly. "She may not have had an opportunity."

"Or," he suggested forcefully, "it's a coincidence and she's here to see me."

Cole said, "We trust you and want you to be involved in the protection detail for the exhibition." He knew he didn't have to say that this job was confidential and no details should be shared outside of the Pinkerton staff.

"I would ask that you give her the benefit of the doubt," Jeremy stated.

Cole sat back and watched him for a long moment. "I will."

Jeremy glanced at Emma, who nodded and said, "I will."

"But that doesn't mean we are not going to work very hard to make sure the collection isn't stolen," stated Emma.

"Agreed," Jeremy said.

"You mentioned you were going to show Abigail around today?" asked Cole.

"Yes," he said hesitantly.

"One of the locations you mentioned was the museum."

Jeremy frowned. "It's a world-renowned museum and is very popular."

"That is correct. Plan on being there tonight. We will be working to set up the security and display cases. The publicity will go out tomorrow to the papers; crowd control will be an issue during the day. There is also a very private party, invitation only."

"Is this the event we are attending tomorrow night?" asked Jeremy, looking at Emma.

"Yes, the invitation said it would be a special limited-time exhibit. Also, Tim and Dora will be there. I think Papa also," Emma said.

"Hmm, I didn't realize," said Cole, frowning. "Ellis is seeing Abigail," he admitted to them.

Jeremy looked shocked. "He is?"

"Yes, they always had a close relationship, and I haven't seen him much since she got back into town."

"She hasn't mentioned him," Jeremy said awkwardly.

"No, they're keeping it private and uncomplicated."

"Do you think it is serious?" asked Emma.

"For Ellis, I think it probably is," Cole commented.

"And Mom?" asked Jeremy.

"I don't know for sure. When she came back, before we got married, she came back for him. Not me." Cole sounded a bit bitter about the situation.

"Pops?" Jeremy asked, worried about him.

"I just felt she only married me because Ellis was settled with Mary."

Emma tried to pull them out of the past and asked, "Do you think he will bring her to the event?"

"Yes," he said simply. "I haven't seen him this happy since your mama."

Emma sat back and said weakly, "But it's only been a week."

"Their shared history creates shortcuts."

"I'll need to mention this to Dora. Should we be worried about him?" asked Emma.

"No," Cole said emphatically before Jeremy could. Jeremy looked a bit surprised at the strength of the comment. "No, Ellis is the one she really wanted."

Jeremy sat and absorbed that but didn't say anything.

Cole realized how that might sound to Jeremy and said, "I was the second choice, Jeremy, not you."

"I know that." The time he'd spent with Abbey had proven that she loved him and bitterly regretted her time away. He looked at Emma and Cole and asked, "Are we going to the museum?"

Cole stared at Jeremy, realizing the time Jeremy had spent with Abigail had been good for him. He smiled. "We need to cover some details here first."

"How long will the exhibit be here?" asked Jeremy.

"Two weeks," replied Cole.

"Do we have enough men to be on the day and night shifts?" Jeremy pulled out a notebook to catalog the details.

"Yes, I've brought in ten men from around the greater Chicago area. Five will work nights and five will work days. They won't be dressed as Pinkertons during the day; they'll be assigned to walk around. Our men will have their normal roles, looking like nothing out of the ordinary has changed in the normal security."

"Speaking of the event, I do have a dress to finish the details on," stated Emma, standing up.

"Quick lunch first?" suggested Jeremy.

"Yes," she said softly, knowing he would want to talk. "Park?"

Cole stood, too. "I also have a lunch to attend, so I'll leave you both." They said their goodbyes and watched him leave the room.

"Let me get my lunch pail. I see you have yours," said Jeremy. They headed to his office and then down the stoop toward the park. It was a quiet walk.

"Eat first," she suggested as they sat down.

He nodded and they ate. When they finished, Emma asked, "You wanted to talk?"

He wiped his mouth slowly. "I don't think we've ever fought before."

"Are we going to now?" she questioned.

"I'm not sure. Emma, I need you to give her a chance. I need you to spend some time with her. You're usually fairer with people than you have been with her. You and Clair allowed Lily Edwards to come back after she went to jail. You took her at her word that she had changed."

She thought about it and said, "Yes, I'm normally more open about second chances, but I'm concerned about you being taken advantage of."

"You think I went into this with my eyes closed?"

"Yes, at least partially," she admitted.

He looked at her for a long moment and acknowledged, "You're right, but I wouldn't be a party to any kind of theft."

"Have you seen anything that might lead you to believe she's here for anything other than to see you?"

"Honestly, no. When we talk, it's usually about me," he said and reached for her hand, "or about you."

"Oh," she said.

"Oh," he mocked back. "Will you come to dinner with us tonight and give her a chance?"

She tilted her head and considered what he said. "I will, but," she cautioned him, "I'll also be looking to make sure she isn't up to any shenanigans."

"I wouldn't expect anything less," he teased.

"So, is our fight over?"

"I think so."

"Okay," she said, laying her head on his shoulder. "What's this about Papa spending so much time with Abbey?"

"I don't know," he admitted. "We must see her at different

times."

She sat up and said determinedly, "Well, I think we should surprise the happy couple."

"Now?" he asked, surprised at the request.

"Sure, I have a few things I can put off."

"But she isn't expecting me for a while."

"No better time to go," she said, drumming her fingers on her lips.

He saw the move and thought, *Planning*. "Emma, I'm not so sure about this."

"Why not?" She laughed, putting her hand down. "You want me to get to know her, right?"

He laughed back, realizing she had decided to investigate the mystery of her dad and his mom. He held out his hand. "Okay, here we go."

She took it and headed out of the park. They waved for a carriage and had it take them to his mom's hotel. If he had any nerves, they were dispelled by the look of mischief in her eyes. "Come on, let's not give them a chance to hide," she said.

Together, they made their way to the stairs. Jeremy stopped her. "I think we should take the elevator."

Her back was stiff, she smiled and said, "Yes, please." The elevator opened and they approached the door, Jeremy was having some doubts, but this was how Emma worked. If his mom wanted to know who she was, this was probably a good start.

Emma knocked and called out, "Housekeeping."

"Housekeeping?" mouthed Jeremy.

"Surprise," she mouthed back, silently laughing.

She leaned her head on the door and heard a muffled man's voice requesting a moment. The door opened a few seconds later, and Emma came face-to-face with her papa.

"Emma!" he said in surprise.

"Papa!" Emma said, feigning surprise.

"What are you doing here?" he asked.

"I could ask the same," she said, looking at him pointedly. "We haven't seen much of you lately. And, as I understand it, neither has Cole."

Before they could get into further conversation, Abbey came up behind him and said, "Why don't you let the children come in?"

Papa turned around and Emma could see his eyes soften. "You're sure?"

"I am." He moved back and waved his hand for them to enter.

"Good to see you, Jeremy," he said, greeting him warmly.

"Hi, Ellis, how are you?" he asked.

"Oh, I'm good," he said, looking at Emma thoughtfully.

They moved into the living room. Abbey said, "Sit down. What made you want to pay me a visit today?" She watched Emma as closely as she watched her. She worried about Jeremy being with this girl because she seemed to have no drive or want to be anything. *Nothing like me,* she thought again.

"Oh," said Emma, "I heard Papa might be here and I wanted to see him."

Abbey and Emma kept staring at each other. Ellis had said Emma was part of a temporary business, mostly office work. *Is there more to her than that?* she wondered. "I understand you were out of town for a few days."

Okay, she is getting directly to it, thought Emma. "Yes, I went shopping with a friend."

"Shopping, you say. What did you find on your shopping spree?"

"We found some lovely dresses," Emma said truthfully.

"Oh, really? I would like to see them."

That won't be possible, thought Emma, *the dresses were a total loss.* She commented, "Maybe one day."

Hmm, Abbey thought, wondering about this girl.

Emma turned the question back and asked, "How long have you and Papa been spending time together?"

Papa started, "Now, Emma, that isn't any of your business."

"No, it's okay," Abbey interrupted. "We're old friends who are getting reacquainted."

"I think it's more than that. Do you plan on sticking around?" Emma asked bluntly.

Abbey looked her in the eyes and said simply, "Yes."

"All right then," said Emma, coming to a silent decision. "Would you like to come for dinner tonight at the boarding house? You and Papa?" she asked, eyeing them both.

Papa glanced at Abbey, looking for her response. She nodded, and he said, "What time should we arrive?"

"How's 6:30pm?" replied Emma.

"We'll be there," he said.

Jeremy looked surprised and happy. He said to Abbey, "I'm sorry I canceled our afternoon. Would you like to go out now?"

"No, I think we'll wait until a later date."

They talked a bit longer, and Emma indicated she needed to head out.

Jeremy said, "I'll go with Emma. We'll reschedule your tour."

They said their goodbyes and left. Jeremy started to put his arm around her shoulder and remembered her back. He took her hand instead and pulled her close to him. "Thank you for that."

"Anything for you," she said, leaning into him. They stayed close together as they went outside. Jeremy waved down a carriage and as they waited for it, he noticed she looked upset. "What's the matter?" he asked.

"I just invited two more people for dinner and didn't tell Dora or her staff first," she groaned. "I promised to be more considerate."

"I can drop you by there and head back to the Pinkerton office."

She said in a low voice, "Yes, that will be for the best."

"Not to worry," he said. "She won't be too mad. Distract her with Ellis and Mom's romance."

She brightened and said, "You're right. She'll want to see that in person."

As they pulled up in front of the boarding house, she kissed him quickly and said, "Wish me luck."

"I'll see you tonight. Wait I will help you down. You need to put compresses on your back," he reminded her. "Yes," she said, grateful for the help.

He escorted her to the door and returned to his waiting carriage. "Can you take me to the Pinkerton office?" Jeremy asked the driver.

"Yes, sir."

"Thank you."

CHAPTER 23

"*D*ora!" Emma called as she entered the boarding house. She could hear Lottie laughing and followed the sound. She found Dora sitting on the floor with the baby and Patrick. He was using the dancing man to make her laugh.

Lottie wobbled over to her.

Emma laughed and started to bend down to pick her up. She groaned instead.

"It's your back, you need to have compresses applied." She got up to retrieve them.

"Dora, I wanted to tell you something," she called as she eased herself down to the floor next to Patrick, giving his hair a quick tousle.

"Just a minute."

"Hey, Emma," said Patrick. "Can I ride your bike?"

"Well, you're still a bit short. How about when you get taller?"

"Okay." He went back to entertaining the baby.

Dora came back in with ice wrapped in a cloth. "Lay on your stomach," she directed. Emma did as she was told and the ice was placed on her back.

Lottie patted her head. "Thank you, baby," said Emma. "Is Tim working in the study?" asked Emma as she tried to let the ice work.

"Yes." Dora noticed Emma was drumming her fingers on her lips. "What aren't you telling me?"

"Well, a few things," she admitted. "First, I invited Jeremy's mom over for dinner."

"Emma! We talked about this. We need to let the staff know ahead of time. But," she said begrudgingly, "it is family, so I'll let them know."

"Oh, and Papa will be here also," she said nonchalantly.

"So, two more. Watch the baby, I'll go tell Amy and Ethyl that two extra people will be here for dinner." She was almost to the kitchen when she realized what Emma said. She turned back without telling them about the additional people and rushed back. "Emma, did you say Papa and Jeremy's mom would be here? They're still seeing each other?"

"I'll tell you all about it, but you might go ahead and mention the additional people to Amy and Ethyl."

"Yes," Dora said distractedly. "I'll be right back." As she walked back into the room, she called, "Tim, come play catch with Patrick."

Tim came out and said, "I would love to. Patrick, get your ball." He ran to get it, always wanting to spend more time with Tim. They went outside.

Dora sat back on the floor and gave the baby some blocks and dolls to play with. She leaned back against the settee and said, "Okay, what's going on with Papa and this woman? Is it serious?"

Emma looked over and said, "Very."

"Is she still a thief?" Dora knew about her background.

"I can't tell."

"You can always tell," Dora scoffed.

"Not this time. She's good."

"So, why invite her over?"

"Because we need to get to know her. And, if Papa's serious, we need to know if she's manipulating him."

Dora saw something else in her expression. "Emma, do you have something else to tell me?"

Emma laughed suddenly. "She is fascinating. She's done so much."

"Emma, she's spent time in prison for some of those fascinating activities."

"I know," she admitted, "but I'd like to speak with her frankly about some of them."

"Just watch how you do it," Dora cautioned.

"I will," Emma said, drumming her fingers on her lips once again.

CHAPTER 24

DINNER THAT NIGHT

The ice had helped with Emma's back and Dora had allowed her into the dining room. She watched Dora fuss with the table setup.

"Does it look all right?" she asked, worried.

"It looks lovely," Emma assured her.

"I will need help serving. I asked Amy to help out with the baby tonight," Dora said.

"I am sure we will have lots of willing hands."

Jake came in at that time and said to Emma, "I have your pictures ready if you want to come to the basement and view them."

Emma looked a bit distracted and said, "Jake, put them away for now; we'll review them after dinner." He nodded and moved to the basement to clean his workspace. "Oh, Jake, please don't mention the pictures at dinner."

"Why would I?"

"You're right. I'm sorry," she replied.

Dora asked, "Are we ready for dinner?"

"Everyone's here. We're just waiting for Jeremy, Papa, and Abbey," said Emma.

They heard the door open and Jeremy's voice call out, "Em, we're here!"

"Ready," said Dora, taking a deep breath. Their papa had not been serious about anyone but their mama.

Emma offered her hand to Dora. "Let's go." Dora took it and they made their way to the foyer.

As they entered, they saw Papa was more put together than they normally used to seeing him. His shirt had been pressed and his vest was buttoned under his jacket. His hair had also been meticulously combed. Emma's mouth quirked up and she sent a wink toward Dora as they greeted them.

Tim entered from the study with Patrick. "I'm Tim, this is Dora and Patrick, and I believe you already know Emma," he said to Abbey.

Emma watched as Abbey was introduced. She was dressed very elegantly, wearing a dark skirt and a lovely blue blouse. She also appeared nervous. Emma saw the smallest shake of her hand. She knew she had to make good on her promise to Jeremy and stepped forward. "Yes, we got to spend some time together this afternoon. Welcome, Abbey, to our home."

Papa looked over at Emma and smiled, happy she was making an effort.

Abbey nodded graciously. "Thank you for inviting me."

Dora said, "Why don't we move into the dining room? Dinner is ready, and we can finish the introductions there."

Their group followed her direction. Savannah was coming down the stairs as they made their way there. Jake was already in his seat, waiting for dinner to begin.

"Where is Lottie?" asked Papa.

"Amy has her upstairs. You can go up later and see her," suggested Dora.

"That would be nice." He looked over at Patrick and said, "Would you like to spend the day with me tomorrow? I'm looking at several job sites." He saw Dora's expression and said, "Not to worry. He will stay with me."

Tim said, "It's okay, Dora. Didn't he take you to these types of sites when you were little?"

Dora had the grace to turn red. "You're right. Patrick, would you like to go with your grandpapa? Tomorrow?"

"Yes, please," said Patrick. He loved spending time with his Papa Ellis.

"Okay, now that's settled, can we sit?" asked Emma.

Everyone took their seats. Emma completed the introductions and food started being passed around the table. The food was amazing and the platters emptied fast.

Abbey said, "That was wonderful. Thanks for including me."

Dora said, "Thank you. Amy is our cook and she did a wonderful job. I'll let her know how much you appreciated it. Okay, everyone up and grab something to move into the kitchen."

Abbey looked a bit surprised at the demand but noticed the others doing as directed. *I guess I'll help,* she thought and picked up the nearest tray and followed them into the kitchen. Emma picked up a pitcher and Jeremy took it from her with a shake of his head.

He saw noticed Abbey watching them and said, "Emma pulled her back earlier and needs to take it easy."

Abbey wondered about that as she entered and placed the tray on the kitchen table. The area was well done and very professional. Dora organized everyone to their workstations for cleaning and putting up dishes.

As they completed their task, Dora spoke up. "Tim, why don't you take Papa, Jeremy, and Jake into the sitting room with you?"

Tim knew that tone and didn't hesitate to say, "Let's move into the sitting room."

Abbey started to move with Papa, but Dora said, "Why don't you stay here with us?"

Emma said, "Yes, please."

Papa looked like he was going to say no.

Abbey looked at them and said, "Yes, I'd like to stay."

Savannah smiled." I have a late date. Don't wait up."

"Sounds like fun," said Emma. Savannah headed to the foyer and then they heard the door open and close

"Would you like some dessert, Abbey? It's a Kuchen."

They didn't talk right away. Dora cut slices of the desert and placed them on a tray for the men. She opened the kitchen and called, "Tim, please come get the dessert." He came to take the tray and thanked her for the treat. He kissed her on the cheek, picked up the tray she'd prepared, and went back into the sitting room.

Cutting additional slices for Emma, Abbey, and herself, she sat down with them. She gave Emma a long look.

"Okay," Emma mouthed, "I will."

"Abbey," Emma started, "we wanted to meet with you by ourselves. We understand you and Papa knew each other a long time ago."

"We did," she confirmed.

"We also understand that it was Papa you were coming back for, but you ended up marrying Cole."

"Also true," she confirmed, wondering where this was going.

"We want to know if you plan to stay and if you are serious about him."

She looked at both of them and said coolly," I wouldn't normally share my plans, but yes, I do plan to stay. At least, as long as Ellis will have me."

"You realize our hesitation in believing what you're saying. You made a similar commitment with Cole, and you ended up returning to your previous field."

Abbey frowned. "Now, that is overstepping. What happened at that time is between Cole and me."

"And Jeremy," Emma reminded her.

"Yes," she acknowledged," and when *he* asks, I'll tell him. "

"That's fair," Emma said. "But I do have to ask the hard question. Are you out of the thievery business?"

Abbey gave her a long hard look. "I'm definitely out of the business."

Emma watched her closely, looking for any tells that would give away a lie. Abbey's gaze was steady, her voice even and her manner a bit defensive. But that last one was to be expected.

Emma nodded and said to Dora, "I think we should give her a chance."

Dora reached over to touch Abbey's hand and said, "Please, forgive us. We're very protective of our papa."

Abbey released the breath she didn't realize she was holding. Ellis' girls were fierce and she wanted them to know she wouldn't do anything to hurt him. She also wanted to be with Ellis for a long time.

"I hope we can move forward from here," said Abbey.

"As do we," said Dora, answering for them both.

"Emma," Abbey said, moving them on to another topic, "Is that an example of your lacework?" She nodded at Dora's lace overlay.

"It is," she confirmed.

Dora fingered the lace. "Isn't it lovely? I have several that she has made me."

"Really? Could I see them?" Abbey asked, a real interest in her voice.

"I don't see why not. I have them in a room upstairs," Emma said.

"I don't want to disturb your baby," Abbey said, looking at Dora.

"Oh, you won't. I have them in another room. Emma uses the attic for her final lacework. Would you like to follow us up?" Dora asked, pushing back her chair in anticipation of standing.

"Yes, very much so," Abbey said sincerely.

They headed upstairs and, as they passed the men in the sitting room, Dora said, "We're heading up to look at some of Emma's lace designs." Papa looked happy that his girls were getting along with Abbey.

They walked up to the fourth floor and entered the attic. It contained twin beds, a desk, and an area where drawings were displayed, showing intricate lace designs. Abbey immediately went to the drawings. "These are just lovely. Have you started them yet?"

"The one on the left is the one lying on the bed."

Abbey went over to examine it and picked it up. "This is so intricate; it must take a huge amount of time to get the detail right."

"It does. I work on it between jobs and in the evenings," explained Emma.

"Ellis mentioned you were a temporary worker," she said absently.

"Well, not exactly. We own a temporary business and I also work jobs for our company," explained Emma.

"That sounds interesting," she said. "I do wish I had seen these before. I would have loved to have some lace additions to the dress I'm wearing to the event at the museum."

"Oh," said Emma nonchalantly, "are you and Papa attending?"

"Yes, we're looking forward to it. As I understand, a new exhibit is the reason for the event." She said, just as casually, "Will you be there?"

"Yes," said Emma. "We're going also."

"I had hoped to see the museum before the event. I understand there are some wonderful paintings and photographs."

"There are," said Dora, not realizing she was telling more than Emma wanted. "A close friend is the assistant curator. He's in charge of the new exhibits."

"Well, that is interesting. You must introduce me."

"We will," murmured Emma.

Abbey continued to study the lace and said, "I would love for you to design something for me. Can we get together next week and talk about it?"

"I would like that," said Emma honestly. She did enjoy her lacework.

"Well, I must be going; I'll see you both at the event."

"We'll walk you down," offered Dora.

As they left, Emma said to Abbey, "I was thinking, I would love to hear about your past adventures."

Abbey paused and said with a faint smile, "I might just do that." She eyed Emma contemplatively and turned to continue walking down the stairs. Emma seemed the opposite of her. *Why would she want to hear those old stories?* She shrugged and put it out of her mind.

They heard the men talking as they entered the foyer. The ladies entered the sitting room, and Papa looked up. "Hello, dear. Are you about ready to go?"

"I am," she said and turned toward Dora and Emma. "Dora, thank you for the lovely meal. I look forward to seeing you both soon."

Jeremy was watching the interaction closely and decided it had gone well. "Mom, would you like to tour tomorrow?"

"I'd love to see you for lunch, but I think we can wait on the tour until after the event."

"Okay," he said and leaned over to kiss her on the cheek.

Papa and Abbey said their goodbyes and left.

"Where's Jake?" asked Emma, looking around.

Tim said, "He went down to his basement workroom to check on some things. Dora I am going upstairs to check on the kids."

"I should be up soon," she said watching him go up the stairs.

"I need to check with Jake," said Emma starting to head toward the basement.

"Hey, wait a moment," said Jeremy, stopping her before she could leave the room. "I'd like to hear your and Dora's impressions of Mom."

Emma hesitated. She wanted to look at those pictures, but she allowed herself to be pulled to the settee. She sat down and watched as Dora joined them

Jeremy didn't wait and asked abruptly, "Did you like her? It looked like you got along okay."

Emma answered, "We got along surprisingly well."

Dora said, "She's a very interesting woman. I think I could like her." She glanced upstairs again and said, "I need to go help Tim."

"Thanks for staying a moment," said Jeremy.

She smiled and headed upstairs.

Jeremy turned his gaze to Emma. "Well?"

"I like her."

"Do you trust her?"

"Trust needs to be earned," she said cautiously, "but I'm giving her a chance." He nodded. She glanced into the foyer and said, "Would you like to accompany me downstairs to check with Jake?"

"No," he said. "I think I'll go up and read for a while before bed."

"Okay, I'll see you soon." She kissed him warmly.

He escorted her out and headed upstairs as she approached the door to the basement. She descended the stairs and called out, "Jake!"

When she didn't get a response, she called again, "Jake!"

He stepped out of his photography room and saw her. "Yes, come down. We need to review your photos."

"On my way." He had the gas lights turned up in his lab and her pictures laid out on the table. He had grouped them by family.

"These are excellent," she murmured as she picked them up to examine them. "They're so clear."

"You did a good job taking the pictures," he acknowledged.

"Thanks!" She smiled and asked, "Can I take these with me?"

"Yes, they are dry. Will you be using them tomorrow?"

"Yes, the lawyer and client will be very happy with these." She gathered them up and said, "Thank you so much."

"Just let me know when you might need the camera next."

"I will." She leaned over and kissed him on his cheek. He didn't change his expression as he looked back at his table, gathering up supplies to put away.

She headed upstairs, looking at the pictures. She knew Jake would make one last sweep through the house and turn off the gas lights that remained lit.

She opened up her door and saw Jeremy already settled in the bed reading. "The pictures came out amazing," she said, jumping onto the bed.

"Let me see." He laid his book down next to him.

She set them out for him to review. As he looked at them, he saw what she had. "It's odd that the women are so similar and the houses seem to be identical."

"Yes, I saw that also. I would assume it makes it easier to find things." She looked at him and said teasingly, "Do you think he ever forgets which house he is in?"

He nodded and said seriously, "It could be confusing. Will you present these tomorrow?"

"Yes, I think Mr. Pennington is going to use them to put some pressure on the case's star witness."

"Well, enough of that." He moved his book to the nightstand and said, "How about less talking?"

"I'm agreeable to that." She moved the pictures to her desk and returned to the bed. Burying his hands in her hair he pulled her to him. She went willingly, enjoying their time together.

CHAPTER 25

The next morning, Emma was getting ready and could hear Jeremy next door. With her tie in place, she finished lacing up her boots and placed her knives in her leg strap and her hat. She was ready for the day and reached for the portfolio containing the pictures for her meeting that morning. Moving to the door, she opened it and stepped out. Jeremy was waiting and said, offering his elbow, "Ready?"

She nodded and took his elbow.

"Good morning," he murmured as he kissed her cheek.

"Good morning,"

"Headed to the lawyer's office this morning?" he asked, indicating her portfolio.

"I am, what about you?"

"I'm headed to the museum; we're going to be there all day to help with security and setup."

"Good," she said. "We need things to go smoothly. I'll be there this afternoon and evening."

They headed downstairs and had a nice breakfast. Jeremy walked her bike to the cable car. He handed it to her as they saw it approaching. "Have a great day. Send me a note if you won't be there today."

"I will," she promised.

She waved at him as he ran to catch it. She hopped on her bike, holding her portfolio in one hand and steering with the other. She headed over to the lawyer's office, carried her bike in, and stored it in the closet.

"Is he in?" she asked Ethan.

"Not yet, but soon," he responded, not looking up from the files on his desk.

"Do you know how he plans to deliver the evidence?" she asked.

"I think he's set up the meeting for this morning." He heard the door and said, "There he is now."

She turned in response to his statement and watched Mr. Pennington enter the office.

"Hello, Emma. I hope that's my photos," he said, eyeing her portfolio.

"It is," she said with a wide smile. "You'll be happy with the results."

He nodded, thinking it was going to be a good day. "Come in and let me get settled." She followed him into the office and he directed, "Lay them out on the table."

She laid them out, showing the two families. The pictures were eerily similar. He walked over to view them. He was quiet as he took in each house and wife. He straightened and said, "That should do it."

"How will we work this?"

"I have Mr. Banks and his lawyer coming over this morning. I think we'll present this information to him at that time."

"Will we have Mr. and Mrs. Gilmore there as well?"

"I don't think I want them here. It will be less emotional if we present the facts to him this way."

"Agreed. What time?"

He checked his pocket watch. "They should be here within the hour. We need to work on your delivery of the information."

She practiced pulling the files and going over each one and asked questions as she went. He seemed satisfied after a few times through and said, "That should do it. We're ready."

"I'll work on my filing and transcribing until it's time to present these."

He nodded, walked back to his desk, and began pulling out files for another case.

Her mind was on the upcoming meeting as she went to her office and sat at her typewriter. A little while later a knock sounded at her door, she looked up from her typing and called, "Come in."

Ethan stuck his head in. "We're ready for you."

She took a minute to calm herself and checked her clutch knife. The circumstances probably wouldn't call for it, but she wanted to be prepared. People didn't always react as you expected. Feeling more composed, she patted her hair and exited her office to go to the conference room. Ethan nodded encouragingly as she passed him.

She knocked lightly and heard a voice call, "Please, come in."

She pushed on the door and entered the room. Hugo Banks and a man who must have been his lawyer were seated at the round conference table with Mr. Pennington. *Ahh,* she thought to herself, *time for the reveal.*

"I have asked Emma to join us," Mr. Pennington said, "She's done some background work for me on this case. Emma, come in and have a seat." He moved the file to her and said, "Could you start?"

"Mr. Banks, you were married to Elle..." she began.

"We *are* married," Banks interrupted, "not were. *Are.*"

Emma nodded and appeared to agree. She continued, "You can confirm you were married fourteen years ago on this date," she said, showing him the file.

He looked down at it and back up at her. "Yes."

"And after you were married, you immediately left town?"

"I had to leave for work." His lawyer nudged him, and he got the message. "But I stayed in contact and sent money."

Mr. Pennington let that one go by without challenge. They weren't going to argue the small stuff.

Emma continued. "Is this your address in Cleveland?" She set the paper in front of him for review.

"What?" He seemed startled by the question.

"Is this your current address?" she asked again patiently.

"Yes, well…" he said, looking at it. His lawyer looked at Emma, confused about why they were asking.

"My client gave you his current address."

"No, what he gave us was where he worked." She looked at Banks and asked firmly, "Can you confirm that address is yours?"

He finally said, "Yes."

She presented one more and asked, "And this one?"

He went white when he saw the second one.

His lawyer saw his reaction and said, "Maybe we need to stop and let me confer with my client."

"No, we aren't in court," Mr. Pennington said. "We need to continue. Emma," he prompted.

"Yes. To continue, I went to both addresses and met your second and third wives."

Before he could stop himself, his lawyer exclaimed, "His *what?*"

Emma laid out the pictures. "If you will notice, both houses are extremely similar, and there are children."

His lawyer looked like he was going to pull his hair out.

Mr. Pennington took over. "So, what we have here is a situation where I think both sides can help each other."

Mr. Banks' lawyer glared at his client and said, "We're listening."

Mr. Pennington immediately slid a piece of paper in front of Banks. "You sign this letter stating the marriage was never consummated and therefore not valid. We can make this case go away."

"Wait, so they just get a free pass?" Mr. Banks said indignantly.

"I think her living in fear of you returning was punishment enough," Emma commented, wondering how he could be so centric in his logic.

"What do I get out of this?" he asked, shaking off his lawyer's hand on his arm.

Mr. Pennington said smoothly, "We will not disclose the bigamy cases existing in Cleveland and Cleveland Heights."

Emma leaned forward, tapping the pictures, and reminded him, "You have two very nice wives who care for you very much."

He hung his head and his lawyer whispered in his ear. He finally looked up and asked, "Where do I sign?"

"Here." Mr. Pennington pointed to the paper.

Mr. Banks signed and threw down the pen.

Mr. Pennington picked it up smoothly and said, "I'll send this over to the DA. I would assume you will also confirm your mistake with him."

His lawyer prodded him and Mr. Banks grudgingly said, "Yes."

They got up and left. Emma and Mr. Pennington waited for the outer door to close before talking.

He sat back in his chair, looking pleased with himself, and said, "Emma, that was perfect."

"Yes, it went well." She started picking up the pictures and asked, "What will you do with these?"

"Put them in a locked file and, if he ever tries something again, we'll have that to use against him."

"Good idea," she acknowledged.

"Now, I think I'll go see my client and deliver the news in person."

"Would you like me to file that with the court?" she asked, indicating the annulment papers he held. Elle Gilmore had signed them a few days prior in the hopes it would be signed today by Hugo Banks.

"Yes, please," he said.

Emma had done courier work like this before and knew the procedure for delivering papers to the court.

He put them into an envelope. "Directly over, no stops!" he said sternly as he handed it to her.

"Agreed." She took the letter and placed it in her inside jacket pocket. "I'll head there now."

"It's still early. Will you be returning?" Mr. Pennington asked as he checked the time.

"Yes, I have some things to finish up."

"Good, I'd like to let you know how the communication goes with the client."

"I'll be here," she promised and watched him leave. She smiled as she noticed a definite spring in his step.

As she headed out, she told Ethan, "I need to file some papers with the court."

He nodded, acknowledging he'd heard her.

Her bike would be unnecessary, as the court was only a short distance from the office. The filing went smoothly, and she headed out. The day was nice and people were out walking. *Out of the corner of her eye, she saw something, she turned and saw a well-dressed woman with that familiar hair. Abbey.* she thought. Her hotel was located close to the courthouse. She stopped and thought, *That is her. I should say hello.*

Emma started to head over but stopped abruptly when she realized Abbey was speaking with a tall man in a dark suit. She stepped closer and tried to be unobtrusive as she continued to observe them. *I need to be closer to hear them,* and she took a few more steps toward them. She could hear snippets of their conversation and thought, *French.* Though she didn't understand them, she could tell from their posture and facial expression it was an argument. Abbey's head was bowed and her mouth turned downward. She was normally very confident but, in this situation, she appeared to be a bit fearful. The man continued to berate her and Emma watched Abbey wipe a tear as she nodded to the question asked. They seemed to reach some sort of agreement and then departed.

Abbey turned toward the hotel and the Frenchmen went in the opposite direction. Emma decided to follow the man at a distance. His destination was a hotel located about a block down; she continued to follow him discreetly. He went to the front desk and asked for his mail. Emma stood close behind him

"Here it is, sir," said the hotel manager, handing several letters over.

He took them without an acknowledgment, turned away, and headed to the elevator.

"Miss, may I help you?" the manager asked.

"No, I think I have what I need," Emma said and turned to leave. What to make of this? she thought. Is it another piece of Abbey that shows she's not quite out of the business? Is this her partner? Are they here to steal the jewels? She would have to let Cole know about this.

CHAPTER 26

Emma went back to the office and start working on transcribing her shorthand notes. She pulled the last paper out of her typewriter and filed it away just as she heard Mr. Pennington in the outer office. Expecting him to return to his office, she was surprised when he came straight to hers.

"Emma! Did you get the papers filed?" he inquired.

"Yes, they said it would be one-to-two days," she confirmed.

"Excellent, that would make it Friday."

"Yes, that seems about right," she confirmed.

"Emma, how would you like to attend a wedding on Friday?"

She looked at him, shocked.

He grinned. "Our clients would like us as witnesses. They also wanted to thank you personally." He had an idea it would be a monetary thank you, but he didn't mention it. "Can you be there?"

"I think so. I have a few things to move around. Will it be in the morning?"

"Yes, I believe there'll be a small tea service provided. We can meet here and take a carriage over."

"That will be nice."

"Good, good." He watched as she started covering her typewriter and pulled out her courier bag. "Afternoon deliveries today?"

"A few and then off to the museum to set up for a special event."

"The one that is tomorrow evening?"

"Yes, will you be attending?"

"Yes, I think I will be. I'm looking forward to it. See you tomorrow, Emma."

She bade him goodbye and headed to retrieve her bike. As she started to exit the building, she heard Ethan say, "Good job, Emma."

She was shocked. Ethan never complimented her on anything. Turning slowly toward him and she said solemnly, "Why, thank you, Ethan."

He nodded and went back to his paperwork.

She smiled as she exited the building, thinking, *It has been a good day.*

She wanted to go to the Pinkerton office to tell Cole about Abbey, but Jeremy was there. Wavering, she finally decided to keep an open mind about his mother *There could be many reasons for a Frenchman to be speaking with Abbey*, she supposed. It was the timing that bothered her.

She continued to think about that as she rode quickly to the boarding house for lunch. Her commission for some lace patterns needed work before she left for the museum.

Riding around the back, she parked her bike by the kitchen door and entered. "Hello, Amy and Ethyl." They said hello back and Emma inhaled. "Amy, what is that I smell baking?"

Amy smiled. "Kuchen."

Emma grabbed one. It was still hot, and she juggled it in her hand until it cooled. She took a bite and said, "Lovely."

Amy grinned. "It's sweet, so I knew you would like it."

"True," she said as she munched on it. "Dora around?"

"Park," commented Amy. "They went out over an hour ago."

"Nice for them," she said, meaning it. Since Dora had gotten help for the boarding house, she was able to spend more time with the kids. She had everything she wanted, and Emma was very happy for her.

Amy asked, "Staying for lunch?"

"Yes, I'll be upstairs until it's ready."

"I'll ring the bell to let you know to come down."

Emma headed upstairs; *lacework*, she thought. She had some details to add to Dora's dress; her own had been completed for a while. Dora's dress hung on a form so she could attach the lace. The event was tomorrow night and she wanted it to be perfect. The lace overlaid a sleek blue dress. It was a bit fashion-forward and would accent Dora's figure. Emma's was similar but, instead of black lace, there was white lace at the cuffs and in layers on the bottom.

She was working steadily and didn't hear anyone come in until someone tapped her on the shoulder. The mirror's reflection showed her who was behind her, she turned and said, "Abbey, I didn't know you were visiting today."

Abbey smiled. "Ellis wanted to stop by and see Lottie while she was awake."

Emma noticed the strained look she had when speaking to the Frenchman had faded away.

"Are they back? Dora had taken the kids to the park."

"Yes, we came upon them as we were entering."

"Papa loves to spend time with the baby. He said she reminds him of us when we were little."

"Yes," she agreed. Abbey looked at the dress and said, "Can I see what you're working on?"

"Yes," Emma said and stepped back.

"I didn't see the full overlay last night. This is nice. Who's it for?"

"Dora, she's wearing it to the event tomorrow night."

"That will be lovely on her." She made a decision. "I'd like one made just like this for me."

Emma looked at her with a measuring eye and said, "I'd have to make some adjustments."

She laughed and said, "Yes well, Dora is a bit curvier."

Emma laughed also and said, "Just don't tell her. She's still concerned about her baby weight."

"She looks lovely, though."

"She does," Emma acknowledged.

"When do you think you could work on it?"

Emma shuffled her schedule in her head and said, "It would take me more than six months to complete."

"That would be fine," she said firmly.

The completion date didn't seem to faze her, and Emma thought, *Does that mean she's staying? Maybe the Frenchmen was just an acquaintance.*

"When would you like to take my measurements?"

"We could schedule some time this weekend."

"After church?"

"We do a family dinner here, and I can measure you after."

Abbey laughed and said, "I'm not sure after is a good idea, with all of the good cooking around here."

"You'll have a treat; Dora still cooks Sunday dinner."

"I heard she's a very talented cook."

"She is."

"I understand you have some talent yourself," Abbey said without mentioning what that talent might be.

Emma frowned, not understanding, and Abbey said, "Baking. I hear there are several desserts you make that could hurt my waistline."

Emma smiled. "I have several you might like."

"Excellent." She sat on the bed and said, "You can finish your work."

"You don't mind?" Emma asked, knowing she had a short window of time to work on it.

"I'd love to watch."

Emma went back to the dress and kneeled at the bottom to confirm the proper length. She finished the final work and stepped back, saying, "I'm finished. I'll do a final check when Dora puts it on. That way, if there are any pulls, I can fix them."

"I love it." She hadn't moved off the bed and Emma sat in an overstuffed chair across from her.

Emma was curious about this woman and thought this might be a good time to ask. "Papa said you were very good at thievery when you were all running around."

Abbey didn't see any malice, just honest curiosity. "Yes," she murmured, "I was quite good."

Was, thought Emma. She asked, "Better than Papa?"

Abbey laughed. "We had similar techniques. Though he never applied himself to the trade like I did."

Emma focused on that last statement and asked the hard question, "Cole and Papa got out. Why did you stay in?"

She gave Emma a long look and finally answered simply. "I was good at it. I liked it. It was exciting."

"I get that," said Emma. "But it wasn't always good."

"No, I occasionally got caught. When I was young, I could cry and get released most of the time. Then I got older," she said and abruptly stood to walk around the room.

Emma watched her for a moment, picking up items off the dresser and placing them back down. "You decided to go to Europe rather abruptly?"

"I did. I had my reasons." She hesitated before she picked up the delicate silver frame. "Is this Mary?"

"Yes, that was Mama."

"She was beautiful," she said sincerely.

"Yes."

Just when they were getting serious, the lunch bell rang downstairs. They both look startled at the sound.

"What was that?" asked Abbey, putting a hand to her chest.

"The lunch bell," said Emma. "We have plenty if you and Papa would like to join us," she offered.

Abbey looked happy at the invitation and responded, "I would like that."

They headed downstairs talking about fashion. Ellis looked up and smiled, realizing they were getting along. He worried about Emma the most. After Mary's death, he hadn't needed anyone but Emma and Dora, but Abbey coming back into his life made him realize he had been lonely. He still loved his work, but she gave him balance.

"Ellis," Abbey said as she stepped down off the last step. "We've been invited to lunch."

"I could eat," he said.

Emma noticed Papa behaved differently around Abbey; he seemed surer of himself and more aware of his surroundings. "Papa, any interesting jobs going on lately?" she asked as they sat down.

"Yes," he said and reverted at least partially to the papa she knew. He went on to describe a project coming up.

Abbey smiled at him, "I'd like to hear more about that also."

Dora was watching with a small smile and fed the baby as she ate.

Emma noticed that smile. *I need to follow up with her. She knows something I don't.* Lunch went by quickly with lively conversation, and each person promised to see each other at the museum event.

Dora and Emma walked them out with the baby.

After they closed the door, Emma leaned on it and said, "Okay, what do you know that I don't?"

"What do you mean?" Dora asked in a coy voice.

"Dora, spill," she ordered.

"It's just that Mama could do that."

"Do what?"

"Pull him out of his engineering world."

"He seems suave," she said incredulously.

"Yes, I remember he was like that with Mama. He would dance with her; he was fully present when she was alive."

"Why is he different with us?"

"He just is," she said with a shrug. "It doesn't mean he doesn't love us; it is a different kind of love." She changed topics. "I noticed you're getting along with her."

"I am," she acknowledged. "I like her."

"That will make Jeremy happy."

"Yes, I think so."

"So, you don't suspect her anymore or think she is after the jewels?"

"Oh, I'm still suspicious," Emma said, not mentioning the man she saw Abbey with that morning.

Dora looked at her but knew the tone, so she left Emma to it.

"I have to head to the museum to help out with the security," said Emma.

"Will you be back for dinner?"

"Philip is providing it for us."

She walked toward the stairs and Dora said, "Aren't you going now?"

"No, I need to be in my delivery clothes. It should be dirty work."

She ran up and changed before heading back down wearing her black jacket, white shirt, pants, and bowler. *You just never know*, she thought. She went out through the kitchen, saying goodbye to Amy and Ethyl as she exited into the backyard to retrieve her bike.

The museum was a few miles away, she pedaled to build up her speed to get there quickly. When she got there, she noticed additional guards standing at the doors and on the street. She knew them by sight and nodded. They waved her up the stairs and yelled at the men at the door to let her in. "Thank you," she said as she entered. The Pinkerton guards were stationed inside as well. One of them took the bike to store it for her.

She gazed into the expanse of the large main room. It had been completely cleared out of the current displays. *Jake will be a bit disappointed that the photos he loves so much have been moved out,* she thought.

"Emma!" called Tony. He had just exited the office and walked over to where she was standing. "Dressed for work?" he asked, smiling easily.

The engagement has been good for him, she thought. "I am," she acknowledged. "What has been done so far?"

He turned towards the main floor and commented, "The floors were polished last night. We have the rugs to layout and the display cases to move. We also have new art to complement the jewels."

Philip had many contacts in Paris to turn to for paintings for various shows. He already had a good reputation as an art authenticator and as a man who could be trusted.

"What artists will be displayed?" she asked.

"James Tissot will be our main focus; his genre is fashionable women shown in everyday scenes."

"That sounds interesting. Can I see them?"

"Sure, they're over here. Follow me."

They neared some paintings lined up by the walls. As they went to each one, he told her the names: *The Traveler, The Two Sisters, Portrait of the Marquis and Marchioness of Miramon and their children, A Luncheon.*

"These are wonderful," she said.

They walked to the additional art that would be displayed three landscapes and three impressionists. She continued around the room, examining each one.

"You won't find Alairs' initials," teased Tony, referencing the forger they had caught in Paris. One of the ways they were able to distinguish the fakes from the originals on the case in Paris.

Emma glanced back with a wide smile. "I would hope not! Isn't he still in prison?"

"Yes, and not likely to get out any time soon."

"Good," she said, happy the man who had tried to kill Philip was out of their lives.

She looked around the room and saw bolts of purple cloth. "What are those for?" she asked curiously.

"Decoration," he said. "Philip told me the color purple has been associated with royalty, power, and wealth for centuries. Queen Elizabeth even forbade anyone except close members of the royal family from wearing it."

"Why is that?" she asked.

Tony responded, "Purple's elite status stems from the rarity and cost of the dye originally used to produce it."

"What will he do with the cloth?"

"He wants it draped on the walls."

"Has he an idea of what he would like?" she asked looking at the fabric.

"I don't think so," he said, frowning. They were starting to run short on time before the benefit.

Emma was thinking and asked, "Would Philip mind if I sketched some ideas on how the draping could be hung?"

"Let me go check with him. He's in his office with Cole and Jeremy reviewing the final plans for tomorrow night." Tony wanted to make sure Philip didn't have other ideas for the fabric. He headed over as Emma continued to examine the room.

Knocking softly on the door, he heard Philip call, "Come in."

Tony entered and said, "Sorry to interrupt. Emma is here and wants to know if you would like her input for the draping."

"Tell her definitely," he said, relieved. There were so many details still to work out. "I will be out in a few moments."

"I will, thank you." He closed the door behind him and went back over to Emma.

"He said yes and he'll be out in a moment."

"Tony, could get me paper and a pencil?" She knew his office was currently off-limits because it was the most secure room in the museum.

He nodded and got the supplies she needed and a book to support the paper. She walked around the room making notes and taking measurements Next, she checked the fabric rolls to see the amount she had available. "Tony, is there additional fabric for the display cases?"

"Well, they already have red felt in them." He saw she was drumming her lips and said, "You have an idea?"

"I do. We could also use the purple in the display cabinets."

Tony smiled, liking the idea. "That sounds amazing."

Philip walked up and said, "I hear you have some suggestions."

"I do." She showed him her sketch; it detailed draping around the room and long lengths between the paintings.

He studied the drawing and said, "Can you demonstrate what you're thinking?"

She unrolled two yards of fabric and set about gathering them. "It will be easier with a bit of thread," she said. "If you could get me a ladder, I can show you the effect." He did as she asked, and she proceeded with the example.

Philip stepped back and said, "I like it. Do you have time to work on this tonight?"

She studied it and said, "If I can get help with the installation of the hangers."

He smiled. "I think we can manage that. What else do you need?"

"I need an iron, ironing board, and my sewing kit."

Tony was making a list and said, "I can go get those for you."

This will be an easier job one day in the future, she thought. She had heard that sewing machines were being demonstrated for at-home use. *Until that time, it's a needle and thread for me.* "Thanks, Tony. I'll measure out the material while I wait for you."

She was still looking at the fabric when she felt herself being embraced from behind. She leaned back and said, "I wondered if I would get to see you."

"Busy trying to make sure this place is secure. What are you up to?" asked Jeremy. She described her project and he said, "Looks like we'll be here a while tonight."

Their group worked into the evening. Jeremy continued to do security scans, evaluating the space. Emma had gotten the fabric cut into manageable sections and ironed them; she had just started tacking together the folds when dinner arrived.

The food was from a local restaurant; they sat down on the floor and enjoyed their meal together. She was sitting next to Jeremy and asked in a low voice. "Any weak spots in the security?"

"I don't think so; we've combed over every inch of this place."

"Good."

The evening wore on. Emma had the drapes ready to go up on the east and west walls. Jeremy helped her move the ladder to each location and provided a hammer when needed to secure the fabric to the walls. She had designed the display so the art was hung between the drapes. The paintings went up next; the purpose was to use the color of the drapes to accent the art.

Once completed, Philip came out to review the effect. "Perfect," he said. He turned to Tony. "Let's get the floors cleaned off and the rugs laid out."

Tony waved to the men working with them and said, "Time to clean up." They moved the ladders and scaffolding from the room. The floors were swept clean and mopped.

While they were waiting for them to dry, Emma saw Cole had arrived.

Jeremy was speaking with Tony about additional security. He had his back to them and didn't notice his arrival. She walked over to Cole and said in a low voice, "Can we step out for a moment?"

Cole frowned. "Yes, of course."

They walked back out the front and stood under the high

portico roof. Cole leaned on one of the columns and asked, "Do you have something for me?"

"I do," she confirmed. "I saw Abbey today."

"Yes, I understand you had lunch with her and Ellis at the boarding house."

She looked at him with raised eyebrows.

"I spoke with Ellis this evening before he went out to dinner with Abbey," he said by way of explanation.

"Oh, okay." *Makes sense,* she thought. "No, that wasn't the only time I saw her today." She told him what she had seen.

"The timing of this is suspect," he said, mulling over the information. "Emma, let me look into this. Don't say anything to Jeremy."

She agreed.

"Let's go back in. I'd like to check the security and confirm the plans with Philip and Jeremy," said Cole.

As they went back in, they noticed the floors had dried and the rolls of carpet were being moved to the proper locations. The carpets were rolled out and adjusted. Then cabinets were placed in the center of the room.

"Emma," called Philip. "I have the cases opened."

Emma retrieved purple rectangles and squares she had cut to size. They didn't have to be hemmed; they could be tucked under the existing displays.

Each one was opened, and Emma added the draping. After everyone left, they would add the jewels to confirm the final setup. Until then, they would be locked up in Tony's office.

A final sweep was completed and the workmen were dismissed. At that time, it was only Tony, Emma, Philip, Jeremy, and Cole. The Pinkerton men were still on guard around the outside of the building.

"Ready?" asked Philip.

They heard a call from the door. Philip went over to find out what was the concern. He came back with Jake, who was carrying his camera. He explained, "After I saw how nice this was turning out, I thought Jake might take some pictures and document the jewels for us."

Good idea, thought Emma.

The museum was locked back down and the jewels were brought out. Philip and Tony had taken time to polish the stones and settings. They gleamed in the light. "We'll need extra light around the cases," said Jake.

"Of course." Philip had arranged for gas lights on stands to be available. Jeremy and Tony moved them close to the cases.

Philip handled the jewels and placed them in each one. "Should we close the lids?" he asked.

"No, leave them open. Otherwise, they may not turn out clear."

"Good suggestion." He completed the arrangements and stepped back to review. He walked around to see the displays from different angles. "Yes, that's it. Jake, you can start now."

Jake was very serious in his work; he gave instructions to have the group help with lifting when he thought it would make a better picture. Once the process was completed, he said, "Philip, would you like a picture with the display board in front of the museum? We could also send them to the paper."

Philip liked the idea and said, "That's a great idea. Tony, would you please join me?"

Tony went red with pleasure. "Yes, sir, thank you."

Their relationship had always been strong, but this was a big step to include him in the publicity for the museum. He felt valued and honored.

The pictures were taken and the jewels were carefully moved back to the safe before anyone could leave. Final security measures were reviewed and confirmed to be in place.

It was quite late when the team headed home, but they felt it would be a nice event.

"Tony," she called, "will anyone be in for a preview tomorrow?"

"No, we're going to keep everyone out until the evening. Philip feels it would be safer that way."

CHAPTER 27

The next night, the family was getting ready for the big event. Emma and Dora were in the attic putting on their dresses. As Emma helped Dora into hers, she said, "There, I have it buttoned up for you." She put on her dress and walked over to Dora, turning around so she could do the same for her.

Once finished, Emma asked, "Do you want some help with your hair?" Both girls were wearing their hair up and it could take a while to style. They completed their task and added makeup to their faces—a mixture made from oatmeal, eggs, honey, and other natural ingredients.

They heard a call from downstairs. "Ladies, Philip and Tony want us there early."

"Yes, well, that's the best we can do," Emma said and Dora nodded. They headed downstairs. Jeremy and Tim were dressed in their tuxedos, looking very handsome.

All motion seemed to stop when they saw each other.

Tim broke the silence and said, "Wow."

Dora smiled broadly. "Why, thank you, sir."

Jeremy couldn't take his eyes off Emma and said, "Beautiful."

Emma smiled softly. "Thank you."

They headed out to the carriage and made their way to the museum.

CHAPTER 28

They were early since Emma and Jeremy wanted to do final security checks. As they pulled up, they noticed the sign outside now included Jake's pictures from the night before. They paused a moment to review them.

Tim commented, "Jake wouldn't agree to come out with us. He said he has a new camera that he's evaluating."

"The pictures did turn out nice," commented Dora. "I'll tell him tomorrow."

They got cleared through the front door and made their way in. The caterers were setting up the hors d'oeuvres and drinks for the guests.

Emma walked over to the display case to view the jewels with Tim and Dora while Jeremy checked in with Tony and Philip. Dora and Tim were looking closely at them, and she commented, "Royal jewels, who would have thought we would be able to see this? Emma, you got to hold these?"

"Yes, and they're quite heavy. I can't imagine wearing them all night."

The guest started to arrive an hour later. Emma noticed quite a large number of them were the same people they had invited to the charity event. There was a large turnout, and everyone wanted to view the jewels. To keep it organized, groups of ten were allowed into the roped-off display area. Other groups were looking at the art on the walls; it had turned out to be just as popular as the jewels.

Philip approached their small group and said, "This is going well. I have some newspapermen here, so this should be in the paper tomorrow."

"How long will you keep the jewels on display?" Emma asked.

"We'll have them for another two weeks." He looked around and said, "I have to mingle," and he moved away.

Emma was looking around and saw Papa and Abbey enter. *They make a very handsome couple,* she thought. Watching them closely, she saw Abbey surveying the room, but not focusing on the art or the people. She was looking at where the security guards were located. Emma would keep an eye on her.

The evening continued. Jeremy walked up to Emma and Philip and said, "All of the guests have arrived."

"Good. Then the building can be locked down. No one in or out until I say so," said Philip, he motioned to the guards with his hands. They barred the door and stepped in front to keep watch.

He went to the front of the gathering and spoke. "Welcome! We are honored to have the French Crown Jewels with us. We would like to thank Tiffany and Co. for choosing us as the first stop. Please review our new French paintings on display as well as the jewels. I hope you enjoy your evening."

Jeremy stood with Emma. She started to say, "Jeremy…"

At that moment, there was a very loud argument at the front door. She glanced to see what the commotion was. Jeremy immediately waved more of his men in that direction.

"You aren't allowed to leave at this time," a voice could be heard saying.

Then, there was the sound of punches landing. The Pinkerton men, in place as undercover guests and museum guards, moved quickly to the door. Emma watched and thought, *This isn't good. No one is watching the jewels.* She pushed her way through the crowds, trying to get to the display cases.

Everyone's attention was toward the door and their backs to her. As she broke through, her worst fears were realized; the glass was shattered and the jewels were gone. Knowing she had to do something to get Cole and Jeremy's attention, she climbed on a chair and said in a very loud voice, "Quiet! I said quiet!"

The room went silent. "Cole." She nodded her head toward the cases.

He and Jeremy ran over. "Gone!" Jeremy shouted. "Philip!"

When he came over Jeremy continued, "Everyone in here will be questioned and searched." That caused a loud murmur among the attendees.

Philip was worried about the important people's responses, but he was more worried about the loss of the jewels. "There's no other way," said Philip. "Please, follow the Pinkertons' direction."

Cole said loudly, "As each of you is searched, you will be allowed to go." They got the people lined up in two lines, one for the women and one for the men.

There was a lot of grumbling from the crowd. "What right do they have to search us?" someone asked.

Cole responded, "We believe the jewels are still in the room. You are all aware of how important this is not only to Tiffany & Co. but to history."

That seemed to calm them down. Philip had screens brought in from the storeroom to help protect the women's privacy. Dora and Emma helped search the ladies.

"I would never do something like that!" an older lady huffed.

Dora caught Emma's eye and gave her a quick smile. Each woman was searched and released. When they got to Abbey, she smiled and said, "Search me." They searched her thoroughly and found nothing.

The men got similar attention from Jeremy and Cole.

Philip and Tony paced at the front doors.

"What do we do?" Philip asked. "How could this happen after all of our preparations?"

"The simpler the plan, the easier to put into action," Cole said. "We need to start letting people go. If the jewels are not on the guests, then they're still here."

"Agreed," said Philip. He announced to the group, "We are very sorry that this event had to end this way. We will find the jewels and continue with the exhibit." He nodded to the Pinkerton detectives to open the doors. The people that had been searched left quietly. Many were not sure what to make of their evening.

Cole spoke quietly to Ellis, saying it would be best if he and Abbey left also. He nodded and said, "I understand. We will head out." Dora and Tim indicated they would leave with them; they had to go home to relieve Amy.

Cole watched them leave and then turned to the group. "We'll need to separate and search the building top to bottom."

The Pinkerton detectives, Cole, Jeremy, Emma, and Tony searched the museum from top to bottom. It was late and they were all exhausted. Suddenly, Emma noticed something. She asked, "Tony, was your office locked during the party?"

"My office? No, there was no reason to. The jewels were out here," he said.

"Hmm," she mused, drumming her fingers on her lips.

"What are you thinking?" asked Jeremy.

"They had to know we would search everyone," Emma said contemplatively.

"Yes," Jeremy said.

She squinted at him. "What's the last place you would think to look?"

Tony's eyes went wide. "The safe!" He called to the others and they all ran into his office. Phillip went directly to the safe to open it.

They held their collective breath as it was opened. Emma had been right, whoever took them knew they would not check the safe for the jewels. Philip removed them carefully for examination. "They are intact," he said, relieved.

"Who did it?" asked Tony.

"Whoever it is will be back to get them," said Cole.

"Yes," agreed Emma.

Jeremy said, "I think I have an idea."

They listened closely and nodded. Later that night, they left the door to Tony's office open. They agreed to go home, each looking exhausted. As they exited, Cole confirmed he would contact the police and have them at the museum first thing in the morning.

CHAPTER 29

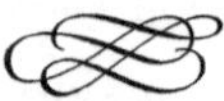

DINNER THAT NIGHT

The guards were making their rounds and didn't notice a figure moving around on the roof. That figure dressed all in black entered through the attic vent on top of the museum. They continued down to the main floor and to the office. The office door was left ajar, allowing access to the safe.

When the figure neared the safe, the office chair swung around, revealing Jeremy. It was a toss-up who was more surprised—Jeremy or his mom. He couldn't believe what he was seeing. She was dressed in all black, her hair covered by a black knit cap. Before he could voice his disappointment, she looked behind her and put her finger to her lips. She motioned for him to turn and jumped behind the door.

He reacted automatically and did as she asked. He heard footsteps, then a man's voice as he entered the office.

"So much easier this way," the man said. He made his way to the safe and opened it with no difficulty. When he looked inside there were no jewels. "What! But..."

"Looking for something?" Abbey asked, coming out from behind the door.

Emma was monitoring the room from out in the museum. She

had taken out the larger man accompanying the smaller thief as he entered the office. While she tied him up, she listened to the conversation. Cole had the place surrounded, so they were letting this play out.

"What are you doing here?" the small man asked.

"Well, it was easy to let you do all of the hard work," Abbey commented wryly.

"Well, *I* have done the work, so you will give me the jewels. Where have you put them?" he demanded.

"Oh, I don't have them," stated Abbey.

Jeremy turned his chair around at that statement. "No, she doesn't. We do, and you're under arrest." He had his gun trained on the small man.

Emma watched and thought, *There are three scenarios. He can give up, run, or attempt to grab Abbey.*

He picked the third choice and grabbed Abbey. Jeremy didn't want to shoot in the small room; he could accidentally hurt her. Jeremy knew Emma was waiting in the museum and that Cole had the area surrounded. Moving slowly, he placed his gun on the desk and held up his hands. "Just don't hurt her."

The man backed away toward the door, pulling Abbey with him. The thief stood in the center of the doorway with his arm around Abbey's neck, a gun at her throat. The small man suddenly looked surprised. "What...?" He looked at Abbey, then slumped into her, then onto the floor. A knife stuck out of his back.

"Everyone okay?" Cole asked as he stepped over the man and into the room. Abbey looked dazed and kept staring at the knife. *Mom,* she thought, looking at it The knife was exactly the type she used to use. She looked toward the door, expecting her to walk in.

Instead, Emma stepped in and asked, "Mind if I retrieve my knife?"

Cole stopped her and said, "Let's get the police involved first, and you can get it from them."

Abbey frowned at Emma. "What is going on here?"

Jeremy asked her, "Are you okay?"

"Yes, but she's under arrest. Turn around, please," Cole stated coolly. Abbey turned meekly and was escorted from the room. Cole looked back and said, "Emma and Jeremy, we will need you to go to the police station with us."

"But—" Emma said, wanting to stay behind and confirm the place was firmly locked up.

Cole interrupted. "Philip and Tony will take care of it. We need you at the station now."

Jeremy took a deep breath and let it out. Whether Abbey was guilty or not, he would be there for her. He followed them out.

Emma watched Jeremy's face and thought, *This will hurt Papa and Jeremy.*

When they arrived at the police station, they took all suspects into separate interrogation spaces. Cole was directing everyone in this event.

Before Cole and Jeremy went into the interrogation room with Abbey, Cole looked over at Emma. "We'll start with Abbey, then we'll bring you in next."

She sat on the bench and waited patiently for them to call her. She nodded to the police chief as he entered the second interrogation room. He was personally handling the interrogation of the henchman. They still had to find the inside person who moved the jewels to the safe.

Cole returned and said, "Emma, please join us."

As she walked in, her gaze was blocked by Cole's back. When he moved out of the way, she looked around, not understanding what she was seeing. Abbey was there but so were Papa and the Frenchman. She sent a shocked look to Jeremy and Cole, then she realized they were all smiling at her.

Her observational ability kicked into high gear. Cole, Jeremy, Papa, and Abbey appeared to be very friendly, with none of the animosity she had witnessed previously. "So, all of you were in on this?" she asked, exasperated, but her eyes twinkled.

"Yes, for this to work, we had to keep the number of people involved low," explained Cole.

"How did you get in without me seeing?"

Cole stood up and moved a curtain back, "A second entrance." She eyed him and her family and said, "So, the three of you are not fighting." She zeroed in on Jeremy. "You were in on this!"

He put his hands up. "I didn't find out until we got here."

She looked around, gathering facts. "And since we're in here without a police officer, that would make you French police?"

"You are right. She is good," the French policeman said.

"Was it also a matter of an exchange?" Emma asked Abbey.

Abbey laughed out loud. She had underestimated this girl. "Yes, I came out of retirement for a small job, and it turned out I was set up." She saw Jeremy glance at her and she responded, "Yes, I did one small job for a friend."

"We set it up so she could be blackmailed. It worked that we had a trade to make," the French policeman said.

"And you," Emma looked at Cole, "you were in this all along?"

"No, not initially," he commented. "I reached a point where I thought Jeremy could be hurt if she was here for the jewels, so I followed her. And I saw the same man you did." He nodded at the French detective.

"Yes," the Frenchman acknowledged. "Cole contacted me and we filled him in on the plan."

She looked at Jeremy and said, "Where's the animosity?"

"I'm just glad Mom isn't going to prison," he said sincerely. In response, Abbey took his hand and squeezed it.

"And you." Emma turned to her Papa. "Is this why you were avoiding me?"

He turned red but said, "Yes, little girl. I was afraid I'd give the game away if I spent more time with you."

She looked at Cole. "The man I intercepted at the museum, he is one of the men who attacked us on the train. You should be able to get him for the murder of the other man also."

"Yes, I will inform the chief so he can add the charge," said Cole.

Abbey said, "Can we get out of here now?" Just being there made her nervous.

Cole stood up. "Yes, they're moving the other man. Let me check to see if we can leave without him seeing you." Cole stepped out for a few moments and then returned. "We can go."

Abbey sat next to Emma in the carriage and commented, "So, you're an investigator?"

"You know that also," Emma said, squinting at Jeremy. He squirmed. Emma was used to being the one who knew all the secrets.

It might be a long night, thought Jeremy.

CHAPTER 31

The following week was exciting. They learned that one of the guest's personal assistants had been bribed to take the jewels and move them to the safe. The henchmen in custody gave up his name. He confessed as soon as he was picked up. The personal assistant had paid other assistants to start an argument and create a distraction. They didn't know why, they were just after the pay day.

The week was ending on a happy note for Emma. Friday morning, she and Mr. Pennington were the only guests and witnesses to Mr. and Mrs. Gilmore's second wedding. It was handled quietly in the judge's chambers. "I now pronounce you man and wife," he said and watched as they kissed.

As they thanked him, Emma and Mr. Pennington stepped forward to offer their congratulations. Mr. Gilmore said, "We would like you both to go to tea with us, to celebrate."

Emma said, "I would love to."

Mr. Pennington responded, "As would I."

"Wonderful. I have a carriage waiting for us."

As they descended the stairs, Mr. Pennington offered Mrs.

Gilmore his arm. She took it and they strode off. Emma and Mr. Gilmore followed at a slower pace.

"Emma, I wanted to speak with you a moment," Mr. Gilmore said. His serious tone caused her to pause and look at him.

"Yes?" Emma asked curiously.

"I have something for you. You saved us from prison. You made it so we can finally have a family." He grasped her hands and pressed an envelope into them.

Emma looked down and back up at him. "Thank you, but this isn't necessary."

"We believe it is," he said firmly.

"Thank you," she said and put the envelope inside her jacket. She would enjoy her lunch and check it later.

Lunch was nice, not just the food but watching two people so in love.

Emma got home before her courier work started and ran upstairs to her room. Sitting on the edge of the bed, she opened the envelope and saw there was a hundred-dollar bill there. What to do with it? She made up her mind and moved to the bed, removing the post, and slipped it inside before she went back downstairs. There might be a project where that money could be useful.

CHAPTER 32

It had been about four weeks since the jewel exhibit and the wedding. The exhibit had been extremely success-ful, and the couriers had picked up the jewels. It was confirmed that they had made it safely to their next stop.

Jeremy was feeling more secure that his mom was going to stay around for a long time.

That evening after dinner, Emma was working on some lace designs for Abbey's dress in the attic room. She had her initial sketches completed and was ready to meet with her.

There was a knock on her door and when Emma opened it, she was surprised to see Abbey standing there. She smiled. "I was just thinking that I needed to show you my designs for your dress."

Abbey looked very serious. "I think it's time we talked." She closed the door behind her and moved into the room.

"No way out, I suppose," commented Emma, wondering what this was about.

"No," said Abbey. "I want to talk about your knife skills."

"Knife skills?" she echoed, bewildered. "Why would you want to discuss that?"

"Who trained you?" Abbey asked, standing still as a statue without answering Emma's question.

Emma didn't know why she wanted to know, but it wasn't a secret. "We had a specialist who lived with us. She taught me."

"This specialist, what was her name?" asked Abbey, her voice low.

"We called her Miss Marjorie, but I believe it was Marjorie Allen."

Abbey walked over to the chair facing Emma and sat down before she continued. "When did she move into the boarding house?"

"She and a friend moved in 1876."

"A friend?"

"Miss Amy. They were inseparable after their husbands passed."

Abbey's face turned white at that statement. "Her husband? He passed?"

"Yes. Miss Marjorie said it was after their last big job. They both went to prison. She got out and he didn't."

Abbey took a shuddering breath at that statement. Emma watched her, letting the pieces of the puzzle build.

"What was she like, when you knew her?"

That made Emma smile. "Wonderfully brash. She spoke her mind. She taught me about knives and how to use them."

"Yes, I was never good at that. It made her angry that I didn't have that talent," Abbey commented.

"Did you know Miss Marjorie? Papa mentioned when she moved in that he'd known her a long time ago, that he owed her for saving his life."

"She was my mother," Abbey said simply, laying her head back on the chair. "We never got along, too much alike, I suppose."

"Your mother," she said, and something clicked. "But that means Jeremy..."

"Her grandson," she finished for her.

"Did she know about him?"

"I'm not sure. I don't think Jeremy knew, but Cole must have. He and Ellis knew her at the same time."

As Emma thought about it, Miss Marjorie always made herself scarce when they visited. She would have a headache or say she just needed to rest. She hadn't thought anything about it at the time.

"Was she happy?" inquired Abbey.

"Yes, I believe she was."

"When I saw that knife—the craftsmanship and the aim—I knew you were trained by her." She sat up and looked Emma in the eye. "So, tell me. What *do* you do, Emma?"

"I work for Pinkerton and independently on other cases."

"A detective." She laughed. "I should have known Jeremy would pick someone interesting. You asked me about my previous life. Now, I want to know about yours."

They sat up that night, talking and comparing the many stories that had shaped the women they had become. They fell asleep talking.

When they exited the room the next morning, they were as tight as thieves. They walked down together and Emma asked, "Would you like our family to take you to Miss Marjorie's grave?"

"I would," she commented softly.

Dora was surprised to see Abbey walk into the kitchen with Emma. "Visiting early this morning," she asked curiously.

Abbey laughed. "No, visited late. I find I'm very tired and should head back to my hotel."

"I can get Tim to get you a carriage and escort you back," suggested Dora.

"I would appreciate that. I'm not used to these late hours anymore." She hugged Emma. "Thank you for last night." She also walked over and hugged Dora.

Tim came in, and Dora asked, "Can you take Abbey back to the hotel in a carriage?"

"I can." He offered her his elbow. He sent a questioning look at Dora, and she mouthed, "Later."

As she handed Amy the baby, Dora said, "Emma, join me in the sitting room, please."

Emma followed her and sat down, telling her all she'd learned about Abbey and Miss Marjorie.

"All that time, and we didn't know?" Dora asked in amazement.

"She must have made Papa promise," Emma speculated.

CHAPTER 33

After Abbey rested, she got ready for her lunch with Ellis. They arranged to meet in her hotel room. She had not fought with him in all the time she had known him, but that was about to change. All of their talks since she had gotten back, how close they had become, and no word about Mama? If they were to move forward together, there had to be no secrets.

Sitting on a chair near the door, she watched the clock and waited.

Promptly at noon, there was a soft knock on the door. She stood and approached it slowly. As it opened, she saw the smile she had loved always. It was hard to hold her face still and not return that smile.

"Abbey, is everything all right?" he asked, instantly concerned.

"Ellis, please, sit down," she requested.

He looked at her and saw her expression had not changed. He moved to the settee and took a seat. "What's wrong? Has something happened?"

She got right to the point. "Mama."

Ellis' face turned white. "Abbey, I was waiting for the right time to tell you. How did you find out?"

"I saw Emma's knife skills," Abbey said wryly.

"Oh," said Ellis and saw the humor. "I guess that would have been a giveaway."

"I was shocked at how similar her skills are to Mama's."

"Yes, they were very similar people. They really loved each other."

"More than she loved me?" she asked softly.

"No," said Ellis, taking her hand, "just a different kind. That shouldn't take away from your feelings for her."

"Ellis, did you tell Cole or Jeremy?"

"Cole knew as soon as he heard her name."

"Did he plan to tell Jeremy?"

"I don't think so; at least, not at that time. She had been gone for so long, he probably didn't want to stir anything up."

"Yes, Cole would want order." For the first time, she wasn't bitter about it. She said graciously, "Thank you, Ellis, for taking her in."

"I was afraid if I didn't, she may have pulled another job," he teased.

"That she would have. Tell me about her."

"Let's order lunch here, and I'll tell you everything I can remember."

They talked and Abbey cried about missing her mama's last days.

Later, Abbey and Ellis sat down with Jeremy and Cole to explain who Miss Marjorie was. Jeremy was disappointed he hadn't been told that she was his grandmother, but he understood she had preferred to keep it quiet.

"That amazing woman was related to me?" he asked Abbey.

"Yes. I'll tell you more about her adventures and your grandfather later."

"Will we have time?"

She smiled at him and said, "We'll have all the time we need."

CHAPTER 34

About a month later, Emma opened the door of the boarding house and picked up the two papers that had been thrown on the stoop—two because she usually ended up cutting up one of the papers for potential cases.

Emma moved to the dining room table to review each page of her paper in detail. The clippings she found interesting were kept in her small black notebook. She went through the pages meticulously, reading and discarding the stories.

Occasionally, she kept the things she found that were amusing. Like today, there was an article about a missing dog and, on another page, another about a dog that was found. It appeared to be the same dog. She made a point to contact the individuals and get the dog to its owner.

She continued reading and found a story about the glass factory. There had been an explosion in a furnace used to make the glass, damaging the area and shutting down operations for six months. Luckily, there had been no injuries.

She tapped that one and checked to be sure the opposite side held nothing of importance. When the other side wasn't found to be important, she tore the article out to add to her collection.

Opening her notebook, she filtered through her clippings collection until she found another one about the same glass factory. Comparing the two articles, she thought, *Two rather serious events happened in the last few months that caused the factory to close short term. Hmm—there might be something there.* She made notes to investigate and see if there was a case.

The society page was next. There was an article there that indicated Mr. Baxton was expected to return from his extended European trip within the next few weeks. He had departed after his wife had disappeared a broken man with no answers as to how she had been taken from him.

That had happened two years ago. Emma had wanted to help with the case but, when Pinkerton offered their services, they had been rebuffed both by Mr. Baxton and the police detective in charge of the case.

The notebook she had made for that case was in her desk drawer. Picking up the paper, she took it upstairs to retrieve it. She opened her desk drawer and found it buried under several other notebooks. Sitting in her chair, she reviewed the information she had gathered at that time:

- The Baxtons were rich, with family money and investments in real estate.
- Mr. and Mrs. Baxton had met when they were young; their families arranged the marriage.
- They were both in their early 40s; there were no children and both were active in the community.
- All accounts said they were happy.

On that fateful evening, the servants found Mr. Baxton covered in his wife's blood. He reported two people had broken into their house and taken his wife. The detectives investigated but could not find a body, and the doctors working the case said the amount of blood indicated she probably had not survived. They questioned the servants and found that the husband and wife were having a quiet evening alone and the staff was out of the house. This was something they did occasionally and the detectives didn't think anything of it.

Over the next week, no ransom request was made and no body was found. The case remained open, but there were no additional leads. Mr. Baxton stopped going out in public and stayed inside the house, mourning his wife's death. He only left to attend the dedication of a memorial fountain in her name. Not long after that, he boarded a ship and moved to Europe. The house had been closed up, and no one expected him to return.

She remembered something from an article a month ago, something about that fountain. *What was it?* Making a note, she thought, *I should go by the library to check on back copies.* There should be time after her morning job.

Emma closed her notebook and headed down for breakfast. Jeremy was already in the dining room adding food to his plate. She leaned down to kiss him before sitting. He noticed her notebook next to her. "Do you have a new case?" he asked.

"I'm not sure yet, but I'm looking into a few things."

"Anything you can share yet?"

"I need more data first." She ate quickly and helped with the dishes before heading to her morning job. Jeremy had some interviews to do that morning downtown, so she wouldn't be accompanying him to the trolley.

Her morning position was still with Mr. Pennington; he had made it a permanent one after the last case wrapped up. That morning, the work was routine and the time went by quickly. After she completed her assigned task, she went straight to the library to look for the article she'd thought might be pertinent to the Baxton case.

She arrived and parked her bike outside and secured it to a

rail. The library was quiet as she entered and headed to the section where older papers were kept. Flipping through the last four weeks, she read through several until she found the article she had been looking for.

"Aha," she said. There was a story a few pages in about how the memorial fountain had a crack in the foundation and would need extensive repairs. The reporter had interviewed the contractor, who said they would have to dig up the wet ground down to at least six feet to repair and replace the piping. The fountain was important; Mrs. Baxton had been a great lady, giving generously to the community. The repairs would have to be delayed until Mr. Baxton returned from Europe. The article further detailed that he wanted to oversee every detail of the repairs.

Emma sat for a moment and reviewed her notes. She drummed her fingers on her lips and thought, *Is it possible he's coming home because, if they dig there, they might find her body?* It was a long shot and no one was paying her to work on the case, but she would investigate anyway.

She hesitated only briefly before she tore the article out of the newspaper. The papers went back into the stacks. Emma glanced around to make sure she wasn't being watched. The area was empty of people and there didn't seem to be much interest in the back issues, as far as she could tell. Amy would be the next one for her to interview, she usually knew the network of servants in Chicago.

Entering the kitchen she asked, "Amy, can I have a few moments with you?"

"Sure."

"Alone?"

Amy knew that tone. She called over to Ethyl, "Could you dust the sitting room and open the shades to allow some light in?"

Ethyl finished wiping off the counters and said, "Yes, I'll go now."

Amy sat at the table and patted the chair next to hers. After Emma sat, she said, "I get to be involved in an investigation?"

Emma smiled; Amy was normally the one sent from the room. "Yes, I need your help. Please, don't share anything I tell you."

"Of course," she said seriously.

"Do you know the people who worked at the Baxton mansion?"

Amy thought for a moment and said, "It's been a few years but, yes, I knew most of the staff. They were discharged as soon as Mr. Baxton departed for Europe."

"All of them? That's unusual. He didn't take any with him?" Normally one or two servants would accompany the family.

"No."

"No one stayed on at the house to have it ready if he returned?"

"No, I believe another company was brought in to manage it."

"Were they pensioned off?" she asked, having experienced that during a previous case.

"No. Again, it was unusual," Amy said.

"Should I contact the cook?"

"No," said Amy, thinking. "In this case, I think you need to speak with the butler, Mr. Amberson."

Emma noted that and asked, "Would you know where he's working now?"

Amy raised an eyebrow and said, "Let me see your notebook."

Emma laughed and handed it to her. She wrote the address and family name quickly.

Emma read the address and said, "I know that area. It's on par with the Baxton's wealth."

"If you would like to write a note, I can have him meet you."

Emma organized the note and gave it to Amy. She asked him to meet her the next morning at the memorial fountain.

She received a note that evening confirming he would meet her there at 8am.

CHAPTER 35

MRS. BAXTON'S CASE — EMMA

Emma arrived at the fountain early and walked around it slowly. It was a large, round structure with stone forming the foundation and the walking path around it.

As she reviewed the area closely, she saw there was something wrong with the foundation; it was uneven in several places. She continued to walk around it until she reached the memorial plaque. It read, "This memorial is in place for Diane Baxton, 1885."

A hand reached around her and laid flowers on it.

She turned quickly and had to tilt her head to look into his eyes. "Mr. Amberson?" she inquired

He nodded and respectfully removed his hat. "Miss Evans?"

"Yes. Would you like to sit?" It was a sunny day, but not too uncomfortable. They sat on one of the benches surrounding the fountain.

There was a long moment of silence, and Emma thought he might be praying. She waited until he opened his eyes. "You miss her," she said.

"Yes," he acknowledged. She thought he wouldn't continue, he looked so solemn. Finally, he said, "She was family. I started working there when we were both teenagers. We played in the house; I helped her with her homework. I met everyone she knew, and I was at her wedding."

Emma teared up for a moment, realizing he hadn't just lost a job; he had lost his family. "I'm sorry for your loss, Mr. Amberson."

"Your note indicated that you wanted to discuss Mrs. Baxton's disappearance."

"I think I found a possible lead, and I had hoped you would help me with it."

He'd heard of her through his staff when she was involved in the Millicent Carlyle case. "Do you think you will be able to get him?"

"Him?" she asked, curious to whom he was referencing.

"Yes, Mr. Baxton."

She studied him and asked, "That was your conclusion-that he did it?"

"I lived with them; I saw everything they did."

She nodded and asked, "Could we discuss the night she went missing?"

"Murdered," he stated forcefully.

"Murdered. Yes, I think the amount of blood found proves that," she agreed. "I understand you and other staff members were out for the night?"

"Yes. Occasionally, they asked that they have time alone in the house."

"Did you go out?"

"I did not. I stayed on site. We have quarters outside the main house, so I stayed there."

"Can you see the main house from your living area?"

Instead of answering, he said, "Would you like to go there and see it for yourself?"

She closed her notebook. "Yes, I would." Walking quickly, she retrieved her bike and rolled it over to him.

He glanced at it with a frown and said, "We'll need a carriage. I don't think we'll both fit on that contraption."

She smiled and said, "A carriage will be fine."

"I have one waiting."

She followed him, walking the bike to a very nice carriage waiting on the edge of the park. The driver got down to help her store her bike and helped her into the carriage. Mr. Amberson gave the address, and the driver pulled away smoothly. The drive took about ten minutes; the house came slowly into view.

"There it is," said Mr. Amberson, indicating the grandiose red brick house sitting far back on a manicured lawn.

"It looks like someone is managing the property and the house."

"Yes, Mr. Wright's will mandated that the house be kept and maintained. It's overseen by a management team. Her father always wanted to ensure she had a place to live."

As the carriage made its way up the long drive, she noticed the ornate courtyard. It was lined with the same brick-like that on the house and was set in a herringbone style. It was a circular shape that allowed them to be dropped off at the main steps.

As she descended the carriage, she saw the steps to the mansion were massive, twenty feet across and on two distinct levels. These led to the main doorway, with multiple windows flanked by columns. The house on either side of the columns was red brick, where greenery climbed in a controlled manner.

She stood back for a moment to take it all in. "Three stories?" she asked.

"Yes, the top floor is the large attic space. It's used for storage."

"Just two people lived here?"

"Yes."

She continued to look around outside at the breadth of the estate.

"Would you like to go in?" he asked.

She turned back to him and said, "I would."

The security guards knew him and allowed them to enter. As they made their way into the foyer, what struck her was the attention to detail. The woodwork gleamed and the tile floor shined. "They're maintaining this as well?"

"Yes." He stopped, lost in his memories

She asked gently, "Is this where it occurred?"

"Where he murdered her, you mean?" he asked in a low voice.

She nodded.

"Yes," he said.

"Would you be able to walk it through with me, what you saw in here?"

He took a deep breath and said, "Of course. Where would you like to start?"

"That night, what made you come up to the house? You were the one to find Mr. Baxton lying near the pool of blood."

He looked at her, surprised she knew that. "I was there because I had been told to make sure all of the lights were turned down at 11pm."

"Was that a usual occurrence?"

"No, normally they would have turned them down without help on the nights they planned to be alone."

So, she thought, *he was chosen as a witness.*

"I was part of the plan," he guessed, reading her thoughts.

"It appears so. Go on with your story."

"I entered the back of the house, through the kitchen, and made my way to the foyer. I usually start there, turning down the lights and making sure doors are locked."

"Was the back door locked?"

He had to think. "Yes, I believe it was."

"Were there guards around the house, like there are now?"

"Not like now, no. We had a full staff and they would not have been necessary."

"Okay, continue."

"I walked into the foyer and saw Mr. Baxton. He was lying on the floor and, nearby, there was a large pool of blood. I had never seen so much blood."

"What did you do?"

"I have to admit I panicked for a moment and wanted to run out the way I had come in."

"But you didn't," she guessed.

"No, instead, I went over to Mr. Baxton to check if he was alive. He was breathing, but had been knocked out."

"There was no sign of Mrs. Baxton."

"None at all," he said.

Emma would have to get the police reports to confirm what Mr. Baxton had said that evening. "Could you show me where the servants' quarters are located?"

"Yes," he indicated with his hand, "if you'll follow me."

They made their way through the large interior, then went down a long hallway. She stopped at a portrait of two people. "Is that Mr. and Mrs. Baxton?" she asked.

He nodded, looking only at Mrs. Baxton.

Emma took note of that. She also studied Mr. Baxton's features closely.

They moved on and exited out the kitchen door he'd mentioned. There was a rock path cut into a beautiful garden. "We lived there," he said, pointing to the brick structures set away from the main house. She walked around and saw that their view was cut off from the front drive.

"If there were a second person or persons involved, you may not have seen or heard a carriage."

"Not from back here," he confirmed.

They continued around the garden area. "Mr. Amberson, I'll have to gather more data. Do you know when Mr. Baxton is arriving?"

"Just what I read in the paper."

"Yes, it indicated we have a few weeks. I understand he asked them to delay any repairs to the fountain until that time? Is it not part of the estate?"

"No, that was Mrs. Baxton's project and was part of the estate that went to her husband."

Three weeks, she thought. She looked at him and commented, "Not much time. I will need to gather information. Would you mind if we meet again, Mr. Amberson?"

"Of course not. I would appreciate anything you can do to help us understand what happened to her."

They went out the front and waved to their carriage driver that they were ready. He dropped her and her bike off at Mr. Pennington's office. She needed to compile her notes for the day and work on her next steps.

CHAPTER 36

It was late in the evening, and Jeremy and Emma were lying in bed relaxing. "Tell me about the case you started today," he said, propping himself on his elbow and watching her.

She looked over at him. "How did you know it turned into a case?" He drummed his fingers on his lips. She lowered her fingers and grinned at him. "Think you know me so well?"

"Yes," he said. "Now, tell me what you're working on."

She went into detail on what she'd found in the paper, the initial investigation, and the interview with Mr. Amberson.

"So, you think Mr. Baxton, did it?"

"The evidence, though circumstantial, looks that way."

"What are your next steps?"

"I'm going to see if I can get my hands on the will. I'll ask Mr. Pennington for help on that. Then, I'm going to see if I can review the police files."

When she looked pensive at that last statement, he asked, "What's the concern with getting the files from the police?"

"The detective involved in the investigation all that time ago, he's still there."

"Can you work with him?"

"I'm not sure," she said, but she was thinking of going to the chief for this. She had been rebuffed the last time she asked to be involved in the case. The best way was to make the request in such a way that no one was aware she was making it. *Carl,* she suddenly thought. The chief's brother could get her message over to him. She did owe him a Berliner; she'd have to make a point to see him in the morning.

Emma lay back, putting together the information she would need tomorrow. When she settled on a plan for her case, she thought of something Jeremy might be interested in.

"Just a moment," she said. Rolling out of bed, she walked over to her desk. She pulled out her current notebook and clippings.

"What's that?" Jeremy asked curiously.

"When I was looking through the paper, I didn't just see Mrs. Baxton's case. I also saw this." She laid them on the bed. Pointing to one, she said, "I found these two, one about six months ago, about a suspicious fire and another one today about a furnace explosion at the same plant."

He read the first article. The fire had started on the second floor of the building on January 24, 1887. Two men and seventy-five boys barely escaped by jumping into snowbanks or running through flames. The plant was repaired and paid for by insurance. The second one noted that insurance refused to cover the second event. All costs would be covered by the owner. Jeremy asked, "Do you think they might be connected?"

"It's highly coincidental that two such incidents could occur at the same facility in that short space of time. It's a glass company and, if the fire didn't wipe the company out, the furnaces are probably the most important piece of equipment in glass manu-facturing."

Jeremy knew something about gas furnaces. They were oven-like structures made for the sole purpose of melting glass in large quantities. The oven could have catastrophic failure due to the design. He mulled it over and asked, "Where's this company located?"

"On the outskirts of town, Wade Street."

"I know that plant, and I believe they supply the local druggist with glass and also ship them to other areas."

"You don't have anything going on right now, do you?"

He thought about his current projects. "No. We're at a stopping point on my cases." He made a decision. "I'll review this with Cole and see if we can approach the owner."

Emma understood. The Pinkertons were a business and would require an agreement to continue.

CHAPTER 37

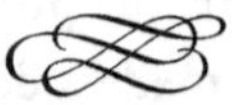

MRS. BAXTON'S CASE -- EMMA

The berliner box was in the basket attached to the front of her bike. Carl had a weakness for them. She stopped the bike and parked it outside before entering the florist shop. The bell above her head announced her entry and she called, "Carl!"

He stuck his out of the back room and said, "Emma what a nice surprise."

The box in her hands took all of his attention and he went directly to her and took it to place on the counter. "Ahh just what I needed today." And took one out, eating it without hesitation.

Once he had his fill he asked, "What can I do for you?"

"I do have a favor to ask," she admitted.

He nodded, his mouth full of another berliner.

"I need a file from form the police station."

"Why not get it directly from my brother?" Emma and he had a good relationship.

"This one might be tricky, one of his detectives be part of the coverup."

"Hmm. In that case, yes. I will get it for you, I will tell him what I am doing, but I will ask him to give you time to investigate."

"Thank you."

"I will bring it over later today," he promised.

They talked long and then Emma headed off to begin her workday.

That evening Dora called her as she walked into the door, "Carl left something for you. It is on the table."

She walked over and opened the file. The biggest surprise was his conclusions -it was not suspected murder but instead, it was a missing person case. *Wow*, she thought. *I wonder about that detective bank account. I will have Tim check it out.*

CHAPTER 38

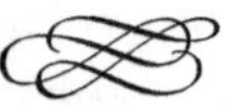

GLASS FACTORY CASE -- JEREMY

The next day, Jeremy met with Cole and showed him the articles. Cole looked at them carefully and asked, "Do you think this is sabotage?"

"I think it might be."

"Okay, make an appointment with the owner. Not on-site, in case any undercover work is necessary."

"I agree." Jeremy sent a note to the owner, using the boarding house as the return address. It would be later that morning when he heard back.

The factory owner suggested an out-of-the-way restaurant for their meeting.

Jeremy agreed and sent back a confirmation.

CHAPTER 39

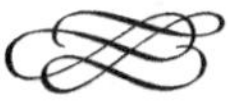

MRS. BAXTON'S CASE --EMMA

*E*mma was on her way to Mr. Pennington's office that morning. She carried her bike in and was greeted by Ethan.

"Hey, Em, how are you this morning?" They were on better terms now that she was a more permanent part of Mr. Pennington's staff.

"I'm good," she said as she stored her bike and started to her office. She stopped and asked, "Ethan, how would I go about getting a copy of a will?"

"What do you need it for?"

"A new case," she told him. Ethan was the soul of discretion and would not mention it to anyone.

"A will may only be viewed after it has been filed for probate, at which time the document becomes a public court record," he said.

"So, I would have access to it?" she asked.

"Possible. Wills are typically filed in probate courts based on the county in which a deceased person lived at the time of his or her death, or the county in which the deceased person owned real estate. Did they die in this county?"

"I believe so. I know his daughter did," Emma commented.

"You just have to fill out a form and submit it to the court," stated Ethan. "Would you like a copy of the form?"

She smiled and said, "Yes, please." She stepped over to get it from him. "I'll complete this and turn it in after I leave today."

"Just to let you know, it may take a while to get this processed." He lowered his voice. "But I might know someone in the clerk's office who could get you the papers to view."

"If you could set it up, I would appreciate it," she responded in a similar tone.

"You know," he said, "you'll owe me."

She looked at him and said sincerely, "Anything you need."

"I'll keep that in mind."

She went into her office to work. It was several hours later that Ethan stuck his head in and said, "I have that clerk for you."

"Come in."

He stepped inside and said, "You need to see Charlie Livingston at the office next to courtroom twenty-two. He'll expect you at about 1:00 tomorrow afternoon."

Emma documented the time and date. "Thanks, Ethan."

She finished her filing and covered her typewriter. Pushing back from her desk, she took her courier bag, said her goodbyes to Ethan, and headed out for the day.

CHAPTER 40

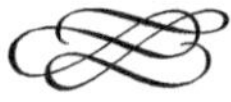

GLASS FACTORY CASE -- JEREMY

Jeremey arrived at the restaurant and gave his name. The host escorted him to a table where an old, rather rotund man was seated. "Mr. Samuels?"

"Yes, are you Mr. Tilden?"

"Yes, Jeremy, please."

"You wanted to discuss the incidents that have occurred at my factory?"

"Yes." He pulled the two articles and laid them down.

"Hmm, yes, those occurred."

"Sir, I'd like to take on the case for you through The Pinkerton Agency."

Mr. Samuels sighed and said, "My boy, I'm going broke trying to stay in business. I don't think I could handle an expense like that."

"Sir, I don't think you can afford not to." Jeremy was thinking and suggested, "What if we agree I only get paid if we find out who the saboteur is?"

As a man of business, Mr. Samuels realized a good deal when he heard one. "That sounds like something I can go along with. What is your plan for getting started?"

"I want to start by seeing the personnel files for that time period and the incident reports."

"I will have that ready for you before you come in."

"Can I have a tour when no one else is there?"

"It is my factory, so yes. Would you like to meet there this evening? The only issue is we run twenty-four hours a day, so there's not a time when there isn't someone there."

"I'd still like to go."

CHAPTER 41

GLASS FACTORY CASE -- JEREMY

That evening, Jeremy dressed in dark clothes and approached the side entrance of the building that housed the factory. They had prearranged the location. He saw a shadow approaching and recognized the owner.

"Let's head in," Mr. Samuels said.

As they entered, Jeremy was surprised; not that they were running at that late hour, but that children appeared to be a large part of the operations. He saw boys as young as nine and ten working near the hot furnaces. They carried materials to the older boys who were blowing the glass.

He would have liked to have investigated the children's working conditions, but he was there for the sabotage case. The owner led the way and showed Jeremy the equipment and explained how his business worked. The children continued to draw his gaze, something had to be done about that.

CHAPTER 42

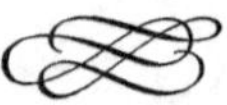

GLASS FACTORY CASE -- JEREMY

The next morning, Jeremy was speaking with Tim in his study about the factory working conditions. "Do you know anything about the glass factories in the area?"

"Some," said Tim. "It's a hard business and, unfortunately, run with a large number of children."

"Tim, there were boys as young as nine there."

"Yes, and behaving like men. Did you notice that?"

"I didn't."

"Watch next time you're there; they drink, they smoke, and they swear like they are adults."

"Why do parents allow this?" Jeremy asked, bewildered. He looked over at Patrick, working on his letters, and realized he was old enough to work in that factory.

"Money," said Tim simply. "Parents can't make it on their own, so the kids have to go into the workforce."

"They're working them day and night. What about labor laws?"

"There's nothing right now. Most unions protect only adults and oppose child labor reform; they fight desperately to keep the glasshouse boys and others hard at work, day and night. The larger industries are opposing any reform to the child labor law because of the cost it will add to have adults in those roles."

"Why don't the parents say something?"

"Unfortunately, the parents are part of the pushback to keep the kids working."

"Even if they're in danger?"

"Yes," Tim asked. "Any theories if this is sabotage yet?"

"Not yet," he said noncommittedly.

Dora came in holding a thick package and said to Jeremy, "This was just delivered for you."

"Here, let me take that." He walked over to accept it. He opened the side of the envelope and saw it was full of the reports he was waiting for.

"Looks like you have plenty to do today," Tim said.

"Looks like," he said wryly. "I better get started on this now. Would you and Patrick mind if I work here with you?"

"No problem," said Tim.

Patrick mimicked his response. "No problem."

Jeremy smiled and moved to the couch. The package contained engineering investigations of the last two events. Separating them on the table in front of him, he picked up the first one and started to read. The rest of his day would involve him going through reports and making notes. He would need to review the data with Emma and Ellis before he came to any final conclusions.

At last, he finished and put away his files, he needed to check with Dora. She was in the sitting room working on her books with Lottie asleep in her cradle. "Dora, would you mind if we added Mom and Ellis to the dinner tonight?"

"That shouldn't be a problem, just make sure Amy's aware. You know how she plans."

"I will and thanks."

"Anytime," she said softly.

CHAPTER 43

MRS. BAXTON'S CASE -- EMMA

*E*mma had a full morning at Mr. Pennington's office then headed home for lunch, entering through the kitchen door.

"Hi," she said to Amy.

She was cutting up vegetables meant for a stew and said, "Lunch is on the table if you're hungry."

"I am," said Emma. "I'll join them now." She entered and found Jeremy, Dora, Tim, Patrick, and baby Lottie enjoying their lunch. Kissing Jeremy hello. "Well, this is a nice surprise."

He explained, "I got the papers from the case delivered here; figured it would be easier to stay and review them."

"Makes sense," she said as she sat down and started gathering a roll, some cheese, and meat.

"Some fruit and vegetables also," Dora reminded her.

"Yes, Mom," she teased and picked out some fruit and vegetables to eat with her lunch.

They noticed she was eating rather fast. Tim asked, "What's your hurry?"

"New case, looking into some information at the courthouse."

"Anything you can share yet?" asked Dora, knowing Emma's

cases could be somewhat secretive.

"Not yet, but soon. Tim, I may need your help looking into something."

"Okay, just let me know."

"What are you doing today, Patrick?" she asked as she watched the boy eat with gusto.

"Grandpapa is picking me up for an afternoon."

"Oh, and what does he have planned?"

"A surprise."

She glanced over at Dora in a questioning manner.

Dora mouthed, "Buildings."

Emma smiled. "I always enjoyed outings with Papa. You should have fun."

"Can I go get ready now?" Patrick asked excitedly.

Dora glanced at his plate and nodded as he jumped up and prepared to run from the room. Tim caught his jacket. "Walk, please. Grandpapa won't leave here without you."

"Yes, Papa," said Patrick and hugged him.

Dora and Emma smiled at how close they had become.

Emma finished quickly and started to do a similar dash when she was also warned by Tim. "Emma, walk, please."

"Yes, Papa," she teased and leaned over to kiss him on the cheek before moving into the foyer. The camera she needed for today was located in the basement. She walked quickly toward it and descended the stairs. The gas lamps were lit, illuminating her path as she made her way down to the locked case where Jake kept his cameras. A key wasn't needed, she picked the lock and retrieved the camera. The camera was kept loaded with film for her to use. Retrieving it, she carried it upstairs and placed it in her bag.

Next, she pulled on her long jacket, and her bowler before she went back through the dining room to access the kitchen door and called out, "I'll be home in a few hours."

"We'll see you then," Dora called back.

CHAPTER 44

MRS. BAXTON'S CASE -- EMMA

Emma grabbed her bike and headed down to the courthouse to meet with Charlie Livingston, Ethan's contact. At lunch, the courthouse was very quiet and a good time to meet someone without a large number of people seeing. Checking her notes for the office number, she avoided the elevator and took the stairs. The room was down the long hallway; she knocked softly on the door and received an affirmative response to enter the office.

Emma entered the room and found it full of filing cabinets. She had seen this type in business offices during her temporary jobs. The man who had called her in was about 5'4", looked to be around 35, and had short, trimmed hair and round glasses. His suit was cheap but well pressed.

"Mr. Livingston?" she asked.

"I am, and you are Emma Evans?"

"I am."

"Good, good. We don't have a lot of time, but you can come through here," he indicated a gap in the long counter, "and view the files on my desk. I'll be over here filing." She noticed he would be across the room and behind additional filing cabinets, giving her privacy.

She smiled and went straight to the desk. There, she found the two wills. The time should allow her to read them closely, but she would be able to take pictures. The sticky gum in her purse would allow her to tack them on the wall to allow for better photos. Taking the pictures quickly, she put the camera back into her bag and removed the tacky material from the back, and replaced them in the folder.

The timepiece pinned to her blouse indicated she had a few more moments. She took the time and started to read through the documents. She saw two things in Mr. Wright's will: 1) all money would go to his daughter and her descendants; her husband would only inherit if there were no children, and 2) he could not be convicted of a felonious act, otherwise, he would be barred from the inheritance.

Hmm, she thought. *What about the daughter's will?* She pulled it up and found the same wording. *He didn't want her to be put at risk because of the money.* She completed her notes and closed the files. Keeping conversations with the clerk to a minimum, she said, "Thanks!"

He nodded, not looking at her as she left.

She thought to herself, *At least I know the reason why he's returning and not just staying in Europe. If his wife's body is found and he's convicted, the money reverts to a trust and it is donated.*

This operation would have taken more than Mr. Baxton. He was knocked out at the scene and, if involved, someone else had moved the body for him. A staff member, perhaps?

She continued her courier duties and swung by Mr. Amberson's house as her last stop.

CHAPTER 45

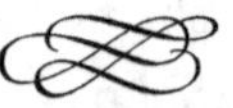

MRS. BAXTON'S CASE -- EMMA

r. Amberson had a limited window of time, so she arranged to meet him at the residence he was working at. "You won't get into trouble with me coming here?" she asked as he let her into the kitchen door.

"No, not at all. Lunch has been cleared away, and I've informed them I would be delayed for some time this afternoon."

"Wonderful."

"Please, sit," he said and watched as she pulled out her notebook. "What would you like to know?"

"Let's go over who was working at the house during the time the event occurred."

"Yes, I can provide that. There was an upstairs maid assigned to Miss Catherine and a man assigned to Mr. Baxton."

Funny, she thought as she noted the difference in the way he said their names. "Kitchen staff?"

"Two helpers and a cook. For big events, we brought in servers."

"Other inside house staff?"

"Two footmen to assist me and a driver."

"What about outside?"

"There were two full-time gardeners; we brought in help as needed."

She nodded. "Were any of these people new to their positions?"

He looked contemplative for a moment and said, "Cassey. Cassandra Woods. She was only here a few months before the event."

"Interesting," she said. Out of the corner of her eye, she noticed he was happy she had written that down. *Why?* she thought again. "Do we have the names and addresses for where the staff moved?"

"Yes, I can provide all except one."

"Which?" she asked.

"Cassey," he said simply.

When she continued to look at him, he said, looking uncomfortable, "She didn't leave a forwarding address and she disappeared at the same time as Mr. Baxton left the country."

"I'll do some checking and see if I can find out if two tickets were purchased for them to come home." *Also,* she thought, *I'll bet the lawyer has their last address. I can check to see if he has remarried since he left. The fact he would remarry isn't suspicious; many men do after their wives have passed. What is suspicious is who he might have married.* "Mr. Amberson, I know this makes you uncomfortable, but were they seeing each other while his wife was alive?"

"Yes, I'm sure they were."

"Did Mrs. Baxton know?"

"No, no. She would never put up with that," he said a little too quickly.

She kept her face blank as she took notes.

He checked the time and said, "I will have to get back to my duties."

"Yes, thank you. Oh, one more thing. You indicated that you

found Mr. Baxton lying near a large pool of blood and that you were inside to turn down the lights?"

"Yes," he confirmed.

As Emma left, she thought, *I need to interview the staff and find out what was happening in that house.*

She grabbed her bike and headed home.

CHAPTER 46

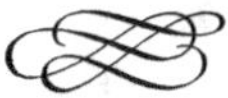

GLASS FACTORY CASE -- JEREMY

The dinner table was full of family and conversations with each talking over one another. As dinner wrapped up, Dora said, "Everyone take a platter and move them to the kitchen." Abbey and Ellis were there for dinner and pitched in to clean up.

As dishes were completed, Ellis looked at Jeremy and Emma. "You have some papers for me to review?" he asked.

"I do," said Jeremy. "In the study."

"Right behind you." He looked over at Abbey and asked, "Will you be okay here?"

"I'll be okay with Tim and Dora." She had picked up baby Lottie and was enjoying the wriggling child.

He smiled at her fondly and followed Jeremy and Emma into the study.

As they entered, Jeremy immediately went to the desk. He had his notes and portions of the furnace inspections laid out.

Ellis picked up the files and studied them. He saw from Jeremy's notes that the two investigations showed similar defects. The manufacturer said the furnaces were fully inspected before leaving and that the defect was not there at that time.

"Were there other furnaces sent out at the same time as these?"

"Yes," said Jeremy. "The files are here." He pulled one out and showed him the report.

"Have you confirmed with the people in this report?"

He nodded. "I sent out the telegrams this afternoon. I should have that information in a few days."

Emma spoke up. "The theory is that, if they don't have any issues with their furnaces, is that they were sabotaged after they got here?"

"Yes."

"How long were these in place?" Emma asked.

"Just a few weeks each. So, whatever happened, it was during a short time period," said Jeremy.

"Is there an employee list available from that time?" asked Emma.

"I can get the list from the owner," said Jeremy.

"Good. Compare the list and see who may have only been there for short durations," said Ellis.

"I will, thanks for the input."

"Can I take these to examine more closely?" Ellis asked, indicating the files.

"What are you thinking?"

"I wanted to look at how the defect might have occurred; how would someone have done it?"

CHAPTER 47

GLASS FACTORY CASE -- JEREMY

eremy received the list the next day with the names and addresses of the employees. Most were located in the Hells. He would need Tim to move easily in the area. That morning, he asked, "Tim, could you accompany me to these addresses?"

"How's tomorrow?"

"I would appreciate it."

They headed down to the Hells early the next morning. There were twenty to investigate. While reviewing the list, they had removed the children who were steady workers. That reduced the list to five temporary employees there around the time of the malfunctions.

They left the first house, feeling dazed after realizing their child had died at the factory.

It was the same for the next three. They went to the fourth house and knocked on the door. A girl of about twelve answered. "Yes?" she asked.

"Can we speak to your mother?" asked Tim.

She looked them over. "She's in the kitchen if you want to

come in." She watched them closely. "Ma, there is someone here to see you."

"Yes?" the woman asked as she walked out of the kitchen. "Henrietta mentioned you needed me for something?"

"Is your husband here?" Jeremy asked.

"No. He delivers ice and won't be back for a few hours. Is there something I can help you with?"

Jeremy nodded and pulled out the paper. "Is there an Aiden living here?"

The woman's eyes filled and spilled over. The girl darted forward. "Ma, sit down."

She took the seat offered and explained, "Aiden died at the glass manufactures."

"We had a second child listed that worked there on these dates, a Brian. Do you have another son?" asked Jeremy.

"No no. We only have a daughter."

Jeremy noticed the girl had looked away when they were asking questions. "I hate to ask, but when did your son pass?"

"It was a little over a year ago," she murmured, looking toward the mantle, where a baseball sat. She went silent.

"I think it would be best that you leave now," the girl said.

They exited and checked their list; there was one more child to check on.

As they exited the last house, Jeremy said, "That was a depressing day."

"Yes, so many children have died at the glass factory," said Tim.

"All of them had parents," said Jeremy.

They silently made their way back to the boarding house. Patrick was running around and saw Tim. "Papa, you are back." Tim swung him up and hugged him tightly. *He will never have to work as a child*, he promised himself. "

"What will you do now?" he asked Jeremy, still hugging Patrick tight.

"Continue watching the workers and see if there are any other issues with the furnaces. I'm also putting in an inspection process to have the entire furnace walked around before each shift starts."

He nodded. "Will they, do it?"

"I'm going to explain the dangers."

CHAPTER 48

GLASS FACTORY CASE -- JEREMY

That night, Jeremy talked to the men and boys on the shift. "We need you to walk around each furnace and inspect it as you come onto your shift."

They were snickering at him and continued to smoke. One of the boys said, "Can we get back to work now?"

"Yes. Just a minute, does anyone remember a Brian working here?" he asked.

One of the older kids stood. "Listen, man, we don't get paid if we don't work. We only know the kids who are around all of the time. The temp kids come in and out when they can't handle the job."

Jeremy was watching children as small as nine smoking and demonstrating mannerisms of much older men. "Ok, you can go, but please check around the furnaces. It could save your life."

"Yeah, sure," commented one of the older boys. They headed back into the factory, immediately going to each of their assigned job areas.

Jeremy watched and saw they didn't inspect the furnaces as asked. He would do it himself; he spent a lot of time going around each one, realizing they were not going to do anything that wasn't productive toward their paychecks.

Jeremy walked home slowly, thinking about the loss of childhood these kids were enduring. *There must be a long-term solution for this.*

CHAPTER 49

GLASS FACTORY CASE --JEREMY

When Jeremy got home, it was late and the house was quiet; everyone appeared to be in bed for the night. He was about to head up when he saw the light on in the study. When he pulled open the door, he saw Ellis sitting at the desk.

"Ellis. What are you doing here so late?"

"Oh, Jeremy," Ellis said absently. "I was waiting for you. I wanted to cover something I found."

"What type of thing?" Jeremy asked and walked over to the desk to look at the materials lying about.

"I think I have the cause."

"Didn't we know the cause was a defect in the furnace structure that allows the flammable material to eventually breach and crack the exterior, leading to an explosion and eventual fire?"

"Yes, that's correct," said Ellis, "but I reexamined the engineering review that described the parts they found. The integrity of the furnace was breached. It looks like it was probably a small defect that someone widened. Notice the hole; see how smooth and completely round the opening appears to be?"

"No one noticed this?"

"No, but I think they should have."

"What kind of tool were you thinking could make this type of hole?"

"An ice pick. They're reinforced and sharp."

"An ice pick. Could it get through the furnace?"

"I believe it could if the defect was already there. It may have been done over a series of weeks or months so the hole was made bigger each time. "

"I did notice the helpers were moving around most of the time and would have access to that area. Ellis, thank you for bringing this to my attention."

"It's not a problem. It's interesting work."

They both said goodnight and Jeremy headed up to bed.

He got cleaned up and climbed into bed with Emma. She snuggled closed. "How was it tonight?"

"Pretty bad," he admitted. "Something needs to be done about the hazardous working conditions."

"It's big business," she murmured, half asleep. "It would also be a political issue."

"Yes." He laid there thinking as she went to sleep.

CHAPTER 50

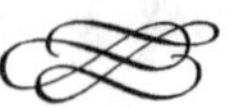

GLASS FACTORY CASE -- JEREMY

*E*mma woke slowly and realized Jeremy wasn't in the bed. She searched the darkroom and saw him standing by the window. "What is it?" He had his hands clenched tightly as he looked out the window.

"The person involved in this is too young to be responsible."

"Who did it? How did you work it out?"

"Ellis came by this evening. He had a theory of what may have occurred to cause the design problem and that led to the explosions and fires. It was an ice pick."

Emma knew where he was going; one of the kids had a father who delivered ice. "Oh, no."

"Yes, I think she was avenging her brother by sabotaging the plant and trying to get it to shut down."

"Now that you know, what are you going to do with this information?"

"The owner will want to prosecute her and send her to the workhouse for most of her life. Emma, he's stealing so much of these children's lives. He already has five deaths directly attributed to his business practices. They're babies," he said helplessly.

Emma was thinking ahead. "Let's go see her, hear her side of this."

"Yes. It's time. I'll go and see if I can get her alone and away from her mom."

"Jeremy, I should probably come with you," she suggested, thinking about the child.

"Yes, you're probably right," he said. The last thing he wanted was to scare the girl.

Emma asked, "What time are you thinking?"

"Can we do this in the early afternoon?"

"Yes. I can meet you here."

The next day, they stood on the child's doorstep, waiting for the door to open. It opened slowly, they couldn't see who held the door.

"Henrietta, is that you?" asked Jeremy leaning forward.

"Yes," came the low answer.

"Can we come in?" he inquired.

She begrudgingly moved back out of the doorway for them to enter.

"Are your parents here?" asked Jeremy.

"Ma is out picking up some sewing, and Papa is due back soon from his job. "

Emma held out her hand. "We haven't met. My name is Emma."

Henrietta did not make a move toward the hand she extended. She just went to a chair and sat down, not looking at them.

Jeremy nodded at Emma to try again. "Henrietta, where does your papa work?"

"Ice truck," she said slowly.

"Have you ever worked with him?"

"Sure, he lets me go sometimes when it's hot. The ice feels nice," she said, looking up at them for the first time.

Emma asked softly, "Have you ever used an ice pick before?"

Henrietta froze at the question, and her eyes darted around the room,

Jeremy said, "Don't run. I don't feel like chasing you down today."

Emma asked again, "Have you ever used an ice pick?"

"Yes, Papa showed me," she said slowly.

Jeremy thought it was the right time. "How did you make a hole like that? The furnaces are brick-lined."

"They have defects when they come in. I've noticed before; the workers installing them are lazy and don't always do a good job. I brought the pick out and started to jab at the defect."

"How long did it take?" asked Jeremy, curious about this girl's commitment.

"Months," she said. "It was slow."

"But you stuck with it. Why? Were you angry at the glass factory when your brother died?"

That got her up, and she said passionately, "He was killed by that horrible boy."

"You mean during an accident at work?" inquired Emma.

"They weren't accidents. They caused those deaths, making those little boys move heavy equipment, and work around boilers that are so hot you can't think straight. It was the older boy, a foreman."

"You blame him. Why?" asked Jeremy.

"One of the other boys told me my brother tripped and knocked over some expensive glass. The foreman grabbed him and threw him at the furnace," snapped Henrietta.

"Are you sure about that?" asked Jeremy. She nodded. "Who was this other boy? Can we speak with him?"

"It's no use. He wasn't held responsible," she mumbled.

"What was his name?"

"Josiah," she said. It was on their list but had no address listed. He would have to speak with him at the factory.

"So, what was your plan?" Jeremy pressed.

"Destroy the business; stop the kids from working there," said Henrietta.

"Henrietta, why didn't you tell your parents? They would have helped," said Emma.

The look she gave them made them pause. "Who do you think makes those boys go there? It is the parents. They don't want reform; they want money."

"Surely," said Emma, "that can't be all true."

"It is," she said shortly.

"You can't continue on this path; you could hurt the boys still working there," Jeremy said.

"I have to go to work," she said, getting up, not wanting to answer any more questions.

"Work?" Emma asked.

"Yes, I work in the cloth factory at night," said Henrietta.

"Okay, we will leave. Don't mention we were here," said Jeremy.

"Why would I?"

They exited with her and watched as she locked the door.

Emma checked her watch. "I have to get moving. Can we head back now?"

"Yes, I have some thinking to do," said Jeremy.

CHAPTER 51

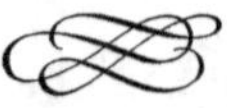

MRS. BAXTON'S CASE -- EMMA

Jeremy dropped Emma off at the boarding house. He needed to head into the office to check on other cases in development.

She tapped her notebook and thought Dora and Amy could help her find the servant on the list Mr. Baxter had provided. She headed into the kitchen to have Amy review it.

Amy saw her come in and asked, "Did you have a good day?"

"Not great," she admitted. "I was hoping you had time to review a list of people with me."

"Well," she said. "I might be able to help."

"Good." Emma pulled out her notebook

"But I'm going to need a dessert tonight. Can we work out a trade?"

Emma smiled. "Amy, you're catching on. Yes, I can help with dessert; what would you like?"

"Heidesand—German Sugar Rolled Marzipan Butter Cookies."

Emma nodded and got to work and the cookies were being placed in the over as Dora entered the kitchen with Lottie walking in front of her. "Emma, you are back?"

"I am."

"How did you get wrapped in making dessert today?" asked Dora, seeing Emma wipe down the table.

"Amy figured out our give-and-take system for information," said Emma with a smile.

Dora grinned and said, "Smart girl," winking at Amy.

Amy sat at the table with Dora and Emma. "What can I help you with?"

"Well, I could use you both."

"Hmm," said Dora, "if I'd known I was part of this, I would've gotten myself in on the dessert deal."

Emma laughed and handed Amy the list first.

Amy looked it over and said, "I can give you most of the locations, except for the gardeners." She handed it to Dora for her review.

"I might have an idea on that," said Dora thoughtfully. "Let me check with Tim."

Emma took down notes on the household staff. "Have you heard anything bad about anyone in particular?"

Amy said, "Not bad but I have heard something about Cassey. She wasn't a maid for very long, and she disappeared soon after Mrs. Baxtons disappearance. I haven't heard of her getting another position."

"Did she have any family here?" Emma asked.

"No, not that I'm aware of. I didn't know her very well," Amy explained.

"Okay, I'll see If I can talk to the other personnel." Emma looked at Dora. "Let me know if you hear anything about the gardeners."

Several people on the list we're working in the neighborhood where Cole and Ellis lived. Notes were sent over to them asking for some time to talk. Once she received a confirmation note back, she headed over to the houses where they were working.

First up were the helpers, Todd and Scotty, who had found a job in the same kitchen. They sat with her. "You said in your note that you are looking at Mrs. Baxton's disappearance?" Scotty said.

She noted the way he said that. He didn't say her first name. "How long were you both at the house?"

"We've worked together since we were kids," Todd said, and his friend nodded.

"That's right. We were there about five years," added Scotty.

"For a long while then," she commented. "Did you see anything unusual with Mr. Baxton and Cassey?"

They looked at each other and back at her. Servants normally kept to themselves and rarely gossiped outside their group. But in this case, they didn't feel any loyalty to Cassey. "She thought she was better than us," said Scotty.

"What makes you say that?" Emma asked curiously.

"Upstairs maids tend to put on airs. They think they're better than the kitchen staff," Scotty explained.

"Did you interact with her socially?" she asked.

"No," Scotty said shortly.

"Not that you didn't try," Todd teased him.

"Yeah, sure, I asked, but she had her sights on the boss," Scotty said.

"In what way?" Emma asked.

"She always did a little extra for him and, if she thought she could catch him outside by himself, she would," Todd said.

"Like where?"

"The gardens, mostly," stated Scotty.

"And her quarters," Todd said.

"Yes," Scotty confirmed.

"Did Mrs. Baxton know?"

"I'm not sure about that," Todd said. His friend shrugged in response.

She thought to ask, "Mr. Amberson, did you know him well?"

"Yes," they said at the same time.

"Was he a good boss?"

"He was fair," Todd said.

"How was he with Mrs. Baxton?"

"You mean Miss Catherine," Scotty snickered.

"I heard him call her that," she commented.

"He felt that he had a close relationship because he was there for such a long time," Todd said.

"Did she feel close to him?" Emma asked.

"She treated him like a servant; he just didn't want to see it," said Scotty.

"Now, that's not fair," Todd protested. "She *did* use a different tone with him."

"What kind of tone?" asked Emma, curious about what they heard.

"Softer, maybe," Todd said.

"He was also the only one allowed there when they wanted to be alone," said Scotty.

Emma thought she heard wrong and asked, "Are you saying on the nights they were by themselves, he was also there?"

"Yes," Todd confirmed. "He would serve them dinner and wait on them until they went to bed and then he would turn off the lights."

"Did you mention that to the police?"

"Oh, we weren't interviewed. Mr. Amberson took care of that."

"He was sure surprised when he lost his job," muttered Scotty.

"Yes," Todd agreed.

Emma thought about that, adding it to what she had learned. She asked bluntly, "Do you think Mr. Baxton killed his wife?"

They hesitated before saying anything. Talking about the people you work for or have worked for could lead to a swift termination.

"I won't mention who told me," she said in a low voice.

Todd muttered, "He just wasn't in the same class as her. He spent too much money and then that whole Cassey thing started."

"He wasn't a bad person but I'm not sure he cared enough about her to kill her," said Scotty.

"He may have cared enough about her money," commented Todd.

She agreed silently with them on the possible motive. She asked a final question. "Was there anything else you would like to share with me?"

"No, I don't think so," said Scotty.

"Me either," said Todd.

"Thank you," she said and got up to leave.

"Did we give you anything important?" asked Scotty.

"I believe you did," said Emma with a slow smile. She thanked them again and exited. *Who next?* she thought, looking down at her notebook.

She located the two footmen and the cook and got similar stories of the household dynamic.

Dora and Tim located the gardeners and they confirmed that Cassey and Mr. Baxton were seen kissing and touching inappropriately in the gardens.

The manservant was the last person she needed to talk to, but it was getting late in the day. The next conversation should be able to provide some direction in the case. After all, who would be more intimate in a man's life, other than the man who helped him dress each day? She had sent a note to the address provided by Amy but had not received a confirmation that it was okay to visit.

CHAPTER 52

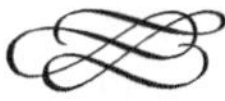

MRS. BAXTON'S CASE -- EMMA

It was the beginning of the evening shift and Jeremy sat in the corner, watching the boys working around him. One of the younger boys waved an arm toward Jeremy and said, "Josiah, that boy isn't working."

Josiah went over to stand in front of Jeremy and said, "You aren't here to sit. You're here to work. Go over there and start helping to move the bottles."

Jeremy stood slowly and asked, "Who me?" He straightened to his full height. "Were you wanting me to do something?"

The foreman realized it was the man that had given them instructions on safety inspections. He said, "No, no. Are you supposed to be here? Does Mr. Samuels know you are here?"

"He does," Jeremy confirmed.

"Well, I'm in charge here," the boy blustered.

"I've heard that," said Jeremy.

The foreman said, "I am going to check and see if you are allowed to be here." When he started to move, Jeremy stuck out his foot and tripped him. He fell on his face and the boys in the area started laughing.

"Stop laughing at me, or I'll…" the foreman threatened as he waved his fist at them.

"You'll what, kill them?" Jeremy asked.

"What? No, I didn't kill anyone." He was starting to look nervous.

"No, but you did make the already hard job more unsafe."

"I was doing as I was told, to keep everyone working. So many of the kids are small and can't do the work," he complained.

"So, you get angry," he guessed.

"Yeah."

Jeremy realized he was just a kid that had come up through the same system these little ones had. "How long have you been here?"

"Since I was nine," he said.

"Did you kill Aiden?"

"Aiden?" His eyes filled with tears. "Mister, I pushed him, and he hit the boiler. The vent pipe was loose and hit his head. It wasn't murder. I didn't mean to hurt him. I have done the same thing to many boys. I had it done to me."

Several other boys walked up and one said, "Mister, that was an accident. We were here. He didn't do it on purpose."

Another boy said, "Yeah, he even picked him up and ran him to the hospital."

Josiah said, "When I realized he was hurt, I got him there as fast as I could. The Sisters there said there was just nothing they could do."

Jeremy let him go. *This whole thing is just so sad. Boys having to make a man's decision.*

CHAPTER 53

GLASS FACTORY -- JEREMY

He met with Mr. Samuels at his office. Jeremy looked around, noticing all of the fine items on display. "Very nice place."

"Thank you. Are you here to tell me the outcome of the investigation?" he asked.

"We examined the furnaces and believe it was localized to inadequate maintenance and installation," Jeremy said smoothly. "Defects in the design combined with blockages inside the furnace can build up pressure over time, causing the furnace to develop holes." He spun the tale. There was no way he was going to disclose Henrietta's part in this.

"What can we do to prevent this from happening?"

"If you don't want to lose the entire place, you will need to clean up all of the areas around the furnaces and start more routine maintenance. When new installations are going in, hire an engineering firm to inspect prior to use. I also have further suggestions about routine cleaning and inspection of the furnaces."

He nodded and said, "If it saves the business, I'll do it."

"I will have Ellis Evans come over for an evaluation," he said smoothly.

He nodded.

Jeremy knew there was not an easy way to get the children out, but he could make the environment as safe as possible.

CHAPTER 54

FINAL GLASS FACTORY CASE -- JEREMY

Henrietta looked shocked at Jeremy's news. "He didn't kill him?"

"It was an accident," he confirmed. "He even tried to get him help at the hospital." Jeremy had confirmed with the Sisters that the boy who had brought him in had stayed with him and cried when he died.

"And you helped the kids that have to go there?"

"Yes, and we will keep an eye on them to make sure they follow through with our recommendations."

She nodded and asked, "You aren't turning me in?"

"No. Henrietta, we would like to help you," said Jeremy.

"I would like that," she said.

"What do you want to do?" he asked curiously.

"I want to be smart enough to stop children from having to work. We have a right to an education."

"I agree. I would like you to meet a friend, her name is Clair. Emma and I think we three can help you take the first step. We can help you with your education and pay you at the same time," said Jeremy.

Henrietta looked like he had handed her the world

We can't save all of the children, but maybe Henrietta can, thought Jeremy.

CHAPTER 55

MRS. BAXTON'S CASE — EMMA

The following day, Emma waited outside the house where the last employee to interview worked. The man she was there to meet had sent word he was not available. The information he could provide was too important to the case so she stayed and waited, in clear view of the front windows. Her patience was infinite, aided by a book and snacks.

He watched from the window and waited for her to leave. When she didn't, he tried to ignore her. *Why is she still here?* he wondered.

"Justin, you should go down and take care of that issue," said his employer.

He would have preferred to leave her sitting there all night, but now he had no choice. He headed downstairs, exited through the kitchen, and called over to her, "Come here, I will see you now."

Emma took a long moment to finish her apple and deliberately closed her book. Standing, she started toward him. His body language was defensive; this would not be an easy conversation.

"Follow me," he said and they walked through the kitchen; she noticed the staff were watching them curiously. They trudged through the dining room to a study, where he closed the doors quietly behind him and turned toward her.

She noticed his clothes and his manners. Servants at this level of society were well educated and could easily pass for the same people they served. Sometimes, that closeness caused trouble. *Like in this situation,* she thought.

He didn't offer, but she went to the long brown couch and sat. He frowned when she didn't wait to be asked. Reluctantly, he joined her there. "What do you want?" Justin asked brusquely.

Lost his manners with me, she thought. "I wanted to ask you about the time you worked at Mr. and Mrs. Baxton's house."

"Why?"

"I'm looking into her murder."

"Someone is actually going to ask some questions?"

"What do you mean?"

"The detective in charge of the case didn't want to talk to us at all."

"Well, I do. I want to hear more about what you saw in the house. What was the relationship between Mr. Amberson and Mrs. Baxton?"

He looked shocked. He had expected another question.

When he didn't answer, she asked, "Who did you think I was going to ask about?"

"Cassey and Mr. Baxton."

"Why is that? Because of the affair?"

"You know about that?"

"Yes, I've interviewed some of the other staff."

"Who?" he asked.

"Two kitchen helpers."

"Yes, Scotty and Todd." He chuckled suddenly. "Yes, they saw everything."

"Back to my original question, Mr. Amberson and Mrs. Baxton," she prompted.

"That was an odd relationship."

"Why use the word relationship?" she asked.

"Because that's what it was. There was always something a little extra. She brought him special things if she traveled; he would be invited to her private sitting room to talk."

"Did he have a similar relationship with Mr. Baxton?"

"No, he felt Mr. Amberson was beneath him."

"What about Cassey?"

He grimaced. "Yes, well, I thought we were going to get married, but she was playing me as much as Mr. Baxton was playing Mrs. Baxton."

"When did you find out?"

"Oh, I found out when everyone else did—when she disappeared at the same time as Mr. Baxton."

"Did you suspect Mr. Baxton of harming Mrs. Baxton?"

"Yeah," he said. "I mean, she disappeared and all that blood and then he leaves the country with Cassey."

"Why didn't you want to see me today?"

"I'm engaged to a member of the staff here and I didn't want any previous gossip about me and Cassey to ruin that."

She nodded. "I shouldn't have to bother you anymore." Standing up to leave. "Oh, one more thing, were you there that night?"

"I was with Cassey; we went out dancing."

She thanked him and he escorted her to the door.

CHAPTER 56

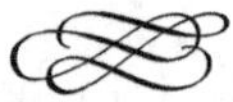

That night, she and Jeremy were at the dining table. She was reviewing her notes and Jeremy was reading. He looked over and asked. "Any updates on the Baxton case? Did you ever get a copy of the file from Carl?"

"I did. It didn't have much in it. Based on my interviews, I believe I have," she said absently, "two suspects?"

"Two? Didn't you think it was the husband?"

"He is suspicious," she conceded. "He was having an affair, and the will gives him the money as long as he didn't kill Mrs. Baxton. No felony, he keeps the money."

"Who else are you considering?"

"The butler."

"Why him?"

"There is something odd about Mrs. Baxton's relationship with him. They seemed overly close."

"Is that all you have? No motive?"

"Well, the butler did lie to me when he said he wasn't in the house when she died."

"That is suspicious. What is your next step?"

"I need to get another look at that fountain. I'll be heading over tomorrow morning."

CHAPTER 57

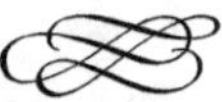

MRS. BAXTON'S CASE—EMMA

It all comes back to this fountain, she thought as she walked around it slowly, looking at the structure and the cement in place around it. The leak was a slow one, and it appeared to be coming out of a long break in the stone. The more she looked at it, she thought, *It is too straight and too clean.* The leak only appeared to be in the one area.

Who built this? Papa would know, she thought. *He could pull the permits.*

She headed over to the house he shared with Cole, his lab was set up in the basement. It allowed him to continue his engineering work without having to go back and forth to the boarding house.

At this time of day, he would be in the basement and wouldn't be able to hear her knocking. She looked around and didn't see anyone, so she pulled out her lockpick kit and went to work on the door. Opening it quickly, she went inside. As she moved toward the basement door, she heard a murmuring coming from downstairs. "Papa," she called, hoping to give him a moment to stop whatever he might be doing that would embarrass her or him.

She paused and heard her papa say, "Emma, is that you?"

"It is, may I come down?"

"Sure, just a moment." She waited, and then he called, "Come down."

Abbey must be here, she thought. As she entered the room, Emma looked toward Abbey and saw not a hair out of place. She smiled inwardly, but outwardly, she said, "Hello, Abbey, Papa."

Abbey sent her a quick smile. "Hello, Emma."

"Hi, little girl. Visiting today?" asked Papa.

"No, Papa, I have a case I need to review with you. Could you access the drawing for the memorial fountain located at Kingston Square?"

He frowned and said, "Yes. What are you looking for?"

"I'm looking for anyone involved in the design and build. If possible, the present management company."

"When do you need it by?"

"Soon would be nice. I'm kind of on a deadline," she said, thinking Mr. Baxton's ship had made it in and he would be there later that week

"It may take some time, but I'll see if I can get it today and bring it by this evening."

"Thanks, Papa," she said and kissed him quickly. He gave her ponytail the familiar tug as she was leaving. She called over her shoulder, "It was good to see you both."

"You, too," Abbey said quietly.

"Lock up on your way out," Papa called.

"I will," she answered back.

CHAPTER 58

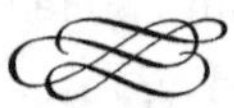

MRS. BAXTON'S CASE—EMMA

Emma was busy for the rest of the day. She had a few pickups to make and some additional deliveries. She pulled up to the boarding house stoop and saw Papa assisting Abbey out of the carriage.

"Emma," he said." I have those items."

"Wonderful, Papa. Hello, Abbey," she said, getting off her bike and kissing him on the cheek. "I'll go put my bike up and meet you in the study."

"We'll see you there." Papa walked up the front stoop with Abbey and knocked on the door. Patrick opened it and shouted, "Grandpapa and Abbey!"

Emma came through the dining room at her customary speed and headed to the study. When she got there, she saw Tim at his desk. "Hey, Tim, can we use the study?"

Tim looked up. "Sure, I could spend some time with Dora and the kids."

He saw Ellis and Abbey in the foyer. "Hello, so nice to see you both. Would you like some tea? Will you be staying for dinner?"

"No, we don't need tea or dinner. We plan to go out after we talk," said Ellis.

Tim smiled and went past them to find Dora.

Emma moved the items on the desk, making room for the papers Papa had with him. He rolled out the design drawings for the fountain, then went on to explain, "The original design was signed off by Mrs. Baxton and Mr. Jeffers."

"Do you have the date?"

"The original submittal was April 1885."

"Well before she died. Had they started the work?" Emma asked.

"The work was started before her death; the holes were dug for the plumbing."

"When was the cement poured?"

"I pulled the permits." He flipped through the pile of papers until he found the right one. "It says here that it was poured August 15, 1885."

"That's the day after Mrs. Baxton disappeared and was presumed to be dead. Hmm… we're getting somewhere. Who was the responsible party for putting together the project?"

"It is Jeffers construction. The owner is Mr. Jeffers."

"I don't think that would be him. He is the owner, I need the man in charge of the project," said Emma thoughtfully.

Ellis looked closer at the signatures of the engineer assigned to the project. He said, "The person who signed the engineering drawings was Mike Smothers. If she is buried there, he would know."

She went to the door and called, "Tim, could you come in for a moment?"

Tim joined them and they gave him some background on the project. "Tim, could you check the bank for payments to Mike Smother's account? I would assume it would be a routine payment."

He said, "I have someone at the bank who can look into any irregularities for me."

"Thank you," Emma said.

"I can let you know tomorrow. If that is all you need?"

"It is."

Papa said, "Emma, you mentioned the leak looked man-made."

"It did," she acknowledged.

"Then he is probably involved, he would know where to cut to have a leak like that."

One last thing, she thought. *I need to check on Cassey's whereabouts.*

CHAPTER 59

MRS. BAXTON'S CASE — EMMA

It was days later and Emma was waiting at the train station for Mr. and Mrs. Baxton to exit. She had confirmed with Cole that there was no employment record of Cassey in town since Mr. Baxton had gone to Europe.

She watched as each person exited the train and did not see anyone who looked like Mr. Baxton. When it looked like the train was empty of passengers, she approached the porter and asked, "Was that everyone?"

"Yes, were you waiting for someone specifically?"

"I'm looking for a Mr. Baxton."

"Oh, he was on board, but he and his family departed at the last stop."

"His family?"

"Yes, his wife and young child."

"Can you describe the wife?"

"Young, blonde hair, and very pretty."

That must be Cassey. "Thank you for your time."

"You're welcome."

Hmm, I will go to the house and see if I can question him, she murmured to herself.

CHAPTER 60

MRS. BAXTON CASE -- EMMA

She organized a note to Jeremy, asking him to meet her at the Baxton estate. She might need some backup if things turned bad. As she rode out to the estate, she went over the questions that she wanted to review.

The guards were not in place at the door. She approached slowly, looking around. At the door, she had her hand raised to knock and heard arguing and a baby crying. She didn't wait; she pushed the door and it swung open. Two men were there struggling and fighting to get a gun. She put a hand into her pocket to access the hidden knife, she heard a shot ring out. Her body jerked back as the bullet entered her arm. She glanced down and saw blood spurt; the room spun for a moment.

As soon as she could steady herself, she ripped her sleeve off and wrapped it around the wound, pulling it tight with her other hand and her teeth. They didn't notice her and continued to struggle. On the far side of the room, Emma saw the woman and baby. She motioned for them to exit the hallway. The woman looked desperate but followed her directions. Another shot rang out, and one of the two men struggling fell to the floor. She recognized the man holding the gun; it was Mr. Baxton.

He seemed in shock as she watched him drop the gun. Emma picked it up and pointed it at him. She said, sensing he would rush her, "Mr. Baxton, I don't like guns, but I do know how to use them."

He decided he would take the chance and went after her; Emma shot his leg, causing him to fall to the floor. She was losing some blood, and she needed to sit. With the gun still pointed at him, she let herself sink to the floor, listening to him scream in pain.

The door slammed open to reveal Jeremy. "Emma, are you okay?"

"Yes, I think so. Feels like a flesh wound," she said, shaking off her grogginess.

He took off her bandage and said, "I think you are right. It should be cleaned, though, and a proper bandage applied. What happened?"

"The two men were arguing, and I got hit by a stray bullet. The man on the floor. Mr. Baxton shot him when they were struggling. It is probably Mr. Smothers, the engineer."

"And who shot Mr. Baxton?"

"Oh, that was me. He wouldn't take direction."

Jeremy laughed.

CHAPTER 61

MRS. BAXTON CASE -- EMMA

*E*mma and Jeremy were transported to the police station by the officers who had responded to Jeremy's note. As they went in, they were greeted by the police chief. It was an important case and one of his detectives might have been bribed to cover it up. His thoughts turned to worry when he saw her arm. "Emma, are you okay?"

"It is just a flesh wound. I'm all right," she said.

He looked her over and she seemed steady on her feet. "Okay, what do you want to do?"

"I have some questions that may lead to who killed Mrs. Baxton."

He nodded, knowing she had the original detective's file. "This way. Jeremy, will you be accompanying her?" Emma saw the detective assigned to the original case, he avoided her gaze. The police chief made note of that and waited for Jeremy's answer.

"I will," he confirmed.

"We have Mr. Baxton and the new Mrs. Baxton. Which would you like to speak with first?"

"The husband," she said firmly. "The man that got injured, that was Mr. Smothers?"

"Yes," the police chief confirmed.

"How is he?" she asked

"He will be fine. The Sisters said he fainted when he got shot," he commented.

"You will want to contact Tim. He has some information about Mr. Smothers' involvement in this and a blackmail scheme involving Mr. Baxton," commented Emma.

He smiled and said, "Didn't I tell you years ago to stay out of dangerous situations?"

She laughed. "I didn't take your advice then, either."

He laughed loudly. The officers in the area looked on in amazement; Emma was the only one who could get him to do that. "Go on in."

She and Jeremy entered the room where Mr. Baxton was cuffed to the table. They had bandaged his leg; his was also a flesh wound.

He had the grace to look embarrassed when he saw her bandaged arm. "I'm sorry about that; I wasn't aiming at you."

"At least not the first time," she commented wryly.

He stayed silent so she continued.

"I know the first one was an accident. I walked in when you were struggling with Mr. Smothers."

"Yes, they haven't told me, is he okay?" he asked in a pleading voice.

"We understand the damage was minimal and he fainted," she commented.

"Thank goodness for that," he said, grateful he hadn't killed him.

Emma looked at her notes and back to him before saying, "We haven't met, but I am Emma Evans and this is Jeremy Tilden. I would like to ask you some questions, and I hope you can be truthful with us."

"I will try," he said, meeting her eyes.

"Did you murder your wife?"

He looked helpless for a moment and said, "I don't know."

"Could you explain that?" she asked.

"No, not really," he said, a bit helpless.

She took a deep breath and said, "Let's go back to the night of your wife's disappearance. Let's go through this step by step. You were having dinner with her. Were you alone?"

As he remembered, he started talking. "It was a special night. Catherine had just told me we were going to have a baby. She was so happy. I had Mr. Amberson open some champagne for us."

Emma knew that part. "What happened next?" she prompted.

"We started to talk about our plans for us and the baby. We wanted to raise her in Europe. It was our dream coming true," he said.

"Mr. Baxton, weren't you having an affair with Cassey during this time?" she asked abruptly.

He had the grace to look embarrassed. "I was," he said truthfully. "It was a dalliance, something to distract me."

"Why did you need a distraction?"

"We weren't able to conceive the baby for years. We started to think it wouldn't happen, and Catherine started to turn away from me."

"So, you found solace with someone else," Emma asked.

"Yes."

"Go on with that night," she told him.

"We drank, danced, and had a wonderful time."

"What happened next?" she asked.

"I don't remember."

She frowned and asked, "What is the very last thing you do remember?"

He thought back. "Mr. Amberson was talking in a low voice to Catherine. He looked upset; I don't know what it was about."

"What would happen to the servants if you went overseas with Catherine?"

"Probably the same thing that happened when she died. We would have let them go and have a management company takes care of the house."

"Hmm. Would Mr. Amberson be upset at being separated from you both?"

"Well, not from me, but he was very close to Catherine."

"What is the next thing you remember?"

"Mr. Amberson woke me up and told me I had killed her," he said, putting his head in his hands.

"Mr. Baxton, you said you were drinking. Is it normal for you to have blackouts or loss of memory for periods of time?"

"Unfortunately, it was at that time," he admitted.

"You don't remember killing her?"

"No, just being woken up by Mr. Amberson."

"Whose idea was it to hide the body?"

"Mr. Amberson," he said, not having thought this through before.

"Who arranged for the carriage to transport her?"

"Mr. Amberson."

"Whose idea was the fountain?" asked Emma.

"That was mine. I involved Mr. Smothers. It was all I could think of. I liked the idea of her there."

"Why did Mr. Smothers agree to help?" asked Emma.

"Money," he said simply. "Money that has turned into a very long agreement."

"Is that what you were fighting about?"

"Yes, he has been asking for more and more money." He hesitated and said, "I think that trouble with the plumbing was him."

"That would make sense," said Emma. "We had a structural engineer review it and determined it was sabotaged."

"Yes, I thought he might do something like that."

"What happened when you got to the fountain?" Emma asked.

"All three of us dug the existing hole at the fountain deeper by six feet and put her in." He was openly crying at this point. He had lost his wife and baby that night.

"If you will excuse us," said Emma, nodding at Jeremy.

"What are you thinking?" Jeremy asked as they left the room.

"Once we confirm the same story with Mr. Smothers, I think I know who to go to next."

CHAPTER 62

MRS. BAXTON CASE -- EMMA

"Mr. Amberson," she said quietly, sitting down on the bench next to him. He was staring at Catherine's fountain, he had been crying. Emma saw the Pinkerton men behind them and waved them back. She started with a blunt question, unsure of how he would answer. "How did you get Mr. Baxton to believe he murdered his wife?"

He didn't look up from where they'd buried his Catherine. "Oh, that was easy. He was a drunk. I had seen him have blackouts and no memory of what had occurred. It was so easy."

"Did you plan it?"

"No."

"What happened?" she asked.

"They were celebrating. I had served them dinner and opened many bottles of champagne for them. They ignored my presence and started talking about moving to Europe. At first, I thought I heard wrong, but they kept going on about closing up the house."

"Did you speak to Miss Catherine?"

"I did. I waited until we were alone, and I asked if I was going to accompany her overseas and be there when the baby was born."

"What did she say?"

"She said only her family would be going. Her *family*. Who did she think I was? After all that I did for her."

"What did you do for her?" Emma asked softly.

"She wanted, a baby so badly, so I helped her," he explained.

Emma asked, keeping the amazement out of her voice, "The baby was yours?"

"Yes, that husband of hers couldn't give her one. Miss Catherine said I was special and I was her family, that it was natural."

"So, she got the baby she wanted and was leaving you behind?"

"I just couldn't believe she would leave me."

"What did you do?"

"I was carving up some meat for the next day's sandwiches when we started arguing. I remember glancing at the knife and picking it up to follow her to the foyer. The rage just overtook me and I reached up and slit her throat."

That explains the amount of blood, thought Emma.

"Where was Mr. Baxton?"

"He was dancing in the sitting room," he said. "I went up behind him and knocked him out and dragged him into the foyer. I woke him up and told him what he did. It was so easy."

"Do you regret what you did?"

He didn't answer her question instead he said, "I miss her so much."

She saw his hand raised but did not see the wickedly sharp knife he was hiding. He brought it up and slit his throat. The blood poured out and she tried to stop the bleeding as he fell back onto the ground. She got on her knees and put her hands on his neck, trying to stem the flow. The men ran up, trying to help. Jeremy also put his hands on the man's neck, but it was no use. He bled out in a matter of minutes.

Jeremy took his bloody hands away, while Emma continued to try to talk to him. "You will be okay; can you hear me?"

Jeremy could tell it was over. "Emma." When she didn't look

up, he said louder, "Emma!" That finally got through and she pulled back, her bloody hands falling to her knees.

"Jeremy, I didn't know."

"No, you didn't."

"Why did he do it?"

"Perhaps he saw no other way out?"

"He missed her so much, considered her his family." She looked at him and said, with tears falling from her eyes, "Jeremy, she was having his baby."

That shocked Jeremy into silence as they watched the men lay a coat over Mr. Amberson's head.

"What will happen next?" Emma asked.

"The coroner will come for his body. There will probably be questions from the police."

"Okay," she said and took a deep breath.

"But not now," he said firmly, seeing she was in shock. "First, we go home and take a long hot bath and a nap. The police can wait until this evening."

She stood and was too calm. He held her close and summoned the carriage home. "Do you think they could add his name to the fountain?" asked Emma drowsily.

"We will ask Clair to look into it for us," he murmured.

He took her out of the carriage and they walked into the boarding house. They must have been a sight, blood on their hands, face, and clothes.

Dora turned white when she saw them. Jeremy shook his head at her and mouthed, "We're okay. Bath."

"Yes, of course. We will get that started now. Ethyl," she called. "Could you draw Emma a bath? Take the back stairs." She didn't need her fainting at the sight of these two.

CHAPTER 63

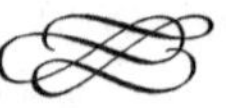

MRS. BAXTON CASE -- EMMA

Emma sat quietly; with the police chief at the police station. He was giving her an update of the events she had missed." Mr. Smothers is at the hospital; officers are with him. He will have to answer for his actions the night Mrs. Baxton went missing." Tim had sent over the bank files confirming the blackmail accusations Mr. Baxton had made against Mr. Smothers. He looked over at her and asked, "Emma. I believe you have something for me?" She nodded and pulled the updated detective's file out of her jacket pocket.

"You will find the actual events the night Mrs. Baxton died in this file," she commented The chief looked across the room at his detective. He squirmed at the attention being aimed at him. The chief asked, "Was there anything else?"

"Yes, Tim asked that I give this to you." She pulled an envelope out and gave it to him.

He opened the envelope and saw it was bank transactions That belonged to his detective. "He was involved?"

"Yes, in the coverup; not the actual murder. What will you do?"

"Oh, I will take care of it." What he did was take the detective into custody with the other conspirators.

Mr. and new Mrs. Baxton were released and allowed to move into the estate. He would still face some charges but probably not receive any jail time. Now that there were no felony charges, his inheritance wouldn't be questioned.

Later that evening she was taking notes on how the case had ended, wishing she could have prevented Mr. Amberson's death, but he was with his Catherine now.

Jeremy sat next to her and took her hands in his. They were still cold. "Do you want to go lie back down?"

"No, I have had all the rest I can take." She shook her head. "Jeremy, I didn't see the signs. I didn't know he was going to do that. I should have known."

"Emma, you are not a mind reader."

"I know, I know. I just wanted to help him."

CHAPTER 64

FINAL MRS. BAXTON CASE -- EMMA

Clair had made arrangements for Mr. Amberson's name to be added to the memorial. Mr. Baxton agreed to the request, but would not be in attendance for the reveal. He asked that it be turned over to the Carlyle Foundation permanently. He would continue financial support for any future repairs.

Emma stood with Jeremy as the service drew to a close. It was only their families in attendance. "I am glad he is with her."

"Me, too," said Jeremy.

CHAPTER 65

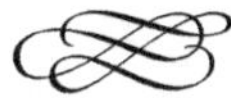

She was sewing the final elements on the dress. "Can I look now?" the bride asked excitedly.

"Of course, turn around."

She turned and saw herself in the mirror. "Oh, Emma, it's so beautiful."

"Thank you. But it is you that looks beautiful."

Dora spoke up and said, as she blotted her eyes, "You hair should go up, and maybe some flowers?"

"Can you show me?" asked Abbey.

They pulled it back to show her. The wedding would be in a few days, and the family would all be together to celebrate the event.

NOTEBOOK MYSTERIES ~ HAUNTED CHRISTMAS (A NOVELLA)

Notebook Mysteries

KIMBERLY MULLINS

PROLOGUE

Clank, clank, clank. The sound of heavy chains seemed to be in concert with the pounding in his head.

He held his hands over his ears and huddled deeper into the bed. The clank of the chains could be heard again. "Marley?" he asked in a whisper and reached out a shaky hand to move the bed curtains back, revealing the dark room. "Marley?" he called again, louder this time.

The clanking seemed to be next to him. Startled, he pulled the curtains closed and sank back on the bed. "Go away, Marley, I don't want to see you."

A long, raspy moan could be heard in the room, and he tentatively stuck out his head again. He regretted it immediately and screamed as the apparition flew toward him.

"I need to get out!" He jumped out of the bed and ran to the balcony doors. "You won't get me!" he shouted as he jumped over the edge.

CHAPTER 1

A FEW WEEKS LATER

*E*mma pulled the paper out of her typewriter and placed it on her desk. She opened the drawer and pulled out the files needing to be updated. They were reviewed for any errors before being filed again. It was her last assignment from Mr. Pennington before the Christmas break.

Her position had started as a temporary one, but Mr. Pennington saw potential in her. In exchange for her investigations, he was teaching her how the law worked. The office would be closed after today for the holidays. *Christmas is approaching quickly; it's only five days away,* she thought.

The holiday was always busy for her family because of all the additional baking. In addition to her regular jobs, she was also helping out at Cousins, the family bakery.

A family party was held on Christmas Eve. Both boarding houses, family, and friends were invited to attend. Emma smiled. She was looking forward to the holidays.

She pulled out her bag to check her courier route for that day. It was open on her lap and she was reviewing the list of locations for document deliveries when a knock sounded on the door.

"Come in," she called absently.

Ethan Worthington, the law office secretary, stepped in. "Emma, you remember that favor you owe me?" he asked.

His tone was serious, and that got her full attention. She looked up and replied in a similar tone, "I do." Ethan had helped her on a previous case and, without him, the truth may not have been uncovered and a murderer might have gone free.

She put her bag aside and watched him as he paced her small office. He finally stopped in front of her. "I need you to investigate something for me, at my family home."

"Oh, if that's all, sure," she said, looking at him closely. She wondered why this request worried him so much.

"No, you don't understand. This house is haunted," he said desperately.

Emma looked at him in amazement. *Ethan is one of the more down-to-earth persons I know,* she thought. *This isn't something he's taking lightly.* She frowned at him. "Haunted? Ethan, what makes you say that?"

He looked around, not wanting anyone who might be in the office to overhear. "Can we meet after work and discuss this matter?"

She understood. He had responsibilities and couldn't take time out of his workday to review this with her. She pulled out her notebook. "When and what time would you like to meet?" she asked.

"Can I come to the boarding house this evening?" He knew her address from the files he kept on employees.

She thought ahead and asked, "Is 8:00pm too late?"

"No," he said, thinking quickly. "That's fine. I'll see you tonight."

He turned and left her office.

A haunted house? she thought. *This will be interesting.*

The clock bell chimed the hour. She looked toward it and thought, *Time is passing quickly.* Gathering her things, she dropped them into her bag. She hurriedly unbuttoned the long row of double buttons on her woolen skirt. It folded over, revealing a split skirt. The dashing design had been Dora's idea to help keep it from getting caught on her bike.

The bag was closed with a snap, and she made her way out to where Ethan's desk sat. Her winter things and her bike were stored in a nearby closet; she retrieved them before moving to the office entrance. Once there, she propped the bike against the door and pulled on her heavy coat, scarf, gloves, and hat. Bracing herself for the impact of the cold, she turned the knob to open the door.

Ethan found his sense of humor as he watched her prepare. He called, "Is that it? Any other layers to add?"

"It's cold out there today," she explained, turning back to him.

"Do you have courier work this afternoon?" he asked, frowning. The weather could be dangerous this time of year, and she normally stayed out all afternoon.

"A few engineering drawings to drop off," she confirmed. "I also told Cousin I would work an afternoon shift to get some orders caught up at the bakery."

"Be safe, don't take any unnecessary chances in this weather," he cautioned.

"I won't," she said as she took the bike by the handlebars to roll it outside onto the stoop. Once there, Emma tried to catch the breath the cold air had stolen from her. She opened her coat to let the air circulate some before buttoning it up again. The wind was brisk and would make her ride harder. The bike was lifted to her shoulder, she carried it down the stoop before jumping on it to go to her delivery locations.

Her teeth were chattering and her arms numb after finishing her deliveries. The thought of the warm bakery made her pedal harder to reach her final destination.

With a final push, she made it to the back door of the bakery. She ducked her head down and pulled her bike toward the door. Grasping the door knob tightly, she pushed it and the wind tore it out of her hands, hitting the wall with a bang. A blast of hot air accompanied the yells from all parts of the bakery. "Shut the door!" she heard someone yell. Hurriedly, she placed the bike on her shoulder, grabbed the door handle, and leaned on it to push it closed. "I'm sorry," she called. There were some grumblings but most of the workers had a smile for Emma.

Cousin spotted her from his workstation and called out, "Thanks for helping out today." He indicated where she would work with his floured hand. "Your list is there," he told her.

"I'll get started as soon as I change," she said and made her way to the storage closet. She put her bike inside and stepped in to change into her bakery uniform. It was a white skirt with a white high-necked blouse and full sleeves. There was also an apron that buttoned on. Her work skirt had also been modified to a split style similar to the kind she wore when biking and was at least five inches shorter than that of the other female bakers.

She exited the room and made her way to her station, pulling on the baker's hat absently as she reviewed her list. The direction says the Apple cakes are to be cut into individual portions. *Not difficult*, she thought. *I just have to make a lot of them.*

She finished baking and moved the cakes from the baking trays to cool. The pastry boxes were lined up for her to fill. As they cooled, she cut them into squares and moved them into the boxes. *These will go out to the events scheduled for this evening,* she thought. The Christmas season had started, and there were parties almost every night.

"Will you be able to work the rest of the week?" asked Cousin as he approached her, his calendar out and pen at the ready.

"Yes, I can. Courier work is light right now."

He nodded, taking notes. "Good, good. Once you get those boxed up you may head out for today. What time can we plan on you being here tomorrow?"

"Let's say early afternoon, for three hours. I have some activities that will probably take up my morning," she said, thinking about her meeting with Ethan that night. *There may be some follow-up to take care of.*

Cousin marked it down and headed back to his office.

Emma cleaned up her workstation and made her way to the closet to change clothes. She called goodbye to the other bakers as she walked her bike out.

It wasn't quite dark when she left, but it would be by the time she got home. She pushed herself to get there as soon as possible. There seemed to be something sinister in the cold that evening.

CHAPTER 2

$\mathcal{D}$inner had been served and the dishes were removed from the boarding house dining room. The remaining people at the table were Tim, Dora, Emma, Jeremy, and Jake. Savannah had a play that would have her getting in late. Jake was preoccupied with a new book he had gotten. It was by Edward M. Estabrook, *Photography in the Studio and in the Field*. His interest in photography had expanded to reading books about new developing technologies.

"Tell us who's coming over tonight and why," Dora demanded. Emma had commented when she got home that there would be a visitor that evening.

"Ethan Worthington, the secretary at Mr. Pennington's office, has a favor to ask," Emma explained.

"Do you have any idea what the favor entails?" asked Jeremy, settling back in his chair with his coffee cup in his hands.

"Yes," she said. She wasn't sure how to tell the group what Ethan wanted her to investigate.

"And?" Tim asked, prompting her.

Emma looked at him and said reluctantly, "He says his family home is haunted."

They looked at her, astonished.

"Haunted? You mean spirits?" Dora asked.

"Or ghosts?" suggested Jeremy.

"Is he serious?" Dora asked. She didn't believe someone would ask Emma for something like this.

"Something has put this notion in his head. He's coming over tonight to review the case with us. He'll be here at eight. I think we should hear him out and take him seriously. I don't want him to feel we are making fun of him," Emma warned.

Dora said immediately, "No, we wouldn't do that."

Tim and Jeremy agreed.

"Emma," Jake spoke up, sounding nervous. "Are there really ghosts in that house?"

She reached over to touch his arm. "Jake, there hasn't been any scientific or photographic evidence to suggest they exist."

He nodded, understanding. "Then why are we going to check into it? To show him they aren't real?"

"That's it exactly. But we will listen politely to what he has to say," Emma stated.

"Yes, we will," he confirmed and lowered his head to read from his book.

Dora stood up. "I need to check on Lottie." She looked over at Tim. "Check on Patrick and see if he's ready to be read to."

Tim reached over to take her hand and accompanied her upstairs. They separated at their bedroom door. She entered her bedroom and walked toward the curtain in her room. Since Lottie had been born, they had added a temporary curtain wall to separate their room from hers, to allow them some privacy while she slept. It would be a while yet before she got her own room. Tim headed next door to Patrick. He pushed the door open and found him sitting up holding a book. "Waiting for me?" he asked. Patrick grinned and scooted over so he could join him on the bed.

After the kids were all settled, Tim and Dora rejoined Emma

and Jeremy, and Jake in the sitting room, talking and waiting for Ethan to arrive.

CHAPTER 3

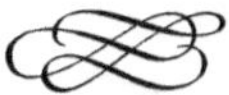

$\mathcal{A}$s the clock chimed 8:00, they heard a knock at the door. Emma put down her book and got up. "He's on time. I'll get it."

She entered the foyer and approached the door. The knock sounded again as she went to open it. Ethan stood in the doorway, wringing his hat like a wet rag. *He's normally so self-assured,* she thought. She looked at him closely. "Won't you come in?" she asked.

He started to enter but stopped abruptly, "Emma, I appreciate you taking this seriously."

"We want to help you," she assured him. "But I want more details before I agree to anything."

"Of course," he said, taking a deep breath to calm himself.

"Would you mind coming into the sitting room? The people here are part of my team," she said, hoping to get him moving.

He walked in slowly and looked at her as she shut the door. "Team?" he asked, his voice sounding hoarse as he started twisting his hat again.

"Would you like me to take your coat and hat?" she asked kindly.

He looked down at it before he handed it over to her. "I'm not sure it could still be called a hat," he said, his mouth twisted into a humorless smile as he shrugged out of his coat.

She didn't comment as she took the garment and laid them on the small table near them. "Are you ready to go in?"

"There'll be more people who know about this?" he asked, twisting his hands he wished he hadn't relinquished his hat.

"Yes, for my cases, it's usually more than just me," she explained, frowning as she continued to observe him.

"Oh, of course. I should have realized," he muttered. He had heard about the many cases Emma worked on and, given their complexity, he shouldn't have been surprised that there were more people involved.

"This way," she said as she guided him to the sitting room. He hesitated at the doorway, his eyes darting to each new face.

"Let me introduce you," Emma said softly, trying to settle him in. "Everyone, this is Ethan Worthington. Ethan, this is my team: Tim Flannigan, my brother-in-law; Dora, his wife, and my sister; and Jeremy Tilden, my close friend," she said with a wink and a smile. She continued, "Jake is our friend and photographer."

"It's nice to meet you all," Ethan said awkwardly.

"Why don't you take a seat?" inquired Dora.

"That would be nice, thank you."

He walked over and sat on the settee; Emma joined him there.

"Ethan, why don't you tell everyone about you first."

He looked around the room. "Well, I work with Emma as Mr. Pennington's secretary. I've held the position for the past five years."

"We understand you need some help," Jeremy stated, hoping to steer the man to reveal the favor.

"Yes. I've inherited my family home. My father passed away a few weeks ago," he said, dropping his head in his hands.

"Ethan, I didn't know..." Emma said, reaching out to touch his arm.

"We are so sorry," Dora commented for the group.

"Thank you," said Ethan sincerely, removing his hands from his face.

"Was it unexpected?" Emma asked as she drew back her hand, trying to approach him slowly.

"Yes." Ethan took a breath to steady himself before continuing. "The police say he jumped off the balcony located just off his bedroom." He leaned forward earnestly. "I just don't think he would have jumped on his own. There is something in that house that made him do it."

"Did your father have any medical problems?" Emma probed.

"No, not that I know of. I had dinner with him once a week and he never said anything was wrong."

"Did he have a personal physician?" asked Emma.

"Yes, Dr. Warner. He's here in town. I can provide you with his address."

"Thank you," Emma said and wrote the information he provided in her notebook.

"Ethan," asked Jeremy, "did your father drink alcohol?"

He shook his head. "No, he never did. He just didn't feel it was necessary."

"Did he exhibit any signs of depression?" Dora asked. She was thinking about the suicide determination.

"No. In fact, he was planning a big Christmas celebration. Does a man making plans like that kill himself?"

"I wouldn't think so," commented Tim.

"Was he seeing anyone, socially?" Jeremy asked.

"No, not that I'm aware of. He didn't want to date after Mom passed," Ethan stated.

"Were there any witnesses? Household staff?" Emma asked.

"We can't keep them. The ones who were there had only been employed a few weeks, but they had run off the day before. The only staff to stay was Mrs. Shephard. She and her son have always been with us."

"What do Mrs. Shephard and her son do for you?" asked Tim.

"Housekeeping and carriage driver. The other staff members were a cook and two maids."

"Did the police question them?" asked Emma.

"I believed they planned to, but since it was ruled a suicide, they didn't follow through."

"I can check on that," Emma commented. "What's the detective's name?"

"Detective Kelly."

Emma noted that fact and looked at Jake thoughtfully, wondering if he had photos of the crime scene. She made a note to follow up with him. Jake would want her to follow protocol when she asked for them.

"You said you had trouble keeping staff. Why won't they stay?" Tim asked curiously. He, Dora, and Emma ran a temporary employment agency, and keeping employees was important.

"They believe the house is haunted. They've complained that they hear and see things, especially at night," explained Ethan.

Jeremy was curious. "Can you describe some of these?"

"At night, you can hear footsteps walking down the halls when no one is there. Windows rattle and knobs turn by themselves. Creaks and moans that can't be explained."

Emma frowned. "How old is the home?"

"More than fifty years old. My grandfather was a carpenter and stone mason. The final design is based on the gothic style. My father continued to work on the house after his dad's death."

"Did you work on it also?" asked Dora.

He looked down at his hands and said, "No. I'm not great with tools. I do better in the business world."

"Ethan," Emma said, "older homes will tend to move with age and the footsteps could be the floors cooling off at night."

"Yes," he agreed. "The house has always had those sounds. As a boy, I would stay up listening for the steps down the hallway before I went to sleep." He paused a moment and said, "If that was the only thing, then I wouldn't have come to see you."

The group sat forward in their chairs collectively, waiting.

"It's my father's room. In the past month, the staff has refused to clean it. We had reports from different maids that they witnessed apparitions there."

"What kind of apparitions?" asked Dora, her voice higher than normal.

"They don't seem to be consistent. I questioned them, but there were no common factors."

Emma looked at Ethan. "Where is the house located?"

"It is north of the main city."

"Did your father always live there, full time?" asked Tim.

"Not since my mom died. He moved to an apartment near mine. We were very close," he said, his mouth drawing down and his eyes dropping.

Dora watched and felt so sad for the man who was now so alone.

"Did your father report seeing any of the apparitions?" Tim asked curiously.

"No," Ethan answered simply.

"How long has it been since you have stayed in the house?" Jeremy asked.

"Last Christmas," Ethan answered, trying to pull himself out of his depressed state.

"Why is that?" Emma asked.

"It's our tradition to stay there over the holiday and have dinner," he explained. "Father had moved back in to get the house organized for the holiday. He wanted a deep cleaning of all of the rooms and wanted to oversee the installation of Christmas decorations."

So, the timeline for this starts just before Christmas this year, thought Emma. "You haven't been there since that time?" she asked

"No, I haven't had a reason to be there."

Emma asked the hard question. "Ethan, why do you think he didn't kill himself?"

The man's face turned ashen at the question, and he replied in a low voice, full of pain. "He wouldn't have done that. He loved his life and would never take it. I know he was killed. Either by a ghost or someone else in the house. Could you look into it for me, *please?*"

Emma looked at him closely before saying, "We will look into it."

Color flooded into Ethan's face and he looked hopeful for the first time that night.

Emma studied her notes. "The house, who owns it now?"

"I do," he said simply. "I'm the last of the family."

"Your father had no brothers or sisters?" Dora asked.

"Well, I did have an uncle, but he died before I was born. I'll be making the ownership official in a probate hearing tomorrow." He noticed the time. "I'm sorry I kept you up so late," he said apologetically.

Just as Emma was about to reply, they heard the front door open and close with a bang. *Savannah,* she thought. That was confirmed when the woman strolled into the sitting room. She wore dark clothes and looked more like a burglar than someone who worked at the theatre. The dark clothes allowed her to move around the set, getting it ready for approaching scenes.

"Hey, the play went well tonight..." She noticed they had a guest and stopped what she was saying.

Emma waved her over. "Ethan this is Savannah Woods. She works as a stage manager at a local theatre and also serves as a member of our team." She looked over at Savannah and continued. "Savannah, Ethan stopped by to talk to us about a case we are taking on."

"It's nice to meet you, Ethan." She looked back at Emma. "You can catch me up tomorrow. I'm going to head up to bed now; it was a long night at the theatre."

Ethan watched her leave the room, somewhat bemused at the sudden appearance and then disappearance of the lovely girl.

Emma saw his attention was elsewhere. "Ethan?" she prompted him,

He dragged his gaze away from the door and said, "Huh? Oh, Yes."

She closed her notebook with a snap. "Why don't we end this here and I'll come by tomorrow morning to review the next steps with you."

"Oh, okay, great," he said absently, still watching the door where Savannah had exited.

Emma smiled slightly and stood, with Ethan following her to the foyer. She got his coat and hat, which he took from her gratefully and walked him to the front door. He slid the coat on and placed his hat on his head.

She laughed suddenly. Covering her mouth quickly with her hand, she said, "I think you need a new hat."

He removed it and turned it over in his hands, commenting wryly, "I think you're right." He stopped and suddenly grabbed her elbow. "Thank you for listening to me and helping me with this matter."

"Don't worry, we'll look into this," she assured him.

With that, he exited into the night, his fists tightly clinched in his pockets.

Emma closed the door behind Ethan and leaned against it.

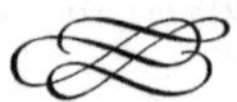

When Emma didn't return, Jeremy went out into the foyer to find her. He saw her leaning on the door.

"What are you thinking?" he asked, watching her drum her fingers on her lips. He knew she was thinking deeply about the case when he saw her doing that.

"Let's go back to the sitting room," she suggested as she lowered her hand to take his.

They walked back into the sitting room and sat down. She pulled out her notebook and said, "Okay, let's go over the examples of haunting he mentioned one by one. First, the windows rattling."

"That could be wind and loose windows," Tim commented.

Emma looked at her list. "Second, footsteps walking the halls at night; could be just the heat cooling off of the floors at the end of the day."

"What else?" Dora asked, fascinated.

"Doorknobs turning at night when people are in bed."

"Explainable as pranksters or an active imagination. Especially in a large, mostly empty house," said Jeremy thoughtfully.

"It might just be the poor man died and Ethan can't accept it," suggested Dora.

"Jake," Emma said suddenly. He looked up from his book at her. He had stayed in the room but remained quiet during the discussion with Ethan.

"Yes?"

"Were you on the scene when they found Mr. Worthington's body?"

"I was called in to take the photos," he confirmed.

Good, thought Emma. "I'd like to see them."

"You will have to get approval first from the detective in charge of the case."

She expected that response and nodded. "I understand, and I'll get the approval and come see you at the station."

"Tomorrow?"

"If I can work it out."

Tim looked at the group. "So, we are taking a case involving a ghost?"

"Yes. I owe Ethan and would like to do this for him," Emma explained. "Additionally, how fun would it be to investigate a ghost during the Christmas season? It has a very Dickensian feel to it," she said, referencing the 1843 book *A Christmas Carol.*

Jeremy smiled slightly. "Where do we go from here?"

"First, I need to get a copy of that police report and then talk to the doctor. We need to know the listed cause of death."

"What about the servants?" asked Dora. Getting information from servants had helped in several of their other cases.

"We need to find them," Emma confirmed. "I'll get a list from Ethan tomorrow and see if you or Amy know them."

"Agreed," Dora said, yawning broadly.

Seeing her yawn and noticing the hour, Tim said, "It's late, let's get to bed. We can pick this up in the morning."

Everyone agreed. Jeremy, Tim, and Jake worked to turn off the gas lamps as Dora and Emma headed upstairs.

CHAPTER 5

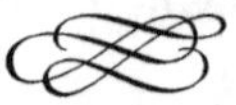

The next morning, Emma and Jeremy were getting dressed in Emma's room.

"Where are you headed this morning?" he asked.

She looked over at him as she slipped on her long jacket. "Police station first, then over to Mr. Pennington's office to see Ethan."

"I thought the office was closed until after the holidays."

"It is," she confirmed, "but Ethan is there closing some cases for the year-end. He also mentioned his father's probate hearing is today. I want to see if I can accompany him. I'd like to see how the process works." She pulled out her notebook. "The rest of the morning, I plan to follow up with the doctor and a few others."

They finished dressing. Jeremy walked into his room and then they walked out of their respective bedrooms and met in the hallway to make their way downstairs for breakfast.

"What will you be doing today?" she asked.

"Not much. It's slow so we'll be straightening up and closing files for the year. We'll also be looking at the caseloads for next year."

As they entered the dining room, they saw Dora sitting at the table with baby Lottie, feeding her breakfast. Dora looked up as they entered. "Set the table, please."

"And good morning to you also," teased Emma, kissing her on her head. She leaned over and gave one to Lottie also. The little girl squealed and grabbed at her hair. "Mama says I have to help set the table," Emma said as she disengaged the child's fingers and moved over to the sideboard where she started pulling out napkins and silverware. Jeremy gathered the plates and carried them over to the table to distribute them.

Amy came into the room at that moment and rang the breakfast bell, located near the dining-room door. Patrick, Dora and Tim's adopted son, came running in and wrapped his arms around Emma's legs in a big hug.

"Good morning, Patrick," she commented as she tried to stay upright.

"Good morning, Emma," he said brightly, tilting his face toward hers, revealing a wide smile.

"Morning, Tim," Emma said as her brother-in-law walked in at a slower pace behind Patrick.

"Patrick, try not to knock down your aunt," the boy's father scolded lightly.

"He's fine," Emma assured him, hugging the boy tightly.

"Emma, I need you to stick around after breakfast to review current jobs."

Tim, Dora, and Emma had been running a temporary employment business for the last six years. It required all three of them to have input into the positions and people available. Emma participated as a co-owner and as an employee of their business.

"That shouldn't be a problem. I have time." She knew the police officers she wanted to speak with wouldn't be at the precinct for another hour. Looking around she asked, "Where is Jake?"

Ethyl answered, "A note came early this morning, he had to go to a crime scene to take pictures." She and Jake had developed a close friendship since she started working at the boarding house.

"Oh, I had hoped to go in with him," Emma said.

"I need help with the trays, please," Amy interrupted her thought and called out from the kitchen door. Her assistant Ethyl picked up the pitchers she had filled and moved them to the dining room.

Everyone got up to bring the food to the table. Dora stayed with the kids.

Breakfast went quickly; the food was always amazing. Emma was concentrating on her plans for the day and let the conversation flow around her.

After breakfast was cleared away, Jeremy leaned over and kissed her. "I have to head in to work a little early this morning. Try to check in with me later, if you can."

"I will," she promised. "I'll be at the bakery in the afternoon today."

"Bring back something sweet?" he asked hopefully.

"I think I can manage that for you."

"Love you," he commented softly.

"Love you, too," she said in the same tone and watched him leave.

Tim cleared his throat. "Ready to start?" He had his books set out.

"Let me get Lottie cleaned up and changed. Can you give me a minute?" Dora asked.

"Of course."

Dora took the baby and headed out of the room.

"Papa?" Patrick got up from his chair and stood by Tim.

"Yes?" Tim asked, giving him his full attention.

"Grandpapa said I could work with him at his house this afternoon if you can take me."

Tim pretended to think about it. "I think I can work that out. Do you want to start your homework soon?"

"Can I start at nine?" the boy negotiated.

Tim smiled and ruffled his thick red hair. "That would be fine. What are you going to do now?"

"I want to go over to Tommy's house. May I go?" Patrick knew he needed permission before going out. Tommy was the grandson of Dora and Emma's Uncle Hans, and he was visiting for the holidays. Their house was only a few doors down from the boarding house.

"Yes, but you must get bundled up and you must pass inspection with your mama. Understood?"

"Yes, Papa," Patrick said before running out of the room to get his coat and a ball.

"Don't forget your hat, gloves, and scarf!" Tim called after him.

"I won't," the boy called back.

Dora came back downstairs, carrying a cleaned-up Lottie. She heard the conversation between Patrick and Tim. "Where's Patrick going?"

"Next door to see Tommy, maybe play some ball. He'll see you before he leaves," Tim said, knowing his wife was protective of him.

Dora looked satisfied with that comment and set Lottie down on the floor next to her chair with her toy blocks. She walked over to the sideboard, pulled out her accounting books, and moved back to the table.

When Lottie started to crawl under the table, Dora called out, "Amy!"

The other woman stuck her head through the door to the kitchen. "Yes, Dora?"

"Could you watch Lottie during our meeting?"

Amy smiled broadly, always enjoying her time with the baby. "Of course." She bent down to look at Lottie under the table. "Come here, baby girl." Lottie crawled quickly to her. She picked up the girl and they went back into the kitchen.

Patrick raced in dressed in his winter gear to stand in front of his mama. "Mama, am I warm enough?"

Dora looked him over and, as she wrapped his scarf more tightly around his neck, said in a serious voice said, "You may not be outside without your hat and scarf on."

He looked down when she made that comment.

"Patrick," she said, taking his chin in her hands and forcing him to look her in the eyes.

"Yes, Mama, but sometimes I get hot with all of this on. Especially if we're playing ball."

She thought about that. "Okay, you may unbutton your jacket for some airflow, but no rolling around in the wet snow. Understood?"

"Yes, Mama," he said respectfully.

"On your way now," she said, letting him go.

Tim watched as Patrick ran off and called after him, "Don't forget your ball. And come back at nine."

"Yes, Papa," he called back.

"I'll come to get you if you forget," Tim warned.

"Yes, Papa."

They heard the front door slam behind him.

"It's been nice with Tommy visiting," Tim said.

"Yes, and more of his cousins will be here closer to Christmas," Dora commented.

"The party is going to be big this year," Emma said, looking forward to it.

"We'll need temporary help to help prepare and serve," Dora reminded him.

Tim looked at his notes. "I'll give you a list of people we have available, so you can choose who you'd like to help out."

"And we'll need to get at least three trees," Dora commented, thinking ahead to the party.

"Patrick and I can go this morning and pick them out. What night do we want to decorate?" asked Tim.

"I think soon; we don't want to wait until the party." She looked over at Emma. "If we get organized, can you help tonight?"

"I don't think Jeremy has any plans, and I'm free," Emma said.

"Good," Dora said decisively. "We'll include Savannah and Jake also."

"Don't forget Abbey, Papa, and Cole," reminded Emma.

Dora nodded. "Yes, of course. I'll send them a note this morning. I hope it isn't too short notice."

"It should be fine. I think the weather is limiting any plans right now," said Emma.

"Do you want me to start pulling out the Christmas decoration boxes this morning?" Tim asked

"Yes, please," Dora said.

"Patrick will be excited, and Lottie will be more aware of the holiday this year," Emma said.

"Oh, dear. We'll have to keep Lottie away from the trees." The baby hadn't been mobile last Christmas, so the concern wasn't there.

"Probably no candles this year," Emma said thoughtfully. Their trees were normally lit with them. She enjoyed the tradition, but it could be a fire hazard, especially with a little one.

"Definitely not," her sister said, picturing what would happen if Lottie pulled down a fully lit tree.

"Agreed," said Tim.

Emma looked around the room, imagining the decorations in place. There would be Christmas wreaths, wood railings festooned with evergreens, and cotton batting for snow. "It all sounds lovely. Do you want me to bring home some sweets to have as we're decorating?"

"That would be nice. I'd rather not spring this on Amy," Dora said. "I'll pop popcorn for the children to string." *And,* she thought, *I'll also make popcorn balls.* Other decorations would include stars cut from gilt paper and lace bags filled with bright candies that would be fastened to the tree's branches.

"And candies strung with the popcorn?" Emma asked.

"Yes, and candies will be strung with them," Dora confirmed, knowing how much Emma enjoyed that tradition.

"I'll also bring some decorative cookies to hang on the trees," Emma promised.

Dora glanced over at Tim; she could see he was getting impatient to start the meeting.

"Ready?" Tim asked with a slight smile.

"Yes," they both commented in a business-like tone.

"We have a larger than normal contingent of employees at the department stores because of Christmas. They've all been notified of their last days. A few stores, along with Marshall Fields and Stubings, have commented that they'd like the employees to stay an extra week after Christmas to do an inventory check."

"Is everyone still available?" asked Dora.

"They should be. I'm hoping we'll have five of the women out of the group apply for business school in the spring." The Carlyle Charity, where they were board members, continued to support women's education. It also helped their business to have more qualified women to work in the engineering offices.

"Has Claire been notified, in case financial support is needed?" Emma asked. Clair Spencer headed the charity and distributed funds to the organizations or people in need.

"I've told her the number, but I need to confirm the names," he commented, taking notes.

"Great."

"Emma, how's the work at Mr. Pennington's office going? Do we need to start training someone to replace you?" Tim asked, looking down at his notes.

"No, I really like it there, and I think Mr. Pennington would like me to work more permanently. We may think about adding a clerk in the future when I'm doing less office work and more investigations."

"We can work on that," he said, making a note in his books.

"Outside jobs are almost nonexistent right now due to the snow."

"Do we have enough inside construction going on to keep those employees busy?" asked Dora. She was concerned that the workers would not have paychecks during the holiday season.

"Yes, a lot of the jobs thought ahead and made sure that the finishing work was going on inside. We shouldn't have to lay anyone off. Any other issues?" He looked at Emma and Dora. They shook their heads. "No? Okay, then." He closed his books and stood up to return to the study.

"I need to be on my way," Emma said, heading to the foyer closet.

Dora followed and watched her bundle up. Emma looked over at her and teased, "Do you want to inspect me also?"

Dora took her seriously, walked over to her, picked up her muffler, and wrapped it around her neck. She looked at her sister and asked, "Pants today?" It was unsafe to be out in the weather without pants and long underwear.

"Definitely during the winter months," Emma said, picking up her bag and placing her winter hat on her head. Her bakery clothes were in her bag for her afternoon job.

Dora reached up and straightened it, tucking in Emma's braid. "Yes, I think you're okay now," she stated as she finished her inspection.

Emma smiled, leaned over, and kissed her. "Have a great day."

She made her way through the kitchen, pausing to give Lottie a big kiss. She sidled out the door as she told Ethyl and Amy goodbye.

Dora called to Tim, "Don't forget we'll need three trees by tonight."

"I want to wait for Patrick so he can go with me," he called back.

Dora looked out the window, letting her forehead rest on the cold glass. The snow didn't look like it was going to abate anytime soon, and she worried about her family being out in it.

CHAPTER 6

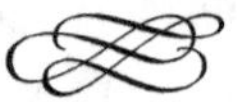

*E*mma rode over to the police station on her bicycle. *Ghosts, Ethan's father, maids running away...she thought. What is going on in that house?*

Sleet rained down her face, and she burrowed further into her muffler. The precinct was close. She increased her pedaling speed, thinking only of getting out of the cold.

Her front wheel hit an ice patch, causing the bike to swerve to the right and hit a large rock. She flew over the handlebars, quickly rolled herself into a ball, and fell into the snow. *I'm going to be in trouble with Dora,* she thought as she lay there. *I'm not supposed to be rolling around in the snow.*

Sitting up, she wiped the snow off her head and shoulders and checked for injuries. The many layers had offered additional protection, so no harm was done. Relieved, she got to her feet, walked over to her bike, pulled it out of the snow, and examined it. The front wheel was damaged. She'd have to carry it the rest of the way to the station. *It's my own fault,* she thought. *I was going too fast on icy streets.* She placed the bike on her shoulder and trudged through the snow to the police station.

Emma kept it with her as she made her way up the stoop and into the station. As she entered, she closed the door quickly behind her, looking around the open entryway. Brushing the sleet off her forehead, she unwrapped her scarf and set her bike down on the tile floor.

The desk clerk, Officer Jessup, watched her walk over to him, dragging the bike with her. He looked at her from his tall desk and said in a cheerful voice, "Hello, Emma. What are you doing out in this cold weather?"

"I stopped by to check on something." She pulled out her notebook. "Is Detective John Kelly here? He is working the Worthington case."

Jessup looked down at his logbook. "Yes, he's here. Third floor. Is he expecting you?"

"No, I got his name from Ethan Worthington. He asked me to look into his father's death."

"It should be okay." The officer knew Emma was friends with the police chief and would be allowed to go up unescorted. "Just ask for him on the third floor."

"I will," she said. She looked down at the damaged bike and back up at the desk officer. "Would it be all right if I leave this here?"

He looked over his desk and down at it. "It looks like it's been through the wars. Sure, roll it behind here. I'll keep an eye on it."

"Well, it doesn't roll anymore."

He gave it a considering look as she dragged it behind his desk.

"Thanks," she said and headed up the three flights of stairs. The door was opened revealing a room full of desks and people. At the first one, she stopped and asked the young detective sitting there, "Can you direct me to Detective Kelly?"

He cocked his head to the right. "Over there."

She looked to where he indicated and saw a tall, thin man standing in front of the desk moving papers and folders around.

She took in his appearance; he had blondish-brown hair and appeared to be in his early thirties.

"Thank you," she said and headed over to him. As she got close, she asked, "Detective Kelly?"

He turned toward her and asked, "Yes, and you would be?"

"Emma Evans."

John Kelly realized he knew that name. He sat on the edge of his desk and folded his arms. "I've heard of you," he said.

Emma was unsure how to take that comment. "I wanted to speak with you about a case you are involved in, Detective."

"Call me John, and that depends on the case you want to talk about, Miss Evans."

"Call me Emma," she responded.

Kelly stood up and moved around the desk to his chair. "Why don't you sit down and tell me what this is about?"

She sat in the chair in front of his desk, then pulled out her notebook. "Louis Worthington. As I understand it, he jumped off his balcony at his property in upper Chicago."

"Let me check. That one was just here." Kelly moved some files around and pulled one out. He opened it, scanning the information.

Emma noticed the size of the file. "Rather thin," she commented.

"Yes," he said absently. "There wasn't a lot to that one. It was clear that it was a suicide."

"Can you tell me about it?"

"Can I ask why the interest?" he asked, looking over at her before sharing.

"His son asked me to look into it. He's concerned there's more to it. He doesn't believe it was a suicide."

"The son. His name is Ethan?"

She nodded.

"Yes, I got that impression from him at the scene and in later interviews with him."

"Can you tell me the details of the case and how you determined it was a suicide?"

He gave her a long look, then glanced down at the file. "We were notified that a body was found at the Worthington house."

"Who found him?"

"It was a delivery person, a young man by the name of Richard Wilkins. He had an early morning delivery."

"Did you get to talk to him?"

"I did. He came straight here to report it and rode back with us."

"What did you find when you got there?"

"The body, lying just as he said," Kelly confirmed.

"What was your first impression?"

"Initially, it appeared to be an accident. It looked like Worthington had fallen off the balcony and hit his head on a rock."

"Appeared?" she questioned.

He looked back at his notes. "We went into the house and to the bedroom. The balcony door's latch was broken and the doors were wide open to the outside. When we went out there, we saw the railing was high—too high to just fall off. We also found a chair on the balcony right at the railing. It was in just the right place to climb onto and jump off."

"So, you changed the focus of your investigation to a suicide," she stated.

"Yes," he said simply.

"Did a doctor take a look at the body?"

"Yes. We notified his personal physician to examine it and confirm our findings."

"Did Jake take any pictures at the scene?" she asked, drumming her fingers on her lips.

He looked through the file again. "Yes, they're here. Are you sure you'd like to view them?"

"I'll be fine," she assured him as she held out her hand.

John handed them to her. She looked at each one, examining the body's position.

"What did the doctor say after he reviewed these?" Emma asked.

"He confirmed that Mr. Worthington fell and his head hit the rock. It was probably what killed him. He can't confirm if he jumped or was made to jump. The only thing he could positively confirm was that he'd fallen, hit his head, and died."

"Did he say anything else?" she inquired, studying the photos.

"No."

"Hmm," she said, thinking that the arms looked fractured. *If he was going to kill himself, would he have this kind of injury?* When she fell off her bike today, her instinct had been to put out her arms, but her training told her to roll herself into a ball before hitting the ground. "I'll follow up with the doctor." She continued her questions. "Did you interview the staff?"

"We had planned to initially, but when the death appeared to be a suicide, there didn't seem to be a reason. It was also hard to locate all of them. Several had run off a few days before. It was reported that they were scared of something."

"Did you find out what scared them?"

He looked a bit embarrassed. "As we understand from the agency that placed them, they believe the house was haunted."

Emma didn't say anything about his comment and asked, "Were there additional pictures of the scene?" She hadn't seen any others in the packet.

"Jake has them. I took the ones that showed the victim for the case file."

"Would you mind if I get a copy of these and the ones showing the house?"

"We can arrange that with Jake." He opened a drawer, pulled out a form, and filled it out. He handed it to her. "Just give this to him."

"Thank you. What about the staff, do you have their names?" she added, thinking that she needed to follow up with them.

"I don't, we didn't need them at the time. Also, Ethan mentioned that two people work there permanently."

"Yes, I have their names. Where were they when Mr. Worthington died?"

He looked at the file and back at her. "Ethan mentioned they were off that evening."

"Hmm," she said. "I'll interview them also."

"Emma," he said firmly. "You need to let me know if anything changes on the case. I don't want to be surprised."

"I will," she promised. She gathered up her things and stood. "Thank you for your time." She took a few steps and turned toward him, "Jake went out to a crime scene this morning…"

"Actually two," he confirmed.

"Would you mind if I take a look at the pictures from these scenes?"

He frowned and ask, "Why?"

"Call it curiosity for now."

"It is Detective Carlson's case, but he shouldn't have a problem with you just viewing them. Hand me the form," he requested.

She handed it to him and he amended it to allow her to view the other scene's pictures. The paper was returned to her and she headed back out the way she came.

He nodded and watched her with a contemplative look on his face.

Taking the stairs two at a time, she exited quickly into the main entrance. Officer Jessup was still at his desk, she headed toward him.

He heard boots clinking on the tile floors, he looked and saw Emma. "Get what you needed?"

"I did. Thanks for the help. Would you mind hanging on to my bike for a few more minutes? I want to see Jake before I leave."

"Go ahead, I'm not leaving the area anytime soon."

She smiled at him and turned to make her way to Jake's lab, located in the basement of the police station. Gas lamps lit her way down to the area he used to develop his film.

"Jake," she called. She heard an immediate reply

"I am developing pictures, please wait."

The development process could take some time, so she sat in a nearby chair and pulled out her notebook to review the details of the case.

It was a few minutes later when he opened the door to his lab. "You can come in now."

She walked in, looking around, curious as to what his new case was. He had pictures hung on a wire above his counter to dry.

He pulled her out of her observations by asking brusquely, "What can I help you with?"

"Detective Kelly said I could pick up the pictures from a case."

"Do you have approval?" He was ready to turn her down if she didn't follow the procedure.

She smiled at him slightly. "Of course." Emma handed him the form. "Kelly also said I could view the ones from this morning."

He reviewed the note thoroughly and nodded. "Let me get this for you. The ones from this morning are there," he pointed to the wire holding the pictures.

As he went to get the items she requested, she studied the drying pictures. "Kelly mentioned that there were two scenes?"

"Yes, two separate ones. We just got back from the second scene," he said, looking at the pictures she'd referenced.

"These are very similar. You said they were two different cases?" She reviewed each one closely.

"Yes."

"When were they found?"

"Both were reported this morning. I was going to develop the film from the first one, but I got called to go to the second scene before I could process them."

"Kelly mentioned this is Detective Carlson's case."

"Yes."

She continued looking closely at the pictures.

"Did you want to review these before you leave?" he asked, pulling out the requested pictures from the Worthington crime scene file.

"If you have time..."

"I do." He made room for her to lay the pictures on his bench. She spread them out.

"Are we still investigating the ghost?"

"Well," she quantified, "we're investigating what happened to Mr. Worthington."

He nodded. "What did you want to review with me?"

She pointed to the picture of the victim's head. "I understand the cause of death was his head hitting a rock."

"Yes," Jake confirmed. "I have a picture of the rock and the wound inflicted." He moved the pictures closer for her review.

She looked closely at them. "That's not a rock that could be moved easily." It was partially buried in the ground. She looked over at him and asked, "Did you go inside?"

"I did."

"Did you take pictures of the room?"

"It is part of the scene," he commented, moving more pictures closer to her.

She studied the room and the balcony carefully. *Smart,* she thought as she noticed Jake had Detective Kelly stand by the balcony to give perspective to the pictures. It was formed out of heavy wood and was over four feet in height. "Going under would have been impossible," she commented.

Jake understood what she was talking about. "The railings were very close together. Going through them would have made that difficult."

It's also too tall, she thought, noting Detective Kelly's height. *The detective was right, it wouldn't have been easy to get over without assistance.* She noticed something in the corner of the picture. "What's that object?" she asked, pointing at it.

He handed her another picture and said, "This one is a better picture." It showed a chair sitting at the balcony rail.

"Detective Kelly mentioned that," she murmured. "Was it in that position when you got there?"

"We didn't move anything; the scene is exactly as you see it."

"Do we think the chair was placed there so he could jump off the balcony?"

Jake had no opinion. He liked to present his data and let police officers make the determination.

Studying the body again, she reexamined the injuries. *The doctor,* she thought. *I need to talk to him.* She gathered all of them up, placed them in an envelope, and slipped them into her bag. Something was bothering her; she glanced at the still drying pictures again. "These are very similar," she said again, studying each one intently.

"Possibly, but that is up to the detective and not me."

"See these marks here?" she asked, indicating the first girl's neck.

He looked over. "Yes."

"And look at the marks on the second girl's neck. Whatever was used to strangle the first one was also used to strangle the second one. These are very distinctive; they appear to have twisted the weapon during the attack."

Jake looked closer, studying the pattern. "Probably some type of rope, and it looks like it was twisted similarly."

"Will you tell the detective?" she asked.

"I will add it to my report when I turn in the pictures."

"Okay, thanks for reviewing these with me," she said, patting her bag that held the envelope.

He nodded and started working on his report.

"Jake." She waited for him to look up. "We're going to decorate the house tonight."

"I will be there on time."

"I expected that," she said with a smile and headed back upstairs. As she ascended, she thought about the information she'd learned. So far, there was no evidence that Ethan's father had been murdered. Just some odd stories about that house and the supposed haunting.

CHAPTER 7

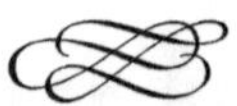

Emma exited the basement and headed to the desk where she had left her bike. She looked around and didn't see Officer Jessup or the bike. Frowning, she studied the area as she slipped on her coat and hat.

"Looking for something?" a voice called from behind her.

She turned around and saw the officer rolling her bike in from outside.

She ran over and knelt, checking the tire. "You fixed it! I damaged it when I fell."

"Sure. It was easy. The front fender was bent against the wheel. I just hammered it out and it's good as new."

She stood up and said gratefully, "Thanks so much for doing that."

"No problem, did you get what you needed from Kelly?"

"I did," she said as she rolled the bike back and forth. She grinned at him and said, "Thanks again, and Merry Christmas!"

"You too!" Jessup said as he watched her roll the bike out of the door.

As she stepped out onto the stoop, she immediately regretted not buttoning up her coat. Leaning the bike against the door, she quickly did so and wrapped her scarf around her neck. She placed the bike on her shoulder and carried it downstairs. The sidewalk glittered like glass in the sunlight. *Best to walk it to the office,* she thought. *I don't want to end up in the snow again.*

It took longer than expected and she was a little late. The office was empty as she entered and parked the bike inside the door. When she didn't see Ethan at his desk, she called, "Ethan, are you here?"

"Yes, I'm in Mr. Pennington's office. Just a moment," he called back.

"Okay," she said and started unwrapping her scarf and unbuttoning her coat.

He came out carrying several files. "Why are you in the office today? Did you have something to work on?"

"No. I'm working on your case and wanted to review some details with you."

He immediately perked up and then frowned. "I can't meet right now, I'm due in court for the probate on Dad's will." He glanced down at his watch. "In about twenty minutes."

"I was hoping I could come with you to observe?" She knew probate of the will meant the document is judged to be genuine. It also allowed heirs to manage the property or money left to them as they liked.

"Sure, the company will be nice," he said, getting his files organized to go over to the courthouse. He walked past her to get his heavy coat and hat. Once he was buttoned up, he slipped on his hat and turned to her. "Ready?"

She buttoned her coat back up, wrapped her scarf around her neck, and added her hat. "Yes. Is it ok if I leave the bike here?"

"Yes, we can come back after and discuss my case," he suggested.

They headed out, and Ethan locked the door behind them.

"Don't you need Mr. Pennington to be in court with you?" Emma inquired.

"No, I've assisted him in a large number of these and reviewed them with him. He approved me going alone."

They walked carefully on the icy sidewalks and made their way to the courthouse. Once there, they continued to the specific court that dealt with wills and probate. When they entered, they saw several people waiting in the room for the judge to begin.

"How does this work?" Emma asked in a low voice.

Ethan replied in the same tone. "We'll wait until we're called, then approach the bench to speak with the judge."

"Okay," she said, sitting back in the chair. They waited and watched as other wills were probated. Simple ones were signed off immediately. One that was contested was scheduled for another day.

"What does that mean?" she asked Ethan in a low voice.

"We're here to confirm that the will is genuine. If someone disagrees with any part and they can prove it, the probate may stop until more evidence is produced," he murmured.

She continued to watch the proceedings. The lawyer for the family spoke in a low voice to his clients. She could see they were visibly agitated. *Wills can be an emotional business*, she thought.

After a long wait, it was finally Ethan's turn. He stood and approached the bench. He waved at Emma to follow him up. She moved to stand slightly behind him, her gaze on the judge. He had a copy of the will in front of him.

"This would be an easy case, Mr. Worthington," he said. "All seems in order."

He moved to approve the probate when an officer of the court walked up to the judge and whispered in his ear, handing him a piece of paper.

"Oh, okay," the judge commented as he read it. He looked out to Ethan. "We will not be able to probate this will today. It seems we've received a note that another party wishes to contest it, and they'll be arriving after Christmas. A caveat has been filed to allow the persons contesting the will to have a hearing. We'll hear testimony from you and the person contesting at that time. You'll be allowed witnesses who may testify on your behalf."

"Judge, who's contesting the will?" Ethan asked. He was bewildered at the news. "I'm the only living relative in the family."

He ignored Ethan's first question and went on, "Be that as it may, we'll be looking at The papers provided after Christmas. Until that time, you may not dispose of the property without the court's knowledge."

"Judge, what does that mean? Can I use the house? Maintain it and hire servants?" Ethan asked, confused at this turn of events.

"You may use and maintain the house. Just keep track of the expenses," the judge directed.

"I will, thank you."

He pulled another file for the next case. "See my clerk for an open date."

Ethan knew he had no other options. "Yes, thank you." He took Emma's elbow and escorted her to the clerk's desk in the back of the courtroom.

" Is this normal?" Emma whispered.

"No," he muttered back. "This should've been simple and taken only one court appearance."

"What will you do now?"

"The only thing I can do is meet with the clerk and schedule an appointment."

They walked over to the clerk as the court continued with the next case. While they waited, she turned to him. "Do you know who could be contesting the will?"

He frowned. "No one that I know of. There are no cousins or other living family members."

They waited patiently for the clerk to call them to the desk to schedule their time. When their turn finally came up, Ethan and Emma walked up to the desk.

"Can you disclose who's contesting the will?" Ethan asked the clerk.

"Not at this time," the clerk replied in a bored voice. He got the same question over and over during the day.

Ethan understood there were rules and confirmed the date for his next appearance. He took the paper with the date and told the clerk, "Thank you."

He was silent as they headed back to the office.

"Are you worried?" Emma asked. She was concerned for him.

"A little," he said. "Sometimes people will try to steal the inheritance if they think no one will stop them. I'll have to contact Mr. Pennington and see if he can find out who might be behind this."

She said, "We can still access the house, which is good for the investigation."

"Yes, thank goodness, that's my priority right now."

"Will you have time to return to the office to review the case with me?" Ethan asked.

"Yes, I do have to be at the bakery this afternoon, but I have time now," Emma confirmed.

They got to the office quickly; Ethan had set a brisk pace for them. They stepped in and stomped the snow off onto the rug at the door. They took the time to dust off their coats and hats, before moving to sit at Ethan's desk.

Ethan pulled out paper and a pen. "Let me write a note to Mr. Pennington to ask if he minds if I stop by about the will today."

"Do you want me to run it by his house while I'm out?" she asked as she watched him write it out.

"Would it be too much trouble?"

"No, it shouldn't be an issue."

"I would appreciate it. Thank you." He finished it and gave it to her.

She put it into her pocket for safekeeping and pulled out her notebook. "Ready to discuss my findings?"

He sat back and took a deep breath, "Okay, so what were you able to find out so far?"

"I met with Detective Kelly. He's assigned to the case."

"What case," he said sarcastically.

"Yes exactly." She sat forward and said, "Ethan, all of the evidence does suggest suicide."

Agitated, he stood up. He realized he had nowhere to go and sat back down. "I just don't think he went out of that window alone."

"I agree," she said calmly.

"He just wouldn't do that," he began to argue until he realized what she said. "What?"

"I believe you're right. You know your father and didn't see any signs of depression or behavior that led to this," she said in a reasonable tone.

"Yes." He felt so relieved someone believed him. "If he didn't do it, who did?"

"That's what we have to find out. I think it's related to the weird activities reported at the house."

Ethan leaned his head back on the chair. "I thought I was going crazy. Talking about ghosts killing my father."

"No, you just knew him. I still need to investigate and get our ghost before Christmas," she teased.

"So, what next?" he asked, ready to help.

She continued to study her notes. "I want to interview the doctor."

"Why?"

"The pictures of your father showed that he tried to use his hands and arms to break his fall. I would expect a person jumping, trying to kill himself, wouldn't do that."

"The pictures showed that?" he asked. He wanted reassurance that his father had tried to save himself.

"Yes. His wrists and arms were clearly broken," she confirmed.

He thought about that. "You're going to follow up with his doctor?"

"I am, just to get his opinion, so I can document it for you. Are you still all right with me speaking to him?"

"Yes, of course."

"The servants, do you have an address for them? The ones who got scared and ran off."

"I have the address for the agency we used. You should be able to get all the names and addresses from them. I'll write it down for you." He handed her the information. "When we couldn't keep people, we started using places that could send us replacements as we needed them. They have a good reputation for placing honest people. It was important because we weren't always living there."

"That makes sense," she said. "We have similar positions within our temporary business." She went back to her notes. "The housekeeper and her son are still there?"

"Yes," he confirmed.

"Why weren't they scared away?" she asked curiously.

"I don't know, you'll have to speak with them. I can send them a note today."

"I would appreciate that. Detective Kelly said they were away when your father died."

"Yes, they were out for the entire evening."

Emma thought about that and said, "I'll head to the agency, Mr. Pennington's, and the doctor's office before I go to the bakery."

"Thanks, Emma."

She smiled as she gathered her gear and her bike to head out into the cold day.

CHAPTER 8

THE KITCHEN AT ETHAN'S FAMILY HOME

A knock was heard at the door.

"Who could that be?" Hannah Shephard asked her son Julian. He sat reading the paper at the kitchen table.

"I'll go find out," he said, as he laid his paper down and stood to walk to the door.

A few moments later, the door swished open as he returned. "Who was it?" his mother asked from the stove. Her soup was starting to simmer and needed to be watched.

Julian was holding a telegram. Reading it, he said, "It's from Ethan. He has an investigator, Emma Evans, looking into his father's death."

Her frown was instantaneous. "Is she coming here?"

His face mirrored hers. "Yes. What will we do?"

A hand moved the vent closed, cutting off their conversation. He sat back and smiled widely. "I know what I'll do. This is going to be such fun!"

CHAPTER 9

Emma wanted to get Ethan's note over to Mr. Pennington first. It was important to her friend. Mr. Pennington lived in a neighborhood very similar to the one in which she lived.

He answered the door on her first knock.

"Emma! What a surprise. Please, come in."

She entered the mostly quiet house. Mr. Pennington was a bachelor and he would be joining extended family closer to Christmas. He led her into his study and motioned to a chair as he sat behind his desk.

"What can I do for you?"

Emma sat and handed over the note. She explained what happened in court with Ethan.

He sat back. "This was not expected."

"Will you look into it?"

"I'll see what I can do."

"Thank you."

"Thank you for helping Ethan."

Mr. Pennington escorted Emma out. She turned to him and said, "I'm not sure how, but this might be wrapped up with Ethan's father's death."

"Understood," he said. He was aware of how her investigations worked. "I'll let you know what I find out."

CHAPTER 10

The next address on her list was about four blocks away. She checked her watch, confirming she had another couple of hours before she had to be at the bakery.

She tried to pedal faster as she noticed the snow picking up. The tires crunched on the ice as she pulled to a stop. Not wanting to skid on the wet sidewalk, she got off and carefully walked the bike the rest of the way.

The sign on the door said, 'Personnel Services.' She entered the office and a man was sitting at the main desk in the middle of the room. It was very quiet and had the air of a library. She placed her bike by the door and quietly made her way to him. "Sir?" she asked.

The man looked toward her, disdain clear on his face. He looked pointedly at the water she'd tracked in. "Yes? Do you plan to stand there and get my floor wet all day?"

"No, of course not." Emma looked around for something to clean up the water with.

He just shook his head in exasperation. "What are you here for, young lady?"

"I'm looking into a death that occurred at a house you staffed with servants."

He looked at her curiously. "Is this about the Worthington house?"

"Yes."

"We've decided to terminate that contract. We're not going to send any more servants to that house."

"Why is that?"

"We are getting reports of odd occurrences."

"What kind of odd occurrences?"

"The servants are saying the house is haunted."

"You can't tell me you believe in haunted houses," she scoffed.

Even though he was sitting down, Emma got the impression the man was looking down his nose at her. "No, young lady, we do not, but we do believe that our employees are scared of something, and we can't in good conscience keep sending people over there to be frightened."

"The owner's son has asked me to speak with the prior servants to figure out why they were scared and get it resolved."

He frowned at the girl. "You're looking into it? Shouldn't someone else be doing that?"

He means a man, thought Emma. "No, I'm the one he wants to look into it. Wouldn't it be beneficial for all of us if we can figure this out and have more opportunities for servants to work?"

"Yes," he said begrudgingly. "Well, get on with it, what do you want?"

"I'd like to speak with the last group that worked there."

"We can do that, it isn't a secret," he said as he looked into his card file and pulled out several cards. He looked at her expectantly. "Do you have paper?"

"I do." Emma pulled her notebook out of her pocket.

"Brook Stevens, Beth Arnold, and Margaret Troy," he stated.

"Do you have the addresses where they currently work?" she asked, looking at him.

"I do, but I don't want you jeopardizing those positions," he cautioned.

"I won't," she promised. He read the address to her.

As Emma looked at them, she noticed all three were working at different homes. *This may take a few days,* she thought. She thanked him and made her way back out. His voice followed her out, "Get someone to clean up the water mess!" Grimacing, she regretted that she'd made more work for someone.

Taking her bike, she pulled open the door and stepped out. The wind pushed her back against the closed door and she huddled into her coat as she struggled to walk down the stoop. The weather seemed to be getting worse, but there was one more stop she wanted to make before heading home for lunch. *The doctor.* The pictures were in her bag, and she had questions that needed answers.

His office was located about six blocks away from her current position in the Mann building. The energy it took to pedal the bike made the blocks feel longer than they were. She was breathing heavily when she finally arrived at her destination. Letting out a sigh of relief, she entered the lobby. A guard spotted her and waved her over to his desk.

"Can I leave this with you?" she asked, indicating her bike.

He looked at it, then back at her. "Yes. Will you be long?"

"I don't think so. I'm going to see Doctor Warner."

He nodded. "His office is 225. You can take the stairs up."

"Thank you," she said as she moved the bike to the wall behind his desk. The doorway to the stairs was visible from her location. She went directly there and up to the second floor.

The outer office was quiet when she entered. There didn't appear to be any staff present.

"Doctor Warner?" she called.

A voice called out, "We're closed presently. You'll need to come back at another time."

She followed the voice and found a man reading papers at his desk. "Doctor Warner?"

"I'm Doctor Warner," the man answered, rather impatiently.

"Would you have a moment for me? I'm Emma Evans, and I'm here about Louis Worthington."

Dr. Warner's expression changed at the mention of Worthington's name. "What would you like to discuss, young lady?"

"I'm investigating the death at Ethan's request. I wanted to review the pictures from the scene with you."

"I have some time. Do you have them with you?"

"I do."

"Hand them over, please."

Emma took the pictures out of her bag and handed them to him. "If this was a suicide, why are the wrists and arms broken? Would he have made a defensive posture like that?" she asked bluntly.

Warner frowned. He had seen the breaks; they were listed in his report. "It is possible that he changed his mind on the way down, or it could be a reflex."

"But, Doctor, couldn't it also show that it might not be suicide?"

"It might," he allowed.

"Can I see the death certificate?" she requested.

He looked over and gave her a long look. "Yes. I've completed it." He reached into a drawer, pulled out a form, and handed it to her.

She read it. "What is Visitation by God?" she asked. "That doesn't indicate suicide."

"No," he said quietly. "That means natural causes. I was trying to spare the family by not documenting suicide." He sat back. "I should have looked closer." He sounded regretful at his quick determination.

"I believe it's possible that someone forced him off of that balcony. I'd like more time to prove that. Can you hold off on filing this paperwork until my investigation is complete?"

"Yes, I can do that." He didn't want to be responsible for giving the wrong information to the family. and perhaps helping a murderer go free.

CHAPTER 11

*L*unch she thought. *It's time to head home.*

The temperature continued to drop, and she pulled her scarf up around her face. The wind pushed against her and made pedaling impossible. The bike would have to be walked home.

Her breath was coming in short gasps, and her energy was drained as she parked her bike by the side of the house. She struggled up the front steps and into the foyer, dropping her outerwear to the floor. The cracking of the fireplace in the dining room called to her; she ran over quickly and stood in front of it with her hands spread. With the feeling slowly returning to them she thought about the interview that morning. *I expected Christmas to be a bit boring this year.*

"Stay over there," called Dora as she entered from the kitchen. "We'll get lunch on the table." She moved to set the table with plates and silverware.

"Thanks," Emma said. She was grateful she wasn't being pulled from the warmth. The bakery job would be casting her out into the cold again soon. She looked around and sniffed. "Are those trees I smell?" she asked excitedly.

"Yes, Tim and Patrick brought them home a little while ago," her sister commented. As Dora watched Emma run out to the foyer to find them, she called, "They're not set up yet."

"That's okay, I just want to see them." The smell drew her in, and she found two in the foyer.

Dora followed her out and stood with her, admiring the trees. "These are for the dining room and foyer. The other one is in the sitting room."

"Perfect," Emma said. "This one is big." She indicated the one on the right.

"That one will stay here," Dora said, looking up at the high ceiling in the area.

"Tim did a good job picking them out."

"Me, too!" yelled Patrick, running up to hug his aunt Emma.

"Yes, you did a great job also," she said and returned his hug.

"Yes, you did," Dora told the boy. "And we'll be decorating them tonight."

"Yay!" Patrick yelled.

"Where's Lottie?" asked Emma.

"Nap. She's lying down in the sitting room."

Emma walked into that room and saw the smaller tree. "Oh, Dora," she whispered. "I like this one the best."

"Me, too. We'll have our Christmas morning in here, together."

"That will be nice. Has Tim gotten down the decorations?"

"Here they are," Tim said from the stairs, his arms full of boxes. "I thought I'd get an early start."

Emma and Dora rushed over to help. They moved them to the corner of the foyer.

"Lunch," Amy said as they set them down. They entered the dining room and saw lunch on the table. They sat down and started passing around the large trays.

Tim looked over at Emma. "Have you found anything out about the haunted house?"

"Some." She told them the updates to the case. "Also, an odd thing happened in court today. Someone is contesting the father's will. Ethan doesn't know who that might be. Mr. Pennington promised to look into it."

"Ethan has no idea who it could be?" asked Dora.

"None. He mentioned the uncle to us when we reviewed the case, but he passed before he was born."

As lunch wrapped up, Emma got her winter gear on and was heading out the front door.

"Emma, are you going to take your bike?" Dora called from the dining room doorway.

"No, the roads are too icy. I was sliding around too much this morning."

Her sister frowned. She was concerned for Emma's safety. "Do you need Tim to see about a carriage?"

"No, I'll be ok," she assured her.

Dora looked worried but knew Emma wouldn't take any chances. She went into the sitting room and found a smiling Lottie sitting up. She grinned at her and asked, "Would you like some lunch?" She nodded and squealed when she picked her up.

Emma walked carefully down the stairs. She carried her bag over her shoulder as she made her way to the bakery. The walk was uneventful; it took her longer than expected, but she made it there for her shift on time.

The door to the bakery flew out of her hand and slammed into the wall again as she entered. One of the bakers ran over to help her push it closed. She fell back against the door. "Thank you."

"Anytime," said Michael and returned to his workstation.

Emma headed to the closet to change into her uniform. As she exited, she went to her station and picked up her list. "Cousin," she called.

Cousin looked up from his baking, "Hey, Emma, good to see you. Any questions about your list?"

"Just one. Can I double this Christmas cookie order and take the extras home?"

"Sure, we have enough ingredients. I'll update our inventory. Is the Christmas party planning underway?" he asked. Cousin knew the cookies she wanted were usually requested for the party.

"Yes," she said and smiled. "We're decorating the trees tonight."

"We can't wait for the party. Chloe is bringing her violin," Cousin said with a grin.

"Wonderful, I'm looking forward to seeing the kids."

Chloe and Cousin had gotten married nearly five years ago and had two little boys who looked just like Cousin. They were very happy.

The ingredients she needed were for anise-flavored German Christmas cookies. She pulled them out and worked steadily, getting the dough made and rolled into balls. They went onto trays and into the oven. For the next steps, she prepped the other trays to go in as those finished. The bakery smelled wonderful, and she let herself think about her mama; baking always brought up pleasant memories of her. The bakery had originally belonged to her.

As the first batch of cookies came out of the oven, she pulled them out to cool while she added the second batch.

Two hours later, all of the cookies were out and cooling. She started putting boxes together and placed the wax paper in each of them. When they were ready to go, she filled three boxes for customers and three boxes for her to take home. *Some for decorations and some to eat*, she thought.

"Cousin, the boxes are ready for delivery," she called, pulling off her apron.

He came over to inspect them. "And three boxes for you to take home?"

"Yes," she confirmed.

"Heading out?" he asked as he looked out the window at the falling snow.

"Yes."

"You're sure it's safe? The weather has gotten progressively worse. The snow is coming down hard."

"I should be okay." *Though,* she thought, *it might be a good idea to wait it out.*

Just as she headed to change her clothes, the back door opened and one of the bakers yelled out, "Close the door!"

She looked over to see who was causing all of the issues. It was Jeremy. She went over quickly and kissed him on the cheek.

"What are you doing here?"

"I thought you might want to take a carriage home."

She leaned into him and nodded gratefully.

"Why don't you get changed. We should leave before the weather gets any worse."

"Okay," she agreed and ran to the closet to change while Jeremy talked to Cousin.

He looked around. "Cousin, you might want to start closing up and getting everyone home."

The other man had been considering that. "You're right. Most of the bakers will be heading out as their orders are complete, which should be soon."

"What about the evening deliveries?" Jeremy asked.

"We have a few. But they should be done by carriage and no walking," Cousin confirmed.

Emma exited the closet dressed in her pants, pulling on her coat. "Jeremy, we'll need to take those boxes home," she said, indicating her workstation.

He nodded and headed over to get them. "What about the others? Will we be stopping for a delivery on the way home?"

"Yes, a quick one. Here's the address," she said, handing it to him.

He slid it into his pocket and looked around at the other bakers who were putting up their work tools and nodded approvingly. Cousin would make sure they got home safely.

"Ready?" Emma asked, wrapping her scarf around her neck and pulling on her hat.

"Yes."

They carried boxes out to the waiting carriage. They went in first and, while she waited, she put her head down into her coat and tightened her scarf. Jeremy finished adding the boxes and turned to help her into the covered carriage. He had a blanket inside; once they were settled, he called up the additional address to the driver and told him to be on the way.

He pulled her close and murmured into her hair, "Better than walking."

"Yes."

"Carriages from now until this weather clears," he said firmly.

She shivered and settled into him. "Agreed."

They made good time to the drop-off. She climbed down and he handed her the three boxes.

"I'll walk this up," she said.

"Are you sure?"

"Yes. It's just down the way."

She hurried down the alley to the side door and knocked. It was answered by a harried-looking cook.

"Thank goodness these arrived. We have guests and no desserts."

"Well, this should help." Emma showed the cook the boxes she held.

"Put them on the table and be quick about it." The cook waved to two waiters to start putting the cookies on the trays. "On your way," she said to Emma, needing to get on with her party preparations.

Emma smiled slightly as she walked back out the door into the alley. Jeremy would be waiting and the driver was probably not happy with the additional stop.

It seemed darker and more oppressive after being in the bright kitchen. She hurried toward the end of the alley, eager to get out of the cold. Something stopped her abruptly, cutting her air off. Gasping for breath, she reached up to loosen whatever was wrapped around her neck. The hold was so tight, that she couldn't break it and found herself being pulled further into the dark alley. When the pulling motion stopped, she was able to get a more stable footing. She tried to suck in a breath, black spots beginning to take over her vision.

Emma felt a foot near hers and stomped down. The rope loosened enough for her to turn. Though her vision was still cloudy, Emma could tell the person's build was a man. She balled her fists and started punching the man's face over and over.

The counterattack wasn't what he expected and the rope fell away as he tried to get away from her. She let him back away from her, she ran toward him, her boots hitting him in the stomach, causing him to fall backward and slide down the ice to the far side of the alley. The exercise drained her, she struggled to get air into her throat and bent over, trying to catch a breath. As her vision cleared, she could see his body and ran toward him. Hearing her boots in the snow, he pulled himself up and made a mad dash out and was gone by the time she reached the mouth of the alley.

Shaking, Emma returned to her previous location and saw the rope that had been around her neck; she bent down to pick it up. Clasping it tightly, she made her way back toward the waiting carriage.

Jeremy saw her come out and jumped down to assist her. He called up to the driver and gave the direction to head home.

"No," she stuttered, "we need to head to the police station."

Jeremy couldn't see her face in the dark carriage but knew from her tone something was wrong. "Emma, what happened?"

"We need to get to the police station as soon as possible," she stuttered again.

Jeremy didn't hesitate and called out, "Police station instead, please."

The driver followed the direction and headed to the station.

Emma shivered, but not from the cold, and huddled deeper into Jeremy's arms.

When they arrived, Jeremy helped Emma down.

"Go get you and your horse warm," Jeremy called to the driver. "We'll need you here in about an hour. Come get us at that time."

He nodded and clicked his tongue to move the horse on his way.

Jeremy continued to hold her close as they headed into the station.

Officer Jessup was still at the desk and he called out, "Emma, you're back!"

When she didn't say anything, he was puzzled. That wasn't like her.

Jeremy looked at her clenched hands and saw something in them. He took them and worked to unbend her fingers. He saw she was holding a thin rope.

"What is this?" he asked and tilted her head up toward him. That was when he saw the marks on her neck. He realized immediately what had happened in that alley. A rage swept over him, but he pulled it back and turned to Jessup. "We need to see Chief Marsh on an important matter," he said stiffly.

"Well, he normally..." Jessup started.

"No! Now!" Jeremy said. He would brook no denial.

Jessup realized it must be important, so he called another officer and sent him to get the Chief. Jessup took a long look at the still silent Emma. "Why don't we move you both inside?" he asked.

Jeremy took her arm and moved to follow the officer inside and into an empty interrogation room. It was quiet and there were chairs for them to sit in. He sat her down in one of them and moved to sit in the one next to her. He took her hands in his and kissed them. They waited.

The door slammed open, and Chief Marsh entered the room. He was frowning heavily and a bit out of breath from the run down the stairs. Something important must have happened for Emma to call for him directly. Going to her he pulled a chair and sat it in front of her, He noted her pallor and asked gently, "Emma, do you want to tell me something?"

"Yes." She unclenched her hand for him and, lifting her chin, said, "I thought you might want to see this."

The chief sat back in his chair and then stood up and went to the door. "Dan!"

Officer Jessup looked up.

"Go get Detective Carlson," Marsh continued. "He'll want to be here. And tell Jake we'll need the pictures from the two cases this morning."

Jessup left at a run, heading to Detective Carlson's desk and then to get Jake. Detective Carlson and Jake met at the door at the same moment.

Carlson said, "Go ahead, Jake."

He nodded and entered the room. His expression did not change as he greeted them. "Hello, Emma. Hello, Jeremy."

"Hi, Jake," Jeremy said.

Jake looked at Emma, but she didn't say anything.

Detective Carlson entered behind Jake and stayed silent. He was unsure why he was here and why the chief was in the room.

Chief Marsh turned to her. "Emma, could you tell us what happened?"

She shuddered. "I was at..." She stopped abruptly and looked at Jeremy in horror. "We need to get someone over to that house! Once they start leaving, the help and the party-goers could be hurt!"

Jeremy patted her hand. "Chief, before we go much further, you might want to send officers over to 6753 Stomp Street and alley. There's a large party going on there."

The chief realized they needed to move quickly on this. "Carlson, tell Officer Demetri to step in."

Carlson left and returned with the officer.

"Demetri, I need you to get ten officers and head over to 6753 Stomp Street," the chief said. "Cover the residence and the alley."

Demetri started out and then slowly turned to ask, "What are we looking for?"

"Someone lurking around," Emma supplied. "It's related to the two strangulation cases from this morning."

Demetri understood the importance. "We'll head over now and keep our eyes open." He exited the room, closing the door behind him.

"Now, Emma, I'm taking you on faith, but I need to know exactly what happened," Marsh stressed.

Carlson looked confused but stayed quiet.

She started again." I was in the alley at the house on Stomp Street, delivering some boxes of cookies for the bakery. I started walking back toward the carriage and someone wrapped this rope around my neck. He pulled it tight and twisted it."

"The mark we saw on the two victims this morning. What did you do?" the chief asked. He knew she had self-defense training and could handle herself.

"I turned within the hold and started to pound his face."

"Good girl. Can you describe him?"

"Not in any great detail; the alley was very dark. He was about 5'11" and had a hat or covering pulled over his face." When Marsh frowned, she explained, "I could feel it as I hit him."

"What happened then?"

"I think I scared him because he ran off." She chuckled suddenly. "He fell trying to get out of there fast."

The men laughed at the picture she painted.

Carlson stepped up to the table. "Emma, did you see Jake's pictures of the two crime scenes?" he asked, indicating the brown envelope Jake was holding.

"Yes, I saw them. Detective Kelly permitted me to view them when I went down to get the Worthington pictures." She looked at

Jeremy. "Two women were found at separate scenes strangled this morning."

Jeremy's face turned white. He could have so easily lost her tonight. He held himself together on the outside, though he felt like his insides were shattering.

"Carlson, have you found out anything about the current cases?" the chief asked.

The detective looked down at his notebook. "We have their names, Brooke Stevens and Beth Arnold. They lived in boarding houses located near each other. We were able to determine this during the door-to-door canvassing."

The chief noticed Emma start at the names. He focused his attention on her. "Do you know them?"

Jeremy frowned at her and waited for the answer.

Emma nodded slowly. "I don't know them, but I did plan on interviewing them for my current case."

"Which case is that?" asked the chief.

Jake answered for her. "It's Detective Kelly's case. The Worthington suicide."

The chief frowned at this. "Have you been in contact with Detective Kelly?"

"I have," she confirmed.

"Do you see a link between these cases?"

"Not right now," she admitted, "but I just started investigating. I believe Mr. Worthington didn't voluntarily jump from his balcony."

"Carlson, where are we in your case?" Marsh asked, looking over at him.

"We think it's someone who knew both girls. And Emma's right," the detective said begrudgingly. "They both have identical rope marks, very similar to those on her neck."

"Emma, would you be okay looking at the pictures?" the chief asked.

"I saw them this morning, but I can look at them again to see if I see anything." She waited while Jake laid them out.

Once the pictures were displayed, Jeremy stood up and went to the corner to lay his head against the wall.

"Emma, do you recognize either of these girls?" the chief asked.

She looked carefully; she was able to push down her emotions. "No, I only know them by name. I do know that they just switched from the Worthington household to other locations." The nervous energy she had experienced was gone and she looked at Jeremy and back at chief Marsh. "Can we head home?" she asked.

"Yes, but I'll want to have someone watch your house," Marsh said.

Jeremy straightened. "That won't be necessary. She'll be well protected tonight. I'll also make sure she has company until we find out who is behind this."

Emma didn't say anything. This time, her assigned role was as the victim.

"Okay then," the chief said, "let's get you home. Emma, we'll need to speak with you as the case progresses. Keep both Kelly and Carlson informed of any changes in the Worthington case."

Jake spoke up. "Emma, can I get some pictures of your neck?"

She understood Jake needed to document it. "Yes. Can we do it now?"

"I will go get my camera," he said and left the room.

Emma didn't know why, but she picked up the roped again and was running it through her fingers.

"Emma," the chief said gently. "You'll need to leave that here. It's evidence."

She looked up, startled at the statement. "What? Oh, yes. I wasn't thinking." She dropped it to the table; the chief took custody of it and handed it to Carlson.

Jake must have run to his work area and back because he was

already in the doorway holding his camera. "Can we move out into the larger area? We need the light."

"Yes, of course," she said and followed him out.

As Jeremy watched her leave, the chief eyed him. "She saved herself."

"Yes, but she could have died, and she was only twenty feet from me," Jeremy said, his voice strained.

He understood and didn't say anything more until Emma and Jake returned.

She walked through the door, her face ashen, and she appeared to be swaying. Jeremy walked over to her. "Ready to go?" he asked in a soft voice.

"Yes, please," she murmured, leaning on him. "Chief, thank you," Emma said softly.

"We'll find this person," Marsh promised, his voice low and emphatic.

Officer Jessup came in. "Jeremy and Emma, your carriage is waiting for you," he said.

Jeremy took her elbow, escorted her out, and lifted her into the carriage. Once he had them settled, he pulled her to him. "Do you want to talk about it?" he asked.

"I'm not usually taken unawares like that. It scared me," she admitted.

"Yeah, me, too."

They sat quietly, listening to the sound of the carriage wheels crunching the icy snow.

"Do we tell the family?" he asked.

"Yes. But we don't let it spoil the night. I need something to keep my mind occupied."

"We can arrange that."

The carriage stopped at their home and he climbed down. He turned to help her out and paid the driver handsomely.

They carried the cookie boxes and headed up the stoop. Loud voices greeted them as they entered. "Everyone is here," she observed as Jeremy helped her take off her coat. She kept her muffler around her neck. Jeremy took both coats and hung them in the closet.

When he returned to her side, he asked, "Do you want to go in? We can go upstairs."

"No, I'm okay," she said and kissed him on the cheek.

Dora came into the foyer. "We're sitting down to dinner. Come in, come in."

Jeremy looked at Emma and she nodded. They went in and, with all the noise of family, no one noticed that Emma and Jeremy were quieter than normal.

Dinner wrapped up. The family was cheerful and looking forward to decorating for Christmas.

"Okay, let's get cleaned up," Dora started. "Emma, why don't you take off that hot muffler."

Emma looked around at Tim, Dora, Abbey, Papa, Cole, and Savannah. "We need a family meeting," she stated softly, her voice strained

"Of course, we'll all be here for the decorating," Dora said, laughing.

"No, Dora, listen. We need to talk first."

Dora realized her sister was being serious and called for Amy to come out of the kitchen. "Amy, do you mind cleaning up?" she asked.

"No, of course not," Amy replied. She went back to the kitchen to get Ethyl. They began clearing the table.

"Everyone," Dora said to the group, "Emma would like us in the sitting room to discuss something."

Papa walked over to Emma. "Anything I should be worried about, little girl?"

"Let's go into the sitting room," she said noncommittally.

They went in. Patrick was sitting with Tim and Lottie. Dora walked over and dropped down next to them, taking Lottie into her arms.

Jeremy looked over at Patrick. "Patrick, could you go read one of your books while we talk?"

Patrick looked at his papa. "Can I?" he asked.

"Yes," Tim replied and looked more concerned when the request was made. "I'll call you when we're ready to decorate."

The family watched Patrick leave and Jake entered carrying a plate. He had just arrived home. They were quiet, waiting for Emma to begin the meeting. She started unwrapping her muffler and Dora saw what she had been covering. She rushed over. "What happened!"

Emma went into detail about the events of the evening. The group was stunned. "I don't mean to depress everyone, especially with our Christmas plans tonight."

They all started talking at once. Cole held up his hand to quiet them down.

"What did the police say?" He assumed they'd gone there first.

"We went there after the attack and spoke directly to Chief Marsh," Jeremy said. "We found out two girls were murdered this morning and they had the same markings on their necks."

They were stunned at this news and began talking at once. Jeremy held up his hands. "Additionally, the murdered girls were also the same ones who ran away from Ethan's house. So far, there's nothing other than their work location to connect them."

The conversation continued and Emma became quieter and her face paler.

Jeremy noticed and caught Dora's eye. He indicated for both of them to go out into the foyer. She nodded and followed as he got up.

Once they were away from the group, Jeremy said, "Dora, Emma would like us to behave as if nothing happened and for the family to enjoy Christmas. Let her deal with this in her own time. Do what you do best: marshal your troops, and get us moving to get Christmas going."

She looked over his shoulder at Emma and came to a decision.

"Yes, you're right." She walked back into the sitting room. "It's time for Christmas decorations, and we're going to get organized now."

Everyone was surprised by this announcement.

"Tim," she directed, "you and Jeremy get the boxes marked sitting room and we'll do this tree first."

"Savannah and Abbey, could you get the cookie trays and the popcorn? Papa and Cole, help move the drinks in here for us. Patrick," she called down the hallway, "get the popcorn and string from Amy."

Everyone fell into line and moved to their tasks. It gave Dora a chance to go sit by Emma. "When you're ready to talk, let me know."

"I will," Emma said as she wiped a tear off her cheek. Dora pulled her close and sat while everyone got organized. When everyone was back from their assigned task, Dora again took control.

"Okay, get the boxes opened, and let's start decorating!"

While the decorations were sorted, the popcorn and candy were waiting to be strung, and the cookies and drinks were set up on the table.

"Who wants to add the first decoration?" Tim asked from his location at the tree. He was holding a box of glass ornaments.

"Me, me!" Patrick shouted and ran over. Tim bent down to lift him onto his shoulder. Patrick placed the ornament and clapped. Everyone looked happy at that moment.

Patrick and Tim moved to sit on the floor near Dora and Emma. Amy brought in the large bowls of popped corn and candy. Dora reached behind her, pulled out the string, and handed it and the popcorn and candy over to Patrick to work on. Papa and Abbey were placing the garland on everything from tables to doorways, to the long staircase, and into the dining room. Dora pulled Emma up and joined Jeremy at the tree to add decorations.

Emma smiled for the first time that evening. She turned to Dora. "Thanks for this." She and Dora hugged.

They hung boxes of decorations and used ribbon to add the cookies to the tree. Once the decorations were up, they sat eating cookies and drinking hot chocolate.

Dora leaned over to her sister. "I think we all needed this." She paused and asked, "Will you be able to sleep tonight?"

"I don't know," Emma confessed.

"Try?" Dora asked. "Why don't you go up and have a nice hot bath and relax," she suggested.

"I'm going to take that advice."

Emma set her cup down, stood up, and kissed her sister on the cheek, then went over to Jeremy to whisper in his ear. He nodded. She told the others good night and headed upstairs. The group watched her go.

Cole looked at Jeremy. "Do you think she was targeted based on the current case?"

Jeremy considered that. "If not, the timing is coincidental."

"Nothing seems to link them?"

"Nothing stands out right now."

"What can we do?" Papa asked.

"Nothing. The police are looking into this. We just have to be here for her and the other ladies in our lives."

"Agreed."

The evening wore down and Jeremy made his way upstairs. He entered his bedroom and quickly made his way to Emma's through the secret door hidden by the bookcase. She was coming into the bedroom door with her hair wrapped in a towel and wearing a robe.

"Better?" he asked.

"Yes, much," she admitted.

He walked over to the fireplace and started the fire. It took a few minutes to get the flames going. "Come over here," he called.

Taking her brush, she went to sit with him. He held out his hand and she passed it to him.

The room was silent, the only sounds were the cracking of the fireplace. The brushing soothed her and she was having trouble keeping her eyes open. Feeling herself drifting off, she didn't object when Jeremy moved her to the bed. The sheets were cool as he slid her into them and pulled the cover over her. He left to get ready for bed. When he finished, he entered the room quietly, climbed in, and pulled her close. "Mmm," she murmured but did not wake up.

A few hours later, her jerking movements and moans woke him.

"Emma! Wake up! You're okay."

She woke quickly and sat up taking deep breaths. *Home,* she thought. *I am home.* And sank back into Jeremy's arms.

"What were you dreaming about?" he asked quietly.

"It was Zeke. In my dream, he was the man who had me by the neck."

Zeke Jones had beaten and nearly killed her when she was ten. When he came after her a final time, they were finally able to stop him.

"He can't come back; we've gotten rid of him," Jeremy said, the satisfaction evident in his voice.

"Yes, I know, but my dreams don't," she muttered into his chest.

"Do you want to talk some?"

"I do," she admitted.

"Do you think this is somehow related to the haunted house case?" he asked.

"I do find it suspicious that Ethan's father died under questionable circumstances and then two servant girls who worked for him were found murdered."

"Do you want to stop working the case?"

"Because of this?" she asked, touching her neck. "No, we just have to move forward on our case and trust the police to investigate theirs."

Jeremy believed the two were related but understood this was her decision. "Where do we go next on the case?" he asked.

"There is the one cook I've yet to talk to. I plan on seeing her tomorrow."

"Emma," he said, his voice deepening, "you can't be by yourself until we find out who is behind this."

She chuckled suddenly and asked, "I assume you think I'll argue?"

"Well, yes."

"No, in this case, I'm not going to," she said, touching her neck again. "Could you set up a Pinkerton man to be around?"

"It's close to Christmas, so I think I can take some time and tag along after you. That is, if you'll have me."

"That I will," she said and lifted her head to kiss him. After that, they fell into a deep sleep.

CHAPTER 12

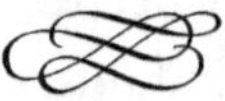

"Good morning." Jeremy leaned over to kiss Emma when they awoke.

"Good morning," she said, stretching.

He moved to the side of the bed and looked back at her. She hadn't made a move to get up. "Are you feeling okay?"

"I'm just taking a moment," she said before she sat up and scooted to the end of the bed.

"How's your neck?"

"Sore," she said, rubbing it.

Jeremy looked over at her but didn't comment. Instead, he stood and walked through the opening behind the bookcase to his room. They got ready and exited their rooms to the hallway. He held out his hand to her. Taking it, she smiled softly as they made their way downstairs.

Breakfast was the normal noisy affair. After they helped clean up, she looked at Amy. "Have you got some time to talk with us?" she asked.

"After I clean up. what can I do for you?" the cook asked as she carried trays back to the kitchen.

Jeremy and Emma followed her in with glasses and plates. "We're working on another case you might help with."

"And you have some servants you need to locate."

"Exactly. But I have to get to the bakery, so would you mind looking at the names and addresses now?"

"Sure," Amy said as she pulled out a chair and sat down.

Jake sat at the table reading his photography book. He had a little time before going to work. Besides, he liked to spend his morning with Ethyl.

"Ethyl, I'll be right with you," Amy told the other girl.

Ethyl smiled, understanding that Amy helped with Emma's cases occasionally. She continued to wash up as the others talked.

"Did you hear about the two maids who were murdered?" Emma asked the two women. Both Ethyl and Amy nodded. "They were two of the girls I was going to ask about, but for now, I need to know about the cook, Margaret Troy," said Emma.

"Yes, I know her," Amy stated. "She should be easy to speak with. But remember what time of the year it is. They'll be quite busy with the season in full swing."

"I will," Emma promised. "What I need is a letter of introduction."

"I can do that. Do you need her work address?"

"No, I got it from the employment agency."

Emma looked at Jeremy, "Would you like to go with me?"

"Just try to stop me."

"I'll write a note for you now," Amy said. She quickly wrote a letter of introduction to explain who Emma was and what she needed. As she handed it to her, she said, "The two girls who died didn't deserve what happened to them."

Jeremy said, "Amy and Ethyl, do not go home without an escort."

"Tim told us this morning, he said he would take care of it," replied Amy and Ethyl nodded.

"Good," he said.

Emma nodded and said, "Thank you."

She took the note, and she and Jeremy left the kitchen.

CHAPTER 13

The two of them reviewed the address together in the foyer.

"It's just a few blocks from here," Emma commented.

"Yes." Jeremy glanced out of the front window. "The sleet has stopped, and the wind has died down. We should be okay to walk."

They gathered up their winter clothes and headed to the first address. When they arrived, Emma looked around. "It's very similar to our neighborhood-working-class, but doing well." The houses were neat and clean, and the sidewalks were cleared of snow.

They arrived at the address and Emma looked around to find the back door. Owners didn't want visitors seeing their servants for personal business. She found it to the left of the building. "This way." Jeremy followed her to the door and stood back as she knocked.

It was only a few moments before it opened to reveal a small woman with her hair pulled tightly into a bun. She had a pleasant expression on her face. "Hello, dear, what can I do for you?" she asked.

"Would you mind if we came in to ask you a few questions?" Emma asked, hoping they could come in from the cold.

"Questions, deary?"

"Yes."

The woman gave them a considering look and finally relented. She stepped back and said, "Please, come in."

They went in and sat down at the table. Each slipped off their hats and scarves. Emma pulled out her notebook and asked, "Are you Margaret Troy?"

"I am," the woman answered cautiously.

"I have this note from my housekeeper, Amy Brown, that helps explain what I need."

Margaret took the note and opened it to read it. She looked a little more guarded but said, "Amy recommends you, so I can take some time. Would you both like some hot tea?"

"That would be wonderful," Emma answered for her and Jeremy.

The housekeeper walked over and filled the kettle, put it on the fire, and then walked back to the table to wait for it to heat up.

"Okay, what is this about?"

"The Worthington's house. You worked there?" Emma asked.

"Not for long," Margaret replied with a shiver.

"Why the short-term position? They need long-term help," Emma observed.

"I really don't want to get into that."

"Can you tell me about Mr. Worthington?" Emma asked, trying to get the woman to open up.

"The job was good and the gentleman a nice enough sort. He needed a lot of cleaning done in a short period of time. We were working very hard on that house. The previous help hadn't done much. And that woman..." Margaret said, her voice trailing off.

"Woman?" Emma asked.

"Yes, Hannah Shephard, she's a manager of sorts. Though I never saw her do much."

Emma knew she had to tread carefully with her next question. "I understood there were some strange things going on in that house?"

"Yes," Margaret said, not sharing any more information.

"Can you tell me about the strange things?" Emma probed.

That seemed to agitate the woman. "I really don't want to talk about it."

Emma pressed, knowing their time was limited. "Did you ever clean Mr. Worthington's room?"

"I think it's time you both left," Margaret said as she stood up with a jerky movement, overturning her chair.

Emma and Jeremy remained seated.

"Margaret, I'm just trying to help Ethan figure out what happened to his father," Emma stressed.

"Please, you need to leave."

"One more thing," interrupted Jeremy. "The two young maids you worked with have been found strangled. Do not leave the house by yourself. Make sure you're accompanied."

This information increased Margaret's agitation; she walked to the door and yanked it open.

"I think you should leave now," she demanded.

"Okay," Emma finally acquiesced. "We'll go, but if you need to talk, this is my address." She tore out a paper with her address and held it out to her.

Margaret took it without saying anything else.

The tea kettle started to whistle loudly.

Emma glanced at the screaming kettle. "Maybe we'll have tea together next time."

They left by the kitchen door. Jeremy hailed a carriage and took her to the bakery for work. Once he walked her in, he turned to her. "Don't leave without me. I'll be back for you."

"I'll wait," she promised.

CHAPTER 14

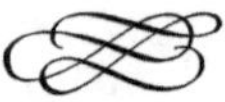

Jeremy picked Emma up after her shift, and the carriage took them straight home. They sat close, enjoying their time together. Once they arrived home, he helped her down and escorted her to the stoop. A person stepped out of the shadows. Emma took a step back and hit Jeremy. "What?" he said as he stumbled into her.

"Someone's here."

Jeremy looked to see who it was. The person stepped forward, the moonlight illuminating her face.

"Oh, Margaret? Is that you?" Emma asked in relief. It was the cook that they spoke to earlier that day.

"Yes," the woman said in a low voice.

"Why didn't you go in? Amy wouldn't mind," Emma suggested, shivering in the cold.

"I wanted to see you without people knowing," Margaret said, rubbing her hands together. They were in gloves, but they must have been bothering her.

"Would you like to come in?" Whatever she wanted, Emma needed some warmth.

"Yes, that would be nice, but not through the kitchen."

"No, we can go through the front, and you can keep your scarf over your face," said Emma.

"Thank you," Margaret said gratefully.

She followed Emma and Jeremy into the house. Emma waved to the group in the sitting room as they walked by and indicated they shouldn't follow. They entered the study and pulled the doors shut behind them. Jeremy walked to the fireplace to stoke the fire and removed his outer gear.

Emma removed her coat and hat and looked over at Margaret. "Please, take off your coat."

She hesitated, not wanting to stay longer than absolutely necessary. Finally, she took off her gloves and unbuttoned her heavy coat. She handed it to Emma and sat down near the fireplace, warming her hands.

"Margaret," Emma prompted, wanting to start the conversation. Jeremy stood by Emma's chair, silent and observant.

Margaret started where the other conversation had left off. "Yes, I was assigned to clean Mr. Worthington's room."

"Wasn't that unusual? Weren't you the cook?"

"Yes. Well, that housekeeper said everyone had to help out. There were no other family members to cook for except for Mr. Worthington or Ethan who were only expected occasionally, so I was told I had to do other things to occupy my time."

Emma nodded and continued with her questions. "Can you tell me about it?"

"Yes. I went in and pulled the curtains open. They were so dusty; the room hadn't been thoroughly cleaned. I knew I would be in there for a while."

"What happened?" Emma asked, knowing something must have.

"I had been in the room for an hour or more. I had the door closed to the hallway and saw something out of the corner of my eye."

"What was it?" Emma asked, sitting forward.

Margaret hesitated again. "I'm not sure, but at the time, I thought it was a ghost."

"What exactly did you see?"

"Something white flying at me."

"Was it a physical sensation? Did it touch you?"

"No, I don't think so. I ran out as fast as I could, but it seemed to follow me down the stairs."

"It followed you?" Jeremy asked.

"I thought it did. I ran outside and stood there for a long time. I was dizzy from the experience."

"Did you go back into the house?" Emma asked.

"Yes, but I refused to go back to that room."

"When was this?" Jeremy asked.

"The night before Mr. Worthington died. I was expecting him to be there the next evening. Mrs. Shephard finished the room, opening the windows to air it out. The room was very clean at that point."

"What happened when Mr. Worthington arrived?" Emma asked.

"He took his bags up and closed the windows. Everything was quiet."

"What happened next?"

"I didn't wait around. The two other girls and I had a plan. We left," she admitted.

"Why did they want to leave?" Emma asked.

"They had reported seeing strange things in that room. The housekeeper just said they were lazy and were telling stories. "

"But you knew that wasn't true."

"Yes, I had seen the ghost for myself," the other woman said quietly, looking down.

"I understand," Emma murmured. Seeing something like that would make anyone question staying there.

"Miss, do you think it was really a ghost we saw?" she asked, wanting the answer to be no.

Emma didn't want to discount her experience and said, "I don't think so, but I do think something is going on."

Margaret looked relieved that her statements weren't being disregarded.

"I will continue to investigate," Emma promised. "Margaret, did you know the two girls…"

"Were murdered?" she finished for her. "Yes. I knew before you mentioned it this morning. All the maids and cooks talk. They were nice girls, just young and excitable. Do you think this is related to the house? Am I in danger?" Margaret's agitation increased.

"I don't know if these events are connected. Right now, they're being treated as two separate cases," Emma said, trying to calm the other woman down.

Margaret nodded and wiped a tear off her face before looking up at Emma. "Could you let me know if you find out what happened to me at the house? I'll feel more settled if I know."

"I'll strive to do just that," Emma assured her.

They stood and walked Margret to the front door. As Emma watched her put on her coat and wrap her scarf around her face and hair, she said, "One more thing. I would like to send someone home with you."

"I'll do it," Jeremy volunteered. "I'll eat when I return."

"Thank you," Margaret said gratefully.

Emma and Jeremy escorted her to the foyer. Emma watched him put on his coat. "Be safe," she said.

He smiled. "Always." He kissed Emma and then took Margaret's elbow and went out into the cold night.

Time for dinner, she thought. She went into the dining room; it was still ongoing.

Dora fixed a plate for her and handed it to Emma. "Long day?" she asked.

"Very busy. Jeremy is going to take someone home. He'll be back soon."

"Anything you can share?" Tim asked.

She looked around and saw people she could trust. Tim, Dora, Jake, and Savannah. She was about to start explaining when Jeremy joined them.

"That was quick," Emma observed, watching him sit. He kissed her hello and rubbed his cold nose on hers. She shivered at the contact.

"She only lives a street over from us," he said.

Dora looked at Emma. "Did you get any more information on Ethan's case?" she asked.

Emma covered the information she had compiled that day. "I've been thinking of ways to disprove the suicide. We have the fact his arms are marked from a defensive manner and the distance he was found from the balcony."

"How far?" Tim asked.

Jake answered for her. "Ten feet."

"Ten? That would mean he had to have a running start."

"Yes," Emma confirmed. "That's what I think also. I think whoever or whatever was in the room caused him to run and jump off the balcony."

"And..." encouraged Jeremy. He knew she had a plan as he watched her drum her fingers on her lips.

"Something is happening in that house. I need to continue my inquiries but, eventually, I will need to go there and spend the night."

The group went quiet, and Jeremy said musingly, "So, at Christmas, we're going to stay in a haunted house and wait for a ghost to appear?"

Dora chimed in. "I know who it is! Marley's Ghost!" she said, referencing their favorite book, *A Christmas Carol*.

"Well, it would be fun to speak to four ghosts, but I only need to find out who the one is. Unless one of you requires redemption," Emma teased the group.

They looked at each other and laughed. "Count me in. Sounds fun," Jeremy said.

Dora and Tim looked at the kids, then at each other. Dora answered for them. "We'll stay here and prepare for Christmas."

Jake was quiet, sitting there with his book. Emma motioned to Dora to tap Jake's shoulder. When he looked up, Emma asked, "Jake, what about you?"

"I don't think I could take pictures of a spirit; it would go too fast," he said, his tone serious.

"No doubt," said Emma, wiping her smile off of her face with her hand.

Looking worried, Jake commented, "We still believe that this can be explained through scientific means?"

Emma nodded. "Yes, Jake."

He looked torn and finally said, "I will go. But I want to share a room."

"I think we can arrange that," Jeremy told him.

"We should let Cole, Papa, and Abbey know in case they want to be included," Dora said.

Emma sent Ethan a note and told him she would like to go to the house on Friday. The plan was to spend the night and experience whatever Ethan's father had.

CHAPTER 15

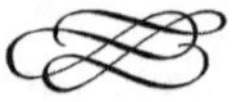

"Ma, they're coming here," Julian said, running into the kitchen. He had another telegram in his hands.

"Who?" his mother asked. She didn't pause her sweeping.

"Ethan's investigators. They're coming here to stay the night!"

That stopped her. She frowned. "Let me see that." She held out her hand for the telegram.

He gave it to her. "What will we do?" he asked, waiting for her response.

She looked at him. "They won't make it through the night."

Julian nodded slowly, waiting for her direction.

CHAPTER 16

The group got organized for the trip. Notes were sent to Ethan, Papa, Abbey, and Cole. Replies were returned confirming that everyone would be at the Worthington mansion the next evening.

Emma and Jeremy checked in with Detective Carlson and found out there had been no more attacks since Emma's. The case had not progressed, and they had no person of interest at this time.

The next evening, the family stood outside the mansion. It was still cold, and their teeth chattered as they made their way up the imposing steps. "A little spooky," Jeremy murmured in Emma's ear.

She shivered from what she hoped was the cold and nodded. The building had something dark about it; the bad weather contributed to the overall feeling.

"Well, it has the look of a haunted house," Cole said, looking around.

"It's the Gothic architecture," Papa confirmed. He pointed out the arches, with peaked windows and diamond-shaped panes.

"It looks like a miniature castle," Jake said.

"It is that," Emma agreed, looking around.

Jeremy walked to the side of the house, frowned, and made his way back. "It appears that it has been added onto over time. The brick appears to start and stop in different color patterns."

"Shall we head up the stairs?" Emma asked.

Each nodded and they walked to the door. As they got close, Emma thought she saw something. She raised her hand and stopped suddenly. "Is that a face?" she asked, looking at the door knocker.

"What's the matter?" Papa asked.

Jeremy leaned in and recognized what it was. There was indeed a face molded into the door knocker. "Why, Marley old man, we were expecting you," he said with a laugh.

"Oh, you. I wonder what else we will see," she commented, raising the knocker and slamming it down with a resounding bang.

The door opened with a creak, adding further to the haunted atmosphere. A shadowy figure opened the door. It was Ethan. Emma released the breath she hadn't realized she was holding.

Not scared of a haunted house, she thought, laughing at her response.

Ethan looked relieved when he saw them. "Welcome all. Please, come in." He held the heavy door open while they went inside.

The entryway was large and dominated by a staircase. The overall look was dark and moody. Heavy paneling covered the hallways and the floor was covered in a dark tile.

Emma looked around. "Is there anyone else here?" she asked.

"Just Mrs. Shepard and her son. Would you like me to show you to your rooms?" asked Ethan.

"Yes. Please," said Abbey, shaking the snow from her hair and coat.

"This way," he said, walking up the stairs.

They picked up their bags and followed him. He showed each

person to their room. When he indicated the rooms for Emma and Jeremy, she held up her hand.

"Ethan, I'd like to stay in your father's room."

Ethan nodded. "This way,"

When Jeremy picked up their bags and started to follow, Emma stopped him. "I'd like to stay in there by myself."

"But why?" he asked, frowning.

"The events only seem to occur when people are alone. I need to see what happens," she explained.

He continued to frown, and she reached up to smooth the lines. "Would it help if you inspected the room with me for any secret openings?"

"Yes," he said begrudgingly, "and I'll be outside the door all night."

"Okay," she agreed softly.

Ethan cleared his throat and guided them to the room. "Here it is."

They looked over at him and headed into the room. "Brr," Emma shivered, "it's cold."

"The windows are open. The housekeeper likes to air out the rooms. Do you want me to close them?"

"No, I'll do that when we come up to bed. I'll start a fire then."

Jeremy started walking around the room, knocking on the walls, and Emma looked under the bed and behind the dresser.

"What are you looking for?" Ethan asked, watching them continue around the room.

"Just ways someone could get into the room."

When they finished, he asked, "Did you find anything?"

"No, and I will be staying in here alone tonight."

Jeremy nodded. He understood this was how she wanted to lead the investigation.

～

Later, before dinner, they split up to investigate the house. The groups set out in pairs, Jeremy and Emma, Jake and Cole, Abbey and Papa.

Jeremy and Emma headed to the basement.

"Can we get drawings of the house? Do they exist?" Papa asked Ethan.

"No, my great grandfather built it himself. So, there wouldn't be any," Ethan said.

Abbey and Papa used a lantern to look around the attic. "How did we get the dusty area?" she asked disgustedly as she picked up the cloths covering the furniture.

"Yes, but better than the basement," Papa said, noting the pictures stacked against the wall. "There does appear to be other relatives," he said, looking through the pictures.

"EEK!" she screamed.

He chuckled. "Abbey, what is it? A mouse? They won't hurt you." When she didn't answer, he walked over to where he had left her. "Abbey? Where are you?"

A hand wrapped over his mouth and he thought, *That smells funny*. Then all went black.

Jeremy and Emma were assigned the basement. Cole and Jake were assigned the main floor, and Ethan was assigned the bedrooms. They went through each, not finding much.

Jeremy and Emma looked around. There was little to see, but he noticed something by the wall.

"What is it?" she asked.

"Chains," Jeremy said, going over to them. "Well, Mr. Worthington loved the book; he may have used them to scare guests."

"Or someone else is trying to scare him," she suggested.

They continued to look around but found nothing.

"It is getting late," Emma said. "We need to head up and see if the others have found anything." She looked at Jeremy and noticed he was focused on a door. "Did you see something?"

"Did Ethan mention what this door leads to?"

"Yes, he said it was a utility tunnel out to the fountains in the front."

Ethan's voice called from above, "Come up, we have dinner waiting."

Jeremy looked conflicted; he really wanted to try that door.

"We can come back and check it later," she promised.

They headed upstairs and went to the dining room to find Cole, Ethan, and Jake.

"Where are Papa and Abbey?" Emma asked.

"They said they would see you in the morning," Mrs. Shephard said.

Emma frowned. "It seems a little early for them to turn in."

"I'm sure they're fine," commented Cole.

"Dinner is in the kitchen. I'll need help with moving it to the dining room," Mrs. Shephard said.

"We can do that," Emma said. They all went into the kitchen to get the dinner trays. Emma looked around and asked nonchalantly, "I understand you have a son."

"I do," Mrs. Shepard replied, not looking up from the glasses she was filling.

"Is he around?" *And is he the man I beat up a few days ago?* she asked herself.

"Yes, he's outside gathering wood for the fireplaces. You should see him later."

"Hmm," commented Emma. "I'd like to interview you both."

"We'll work something out."

They moved into the dining room and as they began to eat, Emma turned to Ethan. "Ethan, did you find out who's contesting the will?"

Mrs. Shephard stood as still as a statue waiting for his answer. Ethan didn't notice the woman's response, but Emma did.

"Not yet. Mr. Pennington is trying to find out. It is odd, though; I don't have any close relatives who could contest it."

"You mentioned an uncle?" Jeremy asked.

"Yes, but he's dead."

"Did he have any children?" asked Emma.

"I don't think so. He wasn't married."

"Do you know where he's buried?" she asked, wondering if the man was in fact dead.

"In a small graveyard, way out in the back. Grandfather's there and I'll place Dad near them."

So, probably not the uncle, Emma thought wryly. That brought her back to Mrs. Shephard and her son. *Did they contest the will? And Julian—was he the one who attacked her? Was that how this case was going to close?*

Cole changed the subject. "Your father rather liked Dickens' books?"

"Yes, particularly *A Christmas Carol.*"

"We saw chains in the basement," volunteered Jeremy.

Ethan laughed. "Yes, he liked to spook people at Christmas with those. It was all in good fun."

"Are there any other things he added?" Jeremy asked, thinking about the chains and the door knocker.

Ethan thought about that. "No. Not really."

They sat together discussing the house and its various eccentricities.

Finally, Emma yawned. "I'd like to go to bed."

"I'll come up with you," Jeremy suggested.

She nodded and held out her hand to him. He took it and the others watched as they ascended the stairs.

Cole looked around. "I think I'll step outside for a cigar. Want to come with me, Jake?"

"No, I think I will head up also."

He went up the stairs and entered his and Cole's room. Turning the knob, he was thinking of reading his camera book. He took a step in and was grabbed by someone behind the door. He struggled, but something hit him on the head. His limp body was drug out of the room and down the hall.

Cole stepped outside and lit up his cigar. The smoke curled up around him. The night air was cold. Moving further out onto the porch, he looked up at the clear night sky. He took the cigar out of his mouth and a cloth was pulled over his face and his hands bound quickly in ropes. No one noticed the cigar as it fell to the ground.

～

Emma stepped out of the bathroom in the hall and saw Jeremy sitting in a hard-backed chair. "You couldn't find one that was more comfortable?" she teased.

"I don't want to take a chance that I might fall asleep."

"I'm sure I'll be fine. I don't believe in ghosts. If something is happening here, there is a reasonable explanation." She changed the topic. "What are your suspicions with the will?"

He laughed. "Caught that, did you? Mrs. Shephard seemed to be frozen solid when that came up."

"We haven't seen the son yet."

"You think he was the one who attacked you?"

"I think he might be," she admitted. "They seem to be the only people in Ethan's life who might have a stake in this house."

"We should find him; the bruises will prove it was him."

"Yes, that's what I'm thinking. We can check in the morning," she suggested.

She leaned in to kiss him goodnight and went into her room, closing the door behind her. "Brr," she said. The windows were still open. No *wood*, she thought. *First things first.* She went to the gas lamps and turned them up. Next, she closed all the windows, hoping that it would be warmer.

Her bag was nearby and she quickly changed into her night-clothes. Glancing toward the bed she noted the heavy curtains surrounding it. *Another Dickens item,* she thought. In *A Christmas Carol,* Scrooge's maid had pulled the curtains around Scrooge's bed down and sold them after his death during the visions with the Ghost of Christmas Yet to Come.

The thought made her shiver, but she shook it off, grabbed the curtains, and pulled them open. When nothing appeared, she chided herself. "I thought you didn't believe in ghosts." She laughed. She was happy to discover the bed was made with thick blankets. Quickly, she walked to the gas lamps, turned them off, and ran back to the bed. She snuggled down and regretted she didn't have Jeremy next to her. The curtains were closed on two sides but open on the side nearest her. Sleep came quickly.

~

"What? What was that?" she asked, trying to pull herself out of her dreams. She shook her head trying to clear it.

"*Emma,*" a soft voice called. "*Emma, you need to wake up,*" it called again.

She frowned in the dark. "*Mama?* No, that can't be right." Though it sounded just like her.

Emma struggled out from under the heavy covers, trying to see where the voice was coming from. There was nothing in the room, and then she felt something brush by her. When she turned toward it, half expecting to see Mary; instead, she was face-to-face with Zeke. She screamed and fell off the bed and onto the floor. "Dead! You're dead!" she screamed again.

Jeremy burst into the room and saw her trembling on the floor. He ran to her and wrapped his arms around her. She was shaking.

"Get me out of here," she said.

He did as she asked and helped her up and walked her to the hallway. He sat her down in his chair and knelt in front of her, rubbing her ice-cold hands. "What happened? What did you see?" he asked.

"Can we go to your room?" she asked. She was scared the ghost would follow them.

"Yes, of course." He brushed back her hands and carried her to his room, setting her on the bed. "Now, tell me," he asked softly as he sat next to her. "Did you see something?"

"First, I heard what sounded like Mama calling me."

Jeremy looked shocked. "Is that what caused you to scream?"

"No. It was Zeke. He was in the room with me."

"Zeke? But, Emma, you know he's dead. He can't hurt you anymore," he reasoned.

"I do know that but, at the time, it seemed real."

"Was it a ghost?" he asked hesitantly.

"You know I don't believe in them. And all my research suggests most hauntings are reported by people either drugged or drunk. Or just someone playing a game. There's also waking dreams and powers of suggestion."

"Well, you certainly weren't drunk or drugged. Were you completely awake?" he asked, trying to follow her reasoning.

"I was asleep, but no, I was awake when I saw Zeke."

"Then what could it have been if that room isn't haunted?" he asked, thinking.

Emma looked around. "Could you hear me scream from out in the hallway?"

Jeremy looked at her seriously. "Yes, scared me so much I almost fell off my chair."

"Then why didn't anyone else come out of their rooms?" she asked as she exited Jeremy's room and wandered down the hallway.

"I don't know," he said. "They should have."

Emma frowned; this wasn't like her family. She tapped on her Papa and Abbey's door. When there was no response, she knocked louder. She looked over at Jeremy.

"Let's try opening it," he suggested.

"Papa? Abbey?" she called. "It's Emma. I am coming in."

She went in first and returned quickly. "They aren't there! And the beds haven't been slept in."

"What?" He ran into the room.

"I'll try Cole and Jake's room; you check on Ethan," Emma told him.

They separated and Emma heard him call out, "Emma, Ethan's not here!"

She ran over. "Neither are Cole and Jake. Where did they go?"

"Downstairs?" he suggested.

"We have to check."

They ran down into the main living room and looked around.

"Nothing," Jeremy observed.

"Kitchen?" asked Emma.

They ran there—no one. They went through every room on the first floor.

"Where are they?" asked Emma, bewildered.

"Who are you looking for?" a young man's voice called from across the dark room.

Emma stiffened and said, "That's Julian, the son. It has to be."

Jeremy called out, "Come out here where we can see you."

Julian stepped into the light. Emma walked close to him and looked at his face. "No bruises," she observed.

"No, I don't have any bruises," he said, bewildered at her statement.

"Where is everyone?" Emma asked.

"The same place you're about to be," he said and reached out to grab her. He didn't realize what was happening until he was face down on the carpet with his arm twisted behind his back.

"Where is everyone?" Emma demanded. "I'm not going to ask again."

"That is something I would like to know," a voice called from a dark corner of the living room. He lit the lamp in his hands and moved toward them.

Emma started violently. It had to be him, the man who attacked her in the alley. His face was covered with bruises.

He noticed her staring and rubbed his face lightly. "You did a fine job on my face, little girl. You caused me to have to hide, and I couldn't continue my fun."

Jeremy wasn't watching the man's face; he was watching his hands. He had a gun pointed at them.

The man saw Jeremy's interest. "Not my normal choice. I much prefer a rope. But sometimes you have to make do."

"Who are you and what have you done with our family?" Emma asked, her voice devoid of emotion.

"Me? We'll get to that later, little girl. I have the same question, though, and I think that young man there might know."

"You won't find them," Julian said.

Emma looked at Jeremy in confusion. *What is happening here?* she mouthed. Jeremy shrugged. He was as confused as her.

"You think not?" The man laughed at them. He seemed to be enjoying the game.

Emma let go of Julian's arm and let him up. Julian faced the man.

"You won't find them" he repeated. "We will stop you *this* time."

The man didn't answer. He shifted his gun to his left hand and pulled out a piece of rope.

Emma paled when she saw it. She already knew he was the man who'd attacked her, but the appearance of the rope made her lightheaded. Bracing herself, she was determined that, if she was going to die, she would die fighting.

"Now, for the girl, I'm going to finish what I started in the alley. For you two, it's a bullet. I'll do you first." He pointed the gun at Jeremy.

"Wait!" Jeremy said.

"What is it? I have things to do."

"If I have to die, I want one last hug from Emma. I don't want to die without her knowing how much I love her."

"Oh, very well, but hurry. I have so little time and so many people to kill."

Jeremy opened his arms and Emma walked toward him. As she got closer, Jeremy turned his body slightly so Emma could see something in his belt. She looked hard at the object. It was her knife! Emma hugged Jeremy and, as she did, she grasped the knife handle.

"I love you," she said.

"I know," he replied.

Emma pulled her knife out of the sheath. Jeremy stepped back and she whirled and threw it toward the man. The knife rotated blade over handle until it tore into the man's shoulder. He looked down at the knife embedded into his arm.

"I'll be damned," he said and dropped the gun to the floor

Emma turned to Jeremy. "How did you…? When…"

He gave her a half-grin. "I picked it up before we left the bedroom to search for everyone. I thought it might come in handy."

"Why didn't you give it to me before now?" Emma asked.

"Obviously, there's no place on you to hide it at the moment," he said, looking pointedly at her nightclothes.

"Good point."

"The little girl has teeth. I'll give her that," the man said as he swayed on his feet and pulled the knife from his shoulder. "That hurt. But not as much as I'm going to hurt you." He began to walk toward them with the knife in one hand. "I'm going to enjoy this."

"You missed," Jeremy chided her, noting the man was still a threat.

"I didn't miss."

"Why's he still walking then?"

"I want answers and a dead man can't provide them."

Emma and Jeremy positioned their bodies into fighting stances. If they were going down, they were going down fighting.

Bang!

Emma and Jeremy dropped to the floor. They watched the mysterious man grasp his bloody hand and fall to his knees.

Emma looked at Jeremy. *"Who?"*

Hannah Shephard walked into the room. She was holding a gun and kept it aimed at the man.

"Ma!" Julian ran over to her.

The man she'd shot was writhing on the floor. Jeremy took custody of the gun. Emma stood and walked over to their assailant, taking the knife out of his limp hand. She was tired and wanted some answers.

"Everyone in the dining room, now," she said. Jeremy and Julian moved the wounded man to chair, tying him up. "Mrs. Shephard, I assume you and Julian know where everyone is located?"

"Yes," she said, "we do."

"I'll let everyone out," Julian said.

"Where do you have them?" Jeremy asked.

"Basement room, off to the left."

Jeremy cocked an eyebrow at Emma.

"Yes, fine. I should have let you investigate that room," she said.

He laughed and went down with Julian to bring everyone up. As they returned, they were all talking excitedly at the same time.

Cole entered first with Jeremy. He looked at Emma. "Got it worked out yet?"

"Almost," said Emma, turning toward the man they had tied up.

Her suspicions were confirmed when Ethan entered and said faintly, "Except for the bruises, he looks just like my father."

"He's your uncle," Emma stated, the one you told us had died.

"Uncle Robert?" Ethan asked, stunned.

Abbey, Papa, and Jake entered next.

"Emma, I would like to go home now," Jake said.

She laughed. "So would I, but first, let's find out what's happening here."

Cole looked at Julian. "Is this the one you told us about?"

"Yes, be careful with him. He's dangerous."

"He doesn't look dangerous to me," Cole said.

Ethan looked at his uncle. "They said you were dead."

Robert winced in pain. "Well, that *was* the agreement. I was to leave and never come back."

"And why was that?" Emma asked.

When he didn't look like he was going to answer, Hannah spoke up. "We were teenagers in the same house. And he started playing his games back then." Hannah pulled back her high-necked blouse, exposing an old rope mark. "He snuck up behind me one night and tried to strangle me. I put up a fight. His father somehow heard us and pulled him off me. I almost didn't survive."

"But there's a grave with your name on it," stuttered Ethan.

"That was our father," Robert said disgustedly. "He wanted to make sure I couldn't come back and claim the house. He wanted your father to have it all."

"Were you responsible for dad's death?" Ethan asked.

"How could I be? Didn't a ghost kill him?" he said mockingly.

Ethan looked confused and turned his gaze on Emma. "I think I can answer that." She had worked it out. The effects she experienced in the bedroom were the same as those when she had been exposed to a gas leak on a construction job. Turning to the group. "The gas lamps in Mr. Worthington's bedroom must be leaking. Not enough to notice, but enough to cause headaches, auditory hallucinations, fatigue, melancholy, and other symptoms if someone stayed in the room for long periods. When did you figure out how to set the gas lamps to leak?"

Robert frowned and looked confused. "What gas leak? I don't know what you're talking about."

"He doesn't, but I do," Hannah admitted.

All eyes turned to her.

"No, Ma! Don't!" Julian begged. He didn't want her confessing.

"But I am responsible," she admitted.

Ethan sat down heavily on a chair at the table. "You? But why did you kill Dad?"

"It was an accident," she said, holding out her hand to her son. He took it. "Julian and I found Robert's hidden crawlspace a few years ago. We've monitored it since that time, waiting for him to come back, hoping he was truly dead. When we found his things there, we knew he was back. We wanted to protect the people in this house. I experienced a gas leak previously and saw the effects and I thought I could control it."

"It worked with the cook and the maids," Emma commented. That must be why the windows were open all the time, even in the cold.

"Not that it helped; he got to them anyway," Hannah said bitterly. "Ethan, I didn't mean to kill your father, only to scare him into remaining in town until after Christmas. That night, Louis was reading *A Christmas Carol* again and drinking some port before returning to his room. The gas leak and the port must have caused him to see something, and Louis ran and jumped off the balcony."

"What was your plan about Robert?" Cole asked.

"With Louis gone, we were going to get rid of Robert, once and for all, so Ethan would never find out," Hannah admitted.

"Why did you take such a personal interest and stay here all of these years?" Emma asked.

Hannah looked down at the hand that held hers.

"It was for me," Julian said.

"Yes, he didn't just strangle me; he forced himself on me. Robert's father stopped him from killing me but not from that. I got Julian." She looked at Ethan and said, "Your father allowed me to stay and raise him here. I did love Louis so much, and I am so sorry he is gone."

Julian and Ethan started to cry at her statement.

"I have a son!" Robert said.

Julian looked at him in disgust. "No, you do not! You are not my father."

That definitive statement seemed to shut him up.

Julian said, "This time, you won't be sent away. You will hang for your murders."

"Just one thing." Emma looked at Robert. "Why did you kill the two housemaids?"

He shrugged. "Seemed like fun and kept me busy until the will was probated."

"You're the one contesting the will!" Ethan exclaimed.

"Yes, it's my house! Not yours!" he shouted. "I came back because it is mine, not some snot-nosed kid! Mine!"

Cole looked at him. "No, sir, it is not your house. Your house will be a cell the rest of your short life."

Robert leaned forward and placed his head on the table.

Ethan walked over to Julian and put an arm on the other man's shoulder. "No, the house belongs to Julian and me. Hannah and Julian can stay as long as they like."

Julian smiled widely.

Cole looked at Jeremy. "Let's take Robert to the police station. It's time to clean this up."

CHAPTER 17

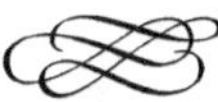

CHRISTMAS EVE PARTY

*E*veryone was dressed in their finest holiday clothes. The house was filled to the rafters with family and friends. Food covered every surface and drinks were delivered by maids. The music was coming from the foyer, Chloe's musical group was playing Christmas music.

Emma and Ethan sat on the couch, watching the room full of people. They were discussing his case.

"Why did your grandfather fake your uncle's death?"

"My theory?" he asked.

Emma nodded.

"He wanted to get Robert away from here. The family name is what he would have been concerned about and he wouldn't have wanted a long, drawn-out trial."

"Do you think he knew he might have continued hurting women?"

He shook his head. "I don't know, but I do know when Grandfather died, he looked drained of life. I think the decision wore on him."

"Will you dig up the grave?"

"No, I don't think so. The police have his statements, so they'll probably not go to that level."

"Ethan, what form do you think your father's apparition took?" Emma asked curiously.

He smiled slightly. "I think it might have been Marley from *A Christmas Carol.*"

"What makes you say that?"

"When Dad mentioned his brother, he always said he didn't want to be like him, make the same mistakes." Ethan saw something that attracted his attention.

Emma glanced where he was looking and saw his gaze was now on Savannah. She leaned forward and whispered in his ear, "You might take Savanah a drink; she looks thirsty."

He grinned at her. "I'll take one over now." He snagged a glass of eggnog from a server and headed toward her.

Dora dropped down next to Emma. "I'm glad you invited Ethan."

Emma looked at him, talking animatedly to Savannah. "I think Savannah is also."

"What will happen to Mrs. Shephard?"

"Ethan is working with the lawyers to prove it was an accident. We believe she'll be exonerated soon. The judge let her be with Julian for Christmas."

"What will happen to his uncle?"

"Trial. Prison for sure. After that, probably hanging."

"Much deserved," Dora said, thinking of all of those women he had killed.

"I wish there had been a way for different cities to compare cases; we might have caught him sooner," Emma lamented

"That's a future view. We can hope that's something we'll see in our lifetimes."

"Yes."

"Merry Christmas, Emma."

"Merry Christmas, Dora."

RECIPES REFERENCED IN THE BOOK

RECIPES

Anise-flavored German Christmas cookies
Ingredients:

- 4 large eggs
- 2 1/4 cups of confectioners' or super-fine sugar
- 4 cups of flour
- 1 teaspoon of baking powder
- ½ cup of anise seed

Directions:

- Beat eggs until thick. Gradually add sugar and beat well until combined. Fold under the sifted flour and baking powder. Roll out dough to about 1/2 inch thick.
- Flour the Springerle mold each time it is used and press firmly into dough. Remove mold and cut the cookies along the outside lines of the imprint.

- Place cookies on a board or cookie sheet that is sprinkled with anise seeds. Let dry in a cool room overnight. Butter a cookie sheet and place Springerle on it.
- Bake at 250°F until light golden on the bottom and white on top (about 15 minutes).

German Apple cake
Ingredients:

- 3 large eggs
- 2 cups of sugar
- 1 cup of vegetable oil
- 1 teaspoon of vanilla extract
- 2 cups of all-purpose flour
- 2 teaspoons of ground cinnamon
- 1 teaspoon of baking soda
- 1/2 teaspoon of salt
- 4 cups of chopped peeled tart apples
- 3/4 cup of chopped pecans

Frosting:

- 1 package (8 ounces) of cream cheese, softened
- 2 teaspoons of butter, softened
- 2 cups of confectioners' sugar

Directions:

- In a large bowl, beat the eggs, sugar, oil, and vanilla. Combine the flour, cinnamon, baking soda, and salt; add to egg mixture and mix well. Fold in apples and nuts. Pour into a greased 13x9-inch baking dish. Bake at

350°F for 55-60 minutes or until a toothpick inserted in the center comes out clean. Cool on a wire rack.

- In a small bowl, beat cream cheese and butter. Add confectioners' sugar, beating until smooth. Spread over cake. Refrigerate leftovers.

NOTEBOOK MYSTERIES ~ SUSPICIONS (BOOK 5)

Notebook Mysteries

KIMBERLY MULLINS

CHAPTER 1

NEW YORK CITY, 1889; JANUARY

Wham!

Something hit Emma on the back of the head, and she pivoted toward the assailant. The old woman stopped her by jumping on her back, pulling her hair, and stabbing at her neck frantically with knitting needles.

Enough is enough! Emma thought as she fell backward on the floor, taking the old woman with her.

Her attacker screamed, trying to get out from under Emma. Emma took the opportunity to flip over and grabbed the woman's hands, holding them above her head.

"Old woman, I have had enough!" she growled at her.

That didn't quell the woman's spirit, and she continued to struggle in Emma's hold. *Who would have thought she'd have so much energy?* Emma thought. The woman was in her sixties!

When she finally appeared to be worn out, Emma wrestled her into a chair. She yanked the knitting needles and yarn from the woman's hands and threw them to the floor. "You stay there or there will be consequences," Emma warned. When she saw the woman's mutinous expression, she continued in an exasperated tone, "Are you going to stay there, or do I have to tie you up?" Her patience was gone.

The old woman kept the same expression but stayed motionless.

"They wanted me to talk to you first because I could keep you calm," Emma muttered. She stepped back and took a moment to pull her long blonde hair back into a ponytail. Once she felt more settled, she got a chair and sat it in front of her suspect. "Okay, let's start again. Your daughter was Mavis Franklin?"

"Yes," the woman answered, hacking a wad of spit her way.

Emma wiped the spit from her face and held out her other hand in warning. "Coreen, stop that."

They stared at each other. The light coming through the windows had started to dim in the small room. Emma didn't want to end the staring contest by turning up the gas lamps, so she stayed where she was.

The tactic worked and the old woman asked in a low voice, "What do you want to know?"

"Your daughter, why didn't you go to her funeral?"

"I was told not to," she answered shortly.

"Who told you not to go?" Emma asked, knowing that was the answer they were after.

When Coreen's response didn't come immediately, Emma followed up with another question. "Was it the person behind the child kidnappings?"

"Yes," Coreen replied, in a clearer voice this time.

"Who is he?"

Instead of answering her question, Coreen asked, "Can I have my knitting back?"

Emma scrunched up her eyes and considered the request. She finally acquiesced, bent down to pick the needles and yarn up, and handed them to her. The sound of the needles filled the quiet room. While Emma waited for her to start talking, she glanced out the window. Something there caught her eyes. *What was that?*

Frowning, she started to stand and investigate. At that moment, the woman started talking. Emma sat back in the chair to listen.

"He's my son," Coreen said, not looking up from her task.

Son! "But he…"

"Had his sister killed? Or I should say, half-sister. Though they were so alike. Rotten to the core, the both of them." Coreen's mouth twisted into a semblance of a smile.

"Like their mom," Emma said. She had a file a foot thick on this woman's criminal activities. She had been the head of a criminal organization long before her children came along.

Coreen sent her a shrewd look. "They followed in my footsteps."

Emma let that go. "Why didn't he want you to go to the funeral?"

"He knew the authorities could link me to her and then to him. He'd do anything to prevent that."

Emma nodded and thought about the census records she had reviewed. "You had a son Christopher. He dropped off the census records at the age of 15. We thought he might have died."

"No, that was his way of hiding. He changed his name. Didn't even want to be called Christopher at home. He changed overnight and moved out to start his new identity. He was never seen with us again."

It was time. "What name is he using?" Emma asked, her voice hardening. A name floated through her head. She shook it, thinking it was impossible. *It can't be him.*

"He'll kill me," the other woman stated.

"We can protect you," Emma said, thinking ahead. They could get her an apartment far outside of town.

"Can you? I don't think you can. But I'm old, maybe I've outstayed my time," Coreen said and continued to knit.

Emma had to keep pressing her; they needed answers. She was their only connection to the child kidnapping case. The people involved had targeted the poor who didn't have the money to advocate for their children. The number of children that had been taken had grown, with new information coming in from all over the country. There was someone behind this, and Emma wanted that name!

"His name!" she prompted loudly.

"John Harden," Coreen stated, not looking up.

Though spoken in a low voice, the sound vibrated through her ears. *John Harden! But he's in prison and has been for a while now.* Memories flooded her mind. John Harden was a known gangster and had been part of her first major case—part of the coverup and murder of her mother. Oddly, at the time, he felt he owed her something by removing the man who had taken over his business. There had been no contact between them since that time.

"Yes, you know the name," the other woman stated and stopped her knitting. She straightened in her chair.

Emma wondered about the airs Coreen was putting on. Her son wasn't famous as much as he was infamous. She continued to watch her.

"Operations have never run so well as when he went into prison," Coreen said proudly.

"Why did he kill Candace?"

"He let her have her way with that business, though he never agreed with it. I think he was relieved when the operation had to be shut down. I think he was also relieved to be rid of her." She looked over and explained, "They never got along."

Emma looked at her, wondering what kind of childhood these two had. She asked, "Did you want them to get along?"

Coreen shrugged, taking up her knitting again. "It was interesting when they fought for attention. I would get nice things from their competition."

Emma just shook her head. *Never a family—only competitors.* Emma stood and said, "Don't move. I'm going to get someone to take you into custody."

Her head still bowed as she concentrated on her knitting,

Coreen replied softly, "Do what you need to, dearie. I'll do what I need to do also."

Emma exited the small room, the needles clicking as she pulled the door closed.

She turned and saw Cole Tilden, the Director of the Chicago branch of the Pinkerton detectives, sitting at a small table. He was dressed in his standard black suit, white shirt, and black tie. He stroked his reddish goatee and considered the cards in front of him. Jeremy Tilden, his son and Pinkerton detective, was sitting across from him. He was dressed in a similar manner to his father but the main difference was his rakish nature. Jeremy's hat was shoved back on his head and his auburn curls fell down his forehead.

"I have some news," Emma commented, waiting for them to turn to her.

They didn't look up. Instead, Cole showed his cards. "Two pairs."

Jeremy laid down his hand and said with a grin, "Flush." He looked over at Emma and asked, "Have some trouble in there?"

"No," she said wryly, "she was perfectly behaved." She grabbed a chair and dragged it up to the small table. "Didn't you hear us?"

"Yes," Jeremy admitted, "but we knew you could handle it." Cole nodded his head in agreement, absently shuffling through the deck.

When he started to deal the cards again, she asked in exasperation, "Would you like to hear what I found out?"

They both turned toward her, giving her their full attention. She gave them the details of the interrogation.

"John Harden! Wow! We lock them up and they get stronger. How's he managing this?" Jeremy asked.

"And how do we investigate someone who's already in prison?" asked Emma.

Cole sat back in his chair. "Someone is carrying out his orders on the outside. We'll go after them."

Jeremy looked contemplative. "Any information we find out about his operations could help us leverage John and find out where the missing kids might be located."

"What leverage?" asked Emma. "Even if we find someone on the outside, how do we use that to push John for information?"

"We'll find something," Jeremy said confidently.

"Hmm." Emma, drummed her fingers on her lips, planning.

"What do we do with Coreen in the meantime?" Jeremy asked, gesturing toward the room where John's mom was located.

"She's expecting him to come after her for talking. She'll need protection," Emma said.

"I noticed an accent. Maybe we send her back to Ireland? That would keep her out of the way," suggested Cole.

"I'm not sure she'd want that," she warned. "She's very stubborn and will have definite ideas on her treatment."

"She'll listen to reason," Cole stated. He stood suddenly and strode determinedly to the door. Jeremy followed closely behind.

"Will she?" Emma muttered to the empty room before following them. She bumped into Jeremy, who had stopped abruptly just inside the door. Cole's voice reached her. "Where did you put her?"

Jeremy moved aside so that she could view the room. "There." She pointed to the empty chair.

"She isn't there," Jeremy said, stating the obvious.

She looked over at him and said sarcastically, "You think?"

They looked around the small room. There were no closets and the windows were nailed shut.

"Where could she have gone? There are no exits other than the one we just entered," observed Cole.

Emma looked around the room and then up at the ceiling. "No, but she could have gone up."

"Spry old lady," commented Jeremy, studying the ceiling. There was an opening she could have gone through.

"You have no idea," Emma said as she rubbed her neck. It was still tender from being stabbed with the knitting needles.

"Do we go after her?" Jeremy asked, looking at his father.

"Probably not; it might be safer for her to disappear on her own. The more people who know where she is, the more likely she is to be found." He looked at Emma. "Do you think she's capable of hiding on her own?"

"Yes, you've seen her file. She used to head up an organization bigger than John's. He must get the instincts from her." She continued to look toward the ceiling. "I think she'll be just fine."

"So, what next?" asked Jeremy. "It looks like we're done here."

"Prison, to see John Harden," replied Cole.

"Where is he located?" Jeremy asked.

"Sing Sing. I kept track," Emma said quietly.

Jeremy walked over, took her hand, and laid his forehead on hers. "Are you up for this?"

She leaned in and commented, "This might be interesting. You know he owes me a favor."

Cole looked over. "A favor? We might use that to our advantage."

Jeremy stepped back and kept her hand in his. "There's no reason for us to stay here. Why don't we head back to the hotel?"

"We need to lock up," Emma reminded him. "Clair is having this building rehabbed for the charity." The charity was started by Emma's team a few years ago to help people make better lives for themselves.

They exited the building, locked up, and headed to their hotel. It was evening and the three of them agreed it was time for dinner. A café was located close to where they were staying and was quiet enough to discuss their plans. Dinner was ordered and their drinks were delivered.

"How do we go about getting in to see John?" Emma asked as she sipped her beer.

Cole had a whiskey in his hand and sat back in his chair. "I'll contact the warden tomorrow. We should be able to get permission to talk to him."

"Will you tell him why we want to see John?" Jeremy asked.

"No, I don't think so. I'll just tell him we want to question him," said Cole.

"Won't he think it's odd, since the man has been locked up since 1881?" commented Jeremy.

"Probably, but he knows not to ask too many questions."

"Agreed," said Emma. "John's mom indicated that he has the run of the place."

"If that's true, why does he stay there?" asked Jeremy.

"Why leave? He has the perfect alibi for any crime committed at his behest," Cole replied.

With their plans in place, the three of them went back to the hotel to gather their bags. They met downstairs to hand over their keys and check out.

"You weren't here long. I still have to charge you for the whole night," the clerk said matter-of-factly from his position behind a desk and windowed wall.

"That's fine," Cole said as he pulled out his wallet. "Our business wrapped up more quickly than we anticipated."

"Where are you headed next?" the clerk asked as he took the money through the opening in the window.

Emma scrunched her eyes at the clerk. "Haven't I seen you somewhere else earlier?" she inquired.

"I don't think so," the man said as he tried to avoid her glance.

She reached through the opening, grabbed his tie, and yanked him toward her, slamming him into the window.

"Let me go!" His scream was muffled by the glass.

"Uh, Emma, what are you doing?" Jeremy asked.

"Jeremy," she said, not taking her eyes off the clerk. "he knows something. He was there this morning when I was questioning Coreen. I saw him on the fire escape outside the window." She paused before tightening her grip. "What do you know!" she demanded of the clerk, keeping her hold on him.

His voice was muffled on the glass.

"Emma," Cole suggested, "I think you need to loosen your hold so he can answer."

She didn't want to let go, but she finally gave him some slack that allowed him to pull his face back from the glass. It freed his hands; he grabbed a pair of scissors and cut the tie she still held. The scissors clanged loudly as he dropped them to the ground, then turned and ran out the back door.

They chased after him. The man was like a rabbit, darting around the alley. He easily evaded them, being more familiar with the area than they were.

"Where did he go?" Emma gasped in exasperation, looking around for the missing clerk.

"Not here," Cole replied, taking out a handkerchief to wipe his brow. "Emma, I'm sorry, I didn't think he'd do that."

"I understand." She fumed, still looking around.

"Who do you think he is?" Jeremy asked.

"Based on his reaction, I think he's a lookout for John Harden," Emma said. "He probably has several people watching Coreen. When we showed up at the hotel, he must have tracked us to the other location and saw me questioning her."

"So, John will know before we get there that we talked to Coreen," Jeremy said contemplatively.

"Yes," said Emma.

Cole looked at the two of them and said, "Let's head back to the hotel. We need to get our bags and arrange for a carriage."

Their bags were where they'd left them in the lobby of the small hotel. They grabbed them, exited, and found a carriage a few blocks away.

"Take me to where I can rent a wagon, please," requested Cole.

The driver mentioned the address and Jeremy said, "We will meet you there Pops. We will get the food for our trip."

Cole nodded and motioned to the driver. While he organized their transportation, Jeremy and Emma left to find a small café to provide their lunches and dinner for that day.

"Some fruit, also," Emma said to the waitress, picking up the bananas from the counter. The waitress nodded and continued to compile their order.

Jeremy held up some cans. "We can use these to take the food."

The waitress took them from him and packed them with their other supplies. The food was paid for and they exited toward the wagon rental location, where Cole waited in the driver's seat, holding the reins for the two horses.

"We got lunch and dinner," said Jeremy, holding the supplies up.

"Climb in. We'll be stopping at a few locations before heading out of town."

The first stop was the telegraph office. Cole called to Jeremy, "Take my place while I go into the office."

"Sure, Pops!" He moved to the driver's seat of the wagon to take the reins.

While Cole was in the office, Emma stood behind Jeremy and wrapped her arms around him. He took her hands in his and held them.

"Will it be a problem for you to see him again?" he asked. The last time she had seen John hadn't been pleasant; she had killed his partner to save herself and a close friend, Thomas.

"I don't know," she said into his back.

They stayed in that position until Cole returned. He climbed up and took the reins from Jeremy so that he could move to the back with Emma. Turning to them, he said, "I got the note sent off to Sing Sing. The warden will be expecting us."

"Do you trust him not to say anything to John?" Jeremy asked.

"Oh, I fully expect that John's aware we're on the way. This was just a courtesy." Cole waited until they were settled and clicked at the horses to get moving. They stopped a few blocks into the trip at a nondescript building. He looked over at Jeremy and asked, "Can you go in and pick up my bag?"

Jeremy had an idea of what they were picking up. "You have a list?"

Cole handed it to him and Jeremy headed into the building. A few minutes later, he returned carrying a large dark bag. He placed it in the back of the wagon without comment and jumped in to sit beside Emma. "Ready," he said and, with that statement, Cole moved the wagon back onto the street.

As they were bumping along, Emma gave that dark bag a long look and thought, *Cole's expecting trouble.* Instead of inquiring about what the bag held, she asked, "How long will the trip be?"

Jeremy answered, "It should be about thirty miles north of New York City on the east bank of the Hudson River. By horse and wagon, we should be there in maybe a day and a half."

She settled down in the back with a bedroll under her head. Jeremy sat next to her and read as Cole drove. They would trade off the driving responsibility as they made their way. The carriage moved swiftly but would take time to get them to their destination.

CHAPTER 2

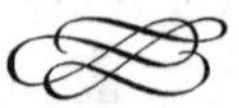

Emma woke abruptly when the motion of the wagon stopped. "Is something wrong?" she asked, yawning.

"We stopped to give the horses time to rest and for us to have lunch," Cole replied over his shoulder.

Jeremy helped her down while his father unhooked the horses and walked them over to a small stream. The lunches were retrieved by Jeremy and Emma. They unrolled a blanket for them to sit on and all three ate, enjoying the quiet.

After a few minutes, Cole broke the silence. "Let's talk about what we want to get from John."

"Our main goal is to find more of the missing children," stated Emma. "I don't care about his other activities unless we can use them to make him talk."

"Yes," Jeremy agreed. Cole nodded.

"So, how are we going to approach this?" she asked.

"Use your instincts in the interview," Cole said. "They've worked well for us in the past."

Emma nodded. They finished lunch and, when the horses had adequately rested, they started on their way again, with Jeremy driving.

"Emma, would you mind if I borrow your lighter?" Cole asked.

"Sure," she said and pulled it out. It was a kerosene repository that had a flint to light the wick. She handed it to him and he placed it in his pocket without comment. When he didn't give it back, she frowned but didn't ask any follow-up questions. She sat back and picked up her book.

"Pull over to the side of the road," he directed Jeremy.

Emma sat up and laid her book down. "What's up?"

"Pops is looking for something," Jeremy responded.

Cole jumped down and ran down the road. He hastened back and climbed into the wagon and opened the bag Jeremy had retrieved earlier. Two pistols were withdrawn from it and he handed one of them to Jeremy.

Emma held out her hand, expectantly.

"Emma, I know you're good with knives…" Cole started.

"I can handle a gun," she said firmly.

"Let her have it, Pops," Jeremy said, checking his gun. "She knows how to use it."

Taking him at his word, Cole handed her a pistol and pulled out several rifles for himself. Jeremy started to move towards them to help.

"No, stay where you are and get us back on the road," Cole said.

Jeremy did as he was instructed and got them moving again.

Emma looked over at Cole, watching him load the guns. She started to do the same and found hers was already loaded. "Did you see something or are you just expecting trouble?" she asked him.

"Right now, I expect trouble."

"The clerk. Could he have sent someone after us?"

"Yes. He's one of John's men and I think we can expect someone soon."

"Or many someone's," she murmured, looking at the road behind them.

For the rest of the day, all three continued to monitor the road behind them. As the sun started to go down and still no one had been spotted, they pulled the wagon over for a dinner break. The horses rested for a long while and then they began their trip in the dark. Emma started to nod off against the side of the wagon. She was startled into full awareness when they heard hoofbeats coming up behind them. It was hard to make out how many men were following them.

Cole snatched up his rifle and yelled to Jeremy, "Keep going!"

Jeremy snapped the reins and got the horses moving at a faster pace.

The sound of gunfire exploded around them.

"Keep down!" called Cole, returning fire with his rifle.

She sent him a side glance and then fired the pistol in quick succession. One of the men fell off his horse. "As I said, I can use a gun. I just prefer a knife."

❧

About a year ago

"I prefer my knife," she complained, feeling the heavy gun in her hand. "Why do I have to learn how to use this?"

"Emma, you might get into a situation where your knife isn't the best weapon," Jeremy explained.

"I can't think of one," she muttered, thinking he sounded like his grandmother, Miss Marjorie, when she'd taught Emma to throw knives.

"I can," he mentioned. "Not everything is going to be hand-to-hand combat."

"I'm not comfortable with this."

"That's why we practice," he reasoned. "Let's get started." He stood behind her and tapped her leg to widen her stance. She had the Colt gripped in her hand. "Remember, this is a double-action pistol. All you need to do is pull the trigger."

She nodded, keeping her fingers away from it. They faced the target; he moved her hands to the proper position and told her to fire the gun. "Brace yourself. There's going to be a kick."

She fired and the pistol spat out the bullet. The kick pushed her into Jeremy. He helped her reposition, and she shot until the gun was empty. Jeremy retrieved the target; her bullets hadn't hit the center but it was close.

"Doesn't seem all that hard," she said, examining the weapon.

~

Back to now

"I guess that answers that," Cole murmured as he switched to another rifle and continued to shoot toward the ever-approaching men.

Emma didn't spare him a glance and continued to fire. The riders pursued them, getting closer. She loaded more bullets and looked over at Cole. He had put his rifle down and pulled out some cans that had a bit of wick sticking out of the top. He lit the wicks and threw them quickly toward the marauders.

The small cans exploded in the distance, and white smoke expanded, overtaking the men. Their horses reared, preventing the men from following them.

Jeremy took advantage of the confusion and pulled ahead of their attackers. They went a couple of miles down the road and he yelled back, "I think they stopped."

"Keep going!" Cole yelled.

He and Emma kept their guns pointed behind them and, after a few minutes, Cole called to Jeremy, "You can slow down and go behind those trees."

He followed his father's direction and pulled behind a group of trees just off the road to the left.

"Are we safe?" Emma asked breathlessly.

"I think we did significant damage; we slowed them down."

"Cole, what were those cans you threw?" Emma asked as the wagon pulled to a stop.

"They were homemade grenades."

"Grenades?" Emma asked, the term was unfamiliar to her.

"A grenade is a small explosive device that was used occasionally in the war. It consists of a can full of powder, old twisted metal, nails, or any other sharp or cutting thing. A wick is added and has to be lit. It works pretty well, mostly as a surprise. Horses get spooked, men get thrown, chaos ensues."

"They were certainly effective."

"What now?" Jeremy asked.

"They may regroup. We need to keep watch," Cole said, looking toward the road. He motioned to them. "Spread out." They entered the wooded area and waited. Emma went to the right and Jeremy to the left. Cole stayed in his location.

"Where did they go?" They heard a man's voice call. "We have to find them!"

"I don't know, but be careful. They took down six of our guys," another man said.

"You go that way," the first man indicated.

Jeremy waited until the men separated; he went up behind the figure nearest him and knocked him out. He pulled his body back into the woods.

"Will, where are you?" the other man called loudly. "Don't hide from me!"

Emma stepped out behind him and pressed the gun to his head. "Drop your gun."

Instead of following directions, he made a sudden move and lifted the gun he held. "I wouldn't," Cole said, as he stepped out of the trees and pointed the rifle at him. "Do as she says and drop the gun."

He dropped it and stayed silent.

"Jeremy!" Emma called. "We have the other one."

He came out of the trees, dragging an unconscious man with him.

"Did you kill Will?" the man asked, his voice shaking.

"No, he's just out," commented Jeremy, nudging the man with his shoe.

Cole said to the man, "We have a few questions for you. Who sent you?"

He looked mutinous.

"You don't have an option here. Your crew's gone and the only person who can help you is unconscious," Jeremy said as he walked over to take the gun from Emma. She stepped back, watching the man closely.

"I have another option," the man said and went for his clutch piece. He turned quickly, pointing the small gun at them. Before he could cock the weapon, Emma pulled her knife and threw it, hitting him in the shoulder.

"I told you the knife was a better weapon," Emma commented smugly as they listened to him scream.

"Now, we want some answers from you," Cole said firmly.

"You won't get any!" the man screamed.

"Stubborn," murmured Emma. "Do you want me to help you with the knife stuck in your shoulder?" she asked and stepped toward him.

His face had a look of terror. He opened and closed his mouth, shaking his head.

"Who are you working for?" Cole asked, using the man's fear of Emma to his advantage.

The man stayed silent. Jeremy prodded him with his gun. "Talk!" he said curtly.

He finally said, "I can tell you who the main guy is, but I don't know who is running things for him."

"Who is it?" asked Emma.

"John Harden."

"One more piece of the puzzle," Cole said.

"What do we do with him?" asked Jeremy.

"Just leave me here. I won't tell them where you are going, I promise."

"And we just take your word?" Emma asked, her voice hardening.

"He's coming with us," Cole said. "Emma, get the rope; it's in the bag." When she didn't move, he said again, "Get the rope."

Jeremy saw her expression and said, "Pops, take the gun. I'll get it."

Cole took Jeremy's gun and kept an eye on both Emma and the man.

Jeremy came back with the rope and tied him up. "What do we do with him?"

"There's nothing we can do. We'll have to bring him with us."

"But where do we put him?" *I don't think he should be near Emma.* Jeremy thought. He looked at the wagon. "We need to adjust the luggage and roll him in the back."

Emma smiled suddenly. "Yes, that's just the location. We don't want him too comfortable."

Cole let the comment pass and said, "Emma and Jeremy, be sure to dress his wound. I assume Emma wants her knife back." He turned to walk back to the wagon to get the horses' food and water.

Her lips curled up in a feral grin; she didn't say anything.

"What's happened to you?" Jeremy asked her in a low voice as Cole left them. "Normally, you have more compassion."

"That person's mixed up in this. The kids have had to survive by any means possible or die. I think he should have the same opportunity; survive on his own or die."

He just shook his head. "Emma, he could be of use later. We need to make sure he's alive."

Emma cocked her head. "That's thinking I can get behind. Get out one of your shirts. I'm not wasting a petticoat on this man."

He hesitated to leave her alone with him and a gun.

"Don't leave me alone with her!" the man screamed.

She saw Jeremy's face. "I won't do anything to him." *Unless I am pushed.*

Jeremy nodded and went to fetch a shirt from his luggage. She could hear the fabric ripping as he returned. He handed her the strips of material and a bottle he'd retrieved from the wagon.

"We need to move him over to that tree." She indicted the large tree behind them. They each took an arm and sat him by the tree. Once there, Emma said, "I need to look at the wound. And I want my knife back. "

He shrank back from Emma. "Stay away from me! You just want to hurt me again!"

"Don't be such a baby," said Emma. "Stay still!" He sat and watched her as she moved closer. Before he could react, she pulled the knife from his shoulder. He screamed in pain.

She didn't spare him a glance as she used the knife to cut his sleeve off to view the wound. He grimaced as she pulled him toward her to check his back.

"It's not that bad," she murmured, "but I will enjoy this part." She picked up the alcohol and poured it on the wound. He screamed again.

She wrapped it quickly. "I'm not doing this for you. We'll keep you with us in case you have other information that can help."

His eyes were glazed, the shock keeping him quiet.

"Tie him back up, Emma," Jeremy said. She did so, none too gently, and pushed him back against the tree.

Cole returned from tending the horses. He had tied them loosely so they could reach the stream and grass.

"Has Will woke up yet?" called the tied-up man as he regained his senses.

Jeremy paused briefly as he set up the fire. "Will didn't make it. He'd been shot during the gunfight." He'd gone back to check on him after they treated the man's wound. Will's injury had been life-threatening and there was nothing he could do for him.

"But you said he was asleep…" The man trailed off. Everyone was gone. What would he do now?

They prepared a late dinner of hard bread, canned beef, and beans. After they finished, Jeremy tossed each of them an apple.

"Hey, what about me?" the man called. "I need to eat."

Emma took a slow bite of her apple and didn't look his way.

"Jeremy, take a roll and some meat over to him," Cole said.

"And some water. We don't need him getting sick on the way. That will just cause delays," Emma said. She really didn't care about the man, unless he got in their way.

Jeremy did as he was asked and held a gun on him while the man ate. He looked at Jeremy and said, "Thank you. My name is Earl Snyder."

"No funny business, Earl," Jeremy warned. "I need to tie you up again." Earl was compliant and held out his hands.

After Jeremy tied the man up, he walked back to the fire and sat by Emma. "Are you okay to continue with this case?" He was concerned about her mood. It had increasingly become more negative. The missing children had affected her; it had affected them all.

She looked over at him. "I'm the same person I've always been. I just don't like to give the enemy too much aid. He's a bad guy who tried to kill us. I understand we need to keep him alive, but if I get a chance to make him uncomfortable, I will."

He gave her a considering look. "Just don't take it too far."

"I won't," she promised and glanced to where Earl was sitting. *Unless he gives me a reason*, she thought to herself.

Jeremy reclined on his bedroll. "What are the plans?" he asked his father.

"I think we should try to get some sleep. We're relatively safe here and the horses need time to rest."

"What about him?" Emma asked, indicating Earl with her hand.

"We take turns keeping watch on him or anything else that might come upon us tonight."

Cole took the first shift while Emma and Jeremy settled down on their bedrolls.

Much later, Jeremy woke Emma for the final shift and wearily went off to his bedroll.

Shaking her sleepiness off, she walked the area and looked at Earl. He was sleeping soundly. They had secured him to the tree so he could lie down. *He looks a little too comfortable*, she thought, resisting the urge to kick him. "Pig," she muttered and continued to patrol the area. When she confirmed everything was quiet, she took her seat about three yards from him, keeping Earl and her team clearly in view.

The hours dragged by and her routine remained the same: walk the parameter and check on Earl. She returned to her base and sat down. *Buzz. . . crack!* A bullet sailed by her ear. She immediately turned toward where the shot had come from, pulled her gun, and started firing. When there was no return fire, she stopped.

Jeremy and Cole ran up, their guns drawn. "What happened?" Jeremy asked.

"Someone was shooting." She indicated the direction the shot had come from with her gun.

"Spread out, we need to see if they're still here," Cole said. They separated and went through the area. They met back and made their reports. They had found no one.

Cole walked over to check on Earl. "Jeremy!"

He ran to where Cole kneeled with Earl. They turned him over. Blood was spreading quickly. He had been shot, and the bullet had gone into his chest. There was no hope for him, his eyes wide open in death.

They looked at Emma.

"I didn't do it," she responded heatedly.

Cole and Jeremy's faces held no expression. "Hand me your knife," Jeremy said, not responding to her statement.

She took it out of her pocket and walked it over to him, handle up.

Taking it carefully, he moved Earl's body away from the tree. He traced the bullet's exit to the tree behind him. After he dug it out, he said, "Definitely not Emma's. This was a different caliber."

Cole had suspected Emma may have become impatient with their guest. He was glad to hear she hadn't killed him. "We need to get moving," he said. "They know our location."

"They know we're here," said Jeremy. "Why not kill us?"

"John," murmured Emma. "This type of behavior sounds like him. Take out the informant, but he still wants to know what we know."

Jeremy and Cole looked at her. She knew him better than they did and would follow her lead. "We can't take the chance he won't try again before we make it to the prison," Emma said.

They started to clear the site and got organized. Emma was quiet as she helped.

Jeremy asked, "What's wrong?"

"You didn't trust me," she said simply, not looking at him.

"You're right, I didn't. You'd made up your mind about Earl and I thought you took the opportunity to get some justice for the missing kids."

She nodded. "That's true. But, Jeremy, I would've told you if I had shot him. I wouldn't lie to you."

"You're right," he said, coming over to her. He took her in his arms. "It won't happen again."

She hugged him back. "What do we do with him?"

"We can't take him with us; he'll start to smell," said Jeremy.

"We'll cover him and the other one up with ground debris," said Cole. "I'll have someone take care of the burials."

Jeremy and Cole dragged Earl and lay him next to Will in the brush. Emma gathered up branches and brought them over to cover the bodies.

Once they finished, it was time to pack up the camp. Jeremy gathered the horses while Cole and Emma helped to harness them. Once completed, they climbed into the wagon and pulled out onto the road. Jeremy drove and Emma and Cole held their guns at the ready in case there was another attack. They went on for about fifteen minutes when Jeremy called back. "We might be in the clear for now." They finally set the firearms in the wagon next to them.

We're being allowed to go to the prison. John, what are you up to? Emma thought. She mulled that over as she settled back, stretching her legs.

Cole looked over at her. "Emma, get some rest. We'll wake you when we need relief." They were only about halfway to their destination at that point. "It could take another day."

The rest of the trip was uneventful; only stopping to rest themselves and the horses. By late the next day, they were near the prison and stopped by a local hotel to freshen up. Emma stayed clothed in her pants and long black coat. Her bowler hat was in place but the lace and dashing feather removed. She needed to fly under the radar and not be seen as a woman. Her long hair was tucked inside her black shirt and the collar flipped up to hide it.

Jeremy nodded approvingly when he saw her. He gave one last yank on his boots and stood up. "Time to go meet Pops. Are you ready?"

"I am," she said confidently.

"Keep your head down as we go in. Oh, and leave the knives here. The warden won't be patient if we're found carrying weapons."

She took off her bowler and removed her long sharp knife from its hidden compartment. Next, she reached into her pants pocket and removed her hidden knife. Lastly, she bent down and removed a knife from her ankle boot, then stowed all weapons in her bag.

"Did you get them all?" he asked laconically.

She tilted her head and coyly answered, "I think so, want to search me?"

He laughed. "Maybe later," he said, pulling her to him. A knock on the door interrupted anything that might have happened next. They looked at each other regretfully.

"Ready to go?" called Cole through the door.

"I am," Jeremy called back.

"Me too," Emma called. She picked up her hat and placed it jauntily on her head. She offered Jeremy her elbow and they exited the room. Cole noticed the mood had lifted and was glad to see that they had worked out their differences.

Their horses and wagon had been dropped off at a local stable. They needed rest, food, and the gunfire had also made them skittish. It had been a long trip.

Cole arranged for a carriage to take them to the prison. He had vetted the young driver and felt confident that he wasn't going to try to kill them before they got there. They had a plan on how to approach John and they'd stick to it.

They pulled up to the imposing prison entrance. Jeremy didn't offer Emma a hand as she descended from the carriage. As a gentleman, she was expected to get down on her own. Her walk and mannerisms became more masculine as they entered the prison gate. The air was oppressive as they entered, the gates swinging closed behind them.

As they made the long walk to the main building, Jeremy looked around with interest. "Where did the name of this place come from?" he asked.

Cole answered, "The land was purchased from the Sintsink Indian tribe in 1685. It evolved from there."

Jeremy said, "I heard the prison is trying to rehabilitate the prisoners for new lives when they get out."

Emma raised her eyebrows and said, "Sounds like John isn't taking to the rehabilitation."

They laughed, helping to relieve some of the tension.

"There are plenty of access ways into Sing Sing," Jeremy remarked, noting the railroads and the Hudson River surrounding the prison.

"This is not a small facility," commented Emma, looking at the many buildings inside the fences. They continued to the main administration building.

As they watched the heavy door on the main prison building being opened for them, Cole said, "I wonder if John is being kept in the same cells as the other prisoners. They are not comfortable; the inmates barely have enough room to move around and no windows."

She again thought, *Why does he stay?*

The warden met them at the main building entrance. "Cole, it's nice to see you."

"You too," Cole said, taking his hand. "We appreciate you letting us visit." He turned to Emma and Jeremy. "This is Warden Augustus Brush. Warden, my son Jeremy, and Emma Evans."

The warden nodded and led them into the room where they would be searched. Cole whispered to the warden, reminding him about Emma.

Brush nodded and said, "I've arranged for our head matron to conduct your search." A large woman entered the room and motioned for Emma to follow her. She was suddenly glad she had left her knives behind.

Jeremy caught her arm as she started to follow the matron. "Do you want me to come with you?"

Emma looked over at the rather sturdy woman. "No, I'll be okay."

They moved to another room down the hall. Once inside, the matron spoke in a firm voice. "I'll pat you down and then check your pockets."

"That's fine," Emma commented, following the woman's directions. It was painless and a little embarrassing, but the matron found nothing. When the search was completed, the woman smiled suddenly, changing her whole continence, and said, "There now. That wasn't so bad."

"No, it wasn't. Thank you for doing this for me."

"Just keep that hat pulled down," the woman warned. "We don't want a ruckus in here."

"Understood," commented Emma as she smoothed her hair into her shirt and pulled her hat low over her eyes. She eyed the matron and asked, "Are there female prisoners here?"

"Yes, Sing Sing is the first institution to have one prison with separate housing for male and female offenders. We have women wardens there."

The matron escorted Emma back to the room where the men were located. Cole and Jeremy put on their coats and looked over as she entered. Jeremy raised an eyebrow and she mouthed, "It's fine."

The warden saw her return. "If you're ready, we have Harden in an interview room waiting. This guard will take you." He waved to the man next to him. The guard stood silently and used his stick to indicate the direction they should take.

They walked down the long hallway. Emma didn't know what to expect.

CHAPTER 3

They went into the room indicated by the guard. John was already there and handcuffed to the table. Jeremy stepped from in front of Emma and revealed her to John.

"Emma," he said. She saw real pleasure in his eyes. He focused all attention on her, ignoring Cole and Jeremy

Her confidence showed as Emma stepped forward; she was no longer the same sixteen-year-old girl she had been the last time they were together. It wasn't just age that had changed her, but her life experience.

"You've changed," he observed.

"Have I?" she murmured, watching him as closely as he watched her.

"It's nice of you to visit me," he said as she removed her hat.

"This isn't just a visit, John," she said quietly. They had agreed that she would begin the questioning. Her prior relationship and the fact he owed her a favor would be part of it.

"May I sit?" she asked, motioning to the chair on her side of the table.

"Please, forgive me for not getting up." He held out his hands, showing the cuffs that attached him to the table.

Emma sat. The guard was behind her at the door; Jeremy and Cole stood on either side of the table, observing the persons in the room. "You don't seem surprised to see me," she said.

"I don't?" he said, answering her question with another question.

She let that go by. "John, we're investigating the child kidnapping ring that began two years ago."

He sat back and smiled, "You caught the person in charge, right? I thought she died very publicly."

"That's right." It was time to drop the first fact on him. "We did find out your sister was the person in charge."

All of Emma's attention was on John and his response. He didn't move.

"Sister?" John cocked his head and said, "No I don't think so. What did you say her name was?"

"Candace." Emma gave the birth name provided by Coreen. "And that would make you Christopher O'Leary."

His eyes narrowed. She knew details that were not public knowledge. "If this is true, where did you get the information?"

"I can't share that at this time."

"Can't or won't? How is Ma doing?" he asked, always a step ahead.

"John," she chastened, "you know I can't say anything further on that topic."

"In that case, I'm not sure what I can do for you," he responded, looking bored.

She continued with her questions. "John, did you know that the kidnappings have started again?" This time she sat back and waited for his response.

His face hardened. *Had she told him something he didn't know?* His eyes flickered. *What is he looking at?* she asked herself.

She went on. "I think you didn't approve of Candace's involvement with the children, given the way you took down the first organization. I'd assume your underlings know your wishes and wouldn't go into business for themselves." Emma played upon his ownership of his organization. In prison or not, this business was his to run.

"I don't wish to talk anymore today," he said. His statement was final.

Jeremy stepped forward, intending to say something, to make him talk. Emma held up her hand to stop him; she didn't look away from John.

"We'll be staying nearby when you wish to have another conversation." She stood.

John watched her silently as she placed her hat back on her head and adjusted her shirt collar higher to hide her hair.

"Emma," John said suddenly, "I really did enjoy seeing you again."

She dropped her coin purse near her leg and bent down to pick it up. As she came up, she murmured, "Remember that favor you owe me."

She didn't wait for a response but walked toward the guard. He sent a glance to John and then opened the door for them. The guard on the outside of the room told his companion, "You can take him back to his cell."

Jeremy, Cole, and Emma made their way out and the door slammed shut behind them. That sound stopped them for a moment, then they continued down the hallway. They exited the facility and located their carriage for the ride back.

All sat quietly in the carriage. When Jeremy started to talk, Cole cleared his throat and shook his head. There would be no discussion in front of a third party. Jeremy nodded and settled with his arm around Emma.

It was noon when they arrived at the hotel. Cole said, "Wait here." He strode to the desk and ordered lunch brought to their room. Once the three were back together, they headed up the stairs. It wasn't until the door to their room closed that they spoke. "Finally, we can talk," she said as she took off her hat and jacket, dropping down on the settee.

"Yes," Cole said. "This case could involve almost anyone. If we don't want to be overheard, we'll have to be cautious about what and where we share."

A sudden knock at the door startled them. Jeremy went to it and called back over his shoulder, "Just the food." He allowed the man into the room to set up the cart. Once completed, Jeremy escorted him out.

They filled their plates and sat down at the table. "Let's start the review of the interview," Cole suggested as they ate.

Emma and Jeremy nodded their heads in agreement.

"I can start," said Emma.

"Go ahead," encouraged Cole.

She picked up her glass to take a drink and then put it down slowly. "I am not sure if John's reaction to my question meant he knew about it or not. His eyes flickered when I mentioned the kids. What happened behind us at that time?"

Jeremy smiled. "I wondered if you saw that. His gaze shifted to the guard."

"What did he do?" she asked.

Cole said, "Nothing. He didn't move at all."

"He responds and he's dead. That must be our guy running things on the outside," said Emma.

"Exactly," stated Jeremy. As John's guard, he could move around unmonitored.

"What next?" Emma asked.

"We find out where the guard lives," Cole said.

"We could follow him," suggested Jeremy.

"That we can," said Cole.

"We'll have to keep our distance; he could be dangerous," Emma said.

"We'll be needing to go at 6pm," Jeremy said.

"Why's that?" Emma asked.

"Shift change at the prison."

"Yes," Cole agreed.

They cleaned up the plates and placed them outside their room. "We have enough time to rest and then head back to Sing Sing," said Cole.

Emma walked with Jeremy to their bedroom and Jeremy turned to her. "What was it you said to John just before we left?"

She smiled widely. "I reminded him he owes me a favor."

Jeremy grinned and escorted her to their room for some rest.

CHAPTER 4

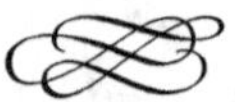

$\mathcal{A}$s they followed the guard home that evening, he took a circuitous route. He stopped at several establishments, exiting each with a bag and a self-satisfied expression on his face.

"I guess he convinced John he wasn't involved," Jeremy suggested, watching from behind his paper.

Cole sat outside the cafe across the road from them.

"Oh, no?" Emma asked. "Take a look at his eye."

Jeremy followed her direction and noticed the man had pulled his hat low; his right eye was blackened.

"John must have been concerned," murmured Emma.

"He's acting normal," Jeremy said, continuing to watch him.

"Is he, though? I think we have a runner," she said in the same tone.

"If he's going to run, he wants something to take with him."

"The bags," murmured Emma.

The guard walked along and they followed, hanging back so as not to be seen. They needn't have worried about being spotted, though; his attention never wavered from his task. Cole gave up pretending and walked boldly over to them.

He seems to be unaware of the parade he's leading, Emma thought.

He has too much on his mind. They continued to follow him into a residential area.

"The area is affluent," Cole commented. "I would've expected something much smaller based on his actual income."

"He's spending John's money and living like he's in charge," Emma observed.

"Hmm, this isn't something he'll want John to know," Jeremy commented.

"No, and normally he may not have led us directly here," Cole replied.

The guard went into an apartment building, they followed and saw him make his way up the staircase. Once he was out of sight, Cole went to see the doorman. Emma smiled when she noticed the handshake and the transfer of money.

Cole left him and approached them. "4th floor—large apartment." They went to the stairs and made their way up.

They studied the door. "Do I pick it?" Emma asked in a low voice.

"No, I think we knock," Cole said, thinking over the man's behavior. "We need to use his panic for our own purposes."

"Think he'll go out the window?" asked Jeremy, running scenarios.

"We'll be ready for that, but I don't think so. The man living here has been taking chances for a while now. He has to know he had a limited time in this role."

They agreed Emma would speak for them. Jeremy knocked and stepped to the side. "Yes, who is it?" the man's voice called. He sounded impatient.

Emma pitched her voice higher and said, "Towels, sir. I was told to bring you towels."

"Towels?" he called back. "You can take them back, I don't want them."

"But, sir, I'll get into trouble if you don't take them."

"Oh for..." he started to say as he swung the door open. He saw them and immediately tried to push the door closed. Cole, Jeremy, and Emma pushed back, causing it to slam into the wall. The man fell backward onto the floor and started to crawl away from them. Jeremy jumped on him to try to secure him, but he got loose and ran to the opened window.

Emma jumped on his back and Jeremy grabbed his legs. The guard stumbled and fell hard, taking Emma with him. She took hold of his hands and began securing them.

"There wasn't an easier way?" she asked over her shoulder.

"Not that I could think of in the moment," said Jeremy, breathing hard.

The man lay groaning on the floor. "Why are you here? What did I do to you?" he whined.

"Let's get him secured," Cole directed.

He and Jeremy took his arms and dragged him to the sofa. Once he was in place, they formed a half-circle around him. The man looked at all three of them but stayed silent.

"We are curious about something," Jeremy started.

The guard looked unyielding and didn't open his mouth.

"How can you live here on a prison guard's salary?" They watched him closely but he still didn't talk.

"Don't you want to brag about your beautiful apartment? The wonderful furnishings?" Emma asked as she stood and walked over to the mantel. She picked up a vase. "Maybe it isn't yours? If I just drop this, would you care?" As she tossed it into the air, he screamed. She caught it deftly and asked. "So, you do care. Are these your things?"

He struggled against his restraints and finally snapped, "Aarg! It's mine, all mine!"

"All yours," commented Cole, stroking his goatee. "Tell us how that's possible."

"I'm not just a prison guard," he said importantly as he sat straighter on the couch.

"You're not? What else do you do?" Jeremy asked interestedly.

"I run businesses. I have many things I'm involved in," he said.

Emma started to look around, opening cabinets and closets. Then she moved to the bedrooms.

"Where's she going? What's she looking for?" he asked, his tone changing to one of desperation as he watched her walk around the apartment.

"Oh, she's just curious about what you might be hiding," commented Cole.

"I'm not hiding anything!" he screamed.

Emma walked out holding several cloth bags. "What's in these, I wonder?" She upended one and dumped it on the table in front of the man. Money tumbled out and onto the floor.

"How much do you think is here?" asked Jeremy idly, picking up one of the bundles.

"Don't touch that," the guard sputtered.

"This?" he said and slipped it into his jacket pocket.

"Put that back! You can't have it. That's mine!"

"What kind of business gives you bags of cash?" asked Cole contemplatively.

He didn't seem to know how to answer that question.

"Do you run the business for John Harden?" Emma asked bluntly.

"If I give you that information, will you leave?" he pleaded.

"His bags are out and his clothes thrown into them," Emma said to Jeremy and Cole.

"Leaving town?" Jeremy asked.

"Yes, I need to leave today," he said desperately.

"That black eye, how did that happen?" Jeremy asked.

The guard moved his hand to touch his face, but the restraints stopped him. "Just an altercation at work. It happens occasionally."

~

The day before:

Jeremy, Emma, and Cole planned out their confrontation with the security guard.

"Tomorrow in his room, what are we looking for?" asked Cole.

Emma stood and walked around, thinking. "First the businesses, there'll be accounting books."

"They'll be hidden. Under a floorboard, inside a wall, or a safe," suggested Jeremy.

"Emma, you look for those and any other hidden papers," directed Cole. He looked over at Jeremy. "You'll be the primary interviewer."

"This will be quick; we won't have time to build a case on him," Jeremy said, frowning. "Questions will have to come through observations." Emma was better at that than he was. He looked over at her, and she sent him a smile showing her support.

They nodded, set in their plans for the next day.

~

"Was the altercation with John Harden?" Jeremy asked, his eyes narrowed.

"Him? Why would he hit me? Untie me!" he demanded.

Jeremy ignored that and continued to question him while Emma returned to searching the rooms.

"What's she doing in there? What else is she looking for?"

"She's just looking around," Jeremy replied.

"She won't find anything." The guard swallowed and his eyes darted to catch a glimpse of Emma.

"Hidden that well?" Jeremy asked, seeing the doubt in the man's eyes.

"Nothing's hidden," he said, but he didn't sound so sure this time.

"Ah ha!" Emma's voice floated in from the other room.

Cole stood up and went to see what Emma had found. The

man's panic increased and he struggled with his bonds. He moved around until he threw himself on the floor.

"Hey now, what's the matter?" Jeremy asked as he gripped the man by his collar and dragged him back to the sofa. "We still have more to talk about."

The guard growled.

"You think you scare me?" Jeremy asked, his voice low and threatening. The man must have seen something in Jeremy's eyes and sat back, looking away.

There was a delay, then both Cole and Emma exited the bedroom, their hands full of books.

The guard froze and stopped struggling.

Emma started opening up the small books first. She read the owner's name and said aloud, "The bank accounts are all in your name. That is your name, isn't it? Jacob Smith?"

He screamed, "It was him and not me! I only took orders!"

"John's orders?" asked Emma, her voice ringing through the room.

"Yes," Jacob said desperately. "This is all him! He had me do it! He said it had to be in my name!"

She tossed the bank books down on the table in front of him. "I don't care about those. What I want is the children, the ones taken before and the ones you've taken since that time."

"Kids? No, no. That was finished when Candace died. I've no involvement in anything like that. That was all her."

Cole was reading through the journals. "This one is the one John must see. It's related to businesses and other types of deals." He picked up another one and read through it. " This one has information concerning events you claim to know nothing about."

"The kids?" asked Emma, her voice going high.

"Yes."

The blood drained out of Jacob's face. "There was too much money involved. They kept throwing it at me and I just gave in and set the networks back up," he said, his tone dull.

"You aren't using schools to find the kids now?" Jeremy asked. The prior kidnappings had been related to Candace masquerading as a school nurse.

"No," Jacob said, "became too hard after you caught her. We had to start grabbing them as they walked to school, went to the park, or played in the streets. It was extremely easy. No one lifted a finger or took notice when one child would go missing. How did you know it was going on?"

"Your people got greedy and took a group of children all at one time. They were reported immediately. It started us on the path here," said Emma.

He grimaced. "I told them we have to lay low, take one at a time."

"Where are they?" she demanded. They all leaned in toward him, their patience at an end.

"No, no, that will get me killed," he said and shook his head.

Emma reached into her pocket, pulled out her knife, and grabbed him by the hair. "This time," she growled, "we will kill you! Right here and right now! I could take care of you and no one would lift a finger to stop me. So, I want you to think long and hard about that answer."

Cole started to move toward her, worried about what she might do; Jeremy took his arm and held him back. "She knows what she's doing," he said in a low voice.

Jacob looked into her eyes and saw she would follow through with her threats. "I have a list of locations where the children might be," he admitted.

"Might?" she echoed, pulling his hair again.

"Yes, *might*. They could be almost anywhere after a few days," he explained quickly.

"Then you will give us the locations you know of," Cole demanded.

Jeremy looked at Emma. "I think he's ready to help us."

Emma slowly released his hair and reluctantly withdrew the

knife. She glared at Jacob and said, "People who do this to kids deserve no mercy. Tell us a lie and I will cut you."

His eyes followed her to the chair where she sat down.

Jeremy cleared his throat to get his attention. "The locations you mentioned?"

"Yes," Jacob said, pulling his eyes from Emma. He listed a number of bordellos located from New York to Chicago. "That'll be your first stop. From there, they could be sent anywhere, including overseas."

Emma's expression didn't change, but her spirits dropped. They may find some, but not all.

"Who are your people on the streets, taking the children? We also need the holding facilities," Jeremy directed.

Jacob was hoping to keep those to himself. Wait until the heat was off and start again. The money available in this business was too good to not start again.

Jeremy waited for the answer to his question. When it didn't come, he turned to Emma. "Emma," he said. She started toward Jacob.

Jacob saw her face and the knife in her hand and immediately started to provide the answers they were looking for. Warehouses were the building of choice as holding spots before moving to bordellos.

Cole spoke up then. "We need specific names of your groups at each location."

"Wait," Jacob said suddenly. "What am I getting out of this?"

Emma and Jeremy sat back; it was Cole's turn to talk.

"You'll be going to prison, probably the one you work at now," Cole said bluntly.

"How is that fair?" Jacob asked indignantly.

"Fair?" Cole said. "Fair is not putting you in the general population and, if you keep pushing, we'll make sure that is where you end up."

His face whitened considerably at that remark. *Yes, that would be worse.* He gave them the names and locations. He had to try one more time. "You could just let me go."

At that moment, there was a knock on the door. Jacob tried to get up from the couch and run. They grabbed him and sat him back down.

Emma said, "I'll get it." She went to the door and opened it.

The local police came in. The lead man looked around. "Nice place."

"Jenkins," Cole said and walked over to him.

"What is going on?" Jenkins asked. "I got your message to meet you here."

"You're right on time," Cole responded.

The two men talked in the corner while the other officers took Jacob into custody.

Cole and Jenkins returned to the group. "We'll book him with this evidence," Jenkins said. "You'll retain the other information on the missing kids?"

"Yes, we'll continue to investigate the children," said Cole.

Jenkins nodded and turned to his men. "Let's take him in. We'll need to sort the charges out."

"But what about John? Will he be charged also?" Jacob cried, distraught at being taken into custody.

Jenkins looked at him. "John Harden is in prison. There's nothing on these papers that indicates he was involved. I don't think we need to bring him into this."

Jacob looked at him in terror and screamed, "He's one of John's men! You have to listen to me!"

Emma, Cole, and Jeremy watched as Jacob was dragged from the room. "Do you think he is one of John's men?" Jeremy asked.

Cole shrugged, "There was nothing that pointed in that direction. Jenkins will use the evidence he has to convict him."

Emma wondered how far John's reach was. In the carriage on the way from Jacob's apartment, Emma looked at Jeremy. "Were we played? Did John use us to get rid of someone who was getting too strong in his organization?"

"Does it matter?" asked Jeremy.

"No, not really," Emma said as she sat back. "The kids are all I care about."

CHAPTER 5

$\mathcal{C}$ ole had arranged for John to be moved to a room for them to speak to him at Sing Sing. The guard accompanying him kept his head down and secured John to the table. *Is he Jacob's new replacement?* Emma wondered.

"Well, this is a surprise. I didn't expect to see you here, Emma. Are you back for that favor?" Harden asked mockingly.

Her head whipped toward him when she heard her name. "No," she said quietly. "It turns out we didn't need your help after all."

He laughed out loud. "How can I be of help from here?" he asked. "After all, I am in prison."

Cole spoke next. "We know that your business activities have continued since your incarceration."

Harden turned his gaze from Emma to Cole. "And you are?"

"Cole Tilden."

John looked at Jeremy.

"Jeremy Tilden," he supplied.

John tilted his head. "Now we know who we are, what do you want?"

John's conversation with Jacob the day before.

Once Emma and the Tildens exited the room at the prison, Jacob stepped up to John to disengage him. "It's time to go back to your cell."

John sent him a look and didn't address the comment. The guard got impatient and grabbed John by the arm. "I said it is time to go."

John appeared to have had enough rough handling and reached up to take him by the collar and pulled him down to his eye level. "You think you're in charge now? That you have something to hold over me?"

Jacob went still. "Yes, until we get what we want."

"Take me back to my cell," John said releasing him. He had settled and looked almost relaxed.

Jacob took a deep breath and released it before undoing his bonds.

John took the opportunity, rolled his hand into a fist, and hit Jacob in the eye.

"You can't do that!" Jacob cried, holding a hand to his eye.

"You will regret trying to take over my business. And if *she* is hurt in any way, you will not survive," John promised.

Taking her had controlled John, but was it worth it? It's time for an exit strategy, thought Jacob.

John had an idea of what the other man was thinking and would not stop Emma and her team from taking him into custody. Jacob would pay for taking someone who meant the world to him.

Present day

The new guard moved Harden back to his cell. Once he was secured inside, he said, "I have taken over all of the businesses."

"Then we lay low for a while," said John. He wanted to wait for news on the children. *She must be found.*

CHAPTER 6

Back at their hotel, Emma was studying the information they had gotten from Jacob. "Where do we start?" she asked.

"We map it out and get the Pinkerton offices in those areas to begin their reconnaissance," Cole said.

"Will we be involved?" asked Jeremy.

"Yes, we'll see this through."

"I'll notify Clair that we'll need safe houses in each area fully staffed with medical professionals," Emma said.

Cole nodded. "We'll start with travel to the closest location and then we'll send telegrams from there."

"Not from here?" asked Emma.

"No, it's better that we're far away from this area before we send anything. Get organized; we'll be leaving soon."

They retrieved their gear and went down to the lobby. Their wagon was parked out in front of the hotel; they would drive themselves.

"Dinner?" Jeremy asked.

"We will get food for the road. Better to camp out. It'll probably be safer," said Cole.

They took turns driving the wagon. While Cole was handling the horses, Jeremy and Emma sat in the back talking.

"You were pretty angry back there," he commented.

"I know. It's the kids. Their involvement heightens my emotions."

"Are you sure you want to be in on the raids?" He was concerned about the things they would see.

"No, I want to be there. And the others…" Her voice trailed off.

"Others?"

"The ones who have been sent outside the country," she explained.

Jeremy shook his head. "We don't have the resources for that. We'll turn that over to the agencies in those locations."

"Jeremy, even if it's only one child at a time, we need to continue."

He took her hand tightly in his. "We'll do that," he pledged. "We'll follow every lead we get from our raids."

"We need the other teams to be briefed on what we're looking for. If we waste this opportunity, we may never find them."

They mulled that over and when they stopped for the horses to get a break and for them to have a snack, they discussed the information with Cole.

He nodded. "This may take years."

"Yes," Emma said as her eyes teared up. She wiped them away quickly and took the sandwiches Jeremy handed to her.

"Pull out the list," Cole said. They looked at it. All the towns outside of New York City were listed; those would be their first stops.

At the first town with a telegraph office, they stopped and Cole arranged for Pinkerton agents to start watching the houses they were targeting. They arrived at the first location in Newark, NJ, an empty warehouse a few blocks from the bordello, for a meeting with the area Pinkerton agents.

Emma dressed as a boy and kept her hat pulled down low.

These men didn't know her and she didn't want any arguments about her role in the raids.

"Patterson," Cole started, "where do we find them in the house?" The men had been watching the bordello.

"Cole, it is good to see you," Patterson said and pulled out his notebook. "We could use the support. We have a large number of areas to cover. The bordello we are targeting has a basement. The only way in is through windows. We think it might be where they are keeping the kids. But there's a problem."

Cole frowned. "What's that?"

"It's the size of the windows. We don't have any men small enough to get in," Patterson explained.

"I think I have the right person for that." Cole looked over his shoulder and he waved Emma over to them.

"He is the right size," Patterson said. He then realized the person in front of him was not a man. "But…"

"Yes?" prompted Cole.

Patterson lowered his voice and exclaimed, "But he is a she! How can we send a woman into that environment without backup?"

"You'd be surprised; she's quite capable," Cole replied.

"And she won't be alone," Jeremy said, walking up beside her.

"I am Jeremy and this is Emma."

"Patterson," he said. If Cole recommended them, he wouldn't question them. "We'll wait for you to report back before we make any plans to enter."

"Do you have drawings of the building?" Emma asked.

"We were able to get them." Patterson turned and pulled out a set of drawings and walked to their makeshift desk. He pointed to it and said, "You see the basement windows here? They're located at the base and go around the building."

"They'll be locked," said Jeremy.

"We should be able to take care of those," Emma commented.

"Has anyone tried to look into the windows to see if anyone is there?"

"They keep them covered or painted," admitted Patterson.

"Then how do you know Emma and Jeremy won't be crawling into an area where people will see them?" asked Cole.

"We don't," Patterson admitted. "We are hopeful, given the nighttime entry, that we will not have any trouble. Also, this is not a rescue mission—reconnaissance only. Once we have the information, we will return and get any children out."

Cole considered this plan without comment.

"Are we ready?" asked Patterson.

Emma looked at Jeremy and held out her hand. Jeremy took it; they would do this together. "Yes," Jeremy said. "We're ready."

They looked at Cole. He didn't like the plan, but he wouldn't stop it. "Okay."

Patterson, Cole, Emma, and Jeremy approached the targeted bordello. Emma and Jeremy had their hats pulled down low as they got their final instructions. "Go over the back fence; there's a spot where the guards don't walk. There are four windows in that area at ground level." Patterson handed them a rope with knots to help with climbing.

Emma and Jeremy nodded and started toward the fence.

Cole stopped them. "If it gets dangerous, stop and back out. We can take it from there."

Emma and Jeremy nodded, understanding his concern, as the Pinkerton agent wished them good luck.

The agent had told them there were guards on the front door but this side was unmonitored. As they reached the fence, Jeremy cupped his hands to allow her to stand and get a view over the fence into the small yard.

"We're good," she whispered.

He took that as an okay to give her a push up and over. She grabbed the top, swung her legs over the tall block fence, and jumped down. The rope weighed heavily on her shoulder; she took it off and threw it over for him. Bracing herself, she held onto one side of the rope while he climbed over. Once he was on top, she retrieved the rope. He jumped down and helped her gather it up.

Keeping their heads lowered, they looked around for any additional guards. They heard voices and stayed close to the fence, but the guards didn't walk into the area where the two were hiding. When the voices could be heard drifting away, they moved silently, crouching down, staying in the shadows as they made their way to the house. Bushes were bunched up around the base of the home. Emma put her hand behind them to see if she could find the windows. They went about five feet from the back left corner and she whispered, "Got it. That means the next one is probably about five feet down."

Jeremy nodded and knelt to look. "Help me pull this back," he said, indicating the bush. They gripped it and pulled it toward them. It gave her enough room to check out the window.

"What do you think?" he asked, still holding the bushes away from the window.

She pressed her ear against it. "I don't hear anything."

"Let's check the ones down this wall," he suggested. They went to each one and she checked—still nothing.

"The front is quite busy. They may be keeping them quiet with drugs."

"Shall we chance it?" he asked.

"Weren't we supposed to let Pinkerton know before we go in?" Emma reminded him.

"We don't know anything yet," he reasoned. This was supposed to be a fact-finding mission.

"We'll go in." They went back to the first window and she looked at it. "It isn't meant to open," she observed.

"No lock?"

"No." She pulled out her knife and dragged it around the sash to remove the paint sealing the window. The glass was old and it popped out rather easily. "Shh," she whispered and reached in to pull the inside covering back. The room was dark and she couldn't see much from her location. "I need to go in." The window would allow someone her size, but Jeremy wouldn't fit.

"I'll be here. Don't take any chances. Just get information and come out. Our men are waiting."

Kissing him quickly, she said, "I will." Jeremy handed her the rope, and she dropped it inside the window and climbed down into the dark room. As she lowered herself, she tried to find a foothold when she felt something soft. She eased back, trying to find something more stable. When a solid surface was found, she bent down and felt the soft material. She took a moment to light her portable kerosene lighter. When the room was illuminated around her, she was shocked at the number of children. There were so many that there were no pathways to walk.

Are all of them sleeping? she thought. Then the smell hit her. She wrinkled her nose. The odors in the room were not pleasant: urine and other bodily waste smells. The kids were so drugged they were messing themselves. *Horrible people,* she thought again.

"Are you here to help?" a small voice reached her ears.

She turned toward it and found a tiny girl. Emma made her way over to her, careful not to step on the other children.

"Hi, little one," she said, kneeling down and pushing the girl's brown wispy hair back on her forehead. "How are you not asleep?"

"The medicine they give us makes me throw up." The girl started to cry softly. "They'll be mad and hit me for throwing up again."

"No, little one, they won't. We'll be taking you out tonight."

She stopped crying suddenly. "Tonight?"

"Yes. I'm going to go back out through that window and we'll come back for all of you."

"No!" The girl started crying again.

"Shh, we don't want to be heard," Emma cautioned softly, looking around.

"*Please* take me with you!" she begged in a rush. "I can hang on tight. My brother could tell you. I clung to his back all the time when he was climbing trees."

Emma looked doubtful but said, "We'll try." She pulled the cover down, looking for restraints on the girl. *They don't appear to tie them up; the drugs must be very strong.* Emma sat the girl up and turned her back to her. "Wrap your arms around my neck," she said softly. The girl did as she was asked and Emma wrapped her legs around her body.

"I'm going to stand up now, and you must hang on tight."

"I will." The little girl's grip tightened, almost strangling her, but Emma didn't stop.

Emma pulled twice on the rope to let Jeremy know she would be climbing up. He would start pulling when he felt the rope go taut. It was harder with her added companion, but Emma resolved to get them both out. Her muscles strained as she reached the window. She said over her shoulder, "I'm going to boost you up. The man's name is Jeremy. Give him your hands."

Emma stopped and boosted the little girl on her back up to the window. Her muscles strained as she clenched the rope with one hand and pushed the girl up with the other.

Jeremy saw movement and reached in to help Emma come out. The size of the hand surprised him, but he didn't question it and pulled the little girl through the window. He moved her behind him and held a finger to his lips. She nodded and waited. When Emma's hands could be seen, he grabbed them and pulled her through. Once she was out, Jeremy bent down, took the girl onto his back, and whispered to Emma, "Ready?"

"Yes," Emma said and rolled up the rope.

They ran for the fence, where Emma threw the rope over and looked at Jeremy.

"You first," he told Emma. He boosted her to the top. Once she was there, he held up the little girl to have Emma take her. She reached out and pulled the girl up and put her on her back. Next, Jeremy jumped up. She swung the rope over and climbed down, with Jeremy holding the rope taut for support. They pulled it down and the three of them made their way down the long alleyway. They ran the blocks back to the warehouse. The men outside opened the door and let them in.

"Mr. Patterson!" Emma called. He turned with a smile on his face, happy to see them. That smile faded when he saw who was with them. "Emma, we told you to look around only!"

"I couldn't just leave her." Emma knelt to put the girl down and moved away so he could see her.

Patterson ran over to them. "Sophy!" he said in disbelief.

"Uncle Lucas?"

"Oh, Sophy," he said crying and taking her into his arms.

"Uncle?" mouthed Emma.

Cole had walked up and seen the reunion. "Yes. He's been looking for her and volunteered for this position."

Emma watched them. She looked over at Cole. "We have to move soon," she said. "There's a limited window of time to get the kids out."

Mr. Patterson hugged Sophy to him tightly and then called out, "Ted, come take her. Have the doctor check her out."

There were medical services arranged in the warehouse so the children could be cleared before being transported to a safe house. Cole had gotten in touch with Clair and she had quickly arranged homes in the areas where the children could be housed safely until their parents were found.

"But I don't want to go," Sophy said. These people were strangers to her.

"Just for a little while and then we'll get you home. Okay?" he implored.

Sophy nodded slowly and went reluctantly with Ted. They

only made it a few feet when she stopped and turned. "Wait!" she called. "Emma!"

"Yes?" Emma asked and went to her. She bent down and listened intently.

"The woman with the tall hair, with white running through it and a large bosom. She's in charge. And she's mean."

"Is she the one who did this to you?" Emma asked, touching the bruises on the girl's arms.

"Yes. She likes to hit us."

"We'll look for her. Thank you, Sophy," said Emma sincerely.

"I held on tight," Sophy said.

"Yes, you did, little one, you did," Emma said and touched her face. "You go with Ted now."

Sophy nodded and took his hand. Ted's nose wrinkled as he got a whiff of her. Emma's mouth turned down and she mouthed, "Throw up and urine."

He shook his head and took her to the doctor.

Patterson looked at Emma. "Why did you bring her out? Why her?"

"She was lucky. She couldn't tolerate the drugs. She was the only one awake. I don't think she would've survived the night."

"Thank you for going against my orders and bringing her here," he said sincerely.

Emma nodded.

He shook off the worry for Sophy and said, "Tell me how many."

"At least twenty boys and girls, various ages. They're being kept heavily sedated. Maybe with morphine."

"Are they restrained?"

"No, I think they're counting on the drugs to keep them quiet."

"Guards in the room?"

"No. Again, I think they are counting on the sedation." She frowned.

He noticed and asked, "What is it?"

"The last kidnapping case, several overdosed. I hope we get all of them out alive."

Plans were made and the men dispersed around the house. "Once we get through the front doors, here," Patterson said, pointing to the drawing, "Emma and Jeremy, you'll need to get to the basement door. You'll have a team with you."

He eyed everyone. "One thing, there might be children upstairs in the rooms."

"Horrible, but you're right," agreed Cole. "Once we get the basement under control, Emma, you, and Jeremy search the rooms. We'll hold everyone downstairs."

Their plans in place, they approached from the front and the back of the house, expecting guards at both entrances. Emma, Cole, and Jeremy were with the group entering from the front. A large group of armed men went in first, crashing the door open.

The door splintered open and they rushed in. The foyer and sitting room were full of couples, some dancing, some talking. At the first sound of the door, the people stopped and stared before running toward the exits. The agents grabbed them easily and contained them in the room. The other agents could be heard coming in through the back of the house, gathering up people as they made their way forward.

Emma and Jeremy came in behind them and ran toward the basement door.

"Wait right there, this is a private residence!" called a voice.

Emma turned slowly toward the voice and saw a woman with a tall head of hair and a white swatch running through it. Her gaze shifted to her chest. *Sophy was right, that is an impressive bosom.*

"You think so?" Emma asked as she strode three steps toward her, then jumped and kicked her in the face. She went down like a rock. One of the detectives nearby whistled and went to take her into custody.

"Let's go," Jeremy said.

Emma went in first and the others followed her down. She turned up the gas lamps and saw there were more than twenty children.

"We need to get them out of here. The doctor can check them at the warehouse." They had twenty men but would need at least ten more.

"I'll go up and tell Pops we need more people," Jeremy said.

"I'll come with you." Emma followed him upstairs and saw Cole was speaking with local law enforcement, directing them.

"Pops!" Jeremy called. "We need ten more men to help move the kids."

"We have additional officers from the local police station who can help with that," his father called back.

Jeremy nodded and waved the men over to the basement. As the children were brought up, the people in the room watched in horror as babies were moved past them.

"We need to get upstairs," Emma told Jeremy, distracting him from the children.

"Yes. Have you got your gun?" he asked.

"Yes."

They approached the second level and split up. The adults appeared to have exited. *Probably due to the ruckus downstairs.* What they were looking for were scared children.

They checked in closets and under beds, speaking softly, trying to find anyone who might be hiding. There were none on the second floor, so they headed up to the third floor and split up again. Jeremy called down the hall, "Emma, over here." When she entered the room, she saw him holding up a bed skirt.

"There's one under here," he directed.

"I'll take care of this one if you want to check the other rooms," she said.

Emma bent down and what she saw broke her heart. It was a girl of about seven wearing a negligée meant for an adult. She was huddled in the corner, shaking like a terrified rabbit.

"Honey, come on out," Emma called softly, lying on her stomach to slide under the bed.

"Don't call me that. They call me that," the girl stuttered.

"Okay, can you tell me your name?" Emma asked, her voice soft.

"Mary," she said, her answer so low, Emma had to strain to hear it.

"My mama's name was also Mary." When she didn't move, Emma started again. "Mary, I'm not with those terrible people. I'm with the Pinkertons and the police. We've found the other kids downstairs and we're moving them to a safe place."

"Safe place? Away from here? Away from those men and women?" Mary asked, hope sounding in her voice for the first time.

"Yes, away from them. Can you come to me?" Emma asked and put out her arms.

Mary crawled to Emma and allowed herself to be pulled out. Once she had hold of her, Mary plucked at her garment "Is there something else I can wear?" she asked. "This is the only thing they would give me."

"I think there must be something. Let me check." She looked in the closet and found a man's shirt. "I think this will work."

Emma walked to the bed and, while she helped Mary change, she noticed the bruises covering the girl's body. She so badly wanted to cry but she held it in as she helped her put on the large shirt. It reached past the girl's knees. She rolled up the sleeves and asked, "How is that?"

"Better," Mary admitted.

"Let's head down."

Mary gripped Emma's hand tightly and kept her face buried in Emma's side. "Don't worry, they won't get you," Emma reassured the girl.

"You think not?" said a male voice from behind them. Emma kept her hand in her pocket and turned, keeping Mary close.

The tall thin man demanded, "Give her to me."

Mary was muttering into her side, "Not him, not him, not him!"

Emma just pulled her closer. "I will not give her to you. I suggest you leave while you can."

"Or what," he sneered.

"I'll have to kill you," she said fiercely.

"You kill me? I don't think so." He pulled out a knife and started toward her.

"Don't think you weren't warned," Emma said and fired through her pocket. The bullet met the mark and the man went to his knees with a startled expression

"You shot me!" he said, looking at the bloody hand he pulled back from his chest.

"Yes." Emma made no move to help him as he fell forward. She didn't stop to see if he was dead; she didn't care.

"Jeremy," she called and when she didn't hear him, she and Mary went room to room. They found him in the last room with a little boy of about five. The boy looked dazed, not quite aware of his surroundings.

"We'll have to carry him. I don't think he knows what is going on," he said and picked him up, motioning for her to go in front of him. They made their way out.

"What about the fourth floor?" Emma asked, looking up at the next set of stairs. She didn't want to put the kids they had with them in additional danger. "Do we leave them here in a room?"

"No! I want to go with you!" Mary cried out and the boy with Jeremy clung tightly to him.

"We go up together," said Jeremy.

They headed up and found several locked rooms. Jeremy kept the children and watched as Emma picked the locks and opened the doors. There weren't any children, but there was morphine and a lot of it. Each room contained more supplies but no more children. Emma let out the breath she was holding. "That's all of them. Let's go."

"No," Mary protested. "There's one more. I hear it at night."

"What do you hear?" asked Jeremy.

"A baby crying."

Emma looked at Jeremy, her eyes wide. She bent down to Mary. "Do you know where the baby might be?"

Mary walked to the closet, tapped the wall, and knelt down in front of it. Emma went to her and asked. "What is that room?"

"It's the punishment room. If you don't do as they ask with the men, you got put in there."

"Emma, Mary, come away from there." Jeremy handed the boy he was holding to Emma and directed them to back up. He kicked the door and kicked again. It came apart and he removed the remnants. It was a small closet, and dark. He stepped a few feet in and Emma handed him her kerosene lighter.

He lit it and examined the room. It was covered in feces and there was a small pile of rags in the corner. "Nothing here," he said, "just rags."

She peered in and saw something. "Jeremy! The rags moved!"

He stepped carefully, trying to not step on them. He moved them around and found a tiny girl who appeared less than a year old.

"Emma, there's a baby girl here." *They must have left her here to die*, he thought. He picked her up carefully and she whimpered. "It's okay, we'll get you out."

They walked downstairs with their bruised and broken children. Emma and Jeremy were barely holding in their emotions as they cradled them. Mary had become a permanent appendage on Emma's side.

Cole saw them on the stairs and ran up. "Any trouble?"

"I left a man on the third floor," Emma reported.

"What happened?"

"A gentleman had a notion to keep little Mary here with him."

"And?"

"I disabused him of that notion."

"I will check it out." Cole headed upstairs.

Jeremy looked over with raised eyebrows.

"Later," she mouthed and hugged the two children close to her.

Jeremy continued to cradle the baby.

A detective downstairs was taking names and arranging for transport to the safe houses. "Three more?" he asked. "Do you want us to transport them?"

"No," Jeremy said, surprising Emma. "We'll take these three over."

"Okay." He noticed how small the child was that Jeremy carried. "How old?" he asked.

"I think less than a year."

His face twisted. "And this is just the start." They had been told there would be many more raids that night, possibly more after that.

"Yes," Emma said. "See if you can find any accounting books in the manager's office. I'd expect these transactions had to be recorded. There'll be a significant amount of money to be tracked."

Jeremy stayed quiet, holding the baby close as they headed to the warehouse. The children needed a doctor's care.

"You heard the guard, Jacob, say they didn't even have to use the schools, that kids were just there for the taking," muttered Jeremy.

"So many immigrant communities don't trust law enforcement, so they may also be under-reporting the kidnappings."

"Yes." They finished the last block and the men at the warehouse door held it open so they could enter.

They were waved over to the large area where the children had been staged. The doctor was shaking his head and covering one of them as they walked up. Emma and Jeremy averted the children's eyes. The body was moved out of the area.

The doctor walked over to them. "Who do we have here?" he asked in a kindly voice, his eyes showing worry.

"This is Mary," Emma said. "She is a brave girl."

Mary kept her head hidden in Emma's hip. "Well, Mary, will you come to me?" The doctor asked, "I need to make sure you're okay."

Emma leaned over and whispered in the doctor's ear. He started visibly at the news. "Yes. I'll have to check that." *Sexual activity in a child that age could be damaging.* He could only hope she would be able to have children later. "And the other two?" he murmured.

"We aren't sure. They'll have to be checked," she said.

"Can you stay so they feel secure? I don't want to scare them."

"Of course." The small boy she held was coaxed away by a nurse.

Mary went with the doctor and another nurse.

Jeremy continued to hold the baby. Emma watched him, concerned about his intense concentration. The doctor distracted her and called, "Emma, can you follow me? Mary is asking for you."

"Of course." She went over to the room where they were going to examine the girl.

Mary looked at Emma. "Will you stay with me?" she asked. She had been left alone with too many men to trust the doctor. She held her hand and Emma took it. The doctor walked over to them and gently asked, "Mary, can you tell me what happened to you?"

"No, no, no," the girl moaned.

"Did the men touch you?"

She nodded, not raising her head from Emma's chest. "Can you tell me where?" She pointed to her chest and between her legs.

"Just touch?"

"Yes, they said something special was planned tonight."

Emma wanted to crush the girl to her. She held off. All she

could think about was, *What if we had delayed our arrival by even a day?*

As they finished up, the doctor asked, "Mary what's your last name?"

"Connelly."

"Do you know where you were taken from?"

"I was in the front yard of my house. They grabbed me and put a bad-smelling rag over my mouth. I woke up in a building like this one."

"Do you know what city or town you were taken from?"

"Buffalo, New York."

"Do you know your parents' names?"

"Mama and daddy," she said and sniffed.

"That's all I need for now. I understand there's food if you're hungry." Her stomach rumbled in response.

"Yes," she said, turning red. Mary and the nurse went to find some food.

Emma went back to where Jeremy sat. He still had the baby in his arms.

The doctor walked up to them. "Let me see the little one." Jeremy's eyes were wet and he continued to rock the baby.

"Jeremy?" asked Emma quietly.

He shook his head and said hoarsely, "She isn't breathing."

"Jeremy, can you bring her over here? I need to check to make sure she is okay," suggested the doctor.

Jeremy cradled the girl to him and walked to the doctor. There was a bit of a struggle to get the baby from him. Once he released her, the doctor laid her on the table. He listened for her heartbeat and started to palpitate her chest.

Jeremy couldn't watch and put his head on Emma's shoulder. There was a sudden gasp from Emma. Jeremy lifted his head and turned back toward them. The girl's chest was rising and falling.

"Is she ok?" asked Jeremy, wiping the tears from his eyes.

"This young girl has had too many drugs, and it depressed her respiratory system. We will have to monitor her and give her a number of massages. Nurse!" he called. He gave her instructions. "And make sure she is fed."

"Thank God," Jeremy whispered, shuddering against her.

"Yes," Emma said, crossing herself.

They went to help monitor the other children. One had perished but they had managed to save so many.

A couple walked into the warehouse. "Emma! Jeremy!" They heard a voice call out. Turning toward the doorway, Emma called, "Clair! Thomas! When did you get here?" Jeremy and Emma ran over to greet the new arrivals. Even in these circumstances, Clair was elegantly dressed and her hair coiffed.

"We were here earlier but we wanted to get the safe house ready," Clair explained.

Thomas said, "We have staff coming in from our New York residence until we can staff locally."

"How many?" Clair asked grimly, looking around.

"Close to thirty," Emma replied.

"Any deaths?" she asked quietly.

"One," Emma said bitterly. "The others will have to be monitored closely as they are coming off the morphine."

"Yes," Clair murmured. "We have a group of five nurses secured for the house."

The doctor walked up to the group. "I'll be accompanying them. I'm Dr. Phillips, and you are?"

Clair held out her hand. "Clair Callahan and this is my husband, Thomas. We run a charity that helps people who need it."

"These kids will need it. How far is it from here?" Dr. Phillips asked.

"We managed to secure a location in residential areas, about five miles from here," said Thomas.

"Will there be enough room for all the children?"

"Yes," said Clair. "We hope to keep them together in case the older children may be able to identify the younger ones."

Dr. Phillips nodded and said, "We will let you know when they are stable enough to travel."

"Thank you, doctor," said Clair sincerely. They watched him go back to caring for the children.

"I'm so glad you were local," Emma said to Thomas.

"Us too."

"Is Mary Elizabeth with you?" Emma asked. They had a baby the same age as her niece.

"Yes, she is with her nanny at the house"

"Oh, nice—how is she?"

"She's busy. Running everywhere. Running all of us ragged."

"And she has you wrapped around her finger."

"Yes," he admitted with a laugh.

It was nice to have a conversation not related to kidnapped children. Jeremy seemed to relax as he listened to the news. They hugged and said they would see them soon. At that time, Clair and Thomas departed to the house to meet the first group of children. Jeremy and Emma stayed behind and only left when the final child was moved to the safe house. The children would stay there for weeks, possibly months, until the families could be located.

The two couples met the next day at Emma and Jeremy's hotel. It was safer for them to meet away from the safe house. The fewer people coming and going, the more likely they could keep its location a secret.

"Thomas and Clair, come in," Emma greeted them. "I've ordered tea for us."

"I'm missing home, but we need to be here," Clair said, sitting down.

"How did the other raids go?" Thomas asked.

Jeremy sat back. "Cole sent several telegrams, and more kids were found at the different locations. They're being moved to the safe houses you have set up." He then added, "We expect that they'll have similar setups. You got the list we sent?"

"Yes," Clair said, "Thomas is managing that for us."

Thomas took over from there. "I've located houses in each of the areas. We've dispersed staff to those cities to do the setup and wait."

"If they're not needed?"

"We'll close down and move to the next location."

A knock sounded at the door and Jeremy got up to answer it. He showed the waiter into the room with a tray of tea and cakes. When the waiter left, they began to speak again.

"These are just lovely," Clair remarked as Emma poured the tea and handed the cakes out. "I'm hoping we don't have any cases involving children in the future."

"Agreed," Emma said, watching Jeremy. She was concerned about his reaction to the baby last night.

Jeremy said, "The baby…"

"The small baby girl?" asked Clair.

"Yes. How is she?" he asked, averting his eyes.

"The nurses stayed with her all night. Her breathing became steadier and they got some milk into her. The doctor thinks she'll make it."

Jeremy let out a breath he didn't know he was holding. "Good."

The conversation moved on to other things. Thomas and Clair said, "We need to head back to the house to check on the kids."

"Oh, we'll be in the area for at least a few weeks. Can you send Jake to us?" Thomas asked. "Pictures would help with the child/parent identification."

"I don't think Jake will be able to be away from home that long," Emma replied.

"Even if Tim was with him?" asked Thomas. Tim, Emma's brother-in-law, could be a stabilizing influence on Jake. When circumstances changed beyond Jake's control, Tim could settle the young man down and help him accept what was happening.

"I don't think it would be fair to pull Jake from his work for that long. Can we find someone local?" Emma asked.

"Is there someone Jake can recommend?" asked Clair.

"He might. I'll see if he can recommend anyone or several people so there won't be a delay," Emma said.

"I'll be happy for this to be over," said Jeremy.

"Yes, but I'm afraid it's just beginning," Clair said, thinking of the damage that had been inflicted on the children.

"Clair," Emma said thoughtfully, walking her out. "Where did you get the people to run the safe-houses on such short notice?"

"My women," Clair said simply.

"From your previous employment?" Emma asked, surprised. Clair had been a Madam at a bordello in the past.

"No." She chuckled. "Though some of them might help if we need them," she said thoughtfully. "It's the women we've helped in our Chicago safe house."

"How did they know we needed them?"

"I told them. As soon as I found out we would need support, I sent telegrams."

"Some of them said they would help?" asked Emma.

"All of them. There was no hesitation. They just needed to be told where to go."

Emma's eyes teared up. "I can't believe it."

"I can. They're strong women who got through something horrible and want to do the same for these kids."

Jeremy stood at the door with Thomas, "Everything's in place?" he asked.

"Yes. We'll handle this one and, hopefully, get the kids home."

Clair and Emma joined them. Jeremy asked quietly, "Would you mind if we check in on the girl?"

"Of course. This is the address." Clair wrote it quickly and handed it to him.

After they left, Emma turned to Jeremy. "Are you still worried about her?"

"Yes," he admitted. "I want to see her for myself. When that little body went cold," he began. He sat down heavily and cried. She went to him quickly and took him into her arms. They sat like that for a long time.

After a while, she said, "We need to do something fun after this. Just for us."

"What?" he said, laying his head on her shoulder. "Murder and kidnapping are not fun?"

She laughed shortly and said, "It certainly has its moments."

"I'll think about it," he murmured.

Emma sat back away from Jeremy and asked. "Did Cole go to the other locations?"

"Yes," he commented.

They didn't sleep much that night, waiting for word on the raids being orchestrated. The next morning, a knock sounded at their door. Emma looked hopeful. Jeremy walked quickly to the door and opened it. A bellman was there with a telegram. Jeremy tipped him quickly and opened it.

"Well?" she asked, following him.

"They were able to get into the targeted houses."

"Kids?"

"Found." He crunched up the telegram. "More dead and abused."

"Jeremy," she said carefully, "we were lucky. We only lost one here."

"One that we know of," he muttered.

"We've gotten into the operations and shut them down," she reminded him.

"They're like cockroaches. They keep showing up, even if we kill their nest."

"Yes," she admitted. "This is horrible and we will do what we can to stop them. Clair will continue to open up activity locations to keep children off the street."

"And still that will not be enough," he said bitterly.

"No," she agreed. "It won't be."

They got some rest before they headed to the safe house. On their way there, he stayed quiet, his mind on that baby girl. The location was in a neighborhood with older homes. There weren't any crowds or noise. It was chosen due to its quiet nature. Emma was dressed in her boy's clothes. She and Jeremy pulled their hats down and approached the door. They knocked. "The guards are well hidden," Emma murmured.

Jeremey nodded and said in the same tone, "Yes, one at the corner, a lady with a baby carriage in front of that house."

The curtains moved on the side of the front door. It opened quickly and Clair said, "Come in."

They followed her direction.

Emma smiled suddenly when she heard children's voices. "They're awake!" she said.

"Yes, and boisterous. All have eaten several meals. We've had to send out for more groceries."

"That is wonderful," commented Emma, relieved.

Thomas called from the stairs, "Were you wanting to check on this little girl?"

They turned quickly and saw the small girl turn and grin at Jeremy. She held out her arms to him and he immediately took her from Thomas. Emma grinned when she saw her grab Jeremy's hair and pull.

Clair watched them as she put her arms around Emma's shoulder and pulled her close. "That seems to be helping him."

"Yes," she murmured. "This has been hard on him. He thought the baby died in his arms. It just wrecked him."

"I'm glad you came by," Clair said as they watched him. "Come in and sit down," she requested.

"Have you started to compile the names and locations where the kids came from?" asked Emma.

Jeremy sat across from them, still playing with the baby. Clair started to speak when a loud argument interrupted her. "Just a minute," Thomas said and he left to settle a fight that had erupted between the children.

"Yes," Clair continued, answering questions about the children. "I have them here," she said and handed it to Emma.

Emma flipped through the pages. "Most are from around here. That's good."

"I wish we could contact the families now."

"We need the pictures," Emma commented. "We want them to end up with the right families."

"Yes," Clair said regretfully. She was a parent and knew any delay could be heartbreaking.

Mary Elizabeth ran out of the kitchen toward Emma. She picked her up. "How wonderful to see you!" Emma exclaimed.

"Where are you headed after this?" asked Clair, watching her play with the small girl.

"It sounds like Cole and you have the other houses under control and I think Jeremy needs a break from cases involving children."

"Yes, do you have something in mind?" her friend asked, thinking it would be a vacation.

Emma said, "No, I was looking at this." She juggled the girl and reached into her pocket for a folded article.

Clair took it and began to read. "A serial killer, Jack the Ripper, is under investigation." She noticed where it was and asked, "In London?"

"It wasn't that. I saw that they're using new investigative skills. I thought we could look into that."

"And this would be a vacation with you not getting involved in the case?" Clair asked doubtfully.

"I need a break also," Emma said.

"What will you do first?"

"Go home," Emma said simply.

"When will you bring this up to Jeremy?"

"On the way there. A nice long train ride where he won't be able to avoid me."

"Good luck with that."

Jeremy was playing with the baby and Thomas sat down next to him. "The women are talking," he commented.

Jeremy looked up. "I see that."

"You think it's about us."

"Maybe," he said, watching Emma smile and put her fingers to her lips. *She's planning something*, he thought.

Clair and Thomas went to look in on the children. Emma and Jeremy sat in the sitting room. "Where are you thinking after here?" he asked

She had thought to wait but told him her plan. "I was thinking we might go to London." She went on to describe the trip.

Jeremy listened. Normally, he was on the same page, but an overseas trip was not what they needed. "Emma," he said stopping her. "No."

"No?" she asked, confused.

"No. I want to go somewhere secluded, a beach or something like that where we can just hang out, watch the water, and be together."

She thought about it. "I think you're right. Do you have a location in mind?"

"No," he admitted, "but Pops might."

"Hmm, I think it sounds wonderful," she said sincerely.

He grabbed her in a hug and swung her around. "I'm so happy you are with me," he said.

"Me too," she said, returning his hug.

The nurse listened to the conversation and stepped back with a small smile.

CHAPTER 7

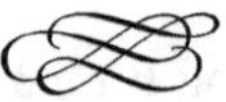

Jeremy and Emma finished up their day and headed back to the hotel. They had just settled in for the evening when there was a knock on the door. She looked over at Jeremy and saw lines had set around his mouth where they hadn't been before. Emma's mood had improved with the raids and the news that more children had been found.

She shook her head. *I have to get him away soon.*

"I'll get it," said Emma and went to the door, finding a bellhop with a package for her. She took it and gave him a tip. Turning it over in her hands, she walked back to the sitting room.

Jeremy sat up and rubbed a hand through his hair. "What is it?"

"I don't know, but I am going to find out." She tore it open quickly.

He closed his eyes again as he listened to her rip open the envelope, his mood still down.

"It appears to be a vacation," she said, looking through the papers. Included in them were train tickets and an address of a cottage on the beach.

"What?" he asked and moved to her side to read the documentation.

True to her word, it was a beach vacation.

"This is perfect," said Jeremy as he read the documents. It was just what they needed.

Emma frowned; it was too perfect. Everything was prearranged. *Why?* She looked over at Jeremy; his hands holding the package were shaking. She knew at that moment that it didn't matter where the trip had come from. She would do what he needed and go away with him. Smiling brightly, she asked, "Do we pack?"

He smiled back genuinely for the first time since the raids had started. "Yes, I do believe we do."

Once they made their decisions, their plans came together quickly. They sent a telegraph to Dora and Cole to let them know they would be going away for a week. In a few days, they were on a train to their destination. They eagerly jumped down from the train when it stopped and went to get their carriage. A man held a sign indicating he was there for them.

"Who arranged this?" she asked herself, not realizing she had said it aloud.

"Must have been Pops," he said, not willing to probe any more deeply. He wanted to just relax and not think for a while. The driver had been arranged and headed out to their rental house.

As they passed a grocer, Emma asked, "We should stop before we become hermits. We'll need food."

"True," he said. He directed the driver to the grocer. They walked into the small store and picked up a basket and got food for the week. Mostly sandwich makings and some baking supplies.

"What are you making?" he asked when he viewed her selection.

"I was thinking about bread and maybe a strudel."

"That sounds wonderful." He looked around. "The fruit is over there."

They finished gathering their items and walked to check out

with the cashier. She was an older woman and had a pleasant smile. "Are you visiting the area?"

"We are," said Jeremy. "We'll also need ice delivered and milk and butter for the week."

"Where are you staying?" the cashier asked.

Emma bumped him when he started to answer. "Sorry," she said. She wasn't sorry and answered for them. "Down at the beach."

"There are several houses there, which one?" the cashier questioned. "I need to know for the deliveries."

Emma turned red and gave her the address.

As they were leaving, an older man moved slowly down the narrow aisle that led to the door and blocked their path. He turned toward them. "Well, hello, am I keeping you?" he asked.

"Just a bit," she answered. "We want to head to the beach."

"Grand day for it," he said. "I hear you're on vacation."

"Yes. We best get going," she said, dragging Jeremy from the store.

"What's the hurry?" he asked.

"Didn't you think they were asking too many questions?"

He chuckled. "No, I think they're very normal for people who live in a small town. They're curious when strangers arrive. Emma, not everything is a case."

"Really?" she teased. "You don't think the cashier had nefarious plans? Or that man outside, was he some kind of undercover spy?"

"Maybe," he responded. "The whole town is a fake, set up for us. Crafted when they heard we were visiting."

"Now that would be interesting," she said, looking back at the town.

He laughed, already enjoying himself. Pulling her with him, he threw an arm over her shoulder and led her to their carriage. "We have our food; now we head to our beach house."

Back in the carriage, they waited expectantly for their destination. As they pulled onto the beach, there were many cottages spread out. "There, that must be it!" she exclaimed. The house looked like it had been there for a while.

"We can only hope the inside is better than the outside," he said.

"Agreed.'"

They thanked the driver and took the food in. He called after them, "I'll return to take you to the station in five days."

They turned back and nodded their agreement, sending him a wave goodbye. They entered the house with their packages and looked around. The house was surprisingly immaculate.

"Wow," Jeremy said.

"Indeed. I expected to spend the first two days cleaning." She laughed. "Let's head to the kitchen and see if a similar job was completed." The door to the kitchen opened easily, revealing an old but clean kitchen. They set their packages on the long wood table and looked around.

Jeremy walked over to the sink and turned on the water. "Running water at least."

"And an ice box," she opened it, "and it has ice."

He walked over and looked into the box. "Well, good."

"It is. Who set all this up?"

"Pop's may have…" Jeremy suggested again, but he was starting to doubt it. He pushed the thoughts out of his head. "Oh well, we're here and it's a vacation."

She put her fingers to her lips and stopped herself. Jeremy needed this week, no matter who planned it. She put on a smile and dropped her hand to her side "Let's go up for a nap."

He caught her meaning and smiled broadly as he took her hand. The bed upstairs was comfortable, and they stayed there for a while.

Afterward, she propped her chin on his chest. "How about a snack and a walk on the beach?"

"Now that's a plan."

She pulled on pants and borrowed a shirt from Jeremy, leaving it untucked. Jeremy pulled on loose pants and left his shirt untucked as well. They headed downstairs, barefoot and carefree.

It was three in the afternoon and there was plenty of time to enjoy a snack and a walk on the beach. The sun was low in the sky and the water was inviting. "Race you to the water," he said. They ran to it, sitting down on the sand to roll up their pants.

Emma splashed quickly into the breaking waves, enjoying the cool water against her legs. "Come on in!" she called. "The water's amazing." He didn't move; instead, he watched her. The picture she made with the ocean at her back.

"Come on!" she called again.

He ran down to join her in the water. It was perfect as he took her hand and walked down the beach. They stayed until the sun started going down. After, they were pleasantly worn out and returned to the cottage. Once on the shaded porch, they collapsed on the old wooden chairs that must have been there since the house was built.

"That was fun," she said, throwing her arms over her head and leaning back against the wall.

"It was," he agreed, "and something we needed."

"Yes." She knew it was too early to talk about the events they had witnessed and she wanted to rest and relax. Instead, she looked over at him and asked "Want some lemonade?"

"Yes, I do," he stated.

When she made to stand, he stopped her, "No, stay here, I can get it."

"If you're sure…"

"I am." He pulled himself up and headed into the house. The lemons and sugar were with the supplies they'd brought from the store. He made it quickly, juicing the lemons and adding water and sugar, tasting it as he went. Once satisfied, he organized the pitcher and two glasses for the porch

She rose when she saw him and went to help him put the tray on the table between the two chairs.

"Thank you," he said.

She poured him a glass and he took a long drink. "Thank you," she replied. "I needed that."

"We have to remember to stay hydrated this week; we aren't used to the heat."

They sat watching the sun slowly make its way down. Jeremy looked over at her. "Dinner?"

"Yes."

"I'll go," he said and got up to head to the kitchen.

She didn't argue, just smiled and sat back. It was nice to have a place to themselves. The boarding house was wonderful, but it was a shared home. She would have to encourage Jeremy to do this a few times a year. Looking around, she didn't think he would disagree.

The door slammed as he exited the house with sandwiches overflowing with ham, tomatoes, and lettuce.

"Yum," she said. "That looks amazing."

He handed her a sandwich and took his. He chewed and watched the water. "You know, I could get used to this," he said, mirroring her thoughts.

"I was thinking we could do this a few times a year," she said.

"Hmm," he said. "I was thinking we might buy a bungalow like this. For us to rent out when we aren't here."

"It would be amazing to have a place like this that's all ours."

CHAPTER 8

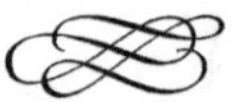

The next morning, Emma left Jeremy to sleep and took her coffee out to the porch to watch the sun come up. She sat and enjoyed the sounds of the water. Stirring herself, she stood and noticed something out of the corner of her eye. *What is that?* she wondered and headed over to investigate it. Bending down, she found a basket of baked goods and fishing poles, and—from the smell—she deduced what was probably a bucket of bait.

She straightened and went over to the basket. There was a card attached to the top. She opened it and read, "Welcome to our small town. Enjoy these. And try fishing today!"

So thoughtful, she thought. It was so nice the townspeople would do this and provide the fishing poles. The bait can wait until later. Baked goods first. She headed inside, where Jeremy was leaving the kitchen.

"What's that?" he asked.

"This?" She held up the basket. "Someone left it outside with fishing poles and bait."

"Fishing poles?"

"Yes. I guess they have our activity for today laid out for us." She started toward the counter with the basket.

"Let me help you with that," he said. He took the side opposite her and helped place it on the counter. "There's a lot of food here," he commented, looking at the variety of baked goods. He picked up a muffin.

"Yes, it was nice of them to send it," she commented but continued to study it thoughtfully.

"Emma? What are you thinking?"

She shook it off. "Nothing, just that I want that exact muffin." She smiled and took the one he was holding.

"Hey!" he protested, laughing.

"I told you, I found the perfect one!" she teased, keeping custody of the muffin and backing away.

He lunged for her and she dodged him, running into the living room. "You better not eat that," he warned.

"This?" She pretended to take a bite. Taking pity on him, she tossed it back and he ate it in one bite. She walked to the couch and dropped down. "Do you want to try fishing?"

"Have you fished before?" he asked.

"No, have you?" asked Emma. She hadn't had much interest in the sport.

"I'm a city boy. We get our fish from the market. But I guess we can try. Do we fish from the shore?"

"I think so. I don't think I'd want to be in the water with a hook."

"Okay then, we go fishing."

Emma went to the kitchen and grabbed some more muffins and scones. Lastly, she added a bottle of lemonade to her full bag.

"We need towels," Jeremy called from upstairs.

"Yes," she called back. "And wear the same clothes as yesterday; we don't want to get burned."

"Okay."

She gathered her items and walked out to the porch. Jeremy came out dressed in the same outfit he'd worn yesterday. He carried the towels. "Ready?" he asked.

"Yes." She picked up one of the poles and handed the other to him. She also handed him the bait bucket.

"What is this?" he asked. "And what is that smell?"

"I think it might be the bait. I'm not sure what type it is. "

"I guess we'll find out."

They walked down to the water, laid out the towels, and opened up the bait bucket. "That's what I smelled," he commented, his nose wrinkling.

The bait was added to the hooks on the fishing line. "Careful with that," he said as she went to cast it into the ocean.

"You're right." She walked a few yards away and cast her line into the water. Jeremy went next and they waited.

"You can move back and sit," he called.

She nodded, watching her line. When nothing seemed to take the bait, she walked back to the towels. They put the poles in the sand, watching the lines bounce in the water.

"I'm not sure I want to catch a fish," said Emma.

At that moment, her line went taut.

"It's too late to stop now!" He laughed. "Get your pole before it's pulled in."

She did as she was told and wrestled the large fish onto the beach. "That was great!" he said. They looked at it flopping on the sand.

"Now what?" she asked.

"Can you cook it?"

"I don't think so, can you?"

"No. Let's put it back into the ocean."

"Good plan." She reached down to pick up the wiggling fish. She removed the hook and tossed him back into the water. It swam away quickly.

"I think we're done fishing," he commented and removed his pole from the water and placed it beside hers on the sand.

"That's better," she said.

He nodded and watched the water.

Emma took that moment to ask, "How are you?"

He knew what she was really asking and said, "Better, I think."

"What happened back there?"

"My reaction to the baby?"

"Yes."

"When the life seemed to drain out of her… I just thought I was dying also." He looked over at her and said, "You seemed better the minute we got Sophy out. Why?"

"I think my frustrations were relieved when we started to find and rescue the children. And I did get to take a few of the bad guys down in the process."

He nodded and sat quietly. There was a subject he wanted to broach. "If the baby's not claimed, I would like us to take her."

"Us?" Emma had not expected this and turned her gaze toward the ocean. *What does he mean? Marriage? Adoption?* "Are we getting ahead of ourselves? She must have a family looking for her."

"I want you to know, that if she doesn't, I want us to adopt her."

She turned tear-bright eyes toward him and asked, "Are you unhappy with how we are now?"

"No, not at all!" He took her chin when she tried to turn away from him. "I just feel that I want to be there if no one else is. This isn't about our life or our decisions."

"This is about her."

"Yes."

She took a deep breath and said, "If this is what you want, I will support you."

They held hands and thought about their possible future.

CHAPTER 9

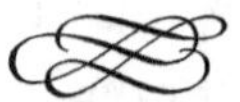

"This week has been ideal," Jeremy said. He and Emma sat on the porch, enjoying the sunset on their final day.

"I agree," she said and let the silence settle around them. A single thought was in her head. *Who set this up? Who was responsible for this ideal holiday? Could this really be Cole? He was busy closing down the houses.* She glanced over at Jeremy and thought whoever did it was worth it. "Jeremy, what are you going to do next?"

"You mean can I handle going back and helping get the kids home?" he asked, knowing she was asking a deeper question.

"I wouldn't have said it that way, but yes," she agreed.

"I just needed some separation, and this week was perfect. I also want to check on the baby girl."

"If her family has been notified and wants her?" she asked softly.

"I only want her to be safe and happy."

"Hmm." She smiled. "Let me know if any arrangements need to be made."

"What about you?" he asked.

"I need to head home. I have some things to work on, and I bet Mr. Pennington has some cases for me."

"Our tickets are for the morning," he mused, looking back out at the water, wishing they could stay longer.

Later, when she put Jeremy on his train, she headed into the town. Her train wouldn't be for a few hours. The town appeared abandoned; there wasn't anyone in the streets. *The store,* she thought, and walked quickly to it. It was locked down; she pressed her face to the window. "Empty? Where are all of the groceries?" she muttered and walked around, peering into different shop windows.

Who could have set something like this up? Who would have the resources to do this? Only one name came to her mind—John. But why the elaborate ruse? He got nothing out of it. She and Jeremy did, but John? She mulled that over and walked back to the train station.

John set this up. I know he did. He set the whole town up. Appeared and disappeared. What does it mean? Why do it?

She was still mulling when she arrived at the station. Her gaze found the ticket booth and she had an idea. "Hello?" she asked.

The clerk walked over. "What can I do for you?"

"Can I exchange my ticket for one to Manhattan, New York?"

"Of course." He processed the ticket and told her the new price. She nodded and pulled out the money. What was her plan? She had no idea. "The town here, is it normally empty?"

He didn't answer. Instead, he motioned to the train. "It's boarding soon," he said. She heard the train whistle.

"Oh, thank you. I'll go now."

She had a ticket in one hand and a bag in another and rushed to the platform. The trip would be longer than her trip home, nearly two weeks. Is *this a bad idea? Too late now,* she thought as she felt the jerk of the train pulling away.

Once she was settled in her private room she thought, *There's a connection. This wasn't about Jeremy and me needing time off. Why had*

John wanted them out of the picture? What didn't he want them to see? She thought about where she'd been when she received the vacation information. They were in a hotel in the same city as the raid. What had happened? Who had she seen? Was there anything unusual?

One thing came to mind: the baby girl Jeremy had rescued. She was just a baby and very different from the typical children the kidnappers were known for taking.

Was the baby John's? The age of the child didn't fit for the time he had been in prison. Did he know something about the parents? It was one thing for him to run things from prison, but he wasn't free to leave.

She leaned her head back on the seat. *Could the girl be a granddaughter? His son or daughter would have to be young,* she thought.

She pulled a book out of her bag but couldn't concentrate on it.

Almost two weeks later, she stepped down off the train, wearing her boy clothes, and pulled her hat low. This time, she would be by herself and she didn't want any trouble. She would still have to contact the warden and request a special search.

The large gate swung open, leading to the foreboding buildings at Sing Sing. When she was led into the administrative building, she requested a meeting with the warden. There was a small room with wooden upright chairs near his office, and she was told to wait.

"You're back," Warden Brush said warmly, recognizing her. "Cole didn't let me know you were coming."

"No, I wanted to follow up on something on my own," Emma murmured. "Can I have the same person who searched me the last time?"

"Of course. Are you sure you want to see him alone?"

"I am," she said. "I also have a favor to ask. I need to leave my things with you until I come out."

"Of course. I can keep them in my office." He bent down to pick them up.

"And," she warned, "there are several knives and a gun in my bag." He looked at her in surprise, then down at the bag.

"Oh, okay, I'll lock it up." He took the bundle to his office and she heard the door click as the lock engaged.

He returned and motioned for her to follow him. Brush had sent for one of the lady officers to conduct the search before Emma went in to see John.

The search was completed quickly and she was escorted to the private visitor room. She entered and saw him at the table, looking much the same as last time. The same guard as last time was in the room with them. She nodded to him as she moved to the table.

"Emma, what a pleasant surprise. You look well rested," John observed.

"Yes, about that. Why? John, I just can't figure out why you did that," she said as she sat down across from him.

"The vacation?" He waited until she nodded before he admitted, "I thought you needed it. After all, you had just been exposed to a traumatizing event. I heard Jeremy especially had a hard time."

"One that was created by you," she accused.

He raised an eyebrow. "As you know, I had nothing to do with that business."

She sat back, took off her hat, and tossed it on the table. "You were involved initially," she stated.

"Was I?" he asked. "I thought we agreed that was Candace."

"Your sister," she reminded him.

"I had no idea she was involved in something like that. We haven't talked in years."

Knowing this line of questioning would not go further, she changed the topic. "Why the ruse?"

"Can't I just be nice?" he asked lightly.

"No, you have an agenda," she said, looking him in the eyes, trying to read his responses.

"Maybe I just want my favor canceled," he suggested.

"Is that it?" she asked and sat back in her chair.

"Yes, I find that it's like the sword of Damocles. I'd rather not wait for it to fall at an inopportune time."

She narrowed her eyes as she evaluated his statement. She didn't believe him; there was something she wasn't seeing. "I'll let that go for now."

He watched her but didn't offer anything more.

"I guess that's it then," she said, reaching over for her hat.

His voice stopped her. "I understand my previous guard got his hands dirty in that mess with the missing children."

She took the hat into her hands, dropped it on her head, and said, "As far as I know, that's under investigation."

"How is my former guard?"

"I don't know anything about that," Emma said noncommittally.

John laughed suddenly. "Will he be joining us here soon?" he asked.

She didn't answer this time and stood. "Bye, John. I hope we don't see each other for a long while."

She hesitated at the door, looked back, and said, dropping the information on him with deadly accuracy, "You have a lovely granddaughter, John."

His eyes widened, showing true emotion. She saw what she wanted to see and left the room. The heavy door closing punctuated her exit with a BANG.

Home, she thought.

Back in the room, John murmured, "Good." He looked at the guard. "Ma did good."

"Yes, she did. She played her part perfectly."

"Did Lidia have any trouble getting the baby and moving to your new home?"

"They are on the way and our baby is well," he said with a grin. "The nurse took care of her at the safe-house until she could be retrieved."

His gaze moved to his son-in-law/guard and said, "I think it's time for us to exit this locale." As he stood, he mused, "I still owe her a favor; this one was significantly bigger than the last one."

The son-in-law nodded his agreement. "Just let me know when and where boss."

"Though, thinking about it, we might wait—just a bit."

"What for?" He was eager to get to his family and away from the prison.

"Jacob is due here soon."

"So, he is. Yes, we should wait."

CHAPTER 10

There was nothing left for her to do but head home. Emma went to the train station and waited for it. *Another week by train*, she thought as she waited to board.

I need to send a telegram. She glanced at the time; it was 3:00, and the train was scheduled to leave at 4:00. *There has to be enough time.* The clerk was at his desk, and she ran and asked him for directions to the telegraph office. "Down there about two blocks. Don't be late," he called, watching her run in the direction he indicated.

She ran until she spotted the small shop, surrounded mostly by dusty roads. She went in and up to the desk. "I need to send a telegraph, please."

"Go ahead," the clerk said. He held a pencil to paper and waited for her response.

She realized where she was and thought about John's reach. *I'll have to send a specific one later.* "Yes, I would like to send it to Clair Callahan. It will read: Jeremy is on the way to you. Stop. He'll be on the evening train in two days. Stop. Please meet him. Stop."

He put down his pencil and asked. "Is that all?"

"Yes, thank you." She glanced at her timepiece and saw she

should be heading to the train station. Paying him quickly, she hurried back in time to board the train before it departed.

Once settled, she thought about the events. *Why did Jacob take the baby? Blackmail? Was that the only way to control John and have the kidnapping operations stay ongoing?*

That telegram would need to be sent as soon as possible. At the next stop, she jumped off the train and ran to the ticket clerk. She found that they also were a telegraph station. "I need to send one out."

"Tell me what you want to say."

"Clair, the baby girl, is she still there? Stop. I think she's related to John, a possible granddaughter. Stop. It's important that I hear back. Stop. On my way home. Stop. Send information there. Stop. Emma."

The clerk took it down and read it back to her.

She nodded and asked, "How much?"

He quoted the price and she paid. *That will do it,* she thought and headed back to the train. Normally, she enjoyed the time alone reading and relaxing, but this time she wanted to know what was happening with that baby. *John must have someone on the way to get her. Jeremy! He got attached—how will he feel? Relieved she got her family or upset we couldn't adopt her? Could it be any baby or just this one at this time?* They would have to talk.

Days later, the train pulled into Chicago. Emma grabbed her bag and ran for the exit. She jumped the steps before anyone could start down. "Young man!" called the porter.

She didn't stop as she ran for the carriages. At the first one she saw, she jumped in and gave him her address. "There'll be a large tip if you get moving quickly," she told the driver. He immediately pulled out and started toward her home.

When they arrived, Emma paid the fee and the promised large tip. She took her bag, jumped out, and headed up the front stairs. She swung the door open and slammed it closed, announcing her arrival.

"What is all the noise?" complained her sister Dora as she came into the foyer. "Emma! You're home!" Dora ran over to hug her sister. After the hug, she pulled away and crinkled her nose. "Ugh. You need a bath."

"I agree," Emma said. "And I need to wash my hair!" She looked around. "But first, have I gotten any telegrams?"

"Yes," her sister said, walking over to a small table located by the staircase. "These came last week." She handed them to Emma and watched as she tore open the one on top.

"Who's that from?" Dora asked. She'd wanted to open them but had respected Emma's privacy.

Emma saw the first one was from Clair. She read quickly and looked at Dora. "I'd inquired about a baby we rescued. We were worried about finding identification on someone so little. Clair said the mother and father were able to identify several birth-marks on her. They took her almost immediately. That's a relief."

It seems *John can make things happen,* she thought.

Dora was frowning and asked, "What was a baby doing as part of this type of operation?"

"I thought the same thing, and I have some further news to share," Emma murmured. Before Dora could follow up, she opened the next telegram. "It's from Jeremy. He got back to the Pinkerton's base and started taking down the areas where the children were kept before moving them to the safe-houses. Looks like a very successful operation." *I wonder if he got to see the baby?*

"Good," said Dora. "These people are like bugs; they keep coming back."

"Yes. Clair has some ideas about that. Community centers like the ones we did here. More important is communication with the parents, especially the poorer ones who don't have anyone to watch their kids. We are also talking to the kids and telling them to stay in groups and watch out for one another."

"Will Clair and Thomas be gone long? That sound like a large project."

"The setup will take a while," Emma admitted. "Her people are in place at the houses and hopefully the identifications won't take long." She looked over at Dora with sudden tears in her eyes. "Do you know who helped set up the houses and take care of the kids?" she asked.

"No, who?" Dora asked, wondering why Emma was crying.

"The women we've helped at Clair's house. She just had to ask and they came. All of the safe-houses are being looked after by them. They're helping get the kids home safely."

Dora wiped her tears. "That's a good thing. Passing on the healing."

Emma dried her face on her sleeve and opened the final telegram. It was from Cole.

Dora noticed the telegram she was opening. "That one came just this morning."

Emma unfolded it. "There's a lot of information in this one," she said as she read. "John Harden was released!"

Dora gasped. She was aware of who and what he was.

"And," continued Emma, "Jacob Smith, the man behind the entire operation and John's man on the inside, was found hanging in his cell."

"Could John have been involved?"

"Yes, I think so." She looked up from the telegram and said, "Dora, that baby was John's granddaughter." Dora gasped in shock and Emma continued to ponder the timing of John's release and the death. She tapped the telegram on her hand.

"Well," said Dora, "good riddance. He was a horrible person!"

"Agreed," her sister said and grinned a slightly evil grin at Dora. "You know, if Cole and Jeremy were here, they'd say the process should have included a judge and jury to find him guilty and punish him."

"Blackmail with a baby. He deserved nothing less," Dora said matter-of-factly.

"Yes."

With that statement, Emma started to climb the stairs and Dora called out in frustration, "You can't leave me with no more explanation than that."

"After my bath," her sister said, not turning around. "Then I'll tell all."

Dora watched her go up and shook her head. *I'll corner her this evening.*

Emma hurriedly undressed and prepared her bath. All she could think of was getting clean. The water was hot and she reclined in the tub with her eyes closed. Time passed quickly and the water started to get cold. She grimaced and admitted to herself that it was time to get out. The towels were fluffy and warm, and she wrapped one around her hair and another around her body before pulling on her robe.

Emma moved slowly to her room and onto her bed. Once there, she took her time to towel dry her hair and brush it. Her energy had drained with each stroke and, when she finished, she laid down. She only meant to take a light nap, but when she woke up, she saw hours had passed.

Time for lunch, she thought. After pulling on a dress and petticoat, she pulled a brush through her hair and braided it, tying it with a red ribbon. Lastly, she pulled on her stockings and boots and headed downstairs.

Dora heard her coming down the stairs and went to wait for her at the bottom. "I have lunch ready; come into the kitchen."

"I wanted to send a telegram," Emma said, looking distracted as she headed toward the door.

"No." Her sister stopped her with a hand on her arm. "Eat first."

Emma looked at Dora's hand and then her face. She could see the beginnings of a slight frown and tightening lips. She wanted to pull away, but then her stomach growled. "There's your answer. Food first," Emma acknowledged as she followed Dora into the kitchen.

Ethyl, a kitchen helper, was wiping down the counters. "Hi, Ethyl," Emma greeted her. "Where's Amy?"

"She's upstairs changing sheets and putting clean towels in the bathrooms."

Emma sat at the table and Dora brought her a thick sandwich and an apple. While she ate, Dora asked, "What happened that made you believe John's related to that baby?"

"It's the only thing that makes sense. John told Jacob to shut the operation down and kill his sister. It should have ended there."

"But?"

"But it continued and John didn't want it to."

"But he was forced to accept it."

"I think so. It was obvious, when we caught Jacob, that it was his operation and not John's."

"And you think the baby was being used to keep John in line?"

"Yes. But I wonder why not kill Jacob sooner? The baby must have kept him in their control."

"And once the baby was safe?"

"He got rid of Jacob."

"How did he find out that she had been rescued in the raid?" her sister asked.

"It could have been anyone; John has a far reach," Emma said simply.

"And you think he used the vacation for you and Jeremy to keep you from realizing what was happening?"

"Yes."

"Did you know it when you went on vacation?"

"I suspected something," Emma admitted.

"Then why go?"

"Jeremy and I needed the time away. The entire operation was weighing on us."

Dora nodded. "Why kill Jacob now if they had him in custody?" she asked.

"John doesn't like loose ends."

CHAPTER 11

$\mathcal{J}$eremy stepped down the steps and off the train. Looking around, he saw Thomas walking toward him.

"Thank you for picking me up," he called.

Thomas smiled. "We received Emma's telegram. It's good to see you. How was the vacation?"

"Good."

"Ready to go to the house?" he asked.

"Yes."

"Want help with your bag?"

"No, I got it."

Thomas had a carriage waiting for them. He was driving, as they wanted to keep people from knowing what the house was being used for. They kept the conversation light as they made their way there. He pulled in and they made their way to the front door. It opened, revealing Clair.

"Jeremy! How good to see you!" He leaned in and kissed her on the cheek. She smiled softly and stepped back to let them in.

The house was significantly quieter than the last time he'd visited. "How many kids are still here?" he asked, looking around.

"Once we got the pictures, the kids were identified quickly. Almost all were picked up," she said.

Jeremy was afraid to ask but forced himself to say, "And the baby?"

Thomas looked at Clair. She answered, "Why don't we go into the sitting room." Jeremy and Thomas followed her and they sat. Tea and cakes were set up on the small table.

Jeremy didn't want food; he wanted to know if the baby girl was alive. "Did she not survive? I thought she was stable when we left."

"Jeremy, no!" Clair said as she moved to sit by him. "We just wanted you to relax before we told you." His eyes went wide and she blurted out, "She's been picked up by her parents."

"Picked up," he said. He was set on the idea of adoption but felt a sense of relief that she'd gone home to her family. A smile returned to his face and he inquired, "Could I have some tea?"

"Of course," Clair said as she took a cup and saucer and poured it for him.

They watched him drink. Thomas asked, "You're all right with the news? You had wanted to see her?"

"I did, but I'm happier that she's with her family. How were they able to prove who they were?"

"We were nervous about that," admitted Thomas, and Clair nodded. "Per Emma's direction, we checked the baby for any identifying marks."

"She had a birthmark, almost perfectly round, located on her upper right leg," supplied Thomas.

"The people that took her were able to identify it?" Jeremy asked.

"Yes, and other things like hair and eye color," Clair added.

"And the baby's reaction to the mother, she laughed when she took her into her arms," Thomas reminded her.

Jeremy felt a weight lift off his shoulders. "So, tell me who's left to be picked up?"

Clair said, "Two little boys. The Pinkertons found their parents and they're on their way to pick them up. They should be here in a few days."

"What will you do then?" asked Jeremy.

"Close the house and head home," Thomas replied.

"You've done an amazing job here."

"Thank you."

"Will you be staying with us long?" Clair asked.

Jeremy looked contemplative. "No, just a few days, and then I think I'll go to the other houses and see if anything else is needed. I'll also check in with Cole and the other Pinkerton operatives."

"We love having you," said Clair, and Thomas nodded his agreement.

"Would you like to meet the boys?" Thomas asked and stood up.

"Yes," Jeremy said and followed his lead.

Thomas took him outside to where the boys were playing in the yard.

The days passed quickly and, as Jeremy was in his room packing to leave, Thomas entered.

"We just got a telegram from Emma."

Jeremy looked up curiously. "Is it from Chicago?" He hoped she had made it back home safely.

"No," said Thomas. "It looks like it's from New York."

"Here? Why wouldn't she tell me she was coming here before going home?" Jeremy asked. "May I read it?"

"I don't think Clair would mind," he said.

"Mind what?" Clair asked, walking the baby Mary Elizabeth in with her.

"A telegram from Emma," explained Thomas.

"No, go ahead and read it," she said as she moved to sit in the chair nearest the bed.

"Emma says the baby girl is John's granddaughter!" Jeremy read aloud.

Clair felt faint. "The mother is his daughter?"

"It appears so."

Clair asked, "Did we do the wrong thing, giving the girl to her?"

"No," said Thomas. "It's her baby. Who her father is shouldn't matter."

"I think it might," mused Jeremy. "She may be the reason the operation was allowed to go on as long as it did. John didn't like it and wanted it shut down. He would have known what was happening in his business. It must have been blackmail."

"It was a good thing we found her and got her back to her mom?" Clair asked.

"Yes, I think the abductions will finally be shut down."

CHAPTER 12

$\mathcal{J}$eremy got to the next safe house and found a similar situation; they were getting ready to close it up. The children had successfully returned to their homes. It was at the third house that he found Cole.

"Jeremy, finally! I've been trying to locate you for the last week."

They hugged. "It's good to see you, Pops. Is there news? Something I missed?"

His father communicated the information he had sent to Emma, that John Harden had been released and Jacob had hung himself in the prison.

"That's a lot of information," Jeremy acknowledged. "Emma sent me a telegram; she indicates the baby girl was probably John Harden's granddaughter."

"Hmm," said Cole contemplatively. "I hope that truly shuts down this type of operation."

"Me too."

What does this mean for John? Cole thought. *Will he start up somewhere else now? I think he may be a focus in the future.*

CHAPTER 13

$\mathcal{A}$ few weeks later, while Jeremy and Cole were busy closing out the case, Emma was settling back into her work and family life.

Breakfast that morning was ongoing and noisy; Jake was talking about his latest photography project, and everyone else was talking about their day. A knock sounded at the door. Emma wiped her mouth and stood, "I'll go get it." She hoped it was news that Jeremy and Cole were headed home. A knock sounded again and she quickly opened the door, finding the very thing she had hoped for: a telegram. She took it and tipped the courier and, once the door was closed, tore it open and quickly read it.

"Please come. Hugo took mine and Evelyn's youngest daughters and will not say where they are. Don't contact me, just come. Please afternoon only, will have a bike on the porch if he is gone. Signed Mrs. Banks." Emma had expected this communication at some point. The offer had been made a couple of years ago during another case. She wanted to give her a way out of her situation if it was needed.

And here it is, she thought. *He shouldn't have involved the children.*

She walked back into the dining room to finish her breakfast.

Dora and baby Lottie were the only ones still at the table. "Who was it from? Jeremy?" she asked.

"No," Emma murmured, thinking about the telegram. "It's from the woman I visited in Ohio a while back; the bigamy case."

"I remember. You didn't expose the husband at that time?"

"No, we got what we wanted: a divorce for our client. At that time, the arrangement with the other two wives seemed to be working for them."

"Didn't only one of them know that?"

"Yes, and she's the one I gave the card to, in case something changed."

"Did you think she might change her mind?"

"Yes," Emma said, thinking about that time and the woman's reluctance to take her card. "Hugo Banks seemed too volatile to keep something like this a secret."

"Did she mention anything else?"

"Not much, but he has taken the two youngest girls. My theory? A new wife."

"A third?" Dora said, astounded at this man.

"No, I think an *only*. Mrs. Banks wants me to go there as soon as possible." Something just occurred to her. "The other wife must also know what's going on."

"When will you leave?" Dora asked, knowing that her sister would help anyone who needed her. *Another case involving children*, Dora thought. Will *this be too much for her after the previous case?*

"As soon as I can get a train ticket," Emma said absently. "And I'll have to notify Mr. Pennington that I've been called out of town."

"Do you have anything pressing?" Dora asked, wondering if Tim would need to fill Emma's position temporarily.

The lawyer's office where she worked as an investigator was involved in a divorce case. Emma had completed her background checks and wouldn't be needed until they went to trial. "I should have a few weeks to spare. You might ask Tim to check if clerical work is needed while I'm gone."

"I'll do that," Dora said. Tim was out meeting with new clients for their business. "When is Jeremy due back?"

"Not for another week or two, depending on travel."

"Did you want to take Savannah with you this time?" Savannah had been involved in this case previously.

Emma shook her head. "No, there's no need. I will go by Clair's office on the way to pick up my train ticket."

Dora reached out her hand to Emma and asked, "Is there something dangerous going on?"

Emma pressed her lips into a thin line. "Maybe, but I need to keep this quiet for now. Mrs. Banks said no contact, so whatever the situation, her mail might be monitored."

Dora slowly dropped her hand. "Will you contact the local police in case you need help?"

"I will," Emma promised and headed upstairs. Once there, she changed into her split skirt and descended the stairs. She went through the kitchen where baking was ongoing. Amy and Ethyl were busy with dinner preparations. Dora was keeping baby Lottie busy with some dough.

She kissed Dora on the cheek and grabbed an apple on her way out. Her bike was stored in a small building near the back door. Walking it around to the front, she climbed on and headed to the telegraph office. A hotel room would be needed as well as a train ticket.

The sun was bright and it warmed her face as she rode. It was early spring, the snow had finally melted, and the roads were fairly easy to navigate. She could see the trees were starting to get their leaves back. The sky was blue and the air clear. It was still early afternoon and it was a wonderful day to be out.

As she rode, the case details ran through her head. The two wives involved were in their thirties and each had two girls each of about the same age. One thing she'd learned about the husband,

Hugo Banks, was that he liked things to stay the same. Same types of wives, same layouts on houses, same everything.

Her errands completed, she headed to Mr. Pennington's office. She entered quickly and waved to Ethan. He was reviewing files on his desk and didn't look up to greet her.

"Is Mr. Pennington in his office?" she asked, stopping in front of his desk.

"He is," he commented, and when she headed that way, he stopped her. "He has someone in there with him."

She nodded and moved back to put her bike in the closet. Reaching for the handle on her office door, she heard Mr. Pennington's door open. She glanced over quickly and saw who the client was. *Well, what a coincidence.*

The gentleman noticed her and walked over. "Emma, it's good to see you."

She looked over at the client. "Mr. Gilmore, how are you and your family?" Mr. Gilmore's wife was the first wife to Mr. Banks and the one who had started it all.

He smiled broadly. "We're doing well."

"Please send Mrs. Gilmore my regards."

"I will, goodbye." Mr. Pennington walked him to the office door.

She waited until he had closed it and approached him. "Mr. Pennington, do you have time to meet with me?"

"Yes, of course, follow me."

"I will get my files and join you."

She retrieved the files and, once they were in his office, she closed the door behind them. He sat at the round table in his office, and she joined him there.

"Do you have an update on my case?" he asked.

"Yes, I have the background with me." She pulled out the reports and handed them to him.

He looked through the information. "This looks complete. We'll be doing voir dire in another month."

She marked the date in her notebook. When she didn't leave, he looked over and asked, "Is there something else you want to discuss?"

"Yes, sir. The Hugo Banks case we were involved in." The case had been settled by Mr. Pennington, where he had used the threat of exposing Banks' other two families to get him to sign the annulment papers for their client, Mrs. Gilmore.

"Involving Mr. and Mrs. Gilmore?" he asked. When she nodded, he continued. "We didn't disclose the bigamy to the police or his current wives. Has there been a development that could affect the Gilmores?"

"Not directly," she said. She took a deep breath and started again. "This is about one of the other wives. I gave one of them my card if she wanted out."

"Did she?" he asked.

"Not at that time," she admitted. "But this morning I received a telegram asking for my help."

"May I see it?" he asked, holding out his hand.

"Yes, of course." She pulled it out of her pocket and handed it to him.

He read it silently, then he looked up at her and said, "Mr. Banks is not a nice man."

"No, and sadly, both women seemed happy with him."

"What do you think is happening?"

"New start, new wife," she said simply.

He nodded and sat back. "Are you concerned I'll try to stop you?"

"No, sir, but I wanted to let you know my plans. And the Gilmores shouldn't come up in this case. It should be specific to the current wives."

"Yes, that divorce is final. Once she married Mr. Gilmore officially, society gave a pass for any indiscretion. Go get those kids and women out of that situation. You let me know if there are any legal concerns that need to be resolved."

"I'm not sure there'll be any divorces, but I think the property settlement will require some assistance."

"Give me both ladies' names and addresses. I'll be waiting for you to contact me once they have Banks in custody. Oh, and you might need these," he said and walked over to his desk to retrieve a file from his drawer.

"Thank you, Mr. Pennington," she said, taking the papers. She opened the file and saw it was the marriage licenses they had obtained in the first case. *This will come in handy.* She reached out her hand to him.

He took it and said warmly, "Be safe. Keep us up to date as you can."

"I will." She was going anyway, regardless of his wishes, but she was glad he agreed with her plan.

She went out to the lobby and was surprised to see Savannah with Ethan. They had met on a case at Christmas and had been inseparable ever since.

"Savannah, hi!" Emma greeted the woman. "Are you out during the day?" she teased.

"Yes, we vampires have to get out occasionally." Savannah worked at a theatre as technical staff. While a show was going on, she would sleep until late into the day.

Emma smiled slightly and moved back to her office.

"Emma," Savannah called, "I'm actually here to see you."

"You are? I thought…" Emma started.

She smiled at Ethan and said, "Him? No, he's just a bonus."

Ethan's face flushed but he looked happy.

"Come into my office," Emma directed. Savannah followed her in and sat down on the corner of her desk.

"Dora told me where you're going," she said, no expression showing on her face.

Emma frowned and Savannah added hastily, "She told only me since I was involved last time. She thought I might want to know. I want to go with you. I know I can help."

Emma thought about that and admitted, "It would be nice to have someone along; you were invaluable last time. But I also don't want you to have to leave your show mid-run." She knew Savannah was running a rather large show at this time.

"Yeah, there is that. Are you sure it's okay to go alone?"

"Yes," she said firmly.

"But if something changes, you'll let me know?"

"Of course." Emma was drumming her fingers on her lips and said, "You know, I could use some support. If we need to take the older kids or need to hide them, having wigs would help. Change them into boys when everyone is looking for girls."

"How old are they?" Savannah asked, thinking about her wigs. She had seen the girls at the time but didn't remember much about them.

"Ten and eleven, petite," Emma replied, trying to remember what they looked like.

"That'll work. If they're a little loose that's okay. I'll include pins to help keep them on. When will you be leaving?"

"I was hoping today, but if needed I can get a ticket for the morning."

"Tomorrow would be easier for me and, with the extra time, I can provide pants and shirts from our costume department."

Emma thought about that. "Okay. I want to get there fast, but I need to be prepared." She reached down and picked up her bag. "I'll walk out with you."

They exited her office and Emma went to retrieve her bike. Ethan watched. "Leaving early?" he asked.

"I have some work out of town. Mr. Pennington knows where I'll be," she confirmed.

He looked at her and then at Savannah but didn't ask any questions. "Safe travels," he commented.

"I have to go also," Savannah said. "I have to go get some things organized for Emma." Ethan knew she was one of Emma's specialists.

"See you tonight after the show?" he asked.

"Yes," she said, walking over to him. "Meet me backstage." She leaned over and kissed him quickly.

Emma and Savannah left together and as they walked downstairs. Savannah asked, "Do you think the other wife knows now?"

Emma nodded. "Yes, I think so. He's taken the youngest girls from both families and hasn't told the mothers where they are. I'll find out more when I get there. The Mrs. Banks who contacted me doesn't trust their telegraph office."

"What are you thinking? What's going on?"

"He took the little ones and is starting a new life."

"Any evidence so far?"

"Not yet, just a feeling at this time. It does sound like a restart."

"Why now, I wonder? Did something happen?"

"I don't know," Emma said. Once they reached the bottom of the stoop, she set down the bike and walked it as they continued to talk.

"I'm going to get the items you asked for and then head home," said Savannah.

"I'll see you there. I need to go to the telegraph office to secure the hotel and the train station."

Savannah waved and headed to the right, Emma directed her bike to the left and rode the few blocks to the telegraph station. She parked it outside and entered.

"May I help you?" the clerk asked.

"Yes. I have to send a telegram to a hotel in Cleveland, Ohio. The Weddell House at Bank and Superior."

"Got it. What's the message?" he asked, pencil ready.

"Arriving tomorrow night. Stop. Will need a room for three days. Stop."

"Is that all?" he asked.

"Just my name. Emma Evans."

She had stayed at the hotel before this and knew they wouldn't share her information.

Next was the train station. The clerk confirmed a ticket was available for the next morning. There would be no return ticket, as she wasn't sure how long the case would take. He told her the amount, and she paid it. The cashier thanked her, and she pocketed her train ticket. *I'm all set for tomorrow.*

At home, Emma went into the house through the kitchen. Ethyl and Amy sat at the table, taking a break before dinner. "Hi," they greeted her.

"Savannah got home a few minutes ago; she said to tell you she is in the attic sewing room," Amy told her.

"Thank you!" She went quickly into the foyer and up the stairs to the fourth floor.

Savannah looked up from the wig she was holding. "I've fashioned the wigs so we can put the hair up in them." She showed Emma the netting on the inside.

Emma went over to examine what she had added, "These are perfect. You won't get into trouble for loaning me these?"

"No, of course not, I'll put the things back when you return." She checked the time. "I have just enough time to finish these. Why don't you take a look at the clothes over there on the bed?"

Emma went over to them and evaluated the sizes. "I think these are just about right."

"Great, I'll put these in a bag as soon as I am done."

"Thank you for helping out. I'll go get my items organized."

She headed down to her room to pack. A variety of clothes would be needed for this case; the situation could require pants, skirts, or a business jacket.

A knock sounded at the door. "Come in," Emma called.

"Getting organized?" Dora asked as she entered. "Will you leave tonight?"

"No, I'll leave on the early train tomorrow. That way I can get in after Hugo has gone to work."

"How will you make sure he isn't there?"

"If a bicycle is on the porch, that means Hugo isn't home."

"Be careful."

"I will be and I won't make a move without data. There are kids involved and the wives need to be protected."

Savannah dropped the bag off on her way to the theatre. "Did you get enough sleep?" Emma asked her friend, watching her closely.

"Yes, plenty. Don't worry about me. Let me know if I need to make a quick trip to see you."

"I'll let you know," she promised.

Dinner was still an hour away and Emma finished getting organized for her trip. She looked around her room, at hers and Jeremy's things. The bookcase separating their rooms was just in place to protect their privacy from anyone who might get curious. She laughed and thought, *Anyone who knows us would know this room is shared.* Jeremy didn't keep his clothes on her side, but the table on his side of the bed contained all of his current reading — novels, case studies into criminal minds. *We do have a lot in common*, she thought.

On the dresser were pictures of Mama, Abbey, and Papa. And one of Papa and Cole. She missed Jeremy so much. Separation was hard, especially after they had finally had a long break together. She'd never expected to want to be with someone every night, but he was her family now.

The evening went by quietly and Emma read and went to bed early. The next morning, she dressed in a dark skirt and a pink blouse with lace at the cuffs, then shrugged on a longish pink jacket. She sat on the bed and pulled on her black boots. Her knives were in place in her leg scabbard and the larger one was hidden in her hat. She had replaced her bowler with a more feminine basic black one. The key feature was that it could be outfitted so the knife could be stowed in the side and easily accessed.

Her bowler hat, made for her by Miss May and Miss Marjorie, was a treasured item and when it had started to show wear, she had retired it. It sat on the table across from her bed. She would forever be in debt to the two ladies who'd taught her how to throw knives and get out of tight situations.

Her bag was ready and by the door. She grabbed it and made her way downstairs. Once in the foyer, she set it by the door and headed to the kitchen.

In the early morning hours, Ethyl and Amy were already busy baking pastry for breakfast and getting organized for the day. Amy heard her come in, "Emma, good morning." Ethyl nodded from the stove. Her attention was taken by the frying bacon.

"Would you like some breakfast?" Amy asked.

"I should," she said. "I have a train to catch this morning."

"Sit down, sit down," Amy said and brought her bread, butter, and fruit to eat. They were Emma's favorite breakfast. "Dora left a note to make you lunch for the train. It's in that bag on the table," she said, nodding to it.

Emma looked over at it. "Thank you, I'll take it with me."

She finished her breakfast, took the bag, and headed toward the dining room. She called over her shoulder, "Tell Dora I left."

"You can tell her yourself," her sister called from the dining room doorway.

Emma ran over and hugged her. "I didn't want to wake you," she said.

"I didn't want to miss you," Dora countered, smoothing Emma's hair back. "You're sure you want to go on your own?"

"I am," Emma assured her. "Savannah helped me with disguises for the girls, in case I need them." She glanced at her watch and said, with a bit of worry in her tone, "The situation may require me to transport them to Chicago."

"You think it'll be necessary to bring them back here?" Dora asked. She was surprised that the girls wouldn't be taken home to their mothers.

"Not here," Emma qualified, "but close. I want them to have access to Mr. Pennington. I think the best place will be the safe house. I'll need to check there and make sure I don't surprise them with visitors."

Dora nodded. "Yes, you're right." She glanced at her timepiece and said with a frown, "But the time. If you go there, you won't have time to make the train. Would you like me to go for you?"

"I'd appreciate that," she said, glad to have that off her list.

"Who should they expect?" Dora asked.

"Right now, I'm not sure. I am hoping that we get all the girls and their mothers out of Cleveland safety. We need to get them away from Banks."

"Then that's what I'll tell them," she said firmly.

Emma kissed her sister on the cheek and walked quickly to the foyer. She put on her hat and picked up the bag and headed down to the stoop. Her bike would be faster, but she had nowhere to leave it at the station. Regretfully, she left it behind and walked the few blocks to access the trolley to take her to the train station. Jumping off at her stop, she checked her pocket for her ticket.

She didn't have a cabin assigned for this short-day trip and moved to settle into the seats in the third-class section. On the way to Ohio, she made notes of what she wanted to ask the two Mrs. Banks in her notebook.

The train arrived and she disembarked dressed in her female clothes. *Hotel first*, she thought. She wanted to settle in and wash up before heading over to the second wife's house. The telegram had specified she should arrive before the afternoon.

Hugo must come home for lunch, she thought.

The hotel she'd chosen was large and she could blend in with the crowds. It would provide the anonymity she needed. They had her room ready and would send lunch up. She took her bag and went to the room. There she washed, ate, and took a cab over to Mrs. Banks' house.

As she approached the neighborhood, she remembered the house clearly. It was the same. *The man likes things the same,* she thought again as she looked at the perfect yard and the bright colors on the house. *I bet the other house has also stayed similar.*

The main difference from her last visit was the children weren't in the yard. It gave a more solemn look to the home. *The bike is there*, she thought and moved toward the stairs to the front door. She knocked a few times and waited.

It opened suddenly, revealing the second Mrs. Banks. "You came!" she exclaimed and pulled her into the foyer.

"Of course, I told you I would," Emma said and allowed herself to be guided.

"Yes, you did." She hugged her tightly. "I'm so happy you're here."

Emma stayed where she was for a moment and then pulled back. "We have a limited time. Talk to me."

"We'll be more comfortable in the sitting room," the other woman said, leading Emma into the room.

They sat on the couch. Emma pulled out her notebook and laughed suddenly. "I don't know your first name. You were Mrs. Banks on my last visit."

The circumstances of their visit were serious, but this comment also made Mrs. Banks laugh. "Yes, that's true. We didn't have to get to know each other. I'm Isabella or Izzy."

"Okay, Izzy, let's get started. What's going on that changed your mind so suddenly?"

Izzy sat back and began to explain. "I was so settled, even with having to share him. I could get used to the limits on our relationship and NO changes to the house. I kept telling myself that the kids are happy, so I'm happy."

"So, what changed?"

"It was little things at first: out-of-town trips, money being tighter than we were used to. And. . ." She paused and her eyes filled with tears.

Emma gave her a moment to gather herself and then prompted, "Go on."

"The mail. We started getting mail from an unknown woman."

"Did you ask him about it?"

"I did, but he said it was just a mix-up. He brushed me and my questions aside."

"Was it a mix up?" Emma asked. It was doubtful from what she knew of the man.

"No, I don't think so. And it went on for a few months."

"Do you have any of the letters that were sent here?"

"No, that's another thing. Hugo took them immediately and I couldn't locate them later."

"Couldn't you have looked at one when it was delivered?" she asked, thinking he would be at work.

"No, he started coming home at the time the mail was delivered."

"What was his excuse for being here during a work day?"

She sighed and said, "The mail is delivered at lunchtime."

"Giving him the perfect excuse. What names were on the letters?"

"*Catherine Banks.*"

"Hmm," she said. *Another clue about a new wife.*

Izzy had seen the same thing and started to cry again. "I think he's starting over with another family."

"Why?" Emma asked, even though she'd thought the same thing.

Izzy sniffed and put her tissue to her eyes. "Our relationship has changed; he makes time for the kids but not for me."

Emma asked the hard question, "Why not just let him go?"

"That's what I called you here for. It's time."

"What about his other wife? Is she aware of you and your family?" Emma asked. The other Mrs. Banks would need to have input if she was going to help with both children.

"Evelyn!" Izzy called, rather than answering.

The other Mrs. Banks walked out of the kitchen, wiping her hands.

"You!" Emma said. "You do know?"

"Yes," Evelyn said quietly as she sat down across from them on a powder blue chair.

"How did this happen?" Emma asked, waving her hands at both of them.

They looked at each other and back at her. "We've known for a while. It was our older daughters; they became friends at school and started to visit with us. The similarities are striking between the two."

"The houses! Did they notice?"

"Yes. They immediately saw the houses were the same and mentioned it to us," explained Evelyn. Izzy nodded.

"How did you keep this fact away from your husband?" Emma asked incredulously.

"He travels," Evelyn said, her mouth dipping downward. "It was easy. Once our daughters told us how similar our houses were and I saw the girls together. I called Izzy and asked her out to tea."

"It just came out," Izzy said. "I was tired of being the only person who knew what was going on."

"Did you know Izzy knew before you?" Emma asked Evelyn. *Had she been angry?*

"No. I found out that day," she confirmed.

"Did you have any anger about being the only adult not to know?" Emma asked.

Evelyn held out her hand to Izzy, and Izzy took it. She clasped it tightly. "No, it's hard enough for women today and we don't want to fight each other."

"How long ago was this?"

"About a year," Evelyn admitted and Izzy nodded in agreement.

"We agreed to try to make it work for the sake of the kids," Izzy said.

"Still keeping everything separate?"

"Yes, but now we could track his movements," Izzy said.

Emma raised her brows in question.

Evelyn explained. "We started keeping schedules of when he was with one family or another."

"Did you find anything out of the ordinary?" Emma asked, wondering how they were willing to live this very different kind of life.

Evelyn replied, "At first, the traveling could be confirmed as being at each of our homes."

"Then, what happened?"

"We started to notice longer trips, ones that included neither home," Izzy said.

"How long was this going on?"

"We worked it out about four months ago," Evelyn said.

"And why now? Why call me at this moment?"

"Hugo's taken our younger daughters," Izzy and Evelyn said at the same time.

"Both of them?" she confirmed.

"Yes," Evelyn answered, her tears starting to fall.

Emma mulled that over. "Legally, he can take them anywhere. He *is* the father of both girls."

"Yes," Izzy said.

Emma continued. "And the police will say that as well." She stood and walked to the mantel and turned back to them. "When was this? When did he take them?"

"It was a few weeks ago. He said he wanted to take my daughter on a trip to New York. She was so excited and wanted time alone with her dad," Evelyn said.

"Did you know he was taking both girls at that time?" Emma asked Evelyn.

"No! I had no idea."

"Has he ever done this before, taken the girls together?" she asked, looking at them both.

"No, he always kept the families separate," Izzy said.

"Did you talk at that time? Were you aware that both girls were leaving with him?"

"We didn't know both were going; we had drifted back to our own homes and lives. We didn't keep regular contact at that time."

Emma understood and asked, "What happened then?"

"Then he came back without my daughter," said Evelyn.

"And mine," Izzy said.

"Who did he say he left them with?" Emma asked.

"He didn't," Izzy muttered.

"What?" asked Emma, surprised.

"He said he just left them with a relative," Evelyn clarified.

"He wouldn't say who it was?"

"No, he wouldn't. Only that she was happy there. And that he wouldn't bring her back," Izzy said.

"When he refused to bring my daughter back, I went to see Izzy," said Evelyn.

"And you confirmed that both daughters were gone?" They nodded, and Emma continued. "What about your other daughters? Where are they now?"

"They're away at school, the same school," said Izzy, answering for both of them. "I'm happy they're not here."

"That won't stop him," muttered Emma. She looked at them. "You will need to notify the school that they're not to be removed without your permission."

"I'm not sure that will work," Evelyn responded.

"Why?"

"Because they won't stop my husband from picking them up. As you said, he is their father."

Emma drummed her fingers on her lips, planning. "Then we need to get them before he can."

"You're going to get them?" they asked at the same time.

"Yes, it's the only way; if Hugo is starting a new family, he'll also want those two."

"Will there be concerns with the law on this? Even with our permission?" asked Izzy.

"I wouldn't think so, not if the school recognizes your authority." She checked her timepiece. "You mentioned we have limited time today?"

"Yes," Izzy answered, looking at the watch pinned to her dress. "He'll be here at noon, right on the dot."

"Then I'll leave now. Can you give me the address and each of you write a letter so I can pick the girls up from the school?"

Both women agreed and Izzy went to get writing paper for her and Evelyn.

"Be sure to use Molly Cooper as my name," Emma directed.

They both wrote quickly and handed her the letters.

"Where will you take them?" Izzy asked, suddenly worried.

"It's probably best I don't tell you now. I will keep them safe."

"What should we do in the meantime?" asked Evelyn, worrying the handkerchief in her hands.

"Act like nothing is wrong, be as normal as possible," Emma directed.

"That will be hard," Izzy said.

"Just remember who you're protecting," Emma suggested.

"Yes, you're right. Will you be, okay?" Izzy asked Evelyn.

"Yes, I am, knowing you're with me," Evelyn said, taking Izzy's hand. They had bonded over their circumstance and had become friends.

Emma took the notes and placed them in her pocket. "I'm cutting it tight on time."

"Me too," Evelyn said.

"Too close, I think," Emma said as she looked out the window. Hugo was walking up to the house with a smile on his face. He stopped by the mailbox and seemed to be waiting for someone. It wasn't long until a postman showed up. Emma kept watching. The postman walked up and handed over his mail. Hugo flipped through the pile quickly and removed a letter.

Placing it in his pocket, he grinned and continued talking to the man.

"Go," whispered Izzy.

Emma walked quickly out of the back of the house and pulled her hat low over her face. Evelyn exited with her, took Emma's hand, and pulled her along through the back of several houses. She seemed to know her way around. Once they slowed, Emma turned to her. "Have you done this before?"

"More than a few times," she admitted. Emma followed her closely.

"How did you know he wouldn't go to your house?" she asked.

"It isn't my day. He has all of that special mail delivered to Izzy's place, so I don't see him much during the day."

They made it a few blocks and were able to move to the main streets as they got closer to her house. Emma said, "You're brave, the both of you."

"No, I'm not," the other woman said, "but Izzy is. And smart. She figured this all out first."

They made it to her house. Emma stood studying it. Again, it surprised her that Evelyn's house looked identical to Izzy's.

"Weird right?" Evelyn asked.

"A little," she admitted as they entered the house. Green! The inside of the house had a different color from the other one! She was shocked and looked toward Evelyn. "Green?" she asked.

"Yes, a lovely shade, don't you think?" Evelyn looked around with a rather evil smile.

"When did you do it?" Emma asked. The light green color was in the foyer and went up the stairs and into the sitting room.

"Back when I found out about Izzy"

Rotating, she looked at everything. "I love it! What did Hugo say?"

"What do you think he said?" she asked wryly.

"He didn't like it," she guessed.

"No, he wanted it fixed immediately."

"But it's still green."

"It is and it will remain so," Evelyn said, showing backbone.

"Even when the children are returned?" Emma asked, wondering about the upcoming changes.

Evelyn turned to face her. "Change will take place and the biggest change will be the removal of my husband!"

Emma didn't say anything. Instead, she checked her pocket. "I need to find a place to rent a wagon."

"Why not a carriage? It would be faster."

Emma didn't answer, not wanting to share more details. When she didn't answer, Evelyn walked over to her writing table and scribbled out an address, and handed it to her.

Evelyn hugged Emma. "Be careful," she said.

Emma hugged her back. "I'll be in touch once the girls are safely away."

"Once you get the older girls, what will you do next?"

"I'm not sure," she admitted. The older girls were her priority now.

CHAPTER 14

Back at Izzy's house

Hugo Banks entered and went to the kitchen, where Izzy worked on lunch. There were no changes in his menu; he would want a thick ham sandwich with fresh fruit on the side and a glass of milk.

He didn't say anything as he sat at the table and waited for her to serve him. It took all of her energy to restrain herself from dumping it in his lap.

He wasn't aware of the tension; he took a bite of his sandwich and casually said, "I'm taking a long trip this weekend. I'll be leaving on Friday."

She did what Emma said not to do and tearfully asked, "How long will you be away? Will you see Marcy? Can you bring her back?" She hadn't meant to say that last statement and, when she saw the anger build on his face, she tried to backtrack quickly. "I, uh, I just miss her, and I'll miss you." She walked over to him and touched his cheek.

The motion of her hand seemed to distract him. He even smiled when he told her, "I'll be back, but Marcy is having a nice time, so I'm going to leave her where she is."

"Whatever you say, dear," Izzy murmured and kissed him. She would do whatever she had to do to protect her and Evelyn's daughters. *Emma, please get them before he does.*

CHAPTER 15

*F*irst the hotel, Emma thought as she left Evelyn's home. *I'll need to check out and get my luggage. And food. I'll have to take some things that will last through tomorrow. Growing girls could be hungry.* With that thought in mind, she approached the desk at her hotel. A clerk stood behind the counter in a crisp white shirt, red vest, and jacket. He looked up as she approached. "Yes, how can I help you?" he asked.

"I'll be checking out," Emma said.

"Your name?"

"Emma Evans," she supplied.

He found her information in his card file. He frowned at her. "You were going to be with us for a few days. Are you cutting your visit short?"

"I am," she confirmed. "I may be back soon."

"Please try to let us know so that we have a room available," he said professionally.

"I will, thank you."

"Will you be gathering your things now?"

"Yes, and I have a list of food items I'd like to order from the restaurant. Could you have them prepared for me? And I'll need it packed for a trip."

He held out his hand for the list, which she supplied, and he glanced at it. "We can have this organized in about an hour. Is that enough time for you?"

"Yes, I'll go up to my room. Can you deliver it there?"

"That should work. Please drop off your key here on your way out."

The elevator was to the left of the desk and she headed toward it. She and two others watched the numbers tick down to their floor. The doors opened and the operator waved them in. Emma stepped into the back and waited as other people filed into the small space. The elevator moved slowly up to her floor. When it reached her floor and the door opened, she said, "Excuse me." The people shuffled around to let her off.

Her room was a few doors down from the elevator. She opened the door and went in. Looking around, she didn't see anything out of place. Her bag was by the door. She picked it up and started to fill it. When she got to her boy's clothes, she thought, *No, I'll need to be dressed as a lady to pick up the girls.*

She pulled out the letters from the moms and reviewed what they wrote.

Molly Cooper will be picking up my daughter Evie. She is needed at home. She has my permission and will act as her guardian.

She opened the other letter and saw it was similar. *Good,* she thought, *keep it simple.*

The hour passed quickly and a knock sounded at the door. Snapping her bag closed, she went to open it. It was her food delivery.

"Your lunch," the young bellman said and handed it to her. She looked at the basket and her bag. "Can you help me downstairs with that and my bag?"

"I can," he said. She did a final sweep through the room and walked to the door with her bag. "Let me take that," he said, indicating the bag she carried.

She smiled and handed it to him. Walking to the bed, she pulled on her light coat and picked up her hat. Turning back to the door, she said, "After you."

The bellman walked toward the elevator with her following closely behind. They stayed together on the ride down and to the front entrance. She handed him his tip and the key to her room.

"Will you need anything else?" he asked.

"No, thank you." The blacksmith was only a few blocks away. She picked up the bag and basket and headed that way. She patted her pocket and headed to find a wagon. She assumed that, if Hugo had the two little girls, he'd want to move the older two as soon as possible. The only thing on her side was surprise; she had to get to them first. She looked at the notes again. The girls were located at the Montgomery School for Girls.

Based on the instructions the moms had provided, she calculated the wagon trip would take ten hours. She could make it in one day, but she'd have to stop and rest herself and the horse. By tonight, she would be close and would be able to go to the school first thing tomorrow. She would have time to move the girls out of Hugo's reach.

The blacksmith sign was visible from her location. She'd have to be careful; she didn't know him and didn't know if she could trust him. The office was located beside the open areas where men were working. The sign indicated they shod horses and provided wagon rentals.

As she walked into the office, it didn't appear to be manned. She wandered out to the area where large open pits were set up and two men were working on projects. They were putting iron items into the fire and pulling them out. She waited, not wanting to disturb the dangerous work.

One of the men finished his work and stepped toward her. "Do you have a wagon and horse for rent?" she asked.

He looked over at her, rubbing his hair and then his large chest. "I might. Where do you want to go? And who's it for?"

"I need it for myself," she said firmly. "And I can't tell you where I'll be taking it."

This isn't the first time someone wouldn't give me a straight answer on what the wagon was needed for, he thought. Mulling that over, he asked, "How long will you have it?"

She thought quickly. "Four days maximum. I'll let you know where to pick it up."

"Hmm," he said, and finally added, "Come with me." They went back into the small office. "How do I know you'll let me know where it is?"

"You'll have to trust me on that," she said, her voice flat.

He sat on his stool. "Tell me what you really want this wagon for."

At that moment, two little girls ran into the room. He hugged them tightly to him. "Why aren't you in school?" he asked, his face transforming with his wide smile.

"Short day," the smaller one answered. "Ma said we could visit." He talked to them animatedly. Both girls shared their news and he sent them home to their mother.

Those girls are about the same age as the ones I am trying to protect. The truth, she thought, *I'll have to take a chance on him.* She made a decision and got up and closed the door to his office. They needed privacy for what she was planning to share. He raised his eyebrows as she took her seat again.

She started. "There are two little girls who need to be picked up before someone takes them."

He sat still at her pronouncement. Thoughts crossed his mind, but all he could say was, "What are you going to do with them?"

"Put them somewhere safe until their mothers can get to them."

"By yourself?" he scoffed.

"It's better if this operation is small. I can get them out and to a safe place."

His thoughts went to his girls and he nodded. "I'll help you, but I want the wagon back and it's gonna cost extra. I won't have it available while you're gone and I'll lose money on rentals from it."

"You'll get it back," she assured him, "and I can pay upfront."

He headed out to the back where the wagon and horses were kept. He turned slowly toward her. "Why don't you accompany me?"

Nodding, she followed him. As they neared the stable, she could tell it was kept in good condition, but a stable always had a certain smell. Her nose crinkled but she didn't comment. He walked the horse out.

Emma studied the horse. "Will she be able to make a long trip?"

"How long?"

"Nine to ten hours," she replied.

"Yes," he said as he patted the horse on the flanks. "Just stop for a break every hour or so. Watch her, you don't want to push her too much. She's solid and will make the trip. I will add her feed to the back and you need to make sure she has plenty of water."

"I'll keep that in mind," she promised him.

They exited the stable with the horse and he connected her to the wagon. Emma pulled money from her wallet and handed it to him. He shook his head. "No, I'll do this for you and those girls."

"But you said—"

"And now I'm changing my mind," he interrupted.

Once the wagon was ready, she asked, "Do you have any blankets?"

"Yes, we have some here." He didn't ask why but knew it was to cover the girls. The blankets were put in the back.

She climbed up, took the reins, and looked over at him. "Thank you." As she started to pull away, she warned, "You might have someone come by and ask if anyone took a wagon."

"I'll make sure they don't know it was you," he promised. "One thing, could you let me know when it's safe and that the girls are okay?"

"I will and I'll let you know where to pick up your wagon." She clicked her tongue at the horse and moved the wagon out.

She watched the horse as she rode away; breaks would be necessary. Once she was out of town, she slowed the wagon and pulled out the map she had picked up at the hotel. Even with additional breaks to rest, she was going to be at the school in the morning.

With late afternoon approaching, she pulled the wagon over into a meadow. There was a stream nearby and she pull down the bag of feed. The horse was unhooked from the wagon and tied loosely to a tree so she could get to fresh water and her feed. The area was covered with grass. The break refreshed both of them and she hooked the horse back up to continue her trip.

The weather was nice and the horse was easygoing. The day flowed into night and she found a wooded area to pull off into for them to rest. There was a stream nearby. She moved the horse's feed from the wagon and then tied the horse near the water. A fire wasn't needed; she didn't want any extra attention. She settled down in the back of the wagon and watched the night sky. *Jeremy, where are you tonight? Are we seeing the same sky?* she thought as she drifted off to sleep.

The next morning, she jerked awake. The morning mist had settled on her face. She wiped it off and sat up, looking around. This should be her last stop. They were just outside of the town where the school was located. The horse was well rested, but she'd need to work harder with the addition of two more passengers.

Her timepiece showed 8:00am. It was early and the school was probably just starting to open. She got up and stretched, her body stiff from sleeping in the wagon. Her baskets of food was nearby, she sat and pulled out a hard roll and some fruit. She grimaced when looking down at her wrinkled clothes. Thankfully, the area she had picked was blocked from the road by trees.

Her bag was in the back of the wagon; she opened it and took out a long black walking skirt, a white lace high-necked shirt, and her papa's jacket. It was oversized on her but would create a more polished image that the school would favor.

Her hair was taken out of a ponytail and pulled into a bun. *There,* she thought, *that should do it.* She checked the time, it was 8:15. The horse was rested and she led the easygoing mare back to her position on the wagon and hooked her up. The letters from the moms were in her side pocket. She patted them absently as she climbed into the driver's seat and then clicked to get the horse moving toward the school.

As it came into view, she saw there was a large area to park the wagon with a tie post to secure her horse. *It's certainly nice here,* she thought, looking around. It was all red brick with white sashes on the windows. The building looked inviting. The gardens looked well-tended and reached around the building. *Their day must have started,* she thought, not seeing any children outside.

The large stoop led into a long hallway. It gleamed, the wood polished and no dust to be found. Pictures of former deans hung on the wall and she glanced at them as she walked by. *A very austere bunch,* she thought. The office was ahead of her. She took a breath before opening the door, ready to be the person she was pretending to be.

Going straight to the desk, she stopped and the man there looked up. "Welcome to the Montgomery School for Girls. Is there something I can help you with?"

"Thank you. I'd like to speak to the director. Please."

The man frowned. "Our director is out and our assistant director is in charge. Do you have an appointment?"

"I do not," Emma admitted, "but it is very important that I speak to him."

"I'll have to see if he has time for you."

"Thank you, I'll wait."

"You may sit there," he said, motioning to the hardwood chairs across from his desk.

Emma walked over to them and sat down to wait. The man frowned at her but went through a door located directly behind his desk. He came out a few minutes later. "He has made time for you, but be aware he is a very busy man."

"I understand," Emma murmured and followed him into the office. Her expression was blank as she entered and got a view of the assistant director. The tall, thin man stood looking at the bookcases located behind his desk.

He turned toward her and smiled easily. "I'm assistant director Lee Baxter, and you are?"

This was not the austere man she had expected. She answered him easily. "Molly Cooper," she supplied, the name they had agreed to and had used in their letters.

He sat and waved her to the chair. "What is this about?"

"I need to pick up two of your students. Their families would like them back for a personal matter."

"Do you have something to show me to prove you have the proper approvals for this?"

She nodded and handed the letters to him from her jacket pocket.

He took his time opening the envelopes and read through each one. "Both families are involved in this personal issue?"

"Yes, their mothers are quite close and share a lot of their lives." *That's putting it lightly,* she thought.

"These seem to be in order," he acknowledged. "I'll need to check their files. Will you wait here?"

"Yes." She watched him exit.

He returned quickly. "There was nothing in their file to prevent them from leaving. Will you be taking them straight to their homes?"

"Yes, I will," she said, trying not to show her relief.

He studied her and then stood. "Follow me, please."

Emma followed him out. They stopped at the desk and he requested the office clerk. "Bring both girls up."

"Yes, sir." The clerk left the area immediately to retrieve the two girls.

They were brought in and Emma blinked when she saw them, trying to hide her surprise. The girls were almost identical: same hair and eye color. No one commented and Emma said, "Hi, I'm here to pick you up. Your mothers would like you to come home." They looked at one another and the assistant director.

The assistant director spoke directly to them. "Evie and Mabel, you'll need to go home at your mother's request. I'm sure you will be able to come back soon."

"Do we have time to get our things?" Evie asked.

"Yes, of course," Emma told her. "I'll be waiting down here." She glanced at her watch. "Try not to take too long."

The two girls nodded and walked back; the sound of their shoes ascending the tall staircase to the dorms could be heard in the office. As Emma waited, she wanted to get them out of here soon. It had almost been too easy.

CHAPTER 16

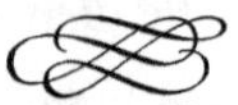

William Darnton, director of the Montgomery School for Girls, arrived back at the school later and entered his office, reading his mail.

The desk secretary entered the office. "Sir, two girls were picked up this morning."

"What did you say?" Darnton asked, still distracted by his mail.

"Two girls went home for a family concern this morning," the secretary repeated.

He frowned, then asked, "Which two?"

"Evie and Mabel Banks."

"Who took them? Was it their father?" Darnton asked in agitation.

This time, the secretary frowned. *Father? Singular?* he thought. "No sir, the mothers of both girls sent a representative to pick them up. A family matter, she said."

"She! Who approved this?" Darnton shouted.

"Well, I didn't. It was Assistant Director Baxter," the other man replied in a huffy voice.

"Tell Baxter to come to my office." His voice was curt. When the secretary didn't move quickly, Darnton yelled, "NOW!"

The secretary jumped up and ran to the assistant director's office. He was out of breath when he entered the other man's office. He asked, "Sir?"

"Yes," Baxter said, smiling broadly and looking up. When he saw the other man's tense expression, he grew concerned. "Matthew, what's wrong?"

"Director Darnton is back," Matthew said, foreboding in his voice.

"That's nice. Will that be all?" Baxter smiled again. He was a happy, easygoing man who wasn't easily upset.

"No, sir, he wants you in his office to talk about the two girls you discharged earlier."

"Why is that?" he asked curiously. "There was nothing out of the ordinary. Except maybe it was two girls from two different families that left."

Were they from different families? Matthew thought, remembering the director's singular use of father and the girls' nearly identical appearances. "You should hurry, sir," he said quietly.

Baxter didn't understand the urgency, but if the director wanted him, it must have been important. Heading directly to the director's office, he knocked a few times and entered. Matthew sat back down at his desk and turned to stare at the door the assistant director had entered.

The director saw him at the door. "Lee, come in and close the door."

"Sure. You wanted to discuss something with me? Everything was in order with the release of the two girls. They had the permission of their mothers."

"Can I see the letters provided?" Darnton asked.

"Of course, I brought them with me," Baxter said and reached into his pocket. He handed them over and the director read each one.

"These are from the mothers. What about the father?" the director asked.

Father? Baxter thought. He heard the same thing from Matthew, a singular reference when he had been expecting a plural. "No, just the mothers. Miss Cooper picked them up at a little after eight this morning and took them home."

The director shook his head. "The one day I decide to take some personal time and what happens?"

The assistant director didn't answer. The question didn't appear to be directed at him.

"These girls were not allowed to be picked up by anyone other than their father!" Darnton yelled.

"I don't understand. There was no instruction in the file."

"No, no, there wouldn't have been," he said in a low voice. The director thought, *I will miss that money.*

"Money?" Baxter asked, perplexed at the turn of the conversation.

The director hadn't realized he had said that out loud. "The father had an understanding with me," he said smoothly. "He would fund the new library acquisitions, but only if we restricted access to the girls."

Baxter just sat in thought. Finally, he asked, "Father? Are the girls related?"

"Yes, he is the father of both children." There was no reason to hide it now.

"But they're in the same grade and both mothers are alive. I haven't heard of a divorce," Baxter stated, perplexed.

"Hmm. That was of no consequence to me. It's their private lives," Darnton said, trying to get himself extricated from the conversation.

Bigamy, thought Baxter. *The director was helping Mr. Banks hide his dual marriages.*

Well, it's too late now, Darnton thought. *I'll need to contact Banks.* "Matthew!" he yelled.

"Yes, sir," Matthew said as he ran in.

"Send a telegram to Mr. Banks and let him know both of his

girls have been picked up. Tell him who was here and when this occurred," he directed.

"Yes, sir," Matthew said and exited to follow his instructions.

As volatile as Mr. Banks is, I hope he doesn't come to the school, thought Darnton as he sat heavily in his chair.

CHAPTER 17

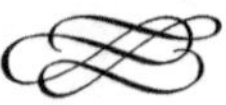

The girls followed Emma's instructions and climbed into the wagon. She told them, "I have some fruit if you get hungry," and gestured to the basket at the back of the wagon.

"We're okay," Evie answered, "we had breakfast earlier."

Before they started out, Mabel stood up. "Where are we going?" she asked.

She is so much like Evelyn, thought Emma. She looked over at the girl and said, "I really don't have time to explain right now. Can you cooperate until we get far away from the school?"

The girls looked at one another and Mabel asked one question. "Did our moms really send you?"

"They did," Emma responded.

"We'll trust you and hold our questions until we're farther away," the girl confirmed and sat down next to Evie.

Emma was relieved. She turned back to the horse and said, "Okay, girl, let's go." They made their way to a fork in the road and drove into it. She pulled up, stopped, and got out to retrieve a large branch with leaves on it. The girls watched without comment as she swept their tracks. She dragged it behind her and jumped back into the wagon and moved them along. Turning around, she told them, "Girls, I need you to use the brush and let it drag behind us to hide our tracks. Can you do that?"

They nodded quickly and took turns holding the branch off the back. After a while, Emma said, "You can stop now." They were on a path that ran through a wooded area and would hide them from the main road.

Chicago was days away and they would be on the road for a long time. Train travel would have been easier but, they needed to stay hidden. They had driven at a steady pace for more than an hour. Rest was needed for both the horse and Emma.

The girls had been quiet as Emma lifted them out of the wagon. "I'll set up lunch if you would change into the clothes in those bags," Emma said.

They followed the direction and looked in the bag. "But these are boy's clothes," Evie said.

"That's right." Emma reached into her bag to pull out her own set. "It'll be safer for us to be traveling as a man and two boys."

"What are these?" Mabel asked as she pulled out the wigs. "It's hair!"

"Yes, those are wigs. Your hair is going to make it obvious who you are. Get dressed and I'll help you with the wigs and hats."

One sister held up a blanket so that the other could have some privacy. Emma changed and was placing her skirt and top back in the bag. "We're ready," Evie called.

She turned and saw the clothes were not a perfect fit, but the baggy trousers and shirts would be comfortable for the long trip. "One at a time," she said and lifted the girls onto the back of the wagon. She got out her wig and pulled it over her hair. The hair color was dark and completely changed her appearance. She felt her head. "I think just one pin will be necessary." The two girls watched her and started to laugh at her appearance. "Now, none of that," she scolded lightly. "It's your turn now."

With their wigs in place, Emma got her revenge by laughing at them. They took the teasing kindly.

"Lunch?" she asked them.

"Yes, please," Mabel said, and Evie nodded.

They ate the hard rolls and cheese. She tossed them apples when they finished.

"Does Father know you have us?" Mabel asked, again assuming the lead for both girls.

"Father?" Emma asked carefully. She didn't want to tell them something that should come from their mothers.

"Yes," Mabel said.

"You know that you share one father?" Emma clarified.

They laughed. "How could we not?" Evie said. "It's like looking in a mirror."

She looked closely at them again; the resemblance had struck her from the start. "Did you know immediately?"

"No. It took some time to work out. Papa was our only visitor. He tried to keep us separated, but we figured it out," said Mabel.

"I followed him and saw him with Mabel," Evie said.

"I did the same," her sister said.

Smart girls! Emma thought.

"Now, where are we really going?" Mabel asked.

It was time to share the truth. She took a deep breath and told them, "Your mothers are concerned that your father may be running away and taking you and your younger sisters with him."

This time, it was Evie who spoke. "Why do they think that?"

"Both of your sisters went on a trip with their father two weeks ago and he returned without them."

Mabel frowned. "We've never been on trips together before."

Evie confirmed that with, "We're always kept separate, even at home."

"That's why your mothers are concerned. They don't want you taken from them."

"What about our sisters?" Mabel asked, holding out her hand to Evie. She took it and held it tight.

"Once we get you to a safe place, I'm going to find them and keep your mothers safe."

"By yourself?" asked Evie incredulously.

"If I have to," Emma said quietly, "but I have a team that will help. I'll need your cooperation and your promise that you'll follow my directions. I need to know you're in a safe place while we find your sisters."

Mabel looked at Evie and then back to Emma. "We'll do as you ask. We don't want to be taken from our moms."

Emma packed up their lunch, got the girls in the wagon, and headed down the road. "Do you have any questions?" she asked over her shoulder at the silent girls.

"Did you know about Dad before this?" asked Evie as she watched the scenery go by.

"I found out a couple of years ago," she admitted.

"You didn't turn him in? Isn't it wrong to have two families?"

"I didn't think there was cause at the time. Both of your mothers seemed happy. I didn't want to tear the families apart. I did leave my contact information with your mother in case something changed in your lives and you needed help."

"Why only her mother?" asked Mabel.

That is a hard one, thought Emma. "I had planned to help both families if something came up."

"Mom knew, didn't she?" guessed Evie.

Smart, thought Emma again. "Yes, she figured it out."

"And she stayed."

"She loved your father and your family. It seemed to be working out. I think she was scared of what might happen if she left."

"Scared of Dad?" Evie asked.

"I didn't think so at the time but scared of the courts finding out about the situation. Bigamy is hard to cover up and harder to recover from. I wanted to make sure the families had options if you needed them."

When Emma said the word bigamy, both girls reacted with a shudder. She saw that and didn't say anything more.

After a few hours and another break, Mabel asked while stretching her arms, "Wouldn't a train have been easier? The wagon isn't built for a long trip."

"I agree, but that would be more traceable. I don't want your father to know where we're going."

"*Where* are we going?" Mabel asked.

"Chicago."

"But Father is from there. Won't people know him or us?"

"Not where I am taking you," Emma promised. They went quiet again.

A few hours later, after their trip had started again, Evie spoke up. "Will we be stopping for dinner soon?"

"I have some houses around here where people know me," Emma said. She and Clair had set up contacts on the various trips when they were moving the ladies from safe houses to their families.

"Will they tell our father where we are?" Mabel asked, her voice shaking.

"No. They'll help protect you," Emma said firmly.

The first house was another few hours away. The time went by and Emma wasn't pushing the horse more than she should. She finally pulled into a long driveway in the country. They got out of the wagon and a woman walked out and greeted Emma and the girls without questions. She walked with them into the house and began setting food on the table. "Go wash up now, through there," the woman directed them down the hall. The girls did as they were told.

"Betty, thank you for taking us in," Emma said, helping to carry food to the table.

"You know we'd do anything for you. Clair was by a few days ago," Betty said.

"How is she?"

"They placed the last child and were headed home. I think this one wore her out."

"Thomas will take care of her, and I hope we don't have any more cases like it in the future." *If Clair is headed home,* she thought, *Jeremy might be on his way also.* She might get to see him in Chicago when she dropped off the girls.

"Would you like to rest your horse a bit before continuing on your trip?" asked Betty.

"We should. It has been a long trip." They didn't talk about her plans, sharing only what was necessary.

After everyone ate, Betty looked at the girls. "Why don't you go lie down?" she suggested. "I have two beds you can stretch out on."

They looked at Emma. She nodded. "Go ahead, get some rest."

Betty took them to the bedroom and after a few minutes came out. "They are out."

"Already?" She hadn't realized how tired they were.

Betty nodded.

"You mentioned Clair and Thomas came by here on their way home?"

"Yes, they had a special request."

"What was it?" Emma asked curiously.

"She wanted to know if I would take in one of the older kids, a boy."

"The family wouldn't take him back?" Emma asked incredulously.

"No," she said, frowning, "I don't understand people like that."

"Where is he?" asked Emma.

"He and Ben went out to work the cattle while you were here. He's skittish around new people."

"How old is he?" inquired Emma.

"Nine, his name is Paul."

"Was he hurt?" Emma asked, not wanting the answer.

Tears formed in Betty's eyes and she brushed them away. "He was, but he'll be safe with us out here. It'll give him time to heal."

"Can I meet him? Do you think that would be okay?"

Betty looked at Emma and said, "I think so. He's shy around anyone but Ben."

"Taken to him, has he?"

She smiled widely. "Yes. He's from the city but seems to fit right into the country." They walked out to the barn and she called, "Ben! Emma wanted to say hello."

Ben walked out. He was a smallish man with dark brown hair; he wore pants and a loose white shirt. He also had a hat pushed back on his head. "Emma! It's so good to see you!"

"I'm glad you were on my path today, Ben," she said and stepped up to hug him. She backed away and said, "I heard you have a new family member?"

"Yes," he said proudly. "He's brushing the horses down. City kid but he has a knack for the horses."

"Will it be okay if I meet him?"

He glanced at his wife and she nodded. "Let's head in slow," he suggested. They walked in talking about family and when they got close to the stall, they heard Paul moving around.

"Son, would you like to come out and say hello to our friend?"

There was a long moment and he slowly walked out and ran quickly to Ben. He hid his face in the man's side.

Emma knelt down to be at eye level with the small boy. "Hello, Paul, how are you?"

He peered toward her and mumbled an answer.

"Louder, boy," Ben said.

Paul took Ben's hand and stepped out. "I'm good."

"My name is Emma, and I wanted you to know that if you ever need anything, you or your parents can contact me."

Ben bent down also and said, "Emma is an investigator. She's one of the ones who saved the kids."

"You helped with that?" he asked incredulously.

"I did," she confirmed.

Paul had used up all of his bravery and hid behind Ben again. Emma took out her notebook, wrote something on a piece of paper, and tore it out. She handed the piece of paper to Paul. "This is my address and my name. I also work closely with the Pinkerton Detectives if you need anything."

Paul put it in his pocket and patted it.

Ben said, "We're going to head back into the barn to see to the horses." Paul nodded his head. "Emma, it was good to see you."

The ladies walked back to the house together arm in arm. "Is he sleeping?" Emma asked.

"Not a lot," Betty admitted. "Ben and I pulled a pad into his room and if he needs us at night, we're there."

"That is wonderful," said Emma softly.

"That woman!" Betty suddenly spat out.

Emma stopped and turned toward her. The bitterness she heard was out of character. "What woman?" she asked.

"His so-called mother. They found her and she said she wouldn't take someone who had been damaged."

"It wasn't his choice!"

"No."

"He has you and Ben now."

"Yes, God brought him to us."

"Let me know if you need anything."

"I will," Betty promised.

Emma checked her timepiece. "We should probably get moving."

"Let me help you get the horse hooked back up. "

Emma thought, *One more stop and then I'll see about a train. It'll be far enough away so that they may not be identified.*

They walked over to the wagon and hooked the horse back up. The blankets were in the back.

Returning to the house, they each woke one of the girls and

helped them put their wigs on. They grumbled a bit but understood the trip had just started.

"You finish with them and I will get you a basket of food ready," Betty said.

"Thanks, Betty."

The other woman smiled and went back to the kitchen. She came out a little while later with a basket. It must have been heavy, as she was using both hands to carry it. Emma took one side and helped her walk out to the wagon.

"Do you need anything else?" asked Betty.

"No, this is plenty. Let's get the girls; we should be on our way."

The girls were lifted into the wagon. She could see Ben and Paul at a distance. She lifted an arm and waved goodbye.

She climbed up into the driver's seat and clicked her tongue to get the horse moving. The girls were still sleepy and lay on the blanket, not saying much. The scenery rolled by at a leisurely rate. She pulled over a few hours later and said, "Break time." She could see a stream to water the horse. "Get out and stretch your legs." She unhooked the horse and took her to the stream for some water. She tied her loosely so she could reach water and grass.

"Can you get one of the blankets down, and we can have a snack?" asked Emma.

Once the blanket was set up, all three sat and Emma tossed each girl an apple. The crunching sound and birds were all that could be heard.

Mabel lay back on the grass and asked, "How much longer?"

"I was thinking about that," admitted Emma. "The horse will make it to Chicago, but I think we might try the train from here."

"I thought you said it was too dangerous," Evie said with a frown.

"I think we're far enough along, and I want to get back to your moms," she explained. They looked relieved that it was going to be train travel for the rest of the trip and no more wagons.

Things were organized and they caught a train about fifty miles from the school. They pulled into the station area and she parked the wagon. She turned to them. "Stay here. I need to get the tickets. Keep your voices down." She went quickly to the ticket office. As she paid for the tickets, she looked around and asked, "Is there anywhere I could stable my horse and wagon until they can be picked up?"

"Yes. A man named Caleb has a barn and, for a price, he'll board them until they're retrieved," the clerk said helpfully.

"Thank you. Also, is there a telegraph station in town?"

"There is," he said and pointed. "It's just down from Caleb's place."

Perfect, she thought. "What time does the train leave?"

"You have two hours, and we'll be leaving on time."

Emma turned and walked away from him and waved to the girls. Joining them at the wagon, they looked at her expectantly as she said, "We need to drop off the wagon first."

She drove the wagon and the girls to Caleb's place. The wagon stopped and she turned to them. "Keep your heads down," she cautioned, "and don't talk. Remember, you're boys. Keep silent and wear these." She tossed them cloth hats.

Jumping down, she headed into the office. A man wearing work pants and a loose shirt was writing something down in a book at the counter. "Sir," she said, deepening her voice some.

"Yes?" Caleb asked, looking up.

"I have a horse and wagon that will need to be boarded. The owner will retrieve them in a few days," she said.

"I can take them. I have room, but you'll have to pay upfront," he said gruffly.

"I can do that," she said calmly. He quoted his fee and she pulled the money out and handed it to him.

"Who'll be picking it up?" he asked.

"Floyd Bentley will be here. I'll send him a note now to confirm the location."

"Okay, I'll board them until he comes by," he said. Caleb walked out to help her move the horse and wagon into the barn.

"Boys, you'll need to get down," Emma said. They understood that they shouldn't ask for help and jumped down. Emma climbed up and retrieved their bags and the basket of food.

The girls helped with the bags while Emma carried the basket. The next stop was the telegraph office. She sent the message to Floyd to retrieve his horse and wagon. She started to leave and thought, they would need to be picked up at the station. "One more, please," she told the clerk.

He pulled out another piece of paper. "When you're ready."

She kept it simple. "This will go to Clair Flannigan at 221 Moffet Street. The message is: Please pick us up at the train station in a few hours."

They exited and headed to the station. She'd considered sending one to the safe house but decided it was best if there was no record of her or their location. The train had not arrived yet and they sat and waited for it. It came in on time and they boarded. Their tickets were third class; they didn't want to call attention to themselves. It wasn't as comfortable as first class but they felt safe. Emma gave each girl one of her books to keep them busy.

Less than a few hours later, they pulled into Chicago. "Keep your heads down," Emma murmured. "I have someone meeting us." They wandered out to where the wagons were picking up passengers. Emma saw Thomas waiting. He waved them over. He jumped down and helped with their bags, and he didn't say anything until they were moving. "The house?" he asked.

"Yes," she said in a low voice. As they drove into an alley, Emma looked at the girls. "Lie down," she instructed. They followed her direction and she climbed in beside them. Thomas got them covered up and pulled out, heading to the safe house Clair and Thomas managed. He pulled into the back and helped them quickly to the door.

Once inside, they found Clair and Katie the housekeeper sitting at the table. "You made good time," Clair said, standing up and going over to kiss Emma on the cheek.

"We did," Emma said.

"Tell me who we have here?" Clair directed. "Sisters?" she asked, taking in their appearances.

"Yes and no. Same father and different mothers. This is Evie and Mabel."

"I'm Clair and this is Katie. Welcome. Come this way," Clair said. "We have rooms for you." They followed the lovely lady quietly; the trip had worn them down. She called back, "Katie, will you bring up a snack to their rooms?"

Katie nodded and gave a quick wink to Emma. "Follow me back to the kitchen."

They got organized with tea and cakes. Emma swiped a few and got her hand swatted. She grinned and helped her carry the trays to the girls' rooms. Once they were settled, they closed the door and headed back downstairs.

"Emma, come sit with me," Clair requested. She hugged Emma's arm tightly.

"How are you?" asked Emma.

"We're better," Clair replied. "The operations lasted longer than expected, and then it turned out some parents didn't want damaged children back."

"Yes, I stopped by Ben and Betty's and met Paul," Emma said.

Clair teared up. "He's a lovely little boy. I'm so glad we found a home for him." They sat down and she noticed Emma grimace. "Are you okay? Would you like me to rub your shoulders?"

"I'd like that," she admitted. "My shoulders are tired from driving the wagon."

"Turn around."

Emma turned and groaned when Clair started to rub them. "Did Jeremy come back with you?" she asked.

"No, he stayed to process some of the paperwork we found and close down a large number of children holding locations."

"But you didn't find all of them," Emma said, disappointment sounding in her voice.

"Emma," Clair said and turned her friend around. "We will never find all of them. We'll just do the best we can."

"What did you find out about the baby?"

"Jeremy stayed with us a few days. He wanted to find the couple that took her. He found the father. Turns out he was paid to be there with the girl."

"What about the mother? Did he find out anything on her?"

"No word yet. Jeremy was concerned he might draw too much attention to her if he kept pursuing the topic."

"What persuaded you to give the baby to her?" Emma asked curiously.

"It was hers," Clair said simply. "The baby responded to her immediately. We also did as you asked and looked for identifying marks on the baby."

"What type?" she asked.

"A birthmark, almost perfectly round."

"So, John's daughter got her baby back and John is out of prison."

"Yes, and probably setting up new operations."

"Will he come back to Chicago?"

"I don't think he will right away. It'll be hard to trace him. He's good at new beginnings." Clair moved to another subject. "These older girls, what are the next steps in this operation?"

"We need to find their sisters."

"The two here, Evie and Mabel look about the same age."

"Yes, and the younger two are also extremely close in age." Emma went on to explain about the two families' houses and how similar they were.

"What an odd man," Clair commented.

"Yes, very odd."

"What about the mothers, will they be at risk if he finds out what's happening?"

"He hasn't been abusive before this, but I do need to figure out what he has planned for the other two wives once he's gone."

"Where he took the little ones, do you think there's another wife?"

"I do. He'll need a new mother for them. I'm also concerned about how he's funding all of this. He makes good money, but a third family is going to cost more and I'd assume he doesn't plan to leave his assets with the other two."

"Losing an asset like a home could harm the wives. They might never recover from that."

"Yes, these two ladies will fight for their homes and their children."

"So, we need to come up with a way to get the girls back and keep them in their homes?"

"Yes," Emma said, thinking. She yawned. "I need to get home and get organized. Who will stay with the girls?"

"I will," Lily said from the door. "I moved my things in today."

She looked over at Lily. The woman had come into their lives in an unconventional way. She had been robbing homes and was caught hiding out at the safe house. As Clair's assistant, she had turned her life around. "Thank you, Lily."

"Anything I could do to help."

"Thomas," Clair called, "we're ready to head home."

Thomas came into the room carrying a cup of coffee. "I'm ready when you are."

"Finish your coffee," Emma said. "How did the baby handle the travel?"

"She's a trooper." Thomas beamed.

"Where is she?" she asked, looking around.

"She's home with her nanny," Clair responded.

Thomas set down his empty cup and saucer on the table. He turned to Emma. "I moved your bags back into the wagon."

Clair, Thomas, and Emma headed out through the kitchen and got into the wagon. Emma lay low in the back until they reached the boarding house. Thomas uncovered her and touched her arm. "Emma."

She woke suddenly and realized she'd fallen asleep. "What?" She looked around. "Oh, yes, home."

Clair was concerned and asked her friend, "Do you want Thomas to help you into the house?"

"No," she said, yawning. "I can make it." Thomas helped her down and handed her the bag and basket. She slowly made her way up to the door and heard the wagon move past as she entered. The foyer was dark and she headed up to her bedroom. As she finally settled into bed, there was a light knock on the door. Dora's voice could be heard through it.

"Can I come in?"

"Yes," Emma called back. She didn't get out of bed.

Dora walked quickly over and climbed into bed with her. "Did you get the girls to Clair?" she asked.

"Yes." Emma settled down with her head on Dora's shoulder. "They're almost identical and they knew they were related through their father."

"Who told them?" her sister asked curiously.

"No one had to. They figured it out when they met each other."

"Hmm. What next?"

When Emma didn't respond, Dora looked over and saw she was asleep.

She slipped out of the bed. "Sleep well. We'll talk in the morning." She pulled Emma's covers up and quietly left the room.

CHAPTER 18

The next morning, Emma was up and trying to determine what she should do next. *Team,* she thought. *I need to run things by my team.*

She dressed and headed down to the kitchen. Tim had returned from his trip and sat at the dining room table. When she walked into the room, he looked up from his books.

"How was your trip? Did you have any problems?"

"No, not really. I'm thinking of next steps."

At that moment, Ethyl and Amy came in from the kitchen and put the platters of food on the table. Lottie ran in with Dora close behind. "Talk after breakfast," he suggested.

"Yes," she said, her mouth already full of a biscuit.

Ethyl called to Jake, "You need to come into the dining room." He came in from the kitchen and sat down. Savannah took a seat and Emma stayed where she was.

"Can you all wait after breakfast? I want to discuss a few things with you," she said.

"Of course," Savannah answered and the others nodded.

The conversation moved on to other topics. Emma turned to

Dora. "Have you heard from Jeremy?" she asked. He knew she was traveling and any updates would have been sent to the house.

Dora looked surprised. "Oh, yes! I forgot about that. Would you like it now?" She made a move to get up.

Emma stopped her. "After breakfast is fine."

The group continued to share their plans for the day, and when they finished the meal, they helped clear the table. Once they had moved all of the platters and dishes, they sat back down at the dining table for the meeting.

Dora was the last to join them. She had retrieved the telegram and handed it to Emma. She took it and said, "I'll read this after." She put it into her pocket and looked at her team.

She updated them with what had happened so far and when she finished, she stated, "I either go after the little girls or I keep an eye on the wives."

"Is Banks dangerous?" Tim asked.

"He can be about some things, but I'm not sure if he knows the wives are involved with the girls being moved," Emma admitted.

"Will he know the kids have been removed from the school?" Dora asked.

"That I'm unsure of," Emma admitted. "It was relatively easy to get them. The director was out and the assistant didn't give me any problems, but the clerk looked nervous about not getting the director's approval."

Savannah looked at her and said, "I want to go with you. I've been there and know both women. I wouldn't mind keeping an eye on them, that way you could see about the other two girls."

Emma looked at her. "I could use your help. Are you sure you can take the time?"

"I can." Savannah was ready to help. "Do you know where he took them?"

"No, but I have an idea of where to start. His place of business. If he's keeping his job, then a notice would be with his current company."

"When would you like to leave?"

"Soon."

"Okay, I just have a few things to do before we leave. I'll need to notify the theatre that a replacement will have to step in for the show."

"Will you notify Ethan?" Dora asked in an innocent voice. The two had been spending all of their time together since Christmas.

Savannah turned red at that. "Yes, I'll tell him I'll be out of town with Emma."

"Make sure you don't tell him why; we need to keep this private," Emma cautioned.

"Ethan will understand," Savannah said. Their team had helped him find out how his father died. He had seen how they worked.

They heard a bang of a door and running feet. Emma put her hand to her lips and her team nodded. Mark Sutherland ran into the room.

"Emma!" he exclaimed. "I hoped to catch you here. When did you get back?" Mark and Emma had met years before in New York City when she stopped his new career as a pickpocket when he was nine. He was thirteen now and his family members were on and off again team members.

"Just last night. Is everything okay?" she asked, suddenly worried.

"Yes, I just wanted to share some news!" he said excitedly. "My uncle is planning a visit!"

"Uncle," she mulled. "Have I heard about him?"

"I don't think so. We don't see him much. He is mom's brother. They were really close."

"Where does he live?" she asked.

"Upper New York State, at least, that is where his mail goes," Mark said as he shrugged.

"Mark, what do you mean? Does he travel for his job?" Emma asked.

"Uh-huh. He goes over the United States and sometimes Europe."

"What does he do?" Dora asked curiously.

"Don't know. Ma says business."

"Was the visit a surprise?" Emma asked.

Mark squirmed and finally answered, "I sent him a telegram and asked him to visit. Mom has been a bit down and this will be perfect for her."

"Is your father looking forward to the visit?"

Mark looked hesitant. "I'm not so sure. I don't think Dad likes him to visit as much as Mom does."

"Do they fight?" Emma asked.

"No. My uncle just takes most of the attention and I think Dad feels a little left out when he's here."

She thought about that and thought she would need to keep an eye on them. "When is he coming?"

"He said a few weeks," Mark replied.

"Be sure to bring him over for us to meet him," Emma said.

He grinned and added, "You'll love him, Emma. I just know it."

Will I? she wondered.

"I have to get back to school," he said.

"Can't miss that," she teased him.

He grinned and ran off.

The group didn't say anything until after they heard the door slam behind Mark. Tim spoke first. "The little girls. I'm concerned about your plan. I don't think it would be legal to remove them from their current location."

Emma frowned and asked, "What would be different from what I did at the school? I'll get the same letters to take them."

Tim explained, "In that case, you went in the front door and I think here you plan something more covert?"

"Yes," she murmured. "The girls are with a new wife who'll probably want to talk to her 'husband' before they're moved. We have to prevent that."

"That could be thought of as kidnapping, even with the mother's permission. You know the authority for the family still rests with the fathers," Tim stated.

She frowned and said slowly, "You're right. The other was different."

"What will you do?" Dora asked. She was concerned that this could get complicated.

Emma looked at her "I'll try to locate the address first at his business."

"Banks has gotten a new wife and a new life?" asked Dora. "Why would he do that?"

"A new start, a new life," Emma confirmed. "I don't know what caused him to want to start again, but my goal is to find out. I'll observe and then approach her when he's not there. If she's like the other two wives, she'll probably listen to reason."

"What if she knows and doesn't care?" Savannah asked.

"That's a chance I'll have to take, but I think she might care. This is getting complicated. I'm not even sure either of the two marriages is legal. He married numbers one and two when he was still married to Mrs. Gilmore."

They mulled that over. Tim spoke up. "The courts will have to straighten that out after the girls are safe."

"Yes." Emma looked over at Savannah and asked her, "Do you still want to go with me?"

Savannah said firmly, "I'm ready to help. When will we leave?"

"In the morning. Will that give you enough time to get things organized?"

"It should. I'll be ready." Savannah thought of the two women and the strain they must be under to get their children back.

"I'll get the train tickets and meet you back here," Emma said, standing.

"I can drive you," Tim offered.

"Will I need to pack wigs and makeup?" Savannah asked, thinking ahead.

Emma nodded. "Yes, and pack pants and dresses for yourself. We'll go first dressed as women, but we'll want the option to change if needed. I also have the girl's clothes and wigs you sent with me. They are in my room."

"I will take them to the theatre with me."

The team started leaving the table. Emma began walking out of the room, pulling the telegram out of her pocket as she went.

Before she could read it, Savannah's voice stopped her. "And Emma?"

She turned back to her. "Do you have more questions?"

"This time, I'd like to ride the train the whole way there," Savannah commented with a straight face.

Emma grinned wickedly. "What, you didn't enjoy the side trip of a train and rolling down a hill?" Savannah had been involved in the case the first time they met Hugo Banks. On the way home, they had been forced to jump off a train or be shot by assailants. They had gotten away, but they had lost two dresses and two pairs of boots rolling down the hill. She assured her friend, "I plan for us to make it to and from without any incident."

Savannah had only been half teasing and replied, "Good. I'll meet you here." She went up to get the borrowed clothes and headed back downstairs and out the door. *Ethan first*, she thought. *Then the theatre.*

The telegram from Jeremy was full of news about the captures and closing of the houses. He would be returning soon. Emma clasped it tightly in her hands and thought, *Soon. We'll be together soon.*

CHAPTER 19

That evening, when all their errands were completed and dinner eaten, the group settled into the sitting room for a quiet evening. A knock sounded at the door. "I'll get it," Emma said. She answered the door and walked back into the sitting room, reading a telegram. She looked over at Savannah. "Good thing we're going in the morning."

"Why?"

"Hugo knows about Evie and Mabel. He's gone to the school."

"What else does it say?" Tim asked.

"Nothing else," Emma said, looking up from the telegram.

"Should we be worried about the girls here?" Dora asked.

"There's no connection to us. I don't think he'll think to look for them here. The safe house is a secret."

Tim stood. "I'll stop by Clair and Thomas' house and tell them that Hugo knows the girls aren't in school anymore." He looked down at the floor where Patrick was playing with Lottie. "Would you like to go with me?" he asked his son. The boy nodded eagerly and got to his feet to follow his papa.

"Thank you, Tim," Emma called to him.

"It's not a problem," Tim said as he and Patrick headed out into the night.

KIMBERLY MULLINS

*E*arly the next morning, they headed to the station. Savannah and Emma were dressed in dark skirts and white blouses and their hair was pulled into buns. Savannah carried her case of wigs and makeup with her. The station was quiet that morning and their train stood waiting. They would only need a day and would share a cabin. They stayed there and enjoyed the day trip to Cleveland.

As they got closer to their destination, Emma said, "I think we should put on the wigs here in case we're spotted."

"Okay," Savannah agreed. She opened her bag and pulled out an auburn wig for Emma. "Your makeup will have to be a bit darker to wear this one." She showed her friend how to apply it so it looked natural.

They prepared for their roles and were ready by the time the train came to a stop. This time, their hotel room would be under aliases. The trip to the hotel was accomplished quickly and they dropped their bags off and headed over to Evelyn's house. The carriage took them close to their destination; they were cautious, not counting on Hugo being away.

"We'll have to keep an eye out as we approach," said Savannah and she pulled a book out of her bag.

"A Bible?" Emma asked.

"Yes, I thought we could use it as an excuse to be at their door if he is still around."

"Good thinking." At that moment, the carriage slowed down and indicated it was their stop. Emma paid the driver and they started toward Evelyn's house.

"It's quiet," Savanna observed as she looked around.

"It is," Emma said.

"How will we be able to tell that he isn't there?" Savannah asked as she bit her bottom lip and held the Bible closer to her.

"A bike will be on the porch if things are safe."

They continued their stroll. They were close but didn't want to rush and bring any attention to their activities.

"The bike's there," Emma murmured.

Savannah looked and saw her friend was right. *Just the same,* she thought and started to move more quickly toward the house.

Emma stopped her. "Slowly," she cautioned.

Savannah nodded and slowed her pace. They strolled together arm and arm toward the home and up the stairs to the porch. Emma raised a hand to knock at the door. They heard slow steps approaching. It opened revealing half of Izzy's face. "Yes, what do you want?" she asked, her voice muffled.

"We would like to share the word of God with you," Emma said.

Izzy's eyes widened when she heard the familiar voice. "Emma!" she whispered, hoping it was her.

Emma nodded.

"Hugo's gone. Come in. Hurry before someone sees you," the woman said and pulled them inside.

Once they were in the foyer, Emma and Savannah saw both sides of her face. The right side was mottled with bruises

"What happened?" Emma asked, concerned. She went over to her and cupped Izzy's face in her hands.

"Hugo is what happened to her and me," came a voice out of the kitchen.

It was Evelyn. She walked over to Izzy with a cloth wrapped around an ice pack. "You need to keep this on your face." She took her friend's arm and walked with her to the sitting room to sit down. She held the ice to Izzy's face.

Emma and Savannah followed and Emma said, "Tell us." She and Savannah sat across from them.

Evelyn started with, "Director Darnton sent a telegram yesterday and informed our husband that Evie and Mabel had been picked up. And that it had been approved by their mothers."

"Hmm," said Emma, "the assistant director was there when I picked them up and didn't give me much trouble."

"Darnton's probably in Hugo's pocket," Izzy said.

"What happened then?" Savannah asked.

Izzy spoke up as she lowered the ice from her face. "Hugo confronted me first and asked where the girls were. I told him if he brought our other girls home, I would bring Evie and Mabel home as well."

"His response?" Emma asked.

"You're looking at it," she said bitterly.

Emma observed Evelyn's appearance as the woman took a seat beside Izzy. "You look relatively unscathed."

She nodded. "That's thanks to her. After he hit her, he went upstairs and she ran all the way to my house and helped me hide."

"Do you think he would have done the same to you?"

"Oh, yes. We watched him storm out of my home. When he left, we went back inside. He had taken the picture of us on the mantel and twisted it and thrown it on the floor."

"I saw a similar reaction when he didn't get his way previously," commented Emma. Hugo's first marriage had been to solely get back at his friend. He felt he was slighted and had stayed married to the woman Mr. Gilmore was in love with.

Izzy couldn't wait and ask, "How are our girls?"

Emma smiled. "They're fine. You know, they already knew that they had the same father."

"But how? I just found out myself," Izzy said, her eyes going wide.

"The girls are nearly identical, so there's that. Plus, they saw their father when he visited. He would meet with each girl separately," she explained.

"They weren't upset?" Izzy asked, worried about what her daughter thought.

"No, just matter of fact about it. They seem very close."

Both of the mothers were frowning and Evelyn spoke for them. "We would like to go to them."

"I think it's best that you stay here," Emma stressed. "They're fine as of now and they're protected until we can work this out."

"How much time do we have?" Savannah asked.

"Not much," Emma replied. "His trip to the school will probably be faster than mine, especially if he pushes his horse and doesn't rest."

Evelyn asked hesitantly, "Will he be able to trace the girls?"

"I told Baxter I was bringing them home, so I don't think Hugo will be anywhere near where they are."

They looked relieved, then Izzy exclaimed, "He'll come back here!"

"He probably will," Emma acknowledged. "We need to make a plan for the younger girls before he returns. Do you know where he has them?"

"We don't," Izzy said.

Emma stood and walked to the mantel. She looked over at them. "I've been thinking about that. If he's changing jobs or transferring, then his work will know. I need to talk to someone in his office." She held up her bag and asked,

"Would you mind if I changed here? I'd like to go straight over."

Izzy said, "Of course. Upstairs first room on the right."

Emma went up and found the bedroom right away. She looked around and thought, *This is the first time I've been up here. I wonder if both houses are the same?* She dressed quickly in the boys' clothes and placed her dress and wig into her bag. Going back downstairs quickly, she twisted her braided hair and pulled her hat over to anchor it down.

Savannah put her teacup and saucer down when she saw Emma on the stairs. "Ready to go?" Emma asked.

"Yes," she said and went over to both ladies and took their hands in hers. "I will find out where the little girls are," she promised. "We'll be in contact today. Be ready to go just in case." They nodded and watched them leave.

They headed out and found a carriage to take them to Hugo's business office. Once they were dropped off, Emma asked Savannah to wait outside on a bench. She pulled her hat down. "I'll be back in a moment."

She entered the building and went to the same person who had given her Hugo's address on the previous case. He had inadvertently given her the two addresses that led to the man's bigamy being uncovered. "Excuse me, I have a question for you."

His head swung toward her. "You!" he exclaimed. "Why are you back? Do you know what happened last time you were here?"

"What do you mean? I just got an address," she said innocently.

"No, you tricked me into giving you confidential information," he said in a loud voice.

"Really?" she asked, her tone dry. "Confidential information? Since when?"

"Well, not at that time," he admitted. "But it is now."

She looked at him consideringly and decided to tell him the truth. "Did you know what the two addresses meant?"

"Not at the time," he admitted in a calmer voice. "But after Mr.

Banks' reaction, I went to both locations. They were eerily the same."

"Did you meet the wives?" she asked curiously.

"No! I didn't want to. I didn't want to be involved any more than I was then," he said. "Why are you here now?" he asked.

"It's bigger than last time."

"How so? What, did he get more wives?" he asked, laughing.

She looked around to make sure they were alone, then leaned in and said, "Yes, I think so. I think that's exactly it. Another family. I also think he's moving his children to that new wife."

He went white at that statement. "There are children involved?"

"Yes. Hugo has four currently, two with each wife."

He pushed his chair back and stood. "What can I do to help?"

"Is he transferring to one of your other locations? Or quitting to move to another job?"

He pulled his files and consulted them. "He's transferring to the New York Office."

She jotted down the information, looked over at him, and asked, "Any idea of his new address?"

"Yes, I have that also." He handed it to her. "A third family?" he asked, bewildered.

"Yes. Please don't tell anyone I was here."

"No worries, I don't plan to tell anyone," he reassured her.

She turned as he called out, "Let me know if I can help with anything else."

"I will," she promised.

She walked outside and went to sit next to Savannah on the bench. "Not only did I get the town he's moving to, but also his new address. Now to see If I can beat him to the little girls." She looked around and commented, "Let's walk some. I don't want to be seen here."

Savannah nodded and, once they started walking, she asked, "Where?"

"New York City."

"Will we go there?"

"Yes. And now that I know where the girls are located, we need to get moving."

When they returned to Izzy's house, they found the ladies in the dining room eating lunch.

"We saved some for you both," Evelyn said, getting up. She brought their plates back; Savannah and Emma quickly ate.

"Thank you," said Emma. Savannah nodded in agreement.

"Did you get his new address?" Izzy asked.

"I did," Emma confirmed.

"Thank goodness! But what if he moves them? Can you get to them in time?" Evelyn asked.

Emma frowned and looked down at the address. "My team at home pointed out that if I take the girls, I could be accused of kidnapping."

"Even if it's for us? Their mothers?" Izzy asked.

"This is still a patriarchy we live in. Though I think Hugo is more scared of being caught for bigamy; it is probably why he hasn't notified the police of the other girls being taken." She turned her gaze to Izzy and Evelyn, "I'm also concerned about something else."

"What are you thinking?" Evelyn asked.

"Hugo may have told the girls that you died and that the move was to start a new family," she said boldly.

Both women's faces lost color; Emma was glad they were sitting. She couldn't have caught both of them.

"Would he do that?" Evelyn asked faintly. "Would he just erase us like that?"

Emma took a deep breath before replying, "Yes, I think he wants a new start."

"Yes, since his first wife, Elle, and her husband announced her pregnancy," Izzy muttered. "He seemed to lose interest in me, in us."

"That's when the trips started," Evelyn confirmed. "I was a naive fool," she said bitterly. "I didn't know any of this was going on."

Izzy took her hand. "No, you shouldn't have to question if your husband has more than one wife."

"You figured it out first."

"Yes, and more the fool. I stayed knowing I was only sharing someone else's husband. And our daughters will suffer because I didn't want things to change."

Emma watched them clean up the lunch. She looked at Savannah and asked, "Do you have time to accompany me on the next part of this trip?"

"You couldn't stop me," she said.

"Good." Emma looked over at the two wives. "I've been thinking about the kidnapping issue. I think what you can do is accompany me and Savannah to retrieve your girls. That way, I know you two are safe and you can take the girls as their mothers."

"Us?" asked Evelyn in a high voice. "You want us to go along on the case?"

"Yes," Emma said. "Definitely. We'll need you to pack. Savannah, go with Evelyn to her house and meet us back here. I'll go get the train tickets. I'd like to leave this evening."

"We can do it," Izzy said to Evelyn bracingly.

"We can," confirmed Evelyn with a deep breath.

They started out and Izzy asked, "Where are we going?"

"The address I have is for New York City," said Emma.

"Will we beat him there?" Savannah asked.

"If Hugo comes back here first, I think we will."

Everyone headed to complete their assigned task. Izzy went upstairs and pulled out her bag and got organized.

Savannah went to Evelyn's house with her, telling her, "Go up and get packed. I'll wait here."

Evelyn nodded and went to her room. She got her clothes

packed in a bag and, lastly, she pulled out a gun from the bottom of her dresser, examining it. *He will pay*, she promised herself and slid it under her clothes. Her bag closed with a snap and she carried it downstairs; they left for Izzy's house immediately.

There, Izzy and Emma were waiting on the porch. "Everyone ready to go?" Emma asked.

Everyone confirmed they were ready. They walked down the stairs to a waiting carriage and climbed in.

"Where to?" the driver asked.

"Train station, please," directed Emma. The group was quiet and, as they entered their two cabins, not a word was said.

"We can sit together for a while," Emma suggested.

The two Mrs. Banks put their bags in their cabin and then walked back to Emma and Savannah's cabin to sit together. There were so many plans and questions, but the group didn't talk; instead, one could hear the sound of fingers drumming on the book Evelyn held. Izzy's foot tapped on the floor, Evelyn's skirt rustled as she struggled to get comfortable, and Savannah's finger squeaked as she drew on the window.

When Emma finally spoke, it startled everyone. "Are you ready to go get your girls?"

The two women nodded.

"Then, now, we plan." She bent her head towards them. They leaned forward, listening intently.

CHAPTER 21

The train pulled into Buffalo and they moved to the day train to be transported to New Jersey. Once there, they disembarked and walked with purpose toward the carriages that stood by for rental purposes at the New Jersey station. Emma gave the address she had gotten from Hugo's work, and the group climbed on board. There was no talking; they had their plan and were concentrating on their individual parts.

The carriage pulled up in front of the house and both women looked on with shock. It was the same house.

"Oh, for God's sake! Couldn't that damn man do something original?" Izzy muttered angrily.

Emma paid the driver, and the women started walking towards the front door. They stopped suddenly when a young girl's laughter reached them. "Bess!" shouted Evelyn.

Emma caught her arm and cautioned the woman, "Remember our plan. We want to approach this logically. We don't want your girls to get hurt." That calmed Evelyn down. They formed a line and continued toward the door.

As they went up the steps, Emma waved them back behind her. She knocked and waited patiently for the door to be answered. It swung open, revealing a younger version of the two ladies standing behind her. Emma could see past her into the house and realized that it was indeed identical to the two Hugo had with his other families. *The man finds a type and doesn't make a change.*

"Hello, can I help you?" the woman asked politely, blocking the doorway.

"I believe so. I'm Emma Evans and these two ladies..." She wasn't able to finish the thought.

The woman stared at Evelyn and Izzy and said faintly, "You're dead. He told me you were dead."

As she started to fall, Emma said, "Great. Another fainter. Quick, grab her!" As the others rushed to catch the woman, she continued. "Let's get her inside before we start attracting attention."

The others helped get the woman's limp body into the sitting room. They laid her on the sofa, and Izzy looked at the others. "How did she know us?" she asked.

Savannah was fanning the woman and said, "Check out the mantel."

The two wives walked over to see pictures of themselves. "Wow, he's mourning us already," Izzy said faintly.

"The girls," the woman muttered as she woke up. "They're out back playing."

"I'll go see to them," Evelyn stated.

"Thank you," mouthed Izzy.

Her footsteps could be heard going through the house and the back door opening. Screams followed.

The new Mrs. Banks kept saying over and over, "He told me you were dead, both of you. He brought the girls here after we married. He said you were dead!"

At the word married, Emma and Izzy glanced at each other.

The woman caught the glance. "We are married, aren't we?" she asked worriedly.

"Well…" Emma began. "You might be the only one truly married to him."

Izzy looked nonplussed and said, "Explain yourself."

"I believe yours and Evelyn's marriages happened while he was married to his first wife. I'm not sure those are valid. We can work that out with a lawyer."

"Well, I don't want to be married to him! I'm the fourth wife?" the current Mrs. Banks asked, looking faint again. She glanced at Izzy. "I'm so very sorry. I had no idea."

"Can I bring the girls in?" Evelyn called from the back of the house.

"Yes!" answered Izzy.

Her daughter, Bess, ran in and jumped into her arms. "Mama! Papa said you had gone to heaven."

"No, baby," Izzy said, pulling her daughter in for a tight hug. She looked over and saw Evelyn carrying her daughter, Rebecca.

The fainting woman sat up and said, "I think we should introduce ourselves. My name is Catherine. And you are?"

"Izzy Banks."

"Evelyn Banks."

"Emma Evans."

"Savannah Woods."

When Emma and Savannah didn't say Banks, Catherine looked relieved. But she had to ask. "You two aren't married to Hugo, too, are you?"

Emma laughed. "No. No, we're not."

"Oh, thank God," she said, relieved. She looked at Emma and asked, "Where do we go from here?"

"*We,*" said Emma, looking at the ladies around her, "have some ideas about that."

CHAPTER 22

The three wives waited together. Catherine looked over at Izzy and Evelyn. "What made you realize your husband had two wives?" She couldn't bring herself to say 'our' concerning Hugo.

"It took a lot," Izzy admitted as she looked over at her new best friend.

Evelyn returned the look. "I didn't believe what Izzy was saying at first. I even threatened her with the police."

"How did you get her to see the truth?" Catherine asked curiously. It was a story she didn't want to believe either.

"I kidnapped her," Izzy admitted.

"Kidnapped?" Catherine asked, fascinated by her fellow wives.

"Essentially. I dragged her to a carriage and made her come to my house."

"Why would that make a difference?"

The other two wives laughed. "Our houses are identical to one another."

"Our?" Catherine asked.

"Yes, *ours*. Your house is identical to mine and Evelyn's."

"Wow," Catherine said. "Hugo had definite ideas on where we were to live and the decorating. Now I know why."

The other two wives nodded.

CHAPTER 23

Emma waited patiently, alone in the sitting room. It could be hours before Hugo turned up. A delay would have meant he'd gone to Chicago before coming here. She sat back with a book, looking forward to the confrontation that would take place.

Bang!

The front door crashed inward. Glass fragments clinked as they rained down on the tile floor. Again, she waited. She wouldn't rush this.

Hugo Banks yelled out, running by the sitting room. "*Catherine!* Where are you!" When he didn't get a response, he softened his voice and called out, "Girls? Daddy's home!" He ran back to the foyer and saw Emma in the sitting room. She wore pants and a shirt; her blonde hair was in a high ponytail. She wiggled her fingers as a greeting.

He looked surprised, then he frowned when he recognized her. "You! What are you doing here? You've caused me enough trouble!"

"Yes, I've heard I have that effect on people. Hugo, it's time for us to talk."

"How *dare* you enter my home and interfere with my family! I don't want to talk! Not to you! I want to know where they are!"

"Not just yet," Emma replied calmly. "I have something to discuss with you first."

He seemed at a loss about how to react to her calm demeanor. He moved to a blue side chair and sat, then stood and sat again; putting his hands in his hair, he pulled at it.

The time it had taken Hugo to arrive had allowed Emma to communicate with Mr. Pennington. The lawyer confirmed something she feared, and it was time to ask Hugo about the information. She shifted in her seat, her hat still in her lap, covering her knife.

"Hugo," she began, "I received a telegram today; it mentioned confirmation of burial plots in Cleveland. Who were those for?"

"Why do you want to know?" His voice went up an octave. "It's none of your business," he muttered. He jumped up and shouted, "*Where is my family?* If you won't tell me, I'll beat it out of you." He stalked toward her and, before Emma could pull her knife, Evelyn's voice rang out.

"Which family are you referring to Hugo?" Shoes clicked, and he whipped around to see who it was. He screamed when he saw her. Emma had told her to keep her distance. *This is starting to get out of hand,* she thought.

"Tsk tsk, you left a mess on the floor. I know how much you hate that," Evelyn scolded him.

"You! What are you doing here?" Hugo demanded.

"You didn't answer her question, Which family are you referring to?" Izzy said as she joined Evelyn in the doorway.

He looked from one wife to another and again seemed to be at a loss of what to say. "You're here also? *Where are my daughters?*" he roared as he finally found his voice.

"They're safe," commented Emma again in a calm tone. They had all agreed to let him be the one out of control.

Hugo's rage took over and he swung his gaze from Emma to his wives as he tried to decide who to go after first. He made a quick decision and charged at Emma, his hands outstretched, She didn't stop him as he landed a fist on her face. Her head went back and she reached for her knife. Before she could pull it, there was the sound of a gun being cocked that caused everyone to freeze. Emma saw the gun and then Evelyn. "Evelyn," she said. "Wait, don't shoot."

Evelyn didn't respond. She kept the gun pointed at Hugo.

"Turn around, Hugo. Slowly."

"I'd do as she says," Emma advised. *This is not part of the plan.*

Hugo turned toward Evelyn and Izzy.

"Now, Evelyn," he said, trying to placate her.

"You don't sound like yourself, why is that?" Evelyn chided.

He gave up trying to reason with her and ordered, *"Put the gun down!"*

"There it is. That's the man I know," she said mockingly.

"We have some questions we would like answered," Izzy said.

Hugo didn't say anything. He just watched them. *I can still control them.*

Evelyn waved her gun at him again. "You were so talkative before. You have something to say?"

Emma decided to let this play out. She got a good look at the gun and didn't think it was loaded. But she couldn't take the chance that Izzy and Evelyn would end up with murder charges.

"I don't want to interrupt, but we should secure him. Do you mind?" she asked the wives.

Evelyn looked like she wanted to say no, but Izzy said, "I think that's a good idea."

"Savannah," Emma called. Her friend came into the room. "Come over here and help me with Hugo," she directed.

Both women took an arm and moved him to the couch. They secured his arms behind him with rope.

Once he was settled, he started with his demands to Emma.

"You bring my older girls to me. I want them with me and Catherine."

"Hugo, you're not in charge here. We are. Ladies, why don't you take a seat?" asked Emma.

Izzy and Evelyn stepped further into the room, revealing Catherine behind them.

Hugo was startled when he saw her but remained silent.

Once they settled, Emma sat down across from Hugo. "You are aware that you're supposed to divorce before taking additional wives."

Hugo looked at her, his mouth turned down and a heavy frown on his forehead. "You said you wouldn't interfere in my life. Once I let Elle free." He was referencing his interference in Mr. and Mrs. Gilmore's lives.

Emma responded, "No, the agreement was for that case only. You went too far when you took the children. They should be with their mothers."

"Bah," he said and looked at his first two wives. "I had plans for them."

Emma decided to play along and asked, "What were your plans?"

"My children would be taken care of by their new mother." His wives didn't say anything; they watched him closely

"I won't be here for that role," Catherine said. "I want out."

"You'll have to divorce me and I will not allow that," he said triumphantly.

"Why me? You had two other wives," she asked, looking at the man who was now a stranger to her.

"Yes," he said, "but my annulment occurred after those marriages. You're the only one I'm legally married to."

"No, that can't be right!" Catherine said in horror. "I'm the only one married to you?"

They looked at Emma. She responded, "We'll have to discuss that with a lawyer." *Though,* she thought, *he's probably right.*

Catherine charged at him, grabbing a lamp on her way. Savannah intercepted her before she could reach him. "Let me go!" the woman raged. "He deserves this."

Emma nodded and said, "I agree, and we'll be turning him over to the police for the pain he's inflicted. But I have one thing I still need to know, Hugo. What was the next step in your plans?"

He seemed eager to share. "Oh, after I get rid of both of you," he said, nodding at Evelyn and Izzy, "I'm selling the houses."

"You would just abandon us? With no home or children?" Izzy asked, her greatest fears coming true.

"No," he said, admitting to the entire plan, "I'll kill you both and that will reduce my wifely count."

Izzy and Evelyn looked at him in horror. He said it so confidently, so sure that he was right, that he would have his children with his true wife.

Hugo sat back and looked at Catherine. *She will see this is the best thing. She is just upset now. I will convince her that this is for the best.*

"Is that your whole plan?" asked Emma. The man was sick. She looked at the wives to see how they felt about his plans.

"Yes, all neat and tidy. The girls would forget you both over time. I'll see to that."

That must have been the final straw for Evelyn and she pulled the trigger. Emma was watching the woman's face and, when it changed, she knew it was time to act. She ran and dove at Evelyn as she pointed the gun at Hugo. There was at least one bullet in it, but her aim was off; the bullet went through the top of the mantel. Emma tugged the gun out of Evelyn's hands. "I think I'll keep custody of this," she said.

Catherine walked over to the mantel to survey the damage. "Well, it looks like you got your target," she said wryly. She held up the picture. Evelyn had blown a hole through Hugo's head.

Evelyn started laughing. The other women soon joined in.

"What is everyone laughing at?" Hugo asked belligerently.

This statement just made them laugh harder.

After a minute, Savannah spoke up. "You mostly." She then handed Emma a scarf. Emma took it and fitted it quickly over his mouth and tied it at the back of his head. "Are you okay?" Savanna asked, motioning to her friend's bruised face.

"I am. Don't worry. Ladies, it's time to take your husband to the police station," Emma announced to the group.

"I'll go see about a wagon," said Catherine. Her part of the plan was to provide transportation. Catherine's neighbor, Ian, had access to one and she knew he could be trusted.

"Oh, before you go, Catherine we will need to secure him," Emma said.

"What do you need?" Catherine asked.

"A couple of blankets, please," Emma said, thinking of the best way to keep him quiet.

Catherine ran up the stairs and looked around. "Found them," she called and ran back down. Izzy, Savannah, and Evelyn shook out the blankets and, with Emma's help, laid Hugo on the floor and wrapped them around him.

"Make sure he can breathe," Emma cautioned. She was watching how tightly they were binding him with the ropes around the outside of the blanket.

"Why?" Evelyn asked bitterly.

"Because we need him alive. He's going to prison this time—no deals—and that will be hard if he's dead."

Hugo's eyes widened. That was always his out; no one wanted to be known to be married to a bigamist. Are *they this strong? Could they testify against him?*

Catherine came back in with Ian. He was a large man who looked more suited to being a lumberjack than city life.

"I'll take it from here, ladies," he said and tossed the blanket-wrapped Hugo over his shoulder. He took him to the wagon he had stationed in front of Catherine's house, then placed him none too gently into the back. "Oops. Sorry about that," he said when Hugo bounced.

Emma smiled and said, "Everyone climb in." Evelyn and Izzy joined her and Savannah. Catherine sat beside Ian on the driver's seat.

On the way to the police station, Catherine turned to Ian. "Thank you for helping."

He stared straight ahead. "Not that it's any of my business, but what did he do?"

"He's married," she said simply.

"Well yeah," he said, "to you."

"Not just me," she murmured.

"What! Who else?" he asked, flabbergasted, stopping them abruptly.

"The ladies with us. Two of them are his wives," she said.

He got them moving faster. She gripped her seat and looked over at him with raised eyebrows. He said, "The sooner he's under arrest, the better."

When they arrived at the station, Ian hopped down and reached up to help Catherine to the ground. Walking around to the back of the wagon, he lowered the gate and assisted the other ladies. Hugo was rolled over and once again thrown onto his shoulder. They went into the station, ready for whatever they might need to face.

The desk officer looked around at the people in front of him; they were all talking at the same time. He called loudly, "Silence! Who's speaking for this group?"

Emma held up her hand. "We have a bigamist we'd like to turn in."

"He's married to all of you?" the office asked incredulously.

"Three of us are," Izzy stated. By agreement, they had chosen not to bring Hugo's first wife, Elle, into this mess.

"Who was married first?" the officer asked, looking at them in interest.

"I'm the first," stated Izzy.

"I'm the second," stated Evelyn.

"I'm the third," Catherine stated quietly.

"Are there any children involved?"

"Yes," Emma replied. "There are four girls. Two from Izzy and two from Evelyn."

He looked at Catherine. "None," she said. *Thank goodness.*

"Let me find someone to take this over and move you into another room."

"Excuse me, sir?" Ian asked.

"Yes?"

"I need to put this somewhere," he said, pointing to the carpet roll on his shoulder.

"What is it?"

"The bigamist, Hugo Banks," Emma answered for him.

He looked surprised and got up to find an officer to take them to a more private location. "Detective Daniels will take Emma and Mr. Banks into one room and the wives into another." He had Ian transfer his load to one of his fellow policemen and the others followed. Ian stayed with Catherine. She seemed grateful for his support and said to him, "Why don't you head home?"

"Are you sure?" He didn't want to leave her.

"I am." He nodded and turned to leave. The rest of their group went into their assigned rooms and Hugo was settled into a chair. Officer Daniels took one across from him and Emma stood in the small room.

The detective sat at the table and reviewed the other officer's notes. "The four children, where are they?"

"They're safe," Emma answered. Ian's mother had volunteered to watch the two little girls until they all returned.

Daniels looked almost regretful as he said, "I guess we'll have to untie him. Why is he wrapped in a blanket?"

"He got rather excited and we had to subdue him for the trip over here," Emma replied.

Daniels stood to untie and unwrap Hugo with a guard standing by. Once Hugo's arms were freed, he removed the binding covering his mouth. Immediately, the man started yelling, "They kidnapped me and held me prisoner! She... she..." he stuttered, aiming his fist at Emma. "She's interfering in my life again."

"Again?" Daniels asked.

"Never mind that," Hugo said, realizing what he had almost disclosed.

Emma smiled to herself. He had started to admit to a fourth marriage. Due to the confidential nature of the previous agreement, she couldn't share any details, but he could.

Daniels looked at her and she shook her head. *I'll have to follow up with her later,* he thought. He directed his gaze back to Hugo. "Now, why would this nice lady hold you hostage?"

"I don't know, but I'd just like to head home now," Hugo said, hoping this was the end of it.

"You won't be pressing charges?" Daniels asked idly.

"*NO!* I'd just like to go home."

"Well, now that that's all settled, there'll be no charges for the ladies here. Why don't we talk about yours?"

"Mine! What charges?"

"Bigamy," Daniels said simply.

Hugo's mouth opened and closed several times, but nothing came out.

"I see you'd like some time to continue gathering your thoughts," the detective said wryly. "We have three women out there who say they're married to you."

"Well, they're lying. I only have one wife." He thought, *I have them now. There's no proof of the marriages.*

"Oh, I forgot. Detective, I have these with me," Emma said as she pulled some folded papers out of her jacket and handed them to him.

Daniels took his time looking at them. Finally, he stood and went to the door.

Hugo watched him and thought, *He's going to tell me I can leave.* He sneered at Emma, *She thought she had me.*

Daniels stepped back into the room with two more officers. "Please take Mr. Banks to booking," he directed.

"*What? NO!*" Hugo started to run out the door. The two officers stopped him and placed cuffs on his wrist. "But you have no proof."

"Your wives are giving sworn statements now," Daniels commented.

"But they're lying!" Hugo screamed again.

"Are they?" the detective asked, feigning interest.

"Yes!"

"You see, Mr. Banks, I have these to back up their stories." He showed him the papers but didn't get close enough for Hugo to see what they were.

"What are they?" There was nothing that would calm him down.

"These are your wedding certificates for all three marriages. I'm afraid, Mr. Banks, that you will have to answer for this in court. You'll be going to prison."

"Prison for getting married?" Hugo asked, desperate for this nightmare to be over.

"Sir, you married more than your fair share," chided the detective.

Hugo seemed to have no answer to that and just stared at them.

"Take him away," Daniels told his officers.

Once he was out of the room, Emma looked at him and said, "You took me at my word."

"The Chicago Police Chief sent me a telegram this morning and said that I should listen to what you have to say. He said you've worked investigations for him and the Pinkerton Detectives."

"We have him this time? Hugo won't get released?"

Daniels nodded. "We'll need to investigate some more but, for now, we'll keep him locked up." He looked at her face and asked, "Did he do that to you?"

She held up her hand to her cheek; it had started to throb. "Yes."

"I assume you'll file an assault charge as well."

"I will," Emma confirmed. She had let Hugo land that punch, knowing the assault charge would keep him locked up until the bigamy could be proven. She provided a statement so the charges could be filed.

"What will you do now?" he asked as he took the paper from her.

"That's a good question. I would like to reunite the families."

"Yes. Banks will be in custody for a while."

"I'll go to the women now. Thank you for your help in this matter."

Daniels nodded and Emma headed out of the room.

The young officer in the hallway asked, "Miss, are you looking for the wives?"

"Yes, do you know where they are?" she asked.

"I do. Would you like me to take you to them?" he offered.

"Yes, please." She accompanied the officer down the long hallway. It was lined with windows that looked into offices and conference rooms. As they turned a corner, the women came into view. Savannah stood looking out the window on the far side of their room. The wives sat together, alternately patting one another's arms.

Savannah turned and saw her first; she called over to the wives and gestured to Emma. They gave her all of their attention as she entered the room.

"We got him," Emma said quickly. "Hugo's in custody."

There was silence and they continued to stare at her.

Emma thought she was delivering good news.

"Izzy, what will we do?" Evelyn said. She looked distraught as she reached out and took the other woman's hand.

Izzy said bracingly, "Evelyn, we do what we planned before. We go forward together for us and our girls."

Catherine looked forlorn. Emma was stirred to ask, "What's wrong?"

"I'm not sure," she said, looking at the two wives and then at Emma. "This morning, I had a home, a husband, and two little girls. Now, I seem to have nothing."

"No!" the other two wives protested. "You have us."

"No. You're family. I think I need a fresh start."

"Will you need help with that? To start over?" Emma asked.

Catherine leaned back and laughed suddenly. "No, on that account, I have no problems. My family left me quite well off."

The other wives looked at each other and Evelyn asked, "Did Hugo know?"

"He knew," Catherine murmured. "I'm the daughter of one of his company's richest clients."

Izzy reached over to her. "We would like you to keep in touch and let us know how you are."

"First thing I am doing is selling that house!" Catherine said. "I never liked it, but he insisted."

The other two wives started laughing. Evelyn answered for Izzy. "We're thinking the same thing."

"What about the older girls, can we go get them?" Izzy asked Emma expectantly.

Emma hesitated. "I think we need them with you and in your custody."

"Will we have to go to Chicago for them?" asked Evelyn.

"I'm thinking you should come back to Chicago with me. I work for an attorney there and he has experience with bigamy cases and, specifically, with Hugo."

"Oh," Izzy said, "I guess we do need someone to work out the legalities of this mess."

"Yes," Emma said.

"What about me?" asked Catherine.

Emma looked over at her. "You concern me the most."

"The fact that I might be the only one married to him?"

"Yes, the fact you were married after his previous annulment. I want to make sure you get the proper legal advice."

"Then," she said, "I'll also accompany you to Chicago."

"We should try to leave as soon as the police say it's okay," Emma told the group.

"What if we need to stay here?" Izzy asked. She was worried about finances for both Evelyn and herself.

"You can stay with me," Catherine said decisively. "I insist." She looked over at Emma and asked, "Can we head home now?"

"Yes," Emma said. "Detective Daniels will let us know when we may leave town." They headed downstairs and she hailed two carriages.

"Aren't you coming back to the house with us?" Catherine asked.

"No, I need to go to the telegraph office to let my boss know what's happened and let him know you'll be coming to Chicago. I'll meet you all at the house."

"Would you like me to go with you?" Savannah asked.

"No, I think we're just about done here."

"Good. I'm ready to return home," her friend said.

"I'll be back soon." Emma watched as they climbed into the carriage and headed to Catherine's. She wanted to notify Mr. Pennington to be ready for them. Lastly, she needed to get her and Savannah's bags and check out of the hotel.

Later, as she entered Catherine's house, she found everyone settled in the sitting room. Without revealing herself to the other ladies, she motioned to Savannah to come into the foyer.

Savannah put down her book and went over to her to help her with the bags. As they got them settled, she said in a low voice, "The detective wants you to go back to the station."

"Did he say why?" Emma asked, her tone similar.

"I'm hoping it is so that we can go home."

"I'll head there now," she said. "Tell them I'll be back soon."

She went outside and hailed a carriage.

"Where to, miss?" the driver asked as he helped her into the carriage.

"Police station, please."

He nodded and climbed back on his seat. He clicked at the horses to get them moving. The trip to the station was short, and he helped her down. As she paid him, he asked, "Should I wait for you?"

"I'm not sure how long I will be. If you're in the area, check here in about an hour."

"I can do that," he promised.

He departed and she went into the station. The officer at the front desk recognized her. "No additional ladies with you this time?" he asked, grinning.

"No, they're at home resting. Can you ask Detective Daniels if he has time for me?"

"Yes, I believe he does." He called behind him and said, "Officer, please take Miss Evans to Daniels."

Emma followed the officer into the offices they had passed earlier that day. The officer knocked lightly on a door and announced, "Miss Evans is here."

Detective Daniels called her to come in. "Emma, I appreciate you returning so quickly."

"We'd like to get the wives out of town as soon as possible. I have an attorney ready to take their case and I'd like to reunite the mothers with their children."

"That is a good idea."

"What will happen now?"

"We have him on the assault charge. We can probably use that as a pressure point on the bigamy case."

"Can we head out of town tomorrow morning?"

He nodded. "It's probably for the best. Can you give me your contact information in Chicago?"

"Of course, let me know if anything changes. Especially if Hugo's released for any reason."

"I will," he promised.

She left and found the carriage outside. "You were able to come back," she said as he jumped down to help her into the carriage.

"Yes. Back to the same house?" he asked.

"Yes, please." They started and she called to him, "On second thought, I need train tickets. Could we go by the station first?"

"Of course." He took her to the train station and waited while she picked up the tickets.

When she returned, he asked, "Back now?"

"Yes, please."

They made it back to Catherine's house and Emma got out of the carriage. "Thank you," she said and waved as the carriage pulled away. She made her way back into the house, looking down at the tickets. *This will allow everyone to get safely out of town while the police build their case.*

She entered and found Izzy and the little girls sitting on the floor together playing.

Izzy saw her enter. "Emma, you're back."

"Yes, and I got permission for us to leave. I picked up the tickets for the morning." She showed her the tickets.

"Good! Evelyn, Catherine, come down. Emma has news!"

Catherine and Evelyn came down the stairs, and Savannah appeared from the kitchen.

"Get packed, we're leaving tomorrow." All of them looked relieved.

"Mama, are we going on another trip?" asked Rebecca.

Evelyn bent down and said, "Yes, baby, we are going to pick up your sister."

"Good. I missed her."

"I'm sure she missed you also."

"Us, too?" Bess asked, tugging on her mother's dress.

Izzy pulled her close. "Of course."

"We have dinner ready," Catherine said. "Why don't we go in, and then we can have an early night?"

"Yes, I think that's a good idea," Emma said, taking Savannah's arm and walking into the dining room. The food was good and the company was talkative. After dinner, she and Savannah were in the living room lying on bedrolls.

"I'm looking forward to the bed back at the boarding house," Savannah said.

"Me, too," said Emma. *And Jeremy,* she thought. She looked over at her friend and asked curiously, "How are you and Ethan?"

Savannah flushed. "Good. We're good."

"Do you think it's a long-term thing?" Savannah was currently working for a theater and traveled three to four times a year with various shows.

She turned to her. "I think it might be."

"But you have doubts?"

"I love Ethan. I want to be with him and marry him."

"Well then, what's the concern?" Emma asked. She didn't believe in marriage for herself, but she didn't force her views on other people.

"I'd like to keep working at the theater and traveling with shows."

"Have you mentioned this to Ethan?"

"No."

"Maybe you should. He might not find this a problem. Be honest and find out. The worst thing you can do is not to say anything."

"You're right," Savannah said as she thought about that.

"Has he asked you to marry him?"

"Not yet, but soon, I think. He's been very nervous as of late."

"He's easy for you to read?" It was like that for her and Jeremy.

"For me. Yes."

"Give him a chance," suggested Emma.

"I will," she promised. "Home tomorrow?"

"Yes, on our way tomorrow."

"Emma?" Savannah asked her friend.

"Hmmmm?"

"You let Hugo punch you, didn't you?"

"I did."

"Ha! I knew it!" Savannah exclaimed. "Why, though?"

"Just in case the bigamy charge didn't hold, I figured an assault charge on a 'poor, helpless' woman would hold him until we could get everyone out of town."

"Helpless? You?" Savannah scoffed.

"Oh, shut up and get some sleep." Emma smiled at her friend.

They woke early and had the girls eat before they left. Everyone was packed and dressed, and Ian had the wagon waiting to take them all to the train station.

"I appreciate you helping out again this morning," Emma said to Ian.

"I want to help." He looked behind her and saw Catherine carrying a bag. He walked over to her. "Are you going with them?"

"Yes. Emma recommended that we see the lawyer she works for to protect ourselves before Hugo goes to trial."

"Good idea," he said, but he didn't want her to leave. "When do you think you'll be back?"

"Soon," she said.

He saw his one chance to say something, and he grabbed her hand and pulled her to the side of the house.

She looked startled but accompanied him. She saw Emma's expression and said, "It's okay."

Emma nodded and watched in case she might need to intervene.

"Catherine, I couldn't let you go and not tell you something," Ian said desperately.

"What is it, Ian?" she asked softly. She had known this man her whole life; he had always been around. When she moved here with Hugo, he'd bought the house next to hers.

Now that Ian had her alone, he looked nervous.

"Ian?" she asked. "What did you want to tell me?"

"I love you," he said, looking down at their interlocked hands.

"What?"

"I love you!" he said loudly

"Love me? But you never said anything," Catherine said, shocked.

"I was finally getting up the nerve to talk to you and then Hugo showed up. He just took you over."

"Yes, I think he did that so I didn't have time to think or make a proper decision," she explained.

"I wanted to ask you to marry me."

"Is that why you moved here? To be near me."

"I wanted to be here, even if you couldn't be mine. I wanted to be able to see you each day."

She touched his face with her hands. "Ian, can you wait for me a little longer?"

"If I knew you felt the same way I do, I would wait forever," he said fervently.

"I'll be back soon and then we can make some plans," she said softly, gazing into his eyes.

He kept a tight grip on her hands.

She smiled softly and said, "We should be going now."

"Okay," he said, not able to take his eyes off her.

Emma walked up and said, "I think we're ready to go."

"Yes." Ian let Catherine go and said, "Let's go to the train station."

They made it to the station and he lifted Catherine out last. They watched each other and she told him, "I will see you soon," she told him.

"I will be here," Ian promised and watched until they board the train before heading home. *Waiting,* he thought. *I can do that. I will wait for her.*

CHAPTER 24

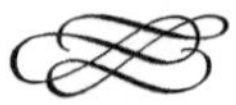

The trip took a week and, when they pulled into Chicago, the group was glad to be off the train.

"Emma!" a voice called out. She looked over and saw it was Thomas.

"Thomas, you got my telegraph!" She had sent it from the station the morning they departed.

"I did," he said as he rushed over. He snatched the hat off his head and said hello to the group. The women responded with grateful smiles.

"What happened to your face?" Bess asked loudly.

"Bess!" Izzy scolded.

"No, that's okay." Thomas bent down to the girl. "I got burned when I was younger. This happens if you get too close to a fire." Thomas had gotten caught in the 1871 Chicago fire.

"Does it hurt?" she asked, reaching out to touch his face.

"Not for a long time," he said. He let her touch the wrinkled skin. He stood and looked at the group. "Would you like to go to the house now?"

"We would," said Evelyn gratefully.

"Savannah!" a man's voice called. She looked over and saw it was Ethan. She ran to him.

Emma looked at Thomas. "Did you tell him we were coming?"

"I had to. He was at our office daily hoping for an update," Thomas explained.

Emma turned to Savannah and called, "Go with Ethan."

"Thank you, Emma!" they both called back, then ran off together laughing.

Thomas helped the wives and girls into his wagon and, when they were settled into the back, he moved back to the driver's seat. He clicked to move the horses. A few blocks from the safe house location, he pulled into an alley. He turned to them. "Ladies, we need you to lie down and be quiet. The house we're going to is special and we don't want people to see who's coming and going. Do you understand?" He looked at the wives first, then the girls. They all nodded. "I have blankets that I'll cover you with." Once they lay down, he pulled the blankets over them and exited the alley.

It was a few minutes later when they stopped and Thomas said in a low voice, "Wait here." He jumped down and tapped lightly on the door. It opened quickly. Katie came out with Clair and they went to the back of the wagon. They uncovered everyone and held a finger to their lips to remind the girls to stay quiet. They got out quickly and made their way inside. Once the door was closed behind them, Clair said, "I think there are people here who would like to see you." The two older girls ran into the room, each of them going to their mama.

"Oh, Mama! I've missed you so much," Evie said.

"Me, too, Mama," Mabel said to her mother.

"What about me?" Bess asked.

"Yes, I missed you also," her sister said.

Mabel had already moved to pick up Rebecca.

"Let's go in into the sitting room," Clair said. She turned to Katie and asked, "Tea and treats?"

"Of course."

The group moved into the other room and Clair walked over to Emma. "You look tired. Can you stay a little while until we get them settled?"

"Of course."

They sat down and introductions were made.

"What type of house is this?" Izzy asked, looking around.

"We call it a safe house. Somewhere we can house women and children who need to be hidden from things in their lives."

"I didn't know places like this existed," Evelyn said.

"We have to keep them hidden, otherwise it would defeat the purpose," Clair explained. "How long do you expect to stay?"

Emma answered for them. "I want to meet with Mr. Pennington. We need his advice on their situation."

"Of course." Emma had briefed her on the case. Clair hadn't expected a third wife, but she understood they needed to be together at this time.

Katie brought in the tea. Once everyone had their fill, Clair told the group, "I'll show you all to your bedrooms. You can tell Thomas which bags are yours."

Once they were settled, Clair came back downstairs. "Thomas," she called. He came in from the kitchen. "Can you take Emma home?"

"Of course."

"Come back for me after. Lily should be here soon to take over for the night," said Clair.

He kissed her and motioned for Emma to follow him out.

CHAPTER 25

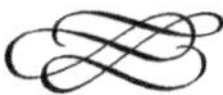

*E*mma was yawning now and said, "Thomas, thank you. Tell the ladies I'll go by the office first thing tomorrow to see Mr. Pennington and then come by here."

"I'll do that," he promised.

She climbed into the back of the wagon and he covered her up for the trip home. When they arrived at the boarding house, he took the blanket off and found Emma sleeping. He nudged her shoulder. "We're here."

She sat up quickly and looked around. "I must have drifted off. This is becoming a habit."

He helped her down. "Do you need help with your bag?" he asked, holding it.

"No," she yawned and reached for it. "I can manage it."

He gave it to her and then watched until she was in the house before he left. It was an old habit he had of watching out for her.

She unlocked the door and as she started up the stairs. Dora met her halfway up with a hug. "Is everyone okay?"

"Yes, I just want to go to bed." Dora nodded and helped her sister with her bag.

Emma didn't turn up the gas lights, but grabbed her night clothes and went to the bathroom. Once there, she cleaned up. She would have liked a bath and to wash her hair, but the tiredness was overwhelming. She made it back to her room and climbed into the big bed, wishing Jeremy was back with her.

CHAPTER 26

*E*mma slept hard and awoke at her normal time. She made her way downstairs and grabbed some butter and bread as her breakfast. "Tell Dora I'll be back at lunch and will tell her everything then," she instructed Amy and Ethyl.

"I will," Amy said, watching her hurriedly eat her breakfast and leave out the back door.

Emma wanted to be in the office when Mr. Pennington arrived for the day. It was early and Ethan had not yet arrived when she pedaled her bike up to the office location. She got off and sat on the stoop waiting for him.

"You're early," Ethan said as he walked up. He had a smile on his face. Emma knew Savannah being back had put it there.

"Yes, lots to do."

"I do have several files for you to review."

"I'll pick them up after I store my bike," Emma said and followed him up the stairs. She got the files and started working on them, listening closely for Mr. Pennington to arrive for the day. When she heard the door open, she hurried to meet him.

He saw her and said, "Emma, you're back. Can you come into my office?"

"Yes, sir. I'll be right with you." She took the files she was reviewing back to her desk, holding back a yawn. She had slept hard but felt like she was still tired from the long trip. There was just no time to rest and the ladies would need some support.

She walked into his office and Mr. Pennington looked up. "Sit down. Tell me what happened."

She sat in the chair across from his desk. "Hugo was arrested for bigamy," she said simply.

"Finally got him," he said with a laugh.

"It's just as we thought," she said. "He has another wife, but this time the charges included kidnapping, possible attempted murder, and assault."

At that last part, he raised his eyebrow in question. "Who did he assault?" Pennington asked.

"Me."

"Your cheek?" The bruise had started to fade.

"Yes. When I was questioning him, Hugo hit me in the face."

"He hit you, or you allowed him to hit you?" Pennington knew Emma could take care of herself and also knew Hugo wouldn't have been able to hit her unless she'd planned it that way.

"Well…" Emma began.

"Say no more. The assault charge will stay."

Emma smiled and continued. "We believe he meant to get rid of the second and third wives." She told him about the stories Hugo had fed to the new wife about the prior wives' deaths, the funeral plots, and trying to sell their homes.

Pennington sat back, watching her speak.

"I have the wives and their daughters with me and they're safe. I could think of no one else who knows this case and this man's history as well as you do."

His eyes glinted and he rubbed his hands together gleefully. "Well, well, so we get another opportunity to go after him."

"Yes. The two wives just want out of their marriages and they want full custody of their girls. The current wife will probably need an annulment."

"It will be complicated with his criminal case. Will the women provide testimony?" he asked.

"They want him stopped so, yes, I believe they will testify."

"Can you bring the ladies here to the office?"

"I think it might be better if you went to them," she said, thinking of the children. "I'd rather not parade them around. We have them in a safe location."

"I'll do what I have to do," he said. "Can you set it up?"

"Yes, I can arrange that, as long as you keep the location confidential. No one can know where they are."

"I can do that. Can you arrange our visit for this afternoon?"

"That works," she confirmed and left his office.

She asked Ethan to send a note to Clair's office informing her of Pennington's visit. She waited for a response. Clair sent back a response and said that would be fine as long as it was just the one person.

She closed the note and went to Mr. Pennington's office. She knocked lightly and was asked to come in.

"The visit has been confirmed for after lunch," she said.

He nodded and she returned to her work. The morning went by and she told Mr. Pennington, "I'll meet you here and then we'll proceed to Clair's office to get the necessary transportation. Is 1:00pm okay with you?"

"I'll be here and ready."

She nodded, retrieved her bike, and carried it downstairs. Riding home, she enjoyed the air on her face; it kept her awake. She made it home, put the bike up, and headed to the back door. Ethyl saw her first. "Welcome back."

Amy saw her and said, "Welcome back. You left so fast this morning, we didn't get a chance to greet you."

"I had a meeting to plan for," she explained.

"Lunch is on the table. Go on in and get some food," Amy commanded.

"I will and thank you. You sound more like Dora every day," Emma teased.

Amy tossed a towel her way and Emma laughed as she entered the dining room. The family was all in place around the table, even Jake and Savannah.

"Jake, you came home for lunch?" she asked, surprised. He never changed his schedule if he could help it.

"Yes, I heard you were home and I didn't get to see you this morning," he explained.

"Well, thank you," she said and went to sit next to him.

"Papa and Abbey want to come to dinner tonight and catch up on the cases," Dora told her.

Emma thought about that. "That should be okay. I do want to keep it within our immediate team for now."

"Can you give us some details?" Tim asked.

She looked regretful. "I want to but I need to take Mr. Pennington to meet the ladies. We have to figure out where they stand in this mess."

"Okay, we can wait until this evening," he said.

Savannah was eating hurriedly. "Do you have someplace to be?" Dora asked.

"I thought I might go back with Emma and see Ethan," she admitted.

Emma smiled at her and said, "I'd love the company. We can take the trolley. I won't need my bike."

Savannah grinned over at her.

After lunch, they got their things and started toward the office. "Ethan, huh," Emma teased.

"Yeah. I think you're right. I need to tell him what I'm thinking about. He means too much to me to leave him out of any future decisions."

They hopped off the trolley and made it to the office. As they entered, Ethan didn't look up when he commented, "Mr. Pennington should be back soon. There are files on your desk for you to work on for now."

Emma grinned at Savannah. "Okay. Oh, Savannah, thanks for walking over with me."

At that, Ethan's head popped up. When he saw who was with Emma, he jumped to his feet and went around the desk to take Savannah into his arms. "It's good to see you," he murmured and buried his face in her neck.

Emma gave them their privacy and went into her office. She closed the door and sat at her desk. Like Ethan said, he had placed new files there.

A light knock on the door pulled her away from her reading. "Come in," she said.

Savannah stuck her head in. "I'm going to the park with Ethan. We should be back soon."

"Okay, is Mr. Pennington back?"

"He is," Pennington called out. "Please come to my office."

"On my way." She waved as she followed Savannah. Her friend ran over to Ethan and they exited the office together. Emma headed over to Mr. Pennington's office. "Are you ready to go?"

"I am," he replied. He walked her out and locked the door behind them. Ethan would open back up when he returned from the park.

"Where to, young lady?" he asked.

"We'll go to Clair's office on Moffit Street and Thomas will take us from there."

He hailed a carriage, as he didn't want to walk the multiple blocks necessary to get to the office building. Once the carriage arrived, he helped her in and they sat quietly enjoying the day. When they pulled up at Clair's office, he helped her down and paid the driver. Just as they prepared to go in, Emma heard a long whistle. She looked over and saw Thomas.

"Mr. Pennington, over there." She nodded to Thomas. They

headed toward him and climbed into the back of the wagon. Once they got within a few blocks, Thomas pulled into an alley. Emma said, "Mr. Pennington, we'll need to hide under the blankets and lay flat."

"I understand." He did as he was asked.

They drove a while longer and stopped. She touched his shoulder and whispered, "We wait."

He nodded and stayed where he was.

Presently, Thomas said, "You can come out now." They lowered the blanket and Thomas helped her down and offered Mr. Pennington a hand as well. They entered through the kitchen. Katie was there cleaning up from lunch. "Well, hello," she said. "We have a new visitor?"

"Mr. Pennington, this is Katie. She keeps the food and the house."

"It's very nice to meet you, Katie. I am James," he said suavely. Emma peered at him; she hadn't seen him around anyone other than clients before.

Katie blushed prettily and said, "The ladies and girls are in the sitting room."

As they walked out to meet them, Emma told him, "They don't have any other guests right now. It's just the wives and their children."

"Hmm, we might need Katie to distract the children," he said.

"Wait here a moment," she stopped him outside the sitting room. "and I'll let her know." Emma walked back and reappeared with Katie.

"Just take them to the study," Emma suggested. "There are books they might want you to read to them."

"I can do that," Katie said, understanding the intention behind their request.

They enter the sitting room. The ladies were keeping busy with sewing and conversation. The kids sat together with dolls on the floor. "Girls," Katie said. "Would you like me to read you a book in the study?" The older girls looked at their mamas and they nodded. They stood and took the small girls by their hands and left the room.

"Ladies, I am James Pennington. Emma asked me here to go over the law and see what help you might need."

They looked relieved.

"Why don't we start with your names and addresses?" he asked.

They each gave their name and address. Emma jotted them down quickly for him. She handed him the paper.

He went over each of their marriages and the timing for each. "I'm assuming Hugo will be going to prison for a long time for the bigamy and the assault charges."

"Good," all three said together.

"I did want to bring up that there is a way to keep this quiet," he said.

"How would that work?" Evelyn asked.

"We could ask him to sign for the divorces and give you the houses as part of a deal."

"Would the deal mean no prison time for him?" asked Izzy.

"I am afraid so," he said regretfully.

"Then no deal. We've thoroughly discussed this and have decided that, whatever it takes, Hugo is not doing this to someone else," Izzy said.

Emma watched them and thought, *They are brave.*

"What about the girls?" asked Emma. She wanted Hugo in prison as much as they did, but she wanted to make sure they knew the children could be affected by all of this.

Evelyn spoke for them. "We talked about that also; we'd like to sell the houses and move far away to start over where no one's aware of our backgrounds."

"That would probably be for the best," allowed Mr. Pennington.

Emma drummed her fingers on her lips and said, "Our charity can probably help you with that."

Catherine spoke up at that time. "No, that won't be necessary. I'll help them. Whatever they need, I'll be here for them. Always."

The other two wives teared up and went to hug her. They were a family, a very different one from the norms of today, but a family nonetheless.

Pennington looked at all three. "So, our goal is to get you your homes and children, am I right?"

"Yes. Do whatever you have to, but keep Hugo in prison," stated Evelyn fiercely. The wives nodded their agreement.

"Can we go back to our homes until this is worked out?" Izzy asked.

"No, I think you should stay here. Emma, can we use your contacts to have officers patrol the homes until we get this finalized?" said Mr. Pennington.

Emma nodded and made a note to contact the Chicago Police Chief for a favor.

As they were leaving, she asked him, "Will you need to go to New York to talk to Hugo?"

"I'm hoping that, given the extenuating circumstances, we can get them to bring him here," he commented.

CHAPTER 27

*E*mma and Pennington confirmed that Hugo Banks would be brought to Chicago for the interview. They used the time he had to travel to strategize how to handle him.

Emma watched Hugo walk into Pennington's office. He looked self-assured and his lawyer had a smile on his face. An officer accompanied him and waited in Ethan's office area. "They think they have us, don't they?" she murmured to Mr. Pennington.

"They do," he said in a similar tone, "but this time I have the wives on our side." She smiled slowly. "Why don't we sit down?" Mr. Pennington said to Hugo and his lawyer,

Hugo's lawyer began, "The only evidence against my client is the testimony of my client's 'supposed' wives."

"You don't think they will follow through with testifying?" Pennington asked.

"Them? No, they won't go against me. They love me," Hugo stated confidently.

Mr. Pennington looked at the man and said, "Love? I don't think that's the emotion they're experiencing right now. Have you talked to them since you were charged?"

"No, but I know what they want." Hugo's voice didn't sound as positive as it did initially.

Pennington looked at him. "I'm afraid when you took the children you played your final card." He looked over at Emma and said, "It's time."

She nodded and stood. She left the room and entered her office. All three ladies were there. "Are you ready?" she asked them.

They looked at each and Izzy spoke for them. "Yes, we're ready."

"Please be aware, Hugo thinks you're on his side and has no doubt of his ability to get through this with no prison time."

"Does he? Well, we'll just have to dispel that notion," Catherine said.

"Catherine, you will wait outside the office."

She nodded and Emma opened her door and walked them to the other office. It was a very proud parade. His two wives stared at Hugo. They weren't demure, and they weren't going to let him have his way.

"Ladies!" Hugo said. He stood to go to them. His lawyer put a hand on his arm and pulled him back into his seat and began whispering furiously in his ear.

"What? No, they love me. NO! I want to talk!" Hugo looked at them, but this time he stayed seated. "Ladies, I was always going to make sure your girls stayed with you. This was just a short vacation for them."

"A vacation with a new wife?" Evelyn sneered.

He looked at the formally submissive woman. "Why, yes. I mean, it's worked out fine so far."

"Has it?" Izzy asked.

"Yes!" His lawyer pulled his arm again and continued to offer him directions. "Fine! Fine! My lawyer says I have to tell you I won't take the children," he muttered.

The lawyer leaned in again and whispered more advice.

Hugo said in a rush, "Or the houses."

The two women started to relax, but then Izzy asked, with a frown, "Are you going to put that in writing?"

"Yes, of course," said his lawyer, "but we would like you to drop the bigamy charges. Say that you were never married."

"Never married? We have marriage licenses and children who need their father's name," Evelyn said loudly.

Mr. Pennington knew it was time to speak up. "Mr. Banks, there will be no deal."

"But the other time..." Hugo started, he noticed the way his wives glared at him and stopped talking abruptly.

"We have found the information that you planned the sale of your wives' homes and you purchased burial plots for each of them."

"Oh, those," Hugo said nervously, "those are for the future. In case anything unfortunate should happen to them." He chose a different tack and nudged his lawyer to speak.

"My client would like to dissolve the first two marriages of Evelyn and Isabella Banks," his lawyer stated.

"What about the marriage to Catherine Banks?" Pennington asked. Catherine didn't want to stay married to Hugo either.

"Oh, I want to stay with that marriage," Hugo said confidently.

"You do?" asked Catherine. Emma had stepped to the door and waved her into the room. She heard his statement.

He looked at her in surprise. "Yes, of course. We've just begun our lives together."

"Well, it's ending here. Mr. Pennington is handling my divorce case also. Though I might get an annulment, given the amount of time we actually spent together."

Hugo hadn't known the meeting would go like this. He expected the ladies to go along with his plans; after all, they always had. They stood in a proud line, together and against him.

Mr. Pennington spoke. "Mr. Banks, we will be invalidating all of your marriages. Once your first one was declared annulled, the other two were not valid."

Hugo tried one last thing; he shook his hand at Izzy. "You knew. You should have to face charges also."

"Did I know?" Izzy asked. "There's no one to testify that I knew anything."

He looked at all three and saw there was no one on his side. His lawyer spoke low in his ear. He finally nodded.

Hugo's lawyer said, "Mr. Banks will sign off on the paperwork to divorce wives one and two and annul the third marriage."

"What about the houses?" Pennington prompted.

"They can have those also," the lawyer allowed. "Mr. Banks will remain in town until the paperwork is completed."

Hugo thought agreeing to the meeting would give him his freedom, but it had not. He was taken into custody and would be remanded to the Chicago jail until the paperwork was ready.

The ladies and Mr. Pennington went to lunch.

"How long do you think it will take?" Izzy asked.

"The paperwork to dissolve the marriages?" Pennington asked.
"Yes."

He looked thoughtful. "A few days. I'll draft them today and arrange for him to sign them tomorrow. I will come by here afterward and get you all to sign yours."

Izzy and Evelyn looked at one another and back at him. "We plan to sell our houses and move away from the area. The girls need a fresh start."

"Can I contact you when it's time for you to return for your testimony? You all must be here."

"We'll come back for that, and we'll give you our contact information."

Evelyn and Izzy walked out with Mr. Pennington. Emma hung back to speak with Catherine. "Will you stay in your current home?"

"No, I'll sell also. We all need a fresh start."

"What about Ian? I noticed he'd like to see more of you."

"Yes, I want that also. I think it was always meant to be Ian."

"Then why Hugo if you felt that way about Ian?"

"You have seen how he is. When he wants something, nothing will stand in his way. I just got swept up. It was exciting," she admitted.

"Yes, I see." Though she didn't. Hugo Banks was all surface and any time spent with him showed what his true nature was.

They walked to the other ladies. They would take the train to Cleveland two days after the paperwork was signed. Catherine had promised to accompany them and set up a money manager to sell the houses and furniture. The packing would be completed and Catherine had set up a house for them to move to in another state.

"We got him," Emma said to Mr. Pennington as they watched them leave.

"Yes, we did. You did a very good job on this. Now, I need to draft that paperwork. Ethan, can you come into my office?"

"Yes, sir," Ethan said and followed him.

Mr. Pennington looked over at Emma. "Take a few days to rest. This whole thing has been trying."

"I would appreciate that. Let me know if any help is needed with the wives' paperwork," she said. She returned to her office to prepare to go home.

As she was leaving, Pennington stepped out. "You did a good thing here. You protected three families when society would have just abandoned them."

"And Hugo will finally get what's coming to him."

"That, too." He laughed.

Emma took her bike and went home.

CHAPTER 28

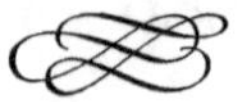

Emma pulled her bike to a stop in front of the boarding house and heard a familiar voice calling her name. She turned toward the sound and saw Mark running over to her.

"Emma! I'm so glad you're home. My uncle arrived and Mom is smiling more now that he's here. You have to meet him!" he told her in a rush.

"I want to," she assured the boy.

"Emma!" called a voice from the stairs.

She looked up in surprise at Jeremy. "You're back!" she exclaimed happily. She got off the bike, laid it against the stoop, and ran up the stairs and into his arms. "When did you get back?"

"Today," he murmured, pulling her in close and lowering his head to kiss her. She sank into him, not willing to stop.

A loud "Hmmf" could be heard directly behind them on the street.

"What?" they said and looked around, their eyes glazed. She shook herself and saw who was there. "Papa! It's good to see you," she said as she accompanied Jeremy down the stoop to kiss him. Jeremy shook hands with Ellis and kissed his mom on the cheek.

"We were invited over for dinner," Papa said.

"Dinner," Jeremy murmured in her ear. "Too bad."

"Papa, I need to clean up. Can I meet you downstairs?" she asked, wanting to spend some time alone with Jeremy.

Mark called, "Emma, I'll bring over my uncle later for you to meet him."

"Thanks, Mark," she called back and waved to him.

Papa looked at her. "Sure, I'll meet you downstairs. Jeremy, will you be accompanying me to the sitting room?"

Abbey punched his arm in warning not to tease them. "Let them be."

He nodded when Jeremy said, "No, I think I'll get something from my room first."

"Fine," Papa said and, as he turned away from them, he smiled broadly and followed them into the house.

Emma and Jeremy continued upstairs. Once they got to her door, he said in a low voice, "Meet you inside."

"Yes," she said and opened the door. They walked purposely to their bedroom doors and went in. She leaned on the door and waited for Jeremy. It didn't take long and the bookcase slid to the side. He came through and strode over to her. "I think we have just enough time for a quick rest," he said, laughing, and threw her on the bed.

She laughed and pulled him to her. A short while later, they heard the dinner bell. It was clanging rather loudly. "I think they want us downstairs," she said, raising her head from his chest to look him in the eye.

"Yes," he groaned, pulling her to him.

"Now, don't start that again. We're wanted downstairs." She got up gracefully and looked over at him. "Come on," she said.

He moved over to the side of the bed, stood up, and headed to his room.

"Throw me my brush," she said.

"Catch," said Jeremy, throwing her hairbrush as he passed her dresser to enter his room.

She caught it and ran it through her hair, finally pulling it into a ponytail. The bell clanged again; she ran to the bathroom to wash up. She was tucking her red shirt into her black skirt when a knock sounded on her door. "On my way," she called. She grabbed her boots and tied them quickly

The knock repeated and Emma rushed over and opened it. "Dinner?" Jeremy asked with a slight smile and offered his elbow.

She returned the smile and took his arm. They walked down together and found everyone already at the dining table. No one mentioned their absence.

Prayers first, and then the trays started making their way around the table. Tim broke the silence and said in a light voice, "Mark's uncle has been over to visit a few times." Emma noticed Dora's face flushed at Tim's words.

Well, well, she thought, her interest tweaked. Mr. Pennington had kept her occupied that when she returned home in the evenings she would eat in her room and go straight to bed. She hadn't been listening to the events going on around her. Now though, she turned all of her attention to her sister and said, "Tell me about him."

Dora's face was still flushed and she said in a rushed tone, "He is very handsome and suave."

"He is that," acknowledged Tim. He wasn't threatened by the other man. He knew his Dora.

"Tell me more," Emma said.

"He's so worldly. He knows about everything, books, business, and clothes," Dora said.

"Clothes?" asked Jeremy.

"Yes. His clothes are tailored and from England," Tim said. He had noticed the cut and asked him about it.

"He sounds very dapper," murmured Jeremy, wondering where the man's money came from. Mark's family wasn't rich; they worked as teachers in the poor districts of Chicago. Jeremy had yet to meet the man since he had just gotten home by train that morning.

"Mark mentioned Elizabeth had been depressed. He was worried and hoped Joseph's presence would help," Emma said, remembering her conversation with the boy before her case started in Cleveland.

"She isn't any longer. Her face lights up when he's in the room," commented Tim.

"Enough of that," Dora said, trying to get them off of the topic of Mark's uncle. "Tell us about your cases."

Emma put the new visitor out of her mind and said, "The evidence is pretty clear for bigamy, and I did press charges to keep him in custody."

Jeremy frowned at her. "You did? What for?"

"He punched me in the face and left a decent bruise," she explained.

"Are you okay?" Papa asked, concerned.

"It has mostly healed," she assured them.

"How was he able to land the punch?" Jeremy asked. He wouldn't have expected someone soft like Hugo Banks to be able to hit her before she could stop him.

She looked down at her hands and then looked him in the eyes. "I let him," she admitted.

"Emma! He could have hurt you," said Abbey.

"It's fine. I rolled with the punch so it didn't hurt as much. Besides, we needed the assault charge to hold him. I didn't want him out where he might be able to threaten the wives or take the children again."

Jeremy nodded. "Good for you, but I'd prefer you chose another method next time."

"Me, too," she said, lightly touching her cheek. Most of the pain and color were gone.

"What about the children, are they sorted?" Tim asked Jeremy, moving on to the other case.

"For the ones we could find," he said. "As you know, some went to new homes."

"Yes," commented Dora. They had been told that some of the families wouldn't take the children back.

"That's just terrible," Abbey said. The rest of the people at the table agreed.

"We did get everyone to a safe location. Clare and Thomas set up a network of homes between here and New York City. Renting some and buying others where they could."

"And the children they haven't found?" Papa asked.

"We have some leads overseas. Officers have been assigned there to search." Jeremy didn't mention that he didn't think there was much hope at this point. The case had so many highs and lows. It still depressed him to think about those they couldn't save.

Emma saw his expression and wanted to help him. She changed the subject. "This is nice, being back home." Abbey and Dora saw what she was trying to do and changed the subject to more newsy topics.

Emma smiled and thought, *Family-they were always there when she needed them.*

After dinner, she headed upstairs for a bath and an early night. Jeremy chose to stay down with his mom and the family in the sitting room.

When her hair was washed, she climbed out of the tub and wrapped one towel around her hair and one around her body before pulling on a robe. She crossed the hall into her room and changed into a night dress. It was cool outside, so she opened the window and sat down to brush her hair. It took longer than expected, and she was still sitting there when Jeremy came into the room. He walked over to her and said, "Scoot over." He took the brush, helping her until her hair was dry. She climbed into bed and watched while he disrobed. After he climbed in with her, she laid her head on his chest.

"It's times like this I miss that beach house," he said softly into her hair.

"Me, too," she admitted. She propped her head up so that she could see his face. "I wanted to talk with you about that." She told him about how their vacation had come about.

Jeremy nodded. "I figured it must be something like that. Pops said he didn't arrange anything."

They let the silence settle around them.

"What are you thinking?" he asked, running his fingers through her hair.

"Having a place of our own, like the beach house, where we can be together."

"Our own place?" He liked the idea. "Are you thinking of the beach?"

"I did like it there." *Though probably not that actual location,* she thought.

"Maybe this summer we find some houses to look at purchasing," he said, mulling it over.

"It would just be ours," she said with a sigh.

"Yes, I think that would be perfect."

CHAPTER 29

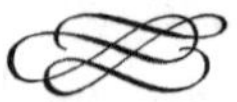

The weekend was spent with Emma and Jeremy locked in their room, getting to know one another after their extended separation. They weren't looking forward to Monday and being apart again.

When Monday came around, Jeremy sat up reluctantly to begin his day and tried to nudge Emma awake. When she burrowed deeper into the covers, he called, "Hey!" and tried to wrestle them from her. She laughed and rolled, trapping the covers under her. Jeremy located the end of the cover and tugged it hard, sending Emma to the floor, laughing.

"Okay, okay, I'm up. Well, sort of," she said, sitting on the floor.

"What a picture, wish I had a camera to remember this moment," he teased, putting out his hand to help her up.

She took it and stood, trying to pull the sheets from around her. Her eyes found the clock. She looked at Jeremy and warned, "Time is slipping by this morning."

"I'll go get ready now. Meet you on the other side," he said and went into his room through the bookcase.

Emma walked over to her dresser and gathered a light blue skirt and matching blue top that buttoned up the front. She thought about her schedule that day. It would be at Mr. Pennington's office. Work had piled up while they had been occupied with the bigamy case. *Time is speeding by.* Dropping her sheet, she pulled on her robe, tying the belt. She walked quickly out the door and to the restroom to clean up for her day.

When she came out, she found Jeremy there, tapping his timepiece. "I'll be quick!" she said, slamming the door open to her bedroom. Closing it, she dressed, yanked on her boots, and finally pulled the brush through her hair. She was slipping it into a low ponytail and bun as she exited. They made their way down just in time for the trays to be placed on the table. Breakfast was a fast affair, as Emma and Jeremy wanted an early start.

"See you later," Jeremy said, watching the trolley come toward them.

"Yes, I'll see you this evening," she said as he kissed her. She watched him run for the trolley, then climbed on her bike and headed to Pennington's office.

She rolled to a stop in front of the office and looked up. The lights were still off. Frowning, she got off the bike and stood there staring up at the door. *Well, I might as well wait,* she thought. Leaning the bike against the stoop, she sat and waited. It was highly unusual for Ethan to be late. *Where is he?* she wondered.

The sound of boots scraping on the sidewalk could be heard from her left. She turned toward the sound and saw it was Ethan, and he was in a rush.

"How did I beat you here?" asked Emma.

"Late night," he muttered, going up the stoop and opening the door. She watched him. Her friend seemed a bit out of sorts. She lifted her bike to her shoulder and followed him into the office. She took it to the closet, watching Ethan race around turning up the gas lamps and opening Mr. Pennington's office door.

"Do you need some help?" she offered.

"No, I have it. Your work for today is here," he said and held out a folder.

She nodded and took it from him. He was already out of sorts and she didn't want to add to it. *Though,* she thought with a smile, *I'll have to ask Savannah what may have delayed him this morning.*

The day was productive, though the time away had increased the work to be completed. Emma took her bike and headed home for lunch. She had several notes from clients that indicated her courier work was back on. At the house, she pulled the bike to a stop and climbed off. She started to roll it to the side of the house when she heard a voice say, "Well, hello. I don't think we have met."

She turned slowly toward the voice and thought, *This must be the infamous uncle that Mark mentioned. Dora was right. A nice-looking man.* She stared at him longer than she should have. She had guessed his identity but asked, "Can I help you?"

"You haven't heard about me?" the man asked, sounding disappointed.

"No, I don't think so," she murmured. She didn't know why she kept up the ruse except that he seemed to get what he wanted without much effort. This man had been given too much based on his looks.

He strolled close to her. "I'm Joseph Black, Mark's uncle, and you are?"

"Emma Evans," she supplied. Joseph seemed to be advancing at a steady pace toward her and, before she could stop herself, she had moved back a few steps and kept the bike between them.

"Emma," he said, "I believe I've heard that name before." He tilted his head as if trying to remember. "Ah, now I have it. You're Dora's sister. You work in a law office?"

"I do," Emma said cautiously. This man was too everything—too suave, too good-looking, and a little too interested in her work. The family didn't share her investigations with strangers. Mark and his parents also knew this and wouldn't volunteer the information without letting her know.

"I want to hear everything about you," Joseph said and, even though he hadn't moved, she fought the urge to back away again.

"I'm not sure that everything would be appropriate, Mr. Black."

Was that a frown? It was just a flash, she thought, but *of what? Annoyance. Did he expect her to just giggle and fawn over him like some schoolgirl?*

Instead of responding, he winked and said, "I'll see you at dinner."

"Dinner? Are you and the family coming over this evening?" This man was being deliberately baffling. She wanted some answers.

They were not forthcoming. Instead, he looked up the stoop and called out, "Hello, Dora." Emma turned and saw her sister had come out to sweep the steps. Dora raised a hand in greeting but kept at her task.

Emma watched Joseph go. She leaned her bike on the stoop and walked up to greet Dora. "That is a handsome man," Emma commented, looking at Dora.

"Hmmm. Yes," Dora said, yet her cheeks didn't flush this time.

What changed? thought Emma. "You're not sweet on him anymore?"

"Was it that obvious?" Dora asked, embarrassed.

"A little,"

Her sister paused in her sweeping and leaned on the broom handle. "I think I was taken in by his looks and charm."

"Did something happen to change that?"

"Well, there is Tim," Dora said dryly. "When Joseph came over this morning, he really wanted a dinner invitation and he seemed a little manipulative. I started to wonder why he wanted one so badly."

"What does he want with us that he had to wrangle an invitation to dinner?"

"I think it's you," Dora admitted.

"That's ridiculous. And how would he know about me? Hold it, he mentioned that he had heard about me when he walked up just now."

"Mark told him all about you, I would expect," Dora said, starting to sweep again.

"Well, Jeremy will be here tonight and that will be an end to that," Emma said decisively.

"You know," her sister said innocently, "if you were married, you wouldn't have these issues."

Emma looked back the way Joseph had gone and said, "No I don't think even that would have stopped him. He's after something."

Dora mulled that over. She didn't like the idea of someone having a hidden agenda that involved her family.

Emma walked back downstairs quickly and said, "I'm going to put my bike up. I'll go in through the kitchen."

"Careful, Ethyl and Amy are canning today. Fruit preserves," Dora called out in warning.

"Yum!" Emma said, hoping to steal some of the treats as she made her way through.

"Yes, but it's going to be hot. They'll be moving the pots around and filling the jars, so be careful."

"I will," Emma said, rolling her bike around to the side of the house.

Dora shook her head and finished sweeping the steps. With her task complete, she headed back in and saw Emma coming out of the kitchen licking a spoon. "Got a sample, did you?"

"I did," her sister said, the satisfaction clear in her voice. She walked toward her and held it out. "Taste?"

"Yes, please," Dora said and took it from her. "You're right, yum!"

"Got any for me?" Jeremy called from the stairs. She looked up, the pleasure evident in her voice as she said, "You're home early."

"Yeah, but not for long," he said, holding up his bag for her to see.

"What? Why?" She didn't mean to sound angry, but they had just gotten to see each other after a long separation.

Dora quietly left the foyer, giving them their privacy.

Emma folded her arms over her chest. He touched her shoulder and she pulled away. "I would prefer to stay here with you."

"I know," she said, her mouth turned down and eyes wet with tears.

"Pops sent me a telegram," Jeremy explained. "They have one more location to check for the missing children."

"Will Clair and Thomas be there also?" She knew they could also use a rest. Both of the cases had required them to be present.

"Only if we get confirmation of children being there. If needed, we can have them set it up and send personnel to help with management and counseling."

"Most of the other locations are closed now?"

"Yes."

"Where are you headed?"

"The location found is about halfway to New York. Everyone is on their way there. We'll be staging a raid."

"You said it's not confirmed?"

"Never a guarantee, but the rumors are pretty sound." Emma had her head down. "What is it, Emma?" he asked, using his finger to lift her chin.

"You just got home," she complained and wiped her eyes. "We haven't had enough time together."

"You could come with me," he suggested.

The excitement was tempting, but she replied sadly, "We finally move past the Hugo Banks case and our trial work will be starting soon. Mr. Pennington would come after me if I disappeared."

"So, you stay here and I go," he said simply. He leaned in and kissed her slowly. Her knees were weak when he pulled back.

She signed shakily. "You're sure you have to go?"

"Reluctantly, yes." He pressed his forehead to hers.

Tim came in the front door. "Jeremy, your carriage is here."

Jeremy pulled his gaze from Emma and responded, "Thank you." He looked back at her. "I'm going to have to run. I'll send you a telegram once we find out if more children were located."

"Okay," she said and watched him go. Dora came back into the foyer and slid her arm inside of hers. "Come on and help me with setting the table."

She nodded and followed Dora to the dining room. She retrieved the silverware while Dora set out the dishes.

"He'll be back," Dora said in a soft tone, watching her.

"I know. I am usually the one running around or leaving at a moment's notice. But I have missed him."

"You got to spend a week alone with him," Dora reminded her.

"I did, and I think we're going to try to make that a normal part of our lives."

"Vacations?" asked Dora.

"A home that would be just for the two of us, to get away."

"You know, that isn't a bad idea, and it's something Tim and I might also want to go in with you to purchase."

When Emma looked alarmed, Dora laughed. "Not to go with you but maybe to use or rent out when you aren't there."

Emma nodded slowly. "I guess you and Tim would also like some time alone occasionally."

"Yes, it would be nice," her sister agreed.

Emma reviewed the table. "Do I have to worry about unwanted attention from Joseph tonight?"

"I don't think so, not with all of us here," Dora said consideringly. "Give him a chance. It may just be a bad first impression. And it'll mean so much to Mark and his mother."

Ethyl called from the kitchen. "The trays are ready."

Dora called out to Tim and Patrick, "Lunch!" They came in with Tim carrying Lottie. Dora took her daughter and sat her down for lunch. The others helped retrieve the trays and the pitchers. After lunch was cleaned up, Emma was putting on her light coat and hat to go out again.

"Courier work today?" Tim asked.

"Yes, I'll be back later."

"Be safe."

"I will," she promised and headed out the door. Emma purposely delayed her deliveries; she wasn't in a hurry to get home that evening. She'd been counting on Jeremy to provide the buffer she might need between her and Joseph. The men in her life weren't normally so forward with their intentions.

What gives him the idea that I'm open to spending time with him? Did someone give him that impression? I'll have to watch him with the other ladies. Savannah will be there. Will he act the same way toward her? Am I overreacting?

Emma walked her bike slowly to the back of the boarding house. When she couldn't wait any longer, she took a deep breath and went to the kitchen door. Ethyl saw her first. "They're just now sitting down to dinner." Emma nodded, slipped off her coat, and laid it on a chair. She took a deep breath before she pushed open the door to the dining room. The first thing she saw upon entering was that Joseph had taken the seat next to where she normally sat. *Who put him there?* She walked to her seat without comment and sat down. Her eyes darted around the table and she quickly noticed Savannah was not there.

She mouthed to Dora, "Where's Savannah?"

Dora mouthed back, "Rehearsals"

No help there, thought Emma with a grimace.

Joseph was attentive and his questions started immediately. "Emma, you have been tied up."

"Yes, just some business to take care of," she said noncommittally.

"What type of business?" he asked, curious about her comings and goings.

"Really nothing too interesting," she said, trying to steer him off the topic.

Dora saw she needed some help and looked to her husband. "Tim, I understand the church is looking for baked goods to be donated for a bazaar this week."

"Yes, I heard the same thing." He knew what Dora was doing and contributed to the conversation. "If you have them ready tomorrow, I can take them."

"Thank you," she responded. The conversation lulled and it moved to the weather and how good dinner was. Emma was relieved to be able to eat in peace.

As they were cleaning up, Joseph asked, "Emma, would you like to take a walk with me?"

The room grew silent, waiting for her response.

"Thank you, but I'm tired and I have to go to court tomorrow."

He didn't argue. Instead, he nodded and said, "Maybe another day?"

She nodded and didn't comment.

After he left, Dora looked at her sister. "He is persistent."

"I know, I didn't know how to turn him down."

"You know," her sister said, consideringly, looking at her hand. She held it up and pointed to her wedding ring. "One of these might help."

"Yeah, yeah, you mentioned that before. That isn't going to happen."

Dora was resolute. "Then *you* have to make it clear to him you *aren't* available."

"I know," Emma said. It wasn't like she could pull her knife and threaten him; this would have to be handled delicately. She would keep Mark's family on her mind as she dealt with him.

The next morning, she was pulling on her coat and Tim called to her, "Emma!"

"In the kitchen," she called back.

Tim came in and went directly to her. "This came earlier. I must have missed you." He handed her a note.

She opened it. "It's from Mr. Pennington. There's an important client he wants me to meet this morning. Thank you, Tim." Inserting it into her pocket, she headed out the back door. Her foot made contact with something other than the step, and she tripped and fell into Joseph's lap. "What?" she yelled in surprise. She struggled to get up, but he held on to her firmly.

"You don't have to leave so soon," he said smoothly.

"Yes, yes I do. I'm on my way to work." She pulled away forcefully and stood. "What did I trip on?" She looked up the stairs and saw a cane. She reached for it and swung it around to him. "Yours, I assume?"

"Mmmmm. Careless, I know," he said. "But I was hoping to see you."

She dropped the cane in his lap and walked over to get her bike from the shed. She looked over her shoulder at him. "Why did you want to see me?"

"You didn't have time for me last night, so I thought I'd walk you to work."

She checked the timepiece attached to her top. "I don't have time for that. I need to be in the office early." Without waiting for his response, she started walking the bike toward the street.

"Emma, are you avoiding me?" he asked, there was an edge to his voice.

His question startled her, not the content but his location. He was so close she could feel him behind her. She had no room to turn and looked ahead when she responded, "No, of course not." She took a deep breath and said, "I don't want to get into this now, but I am with Jeremy."

He walked around her and took her hand. "I don't see a ring," he said, looking at her fingers.

Dora was right, she thought. *Society allows for this type of behavior to unmarried women.* She yanked her hand out of his. "No, no ring. It isn't something I want. But I am committed to him."

He smiled suddenly and said lightly, "There's no reason for us not to be friends, though, is there?"

"No," she said slowly, watching him. His attitude seemed less menacing. *How did he change like that? One moment he's predatory, and the next he's a person you could see as a friend.*

"Well then, friend, I heard you have an interest in old books and I have some with me. Would you like to view them with me after dinner tomorrow?"

That didn't sound too bad, and she'd be with other people at the boarding house where he was staying. *And I can ask Mark to stay with us.* "I would like to see your books," she said politely, "but now I have to go to work."

Joseph walked with her to the gate and held it open for her.

"Thanks," she said, stepping onto the bike in the street. She arranged her satchel over her shoulder and climbed onto the bike and headed to work.

"Anytime," he said and watched her leave. *Bikes,* he thought, *another thing I'll have to get rid of. Why is it that the ones I pick always have to be changed? Why can't they be what I need in the beginning?* He pondered that. Initially, each one seemed to have only small flaws for him to correct. Though, eventually, these flaws turned into something he couldn't ignore. He thought about Emma. Will *she be able to change or will I need to do a final correction on her as well?*

He wandered back to the boarding house he was currently residing.

CHAPTER 30

"*H*ow are you?" Ethan asked as Emma entered the office.

"Good," she replied, not sharing her concerns about her new acquaintance. She glanced over and saw her friend had a wide smile.

"What are you so happy about today?" she asked as she walked her bike to the storage closet.

"I have a lunch date," he said importantly.

"You do? Can I guess who with?" she teased.

"You may," he said, nodding his head.

"Savannah, perhaps?" she teased.

"It is," he admitted and moved around to the front of his desk.

"What are you planning?" she asked, interested.

"Picnic at the park. We have a late day in court and should have enough time."

"Yes, Mr. Pennington sent me a note and said he's going to review a new case with me today. When did it come in?"

"We were notified on Friday. Mr. Pennington worked this weekend to get things organized."

"What are the charges?"

"Murder," he stated simply. "The prosecutor says our new client killed her husband because he lied about his money."

"I would assume the fact he had so little of it?"

"Yes. After she was charged, the creditors started calling and they wouldn't leave her alone."

"Why her?"

"He signed her name over to the creditors and, with the marriage, there was little she could do."

"Did she admit to killing him?"

"No. The prosecutor is going to have to show evidence and there's no body."

"No body," Emma said thoughtfully, mulling that over. "Why do they think he's dead and not just missing?"

"Blood. They found it in their stateroom on the steamer."

"Were they traveling?"

"Extended honeymoon. They found the blood when the ship docked in New York."

"But why are we defending the case? Shouldn't it be someone in New York?"

"Mr. Pennington knows Mrs. Mercer. She's a personal friend."

"Hmm… What do you think? Did she kill him?"

"Mr. Pennington believes that the man is alive and waiting for her to take the fall." His phrasing was to be expected. Ethan didn't voice his opinion, he only voiced Mr. Pennington's.

How to find this man? "Do you think she'd sit down with a sketch artist? I could get Dora to do it for us."

"Mr. Pennington would like that. You could investigate the disappearance while Mr. Pennington's in court."

"Okay, could you let Mr. Pennington know I want to speak to the client?"

Mr. Pennington's door opened and he saw Emma and beckoned to her. "Emma, please come in."

She looked surprised. She hadn't known he was there. "Yes, of course," she said and started to follow him into his office.

"The client's already in his office," Ethan whispered.

She nodded and mouthed, "Thanks."

As Emma entered Pennington's office, she saw a lovely woman of about forty years old. She wore very stylish clothes and had perfectly coiffed hair, but the effect was spoiled by the woman's flushed face and swollen eyes.

"Ma'am," Emma greeted her.

The woman inclined her head but didn't say anything, using her handkerchief to wipe her eyes.

Emma looked toward Pennington and raised her eyebrows in question. He responded with, "Emma, have a seat. This is Mrs. Eloise Mercer. Eloise, Emma Evans is our investigator."

"You have one on staff, James?" Mrs. Mercer asked as Emma took a seat.

"I do," Pennington admitted. "Trials are expensive and are to be avoided. Emma might find us the evidence we need."

Mrs. Mercer nodded stiffly.

"Emma, I assume Ethan told you about the case. What are your initial thoughts?"

She pulled out her notebook and consulted it. "First," she said, looking at Mrs. Mercer, "we believe he is missing and not dead?"

"Yes," Pennington said definitely, answering for Mrs. Mercer.

"What about the blood, how do we account for that?" Emma asked bluntly.

"The blood won't matter—no body, no case," stated Mr. Pennington firmly.

"I think you're wrong there, Mr. Pennington. I think once we find the body alive, then that will make this no case," stated Emma.

He nodded. "You're right, that would be the best. That way, the creditors can go after the right person."

"I think we need to get a sketch unless you have pictures of your husband," Emma said to Mrs. Mercer.

"No, John refused to have his picture taken. I thought it was endearing," the woman said bitterly.

Emma nodded, taking notes. "I can have Dora come over to get the sketch."

Mrs. Mercer sent a worried glance to Mr. Pennington. "James, I would like to find John and talk to him."

Mr. Pennington looked at her. "I think we need to have Emma start investigating."

"I can accompany Ms. Evans to her residence to have the drawing made," suggested Mrs. Mercer.

"I don't think that will be necessary." He looked at Emma. "Can you bring Dora here this afternoon?"

Emma nodded. "I have a few more questions. I can follow up when I bring Dora back."

Mrs. Mercer sniffed. "Yes, I can do that."

"What attracted you to him initially?" Emma asked. Details like this would matter. She needed to know what kind of man she was looking for.

"He was charming, very suave. He said all the right things. He was thoughtful; he knew how to make me happy."

"Tall?"

"Taller than me." Emma looked at her; the woman was about 5'6", so he might be 5'8" or 5'9".

"Dark hair, light hair?"

"Light hair. He loved the sun."

"Was there anything that made you have second thoughts about marrying him? Did you see any money issues ahead of time?"

"No. He seemed to have an unlimited income. He paid for everything. At first."

"When did you realize, he was lying to you?"

"When he disappeared. Then the bills started coming in," Mrs. Mercer admitted.

"How long after the marriage was this? "Emma asked.

"Six months."

"Why didn't you find out about the bills earlier? I would have expected the creditors to come for the money once you married."

"He insisted on an extended honeymoon. We weren't in one place long enough to receive our mail."

"Who paid for the trip?"

"I did," Mrs. Mercer admitted. "I did it as a gift to him. I realize now that he was avoiding creditors."

Pennington said, "Men like this do not do this just one time. It's usually part of a pattern. Eloise, I think you're lucky."

"Lucky? Why do you say that?" she asked in disbelief. She could think of a lot of names for her situation, but lucky wasn't one of them.

Pennington sighed and sat back in his chair. "Sometimes, these men don't run off; sometimes, things happen to their brides."

Mrs. Mercer gave him a long look, almost like she wanted to argue, but she instead turned to Emma. "Will you be able to find him?" she asked.

"Where did you meet?" Emma asked, avoiding the woman's question. She didn't want to promise anything at this point.

"We met at a library auction. We both have an interest in rare books. He bought me a wonderful first edition," she said, lost in her memories.

Emma pulled her out by asking, "How long had you known each other before you were married?"

Mrs. Mercer turned red and looked down at her hands. Pennington prompted her, saying, "Eloise, please answer."

She looked back and mumbled, "One month."

"Who suggested the wedding should occur so soon?" Emma asked.

"I don't know," the woman said helplessly. "He was going on an extended trip and I didn't want to be without him. So, we married."

Emma didn't show her feelings but thought, *She should have been more cautious.* "Tell me about the last time you were with him."

"We were on the way home on a steamer. He said he had a headache and wanted to stay in the cabin. He insisted I go to dinner without him."

"How long were you gone?"

"Just through dinner. I returned as soon as it was over."

"What did you find when you got there?"

Mrs. Mercer shuddered and stood, pulling out her tissue. "There was blood, so much blood. I screamed and everything went black. I woke in the captain's cabin."

"Did they accuse you of killing him?"

"Not initially," she admitted, "though they made me move from my cabin and restricted my movements until we got to port. The local police in New York City took me into custody."

"I can take it from there," Pennington said. "They searched the cabin and found no body. They said the door was not tampered with and she was the only other person with a key."

"But doesn't the room steward also have a copy?" Emma asked, remembering her trips.

"I haven't traveled by steamship before this," he said. "That's a good question. I'll find out who the steward was."

"The blood could be from anything; it even could be animal. There's no way to tell," Emma remarked. "There's some talk that Karl Landsteiner in Vienna is working on the ability to tell the difference between the two, which would have helped here."

That's for the future, she thought. So much was coming up that would help law enforcement. Now, though, it was time for the hard question. "Mrs. Mercer, did you kill him?"

"No," she said immediately. "I loved him. I would have helped him through this mess."

She would have stood by him? "What if we find him? Will you take him back?"

Even Mr. Pennington looked shocked at that question, but he watched Mrs. Mercer for her answer.

Mrs. Mercer stood and walked around not answering.

Mr. Pennington said, "Eloise, you know what kind of man he is now."

"Maybe he was just scared," she suggested.

"Scared enough that you would go to prison or possibly be hung for him?" Pennington asked. He needed to scare her straight. If his friend continued down this path, he didn't know if he could save her.

That statement penetrated and she asked, "Could that happen? I thought we would just find him and this would be over."

This is why I didn't promise to find the man, Emma thought. If he isn't found, the authorities can presume death. It'll be hard to convict her, but not impossible

"Yes, it can happen," he said," and you have to be prepared for it. Even if we find him, he's not good for you."

"You can do better," Emma said quietly.

Mrs. Mercer looked over at the much younger woman and said, the bitterness coming up again, "At my age? No, this is who I attract now. Or I should say, my money attracts."

Pennington decided to let that go. "I'd like to have the sketch done as soon as possible. Can it be done today?"

"Yes, of course. I have some business matters this afternoon to attend to here. Will you let me know?" Mrs. Mercer asked.

"Eloise, remember, you need to let me know where you'll be. That's the only way you can stay out of jail," he reminded her.

"Of course, James."

Emma noticed she didn't look him in the eye as she said that. "I'll check with Dora, but we should be able to be here at two o'clock this afternoon."

"Eloise, can you come back at that time?" Pennington asked.

She nodded. He looked over at Emma. "I need some time with

Eloise." Walking to the door, she left the room. *The creditors,* she thought, *I need to find out who wants her husband to pay.*

Ethan sat at his desk and raised his eyebrows at her. She shook her head and mouthed, "Later."

He nodded and she headed back to her office. Before she could get to the door, raised voices could be heard from Mr. Pennington's office, then it suddenly went quiet. The door opened moments later and Mrs. Mercer exited, looking more frazzled than when Emma had seen her. She went directly to the door and before Ethan could stand, she had left the office.

They turned and looked back at Mr. Pennington. He just glared at the door, then stepped back into his office and slammed his own.

Wow! Emma thought. *Emotional case.* She went back to her office to organize her notes and look at the next steps. *Should I tell him about my suspicions that she might run off?*

When she left her office, she found his still closed. With her hand raised, ready to knock, Ethan said, "I wouldn't do that."

She was conflicted, but lowered her hand and backed away. *I'll tell him when I return this afternoon.*

Going back to her office, she sat and reviewed her notes from the interview. The description of Mrs. Mercer's husband was generic but why did it remind her of Joseph?

CHAPTER 31

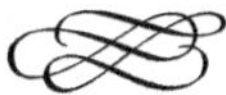

"What time will we need to go over?" Dora asked at lunch. Tim was home. He and Amy could take care of the children while she was out.

"About two o'clock," Emma said.

Dora nodded. "That will work."

They were finishing up when a knock sounded on the front door.

Tim stood, wiping his mouth, and said, "I'll get it." He came back in quickly with a note and handed it to Emma. She opened it and said, "Dora, you don't have to make plans to be out today. Mrs. Mercer won't be available. She had to head home for business reasons."

"Let me know when we reschedule," Dora said.

"Can you tell us more about this case?" Tim asked.

Mr. Pennington knew when she needed to share certain information with her team. The discussion moved to how fast the couple had married, the blood that was found, and the creditors demanding payment.

"What are you thinking, Emma?" Dora asked, seeing that Emma was drumming her fingers on her lips.

"Did it strike you that her description of him was very similar to that of Joseph? Not just the physical, but in the way she described their relationship. How fast it developed?"

"You don't think he's the man involved in this?" Dora asked, alarmed.

"Not really," her sister admitted. "I just had a feeling."

Dora pondered that. "You know, you're right about him rushing you in the same way. Though he can't be after your money; there isn't any. Not the amounts she has, anyway."

"No, I probably had him on my mind when I went into the interview."

"Emma, be careful," Dora cautioned her sister.

"Like you said, Dora, I have no reason for him to want me," she said lightly. Inside, she thought this was the same kind of man Mrs. Mercer had married.

That evening, Emma was home, thinking about Mrs. Mercer. *What business could be more important than the murder trial?* She picked up her lacework while she thought about the woman's sudden disappearance.

There was a knock at the door. Patrick ran to answer it, and Tim followed behind. There were voices and then Patrick called, "Emma! You have guests!"

She walked out of the sitting room and saw Joseph and Mark.

"I am the bearer of a gift," Joseph called out, holding up a package.

"We have a book for you," Mark said, knowing Emma would love this gift.

"Book!" Emma said. "That is nice. Would you like to go into the study?" Tim had finished his work for the day and they had the room to themselves. Books were her favorite thing and she was curious about what he had brought her.

The gas lamps were turned up in the room and Emma motioned to the desk. "You can place it there." Joseph took the book out of his bag and laid it on the table.

Emma picked it up and reviewed the spine, before opening it carefully. It was a first edition. "This is very nice," she said. *And expensive*, she thought. "Daisy Miller, A Comedy in Three Acts."

He told her, "I would like you to have this."

"No, it's yours. You don't have to give it to me," she protested. Though she would have liked to have the book, she didn't want to be indebted to this man.

"I insist," he said smoothly, pressing it into her hands.

She turned it over in her hands and said, "It is a lovely edition. I'll treasure it."

"Mom wants us back soon," Mark reminded his uncle.

"Yes, that's right, I don't want to disappoint her," Joseph said absently. All of his focus was on Emma.

Emma looked up from the book and blinked as she saw his intense interest. "I'll walk you to the door." As she pulled it open for him, she said, "Goodbye, and thank you again for the book."

They left and she shut the door and went back to the study. She picked up the book again and thought, *It is so lovely*. Flipping through the pages, she found an inscription that said, "To TC from LT with all my love".

How wonderful. Books that have a history are so interesting. Thinking about those people who had read and enjoyed the book before her, Emma clutched the book to her and went to her room to read it. The dinner bell distracted her and she saw that she had been reading for an hour. She put down the book reluctantly and got up to go downstairs to dinner.

Something occurred to her as she made her way downstairs. *Didn't Mrs. Mercer say that one of the things she and her husband had in common was rare books? Another connection or another coincidence?*

Mark and his family were already seated around the table. She went over to Mark's mom and kissed her on the cheek. "I haven't had time to come by and see you."

"That's all right, I knew you were busy with work. I'm glad we can spend some time together tonight," Elizabeth said.

She turned to George. "It's good to see you also."

"You, too," he said.

She took her seat, prayers were said and the food was passed around. Dora had sat Emma closer to her so she could help if Joseph made her uncomfortable. Conversation flowed around the table. Savannah was there and talked about her latest show. Emma watched and noticed Joseph wasn't as forward with her.

When Joseph took over the conversation, she saw George's eyes narrow. *Hmm,* she thought, *what's happening there? Not such a loving family after all?*

The topic Joseph chose to discuss was the woman's place in the home. How important it was to the family structure. What he was saying was true, but it seemed to have a second meaning. "Like my sister here, she stays home to take care of Mark and his father. She's a shining beacon to women everywhere."

Emma sent a look to Dora and shook her head. They wouldn't mention Elizabeth's job; evidently, they kept that information from her brother. *He wouldn't approve?* After that statement, she saw George had bent his fork. She casually said, "I'm sorry we gave you a damaged fork. Here's another one." He didn't say anything but exchanged forks with her.

Dinner ended quietly and it wasn't until dessert was served in the sitting room that Joseph approached her. The others had gathered into small groups talking amongst themselves. It was just the two of them on the settee. "I love the book, especially the inscription," she said.

"Inscription?" Joseph questioned. His eyes narrowed almost imperceptibly.

She wondered at that reaction. "Yes, it's from LT to TC with all my love."

"I didn't know someone had done that. I can take it back and give you one that's not written in," he said smoothly.

She protested. "No, I want to keep it. That makes it more valuable to me."

"I would rather take it back," Joseph said, his voice starting to show his displeasure.

"No. I love it as it is," she insisted. *Why the intense reaction? Does this mean the book is connected to someone, maybe Mrs. Mercer?*

"If you're sure..." he said, his voice trailing off.

"I am," she assured him, not wanting to part with the book.

A knock sounded at the door. Emma excused herself to answer it. She stepped back into the room with a telegram.

"Who sent it?" Dora asked.

Joseph watched her open it.

Emma smiled widely. "Finally. Jeremy's on the way home. Business is complete and successful."

"That's great," said Tim. "How soon until we see him?"

"Should be about a week with travel and cleanup," Emma replied in a distracted voice.

"So, I get to finally meet the mysterious Jeremy," Joseph said, suddenly appearing behind her.

She didn't have to hide the note. Jeremy had kept any information about the missing children out of it. "Yes, you'll like him. He reads as much as I do."

"Then I'd say I can't wait to meet the gentleman."

The evening came to a close with Mark's family leaving for their boarding house. Emma couldn't wait to get upstairs to read her book.

Early the next morning, as she was getting ready, she looked at it with regret and thought, *I can't carry a first edition with me. I'll have to leave it here.* She placed it on her desk and grabbed her bag to head down to breakfast.

Her day was rather ordinary, just paperwork at the law office. Mrs. Mercer had not returned for them to get a sketch and Mr. Pennington had managed to get a trial delay. He did mention Emma would receive the creditor's information soon. After a quick lunch in the park, she finished her courier duties and went home and back to that book.

Once there, she barely stopped to say hello to Dora and the kids as she headed upstairs. Going directly to the desk, she didn't find it. The handkerchief she had laid on top of it was still there, but the book was missing. *Did it fall?* She knelt down and looked around the floor. It wasn't there. She stood and continued to her door, at the landing she called, "Dora!"

"Yes," Dora said and came out of the sitting room with Baby Lottie in her arms. "Do you need something?"

"Yes, have you seen my book? The one I got from Joseph?"

She frowned. "No, I haven't."

"It isn't here."

"Let me check with Ethyl; she did dust your room this morning."

Dora took the baby and went to the kitchen. "Ethyl, could we see you in the foyer for a moment?"

The woman looked surprised and glanced at Amy for permission. "You can go, just don't be long," Amy said.

As Ethyl approached Dora, she said over her shoulder, "Of course, I'll be right back."

They walked back to the foyer. Emma had come down the stairs and was waiting for them. "Ethyl, did you dust my room this morning?"

"I did," she said. "Wasn't that okay?" She pulled on her apron, worrying it with her hands.

"Of course, it was okay," Dora reassured her. "Emma just can't find a book that was on her desk."

"Oh!" Ethyl said in surprise.

"What is it?"

"I did leave your door open for a few moments," she admitted. "I had forgotten your sheets. I went down to get them. I wasn't gone long and I didn't see another person other than family in the house."

Emma thought that was enough time for Joseph to take the

book. He didn't want her to have it after she told him what she had found. *I need that book back*, she thought.

"Did I do something wrong?" Ethyl loved her job and didn't want to lose it over something like this.

Dora assured her, "No, you're fine. You may go back to the kitchen."

Ethyl looked relieved and almost ran back to her workstation.

"I didn't mean to scare her," Emma said.

"She'll be fine. Who do you think took it?"

"Who else?"

"Joseph," Dora supplied.

"Yes, he didn't know that inscription was in there and it must lead to something or someone in his life."

"Something bad?"

"Something he wants to keep quiet."

"What will you do?"

"Get the book back," Emma said determinedly.

"Be careful, we don't know if he can be dangerous."

"I will," Emma murmured. *What is his schedule? I'll have to watch him to determine the best time to go into his room.*

Emma took off the next morning at her scheduled time and doubled back through the backyard. She left the bike hidden in a bush. The spot she picked to watch for Joseph allowed her to see the people coming and going on their street. Finally, he appeared. He looked in both directions and she stayed out of sight as he strolled down the street.

Should she chance it? *Yes.* She hurried in through the kitchen and was seen by Mrs. Spencer, the housekeeper.

"Emma, why the rush?" Mrs. Spencer asked, pulling her hands out of the dough she was kneading.

"Dora asked for some linens from the attic; we might need them for tonight."

Mrs. Spencer looked at Emma but didn't ask too many questions. If she was investigating something, then Mrs. Spencer would help however she could. One of those past investigations had helped her find out how her son died. "Let me know if you need anything."

"I will," Emma promised and took the stairs two at a time up to the third-floor room she knew Joseph was using.

Emma looked around and, when she confirmed it was clear, she used her lockpicks to open the door. Entering, she quickly scanned the room; the book was not on any surface. She went to the desk to check the drawers. Next, she went through the dresser and the closet. When the book could not be found, her gaze shifted to the bed. *Mattress,* she thought, and lifted it up. *Still nothing,* she thought in exasperation and she dropped it back into place.

The weather had been unseasonably warm. She cast a gaze toward the fireplace. *Could that be it?* She reviewed the outside of it and did not see any abnormalities. *Inside,* she thought, and crawled in. She stood carefully. Running her hands on the bricks, she found there were several protruding. Her fingers slid around and down the bricks until she found a crevasse; she pried the bricks out and felt inside. *Twine and paper!* She pulled on the item and saw it was a book. "Got it," she said triumphantly and carefully bent down to crawl back out.

She kept the package close to her as she made her way out and locked the door carefully behind her. The stairs creaked as she made her way downstairs. She stayed close to the wall and avoided the sitting room as she made her way into the kitchen. Mrs. Spencer gave her a nod as she went past her with a small wave. Emma walked quickly through the yard and into her home and up to her room. She opened the book quickly to confirm it was the one Joseph had given her. *Where can I put it? He knows all of the hiding places. But not Jeremy's room!*

Emma went through the bookcase into his room. There was a loose floorboard. She crawled under the bed and pulled the board out and placed the book inside. Once done, she crawled back out and looked down at herself. The dress was done for, not only ripped but also stained from the fireplace soot. She heard Dora's voice calling her.

"Emma, you received a note from Mr. Pennington's office. A package came with it," Dora called to her.

Emma glanced down again and thought, *There is nothing to be done now.* The note from Mr. Pennington could be important. She went down to the foyer and took the package from her sister.

She opened it and said, "Oh, this is the creditor information I have been expecting for Mrs. Mercer's missing husband."

"What do you expect to find?" Dora asked.

"His last known locations. The purchases should tell me where he's been. We have no job, no friends, and no family to follow, so we will follow the bills."

Dora noticed the state of her sister's clothes. "What in the world have you been doing? That dress may have to go into the rubbish bin or be torn to make rags."

"I hope it can be salvaged," Emma said, picking at the sleeve. Motioning to the package, she said, "I'll take this up with me while I change."

After she washed off the soot as best she could, she left the garment to dry in the bathroom. She changed into a skirt and top, then retrieved the package and went to the study where Tim and Patrick were working.

Are Mrs. Mercer's husband and Joseph the same person? she thought. *There are similarities.* She opened the packet and started documenting the locations where he had spent money.

She looked at the list thoughtfully. *Would Mark have an idea if these locations were where Joseph was located? It would be a new lead.* Answers were needed about the man who had shown up in their lives. *I need to check with Mark first.*

"I need to get something. I'll be back." Tim and Patrick waved as she left the room. School would be out soon and, if she wanted to see Mark before he left, she'd have to hurry. The ride over was an easy one and once there, she leaned the bike against the fence and waited for him.

The kids started coming out of the large building. When Mark didn't turn up, she locked the bike up to a wood post and headed inside. The school had long hallways that led to classrooms on either side. Each one had a few students working or talking to the teacher. About halfway down, she found him talking to the teacher. When he started back to his desk and glanced toward the door, he called out in surprise, "Emma!" He walked over and hugged her.

Their relationship had always been close. After their first meeting, they had kept in touch by letter, then again a couple of years later when the team had helped his family escape from kidnappers. Eventually, they moved into Emma's family's second boarding house and became part of their larger team. Mark's parents were occasional team members for her investigations. Both were teachers and could provide insight into the children if the case called for it.

"Well, I just couldn't wait to talk to you and I wanted to walk you home. Is everything all right here?" she asked, motioning to the teacher.

"Yeah, I just had some questions about my homework."

"Ready to go?"

Mark nodded and got his things. They walked out together. Emma retrieved her bike and asked him casually, "Do you remember the locations where your uncle has been or lived."

"Yes, of course! I want to travel like him, so I started keeping a journal about it. I want to go to all the places he told me about."

"A journal?" she asked, surprised.

"Yes, but," he said looking around, "don't tell him. He wouldn't like it."

"What makes you say that?"

"He just likes to keep to himself. He said writing these down is the wrong thing to do. It could be incriminating."

"Can you show it to me?" she asked in a whisper.

He looked at her; she was family now and he would do anything she asked of him. "Sure. When do you want to see it?"

"Is today too soon?"

"No, I don't think so. But I'm not sure where Uncle Joseph is today."

"Where do you keep it?" Emma asked, drumming her fingers on her lips.

"The basement at our boarding house," he answered.

"We shouldn't be seen together. How about you go first and I'll meet you?"

He nodded. "I'll see you there."

She stopped and he continued on. If anyone was watching, they wouldn't be seen together.

When she could no longer see Mark ahead of her, she walked her bike to his boarding house. She glanced around quickly and moved the bike to the side entrance. After putting it away, she made her way through the kitchen and waved to Mrs. Spencer. "I need to borrow a book," she mentioned.

Mrs. Spencer nodded, watching Emma from her position at the large pot. *Twice in one day,* she thought. *Who could she be investigating here?* The new addition was Joseph. She narrowed her eyes; she would help out if she could. Her assistant wasn't aware of any undercurrents and continued to roll out her bread dough on the table.

Emma passed through the dining room and into the foyer. *The study first,* she thought. They had set it up so that the boarders had plenty of reading material. She went to the shelf and removed a book. After pretending to read a few pages, she glanced into the hallway; it appeared to be empty. She closed the book and walked to the basement door and opened it.

The lamps were turned up and she followed the stairs down. The noise of papers being shuffled caused her to pause and move more cautiously. On the last step, she saw Mark looking around frantically, pulling open drawers; things were scattered on the floor from his search.

She frowned. "What is that smell?" she asked. *Has something been burned? That could be dangerous in this small space.*

Mark didn't hear her question. He was frantically looking around. "Emma, I can't find it!"

"Well, it must be here," she reasoned, looking around the piles of paper on the floor. "Maybe you left it in some of the other furniture here." Emma and Dora had bought a little too much furniture when they were furnishing the second boarding house. Dora had kept the extras, thinking a third boarding house would require more furniture. *The dresser looks like it might be the place to start.*

"Take that end," Emma directed. She and Marked adjusted the dresser and the burning smell got worse. "It's here," she said and bent down to look at the floor. She felt around and found something warm and picked it up. "Well, I found what was burned," Emma said and held up what appeared to be the spine of a notebook. It was scorched and tattered; there were no pages left.

"My journal," the boy said, running over to take it from her.

"Careful, it's still a little warm. Did Joseph know about it?"

"He did," he admitted. "When he got here, I told him I was writing about his different trips."

"Did he know where it was?" She looked around at the area, trying to determine if anything else was out of place.

"I didn't think so. No one comes down here," Mark explained.

"Did you pull out all of this?" Papers and books were scattered and the furniture had been moved away from the walls.

"Some of it. I emptied the desk. It's where I kept it hidden." He reached down and started picking up the papers he had displaced.

"Have you always kept it down here?"

"I have since his first night here."

"How come?"

"After I told him about the book, I found him looking around my room. I didn't know what to think, but I knew he wanted it, so I hid it. I didn't write anything bad," he muttered.

She pondered this. "How about you go walking at the park with me and we'll try to put the details back together?"

"Do you think we can?" he asked, relieved. He had worked hard on that journal.

"We can try. Why don't we go now?" she suggested.

"Sure."

Emma stuffed the journal remnants into her bag. They headed upstairs together and into the hallway.

"Going somewhere?" Joseph asked, startling them. They looked toward him. He was leaning nonchalantly against the wall, just outside of the basement door.

"Emma wanted to take me to the park and maybe a bookstore," Mark said.

"Sounds like a plan. May I come with you?" Joseph said as he straightened from the wall.

Emma was finally learning how to handle this man. "No," she said firmly. "I think we want to do this on our own today. Don't we?" She looked at Mark for his agreement.

"Yes. We go all the time," he said eagerly.

"Okay then, if I'm not wanted," his uncle said.

Emma looked at him and couldn't read his tone. "We'll see you tonight," she assured him. She turned to Mark. "Ready to go?"

"Yes."

Emma smiled indulgently and thought, *I will be spending some money in the bookstore today. Mark will be a well-paid source.*

They walked to the park, neither of them turning back to see if Joseph was behind them. They reached a bench in the shade and sat down. *Did he follow?* She looked and, when she didn't see him, she pulled out what was left of the leather journal.

Mark reached out and touched it. "Why burn it?" his voice trembled as he asked.

"Mark, do you think you could remember each destination?" she asked trying to distract him.

"I think so, but I wouldn't be as good with the dates."

"Could you guess?"

"I think so. But how do I work on it? If Uncle Joseph finds it, won't he just burn it again?" he said, his tone miserable. "He was my favorite person before this. I prayed for him to visit my mom to help cheer her up. And he does this!"

She hated to see his relationship tarnished. "Maybe he had a reason for the privacy?" she asked. *Were there things he didn't want others to know? What occurred in those places that he wanted to keep hidden?*

"Yeah, are you going to ask him what that reason is?" the boy asked.

"Maybe later, but not now. I'd like to look into the locations and dates that you remember."

"Do you think he did something bad?" Mark asked tentatively.

"I hope not, but I am concerned he went to this extreme to hide the information." She didn't mention her other suspicions about Mrs. Mercer's husband.

"I get that. You could meet me after school like you did today and I can give you the pages that I've put together. He shouldn't be able to search there."

"No, that's true. I'll also keep what you give me at the Pinkerton offices. When do you think you can start?"

"Tomorrow," he said decisively. "Can you be there after school?"

"I'll make time." Her courier duties allowed her some flexibility with her schedule.

"What if you can't always be here?" Mark asked, thinking ahead.

"Leave it on your desk and, if needed, I can get into the school at night," she said decisively.

Mark wanted to move on. "Can we go to the bookstore now?" He was ready for the heavy conversation to be over.

"I think that's a great idea," she said and stood up.

"Can I get two books in exchange for the information?" he negotiated.

She smiled and held out her hand to him. He grabbed it and they rushed to the bookstore.

On the way back, she kept her bag close to her. She still had the burned journal in her possession.

Mark picked out a varied selection but also showed interest in journals describing the 1849 California gold rush. Emma saw them and teased, "Do you have an interest in gold mining?"

"In adventure," he said and grinned at her. She grinned back, knowing they had that in common.

They separated at his boarding house; he carried his bag of books and journals into his home with him.

She watched him enter and started up her stoop; she wasn't watching where she was going and ran into Joseph. He placed himself in her path.

"We must stop meeting this way," he said.

"Yes, you do seem to be everywhere today." When he didn't move, she asked, "Is there something I can help you with?"

"No, no." He stepped to the side and, as she started to brush past, he placed a hand on the bag she held tight. "That's funny," he said, "I smell something burning. Should we check your bag?"

"No, there's nothing in my bag," she said, wrestling it from his grasp. "I have things in there I consider work-related, so I can't show them to anyone."

"You do? Well, now I want to see them even more." He reached for the bag again.

"Joseph, please let the bag go." Her voice was almost a growl. She was tired of his shenanigans and was ready to pull her knife if he didn't move out of her way.

He must have seen that he had pushed too much and let it go.

She didn't comment further and headed into the house, slamming the door behind her.

Dora was walking down the stairs when Emma came in. "Goodness, what is all the noise about?"

Emma looked at her sister and thought about what was in her bag. *All I have is a burned journal; that doesn't prove anything.* "It was nothing, the wind caught it."

"Wind? Do we have any?" The day was settled and the trees didn't seem to be moving with even a gentle breeze.

"Yes, the wind," Emma muttered and headed upstairs.

CHAPTER 32

Mark set to work on his new journal. Emma stopped by each day to gather the pages. She spent hours at the Pinkerton offices going through them. Jeremy was still away, so she was able to use his space. The dates and locations were more numerous than expected. Mark told her that he would be finished with the journal entries the next week.

The door to Jeremy's office was open and, when Cole walked by, he stopped and called to her, "Emma, are you here today?"

"Cole, do you have time to meet with me?" she asked, looking up from the paper she was reviewing.

"Sure, what's up?" he asked, walking into the office and laying his coat on the couch before sitting down in the guest chair at the desk. She handed him the new journal pages and the credit records. She had circled the ones that were identical in location.

"What are these?" he asked, looking at both sets of papers.

"Mark's uncle, Joseph, is visiting and something about him bothers me."

Cole listened intently; her instincts were rarely off.

"He's very similar to the man we're looking for in a murder case. You have heard about Mrs. Eloise Mercer?"

"Yes, they say she killed her husband. You think this Joseph is him?"

"I have no proof. There are no pictures or drawings of the man."

"Why do you think he is the same person?"

"Something happened. Mark was keeping a journal of all the locations his uncle had mentioned he had traveled to. His uncle found out about them and that journal was found burned soon after."

"Burned? Why do you think the uncle is responsible?"

"Because Mark found him looking through his room. Mark had moved the journal to the basement and that's where we found it burned."

"So, he was concerned someone would see his movements, the dates, and the locations. You're thinking there might be possible criminal activities on those dates and times?"

"The dates may not be perfect. Mark had to try to remember each of them and populate a new journal with the information."

"He did all of this from memory?" Cole asked, impressed. There must have been ten pages of dates and locations.

"He's a smart kid."

"That explains the first document. What's this one?" he asked, holding up the credit report.

"That's a credit report that says Mrs. Mercer owes money. It's her husband's bills from various creditors. That might be the first evidence linking Joseph to my murder case," she stated.

Cole studied it and said, "Tell me what these circles mean."

She came around the desk and took both documents and laid them side by side. "The circled ones match almost identically to the locations where Joseph was during the month before the wedding to Mrs. Mercer."

"It isn't enough to arrest him."

"No," she agreed, "but I was hoping we could investigate the dates and see if we have anything that may pop up."

"Like what?" he asked.

"More wives, unexplained disappearances or deaths."

He nodded. "Other wives are possible. I can do that. First, I'll send telegrams to the police precincts in each of these cities."

"Thank you so much! Let me know if you find anything," she said, relieved someone else was on the case.

"I will," he commented, looking at the data.

CHAPTER 33

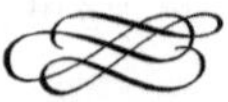

*E*mma spoke to Mr. Pennington. "Will Mrs. Mercer be returning soon?"

He shook his head. "I don't know. I can't contact her. "

"When was the last time you heard from her?"

"A few days ago. She said she would be back soon."

Emma nodded. She had feared Mrs. Mercer would flee.

"Will the case continue without her?"

"Yes. They can try her in absentia. I'm asking for a delay. That should buy us another month."

CHAPTER 34

Things at home had calmed down and Joseph had stopped pressuring her for dates. He had also stopped showing up at inopportune moments. Does *he know the book is no longer in his fireplace?*

Mark was over early one morning, returning a book he had borrowed and Emma asked him, "Is Joseph still in town?"

"He had a trip a few days ago but was back by that evening."

"When was this?" she asked.

"Earlier this week."

"Where did he go?" Emma asked.

"No way am I asking that question," Mark said. He and his uncle were just starting to talk again.

"Hmm," Emma said.

"Thanks for the loan."

"Anytime," she said and watched the boy leave. Her thoughts turned to Jeremy. He was still away and she missed him more each day. To distract herself, she found Dora in the dining room "Where's my paper?" she asked.

"Patrick put it in your chair."

Emma had two papers delivered—one for her to scan for

possible cases and one for the family. When she picked her copy up, pieces fell out. "Who's been cutting up my paper?" she called loudly.

Dora smiled indulgently and said, "It may have been Patrick. He likes to cut the comics out."

She shifted through the pages and said, "No, I don't think so; the comics are here. It's other articles that are missing," she said. "Where's the other paper?"

"I'm not sure," her sister admitted. "I don't remember seeing a second one this morning. Check with the other boarding house; I know they get a paper."

Emma went straight over and into the kitchen door. Mrs. Spencer was sitting at the table making a list for the day. She greeted Emma. "Good morning. What can we do for you?"

"I was hoping you had a paper I could borrow this morning."

"I haven't seen it yet. Have you checked the front stoop? Mark normally gets it for me."

"I'll go check," Emma said, heading that way. She opened the door and didn't find the paper on the stoop. She closed it turned and saw Mark coming down the stairs.

"Good morning, have you seen the paper?" she asked.

"Not yet, I was just going out for it," he said, heading toward the door.

"It's not there," she said, stopping him.

"No? We may have gotten missed. It's happened before."

"Hmmm," she said, doubtful that two papers would be missed. She kept her tone light and said, "I'll check it later."

"Were you looking for anything in particular?"

"No, just reading through it. You know I like to read the news. Have a good day," she said and headed back home to get ready for her day.

On her way back in, she picked up her newspaper again and thought, *I can go down to the paper itself and get a copy.* She checked her timepiece and saw that she had an hour to spare that morning.

She started to rush out, but Dora called out, "You need to eat! And get your lunch!"

Emma wanted to leave but knew Dora was right. "All right, I'll be right there." She went into the kitchen and quickly grabbed bread and butter and her lunch pail.

"That isn't enough!" Dora said.

"It's plenty and I have an errand this morning."

Dora shook her head and watched her sister leave.

Emma got her bike and, once she was on the street, she jumped on and headed to the paper. She got there and pulled up. Wagons that had been out in the early morning for deliveries had returned. Emma called to the boy on the loading dock handling the returns. "Hey, Toby, could you toss me one of those papers?"

"Sure, Emma, but don't you get a delivery at your house?" he asked and tossed her the rolled-up paper.

"Yes, but the only one I could find was cut up this morning," she said absently and opened the paper. She read over it and almost missed the small update about a murder in another state. She frowned and looked closer at it. It gave a location but no specific date. She needed to take it to Jeremy's office and compare it with the journal entries that Mark had provided. Glancing at her timepiece, she saw it was getting close to her start time at Pennington's office. She'd have to stop by Jeremy's office in the afternoon.

The court had approved the delay for Mrs. Mercer. They still had not heard from her. Once Emma arrived at the office, she placed her bike on her shoulder and made her way inside. She was shocked when she saw the office full of people. Mr. Pennington was already in. *It's too early for him to be here*, she thought. There were also multiple police officers and the prosecutor for Mrs. Mercer's case. Taking her bike to the closet, she went over to Ethan and asked in a low voice, "What's going on?"

"Mrs. Mercer is missing!" he said in the same tone.

"It has been confirmed?"

"Yes, the officers went to the house to escort her back and she wasn't there. Her bags were also missing."

"When did they think this was?" she asked.

"A few days ago."

Joseph was also gone during that time she thought. "Why do we think she ran off?"

"Mr. Pennington is sure she didn't go by herself."

"Do we think someone took her or did something to her?"

"That is a possibility," he admitted. "Though, if she is with her husband, I think she went willingly."

Pennington looked around and saw Emma in the room. "Emma, come over here. Officers, I'm sure you all know Emma Evans. She's our investigator."

"Hello, Emma," one of the officers said. "Have you spoken to Mrs. Mercer?"

"Hello, Pete. I planned to have another one, but she had to go home for personal business," Emma responded.

"Do you have any idea where she may have gone?" Pete asked.

I don't she thought but I can bet who she is with, she thought, *but with no evidence, now isn't the time to share.* "No, but I think her husband may still be alive. I've no way to trace him right now."

"What do you know?"

"We just know tall, light hair, slim build."

"That could be almost anyone," Pete muttered.

"You're right," she admitted.

Pete looked back at Mr. Pennington and said, "We'll let you know if we're able to locate her."

"I would appreciate that," Pennington said as he walked the officers to the door. On his way back, he said, "Emma, Ethan, my office please."

Emma looked at Ethan and he shrugged; they were surprised at the request but followed him into the office.

Mr. Pennington shut the door and they sat down at his round table.

Mr. Pennington started with, "We will have to delay the trial, again."

"Yes, until we find her," Ethan commented.

Mr. Pennington nodded. "There could be additional charges."

"Do we think she ran away?" Emma asked. "Or that she was taken?"

"A few days ago, she was still angry but seemed committed to taking this to court to prove her innocence."

"Then why disappear now? Wasn't her money locked up?"

"Yes, due to the creditor's claims, her investments and property were not under her control. All of her business decisions were run through the courts."

"Then how could she leave?" Emma asked.

"There are ways," he said.

When she looked at him questioningly, he said, "Jewels. She had managed to sew a large number into her dresses."

"Oh!" Emma exclaimed.

"Yes. I told her to do that, just in case, but I didn't think she'd use them to run away. Have you made any progress on the creditors and identifying the husband?" Mr. Pennington asked.

"I have some suspicions, but no real proof right now."

"Let me know when you feel there is something to go on," he said.

She nodded. She and Ethan left the office to start their day.

CHAPTER 35

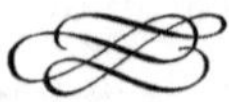

She was home that evening, going over the information they had. They were still waiting for the information Cole had requested from the police officers. The night was cool and she wanted to take a walk and think about what they had in evidence.

She had walked about six blocks and started to turn around when someone grabbed her arm. She reacted and swung her leg around to trip him. The hit was successful and she glanced down at who had taken her by the arm. It was Joseph.

He didn't look hurt but he seemed shocked. He stood up quickly, but this time he didn't touch her. Instead, he leaned toward her and asked, "What do you think you're doing?"

"What do you mean?" she asked, feigning ignorance.

"You think a few articles, an inscription in a book, and my travel locations will add up to something?"

"I don't just think so, I know so, Joseph. Or should I say Benjamin Mercer?"

His eyes narrowed. Then he changed his expression to say pleasantly, "Emma, we could be together. You, at home, and me..."

"While you do what? Run up credit and marry other women? I don't think so," she scoffed.

"I thought you could be like my sister," he said. "I had it all planned."

"What you need to do is turn yourself in so that Mrs. Mercer won't be charged with your death." When he didn't say anything, she said, "Unless you have her somewhere under your control. Did you take her?"

He looked around and said, "I like it here. I think I'll be putting down roots and have a family of my own."

"Not with me!" said Emma indignantly.

"We shall see," he said, walking off.

"We'll get you!" she called.

He stopped suddenly and turned to her. "Will you? I don't think so." He turned back and continued at a leisurely pace.

At dinner that evening, the door slammed open in the foyer. Emma looked at Dora and she shrugged.

"I'll get it," Tim said as he stood.

He didn't make it out of the dining room as Jeremy strode in. Emma jumped up and jumped into his arms. "You're back!"

"I am," he said, kissing her and swinging her around.

"Successful trip?" she asked when he put her down.

"Yes, and a final one."

"Did you find everyone?"

"Everyone that's in the States. The Pinkertons have a line on the ones in Europe."

"I'm glad."

"Me too. I'll be here for a long time."

"Sit and eat," Dora said. "You must have come straight from the train station."

"I did, and I am hungry. I could also use a bath," he said in a low voice to Emma.

"Whew! You sure do!" She smiled back, happy he was here with them.

"Tell me," he said looking around, "how is everyone?"

They all talked and updated him on the activities. After dinner, he said, "I need to go get cleaned up."

"We'll have dessert waiting," Dora said with a smile as she watched Emma and Jeremy head upstairs.

"Meet you in your room," he said, bending his head to hers. She returned his kiss. He reluctantly lifted his head and went into his bedroom to retrieve his towel and a robe. He went back to the bath and ran the water. The bath was so nice, he soaked for a few extra minutes before he got out, dried off, and put on his robe. The towel was used to dry his hair as he entered his room. He looked over toward Emma's room and saw the bookcase door was open. *No need to change*, he thought and went to see her.

She was on the bed reading.

"Want some company?" he called.

She looked up and smiled slowly. "I think I would."

He ran over and leaped on the bed, bouncing her. She was giggling as he dropped down beside her. The giggling stopped as he pulled her into his arms. They stayed like that for some time. After, he sat up in bed. Emma pulled up her sheet and moved with him. He asked casually, "Is Mark's uncle still around?"

"Yes," she said and frowned.

Reading her face, he asked, "Did something happen?"

"Odd things," she muttered. "He just pops up when you least expect him." She told him of tripping over his cane at the back stairs. "He can be nice," she admitted. "It masks the creepy stuff."

"Is that all?" he asked. Now that he was back, he'd make it clear to Joseph that Emma wasn't available.

"No," she said, "I think there's much more." She reviewed the Mercer case with him, the credit comparison with Mark's list, the fact that the first list had been burnt, and the disappearance of Mrs. Mercer. While he mulled all of that over, she said, "I also told him I knew who he was—Benjamin Mercer."

Jeremy sat back. "When I asked if anything happened while I

was gone, I meant this! Emma, he could have hurt you! Well, I'm here now, so that should quell his interest."

"I hope so. Dora said that one thing would have stopped him."

"And that is?" he asked.

"A ring," she muttered.

He caught her chin and tilted it and asked, "Is that something you would like?"

"You know it isn't," she said, looking him in the eye. "I don't need a piece of paper to tell everyone how I feel about you. It's just society's rules, but it may have been enough to keep him away."

The dinner bell clanged.

Emma smiled. "I think we're being called."

"Dessert," Jeremy said.

They cleaned up and headed downstairs. They were talking softly, holding hands.

Emma glanced down and said, "He's here."

Jeremy looked where she indicated and saw Joseph leaning against the sitting room entrance. He straightened as they approached. "Jeremy," he said and walked toward them. He waited at the base of the stairs.

"I am, and you're Joseph?" responded Jeremy.

"It's nice to meet you," Joseph said with that same charm that he could turn on and off at a whim.

Jeremy watched him and saw what Emma saw. This man was not what he seemed. "Come on, Emma, we're going for a walk." They had planned to have dessert, but he didn't like this man.

"I insist you stay for a toast," he said.

He insists! thought Jeremy.

Elizabeth came out of the sitting room. "Oh, please do stay. We'd like to enjoy the evening together."

Emma tugged Jeremy's hand and he told her, "Of course."

Joseph moved to the center of the room, taking his place and telling stories that made everyone laugh. Dora brought in desserts and he turned the conversation to morals.

"Oh, I also forgot to mention he has views on the woman's place," Emma told Jeremy in a low voice.

His tone had shifted from pleasant to no inflection at all. "Women are too free with their bodies, giving themselves outside of marriage. Society has rules for a reason."

"Surely you don't believe that?" asked his sister.

Joseph just shook his head. "Too much freedom. Soon we won't have brides, just working companions. Then what form will the family take?"

"Are you talking about something in particular?" Jeremy demanded.

"Why nothing, of course, just expressing my opinion," Joseph said smoothly.

Emma gripped Jeremy's hand and gave an almost imperceptible shake of her head.

Joseph strolled by Jeremy and leaned down and murmured, "I know about that bookcase in your room."

Jeremy had had enough! He jumped up and grabbed Joseph by the collar and pulled him through the foyer and into the study. He shoved him to the floor and pulled the doors shut violently.

Emma stopped everyone from going after them. "Let them talk."

George sat back in his chair and looked happier than he had in weeks.

"Have you been in Emma's room?" Jeremy demanded, watching as he stood and dusted off his clothes.

"That bookcase doesn't hide the dirty deeds the two of you are doing outside of marriage."

"It's time you left town! Now!" Jeremy said, grabbing him and slamming him into the wall again.

"Leave?" Joseph laughed. "No, I think I'm staying here. After all, my loving family lives here."

"Even with all the loose women?" Jeremy asked sarcastically.

"Oh, I can fix that."

"Is that a threat?"

"No, of course not."

"You *will* leave town and you *will* not threaten Emma or anyone else again. *Do we understand each other?*"

Joseph was silent for a moment. "I feel that I should make plans to leave."

"Good," Jeremy said. "I thought we could get on the same page."

"Can you release me now?"

Jeremy slowly let him go and they rejoined the family.

"Why don't I make a toast?" Joseph said, entering the sitting room as if nothing had occurred. "I will make this my final goodbye."

"What? Why would you leave?" asked his sister. "We've loved having you here. Please, can you reconsider?"

"You know if he has to leave it must be for business," George said. "He can come back some other time." Though he hoped it would be a long time before they saw his brother-in-law again. His wife was almost a different person when he was around.

Mark's mom and dad had privately talked about Joseph a few weeks after his arrival. "Why do you keep encouraging him to see Emma?" George asked.

"I'd love it if they were together; that way our family can stay together here in Chicago."

He shook his head. "What are you thinking? You know she's with Jeremy."

"I haven't seen a ring," she stated, sounding too much like her brother.

George frowned. "You get like this when he's here. You know

Emma doesn't want to be the home and family type. The fact is, you hide your work when he's here and you seem to believe everything he's talking about. It just isn't right."

"I do that," Elizabeth admitted, collapsing on the bed. She stared at the ceiling. "I just don't want him to be disappointed in me."

"Would that be so bad?"

"You never have liked him," she accused, turning over on the bed to look at her husband.

"I did," he contradicted her, "in the beginning. I bought into his charm just like everyone else."

"What changed? He's always been the same," she asked, confused.

"That's it exactly! He's been saying the same things he said ten years ago. The same rhetoric."

"But that's because he wants things how they used to be," she tried to explain.

"Look around," he said, "we tell our students that the world is changing. The industrial complexes will allow more and more women to work and help their families. You're an example of this progress, except when your brother is here."

"You're right," she murmured, realizing she was hiding who she was from Joseph. "Do you think Emma will forgive me?"

"I wouldn't worry about Emma. It's Jeremy who might have the problem with your interference," he stated dryly.

Back to the present

The next morning at the Pinkerton office, Jeremy was still railing about Joseph's actions.

"He has to leave town. He's dangerous," he said.

"We still don't have enough proof. We need Mrs. Mercer for an identification," Emma said.

Cole nodded. "I was thinking we could take custody of him on the train when he leaves. Question him outside of town. I'll have agents on the train and, as soon as he boards, we can take him into custody."

"We'll need to escort him to the train," Jeremy said.

Emma nodded and hoped it would be that easy.

That evening, Emma and Jeremy went to the second boarding house to confirm Joseph's plans. He was sitting on the stoop enjoying the evening.

"We have your train tickets," Jeremy said. "You'll be leaving in the morning."

Joseph shrugged, seemingly indifferent to the plans they'd made for him. He looked at Emma. "Why don't you accompany me to the train tomorrow? Make sure I get off and out of your town."

"Now that, we will do," she confirmed.

"No. Only you," he said and looked at Jeremy.

Before Jeremy could disagree, Emma said, "I'll do that." She looked at Jeremy. "We can take separate carriages and meet you there."

"No," said Joseph. "I want to take the trolley one last time."

She frowned but said, "That should be fine." She just wanted him gone.

Back at their boarding house, Jeremy confronted her. "I don't like it."

"Me either, but you know I can protect myself if he tries anything."

He kissed her and said, "Yeah, I know you can. I'll meet you at the train station."

CHAPTER 38

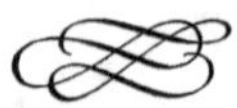

The next morning progressed without drama. Joseph said a grand goodbye to his family and accompanied Emma to the trolley. They climbed on board and watched the city go by.

"You know," he started, "I had plans for you."

"Plans?" she asked, wanting to keep him talking.

"You appeared to be everything I wanted to help me build a strong family. Someone with a solid work ethic that could be used at home."

"There's just that persnickety issue that I don't want to stay home and be a 'housewife'. Oh, and the fact that I don't want to be with you."

He didn't react to that; he just continued on as if she hadn't said anything. "There were also other facts I could not overlook."

"And those would be?"

"Perhaps that you choose to live out of wedlock with Jeremy," he said calmly.

She stopped him abruptly and said, "Nothing I do is of any concern of yours." She was glad the trolley was fairly empty at this hour.

"No, it's women like you that made me the man I am."

"I don't think you can make women as a whole responsible for that."

That statement seemed to get through the blasé act he had perfected. "That is enough," he said shortly.

"Finally. Is this the true you I'm speaking with?" she asked with interest.

"I want to stay here. I'm happy here with my family."

"You agreed to leave."

"You pushed me into it."

She didn't say anything but felt his hand tightening on her arm. As the trolly increased in speed, he started to pull her toward the side, near the exit.

At the speed they were going, she could survive a fall, but watching the carriages and wagons go by, she realized she'd be trampled to death. Pulling back, she found that he was stronger than he looked. His expression showed no strain as he moved her closer and closer to the exit.

He's planning a quick movement, she thought. *Otherwise, people would interfere.*

He leaned into her. "Had you not been flawed, I would have picked you to be my wife."

She felt him readying himself. It was going to be him or her. She worked her feet through his and when he went to push her into the traffic, she braced herself for a fall.

Instead of her being pushed off, an arm came up behind him and pushed Joseph into traffic. He fell with a scream. The milk truck coming up had no time to stop and avoid him. The trolley driver stopped, almost dislodging several other passengers.

Emma caught a glimpse of the person who had pushed Joseph. It was John's new guard from Sing Sing. *Looks like my favor has been taken care of,* she thought. The guard nodded to her and jumped off the trolley.

"What happened? Why have we stopped?" the people grumbled around her.

"Someone fell off," another person responded.

The passengers exited the now-stopped trolley slowly. The local police officer was checking what was left of Joseph. Emma saw him shake his head. She didn't feel anything. Someone had died, a family member of someone she was close to. Mark and his mom would be heartbroken, but if they knew that he was a murderer, they would have been destroyed.

She accompanied the officer to the police station. There were questions, but it was determined to be an accident. Jeremy and Cole were notified she wouldn't be at the station. McGee offered to escort her home.

The hardest part was going to the boarding house where Mark's family lived. It was just her and the officer. For once, she knocked on the door, choosing to have additional time while it was answered. Steps ran to the door and Emma knew it was Mark.

"Emma! Why'd you knock? Come in. We're in the sitting room." It was Saturday and the family was at home.

"Mark, I have someone with me," she said gently. "Can you bring your mother and father to the dining room?"

He looked at Emma and the police officer and said, "Okay. Right away."

Emma nodded toward the dining room and she and McGee went in to sit and wait.

"I don't understand why she's here with a policeman and why she needs to see us," Elizabeth said as they walked out of the sitting room.

"Let's go find out," George replied.

They entered, and Mark's mom was frowning. Her husband's face was curiously devoid of any emotion.

"What is going on?" Elizabeth asked.

"Let's sit," McGee urged.

She nodded and took a seat, not taking her eyes off the officer.

Emma started. "We have some news to share with you."

Elizabeth stood abruptly. "No! No, I don't want to hear it."

"Elizabeth, we have to hear. Please, go on," George said. But he didn't try to make his wife sit back down.

"As we were going to the train station, Joseph fell from the trolley and was trampled by a milk truck," Emma stated.

"What does that mean?" Elizabeth asked faintly.

"That means," McGee said, taking over from Emma, "that Joseph Black has passed away."

Mark began crying and Elizabeth came out of her daze and started crying also.

George walked over and took his wife in his arms. "Where can we pick him up?" he asked.

"That won't be necessary. If you'll let us know the funeral home you would like to use, we'll have him taken there," McGee stated.

"I'll take care of it and get that information to you."

"Let me know if you need any help," McGee offered.

"I think we need time alone now," George said, taking his wife and Mark out of the room.

"Yes, of course," Emma said.

"Thank you for accompanying me. These types of things can be hard," Emma said to McGee.

"Of course."

They parted, and Emma went home.

"Emma, did Joseph get on the train okay?" called Dora from the dining room.

"Oh, Dora!" she cried and ran over to her sister.

"What happened?" Dora asked, taking her into her arms.

Emma explained what had happened on the trolley. Dora didn't say much during the story. "Let's go into the sitting room. There's more to this story," she said, making Emma look her in the eyes.

"You knew?" she asked, sniffling.

"I had a feeling he was a bad guy, especially after the morality speech he made last night."

"Yes, that was pretty horrible," Emma acknowledged.

"It all seemed to be aimed at you and Jeremy."

"It was. He considered Jeremy my greatest flaw—being together without marriage. He had plans for me to marry him."

"Marry!"

"Yes, but my flaw put me on the same list that his other engagements suffered."

"Other engagements?"

"Yes. Jeremy and Cole looked into several cases where he had been located."

"The newspapers?" Dora guessed.

"Yes. He couldn't control that. There were too many bodies and debts piling up. Once the press picked it up, it would be everywhere."

"How will you identify him and link him to all of it?"

"I have an idea on that," Emma murmured.

"Poor Elizabeth," Dora murmured. "She was so proud of him. This must be hitting her hard."

"Yes," Emma said and laid her head back on Dora's shoulder.

CHAPTER 39

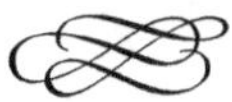

The funeral was small, with only Mark's family and a few other people from both boarding houses. Mark and his mom talked about Joseph and told stories of happier times. They slowly got back to normal with the grief still heavy in their hearts.

Dora had sketched Joseph from memory. Cole and Jeremy circulated it through the different police precincts. Stories started to come back about other marriages, ones that had ended in the bride's death.

Mr. Pennington grew more fearful by the day that Mrs. Mercer was one of his victims. They had confirmed with the creditors that Joseph was the man they were searching for. He sat in his office, reading over briefs when he heard Ethan say, "One moment, please."

"Sir," Ethan said and opened the door to show him who was there. It was Eloise.

He stood and stared at her.

"James, how could I be so wrong?" she asked and held out her arms to him.

He went over to her and took her into his arms. "It's all over now."

CHAPTER 40

"It's taken care of?" John Harden asked his second-in-command and son-in-law, Dan Piper.

"Yes, the man has been removed," Dan confirmed.

"Is it enough?" asked John.

"Enough?"

"Is the favor enough to close my debt to her?"

Dan stayed silent, not sure what he should say.

"I have one more thing for you to do," John said, "and then we will sever our ties with Emma Evans."

"Yes, boss."

CHAPTER 41

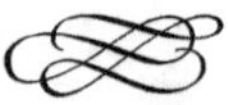

Tim called to Jeremy and Emma, "A package came for you. It's on the table."

Emma frowned and went over to pick it up. "Who is it from?" asked Jeremy.

"I don't know," she said, turning it over. There were no markings, just their names on the front. She opened it, slid out the document, and read it through. "It's the deed to the beach house!"

"What?" Jeremy exclaimed. He took the paperwork and saw the same thing she had.

Emma looked at Jeremy. "I think this is a final favor from you know who. Should we take it?"

He knew who she referenced and nodded slowly. "Yes. Yes, I think we should."

NOTEBOOK MYSTERIES ~ PARISIAN INTRIGUE (BOOK 6)

Notebook Mysteries

Parisian
Intrigue

KIMBERLY MULLINS

PROLOGUE

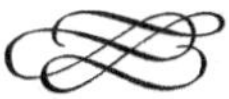

PARIS JAIL 1889

"You just had to get us involved," Jeremy muttered from under his hat, not stirring off the bench where he was reclining.

Emma turned toward him and leaned back against the jail cell bars. "Me? I wasn't the one who threw the first punch."

"Calm down," called Dora's voice from the adjacent cell.

"Calm down? You were the one who punched the police officer!" Emma said, straightening.

"That's how I heard it," Tim said from the hallway outside of the cells.

Dora rushed toward him. She pressed against the bars and held out her hand. "Can you get us out of here?"

He took it and said, "Not me, but I brought someone who can help."

A man in a black suit, black tie, and white shirt walked up.

"Cole!" Emma called.

Jeremy lifted the hat off his face, showing a black eye. He sat up and moved it to a jaunty angle on his head. "Hey Pops, here to spring us?"

"That remains to be seen. There's some confusion about the events you were involved in," Cole said drolly.

"What could be confusing?" Emma asked. "I found a dead body in a trunk. The husband slapped me, then the whole room joined in." Frowning, she looked at Jeremy in search of his support.

He shrugged and said, "Yeah, anyone would have known to check the trunk for a body."

Cole laughed. "Most people come to Paris for shopping and sightseeing."

"Well, not us," said Emma firmly.

CHAPTER 1

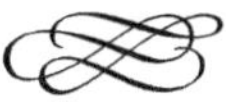

FOUR WEEKS AGO, IN CHICAGO

$\mathcal{E}$mma walked into the dining room where the family was enjoying a late Sunday lunch. Tim, Dora, Emma, Jake, and Jeremy sat around the table with the children. They had gone to church that morning and were enjoying a lazy afternoon.

"Delivery," she said waving an envelope in the air.

"What is it, Emma, a telegram?" Jeremy asked, setting down his fork.

"No, an invitation," she responded, not looking up from it.

"To a party?" Dora asked curiously as she continued to cut up three-year-old Lottie's food.

"No," Emma said, glancing up suddenly. "It's an invitation to the Paris Exposition!"

"Paris!" everyone said together.

"Someone invited you to Paris?" Dora asked. She felt envious. Her sister was always doing exciting things.

"Not just me. All of us," Emma said and gestured to everyone at the table.

Everyone was silent as they digested the information. Finally, Jeremy spoke up. "Can I see that?"

"Yes," she said as she handed him the invitation.

"Who sent it?" Tim asked.

"It says it's from the Art Curator's Society. Have you heard of them?" Jeremy asked Emma.

"No. I can't say I have. It mentions that reservations are in place for us at the hotel and that the tickets for the train and steamer are prearranged." The name of the steamer was *La Bretagne*. *What a coincidence,* she thought. She had been to Paris previously on the *La Bretagne*.

"When are we expected to go?" Dora asked. She was thinking about the kids, the boarding houses, and all that needed to be done to keep things running smoothly.

Jeremy handed the invitation to her without commenting.

Dora read the note quickly. "But this says tomorrow!" she exclaimed. "How can we get organized to leave by then?"

Tim was already thinking ahead. "We have the help here for the boarding houses and our other businesses. But it's the kids I worry about."

"I think we can do it," Emma said in a firm voice. "We just need to get organized. The first thing I'd like to do is confirm the tickets are authentic." *Paris,* she thought. *This time it will be with Jeremy.*

"Agreed," Jeremy said. "We won't be able to firm up the hotel, but we should be able to confirm the train and steamship tickets."

"I can go to the train station and confirm the tickets if you want to handle the steamship," Tim said to Jeremy.

"I think I can handle that," Jeremy responded.

"What about the hotel? Shouldn't we make sure we have somewhere to stay?" Dora asked worriedly. Papa and Abbey were in Paris, and they had heard from them that the area had millions of tourists and the hotels were overwhelmed.

Emma reviewed the letter for the name of the hotel—The Grand Hotel Terminus. It had been constructed specifically for the event. "I know this hotel," she said, "but with this short notice, we won't be able to confirm our rooms."

Tim said, "Let's meet back here this evening and discuss our plans for moving forward."

Everyone agreed and Tim and Jeremy started out of the room.

Dora halted them. "Hold on. You need to stay and help clear the table first."

The two men turned back to her. Tim smiled sheepishly, "Of course." He went back to the table to retrieve the empty plates.

Jeremy followed his lead and took an empty platter from the table. With everyone pitching in, the dishes were carried into the kitchen quickly. Amy and Ethyl, the housekeeper and helper, had the day off, so everyone had a job to do—scraping, washing, drying, and putting away.

After the tasks were complete, they moved back into the dining room. Jeremy and Tim got ready to leave.

Emma hung back and talked to Dora. She teased, "Won't Papa and Abbey be surprised to see us."

Papa and Abbey had traveled to Paris a few weeks prior at the behest of Gustaf Eiffel. The two men were good friends and Eiffel had wanted Papa there for a final walkthrough of the tower that was to be the centerpiece of the Paris Exposition. The celebration was in place to commemorate not only technological advances but also 100 years since the revolution that had changed France's ruling class from a monarchy to a democracy.

Dora smiled as she hid her concern at being away from her kids.

"What's the hubbub?" they heard from behind them.

Savannah and Ethan walked into the dining room, their appearance slightly disheveled. Savannah Woods worked back-stage at a local theatre and was between shows at the moment. Emma used her expertise in makeup and costuming when she needed to be in disguise. Ethan Worthington worked with Emma at James Pennington's law office.

"Savannah, Ethan. Just getting in or going out?" Emma asked with a smile.

Ethan colored in embarrassment. "I just dropped by last night to see how Savannah was doing and lost all sense of time."

"Sure, you did," Emma teased. She was pleased that the duo was dating. There had been hints that big plans were in the future.

"So, what's going on?" Savannah asked again. "Where's everyone rushing off to?"

"Oh. We've been invited to the Paris Exposition. We're finalizing the details," said Emma.

"Sounds exciting. When are you leaving?" asked Savannah.

"Tomorrow," answered Tim from the doorway, where he and Jeremy stood in their coats.

"Tomorrow? Isn't that kind of fast?" asked Ethan.

"It is," Emma agreed. "But I think we can get ready in time. Ethan, I plan to drop by the office and leave a note with Mr. Pennington."

"That should be okay," Ethan replied. "We're a little slow right now."

"Savannah," Dora spoke up, "Lottie is staying here and Amy is going to look after her. I hate to ask, but could you check in with her from time to time?"

"I'd love to," Savannah said.

"Are you going to be okay staying by yourself?" Dora asked. The boarding house was a little empty at the moment. The last family had moved on a few days before.

Savannah slated a glance at Ethan. "Oh, I have a feeling I won't be that lonely."

Ethan turned redder as everyone else laughed.

Jeremy walked over to Emma's chair. "Want to go to the telegraph office with me?"

"Yes," she said and held out her hand to him. He took it, pulling her up. They left the dining room and entered the foyer. Jeremy got her coat out of the closet and, as he helped her put it on, he asked, "Telegraph office first to send a note to the steamship?"

Emma nodded and pinned on her hat as she called, "Tim, are

you coming with us?"

"Yes," he called back from the dining room. He leaned in to give Dora a quick kiss goodbye.

"Just a moment." She moved to the sideboard and pulled out some paper. She wrote quickly, folded it up, and said, "Don't forget to give this note to Amy on your way," she said as she handed it to him.

Before taking it, he moved his fingers to the worry lines showing on her forehead. "This trip will be good for us," he murmured.

"Will it?" she asked, leaning into him.

"Yes," he said firmly. "I have to go, they're waiting for me."

She pulled back and slid the note into his pocket. Patting it, she said, "Don't forget."

"I won't," he promised, kissing her again before jogging into the foyer to meet Jeremy and Emma.

"Trolley?" Tim asked as he put on his muffler and buttoned up his coat.

"Yes," Jeremy said, and Emma nodded.

As they exited the house, they found the cool breeze had picked up. The group held their hats as they descended the stairs and turned toward the trolley.

Dora crossed to the window and watched them leave, her frown back in place. Her preference was to stay right where she was. *The occasional trip to New York is fine, but this trip...* she thought. *Paris sounded wonderful but this trip will be so much longer than I want to be away.*

At that moment, she heard a scream and turned toward it, it was a happy scream from Lottie. The girl had found her doll. She ran over to her mom and said, "Up!" Dora picked her up and swung her around, listening to her squeal.

Five weeks away, Tim wants this. And so do I, she admitted to herself, *I want to see Paris with him. I'll go.* She hugged Lottie tightly. "I'll make sure you're safe while we're gone," she promised.

CHAPTER 2

$\mathcal{E}$mma hung on to the strap on the trolley and turned to her brother-in-law. "Do you think she'll go?"

Tim shrugged. "I'd like her to go. I'd like to see Paris." Emma had talked about it after her first trip, and he wanted to see it for himself. Dora's opinion mattered to him and he would listen to her concerns but he hoped to be able to convince her to go.

"We'll see you back home," Jeremy called when Tim jumped off near the train station. He waved as he left. Jeremy and Emma stayed on for a few more stops.

After they jumped off the trolley and walked the few blocks to the telegraph office, Emma tapped the letter in her hand. "What do you think this is about?" she asked.

"I think someone wants us in Paris," he said in a contemplative voice.

"Nefarious reasons?" she asked. Emma was always up for an adventure.

"Probably. Would that be a problem?" They'd had many adventures but had never traveled to Paris together.

"No, not really, but I do worry about Tim and Dora coming

with us on this trip." She thought about what could happen. There was always an unexpected nature to their adventures.

He mulled that over then said calmly, "They can handle themselves."

She looked thoughtful. "Yes, I believe they can."

CHAPTER 3

A knock sounded at the kitchen door. Dora glanced over and saw it was Amy and waved her in. Amy held up the note.

"This sounded like you needed to see me immediately. Is something wrong? Tim was in a hurry and didn't say much."

Dora smiled. "Nothing is wrong but we do need your help. We're going to Paris."

"Paris?" asked Amy, confused at the news. She pulled out a chair and sat across from Dora at the kitchen table.

"Yes. Lottie and Patrick will be staying here. I'd like you to move in and take care of them for us."

"I can do it. It will be a lot less work with all of you gone," Amy teased.

Dora bit her lip. She was still reeling at the idea of being away from Patrick and Lottie. Amy reached over and placed her hand on top of Dora's.

"You know I care for them like they're my own."

Dora wiped a tear away with her free hand. "I know. I'll miss them so much. We'll be gone four to five weeks with all of the travel time included."

Tim heard her last comment as he came into the kitchen from the dining room. He bent down next to her. "I'll miss them, too, but I'd love some time alone with you."

"Yes, that would be nice," Dora said as she turned in his arms. Amy smiled and discretely left the room.

"Will you go?" Tim asked his wife.

"Yes, I think I will," she said and kissed him.

CHAPTER 4

"So, we're a go?" Dora asked as they sat down at the kitchen table. Sunday nights were informal and tonight they were eating sandwiches.

"We are," Emma stated, shaking out her napkin to place in her lap.

"The tickets are real and we're expected to be on the train tomorrow," Jeremy stated as he built his sandwich.

"Can we get organized and be on that train in time?" Dora asked. Now that she had a plan for the kids, her thoughts moved to the things that must be done before they left.

"We should be able to make it. It's the tight timeline in New York from train to ship that has me concerned. We'll have to go directly to the steamship when we get there," Emma said.

"Paris. Will you be happy to return?" Dora asked. Emma's trip to Paris had involved a close friend's kidnapping and an eventual takedown of an art thief.

"Definitely. Especially with all of the new things there for the exposition. Papa's letters describing all of the new structures, the Eiffel Tower."

"He mentioned there are two sides to the exposition?" Tim asked.

"Yes. The main site is located on the Champ de Mars on the Left Bank. That's where we'll see the Eiffel Tower, the Palace of Machines, Fine Arts and Liberal Arts buildings. The other site is located on the Esplanade des Invalides. There'll be pavilions of the French colonies. We'll also be able to eat there."

"There'll be so much to see," Dora said as she thought about their trip.

Tim heard the wonder in her tone and was glad she had decided to go with them. It wouldn't have been the same without her.

"We'll have to practice our French on the way there," Emma reminded everyone. "They prefer it to English."

They nodded.

"We just need to get the phrases down," she reassured them.

Jeremy hated to interrupt the excitement, but he needed to remind them of a few things. "We need to talk about who may have sent the invitation."

Dora was confused. "What do you mean? It wasn't a group that wanted to reward Emma for her efforts to save the artist's work?"

"We stopped by the museum today and talked to Philip. He didn't recognize the society's name," said Emma. Philip Johnson was the curator of the local museum and a longtime friend.

Dora interrupted, "Does that mean the society doesn't exist, or it didn't before this?"

"We don't know," Jeremy admitted.

"We're still going?" Tim asked, shifting his gaze to Dora.

"We are," Emma confirmed.

"Dora, Tim, we don't want you to go if you're uncomfortable," Jeremy said. He and Emma had decided they should know what they might be walking into in France.

Dora hesitated and took in the picture Patrick and Lottie

made as they played together on the floor. She glanced at Tim. "No, we want to go."

"Yes," Tim agreed.

They continue to discuss the details through dinner. After they split up to begin packing, Emma and Dora filled the trunks in their rooms with dresses and hats. The men would bring smaller bags. Each couple didn't sleep much, anticipating the trip in front of them.

~

Early the next morning, Emma made her way downstairs. The trunks and bags were staged in the foyer, waiting to be taken on the trip. She heard talking in the kitchen and headed toward it. The closer she got, she could hear Amy reassuring Dora. She pushed open the kitchen door and saw Amy holding Dora's hands.

"I have them," Amy said earnestly. "I brought my things over and I have extra help coming in a few days a week to help with the cleaning. I'll be with Patrick and Lottie the whole time."

"Remember, Patrick will want to spend some time with Uncle Otto's grandkids," Dora reminded her.

"I have that written down," she assured her.

"Nearly ready?" Emma said from the doorway.

Dora gripped her bag tightly and almost said no. Instead, she took a steadying breath. "Yes."

"Well, come on." Emma waved to her.

Dora hugged Amy and they followed Emma into the foyer.

Tim came downstairs. "Amy, both kids are still sleeping."

"All right, I'll get breakfast going and get the kids up after."

Jeremy came in from the stoop. "The cab is here."

The assembled group made their way out of the house. The men they had arranged to transport their trunks were in place behind their carriage. The luggage was moved and the four made their way to the train.

A dark figure crept from the alleyway near the stoop and watched as the wagon and buggy pulled away. The figure went up the stoop and tried the door knob. When it opened easily, they entered. The four must have left it open in their haste to leave.

Once inside, they spotted what they had come for. They retrieved it and exited quickly out the same door.

CHAPTER 5

ON THE TRAIN TO NEW YORK CITY

"I'm tired of practicing French," Dora said. "Tell me about what we'll see when we arrive in Paris."

Emma pulled out a stack of letters. "Papa said the design Eiffel built has passed its inspections."

Tim put down his book. "Weren't there some concerns about his initial design?"

Emma reviewed the letter, "Well, mostly from Jules Bourdais, the architect. He called it a 'vulgar' iron structure. He stated that stonework was superior in every way to Eifel's tower."

"He was in competition with Eiffel, wasn't he?" Tim asked.

"Yes," she said dryly. "And that would explain why he'd question the design that was selected. Papa was on the committee that reviewed both designs to help make the decision." His expertise was as a structural engineer and was in demand to review designs of new buildings. He and his wife spent half of their time in New York and half of their time in Chicago.

"How did Bourdais react to Ellis' review?" Tim asked.

"Bourdais was evasive and issued vague assurances that his structure would undoubtedly stand. He was upset that Papa supported Eiffel's statement about structural changes that needed to occur. Masonry had been pushed to its limits and to go higher they would need to use iron and steel. Furthermore, Bourdais had made no provision for the foundations of his masonry tower. It would rest directly on the ground," said Emma.

"What was Eiffel's experience?" asked Tim.

Emma continued, "He has worked all over Europe on some enormous arched bridges. They became the basis for his design for deep foundations supporting heavy structures. Also, given the height of the tower, the force of the wind would be a major consideration. He said, 'It's the wind that determined the basic shape of my tower,"

Jeremy was reviewing some of the hand drawings Ellis had included in the letter and said, "The initial design appears to be an unadorned iron architecture."

"It's a different design for Paris," Emma conceded, thinking of the grandeur of the old stone buildings, cathedrals, and palaces. "I'm not surprised people this structure was ugly, at least initially."

"When did Ellis pick sides?"

"I think after the great fire. Papa wants the buildings and structures to have the proper support. Preventing collapse has been his goal since then. He was happy that it appeared the first battle between iron and stone was over with Eiffel winning a resounding victory."

"The main attraction will be the Galerie des Machines; the building is said to be of similar design to that of the Eiffel Tower," Jeremy commented.

"It will be something to see," Tim said. "Didn't Ellis mention it contained fifteen acres of exposition space and was filled with sixteen thousand machines?"

"Sixteen thousand," Dora repeated, awestruck. "What types of things will we see?"

Emma flipped through her letters and found the one that listed the displays. "Here it is," she said. She began reading. "Daimler and

Benz gasoline-powered motor cars. The telephone and telegraph will also be there."

"Didn't I see where we'll be able to climb the tower?" Dora inquired, reading over Emma's shoulder.

"Hopefully, more than that. I'm hoping Papa can take us higher up."

"What a view that will be—of the entire exposition grounds," Dora said, wondering about the sights they would see.

"It sounds so big. What else will be there?" Jeremy asked.

Tim spoke up. "I read in the paper that Buffalo Bill's Wild West Show featuring Annie Oakley will be there. There are also Egyptian temples and Aztec palaces."

Jeremy shifted his gaze to Emma. "There'll be something that should remind you of our first trip to New York."

"What's that?" she asked curiously.

"Remember the park?" he asked. "The statue?"

"The Statue of Liberty? They finally got it set up in the New York Harbor."

"Yes, we'll see a miniature version of it on the Seine."

They spent the rest of the trip practicing their French and discussing the sights they'd see. They didn't discuss who might have invited them.

CHAPTER 6

ON THE STEAMER LA BRETAGNE TO FRANCE

"We can slow down now," Jeremy said as he restrained Emma and Dora from a run to a walk. He motioned to the ship with his hand. "It appears there's a line at the gangplank."

Tim caught up to them. "I got the steward to take the bags and trunks on board." He took Dora's hand and they got in line to ascend the gangplank onto the ship. When the line started to move, he moved with it, he didn't get far. Dora wasn't moving. "Dora, come on, this is the beginning of our trip."

She was turned away from him. He knew she wasn't thinking of the view in front of her. "Lottie and Patrick will be fine," he assured her.

"Yes, I know," she said, studying the city one more time before turning back and following him. They caught up with Jeremy and Emma as they stepped off the gang plank and onto the ship.

After checking in and getting their door keys, Tim, Dora, and Jeremy were examining the features of the ship. They had never been on a steamer before this. Emma remembered her last time on this ship and hoped it would be a trip with less excitement. She gave them time to survey the area.

"Emma!" a voice called.

She turned toward the voice and saw the ship's captain coming toward her. She smiled broadly and took the hands he extended to her.

"How wonderful to see you," he said. "Will you be with us on this trip?"

"I will," she confirmed.

He leaned in and asked softly, "No excitement this time, I hope?"

"Me, too." She laughed, knowing he was referencing her last trip to Paris by steamer. She had uncovered a plot that involved a wife and her boyfriend who killed her husband and threw him overboard.

Jeremy walked over to Emma and the captain. Emma introduced him. "Captain De Jousselin, this is Jeremy Tilden. We're traveling together."

"It's nice to meet you," De Jousselin said sincerely. "I'd like to have you both in my cabin after dinner."

"We'd like that also," Emma said warmly.

A young ship officer walked up to the captain. The man spoke softly to him and he told Emma and Jeremy, "I must leave you now. We'll be on our way soon."

"It was nice to meet you," Jeremy said.

"You, also."

As they watched the captain leave, Jeremy took her hand. "We should find our rooms and get settled in."

"You're right." She called out, "Dora, Tim, we need to go to our rooms."

Dora frowned but took Tim's offered elbow and followed them up the staircase. "You will have time to see the ship once we are underway," Emma promised her.

They stepped into a long hallway with a red carpet running its length. They went about halfway down and Emma pulled out her notebook. She pointed to the room on the right, "That's your room. Ours is further down."

Tim and Jeremy pulled out their keys and opened the doors. Emma heard Dora exclaim, *"These are our rooms?"*

Emma smiled. She had been in similar rooms on her last trip and her reaction had been the same.

Dora rushed to Emma's door. "Emma, is yours as big as ours?"

"It is," she confirmed, opening the door wide to show her the room. "

"Aren't they wonderful?"

"The rooms are nice," agreed Emma. She raised her eyebrows at Jeremy. He nodded and moved around the room opening and closing the various doors in the room. Dora went back to her and Tim's room; she was ready to enjoy her vacation.

Emma walked around the living area, dropped down on the couch, and shifted her gaze to Jeremy, "What do you make of this? So far, first-class accommodations."

"Yes. I guess whoever's behind this wants us happy. At least, until we reach Paris."

"Do we worry all the way to Paris or do we enjoy ourselves?"

"Enjoy ourselves."

"I'd agree to that."

He dropped down on the couch next to her and teased, "What would you like to do now?"

She stretched out her arms. "I could use a long nap."

He stood up and pulled her to him. "Now, that can be worked out," he murmured. He kissed her for a long moment before he walked her to the bedroom. They closed the door and had a very long rest.

A few hours later, both couples made their way downstairs and entered the dining room. Dora and Emma were dressed in evening gowns; Emma in red and Dora in dark blue. Jeremy and Tim stood behind them in their black suits.

"Would you like a table?" asked the steward.

"Yes, please. Our names are under Emma Evans," Emma responded.

He moved his chart and tapped it a few times before he said, in surprise. "We have a request from another gentleman to join your group. Would that would be all right?"

Emma moved her gaze to each person in her group. When they nodded, Emma said, "That should be fine."

The steward's face cleared and he smiled. He was relieved that there weren't any arguments about the addition to their table.

He moved from behind his podium and motioned to them with his hand, "This way, please." He guided them through the dining room. When they reached a large round table, they saw one person was already seated.

"Must be him," Emma muttered. Dora nodded.

Jeremy and Tim held the chairs out for Emma and Dora.

Once they were settled, the unknown gentleman said, "I hope you don't mind my request to join your group." He spoke with a French accent.

"No, of course not. Welcome," Emma replied. The others nodded.

They sat quietly reviewing the menus in front of them.

"I'll start the introductions," the man said jovially. "I'm Julian Bernard and I'm traveling to the exposition in Paris. "

"So are we," Tim commented for the group.

"Wonderful. Please introduce yourselves."

Tim took the lead. "I'm Tim Flannigan, and this is my wife, Dora. We're also traveling with Emma, Dora's sister, and our friend Jeremy Tilden."

"So nice to meet you all," he said, to everyone at the table. "What do you want to see at the exposition?"

They talked throughout dinner about Paris and the exhibits

they planned to see. When the conversation moved to questions from Julian Bernard about their lives in Chicago, the quieter Emma became. The others laughed at something Julian said, but Emma didn't respond. Jeremy sent her a questioning look. She slowly moved her eyes from Julian to Jeremy.

What has she seen? What am I missing? he thought, watching Julian. Tim and Dora filled in the gap left by Emma and Jeremy.

After dinner, Dora and Tim excused themselves to go dancing. Emma and Jeremy stayed at the table with Julian.

Coffee and desserts arrived and so did more questions from Julian.

Questions. Questions about where we're from, where we're going, and what we do for a living. Why? Emma thought.

Rather than answering the multitude of questions, Emma began, "Mr. Bernard…"

"Julian, please," he interrupted.

Emma smiled slightly, "Yes, Julian. What do you do for a living?"

"Oh, this and that," he said lightly, avoiding her question.

"This and that what?" she asked, trying to pin him down.

"Business, it's very uninteresting; I'd rather talk about you," he said, his voice smooth.

"Have you been to Chicago?"

"Maybe. A long time ago."

Jeremy reached for her hand under the table and squeezed it lightly in a warning.

She ignored him and stated firmly, "Julian, you've been asking us a lot of questions."

"Have I?" he countered, his pleasant expression not changing.

"Yes," she said firmly.

"Well, I find you interesting," he said and smiled at both of them.

"Why is that?" *What does he know about us?*

"Oh," he said leaning in, "I know that you have a more interesting job than the temporary business you mentioned."

Emma and Jeremy tensed. Jeremy took the next question. "What do you know?"

"I know you're both detectives," he said simply, sitting back in his chair and sipping from his coffee cup.

"That isn't exactly a secret," Emma said. *And*, she thought, *we're not currently on a case.*

"No, but I think it's something you don't share openly and with strangers."

Jeremy leaned forward. "Why the interest in us and our work?"

He smiled. "Oh, I was just fascinated. I have been following your career since you, were in France. And," he said as he moved his gaze to Jeremy, "you're with the Pinkerton Detectives."

"All of these questions. Is it just interest?" Emma asked. She clearly didn't believe him.

"Yes, of course." Julian took a drink of coffee, checked his watch, and placed his cup on the table. "Why don't we meet tomorrow and talk some more?"

With that comment, he stood and disappeared into the crowd of people.

Emma shook her head. "That was odd."

Jeremy continued to focus on the direction Julian had gone. "Yes." He moved his gaze back to Emma and asked, "Could he be behind the tickets?"

She took a long moment, thinking about Julian. Finally, she said, "Maybe. He was certainly eager to spend time with us." She glanced at her watch. "We should go. I believe the captain is expecting us in his cabin."

They headed out, passing the dance area where Tim and Dora had gone. "Before we go, should we mention our suspicions to Tim and Dora?" Jeremy asked, nodding toward the room.

Emma glanced around and saw them with another couple,

laughing. "No, they seem to be having a good time." *Who was that couple?* she wondered.

"Ready?" he asked.

She nodded and took his elbow. As they walked off, she had to pull her gaze away from them. She continued to think about them as they made their way to the captain's cabin. The steward assigned outside the door held up his hand to stop them, "Just a moment." He stepped in briefly and returned to tell them, "You may go in."

"Thank you," Emma murmured and stepped in. As the two entered, they saw the room was set up with drinks and desserts.

Captain De Jousselin came into the room from a door in the back. He was more casually dressed and had removed his jacket and hat. "Please, come in. Sit down."

"I assume things have been quieter on your ship since my last trip?" Emma asked.

"Yes," he said, "thankfully."

Jeremy leaned forward in his chair, taking the glass the captain offered. "Do you know the passenger, Julian Barnard?" he asked.

De Jousselin's eyebrows rose quickly. "Julian Bernard? Why yes. He travels often with us." He watched Emma closely. "Is there something I should be concerned about?"

Emma quickly assured him, "No, no. We were just curious. Do you know what business he's in?"

De Jousselin sat back and stroked his beard. "I believe he buys and sells merchandise."

She wondered about what the merchandise might be. "Does he normally have crates with him?"

"No, not that I know of," he replied.

They let the conversation about Julian come to an end and instead talked about their plans for Paris.

CHAPTER 7

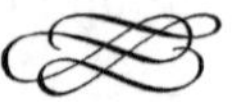

The next morning Dora, Tim, Emma, and Jeremy walked down to breakfast. Dora stole a glance toward Emma. "I hope you don't mind, but the couple we met last night wants us to join them for breakfast."

Emma shook her head. "No, of course not, go ahead. We're supposed to meet Mr. Barnard."

"Julian," murmured Jeremy.

Emma smiled and didn't comment.

Breakfast was served on the deck. As they approached the sunlit area, both couples split off to find their breakfast companions. Emma hesitated at the door and watched as Dora and Tim moved to their breakfast table. The couple they were joining appeared to be a little older than Dora and Tim. They smiled broadly at them, even standing to hug them as they approached. *Fast friends*, she thought. *I'll have to keep an eye on that as well. No one is above suspicion on this trip.*

"You know you need to be more trusting," Jeremy commented, seeing where Emma's eyes were directed. "It's good for them to have friends."

She let out a long breath. "I know I should, but it's hard to trust people to care about them as much as we do."

"Especially with people you love."

"Especially," she confirmed as they made their way to their table and sat. When Mr. Barnard did not appear, she asked, "Do you think we should wait?"

Jeremy leaned back in his chair, enjoying the feel of the early morning sun on his face, and said, "For a few moments." They relaxed breathing in the sea air.

Several moments later Julian walked up to their table. "May I sit?" he asked.

"Of course." Emma's voice was less severe than the night before. She and Jeremy had talked and had decided that they needed to find out more about this man.

"And where are our other companions this morning? Sleeping in?" Julian asked.

"No," answered Emma. She indicated the table across the room from them. "They met another couple and wanted to spend some time with them this morning."

He turned in the direction she indicated and, when he turned back, she thought she detected a brief frown on his face. It disappeared quickly. She wondered about that as they ordered their breakfast.

"Do you know the couple Tim and Dora are eating with?" Emma asked, wondering how he'd respond.

He looked her in the eye and said, "No, I don't think so."

Jeremy narrowed his eyes at her and she let the topic go. They moved on to talk about their day. To Emma's consternation, Julian brought up more questions about their trip. She tried to match him question for question.

"Where are you both staying in France? At the Grand Hotel Terminus?" asked Julian.

"How did you know that?" Jeremy asked. He was starting to think Emma was correct and Julian knew more than he letting on.

He answered quickly, "Oh, it's a special hotel. It was built specifically for the exposition. It's lovely and very grand. You will enjoy your time there." He didn't wait for a comment and moved onto another question. "You mentioned you'd be there for how long?"

"I don't think we did mention that," muttered Emma, not quite answering the question.

Jeremy looked over at her and then back at Julian before he replied. "We'll be in Paris for three weeks. We'd like to spend some time at the Galerie des Machines. We're interested in all of the advancements in technology. We especially want to see the new light display. It sounds amazing."

Julian sat back in a contemplative manner and said, "Yes, you know not everyone is happy that things are progressing. Some people are against change and progress."

"I have seen some articles. I thought their response has been mostly nonviolent demonstrations," said Jeremy.

"That could be changing," Julian responded.

"Why are they against electricity?" Emma asked curiously.

"They believe the dangers outweigh any benefit it could provide," Julian said.

"But we're hearing residential homes will soon have lights. If it were truly dangerous, that wouldn't happen," she protested.

Julian's eyes squinted for a moment before he answered. "Yes, there are those who would rather we stopped moving forward."

"Do you think they'll create a problem at the exposition?" Emma asked sitting forward.

"It's something that should be considered," Julian allowed.

Emma thought about that. "Should the police be notified?" she asked.

He waved his hand in dismissal and said smoothly, "I'm sure they have everything under control. The security is being handled by the Parisian police."

They moved on to lighter topics. After breakfast was finished, they excused themselves to go back to their respective cabins.

Emma realized she still knew nothing about the man. She mentioned this to Jeremy.

"You don't need all of his secrets," he teased.

"I know, but a few would be nice. Do you think there's a concern about these anti-electricity people he mentioned? Could they be dangerous?"

"I can't be sure, but it sounds like the French police are aware of them."

"Yes," she said contemplatively.

He took her hand and suggested, "Let's walk around the deck and enjoy our time together."

"Okay," she said softly. She sent one last look at Dora and Tim's breakfast partners.

"They're allowed to have friends outside of us," Jeremy commented softly, watching where her gaze drifted.

"I know. They want to have other friends," she said softly, "but I would like some time with them."

"Tell her. Maybe ask for their new friends to join us," he urged.

"I will," she promised.

That evening, Emma went to Dora and Tim's room. She knocked softly on their door. Hearing "Come in," she opened the door and saw Dora braiding her hair and pinning it to the top of her head.

Tim walked out of the bathroom. "Hello, Emma. Ready for dinner?"

"Yes. I was wondering if we could all eat together tonight," she suggested.

"All?" Dora asked, pausing in her dressing preparations.

"Yes, your new friends are welcome to join us," Emma offered.

Dora chewed her lips and glanced at Tim.

Tim explained, "Lenora and Michael don't like big groups.

We've asked them before this and I think the question made them uncomfortable."

Odd, thought Emma. "Okay, then will you both meet us for dinner?" she asked.

"Of course, we'd love that," Dora replied.

Emma started out of the room and asked in an offhanded manner, "Do Lenora and Michael know what we do back home?"

Dora glanced over. "Yes, I mentioned it. I didn't think it was a secret."

"Oh, it's not. I just wondered." Emma smiled and said, "Come down to our room when you're ready."

"We will," Dora said as she watched her sister leave.

"What was that about?" Tim asked, putting on his tie.

Dora smiled, walked over to him, and brushed his hands away to take over his tie adjustment. "I think we've been spending time with our new friends and they're missing us."

Emma walked slowly to her door and, when she reached it, instead of opening it, she lay her head on it. It opened suddenly and Emma found herself in Julian's arms. She yelped and struggled before she realized who it was.

"My dear, I'm sorry. I stopped by to see if I could join you for dinner."

Emma pulled herself upright "That's okay. I was thinking about something just now. You're welcome to join us."

"I told him I needed to confirm with you," Jeremy said.

"Now we're confirmed. I'll meet you there," the other man said.

"Dora and Tim will be joining us also," Emma said, watching his expression.

She saw that that bothered him. She continued to watch him closely.

"Will their companions be joining us?" he asked in a curt tone.

"No," she said slowly, wondering what the concern was. "They prefer to be on their own."

That cheered him up considerably. "Good. I'll head out now."

"Julian," she said, stopping him with her hand, "do you have a problem with Dora and Tim's new friends? Should I be concerned about them spending so much time with them?"

"How could I have a problem when I don't know them? I'll meet up with you in the dining room," he said and excused himself, closing their door softly on his way out.

"Hmm," she murmured.

Jeremy sat on the bed, buttoning his vest. "Julian evidently did not want to spend time with Lenora and Michael."

"No, he didn't," she observed.

Jeremy stood. "I wonder why? Are you worried he knows something about them that we don't?"

"I think we need to keep our eyes on Julian, Lenora, and Michael. There's something there."

"Have you ever seen the three of them together?"

"No. Julian seems to be there just before or just after the time they could meet."

"You need to hurry. Tim and Dora will be here soon," Jeremy reminded her.

She nodded and ran quickly to the closet, pulling out her dark red silk gown. The lace was dyed in black and attached to the front of the bodice neckline. She slipped her skirt and top off revealing her combinations. The gown went on and Jeremy came up behind her and started working on securing the closures as she quickly put her hair up. Just as she was adding some lip color, a knock sounded on their door.

"They're here. Are you ready?" he asked as he finished the last closure.

"I am," she said, patting her hair.

Jeremy slipped on his gray suit jacket and opened the door. "Welcome."

"Are you both ready?" Dora asked.

"I believe we are," her sister stated as she searched for her bag.

"Looking for this?" Jeremy tossed the bag at her.

Emma caught it deftly, opening it quickly to check for her clutch knife. She closed it with a click. "Ready."

They started out.

"Oh no!" Dora exclaimed.

"Did you forget something?" asked Tim.

"Yes, I'm sorry. I need my hair clip." She reached up and felt her hair falling in the back. She inquired, "Can we meet you in the dining room?"

"Yes, do you need help?" Emma asked.

"No, I can fix it. We'll meet you." Dora and Tim hurriedly went back to their room.

Jeremy offered his elbow to her. She took it, and as they walked around the corner, they saw Julian down the corridor. They started toward him but noticed he was not alone. He was with Lenora and Michael. Jeremy pulled them to a stop.

"I thought they didn't know each other," Emma murmured.

"It appears they do know each other, but they don't appear to like each other."

"Yes," she agreed. The three seemed to be arguing.

Jeremy tapped her arm to indicate they should turn back. They moved slowly in the opposite direction of the three, trying to not be seen. As they walked, Emma turned to Jeremy. "Do we confront him?"

"About what? A conversation with people we don't know that well?"

She shrugged. "Okay, maybe we don't need a full confrontation."

"Let's go to dinner," he suggested. They walked on and saw the doors to the dining room. They were etched glass, they sparkled from the lights inside. The steward pushed them open to allow them entry. The host stood at his stand and asked, "Would you like to be seated?"

"Yes, please," said Emma. The host took their name and escorted them to their table, they were the first to arrive.

Julian appeared at the entrance and, when Jeremy spotted him, he turned to Emma. "Let's not mention what we saw."

"Maybe just a comment," teased Emma.

Jeremy raised an eyebrow, and stayed silent, he knew she'd make the right decision.

Julian walked over and pulled out his chair, looking like his normal jovial self.

Emma couldn't help herself and asked him, "Did you have a busy evening?"

Jeremy tapped her leg in warning.

"Not really," the other man said. "After I left you, I was able to get some reading in."

She watched him and thought that he didn't owe her an explanation. He was mysterious, but she didn't think he was dangerous. There was something about him that kept her on her toes. She'd keep an eye on him and his relationship with Lenora and Michael.

Dora and Tim arrived.

"Two very lovely ladies for the table. What more could I have asked for?" Julian said suavely. Both women smiled in response to the compliment.

Emma turned to Tim and Dora as she kept Julian within her sights. "Were Lenora and Michael all right with their loss of dinner companions tonight?"

Julian went still, waiting for their answer.

Tim didn't notice. "I believe so. They weren't at their cabin when we went by, so we left a note."

No, they wouldn't have been there, thought Emma. *They were with Julian.*

The evening settled and the five stayed together after dinner, talking about France.

"Emma, you mentioned this is your second trip. Did you enjoy

Paris the first time you were here?" Julian asked. He didn't mention that he knew why she had been in France.

Emma played along with the deception and stated, "The initial reason for the trip was to help a friend, so sightseeing wasn't the main priority. I'm hoping this trip is more relaxed."

"Hmm," Julian commented. He seemed to have no response to that.

~

The rest of the trip was quiet, with Tim and Dora splitting their time between the two couples.

Emma tried several times to have the other couple join their group, but there was always a reason they couldn't meet.

Emma walked with Jeremy and looked at the water. She turned to him. "They aren't even willing to meet us. Isn't there something odd about that?"

Jeremy looked over at her. "Yes, but it might be just as Dora says—they prefer small groups. Tim and Dora are enjoying their new friends; let's just let it lie."

Emma gave one more glance and said decided he was right. But she continued to think about the argument they witnessed.

CHAPTER 8

SHIP DOCKING IN HAVRE, FRANCE

They had arrived in Le Havre, a port city in France. Their trucks and bags had been picked up that morning and would be moved to the train that would take them to Paris. It would be a day until they arrived in Paris.

Emma and Jeremy were waiting in the lobby for Dora and Tim. She turned when she heard Dora's voice. Tim and Dora were accompanying Lenora and Michael down the stairs.

"Where are you staying?" Dora asked the couple.

When they answered, Emma realized they would be staying in the same place as their group.

Jeremy waved to Dora and Tim and called over, "Our luggage is being moved to a wagon as we speak."

Dora and Tim said goodbye to their friends and moved to Emma and Jeremy. The four started to the gangplank.

Boom!

They started at the loud noise and turned toward it. The sound was a large, empty trunk falling onto the deck. The men picking it up must have misjudged its weight. As they watched a young woman rush over and yell at them to get moving. Her much older husband trailed after her. The beleaguered men followed her direction and picked up the trunk. Jeremy, Tim, and Dora turned back to continue down the gangplank.

"Emma?" Jeremy asked, realizing she was still watching the couple with the trunk. "Are you ready? We need to get to the train."

She gave one last long look at the trunk and the couple before heading to join him on the gangplank.

They found the wagon and their carriage waiting to take them to their train. As they climbed in, a voice called out; it was Julian. "Mind if I get a ride in with you?"

"Yes, we can make room," Jeremy said. Emma raised an eyebrow but scooted over to allow him a place to sit.

"Thank you. It has been a marvelous trip and I'd love the company for the final leg to Paris." The trip over to the train was fun with Julian pointing out sites for them. They arrived quickly and were settled into their room just as the train was pulling out of the station.

A knock sounded on their door. When Emma opened it, she saw it was Julian. *Of course, who else would it be?* she thought. She asked in a wry voice, "Julian, what a surprise. Would you like to join us?"

Surprisingly, he declined. "No, that is fine, I have my own cabin. I'll see you all once we get to Paris." He turned and walked down the hall. Emma closed the door behind him and the group stared at it.

"If he weren't so entertaining, he'd be irritating," Jeremy said sardonically.

"It's hard to turn him down when he wants something. Is it the accent?" Dora asked.

"Do you fancy him?" Tim teased.

She smiled softly and said, "I prefer redheads."

Tim grinned broadly in response and his face turned as red as his hair.

The trip was short, and they were in Paris in just under a day.

As they exited the train, Jeremy and Tim located the luggage and arranged carriages. Julian once again joined them.

"Do you have any additional luggage?" asked Emma.

"Just this bag," he said, indicating the carpet bag he was carrying.

"I don't think I could travel with so little," Dora commented as they watched the trunks being unloaded.

Julian commented, "I bet those hold the lovely dresses I saw you wearing on the steamer."

Dora's face turned red.

"Ready?" called Jeremy once all of the luggage was on the wagon.

They headed toward the carriage, climbed in, and headed to the hotel. Emma spoke to the driver. "108 Rue Saint-Lazare, s'il vous plaît."

"That is located in the 8th arrondissement," Julian explained. "The areas are broken up by their numbers. Arrondissements with higher numbers spiral out clockwise from the center. Its shape is like a snail shell. Most of these were former small villages annexed by Paris earlier this century."

"How far is our hotel from the exposition grounds?" asked Tim, thinking of their travel time each morning.

"About 3,701 kilometers. There should be carriages lined up to go to the exposition. What will slow us down is the traffic. It's reported that Paris has more people here than ever before."

"Papa also indicated there's a train once you get to the exposition grounds," Emma said.

"It's needed. The entire complex is 220 Hectares and the Galerie des Machines you mentioned is at the back of the exhibit," Julian supplied.

Emma muttered, "I should have brought my bike."

"We'll walk if we can't get transportation," Jeremy assured her.

"There is a lot to see on the way; the distance will not feel so long," said Julian.

Dora, Tim, and Jeremy were leaning out of the carriage windows and looking around. As they got closer, Julian continued to point out the sites.

"The arrondissements I mentioned previously are all different. Each one has a feeling with different cultures melding and having their own shops, bakeries, and history."

Emma watched from her seat and enjoyed her family's response to their first time in Paris.

"The hotel we're going to, have you stayed there before?" Jeremy asked him.

"No. It's newly built for the exhibit. It just opened in May. I believe Eiffel himself announced the opening from his tower."

They stopped in front of their hotel, a large brick structure. It was four stories and appeared to take up an entire city block.

They climbed out, and Jeremy paid the driver. He looked around, "What type of facade is that?"

Emma answered. "It's a Haussmannian facade and very elegant. Those," she pointed out, "are Corinthian columns."

The group entered the hotel's main door and were surprised at the opulence—chandeliers, balustrades, hand-painted frescoes, and marble and mosaic tiling.

"I understand there is a bar here that we must frequent for a glass of wine," Julian commented.

They looked around and took in the crowds that were in line for rooms. Emma muttered to Jeremy, "I hope we have a reservation."

"Shh, we don't want to worry Tim and Dora. It'll work out," he said, hoping he was right. "And if not," he continued in a low voice, "the couches look comfortable down here."

She gave him a look but didn't comment. She turned to Tim and Dora, "Have a seat. We'll go check in." The two of them found a space and sat down, continuing to observe the grand room.

Emma and Jeremy approached the desk. There was a line and, during their wait, several people in front of them were turned away with no reservations. Emma squeezed his hand and he squeezed back. When it was their turn, she stepped up and said, "Bonjour, monsieur."

Before the clerk could respond, the young woman who they had seen on the steamer with the empty trunk stepped up. "We need a room!" she demanded in English.

The clerk answered in perfect English, "I'm sorry, madam unless you have a reservation…"

"We have a reservation," the woman interrupted.

"That is fine, but these people," referencing Emma and Jeremy, "were next. You will have to wait your turn."

"But… but I'm…" the woman tried again belligerently.

He looked down his nose at her and said quite firmly, "It does not matter who you are. You will get in line."

That statement finally got through to her and she and her husband stepped back into the line. She was not happy and seemed to turn her anger on her husband. He visibly shrank as she spoke.

"Bonjour, monsieur," Emma began again.

"Bonjour, madam. You may speak English," the clerk stated. His tone was softer than before.

"Thank you. I have a reservation for Emma Evans and family," Emma, sincerely hoped she did indeed have a reservation.

He didn't check his book, instead, he said quickly, "Yes, madam, we have that here. You are on the 3rd floor."

That was quick, she thought. *He didn't check his book. He already knew to expect them.*

"How many keys will you require?"

"How many rooms do we have?" she asked, thinking ahead.

Again, without looking he said, "It is a suite with 3 bedrooms."

A suite? In Paris and at the time of the exposition? "Four, please," she answered. "Could you tell us who made this reservation?"

He squirmed and didn't answer. Instead, he moved some paperwork around on his desk.

Emma started to lean in with more questions when Jeremy put a hand on her arm and leaned down to whisper into her ear, "We can do this later. Let's get to our rooms for now."

She nodded and stepped back.

When there were no further questions, the clerk pulled over a large sign-in book "Please, sign here."

As she signed in, he motioned to a bellhop. "Take their luggage to 319."

The boy's eyes widened in surprise at the location and he hurried to get the baggage cart. He called another bellman over to help with the heavy trunks. Emma watched them and turned back to the clerk, "Merci."

He replied, "You're welcome, enjoy your stay." He watched as they made their way to the elevator and headed up to the room.

Another bellman waited by the elevator while they got organized. Emma retrieved Tim and Dora and joined Jeremy when the doors opened. They entered, and the bellmen followed them. He motioned to the men with the luggage to come up on the next elevator. The doors closed, and they watched the operator take them to their floor. The door slid opened, and the bellman waited for everyone to exit before he said, "Follow me, please."

They followed and noticed the custom etchings of iconic Paris scenes hanging on the walls. "These are lovely," Dora said as she stopped to examine them. As they continued to their room, they stopped several more times to admire the wallpaper and wood floors with beautiful braided rugs.

They stopped and the first bellman opened the large double brown door for them to enter. The four stepped into the doorway and a large open space in front of them.

"Wow!" Dora exclaimed. She was impressed with everything she saw in the hotel.

"Yes, wow," Emma agreed. *Whoever is behind all this has money,* she thought. She looked at the large area; there were couches, a dining room, chandeliers, and multiple doors leading off of the main room.

Jeremy was unsure if this was usual for Paris. "Was this similar to the hotel you stayed in on your last trip?" he asked Emma.

"That one was nice, but nothing like this one," she murmured as she took in her surroundings.

The bellman approached a door at the far end of the room and pushed it open. "Just the one room?" asked Dora. She was confused about where they'd sleep.

"No," he said in stilted English. "There are three." He walked quickly to open the door on the far end.

Dora noticed he didn't open the third door. "What is that one?" she asked, motioning toward it.

He didn't answer but, instead, opened it for her to review. She stepped up and said, "There are three bedrooms off the main room and on-suite bathrooms?"

They didn't choose their rooms; the bellman chose for them, Each couple went to examine their assigned rooms. Jeremy called out, "Is your room acceptable?"

Tim stuck his head out of their room and called back, "It's exactly right." Jeremy nodded. He and Emma were also happy with theirs.

The bellman arrived with their luggage and Jeremy directed the bellman to place them in each room. He walked the bellman out and paid him a tip. With the door closed behind him, he moved back to the living room to relax with Emma.

Tim and Dora joined them there.

"Well, I guess the question of 'will we have a room' has been answered," Tim said dryly and the group laughed in response.

"Do we want to stay in tonight?" Jeremy asked. He was thinking about food.

"Well, I was thinking about a walk to see what is in the area around the hotel, " stated Emma hopefully.

"And a snack here," Dora suggested as she held a hand to her rumbling stomach. Though the train trip offered food, the selection was limited.

"Now that is a plan," indicated Tim.

Emma said, "First, I think we need to let Papa know we're here."

"Do you have his address?" Jeremy asked. "I can have him notified that we have arrived."

She pulled out her notebook and showed it to him. His lips quirked up in response to the ever-present notebook.

She quickly wrote a note to have him send to Papa. She handed it to him.

"I'll be back," he said. "While I'm out, would everyone like me to place the order for food?"

Tim and Dora got up and Dora said, "Please. We'll unpack. Let us know when the food is here."

"I'll do the same," commented Emma.

The two groups had their tasks and moved to get them completed.

Dora and Tim took a moment to look out of the tall windows in their room. The stone buildings around them were old but so lovely.

"We should have another hour or two to see some of the areas around the hotel," Tim commented.

Dora sighed. She wanted to stand at that window for a while longer but knew they needed to unpack. She moved to her trunk and Tim followed to open the lock for her. Once it was opened, she shook out her dresses and hung them up. Next came her combinations that acted as her undergarments. When she started folding those to add to her dresser. Tim said teasingly, "I can help with that."

"Oh, you, get your own bag unpacked."

As they were finishing up, there was a knock on the door. "The food has arrived!" called Jeremy. That got Tim and Dora moving quickly toward the living room.

Emma was already in the living area, having finished unpacking her trunk. "Turns out it wasn't food," Jeremy said as he walked into the room.

Emma frowned. "Then who was at the door?"

Jeremy stepped away and revealed who was behind him. It was Papa and Abbey.

"Papa!"

She ran to him; he caught her and hugged her tightly. She closed her eyes, enjoying the moment. She opened them again and stepped back to allow Dora and Tim to say hello. She went over to Abbey and hugged her also. Her affection was genuine for her papa's wife. She had been so good for him.

"Abbey, hello," said Emma.

Abbey hugged her back, "We got your note and had to come right over. What a nice surprise. When did you decide to come to France?"

Jeremy came over and hugged Abbey tightly. "Hello, Mom." He looked at the group and said, "Why don't we sit down and we can discuss the circumstances of our trip."

Papa frowned at the wording Jeremy had used but followed them into the living room. As they made their way over, Abbey glanced around and commented, "This is a lovely suite."

"Yes, and that is part of the story," Emma said.

Everyone sat down on the couch and two side chairs.

"What circumstances?" Papa asked. "Is there something going on?" He turned an intense gaze toward Emma. "Are you here on a case?"

"Papa, we didn't decide on this trip; the decision was made for us," she said.

Papa frowned and started to ask another question when he was interrupted by a knock at the door. Jeremy stood up and went to answer it. This time, it was the room service order. He stepped aside to let the waiters bring in the assorted trays.

"Where would you like these?" the waiter asked in broken English.

"The table would be nice, merci," Dora said.

They moved to the dining table and deposited the trays onto the surface. Jeremy walked them out and tipped them for their service.

"Join us," Tim encouraged Abbey and Papa.

"Yes, thank you," Abbey answered for herself and Papa.

They all sat together and passed around plates with fruit, bread, and cheese.

Jeremy walked over to the side table and pulled out wine glasses. "Wine, everyone?"

A resounding "Yes!" sounded from the group, followed by laughter.

Papa sent a serious expression to Emma and said, "Now, tell me about this trip. How did it come about?"

She explained about the letter, the tickets, and the hotel.

"Should you have made the trip? Not knowing if there were actual reservations once you got here?" he asked, concerned for them.

Jeremy explained, "We did confirm the train and streamliner tickets. We all decided we'd take the rest on faith that we would have a place to stay once we got here. How could we pass up an opportunity for an all-expense-paid trip to Paris?"

"Have you had any trouble on the trip so far?" asked Ellis.

"Not so far." Emma squeezed Jeremy's hand as a warning not to mention Julian.

"Keep your eyes open," he said. *A mysterious benefactor?* What could they want with his family?

"Papa, we will," Emma said. "We're going to check out the Art Curator's Society first. Then we're going to see if we can track down who sent the tickets to us."

Abbey decided to change the topic. "Would you like to hear about the things we've seen?"

"Yes, please," said Dora, eager to hear more about the city they were in.

Abbey started. "The crowds are rather large—so get out early. The bakeries are called Boulangeries. They open very early and the bread is not to be missed. You must try the croissants and pain au chocolat."

"Yum!" said Tim. The others nodded in agreement.

"Also, the sourdough bread we have here is called pain de campagne. The bread has a particular method to eat it. Let me show you." She picked up a round loaf of bread and tore it into pieces with her hands. "Like these."

"I like that," Tim said and picked up another round loaf and tore off a large piece for himself. "Dora, we need to find out how they make this."

Abbey gazed at them thoughtfully. *I'll have to do something about that.* She had several friends who were bakers and would not mind an extra pair of hands to help with the morning baking. She also had a surprise for both Dora and Emma for the next morning. "Please keep your morning free tomorrow. I have an appointment set up for you," Abbey stated. She had acted quickly when she found out they were in the city.

"What kind of appointment?" asked Emma.

"It's a surprise. I'd like to pick you up at 8AM if that is okay?"

"That would be lovely," Dora answered for them both.

"Tell us, more," Jeremy suggested.

Abbey smiled at him and held out her hand for him to take. "I have had plenty of time with friends."

"What she's saying," Papa said, taking her other hand, "is that I have been busy with inspections at the exposition."

"And playing with the toys," she commented.

When the group frowned, not understanding her reference, he said self-mocking voice, "Yes, she calls the machines toys."

She smiled, forgiving him for leaving her. "He's forever over there tinkering and asking questions, but I get to see him in the evenings. I'm happy with that."

While they talked about the exhibits Abbey had seen, Papa stood and motioned to Emma. She nodded and walked with him over to the balcony.

"What are your plans?" he asked, his voice serious.

She answered the surface question. "We plan to see the exhibits and explore the city as much as we can."

"Emma," he said, his voice low. He knew she was dodging the question.

She looked him in the eyes and said truthfully, "Yes, Papa, I understand what you're asking. We, Jeremy and I, are going to investigate the group that may have sent us the tickets."

"How do you expect to start? And what do you expect to find?"

"Initially, we thought Philip could tell us the organization was real. He indicated it didn't exist when he was in Paris, but it could have formed later. I have several of Philip's contacts in the area. We'll stop by and find out if the organization exists. If it does, we'll thank them for the trip."

"And if it doesn't exist?"

"I'd have to assume we have been brought here for a nefarious reason. I'd like to know why here and at this time. What is it that makes us so valuable to them?"

Papa frowned at the way she phrased that question. "Why indeed?" *What was it that Emma, Jeremy, Tim, and Dora could provide that no one else could?* He continued to mull that thought over when Abbey walked up and slid her arm into his.

"Ready to go?" she asked.

He leaned down to kiss Emma's cheek and murmured, "Send me a note when you get the information about who paid for the trip."

"I will," she said softly. "Goodbye, Papa. Goodbye, Abbey. We'll see you in the morning." She watched as they walked back to say good night to everyone.

Abbey said, "Just a moment." She rushed back to Emma and whispered, "I'll arrange a morning in a bakery for Dora."

"That would be perfect," she said and kissed her cheek.

Abbey rejoined Papa, while Dora and Tim walked them out. Emma turned back to watch the scenery from the window. Jeremy came up to Emma and pulled her back to him. "Everything okay?" he asked.

"Yes, Papa was just concerned about who might be behind this trip."

"Aren't we all? Would you like to check Philip's contacts out first thing tomorrow?" he asked.

"It'll have to wait until after the surprise trip in the morning," she said regretfully.

They stayed there for a few more minutes, enjoying the view.

"Are we going out?" Dora asked impatiently from across the room. They had eaten and she was eager to see some of Paris.

Emma turned to her. "I think we can manage that. Though we should stick to this neighborhood for tonight."

They put on their coats and hats and made their way to the elevator. They exited the crowded lobby and walked down to the Avenue Montaigne, Rue du Faubourg Saint-Honoré, and Élysée Palace enjoying everything they saw.

They walked for a long while and when it started getting late Emma said regretfully, "We should head back. We don't know the area that well."

The group agreed and they headed back to the hotel. It was about the time the exposition was closing and a huge boom could be heard.

"What was that?" asked Dora, looking panicked.

"I heard about that," Jeremy said. "At each opening and closing of the exposition, they set off a cannon."

"Every morning and evening?" Dora said faintly.

"We'll get used to it," Emma assured her.

CHAPTER 9

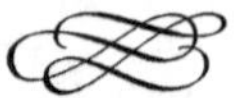

The next morning came around quickly. Jeremy and Emma heard a soft knock on their bedroom door.

"Emma," Dora called through the door.

Emma called, "Come in." She and Jeremy were lying in the bed.

"We want to get going early to the bakery. Would you like to get dressed and join us?"

Emma looked at Jeremy, then back at her sister. "Our first trip to a boulanger? Of course, we want to go."

"We can't miss that!" Jeremy said and sat up.

Dora excused herself to allow them some privacy as the two got dressed. They were ready quickly and met Dora and Tim in the living room. The group headed out.

"We should have plenty of time before we're supposed to meet Abbey," said Dora. The sun was just coming up as they made their way downstairs to the lobby.

"Do we need to stop and ask the concierge for a recommendation?" Tim asked.

"No," Dora replied. "Abbey gave me the name and location of several of her favorite boulangerie. She said the first one is about two blocks from here on the right."

The area was quiet in the early morning. They strolled along the sidewalk, looking in the windows of many small shops. When Emma delayed a bit in front of one, Dora called, "We need to hurry; there'll be a line."

"Oh, of course, let's keep going."

They turned the corner and saw why they had to arrive early. A line had already formed, though it moved quickly with persons exiting the shop carrying delicious-smelling pastries.

They waited patiently, leaning close to the window as they tried to get a view of the varied pastries available.

"What should we get?" Emma asked.

"Croissants, they're buttery goodness and Abbey said not to be missed," said Dora.

"What about some pain au chocolat?" Tim asked. He remembered the description from the night before.

Jeremy nodded. Chocolate was also a favorite of his.

They entered and the smell of bread washed over them. Emma paused in the doorway, thinking of Mama and her bakery. *She'd have loved this*, she thought. There turn had come and as they stepped up to the counter, the clerks were in a rush, their morning spent baking and then selling. She asked, "Dora, would you like to order for us?"

Dora looked nervous but asked for the croissants and pain au chocolat in French. The baker smiled and handed her the pastry bag in exchange for their money.

"I hope you enjoy it," he commented in accented English.

Dora blushed and they shuffled out so the next person in line could get their order.

They stepped out with their wonderful-smelling treats and could not wait for a second longer to take a bite. The pastries were handed out. Emma took a minute to pull her croissant apart.

"Dora, look at these layers."

Dora mimicked her move. "I'd love to find out how they can do that."

Emma took a large bite and moaned. The butter and the layers were lovely. Dora reacted the same way. They glanced at the men, their hands were empty. "Where are your pastries?" Dora asked.

"We have a problem," Tim said.

"A problem? What kind of problem?" Dora asked worriedly.

"Our pastries are gone," Tim said sadly.

"Already?" Emma asked.

Jeremy answered for both of them. "Yeah….we didn't take the time to investigate the pastry; we just ate it."

Emma finished her pastry. "How was it?"

"We should have gotten two," Tim answered unhappily. He looked longingly back at the bakery but the line had grown even further.

"Why don't we walk to the Arc de Triomphe?" Jeremy suggested.

Emma teased Tim. "We might find another boulanger on the way."

Tim grinned and instantly cheered up. They began their walk. It was easy to spot the boulangerie; the lines were long. They waited in one more line to get more pastries. This time they waited to eat them.

Their destination stood at the western end of the Champs-Élysées at the center of Place de l'Étoile. Signs in the area stated that this was the meeting point for the 17, 8th, and 16th Arrondissements. They counted as they went around it and saw there were twelve radiating avenues. After they went around twice, then found a bench to sit on. The boys ate croissants this time and the girls ate Pain au chocolat. All agreed both were delicious.

After they finished, they walked around and read the writing on The Arc de Triomphe. Emma read aloud, "It honors those who fought and died for France in the French Revolutionary and Napoleonic Wars, with the names of all French victories and generals inscribed on its inner and outer surfaces."

"Doesn't the exposition also honor the revolution?" Dora asked.

"Yes, the 100 years since the event occurred," commented Tim. They were silent thinking about how many deaths occurred during that event. The four continued around the structure.

"I believe you can go to the top of the structure and look out at all of Paris," Emma said.

Jeremy walked around until he located the stairs and called, "It's over here." The monument had opened for viewing a few minutes earlier.

A man stood at the entrance and directed them to the top. "The area you're walking in changed only thirty to forty years ago. Napoleon III changed the tree-lined boulevards and wider streets were added."

The group made their way to the top and took in the view. Paris was laid out in front of them. It was a wonderful site, a fashionable avenue with trees on either side that formed rectangular groves. There were also footpaths, fountains, and gas lighting.

Dora nudged Emma. "We'll have to come back and shop here."

"I'd also like to see the Élysée Palace," commented Emma.

"Countries with monarchs are staying away from the exposition," commented Jeremy, continuing to look out at the sites.

Emma said, "They don't want to foster the idea that it's a good thing to dissolve their countries' political systems."

"The revolution was also quite violent," Tim mentioned, "I'm pretty sure the kings and queens left in Europe would like to keep their heads in place."

The rest of the group laughed and Dora punched him. "None of that, we don't want to be rude."

"Who me?" he teased back and grabbed the hand she had punched him with and kissed it.

"Emma," Dora asked, trying to change the subject, "what is the architecture we're looking at?"

Emma said, "It's an old city. You'll see examples of architecture from every period, from the Middle Ages to now. Paris was the birthplace of the Gothic style and has important monuments of the French Renaissance, Classical Revival, and the flamboyant style of the reign of Napoleon III. We're also lucky to see new landmarks that will be around for a long time, like the Eiffel Tower and Grand Palais. I do wish we had a map; we could explore more of the area."

"I got one from a man at the desk downstairs," said Dora as she pulled it from her pocket. "It's called the chromolithographic tourist pocket map. We should be able to use it to get around."

"We could have used this earlier," teased Tim, reviewing it.

"I forgot I had it," she admitted.

They studied it and pointed out sites that appeared on the map —the Eiffel Tower, the Pantheon, and others.

Jeremy noticed the time, "We should get back. Mom will be picking you up soon."

The four of them headed down the stairs, being careful of the tourists passing them on their way up.

"Our surprise," Dora said happily.

"Yes, of course, the surprise," muttered Emma.

Dora caught her by the arm and pulled her to a stop. "Aren't you looking forward to it?"

"Not really. I just had some things I needed to get done this morning," Emma said. She was thinking of the questions she needed to ask the museum curators.

"But you will try to have a good time?" Dora asked, feeling a little disappointed.

"I will," she promised and smiled at Dora. She appeared cheered and they continued to walk arm and arm to the exit.

"The exposition will be opening soon," Emma commented.

"Oh, yes, we'll have plenty of time to go once you return," Tim told her.

They walked through the tree-lined streets, admiring the

magnificent homes made of stacked stone. Emma stopped and commented, "I'd like to see the inside of some of these."

Jeremy looked around. "Mom may know some of the residents; we could ask if it's possible." Abbey had lived in France for many years.

Emma nodded and said a bit dreamily, "That would be amazing." *What a dream,* she thought, *to be able to live in this amazing city.* She thought of something else. "You're sure she knows them, right?" she asked Jeremy. His mother was a very skilled cat burglar and had been known internationally for her skills.

He smiled. "I'm sure the visit will be conducted through the front door and not a window."

They got back to their room and freshened up. When they heard a knock at the door, Emma rolled her eyes but got her hat and headed to the door with Dora.

It was Abbey, and she was smiling brightly. "Are you ready for your surprise?"

Emma smiled, understanding this was family. "Yes."

"Me also," Dora said.

They followed her down to a waiting carriage. Abbey instructed the driver to go to an address that was in the opposite direction of the exposition. When they pulled up in front of a very elegant clothes shop, Emma sucked in her breath. *Definitely a surprise,* she thought.

"Emma, it's clothes," Dora said excitedly.

Abbey saw their reaction and grinned. "A good surprise?" she asked.

They grinned back and then climbed quickly out of the carriage.

"We have appointments for you both. Let's go in," Abbey said and they followed her into the shop. The garments hanging in the room were so beautiful. Emma would have loved to look at the structure of each one. *How are these wonderful gowns put together?* she wondered

"Abbey," a woman's voice called. "Are these your two daughters?"

"They are. This is Dora and Emma. Girls, this is Madam Sucrest, she's an amazing designer."

"Hmm," Madam Sucrest said as she walked around the girls. "You're right, they have lovely figures. But the foundation garments. Tsk tsk. Ladies, you need support. It makes the dresses fit so much better." She clapped her hands loudly. Two assistants appeared and escorted Dora and Emma to the dressing rooms. Madam Sucrest followed and commented, "First, we'll need to fit you for corsets. We may have some we can adjust for you to take home today."

"But," protested Emma, "we don't wear corsets."

Everyone stopped at once and Dora ran into the assistant in front of her. "And why not?" Madam Sucrest asked.

"Mama said they'd be bad for us and lead to medical problems," Emma responded.

"Bah! Medical problems only occur if you put them on incorrectly or use the wrong materials. A good corset will fit and provide structure."

Emma continued to offer facts. "Isn't whalebone used to stiffen it? Won't that cut into me?"

"No, if anything, whalebone is flexible and will fit better with the heat of the body." The woman reduced her voice level. "Will you give it a chance? We can put you in one and show you what a difference it will make to the dress."

Emma was still worried and looked at Dora and said in a low voice, "Mama didn't approve of these."

Dora was more reasonable and answered her in the same low tones. "But, Emma, that was over fifteen years ago. Let's see what has changed."

Madam Sucrest studied Dora. "You have had a child?" she asked.

"Yes," Dora said. She was embarrassed that it was visible on her figure.

"The corset can offer support, especially during the time of heavier breasts."

Both girls were resigned to trying the corset and moved into their dressing rooms. Once they undressed, they stood in their combinations while the assistants measured both women and went to get a corset that would fit.

Emma's assistant said, "The fasteners are in the front now, so you may dress yourself. I'll show you how to put it on. Do not overtighten; we can pad you out to make your waist look smaller." The assistant tightened the stays in the back. "I will only tighten it to give you a shape, we want you to be able to move around and do things you'd normally do."

Emma paced and realized it did offer support to her chest and back. *This does feel pretty good,* she thought. She moved and kicked out with her leg. She lunged forward and then tried to lean back. "Okay, so there are limitations," she murmured.

The assistant frowned. These were not the moves normal customers did to check to see if they could move in a corset. "The dress is next."

Emma watched as the assistant went to the beautiful gold dress hanging in the room.

"That one?" Emma asked, holding her breath for the answer.

"Yes," the assistant said as she took it off the hanger and walked it over to Emma. "Arms up, please."

Emma placed her arms through the dress and the assistant pulled it over her head. The dress settled on her hips and was fastened in the back.

"You may turn around now."

She turned and saw her image. "Oh, that is lovely." The gold and brown tones were deep with a square neck. She looked at the structure of the garment and saw that the corset did its job. It didn't impede her breathing.

The assistant saw her examining the garment and said, "The

stays give structure to the top, and padding attached inside the skirt and top help to fill out the garment."

"Emma! Come out," called Abbey. "Dora has come out already."

She walked out of the door and Abbey said, the satisfaction clear in her voice, "Perfect."

Emma turned and saw Dora standing on a wood block to allow her assistant to hem the skirt. She was wearing a dark blue color that was similar in style to her own. A full skirt with a structured top. The difference was the necklines. Dora's was scooped and Emma's was a bit higher and square.

"Oh, Dora, you look lovely," Emma said.

"So do you," her sister responded

"Do you approve?" Abbey asked them.

"We do!" they said at the same time and grinned.

Madam Sucrest came out and walked around both girls and nodded her approval. "We need to do some fitting on these, but we have some day outfits you may take with the corsets."

They changed into the other outfits, which were quickly fitted to them. An hour later, they were having tea and cakes while they waited for their dresses to be finished. Madam Sucrest called, "They're ready." They went back and put on the suit dresses; they were perfect.

They exited the shop and hugged Abbey. "Your other dresses should be ready later in the week."

"How long have you known each other?" asked Emma.

"Oh, for a long time," Abbey said, not sharing anything else.

"Was Madam Sucrest always so talented with her hands?" Dora asked.

Abbey unexpectantly said, "She had to do something after retiring from stealing jewels."

"She was a…" exclaimed Dora.

"Yes, she was once a famous thief. Almost as good as me," Abbey said, then laughed.

"Did you work together?" asked Emma.

"We have," said Abbey. She changed the subject. "Now, tell me, did you like the dresses?"

"Thank you, these are so lovely," Emma said.

"I'm glad you enjoy them. I need to get you back so you can start your investigation,"

They returned to the hotel close to noon and Dora asked Abbey, "Would you like to eat lunch with us?"

"Thank you, but no. I'm meeting Ellis and going to see some of the exhibits with him this afternoon. We'll see you soon," she replied.

"Abbey, thank you," Emma said. "We had a nice time and the garments are gorgeous."

"You're welcome," she said as she watched the two women climb down. She told the driver to take her to her apartment.

They watched her go and Emma turned to Dora. "That was amazing. Who would have thought corsets could be comfortable?"

"I agree," said Dora. "This really helps my back. Since I had Lottie, I've felt strained."

"I didn't know. I hope it helps, but don't wear it too often; your muscles need to be allowed to work without it," Emma suggested.

"I will. Ready to go up and let the boys see the new dresses?" Dora asked.

"Yes, let's go up."

They headed into the crowded hotel and waited for the elevator.

"Will you head over to the exposition this afternoon?" asked Emma.

"Yes," Dora answered. She mentioned lightly, "Lenora and Michael will be meeting us here."

"When was this arranged?" asked Emma, carefully keeping her tone even.

"As we were leaving the ship."

"They must be close by," Emma said, not revealing she knew where they were staying.

"They are staying in the same hotel we are."

As they entered the hotel lobby and heard a voice call, "Dora!" They looked over and saw Lenora and Michael calling her.

Dora raised her eyebrows at Emma, who commented without expression, "I'll wait here."

"Thank you," Dora said softly.

Emma watched as her sister hurried over to them.

They hugged and talked animatedly. *Plans for the exposition,* Emma thought. She continued to watch Dora interact with the couple.

When she didn't come back, Emma walked over to the elevator. Just as the doors opened, Dora rushed up. They gave their floor number to the operator.

"Just caught it," Dora said, out of breath.

"Plans all worked out?" asked Emma. She tried to keep any emotion out of her voice, looking at the top of the elevator.

"Yes," Dora said, smiling. She didn't realize Emma was unhappy. "They have a carriage and we'll start over as soon as we have lunch and freshen up."

Emma continued to dwell on that sudden friendship. There were too many unanswered questions about these people. They were both silent as they waited for their floor. The doors opened, and they stepped out together and made their way to their hotel room.

They opened the door and called out, "Tim, Jeremy!"

"We're in here and we ordered lunch; chicken and vegetables with bread and fruit. Come on in."

They walked in and the men viewed the outfits for the first time.

"Wow, those are nice," Tim said.

"Do you notice anything different about us?" Dora asked.

"No, not really," both men said.

Emma and Dora laughed. Dora said, "We'll show you later."

"Hmm," Jeremy teased, "now I'd like to know what's different."

Emma laughed and said, "Later."

They started to eat and Emma grew quieter.

"Is anything wrong?" asked Jeremy.

"I am just thinking about the people we need to meet this afternoon." Philip had given her a letter of introduction to meet with several museum curators. *The investigation into who brought us to Paris must come first,* she thought.

They ate quickly and got their coats and hats from their rooms. "Is everyone ready to head downstairs?" asked Jeremy, pulling on his coat as he exited the bedroom. Like Chicago, the weather during September could be chilly.

"I just can't wait to see the tower and the opening into the exposition; there are supposed to be fountains and statues the entire distance from the entrance to the far central dome," commented Dora.

Emma wanted to go see it but knew they needed some answers first. "We'll get there as soon as we can," she said, "I can't wait to see it also. Will we be able to meet you for a late tea?"

Tim cleared his voice and Dora said apologetically, "I'm not sure. We promised the rest of the day to Lenora and Michael. How about dinner instead?"

Jeremy nudged her and she responded begrudgingly, "That will be fine."

The two couples headed out of the room and down the elevator into the lobby, where they immediately saw Lenora and Michael. She noticed they didn't approach their group but called to Tim and Dora to join them. *Why do they avoid me and Jeremy?*

Jeremy watched them leave and turned to Emma. "Okay, let's have it."

"They don't want us around," she stated.

"Yes, they do, but their new friends want some alone time. It's not that unusual," he reasoned.

"I know, I just thought we'd be with them at the exposition. That was the plan."

"We'll have two weeks," he pointed out. "Just let Dora and Tim know how you feel. I'm sure they'll make time for us."

"You're right." She knew he was right but she turned to stare at the group of four.

He wanted to stop her from dwelling on Tim and Dora's new friends. "Do you have the curator's name and address?"

"Yes, we'll need directions."

He looked around and saw the concierge at his desk. "Over there," he said, indicating the desk.

They made their way over. The man spoke English and gave them directions to the museums. "You will need a carriage to get there."

"I hope it isn't in the direction of the exposition," Jeremy said dryly as they exited. The crowds already forming in the streets and traffic didn't appear to be moving.

"Me, too!" she said, looking around.

"Do you have the letters Philip wrote?" asked Jeremy.

"Yes, I have them here," she said, tapping her pocket.

"We need to walk a few blocks to get away from this crowd," Jeremy said.

"You're right."

They crossed the street and walked to a less crowded location to locate a carriage. They found one and gave him the address. It was located in another arrondissement. They looked around as they traveled and enjoyed the view of the different neighborhoods going by.

The carriage pulled to a stop in front of a large stone structure. The building's appearance was that of a palace. A large number of the monarchy's homes had been turned into buildings for the public good. They paid the driver and got out of the carriage. He drove away as they turned and stared at the large building with many different floors.

Management will not be easy to reach in an establishment this big, Emma thought. They needed to speak with the top person. She hoped her letter would get them to the person they needed. She took a deep breath and they ascended the imposing stairs.

The museum had been open since 10 am that morning. They entered through the main double doors and into a large entryway. There was a security station there; they paused and inquired about the manager. The guard said he was unavailable. They weren't getting anywhere with the large imposing man.

"The letter," muttered Jeremy.

"Oh, yes." She pulled it out and said, "I have a letter that might help."

The security guard took it from her and carried it over to a closed door on the opposite side of the gallery. It seemed like an eternity, and then the door opened again. This time, the guard was accompanied by a man of about fifty.

"Bonjour!" the man called to them. He had white hair and a full beard. His suit was burgundy with white lace at the cuffs.

"Bonjour," they replied.

"Je suis, François Le Burke, le réalisateur."

"Je suis Emma Evans et Jeremy Tilden," Emma said.

"You may speak English. Would you like to come to my office?" the director said, indicating the way with his hand.

"Thank you," Emma said gratefully.

They walked through several exhibits. Emma had to concentrate on why they were there and not get distracted. They entered the director's office. It was a large space that was different from the main museum in that it had windows. Normally, museums didn't like natural light; it could wash out the art. Gas lights were used to illuminate the areas.

Le Burke moved behind the large desk and indicated the chairs in front of his desk. "Sit, please. I read your letter of introduction. I have known Philip for years. What can I do for you?"

"Yes, we met with Philip because of an invitation we received." Emma handed the invitation to him.

"Hmm," he murmured as he read it. He said in a distracted

manner, "Yes, Philip, was tied up with that mess a few years ago—forgeries involving paintings." He looked at her in surprise when he realized with whom he was speaking. "You said Emma Evans?"

"Yes," she responded.

Le Burke got up and came around the desk and took her hands in his. "My dear, we're so grateful to you! So many artists' works could have been lost forever."

He went back to his chair and picked up the invitation again. He studied it carefully and said, "You'd like to know if this is authentic."

"Yes," Jeremy said. "We haven't received any follow-up and we're concerned about the reason for wanting us here."

"I can tell you this. This is not an authentic organization. I'm involved on the boards of the main art societies here in Paris. I'd have at least heard of it if it existed."

Emma let out a long breath. "So, the reason given for our being here is fraudulent. But why?"

"Have you seen anything suspicious since you arrived in Paris?" he asked.

Emma thought of Julian, Lenora, and Michael, but said, "No, but we're concerned that we're being manipulated."

Le Burke picked up his pencil and started writing. "I'll keep the name and ask around to see if anyone else has heard of it."

"We'd appreciate it," Emma said. "We're staying at the Grand Hotel Terminus."

He wrote that down and thought he'd have to send notes to other museum curators in the area. He asked, "Have you been to the exposition yet?"

"We'll be going after this. We wanted to see you first," said Jeremy.

"I'm honored. You must stop by the central dome. It's at the far end of the fountains after you get through the tower. Inside of it are arches and murals that are wonderful in their detail and artistry."

"We'll keep an eye out for them," Emma assured him. "Thank you for taking time for us today."

"I'm pleased you brought this to me, and I'll follow up as soon as I know something." With that, Le Burke stood and accompanied them to their carriage. "Au revoir," he called.

They climbed into the waiting carriage and requested to be taken to the exposition. As they started moving, Jeremy looked over at Emma.

"Who are you thinking of for this?"

"The same as you, I'd expect," she said, glancing over at him.

"Julian, Lenora, and Michael," he confirmed.

"Yes," she said contemplatively. "They've shown up seemingly out of nowhere, and now they've interwoven themselves into our lives."

The trip to the exposition grounds was indeed taking a long time. The driver had warned them that the trip would be longer as the streets were very full.

He was correct as they got closer to the bridge, they were surrounded by other carriages and people walking. The Eiffel Tower, the main entrance to the exposition could be seen from where they were. The anticipation took Emma's breath away and suddenly she couldn't wait to get there.

Jeremy felt the same and looked around. "It would be simpler to walk," he pointed out. Emma agreed and started out of the carriage.

Jeremy laughed and stopped her. "I think we should tell the driver first."

"True." She called to the driver, "We'd like to get out here."

He nodded and told them their price. It was not necessary to pull over; the crowds had brought them to a stop. They paid him, climbed down, and took the footpath across the bridge. Walking up to the entrance, they stood for a long moment and marveled at the size of the structure. It distracted them from anything around it.

"Jeremy, come over here," she said, moving through the crowds to get to the tower. She moved until she stood where one of the interlocking joists connected to the ground. Spinning in a circle, she took in the four massive pillars that held the tower's shape. "It's tall!" she said.

"You know, it's 57.64 meters just to the first level," commented Jeremy. "Give me your hand." She gave it and he pulled her back out of the crowded entry into the Exposition.

"We just got here! Where are we going?" she asked, laughing at his excitement.

He kept pulling her and she realized why; he wanted to get a view of the entire structure. "It's rather like a triangle," said Jeremy.

She studied it, "Except that it appears to be curved on its sides. It has different levels and different platforms."

"Didn't Ellis say Eiffel designed it because of how it would handle the wind?" Jeremy asked.

"Yes, the design causes the air to flow through and not push or pull on it. The actual placement of the supports and platforms took this into account."

"How long does something like this take to build? Was it being constructed when you were here last?"

"I believe the pillars were going in when I was here, but I don't remember seeing it in person at the time. I think I just wanted to get home to you." That period was full of personal turmoil for Emma and Jeremy. Each had faced challenges that required them to act without each other.

He leaned back, shielding his eyes to see the top. "How far is it to the top?"

"At its highest point, it's 324 meters. Papa says there's an apartment at the top for Eiffel."

"I'd love to see that!"

"Me, too," she said. She'd have to ask Papa if that were possible.

They continued to look around the base and Jeremy said, "Didn't Ellis say there were only stairs?"

"Initially," she confirmed. "The elevator didn't work at first, so only the stairs would be utilized to climb to the top. Papa wasn't thrilled; it was 328 steps to the first floor and 674 steps to the second floor. In total, there are 1,665 steps from the esplanade to the top of the tower. "

"What's on each level?" he asked curiously. "Is it just empty?"

"No, each level is something special. The first level has four majestic wooden pavilions designed by Stephen Sauvestre. The second level has an observation deck and, finally, the summit where Eiffel's office is located."

Jeremy laughed. "I'm not so sure I'm that good with heights. Did you want to go up today?"

They looked at the long lines for both the elevator and the stairs. Though the lines were significantly shorter for the stairs, Emma shook her head and said regretfully, "No, maybe next time. Why don't we wander around the exposition ground and see what else is here first? Plus," she said, sending a grin his way, "we have an in."

When he raised his eyebrows at that, she answered the silent question. "I'm sure Papa can get us up faster."

"And probably higher," he said and laughed. "Okay then, we're going to the exposition."

Though it was her suggestion to leave, it was hard to tear her eyes away from the iron structure. Jeremy had to tug at her hand as they made their way through the crowds.

The tower had taken up all of her attention and she hadn't noticed anything past it. But now, as they made their way through, she saw the large white fountains surrounded by lush grass. The water feature had numerous statues around it and at the main water supply. There was a wide walkway on each side and buildings boarding it.

"It's wonderful."

"Let's move away from this crowd," he suggested.

The entire world seemed to be trying to get into the exposition that day. They walked to the grassy area and paused to take it all in.

"Before we go any further, we should review the map," Jeremy suggested. The concierge had given it to them when they mentioned they'd also be attending the exposition. He pulled it out of his pocket for them to examine.

She looked down at it and then glanced around the area and the many buildings. "That must be the central dome is there," she said, pointing toward the far end where a gold dome could be seen.

"What are the ones on the left of the dome?" he asked, looking over her shoulder at the map.

She read it out loud, "The Palaces of Liberal and Fine Arts, each with a richly decorated dome, facing each other across a garden and reflecting pool between the Eiffel Tower and the Palace of Machines. Both were designed by Jean-Camille Formigé. Both buildings had modern iron frames abundance of glass but were completely covered with colorful ceramic tiles and sculpted decoration." She studied the grand structures. "What will they do with it once the exposition is over?"

"I don't know," he said honestly. He studied the map and said, "The crowd seems to be coming in through this one point. According to this map, there are twenty-two different entrances to the exposition around its perimeter."

"Good to know if we need to get out quickly," she teased. She looked at the map and around the area and asked, "How long do we have to view everything?"

"They're open from 8AM until 6PM for the major exhibits and palaces, and until 11:00 in the evening for the illuminated greens and restaurants."

"What is that there?" she asked, pointing to the map.

He looked on and said, "They're certainly ornamental. It says it's Les Invalides. It's the major ceremonial entrance. The two tall pylons with colorful ornaments, like giant candelabras."

Emma continued to review the map. Suddenly, she frowned, looking down and then up again, and drummed her fingers on her lips.

"What's wrong?" Jeremy asked. He knew she only did that when she was planning something.

"I don't know where to start; there's too much to see."

"Now, that is a good problem," he said with a wide smile. "Why not start at the back and work our way forward?"

She squinted at the map and said, "Galerie des Machines." She looked back at him. "Excellent idea."

As they started out, a voice rang out. "Would you like to take the trains? They're supposed to be very efficient."

They stopped when they heard the familiar voice.

"Julian," she muttered, with a frown on her face. She put a smile on her face and then turned. "Julian, how nice to see you again. How did you find us?" she asked lightly, but there was a bit of steel in her eyes. She really wanted the answer to that last question.

"Oh," he said, "I just happened on you. May I accompany you?"

When Jeremy started to say no, Emma bumped him with her hip. Instead, he said, "Yes, please do."

She leaned in and said in a low voice, "It'll give me a chance to question him." She looked over at Julian. "You mentioned you were here for business. Is it at the exposition?"

Julian wasn't forthcoming and instead murmured noncommittally. When he didn't continue, Emma pulled herself together and decided this would take some time.

"Have you had a chance to see anything yet?" Julian asked.

The question was broadly asked, but Emma decided it involved the exposition. "Oh, not yet. We just got here."

"I just got here myself."

She didn't believe him; the man had too many secrets.

"Where are Tim and Dora this afternoon?" Julian asked curiously as they started to walk further into the exposition location.

"They left for the exposition after lunch," said Jeremy.

"Alone?" he asked lightly, seemingly uninterested.

"No," replied Jeremy. "They're with Lenora and Michael."

"Hmm," he commented. "They have formed a friendship and are continuing to see each other?"

"Yes," Emma said. She tried to not let her worry show in her voice.

Jeremy wanted to pull her out of her thoughts and took her hand. "Let's look around," he suggested.

"I heard the cultural areas are interesting," she mentioned as they walked.

Looking at the area around them, Julian commented, "A separate, smaller site is located on the esplanade of Les Invalides, which is where the pavilions are. The exposition is showcasing villages inhabited by natives of the colonies. That is where you can go to a large number of outdoor restaurants and cafes with foods from Indochina, North Africa, and other cuisines from around the world."

Emma forced her gaze away from Julian. The three continued to stroll toward the central dome. The fountains were turned on and the water flowed and the sound drowned out the noise of the crowds around them. They paused and took in the area. The water flowed from a large white statue; other statues were lined up around the water.

They moved past it and climbed the steps up to the gold dome. As they entered, they immediately stopped to view the amazing sight in front of them. Even Julian seemed affected; his questions stopped as he took in the interior.

The people that entered behind forced the three to move further into the building. Julian pulled them over to the side to allow the others to enter. They continued to gaze at the murals and the gold that seemed to engulf the room. The artistry of paintings and panels located on every wall fascinated them. The sun shone in through the high windows and the chandeliers caught it and gleamed, throwing halos around the room.

Julian seemed to have found his voice and said, "We should move along."

Emma and Jeremy continued to look around. The dome was the entry hall for the Palace of Fine Arts, Liberal Arts and was the axis and entry for the Galerie des Machines.

"It appears this is only the beginning and opens up into other areas." Emma turned her gaze away from the ceiling and realized what was in front of her. It was the Galleries des Machines. At that moment, she could only marvel at what she was seeing. The structural supports pulled her in; she looked back to motion to Jeremy and saw he was distracted by the fine arts wing.

"Tony would have wanted to go there first," he commented. Tony was someone they were both friends with. Her first trip to Paris was to help him with an art heist/kidnapping case. He studied art and was the assistant curator of the museum in Chicago.

"Yes," she agreed. "We'll have to go through it so we can describe it to him later." She desperately wanted to go into the gallery of machines but understood the draw of the art.

"I just hope we have enough time to see it all," Jeremy said.

"We will," she said confidently. They had two full weeks left of their trip.

They moved forward, not looking back to see if Julian followed them. "The construction from the tower is being used throughout this building," Jeremy commented.

"I think Papa mentioned the design was initially used in bridge construction and this is the first time it's been used like this."

"Think about how many more things are displayed here; so many new inventions, so much new technology has been evolving."

'It doesn't seem that it's unpopular." They walked into the

gallery; again, the crowds wouldn't allow for long observation and they had to move to the sides.

"Edison's lights are being used to illuminate the whole thing," Emma said in wonder at the bright interior.

"I didn't expect the area to have decoration," Jeremy said, pointing out paintings, mosaics, and ceramic bricks that formed part of the cladding on the walls.

"Yes, the decoration continues from the dome," she marveled, spinning around. "It's so big."

Julian's voice startled them when he said, "It's 370 meters long."

So big, thought Emma and she continued to review the space. *It's difficult to know where to start; there are three separate walkways surrounding the machines.*

"So many new things. What is that up there?" Emma asked as she pointed toward the platform located far above them.

"That, I believe, is a train track," Jeremy commented, watching it move up and down the gallery. They walked up to the stairs that lead to the train. Jeremy read aloud from the display. "Bon and Lustremont Paris are builders for the rolling carriage over the Gallery des Machines."

"It's so high up in the air!" she exclaimed, anticipating the ride. *It really is the best way to see everything,* she thought, continuing to study the sheer size of the space. The trolley appeared to roll the entire length of the gallery, allowing people to see things from a different angle.

"I understand that Edison's inventions are displayed here and in some of the other pavilions," said Jeremy, as he looked around.

"We'll have to get over to the different exhibitions after we finish this gallery," stated Emma. "Though this one feels like the one where we will spend the most time."

"Yes," said Julian, his voice going low. "It is an important exhibit, one that will change the world. Too many people are trying to fight the use and expansion of electricity. Without it, none of these marvelous inventions would exist."

Emma was distracted for a moment and said, "You mentioned that before. Do you think we have cause for concern at this event?"

His face went dark momentarily. He laughed, trying to cover, and said, "How would I know? I know only as much as has been in the paper."

She looked at Jeremy, and he shrugged his shoulders. They needed to keep an eye on him; something was going on here. He seemed preoccupied with the anti-electric group.

They had only passed a few exhibits when they saw Tim and Dora. *And of course*, thought Emma, *Lenora, and Michael.*

Emma called out to her sister, "Dora!"

Dora heard her voice and turned toward her. She smiled, quickly running over with Tim following closely behind. Emma noticed Lenora and Michael stayed back.

"Isn't it just marvelous, all of these new things?" Dora asked.

"It is," Emma agreed.

"Julian," asked Dora," how are you?"

"I'm good. I heard you both were here already," he said. "Have you been in the exhibit all since you arrived?"

Emma, too, noted the question and her response. Julian's questions were clues. She needed to start documenting these and reviewing them with Jeremy.

"We started after lunch and then we meant to come here first but Lenora and Michael wanted to see the lighting display first," Dora answered.

"Which part in particular?" Julian asked.

Tim answered, "Oh, the layout and where everything was being managed from. That sort of thing. It was interesting to see how the electricity has been brought into the exposition."

"Really," Julian murmured.

Emma sent him a sharp look at that question. *What is he*

implying? Another voice distracted her. She glanced over Dora's shoulder and saw Papa. "Papa," she called and went over to him quickly to give him a hug and a kiss on the cheek. Dora followed closely behind and also kissed him on the cheek.

"Emma, I thought I'd find you here—among all of the new technology."

She grinned, "It's marvelous."

"Jeremy, is she wearing you out?" Papa asked as Jeremy and Tim walked up.

"Not just yet." He smiled broadly. "How much time have you spent here since you arrived in Paris?"

"I think that the answer given by me would be different than that given by Abbey," Papa said drolly.

Emma looked around, "Is she here with you?"

He smiled, "She said she's spent all of the time she'll ever spend in here."

"So, you have been here a lot?" Emma teased.

"Yes, I find it infinitely fascinating," he admitted. His gaze moved to Dora and Tim. "I didn't expect to see you both here. Is there something that interested you in particular?" Emma wondered about that; it was almost like a warning.

"We're enjoying everything," Dora commented. "We'd probably be spending more time in the other exhibits, but our new friends really wanted to see the Edison exhibit and the Galerie des Machines first."

"Try to see other things as well; the time will fly by," Ellis commented.

"Yes, Papa," said Dora. Tim had been thinking along the same lines. He enjoyed their new friends, but he and Dora had a list of things they'd like to see.

Papa looked around and said to their group, "Would you like to go to the highest level and ride the suspended carriage? It will give you a bird's eye view of the entire gallery."

That was exactly what Emma wanted. Her eyes lit up and she

said, "Yes, please." She put her hand out to Jeremy's and he took it; they were eager to see the gallery from the height of the suspended carriage.

"Dora? Tim?" Papa asked as he noticed them hesitate.

"Please include us in that. Let me check with…" Dora's voice trailed off as she turned. She looked back at them and said, "I'll be just a moment." She walked a distance from their group. When she came back, she was wringing her hands, "They aren't there. I hope they don't think we left them."

Tim frowned, "I'm sure they'll find us later." Though he continued to stare in the direction Lenora and Michael had gone.

Emma said, "We also have someone with us." She turned and called, "Julian!"

He wasn't there either. "Jeremy, do you see him?" she asked.

Jeremy observed, "I guess our company has also disappeared."

"Should we…" She let it go as she followed her family up the stairs to the carriage. She continued to look around as they climbed, trying to see everything. They made it to the top and stood in line to take their turn.

She spotted someone familiar in the crowd. *Is that Julian?* she thought as she leaned across the railing. *It is him. What is he doing?* She could only see his back; the persons he was talking to were blocked by the machines. Two people stepped closer to Julian and she could see who he was talking to. *It is Lenora and Michael. Just like the last time, they're arguing again.* Whatever the topic, both sides were taking it seriously. It almost came to blows until Lenora stepped between them to separate the men.

"What are you looking at?" Dora asked hugging her from behind.

"Over there," she murmured.

Dora followed her direction and said, "Isn't that…?"

"Yes, it is," Emma commented quietly, not wanting to share her opinions about her new friends.

"That's odd. I didn't think they knew each other. I never saw them interact before this."

"We saw them have a similar conversation on the ship," Emma said.

Dora turned her around. Once they were face-to face, she said, "You did? You didn't mention it."

"No, I wanted you to enjoy your new friends. One argument didn't seem pertinent."

"No, one wouldn't have been a concern," said Dora as her eyes moved back to the argument. It seemed to have no resolution and they stormed off in different directions.

"Should I be worried?" Dora asked.

Emma was quiet for a long time before saying, "I don't trust them."

"Which ones—Lenora, Michael, or Julian?"

"All three. I feel they're involved in something. I'm just not sure what," she admitted.

"It doesn't appear that they're on the same side."

Emma looked over at her. "You don't sound too disappointed that there may be something up with your new friends."

Her sister smiled, "It's getting to be a little too much. They're always around."

"I thought you liked them."

"I do but in smaller amounts. It's like strudel; I like it, but I don't want it for every meal."

Tim and Jeremy heard that last part as they walked over to where Emma and Dora were standing. Tim pulled Dora to him, "Are you talking about Lenora and Michael?"

She nodded.

"You told them?" Jeremy asked Emma.

"Yes, it was time. And Dora and I just witnessed another fight between the three of them." Dora quickly explained to Tim what they had just seen.

Tim asked, "This has happened before?" He didn't know if he

should feel upset that they had left him and Dora out of the conversation.

"Yes," Emma admitted.

"We didn't know if they were arguing over something petty on the ship and we didn't want to influence you about your new friends," Jeremy said.

Dora frowned, knowing how Emma could keep secrets from her. Her sister tended to make too many decisions on her behalf.

Tim watched the expressions on his wife's face and knew where her mind was headed. He leaned down and whispered in her ear, "Don't be upset. They told us when a second event happened."

She nodded but felt she needed to ask another question. "Is there anything else we need to know about?"

Emma hesitated and Dora saw it. "Well?" she demanded.

Emma looked at Jeremy and then back at Dora. "We..." she began, only to be interrupted by Papa.

"We're next," he called.

They hurriedly moved toward the opening of the trolley and, while they were waiting to board, Dora took Emma's arm and turned her until they could see in each other's eyes. "We'll talk about this later."

"We will," Emma replied softly. The line started moving and their group boarded the trolley. They headed toward the far side to take their seats until it was full.

The trolley engineer said loudly, first in French, then in English, "To ride safely, please do not stand or rock the vehicle."

They listened to his instructions and prepared themselves for the trip. The excitement removed all thoughts of Lenora, Michael, and Julian from their minds. She held Jeremy's hand tightly as she observed the sheer expanse of the gallery. "So many new things," she said.

Papa heard her and started pointing out the machines below.

"Little girl, look over here." That was something he had called her since she was a small child.

The trolley made its way down and back again. It just wasn't long enough for her, and Jeremy could see she was disappointed at having to get off.

"We'll come back. I promise," he said softly.

"Yes, definitely," she responded.

As they exited the trolley and made their way downstairs, the group agreed that they'd spend the rest of the day together—eating at the exposition grounds and heading home that night. Papa enjoyed the day with his daughters and their husband/companion. No one had mentioned that Julian, Lenora, and Michael had disappeared. Each felt relieved that they were together as a family.

After the long afternoon of walking, they had a late dinner with Abbey and Papa at their hotel.

"It's getting late. We must go," said Abbey. She noticed Ellis looked tired and thought it best to get him home for some rest. The hours he was keeping on this trip were strenuous, up by 6AM and usually down at the exposition grounds with Eiffel until late in the evening. She wanted to make sure he didn't do too much.

They made their goodbyes and the door closed when Jeremy said, "Emma, didn't you mean to ask Abbey about something?"

She glanced toward Dora, "Yes. I forgot."

"I think you can still catch her if you take the stairs," he suggested.

Emma thought quickly, "I'll do that." He held the door open for her and she dashed to the stairs. As she exited the door into the lobby, she looked and saw the elevator was standing open. *Where are Papa and Abbey?* she thought to herself, glancing around. Not seeing them, she went to the main entry doors.

Papa's outline was seen easily through the glass. *There they are,* she thought and put her hand on the door and started to pull them open when she saw them speaking with someone. She released the door when she saw who it was. *It's Julian. Do Papa and Abbey know him?* She decided to find out, but before she could, a crowd came through the door, pushing her further into the lobby. She untangled herself and made her way back to the door and opened it. *Gone!* She ran down the street, but there was no sign of them.

Odd, she thought. She didn't think Papa and Abbey knew Julian. Had he just happened to be in the area? *Unlikely,* she thought. *I'll need to ask Papa about this.*

She glanced again toward the front desk, wondering if the crowd that had pushed into the lobby had gotten rooms yet. She studied the people in line and saw a lovely young lady and what was perhaps her mother, though she only saw her back. The daughter appeared to be of negroid descent. They both looked tired, the older woman with her back to Emma was leaning onto the younger woman. A long trip probably. *Hopefully, they have a reservation,* she thought and headed back upstairs.

She knocked lightly and Jeremy opened the door. He asked, "Were you able to catch her?"

"No, I wasn't," she said, meditatively. "Where's Dora and Tim?"

"They went to get ready for bed but said they wanted to talk when you returned."

He could tell something was bothering her as she took a seat on the couch. He sat down next to her, took her hand, and asked, "What's wrong?"

She looked forward for a long moment, "When I found Papa and Abbey, they were talking with Julian."

"Julian! I didn't realize they knew him."

"I'm not sure they do," she said thoughtfully. "It's possible they ran into each other."

"That's a lot of coincidences."

"I agree. I'll follow up with Papa tomorrow."

She continued to be preoccupied and Jeremy asked, "Was there something else bothering you?"

"Yes, we have so many new people in our lives; people who seem to keeping secrets from us."

Dora and Tim walked in and heard the word secret. Dora had gotten ready for bed and was in her robe, her hair loose on her shoulders.

"Yes, secrets. Emma," she started, "I'd like to know what's been kept from us."

Emma jumped up and said defensively, "That isn't fair. We were trying to give you some space and time with your new friends."

"Who you didn't trust," Dora accused.

Jeremy stepped between the sisters, "Dora, I discouraged her from interfering in your new friendship. We really only had some suspicions."

Tim, always the peacemaker, said, "Let's sit down and discuss this calmly."

After they sat, he looked toward Emma and Jeremy and asked, "Can we hear the suspicions so we can make our own decisions?"

Jeremy's mouth quirked when Emma pulled out her notebook. She reviewed her case notes, "It's a lot of little things. The fast friendship, not just yours with Lenora and Michael, but also Julian's with us."

"We also had the added issue of us being brought here for reasons we're not sure of," added Jeremy.

"And the confirmation from Philips' friend that the organization that brought us here does not exist," she explained.

"When did you see the first argument?" Dora asked, remembering they had mentioned another altercation.

"It was the second night on the trip when your hair had come down. You went back to your cabin and we continued on," she said.

"Could you hear anything?" Tim asked.

"No, unfortunately, we only saw them talking," Emma replied.

"What else?" Dora asked.

"There isn't a lot more," admitted Emma.

"Well…" started Jeremy.

Emma nodded, encouraging him to go on.

"There is the electricity thing," he finished.

"Electricity?" asked Dora.

"Yes, we have nothing solid, but Julian has mentioned the anti-electricity people more than once, and when coupled with the arguments…" Emma explained.

Tim glanced at Dora. She nodded, and he said, "We might have something to share."

Emma frowned and leaned forward. "Tell us."

"Today, we mentioned the time we spent at the Edison exhibition?" Tim explained.

"Yes," said Jeremy.

"We didn't just look around. We also got special access to the rooms where the electricity comes into the building," Dora explained.

"How did you get access to that?" Emma asked, knowing how tight the security was around the technology exhibits.

"Papa," admitted Dora. "We used his name and were allowed into all of the secure areas."

"What were Lenora and Michael doing during this time?" asked Emma.

"They were extremely interested in where the electricity came in and how it could be turned on and off," Tim admitted.

"They also explained all of the security to us," commented Dora.

"But we still have no real connections of anything bad to any of them. We just have conjecture," Emma said,

"What do we do?" her sister asked.

Jeremy stood and walked to the mantle. "For now, we keep a watch for anything suspicious."

"I'd recommend you curtail your exposure to Michael and Lenora for now," Emma said firmly.

Dora frowned, "I'd like to make my own decisions, but yes, I think you're right."

There was a knock at the door and the group jumped in response. Jeremy walked over and opened the door. It was a bellhop. "Yes?"

"I have a note for Dora Flannigan."

Jeremy held out his hand, "I'll take it."

He handed it over, and Jeremy pulled out some coins and tipped him. He closed the door and went back to the living room. He walked over to Dora and handed her the note, "It's for you."

Emma frowned. She watched as Dora opened it slowly while the group waited.

She read silently and laughed abruptly. "Abbey sent me a note; she's arranged for me to work in a bakery in the morning."

Wonderful, thought Emma. *She didn't forget.*

"Early?" Tim asked, knowing baker's hours because of the family bakery back home. The dread in his voice was evident.

"Yes." She laughed. She knew Tim was not looking forward to being up with her at that hour.

"What time?" His tone hadn't changed.

"It says 3AM," she supplied.

Emma lay her head back on the couch, "I'm glad I wasn't included in this 'surprise'. What will you learn to make?"

"The rounded bread and croissants. The types of bread we've had since we have been here," Dora said, looking at the note and thinking about the bakery.

"You must make those once we get back home—since we tried them here, I don't think I can live without them," Emma said with a laugh.

Tim stood up holding out his hand to Dora, "We need to go to bed. If you have to be there at three, we'll have to be up earlier."

"You're right," she said, taking his hand to help her stand. "Can we meet you at the exposition tomorrow?" Dora asked her sister.

"Are you sure you won't be too tired?" Emma asked, concerned that she'd wanted to do too much.

Tim answered for her. "She should be back in time for a nap before we head over. We can meet you after lunch." *And I'll also be taking a nap*, he thought.

Jeremy poured himself a glass of wine and brought one to Emma. "Knowing Emma, we'll be at the Galerie des Machines or in the science pavilions," he said smiling at her.

"This's true—I also want to see the new telephone demonstration and lighting exhibits," said Emma.

Dora thought again of Lenora and Michael's fixation with that pavilion. "You might want to watch out for Lenora and Michael," she commented.

"We will," Emma promised.

Before the conversation could continue, Tim pulled on her arm and reminded her of the time.

"I'm being reminded we must go to bed. Goodnight," she said, allowing Tim to lead her to their room.

"Goodnight," Jeremy and Emma called, watching them leave.

Emma took a drink of her wine, "I enjoy baking, but not that much!"

He laughed. "I'd much rather wake up at a reasonable hour."

She thought about how many people were still arriving for the exposition. "So many people," she said, "in one place."

"Yes, the hotel has stayed busy."

"I noticed that. While I was downstairs, there was another large crowd checking in."

"People from all over the world are in Paris."

"Yes, I'm finding the people as interesting as the exposition," she said, drumming her fingers on her lips.

He knew that meant she may have seen something and asked, "What did you see?"

"I don't know," she said but continued to drum her fingers.

"What was it?" he asked, prodding her.

"It was a young girl of about sixteen and a companion—her mother, I believe," she said and didn't add more.

"What bothered you about them?"

"The girl seemed to be worried and anxious."

"It may have been the crowds or from traveling," he said reasonably. "Did the mother seem anxious?"

"No, I didn't see her directly. She was facing forward the entire time."

They let the silence settle around them as they finished their wine and went to bed.

Emma woke from a sound sleep and looked around the dark room. She heard Dora's voice next to her. "Emma, can you get up? I need to speak with you."

"Yes," she said softly and got up, careful not to disturb Jeremy. She followed Dora into the living room. She could see Dora was dressed and ready to leave for her bakery job.

Emma rubbed her eyes, "What's wrong?"

"Tim is sick. He needs to stay here."

"You can't go on your own," Tim said from their bedroom door. Emma could see him pulling up his suspenders. His face had no color and he seemed to be swaying on his feet.

"Tim, go back to bed. I'll take her," Emma said firmly.

He was conflicted but knew Emma could handle herself. "You don't mind?"

"Of course not," she assured him.

He started to object and opened up his mouth to say something. Immediately he regretted it. He covered his mouth with his hand and ran to the bathroom.

Dora bit her lip, watching him. "Should I stay?"

"No," Emma insisted. "You should go. I'm going to get changed. I'll be just a moment." She went back into her room and pulled out her skirt and top.

"What's up?" asked a sleepy Jeremy from the bed.

"Tim's sick, probably something he ate. He's staying here. I'll take Dora over to the bakery."

"Want me to go with you?" he asked and stated to sit up.

"No, you stay in bed. Someone should get some rest. I should be back soon."

"Okay." He didn't argue as he lay back and watched her pull her long hair into a ponytail.

"Don't forget your hat," he reminded her.

"Yes, I might need it." She checked it for her knife and, once she confirmed it was in place, she also attached her thigh scabbard. She grabbed her coin purse and her notebook and went to kiss Jeremy goodbye.

"Hey," he said, yanking her ponytail a bit, "stay safe, and don't take any unnecessary chances."

"Who, me? Would I do that?" she teased.

"Yeah, you would," he said. "Now promise me?"

"I promise," she said softly before she kissed him and headed to the living room. She closed the door softly and saw Dora waiting for her.

"Are we still okay on time?" Emma asked.

"Yes, but we should be going."

Dora saw the hat, "Are you expecting trouble?"

"Not expecting no, it's just a precaution," she said, placing the black hat on her head. Dora pulled on her coat and Emma her black coat, fashioned to look like a cape.

They walked to the door and out into the hallway. Once they were at the elevator, Emma pushed the call button. They heard it engage and, while they waited for it to arrive, Emma turned to Dora, "Did you get Tim back to bed?"

"Yes—it's probably something he ate. He seemed to get most of it out of his system."

"He should be better after some rest."

"I think so."

They got into the elevator and watched as the operator operated the lever that would take them to the lobby. Dora said, "I need to see if the doctor is available to go to our room."

"There should be one on call. Check with the desk manager in the lobby," Emma suggested as they exited the elevator.

Emma watched as her sister went to the desk; it was quiet and there was no line. It should only take her a moment. While she was doing that, Emma looked around the ornate lobby. The furniture, normally covered with people, could now be seen. It was a tasteful selection that went with the tile floors and painted walls.

She heard the elevator bell sound, then glanced toward it and saw the young girl from earlier in the night exit into the lobby. There was no companion with her this time, and she was obviously upset about something.

Emma hadn't noticed Dora was next to her and was startled when she heard her say, "We need to get going, Emma."

"Of course. On our way." As they turned to go out the doors, something hit them in the back, pushing them forward. Dora caught herself before hitting the ground and turned to check on Emma, who had fallen on her knees. Dora went to her and they both watched as the girl who ran into them didn't slow her pace as she sped out of the hotel. "Well, she certainly was in a hurry," said Emma dryly.

"Are you okay?"

"Yes, it was just unexpected," she said as she took Dora's hand. She straightened up and dusted herself off. "I hope she finds what she's looking for."

They stopped the bellman outside and asked for directions to the patisserie. He told them it was only a few blocks from the hotel. They put the event out of their minds and headed there. It was early morning and the chill made them sink into their coats as they walked arm and arm. Emma pulled out her portable gas light and used it to banish the shadows on the narrow roads. She paid attention to the path so she could make her way back to the hotel.

"Will you bring back some treats?" Emma asked, teasing.

"As many as I can carry," Dora promised.

"Wonderful. What time should I pick you up?"

"I should be on my way back about 8AM at the latest, but it'll be daylight. I'll be fine on my own."

"If, you're sure?" She wanted to be there if Dora wanted her, but sleep would be wonderful.

"I'm sure." They continued to walk and Dora asked, "Where will you and Jeremy be today?"

"The exposition. I want to spend a few more days exploring there and then I'd like to see the different arrondissements."

"Will Jeremy be spending some time with Abbey this trip?" asked Dora.

"I believe there are some people she'd like to introduce him to," Emma commented.

They got to the patisserie, and Dora noted, "Abbey said I'm to go to the back door." They went round the corner and found the door. Dora knocked, and it immediately opened. A tall man in white pants and a white baker's top with a bandana wrapped around his head.

"Bonjour," Dora said.

"Bonjour. You're Dora?" he asked in English.

"Je suis Dora et Emma," she said, indicating her sister.

"Will you be staying, Emma, to help us bake?"

"No, I'm here to make sure Dora arrives safety."

"I'll take care of her," he smiled.

She grinned, "Just be sure she brings some of the items you bake home!"

"She will," he said, grinning back.

"Bonsoir," Emma said.

He saw that Emma was alone and was concerned that she would be walking back by herself. "The area is more dangerous with so many people here for the exposition. Should you go by yourself?"

Dora knew her sister could take care of herself, "She'll be fine," she told the man.

Emma tipped her hat at them and made her way back down the alley. She pulled out her small gas light to help her find the way back. Some shadows seemed to move behind her, but she didn't think they were threatening. She kept going, listening intently to her surroundings. The shadow seemed to be keeping up with her. *Not a professional,* she thought. *The footsteps are loud.* They also started to speed up toward her. Rather than running from her pursuer, she let them get close and then she side-stepped and they ran past. Her pursuer noticed their mistake immediately and doubled back. She extinguished her light and stepped into the shadows. As she studied her pursuer from the shadows Emma noticed something over their face. *A mask* she thought. *Hmm.*

Her pursuer couldn't find her and looked to be increasingly frustrated. So much so that they pulled off the mask.

It's Michael! She stayed where she was until he left. *What was that about? Is he after me or Dora?*

She was thinking about the encounter as she entered the hotel lobby; the doorman opened the door for her. She nodded to him absently as she entered. Her eyes automatically searched for the girl who had knocked her down in such a rush earlier. The girl didn't seem to be around. *That's probably a good thing,* she thought.

She yawned and walked to the elevator, pushed the button, and waited for it to arrive.

Her time piece showed 4AM. *Still time to sleep,* she thought. She was too tired to try to make any connections between Michael and her other clues.

Emma got to the hotel room and opened the door quietly. Her eyes moved ward Dora and Tim's door. *How is he?* The door was cracked open and she pushed it until she saw him on the bed. He was there and snoring loudly. *He must be better,* she thought.

She smiled and went to hers and Jeremy's room. He was lying

on his back; she undressed quickly and crawled in, snuggling close to him.

"Hmm," he murmured. "Any concerns?"

"Dora got there okay. We can talk about my run-in in the morning," she murmured, going right to sleep.

That last comment shook him awake. "Wait! What run-in?" He started to sit up but realized she was out. It must not have been something that worried her too much or she'd have woken him to discuss it. He lay back down and went back to sleep.

Hours later, they heard a light knock on their bedroom door. Emma sat up, pushed her hair out of her face, and called out, "Yes?"

Tim stuck his head in, "I'm off to get Dora."

"Are you feeling better?" Jeremy asked.

"Much. Though now I feel hollow," the other man replied, rubbing his stomach.

Emma laughed. "I'd expect so. Make sure she brings home some of her work."

"I will," he promised. He closed the door and headed out, thinking of those pastries.

Emma fell back into Jeremy's arms, taking advantage of the time they had together.

"We need to talk," murmured Jeremy as Emma began running her hands over his body.

"I think there's something else that's much more fun that we could do instead," she said, raising her face to his for a long kiss.

"We still need to talk," he said, trying to be firm but not having any luck.

"Mmm, later."

Much later, as they were getting dressed Emma turned to him, "You'd better hurry. There'll be bread and croissants here soon."

Jeremy paused as he was buttoning his shirt, "You know we need to have that conversation now."

Emma wasn't ready to talk and walked over to Jeremy and started kissing him lightly to distract him.

He was enjoying the kissing but knew what Emma was doing. He backed away from her. "Emma, what did you mean this morning when you said 'run-in'?"

She opened her mouth to tell him, but there was another interruption—a knock on the door. "Tim must have forgotten his key," she said, relieved she didn't have to go into the details just yet.

"I'll get it," he said, finishing buttoning up his shirt. He pointed at her, "When I get back, you will talk to me. And no distractions. I'm on to you missy."

She smiled but didn't say anything.

Jeremy shook his head and headed into the living room to open the door. As he turned the knob, he said, "What, did you forget your key?"

Emma busied herself putting up her hair when she heard Jeremy call out, "Emma!"

"Is it breakfast?" she asked as she came out of the bedroom, pulling her hair into a ponytail.

"It's not breakfast." He stepped back and revealed who was at the door.

It was the girl from last night and she appeared to be about to fall!

"Jeremy!" Emma called. He caught her before the girl hit the floor.

He hefted the unconscious girl into his arms and looked at Emma. "Where do you want her?"

"For now, the couch." She indicated it with her hand. "Is she okay?" She didn't ask the question she wanted to. *Is she dead?*

"Looks like she's just unconscious," he said lying her on the couch, "What do you want to do?"

"Could you go downstairs and see if the doctor's available?"

"That's probably best. I'll go see if I can get him to come up."

He walked to the door and opened it, but was surprised again. This time, it *was* Tim and Dora.

"Hi," he said as he hurried past them

"Where are you going?" Dora asked. "We have breakfast." She and Tim held large boxes.

He turned back to them at the elevator, "Save some for me. We have a guest, and I need to go for the doctor."

"The doctor! Why?" Tim called.

"Is Emma okay?" asked Dora worriedly.

He didn't wait to answer them and got on the elevator.

"Come in and I'll explain," Emma called out to them from their hotel doorway.

Dora and Tim moved toward the room slowly and entered, not sure what to expect. They saw Emma had moved back to the couch and was sitting beside a young girl. She didn't appear to be awake.

Dora handed her packages to Tim and ran over. She knelt next to her, "Is she okay?"

"I'm not sure," Emma admitted. "She just showed up at the door and then passed out."

"Let me get a wet cloth for her head," Dora said, standing to retrieve one. Emma continued to stroke the girl's long, dark curly hair off of her forehead.

Dora brought over the wet cloth and placed it on her forehead. She looked over at Emma, "Poor little lost lamb. What do you think made her come to our door?"

"I'm not sure."

Dora looked closer, "Isn't that the girl who ran into us this morning?"

"I think so. I had seen her earlier last night with a woman who might be her mother."

"Why come to us?" asked Tim.

"I don't know, but she was upset last night."

There was a knock on the door. "We stopped and asked for

some tea and coffee to be delivered by room service." Tim said, "That should be them."

"I could use some tea," Emma admitted.

Tim got up and let room service in. They moved the tea and coffee to the dining table. He tipped them and they left. He and Dora busied themselves with coffee and tea. He also moved some of the pastries to a tray and brought them to the living area.

They started to eat when Jeremy came in a few moments later. He picked up a pastry before dropping into a chair. "They're sending the doctor up in a few minutes; the hotel's full and there's only one."

"It's probably the same one who came by here early this morning," said Tim, rubbing his stomach, remembering the pain from the night before.

They nodded and continued to eat their breakfast while they watched the girl sleep. A little while later, there was a knock on the door. Jeremy put down his coffee cup and stood, "I'll get it."

He came back into the room with a rather rotund man. The man's jacket was opened, showing his vest and shirt. He immediately headed over to Tim. "Bonjour, Tim. I thought we worked out your problem last night."

Tim held up his hand, "Oh no, doc, it isn't me this time." He motioned toward the couch.

That was when the doctor saw the unconscious girl. He walked over to her and knelt next to her. "What has happened here? Too much dessert, like our friend here?" he said as he referenced Tim.

Tim turned red as Emma answered, "We're not sure. She showed up in our doorway and passed out."

"Fainted, you say. Did she say anything before losing consciousness?"

"No," said Emma, wondering why he asked that question.

"She did say one word," Jeremy corrected.

"What was it?" asked Emma, not realizing she'd missed something.

"She said 'Emma,'" he commented.

"Well, I didn't expect that," Emma said in surprise.

"Do you know her?" asked Dora, looking at her sister.

Emma frowned, "No, not exactly. I've seen her in the lobby a few times. I've never spoken to her."

"I'll need to examine her," stated the doctor.

Dora turned to the group, "Let's give them some privacy." They agreed and moved to the dining room.

"You mentioned you saw her more than once?" Dora prompted.

"Yes, yesterday when I tried to catch Papa and Abbey, and again this morning when she ran into us."

"You've never talked to her?" Tim asked.

"No."

"How would she have known your name?" wondered Dora.

"No idea," Emma said honestly.

"Didn't you mention she was with someone?" asked Jeremy. *Normally, girls don't travel alone. There were exceptions,* he thought, looking at Emma.

"I did see someone. I had thought it was her mother, but I never had a clear view."

As they thought about that, the doctor called out, "You may come over."

"Will we disturb her?" asked Dora.

"No, she's in a deep sleep."

"Is there anything wrong with her?" Emma asked.

"No, I think it is just exhaustion. She'll need to sleep a long while before she can answer any questions. I'd put her somewhere comfortable, loosen her clothes, and let her rest."

"How long will she be out?" Emma asked.

"Probably a few hours," the doctor admitted. "I have to be going now. No rest for me."

"Will you come back after she's awake?" Dora inquired.

"Tell the front desk to send for me when she wakes," the doctor instructed as he walked to the door.

"Thank you, doctor, for a second visit," Tim said as he accompanied him out.

Dora, Tim, Emma, and Jeremy moved to the living room and stood over the girl. "Until we can find out who she is and why she wanted to see me, we should move her into the extra bedroom," Emma suggested.

"Agreed," Dora said.

Tim lifted the girl and moved her to the spare room. Dora and Emma pulled down the bedspread and sheets. Tim laid her down, and Emma and Dora slipped off her boots and loosened the top of her dress.

They looked at each other and Emma motioned to the door; they moved to the living room pulling the door closed so the girl could get some rest.

Emma saw Dora check the time, "You can rest if you need to. Jeremy and I'll keep watch," she said

"I could use a nap," her sister admitted.

Tim who was also looking a bit pale said, "I'll join you."

Jeremy and Emma settled on the vacated couch. He looked over at her teasingly and said, "I think there's more pastry."

She jumped up and he pulled her back; he wanted to get to the box first. He crossed the room to the box, she caught up quickly, laughing. He opened the box, "Wow, Dora brought more than bread and croissants." There was also decorative pastry; each had a label.

"I'm going try the eclairs," Emma said, reaching for the chocolate-covered pastry.

"I think I will, too," said Jeremy as he watched her take them from the box. He took the pastry Emma offered him, and they returned to the living room to sit down. As they bit into the pastry, the cream oozed out. "Yum!" she said.

"Definitely yum," he mumbled as he took another bite.

They ate slowly, enjoying the treat.

Jeremy finished his and wiped his mouth with a napkin. He looked at Emma, "What do you think about the girl? Why is she here?"

"Not much to think just now; though I do wonder where her companion is and where she was going in such a hurry last night."

"All questions that must wait until she awakens."

"Do we call the police?" she asked. They were in a foreign country and she didn't want to make any missteps.

"And report what? A girl shows up and collapses on our doorstep? No, no, I don't think so; at least not yet. Let's wait until she gets some rest and can talk to us."

"So, what do we do in the meantime?"

He reached past her and grabbed some books off the table. He tossed one to her and said, "Read."

She caught it and saluted him with it.

They relaxed and waited.

Several hours later, Tim and Dora woke and walked into the living room. "Has she stirred yet?" Dora asked with a wide yawn.

Emma glanced over to the door where the girl slept, "Not yet. We've checked on her, but there's been no movement. It may be hours yet."

Dora frowned. Emma noticed and said, "You don't have to stay. We'll wait for her to wake up."

"Are you sure?" Dora looked worried; this was their vacation and she didn't want to say cooped up in the hotel.

"Yes. Do you have plans?"

"Well, yes," her sister answered hesitantly. She glanced at Tim and then back at Emma.

"With Lenora and Michael?" Emma guessed, squinting her eyes a bit. Jeremy glanced over sharply.

"Yes," Dora admitted.

Tim squirmed a bit but said, "There was a note waiting for us at the front desk this morning. We picked it up on our way in. They said they missed our company and would like to see us this afternoon."

"But what about what we saw?" Emma asked. There was also the added complication of Michael. *Why was he following me this morning? What did he want?* She still didn't know what it might mean. There was no reason to bring it up now and further antagonize Dora and Tim.

"We've been getting to know them. We know about their families. I know Michael is worried about Lenora's brother. I've told her about the loss of our mother. I want to ask them, to their faces —What is going on." Dora wanted Emma to hear her out. She and Tim wanted to make the decision based on facts. Right now, they didn't have many.

"You're right. You know them better than we do," Emma conceded. She still had her concerns, thinking about Papa and Julian's conversation. "Where are you meeting them?"

"They want to meet at the Edison exhibit," Dora replied.

Again, thought Emma.

She saw Emma's look and said, "We'll be okay."

"I'd try to stay with other people. Don't be alone with them."

"We can do that," Tim said, thinking of the crowds at the exposition.

"Will you be leaving soon?" Emma asked.

"Yes, in a few minutes. Did you want us to get you some lunch before we go?" Dora asked, concerned that Emma and Jeremy wouldn't be able to leave the suite.

Emma moved her gaze to Jeremy's; he shook his head. She responded, "No I think we're okay. As long as one of us is here, we should be fine."

"As long as you're alright." started Dora.

"We are," she said firmly.

Dora and Tim got their jackets and hats and headed out to start their day at the exposition.

Jeremy and Emma watched as the door closed behind them. Jeremy turned a steady gaze to Emma, "Are you worried?"

"Yes, remember the run-in I mentioned?" she said.

Jeremy frowned, "You never did explain that."

"No, it was odd." She explained what had happened.

"What was he after?" Jeremy asked, confused.

"Who is what I'm wondering-me or Dora?"

"Why not tell them?" he asked.

"You heard them; they want the couple to tell them directly what they're involved in."

They sat in silence.

"We can't protect them from everything," Jeremy said finally.

"I know. I just don't normally have to worry about Dora. She's always so busy with the boarding house and family."

"Her only excitement is usually when we've included her in one of our cases. You know she has good instincts and Tim will always be with her," he reminded her.

"I know, you're right," she admitted.

They settled back down and waited, not only for the girl to wake up but also for Tim and Dora to return safely.

CHAPTER 10

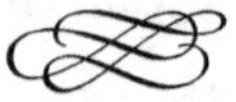

Tim and Dora walked down the hallway to the elevator. It was crowded with people heading to the same place they were. He inquired. "Stairs?"

"Yes, please." They found the door, descended quickly, and entered a crowded lobby.

"We should get lunch before we go over to the exposition," Tim suggested, anticipating the crowds.

They walked a few blocks, looking for an open café. They found one with outdoor seating.

"This is pretty," Dora commented, taking in the area around them.

He nodded and pulled her chair out for her. He sat and picked up the menu. "What would you like?" he asked. "Poulet?"

"Yes." She nodded. "Add carrots and a round bread."

The waiter came over and they ordered in broken French.

"Did we get the order right?" he asked as the waiter left.

"We'll see," she said with a smile. "I hate that Emma and Jeremy have to stay at the hotel,"

"Yes, who would have thought a girl would just show up at our door?"

Dora sent a side look to Tim. He laughed and said, "I know, I know. If a strange girl was going to show up anywhere, it would be at Emma and Jeremy's door. Those two are never short on adventure."

"I hope the girl will be okay," Dora said.

"Yeah, me too."

Their lunch was delivered; they viewed it happily and ate quickly.

Tim wiped his mouth and placed his napkin beside his empty plate. "That was good."

"It was," she said as she mimicked his movements.

He sat back, "I kind of missed seeing Michael and Lenora."

"Me, too," his wife admitted. "But Emma's right; we need to try not to be by ourselves, in case there *is* something to all of her observations."

"I'm hoping this is just a big misunderstanding. I like them," he said.

"Me, too."

Tim paid the bill, stood, and offered her his hand. She took it and stood. They walked outside and found a cab to take them to the exposition. "Where do we start?" he asked.

"They said the Edison exhibit."

"They really have an interest in the electricity exhibits. It seems we're always being pulled there."

"That's one of Jeremy and Emma's concerns," she murmured.

"That's true, but people have interests; maybe this is theirs," he commented.

"The exhibit is the talk of the exposition," she agreed.

They were quiet, listening to the rattle of the carriage as they made their way to their destination. She reached out and gripped his hand; he squeezed it back.

The carriage pulled up to the entrance, they got down, and headed to the science pavilion.

"Remind me of the location of the science pavilion?" he asked in exasperation.

"Just a moment," Dora said. They moved to the side to let other people pass and she pulled out the map. She pointed to the building to the right of them, "It's here."

"Okay, let's head that way," he said.

"Maybe we can get them to go to other areas. I heard there's a furniture area. I'd love to see it," Dora said hopefully.

"If not, we can break away from them and see it by ourselves." Tim asked, "Would you like that?"

"Yes, I would," she replied softly.

They headed toward the building.

As they entered, they looked around for the other couple. Dora saw that Tim was frowning and asked, "Is something wrong?"

"No, I just saw Lenora, she appeared to be upset."

"Where did you see her?" she asked, concerned for her friend.

"Over there." He motioned to the far wall with his hand. "Wait a minute. I see Michael. We can check with him."

"You do that. I'm going to see if I can find her."

"Okay."

He leaned down and gave her a brief kiss. She squeezed his hand and headed toward the wall where he had seen her. There was a door there, opened slightly. She reached her hand into it and opened it enough to go inside. "Lenora?" she called.

Dora heard a sound. She listened closely and called again, "Lenora!" When she got no response, she stepped into the dark room and headed toward the sound. Something caught her foot, and she fell to her knees. Picking herself up, she tried to find the lights. Before she could go too far, she felt something on her ankle again. She reached down and felt a hand.

"Oh my." The hand felt rough with calluses and seemed to belong to a man. "Let me find a light." She tried to remember where the lights were during their tour. *The door*, she thought, and turned back, trying to avoid stepping on the man. She opened the door to bring in the outside light and found the switch. She flipped it and turned toward the person on the floor. It was Julian!

"Julian!" she called frantically and ran over to him. She knelt and realized he was bleeding from his chest. She put her hands on it to stop the flow of blood. "Hold on Julian, you'll be okay. I know you will."

She looked around desperately and said, "I need to get someone to help you."

His hand gripped hers and he said in a low voice, "Wait, Dora. I need to tell you something!"

She had to lean in to hear his low whisper.

"Bomb, Cervantes," With that, his eyes widened and he went limp.

"Julian! No! *No!*" Dora screamed, putting her bloodied hands on his face.

"You just had to leave him alive."

Dora went still as she heard a man's voice from the door. She removed her hands and sat back on her knees, stunned. It was Michael!

"He did die," Lenora said defensively, stepping from behind him. The look on her face was not one Dora had seen before. This was not the same woman she had gotten to know and called friend.

"But not soon enough," said Michael. "He was able to tell her something."

"Really? What did he tell you?" she asked Dora.

All that Dora could think was, *Bomb, he had said bomb and Cervantes.* Her eyes wide, she said nothing as she stared at them. The hand she absently raised to scratch her cheek left bloody streaks behind.

"She isn't going to answer. Instead of arguing with me, grab her!" Michael demanded.

Lenora did as she was told and took Dora by the arm, trying to haul her up.

Dora felt like she was swimming through the air.

At that moment, Tim walked in, "Dora, I couldn't find Michael…" He stopped when he saw Michael with a bloody Dora. "What happened? Are you okay?" He didn't notice Julian on the floor in his rush to Dora's side.

"Stop right there," Lenora demanded. She had a gun, and it was pointed at Tim.

He followed her direction and stopped just before he got to Dora. "I don't understand," Tim said, shaking his head as he tried to take in everything.

Tim's appearance helped pull Dora out of her fog. She spoke up and filled in some details. "Tim, they killed Julian. He's there on the floor."

His gaze followed her pointed hand and saw the body prone on the floor. "Julian?" he asked incredulously. Tim stared at the body, how had he missed that? He looked back at her. "Is that blood on you?"

"I'm not hurt," Dora said to him, knowing he was in the same fog she had just exited. "It's Julian's blood."

Tim had more questions and when he opened his mouth, Lenora snapped, "That's enough! We need to get out of here before he's found."

"A large part of this is your fault," Michael told her.

"My fault? How is this my fault?" Lenora demanded.

"Wasn't he supposed to be electrocuted?"

"It got complicated," she said. "I had no choice." She paused and studied Dora. "Clean her up. She's conspicuous."

Michael pulled out his handkerchief and roughly wiped Dora's face.

"Stop that!" Tim said. He stepped toward Dora, not wanting to see his wife get hurt.

"You can stop there," Lenora said pointing her gun at him. She said to Michael, without taking her gun off of the couple, "We need to go."

Michael looked helplessly at Dora's blood-soaked hands. Lenora got exasperated with him, "Dora, put your hands in your pockets." Dora did as she was told and continued to watch the two people who were their friends just hours ago.

"Let's go," Lenora said, waving her gun at them.

Tim didn't move, "Where's the guard? Why wasn't he at the door?"

"Oh, you don't have to worry about him," she said and glanced toward the wall. Tim's eyes followed hers and found the guard. He was slumped on the wall.

"Is he?" Tim asked.

"He is," she confirmed. She gazed at Michael and said smugly, "*He* was electrocuted."

Tim wanted to fight back and started to make a move. She grabbed his hand and shook her head, knowing what he was thinking.

Michael said to Tim, "I will kill her if you make any sudden moves."

Tim reluctantly nodded his head.

They left the area and took one of the many exits out of the exposition. The crowds made their movements harder, to control Tim they kept an arm around Dora, with a gun at her back. They had a carriage waiting for them. They climbed in and Tim sat next to Dora. "We're not heading toward the hotel," he muttered, watching the scenery go by.

"No," she said as they got further away from the exposition grounds.

When they arrived at their destination, they were told to get out.

They climbed down and entered what appeared to be a very large apartment building. Michael led them down the hall to an apartment on the first floor, with Lenora following closely behind. They entered a small room with a kitchen on the far wall. The furniture was older and was more patches than the original fabric. A small table and four chairs were in place near the kitchen.

"Wash up," she told Dora. Once her hands were clean, she ordered them, "Sit!" Lenora said, indicating the chairs around the table. They did as they were told, wondering how this was going to play out.

"Julian told me what you were planning to do," Dora told the duo boldly.

"You talked to him," Tim muttered.

"Just before he died," she muttered back.

"What did he say?" Lenora demanded.

"I know about the bomb."

Tim started at this statement. "Bomb? What bomb?"

"So, Julian got talkative, did he?" Lenora asked.

"Yes," said Dora, not sharing anything more.

"It's probably good that you know; that way, you don't accidentally share something you shouldn't."

"You don't think we're going to help you with this?" Tim asked incredulously.

"Yes, I do. At least until we have time to place the bomb," Lenora said.

"Why are you doing this? There must be a reason," said Dora.

Michael spoke up, "Electricity is dangerous and has no place in our society."

"You're one of those extremists against electricity?" Tim said. They didn't know these people at all. "Was it all fake? The family stories, the sharing?"

"We're not extremists!" Lenora shouted.

"Lenora," Michael cautioned.

She listened to him and said more calmly, "We're not extremists. Electricity kills; if a person touches it, they could die."

"Doesn't that make you a hypocrite?" Dora asked, "You killed two people in your effort to prove electricity is dangerous."

"I'll do what I have to. I'll prove that this technology cannot be utilized safely. And," she said, looking at them both, "you will both be active participants in our efforts."

"You can't make us do that," stated Dora.

"Really?" the other woman said, turning the gun on her.

"Do you want more deaths on your conscience?" Dora asked.

"Oh, I don't think I'll have to kill you, I have something else planned," Lenora pulled something out of her pocket. She held it up. It was a red ribbon and a lace hairpin.

Tim and Dora knew instantly what she was holding. "Lottie! You have Lottie!" Dora shouted. Tim wanted to respond in the same manner, but they had to hear more.

"I do and if you do not do what I want…" Lenora said, letting the words hang in the air.

"Where is she? Is she in Paris?" Tim asked in an oddly calm voice.

"She's in a safe location. That is all you need to know for now," stated Michael.

"Why us? Why involve us in this?" asked Dora desperately.

Lenora laughed a bit hysterically, "What better way than to have the great engineer's daughter help us take a closer look at how the security is set up around the electrical transformers?"

"Papa?" questioned Dora.

"Yes. Who else would have access to areas where regular people cannot go? You, as his daughter, can get access."

"We won't help you kill more people," Dora said, knowing she couldn't do what they asked.

"I think you will. In fact, I'm so sure you will that I'm letting you go back to the hotel," Lenore commented.

Michael said, "What!"

She explained, "They're going to find the bodies and we may need an alibi. You will provide that for us, in case there are any questions," Michael nodded, understanding her reasoning.

Emma, she thought. *We can get help with this.*

Lenora read her easily. "No, you won't tell Emma. You will

follow our instructions to the letter or we'll have to do something we don't want to do," she said holding up the ribbon again, to remind her.

"Will you follow our direction?" asked Michael, ready to get them out of the apartment.

Tim knew the best thing for them was to agree. "We agree," he answered.

"But..." stuttered Dora, ready to speak up again.

"We agree," Tim commented again and looked her in the eyes.

Finally understanding, Dora said, "Yes, we agree."

"We'll transport you back to your hotel," Michael said.

"Don't bother," Tim said. "We'd rather walk."

Lenora reluctantly lowered the gun and didn't stop them from exiting the apartment. Once they were on the stoop, Dora looked at Tim, "Which way?" She hadn't paid attention on their way there.

"We need to head this way," he said, indicating the left. They walked for a while and stopped when they came to a park. "Would you like to go in?" he asked.

She nodded, keeping her head down, not saying anything. They went in and she started to cry uncontrollably. He guided her over to an empty bench near the fountains. As they sat, she continued to cry. With tears in his eyes. *Lottie,* he thought, hugging Dora tightly.

"Do they have her?" she asked.

"They showed us the ribbon and lace that Emma made her. Lottie kept it with her always," he said in a low voice.

That made her cry harder; his face was wet as he continued to hold her tightly. They sat there for a long time until, eventually, their tears dried up.

"We can't tell the family," Tim said wiping his eyes and pulling away from Dora.

"I know," she said miserably. "What are Lenora and Michael going to involve us in?"

"It appears to be murder. Maybe multiple murders."

"The bomb will kill more than a few people," she agreed. They both thought about how many people were attending the exposition.

"We can't just wait for them to tell us what to do," he said, thinking about how to move forward.

"No, no, you're right," she said and pulled out a tissue. She held it to her nose, "What are we going to do?"

That glimmer of determination reminded him of Emma when she had a new case. They were more alike than people realized. "I guess we ask what would Emma do?"

"Pull out her notebook and start making plans," Dora said, thinking of her sister.

"Well, we don't have one—let's think. What would be first on the list?"

"The hotel! They're staying at our hotel!"

"Yes, we can head there first."

"What do we do when we get there?"

"We need to get into their room and find some clues."

"What kind of things are we looking for?"

"I don't know," he admitted, moving his gaze from hers as he tried to hold his emotions together.

"Tim, we'll get through this," she said, taking his hand, tears filling her eyes again.

He didn't say anything but squeezed her hand. They couldn't just sit. Tim stood, "I think we need to head over now and get there before they can destroy anything that proves they're related to the murders in the transformer station."

"Could those be accidents and not on purpose?" She was grasping at straws. How could they have been so wrong about them? They were supposed to be their friends.

"Yesterday, if you'd asked me the same question, I'd have said no. But today, when I saw Lenora's face..." Tim said, his voice trailing off.

"I didn't recognize her at all," said Dora still dazed by it all.

"And even if the guard was an accident, Julian seemed very deliberate, they wanted to use him to prove a point."

"We still don't know what their relationship was with him and why he was the one they chose to show the dangers of electricity."

Tim nodded at her statement.

"You know," she said, thinking, "he might have been some type of investigator."

"He did remind me of Emma, the way he always had questions and turned up when least expected."

"We should go," she said finally.

Tim took Dora's hand in his and went to find a cab. They found one easily; there were many around to transport people to and from the exposition. They asked to go directly to the hotel. "Could you stop about a block away, please?" she asked the driver. "We should be carrying something. Some food, maybe flowers."

Tim nodded, "Props, to help with our story."

"Exactly," she said. "The patisserie I worked at this morning, let's run by there."

When they arrived, they climbed down, paid the driver, and went quickly to get croissants and baguettes. The florist was on their way back and they bought a bundle of flowers.

They carried their items, not saying anything, and headed directly to the desk to try to get the room number. "Bonjour," the hotel clerk greeted.

"Bonjour," they responded.

Dora smiled, trying to put him at ease. "We're trying to locate our friends. They asked us to meet them at their room for a snack."

"Can you give me their names?" he asked and smiled back at her.

"Lenora and Michael Cervantes," she supplied.

"Yes, of course. Here it is," he said, pulling a card out of the file.

"They're in room 412. It's up the elevator and to the right. I hope you enjoy your pastry."

"Thank you," she said, smiling at him again. They headed to the elevator and, once boarded, they stood quietly, not wanting to say anything in front of the elevator operator.

The doors opened and they headed to the right. Almost immediately, they saw the housekeepers in that area. They stepped back into the shadows to plan.

"What if they've already been to their room?" she asked worriedly.

Tim saw a maid enter the hallway from one of the rooms and he put his hand up to Dora's mouth. "Shh."

They watched quietly as the maids entered the next room to the right and left the cart in the hallway.

"Stay here," he said and slipped behind the cart to see what room they were working on. They appeared to have a few more still to clean before Lenora and Michael's.

He waved at her to walk to the room. He went back to the cart quickly and grabbed the keys, located on a hook. He took them and tossed them to her. She caught them deftly, opened the door, and tossed them back. She went inside and Tim immediately came in behind her. He put out the privacy sign and shut the door softly behind them.

"What would Emma look for..." Dora muttered to herself, taking in the room. "Trash," she said, spotting it.

Tim continued to study the room for letters and anything paper. "The desk," he said He went over to it and started opening the drawers.

Dora directed, "Okay, let's start there; I'll get the trash." She dumped the trash quickly on the floor. "Well, they've been eating a lot of chocolates," she said as she pushed the wrappers out of the way. "What is this? A brochure?" she murmured. She unfolded it. "Ah-ha!"

"What is it? Did you find something?" Tim asked. He dropped the papers he was holding and walked over to her.

"Remember the anti-electrical people Julian mentioned to Emma and Jeremy?" she asked, holding up the cartoon.

"Yes, I remember. We heard about them—are they part of that group?"

"This's why they wanted us here. You heard them earlier."

"You think they paid for this trip?" asked Tim.

"It makes sense. *IF* they took Lottie, she's the leverage to get us to do what they want. The papers on the desk—anything there?" Dora asked.

Tim went back and pulled out a letter he had found. He said, "Just this. It mentions… a woman named Janna who is holding something for them."

"Could it be?" she asked, excited to have found something.

"Let's not get our hopes up," he cautioned.

She walked over to him, "Does it give a location or a return address?"

"Yes, in the 3rd Arrondissement."

"So, we go there next and talk to this Janna."

"Just like that?" he asked, "You think it will be that easy?"

"No. I don't think it will be that easy, but it may help us figure out what her role is and if she has Lottie. Tim, what if she does?" she asked, reaching out a shaking hand toward him.

He took it, "I don't know. But if Lottie is there, we'll get her back."

"If not?" Tears welled in her eyes.

"Then we continue investigating. And in the meantime, we do as they ask."

"We can't allow anyone to get hurt because of us!"

"NO!" he lowered his voice and said, "No, of course not. We have some time to figure this out. If you'd like to go back to our room while I go over…"

She interrupted, her tone firm. "Tim, I'm coming with you."

He smiled, "I wouldn't have it any other way." He pulled Dora into his arms and gave her a long slow kiss. As they parted, he offered her his hand and she took it. They walked together to the door and picked up the flowers and pastries on the way. He held up his other hand, slowly opened the door, and stuck out his head. He pulled back in and said in a low voice, "The maids haven't finished the room next door yet."

She nodded and removed the privacy sign as they slipped out and locked the door behind them. They walked casually down the hall, back to the elevator, and pushed the call button.

It arrived and, when it opened, they were surprised to see Jeremy standing there.

As they boarded, he asked, "Hey, are you back from the exposition already? We weren't expecting you until much later."

They avoided his eyes and Tim replied, "No, we need to do a few more things today. We aren't coming back to the room just now."

Jeremy frowned, "Why were you on this floor? Did you get off in the wrong location?"

"No, no, we wanted to go to Lenora and Michael's room," Tim said truthfully. He just didn't mention they weren't there when they went in.

It was their turn to ask the questions. "Are you going downstairs?" Tim asked.

"Yes, I need to get a few things."

"How is the girl?" Dora asked, finding her voice. She wanted so badly to tell him what might be happening to Lottie. He and Emma could figure this out faster than them. Not thinking she took a step toward Jeremy. Tim intercepted her and pulled her to him.

"She woke briefly and told us her name and her room number. I'm going to get her clothes and things."

"Good idea. She'll want those when she fully wakes," Dora said softly.

The conversation stopped when the doors opened. They entered the lobby, and Jeremy turned to them both.

"Is everything okay?" he asked.

"Of course. Why wouldn't it be." Time replied.

"I don't know. Something seems to be up with you two."

"We're fine," Dora said.

Jeremy wanted to push the issue but instead said, "You know if something's wrong, you can tell me and Emma."

"We know that," Dora assured him not looking into Jeremy's eyes. She felt that if he saw her eyes, he would know what was going on. If that happened, he would want to involve Emma and himself, go against the directions they were given.

Jeremy finally decided they weren't going to tell him what was going on. "Okay," he said, "We'll see you later." He headed to the desk.

They waved and headed outside. Tim pulled her to the side of the building. He took the flowers and food from her hands and threw them in a trash can. "You were going to tell him," he accused her.

"I wanted to," she admitted, staring down at her hands now empty hands. She clinched them tight.

He saw her anger had overridden her worry, but he had to make her see reason. He tilted her head up to him. "I'd like to tell them also, and I'd like to go to the police and let them handle this. But this is not something we can get help with. *WE* have to do this on our own, for Lottie," he stressed.

She was quiet for a long time, thinking about everything. She'd been thinking about herself and not Lottie. "You're right. I'm glad you stopped me. We need to do this on our own, for Lottie."

He pulled her to him in a tight hug. They slowly moved apart, knowing they must take the next steps. She asked, "What's the plan?"

"We don't go straight there. We investigate the area first."

She nodded and they walked to a nearby cab and asked to be taken to the address Tim had found. The carriage ride was tense and they huddled together. When they arrived, he helped her out after they paid the driver. They hadn't been in this arrondissement before. It had older buildings and stone roads. They walked around the building they were investigating. Dora commented, "It's a church."

"Or a school," said Tim, watching a group of children come down the stairs.

"Well, do we go in and ask for Janna?" inquired Dora. He nodded. She was apprehensive but followed his lead.

They made their way up the stairs, and Tim pulled the large, heavy double door open. They entered an area that had many closed doors. "Where do we start?"

As they were walking by, a young girl came out of one of the doors and Dora took a chance and asked, "Are you, Janna?"

"Yes, can I help you?" Suddenly, a baby crying could be heard from the room she had exited. "Tim!" Dora exclaimed.

He ran to the door and in the direction of the crying.

Janna looked wildly to the left and right and ran off. Dora ran after her. She chased her down small hallways and into a larger room. Dora stopped and realized the woman had just disappeared. *Where did she go?*

"Dora!" Tim called. "Where are you?"

"I'm here!" she called back. She ran back to him and asked, "Did you find her? Was it Lottie?"

He was angry and frustrated, "There were children, but Lottie wasn't one of them. Were you able to talk to Janna?"

"No, she just disappeared. This place is a maze," she said, observing the stone walls and many doors.

"We need to find an administrator; there must be someone in charge here," he insisted.

"Let's go to the sanctuary," she said. They went toward the large doors surrounded by glass. She peered in and said, "This must be it." The pews were still in place and the altar was set for services.

Tim pulled the door open and held it for her to enter. "That must be the man in charge," he said, indicating a man in a black suit with a white collar. The man raised his hand and walked toward them.

"Bonjour," they said as he neared.

He held out his hand toward them and said, "Bonjour, comment puis-je vous aider?" *Hello, how may I help you?*

Tim held out his hands to take hers and said, "Jes suis Dora et Tim Flannigan."

"I understand English, if it's easier for you. I am Pastor Franc," he said in a kindly manner as he released Tim's hand and took Dora's.

"Thank you. We have something important and private to discuss with you," said Tim in a firm voice.

"Let us go over to a quieter area." He indicated the alcove by the sanctuary. They nodded and followed him.

They entered a more enclosed space. He turned up the gas lights and asked them to sit on the low wooden benches. "Pastor, what is this place? A church, a school?" asked Dora, wanting to put him at ease.

"It's sometimes a church, a school, or whatever the community needs."

"You have employees working here?" asked Tim.

"Volunteers," he supplied. "We don't have a large operating budget; we make do with what we can."

Tim finally asked the one question they wanted answered. "Is a young woman named Janna one of your employees?"

That question seemed to give him pain. He stood and seemed to be saying a prayer before answering.

"You know her," stated Dora, her voice soft but accusing.

"I do. She's my daughter. What is she involved in?" They could hear the implied "now" at the end of the sentence. It was apparent this wasn't the first time he'd had this conversation.

"We believe she's part of an abduction of our small daughter," Tim said bluntly.

He frowned. "You're from America?" he asked.

"Yes," Dora answered.

"Did you bring your child here with you?" He seemed to be trying to put the pieces together.

"No, she was taken in Chicago."

The pastor shook his head, "Janna hasn't been out of Paris in a few months. Are you sure she's involved?"

"We think she's involved with a couple, Lenora and Michael Cervantes. They're American."

"I do not know those names. Can you describe them to me?" Janna's father asked, trying to help.

Dora started. "Michael's about this tall." She used Tim to measure, putting her hand on his shoulders. "He has lost most of his hair."

Tim interrupted. "There's still some in the back, dark brown," he supplied. "And I believe he's in his late thirties. He has some weight around his middle. She's about the same age."

Dora stated, "Lenora has reddish-blond hair."

That last part seemed to spark something in him. "Yes, they're familiar. I've seen them here, but they have not been introduced to me."

"When did you see them last?" asked Tim expectantly.

"Yesterday," the other man admitted. "They were speaking with Janna and they seemed upset with her."

"Do you know all of the children in school here?" Tim asked.

"We have so many," he said regretfully. "My daughter runs the program."

"Is there anyone who helps her, someone who might know the children brought here?" Dora asked, trying to be hopeful.

"Yes, Marcella. Would you like to meet her now?"

"Yes, please," Dora answered for them.

"What are you thinking?" Tim asked in a low voice as they followed the man.

"I'm thinking I can give them a sketch of Lottie and see if they've seen her. We need to know if she's in Paris."

They followed him to the room Janna had come out of. It was a long, narrow hallway with several doors to the left and right. The pastor pulled open the door and a young woman in the room screamed and pointed at Tim.

"Du calm. Leur enfant est porté disparu et Janna pourrait être impliquée," the pastor said with a raised voice.

"Non non, elle ne ferait jamais de mal à un enfant." She shook her head to prove the point.

The pastor turned back to Tim and Dora. "What is the child's name?"

"Lottie," they supplied together.

"Son nom est Lottie et elle a les cheveux blonds rougeâtres."

She started to wring her hands and said, in fast French, "Janna a mentionné son nom. monsieur je ne l'ai jamais vue, je vous le promets."

He told them, "She has heard the name from Janna, but there hasn't been a child brought here

"I don't know whether to be relieved or more worried," Tim muttered to Dora.

"Do you have some paper? I'd like to give you a drawing of Lottie. That way, if you may have seen her but they called her by another name," said Dora.

The pastor left them and returned with some paper and a pencil and handed them to her.

Tim looked around for a place for her to sketch. He saw a small table and chair and said, "Over here." She sat in the chair he pulled out and began sketching quickly on the paper. Within a few moments, she finished. She held it for a moment, fighting tears. *My baby.*

"Dora?" Tim prompted softly.

"Yes," she said, "here it is." She handed it to him.

He didn't look at it, he needed a clear head. He handed the drawing to Marcella. "Could you ask her if she's seen this child? It would mean so much to us."

She nodded, albeit reluctantly, and took the paper. She examined it. "Non! Je ne l'ai pas vue! Cet enfant n'est pas venu ici."

The pastor interpreted. "She has not seen her. This child has not been here."

Dora responded to this by taking Tim's hand in hers and asked the pastor, "Can you ask if she knows the couple?"

He looked at Marcella and asked, "Êtes-vous là où elle pourrait être?"

Her eyes were cast down and didn't respond.

The pastor eyed her sternly. "Vous devez me dire!"

"She'll have gone to a building, in the arrondissement—that is where they meet," she admitted in halting English.

"How do you know?" Tim asked.

"I was there once," Marcella said.

"Have you been back?" Janna's father asked.

"No, they are too revolutionary for me. I don't understand why they're so against new things."

"What types of new things?" asked Dora.

"Electricity."

Tim and Dora looked at one another. It was bigger than they'd thought. How many people were involved?

"Where do they meet?" Tim asked.

She answered, "In a basement at St. Thomas Place." She gave them the address.

They immediately turned, planning to go straight there. Janna's voice stopped them.

"They will not be there now," she said slowly.

"When will they be there?" Dora inquired rather desperately, her patience evaporating with every moment they believed Lottie was in danger.

"They meet tomorrow at 9PM."

Tim said to the Pastor, "We need to ask you not to say anything to them. It might jeopardize our daughter's life."

"We'll honor your request and I'll find Janna and question her."

Tim gave them their hotel to contact them with any further information.

"Thank you."

They headed out and Dora said, "Oh, Tim, we still don't know anything."

"We have a lead, and we'll go to that meeting tomorrow," he promised.

"What if they see us?"

"I am not sure," he admitted. "It is our only lead."

CHAPTER 11

BACK AT THE HOTEL—PATRICE

few hours had passed when Jeremy and Emma heard something coming from the room where the mysterious girl slept. Jeremy glanced at Emma, "Finally," he said. She stood and walked with him to the bedroom door. He knocked lightly and pushed it open.

They found the girl sitting up on the bed. Her eyes widened when she saw Emma and Jeremy enter the room. "It appears that she may stay awake this time," commented Jeremy with a twisted smile. The previous time she had awakened, she had only said Emma's name again before losing consciousness.

Before they realized what the girl was doing, she had thrown off the covers and ran toward Emma. Jeremy started to react, but Emma held up her hand to stop him. She caught the running girl in her arms and held her tight. "You wanted to see me?" she asked.

"You have to help me!" the girl said frantically.

Emma held her for a moment, then pushed her back, "Why don't we move into the living room, sit down, and you can tell me what you need help with."

That seemed to calm the girl, and she followed Emma into the living room. She continued to hold Emma's hand in a tight grip.

The three sat. Emma held onto her hand, "What's your name?"

"Patrice Lanier, my mum is Catherine Lanier."

"You know my name," said Emma, "and this is Jeremy."

Jeremy leaned toward them and asked the first question, "Why did you come to our room?"

"For Emma," Patrice said, looking at Emma beseechingly. "I was told you were a brilliant detective, and I need someone to help me find my mother."

"Your mother? Was she the woman who accompanied you at check-in?" Emma asked.

"Yes." That confirmed Emma's guess.

"And you said she's missing? When did you see her last?" Jeremy asked.

"Last night. She got sick and I went down to the lobby to get a doctor."

"Was that where you were in such a rush too early this morning?" Emma asked.

"Yes, the man at the desk gave me an address to go get the doctor," she explained.

Emma frowned and moved her gaze back to Patrice. "The doctor should have been at the hotel. It's strange they asked you to go get him."

"Was he at the address you were given?" asked Jeremy.

"No, that was odd also. When I finally arrived at the address, there was no one there."

"What did you do then?" Emma asked, already caught up in the story.

"I came back, and I went to the desk to find out if I had the wrong address," Patrice explained.

"What happened then?" Emma asked.

"The man at the desk was different than the one who gave me the information about the doctor. The question seemed to confuse him and he said the doctor could be available from his room at the hotel. He said there was no outside doctor."

"And?" Emma prompted when the girl went quiet.

Patrice pulled her hands out of Emma's and started to wring them. "They sent someone for him and we headed upstairs. When we got to mum's room, it was locked."

"Where was your key?" Jeremy asked. He already knew part of this story. When he went down to get the girl's clothes, the desk clerk said she did not have a room there. He had hoped it was because the room was under the mother's name.

"I had it with me; it didn't work. We tried it several times. We also knocked, but Mama didn't come to the door."

"Was it the right room?" Emma asked, thinking Patrice had been so tired that she went to the wrong room.

She frowned. "So much of last night ran together, I thought the same thing. We went back downstairs and told the clerk. He checked for our room and he said I didn't have one in that hotel."

"No room?" Emma murmured. *Is this girl just confused and lost or is there a mystery to be solved?* "Jeremy, could you go inquire at the desk?"

"I can do that," Jeremy said and stood. "Could I talk to you for a second?" he asked Emma.

"I'll be right back. Will you be okay?" Emma asked Patrice.

Patrice was uncertain but said in a shaking voice, "Yes."

Emma nodded and stood to follow him to the door.

"Is she at the right hotel?" he asked. "Her story sounds incredulous."

Emma commented, "She was in line for a room with her companion when I saw her last night."

"They're very crowded," he murmured. "I hope it's just a mix-up. I'll also notify the doctor she's awake."

"Good idea," she replied. She watched him leave and closed the door behind him.

She returned to the living room and stood in front of Patrice. "Would you like something to drink and a pastry?"

Patrice nodded.

"Stay here. I'll bring it to you."

She returned with the pastry and some water.

Patrice ate the offered pastry and her cheeks flushed rose with pleasure.

CHAPTER 12

$\mathcal{J}$eremy headed down the stairs and exited into the lobby. The check-in line was long, as usual, and he avoided it and went to the far side of the desk. A young man walked up and asked, "Bonjour, may I help you?"

"Bonjour. Yes, can I speak to the manager, please?"

The clerk studied him, "Yes, Monsieur. I'll get him for you." He waved for another clerk to take his spot at the desk. He spoke in a low voice to him and headed into the back room.

Moments later, another man accompanied him out of the back room and went directly to Jeremy. He was older and appeared to be a senior member of the staff. "Bonjour," he greeted.

"Bonjour," Jeremy responded.

"Monsieur?" The manager asked.

"Tilden."

"Monsieur Tilden, you wish to talk to me?"

"Yes, I wanted to ask you about a guest."

"My answer will depend on what information you're requesting," he explained.

Jeremy nodded, understanding his limitations. "Of course. Her name is Patrice Lanier and her mother's name is Catherine Lanier."

The manager frowned and turned to the young man next to him, "Isn't that the young woman who said she has a room?"

The young man answered, "Yes, first she accused me of sending her to the wrong doctor then she demanded we take her to her mother."

"What was your response?" asked Jeremy.

He looked over at his manager, who nodded for him to answer. "I asked her for the room number and accompanied her there."

"What did you find?"

"An empty room and no mother," the clerk replied. "When it appeared that her mother wasn't in the room, I couldn't calm her down. She kept insisting that I had done something to her mother. I had planned to call the police if she didn't leave the hotel."

He asked, "Can I see your book from that night?"

The manager answered that question, "Of course, follow me."

He and Jeremy walked over to where people were checking in and the manager retrieved a large book. He placed it in front of Jeremy and flipped the pages until he found Monday night. He turned the book toward Jeremy and showed him. "She isn't listed. Neither of them is in the book."

The young clerk who had stood nearby spoke up, "That is what I told her."

"I understood Miss Lanier had two rooms. Both singles," Jeremy said.

"That is what she said."

"What about *her* room?"

"It was also empty," the young clerk confirmed.

Jeremy thought about that, "Could you check and see when the current people moved in?" he requested

"Yes." The manager turned the book back to himself and checked. "Those rooms were taken that next morning."

"Okay, thank you."

"Monsieur, will you make sure she doesn't cause concern in our lobby again? It was very disruptive."

Jeremy understood the man's dilemma; this was a very nice hotel. "I think we can manage that. Can we have the doctor sent to our room?" He confirmed his room number and headed back upstairs He opened the door and saw Patrice. "Feeling better?" he asked her.

"Somewhat," she commented quietly, afraid to ask what he had found out.

"I contacted the doctor to come up."

"For what reason?" Patrice asked, losing the color that had finally entered her face.

Emma reached over to her, "Your health must be considered. We can't find your mother if you're not able to participate. Do you understand?"

Patrice frowned; her experience with doctors at that facility had not been a pleasant one, but she understood their reasoning. "I'll see him."

A little while later, there was a knock on the door. Jeremy went to answer it and brought the same doctor who had attended her earlier into the room. His face was cheerful. "It's nice to see you awake, young lady," he said, looking at Patrice.

"Yes," Emma said, answering for the girl.

Patrice asked in a confused manner, "Who are you?"

"I'm the doctor," he explained kindly.

She frowned and shook her head vehemently. "You weren't there when I went to get you last night. I drove a long way to find you."

"Why would you have gone somewhere other than the hotel to get me?"

"No, that can't be right," Patrice muttered, sounding more confused.

The doctor commented, "I need to examine you."

"You won't leave me, will you?" Patrice said as she grabbed Emma's hand and held it tightly.

Emma patted it and reassured her. "I will stay with you. Why don't you let the doctor examine you?"

The girl nodded and quieted down. Emma looked around, "Why don't we move to your room?"

The doctor said, "Yes, of course. I'll follow you."

They moved to Patrice's room to begin the examination.

Jeremy remained in the living room and was reading when Emma and the doctor came out of Patrice's room.

"Is she doing all right?" he asked.

The doctor answered, his tone grim. "Yes. She needs rest and food and, hopefully, some of her confusion should be reduced."

Jeremy asked, "That is good right?"

The doctor answered him, his tone serious, "The confusion concerns me. What is this about her room not being hers and her mother being missing?"

"We're investigating," Emma answered "We don't know what's happened, though I did see someone with her that first day,"

"If your investigation does not turn up anything or if her confusion gets worse, you will need to notify me. We may need to have her hospitalized."

They both nodded, understanding what he meant.

"Thank you, doctor. Can I see you out?" Emma asked.

"No, thank you. I've been here enough, I think I can find my way out," he said and left their suite.

"Why don't we go check on Patrice? Then we can discuss what I found out," suggested Jeremy.

Emma nodded and accompanied him to Patrice's door. They knocked lightly and pushed it open. They saw her taking something.

"Patrice! What are you taking!" Jeremy exclaimed.

"Pills," the girl said, swallowing the ones in her mouth.

"Where did you get those?" Emma asked, running over and taking the remainder from her.

Patrice frowned at them, "I got them here in my room."

"From the doctor?"

"No, it was the little ghost. He said I must take them."

Little ghost? Emma looked at Jeremy and he shook his head.

CHAPTER 13

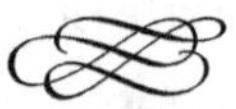

Tim and Dora returned to their hotel, feeling quite down at the events of the day. The loss of new friends, the suggestion of a bomb, threats on their lives, and finally Lottie.

They stood pensive outside their hotel door, not wanting to go in. The idea of hiding something from Emma and Jeremy was so foreign that it was making Dora physically ill.

Tim frowned, watching her lean against the wall, looking pale and unhappy. "We have to go in."

"Yes," she said softly. "Would Jeremy and Emma have seen something we didn't? Could they have figured out their attitude on the steamer and prevented the deaths that have occurred?"

"I was thinking about that, the way they avoided her and Jeremy. They seemed to know they couldn't let them get close or they'd be exposed." He started at the door and said again, "We need to go in. Can you manage?"

She straightened and said bitterly, "You mean lie." She thought of Lottie and took a deep, stabling breath.

"Ready?" he asked, not commenting on her statement.

"Ready."

They walked in, still so wrapped up in their own problems that they had forgotten about the girl who had shown up in their room that morning. Emma and Jeremy had been dealing with it on their own.

The girl they had only seen unconscious was walking around the room at a brisk pace and talking. "And then we came here," they heard her say.

Emma saw them in the doorway and called, "Come in, please."

They looked questioningly at the girl, who continued to talk and seemed manic. Emma ignored her and asked them, "How was the exposition?" She was eager to hear about what was happening outside the room.

"Emma, what's up with her?" asked Dora, watching the girl continue to pace and hold conversations no one was listening to.

"She took some pills someone gave her last night. I got her to purge them, but some managed to get into her system. We're just trying to keep her company until it wears off."

"She's talking. Is it important?"

Jeremy walked in with a glass of wine for Emma and sat down. He informed Dora and Tim, "This is all stuff we have heard a dozen or more times. She's stuck on a repeat of the scenario. We're hoping we can move forward again once she winds down."

Emma wanted to talk about the exposition, "Did you get to see the phonographic demonstration?"

"No, we didn't stay in the Gallery of Machines very long today," Dora said truthfully.

Emma's eyes widened in surprise. "Oh, did you go somewhere else?" she asked, glancing over at Patrice. She pulled her attention away from the talkative girl, who continued to pace and focused on Dora. She noticed Dora didn't look right—her face was pale; her eyes had the appearance of crying. "Is something wrong?" she asked, walking over to her sister.

"No," Dora answered quickly, holding shaky hands to her pale cheeks. "It's just all the people and sites. I got overwhelmed."

Tim thought this would be the best time to leave and go to

their room. He took Dora's hand and started leading her away, "She needs to rest," he said. He needed to get her away from Emma's prying eyes. He didn't know how long Dora would hold up to her questions. They had always been extremely close and their feelings could be read easily from one to the other.

"Can we talk later?" asked Dora as she was led away.

"Of course," Emma said, watching them disappear into their room. She glanced over at Jeremy, "What's happening there?"

He looked toward the door speculatively recalling the talk he had had with Dora and Tim earlier, "I don't know, but I think we need to watch them."

A knock on the door distracted them. Jeremy went to the door and was relieved when he saw who it was. "Doctor, thank you for returning." He had been unavailable when they tried to contact him earlier.

"Has anything changed?" he asked, entering the room.

"You could say that," said Jeremy in a lightly sarcastic voice, indicating the still agitated Patrice with his head.

The doctor followed his direction and saw the girl he had examined earlier was definitely more animated. He walked over to her and had to take her by the arm to stop her from moving about the room. "My dear, can we go back to your room?"

Emma walked over, "Yes, let's go let the doctor have a look at you."

"But," Patrice began rapidly, "my mum is still missing and I need your help."

"Yes," said Emma soothingly, "I know. And we'll find her, but we have to take care of you first."

Jeremy watched as Emma and the doctor accompanied Patrice back to her room and shut the door.

Emma watched as the doctor checked Patrice's eyes and heartbeat. He finished his examination. "Have you taken anything?" he asked her.

"No, I don't think so," she answered and started talking about her mother again.

Emma answered for her. "Yes, we found her taking these pills after you left. She said a small ghost gave them to her last night."

"Did this reaction start at that time?"

"What reaction? I'm fine," Patrice muttered and tried to stand up.

"No, you're different than the last time I saw you. Your hands and arms have tremors and your eyes are dilated," stated the doctor, holding her by the wrist.

"I don't know what you're talking about," she said defensively. "I took the pills, but first I took the drinking potion."

"What drinking potion?" the doctor and Emma asked at the same time.

"I was asleep, and I had a dream about a boy in my room, here."

"You're talking about the little ghost you mentioned earlier," Emma said, frowning. "What did he do?"

"He says I must drink this drink. He said he was a ghost," she said to Emma.

"Did you take the drink?"

"He said I had to. I didn't feel I had a choice."

"How did you feel after the dream?" asked the doctor.

"So sleepy," she said and started to get agitated again. "Then I woke."

"Was he still there?"

"No—he was a dream."

"Was he, though?" asked Emma, doubt clear in her voice. "I'm not so sure." Wondering about this, she stood and directed, "You stay here with the doctor."

She made her way to the door and into the living room.

"Is she okay? Can he tell what happened to her?" Jeremy asked.

Emma continued to search the room. She finally located, what she needed – an umbrella.

He frowned at it and glanced toward the window. It was a clear day. "Uhm, are you planning on going somewhere?"

"Maybe," she admitted. "Can you join me in Patrice's room?"

He continued to frown at her statement, but he followed her into the room. "We haven't spent much time in here," he commented.

Emma motioned to the doctor and Patrice. "Can you go into the living room for a moment?"

The doctor was curious but he understood his job was to care for Patrice. She was animated again and was easily led out.

"You know we didn't pick our rooms; we didn't get an option," commented Emma, thinking of the day they arrived.

"That's true," Jeremy said and looked around. "They took us directly to the rooms—we didn't question that at the time. They didn't mention this room, except to say it was extra space. Do you think something was planned about Patrice being here?" he asked.

"I'm beginning to think so. This whole thing seems planned. Her showing up on our doorstep, this empty room."

He questioned the umbrella, "Are we looking for hollow spaces?" In a previous case, she had used one to find a hidden compartment in wood flooring. It guided them to a key piece of evidence that helped close a case they were working on.

"Yes, I was examining the room and saw that the size is smaller than ours." Jeremy left the bedroom and stepped out the distance between the rooms. He came back into the room. "I think it's on the left side," he said.

She walked over to the wall and used the base of the umbrella to tap across it. She listened for any changes in tone. About five feet in, she found what she was looking for—a hollow-sounding spot. "Here," she called to Jeremy.

They ran their fingers over the wall, feeling for the seam. "I know it's here," said Emma.

"Wait, I know what we can do," he said and left the room again. Emma waited and Jeremy came back in with a cigar.

"Is this the best time to be smoking?" Emma joked. Watching him light up, she had an idea of what he was thinking. If there was any air movement behind that wall, the smoke's movement would show it. He puffed and blew on the part of the wall they were suspicious of. Within moments and a few more draws on the cigar, they found the opening. "We need something to pry it open," Jeremy said, laying the cigar down on a plate.

"I have just the thing." Emma exited and returned with her long knife. It was something she kept with her always. She inserted it into the location where the smoke had been dissipated and pulled back. The knife was strong enough not to bend and created an opening where they could insert their fingers. They both pulled and the door opened, revealing a staircase.

"Ah-ha," said Emma.

"Hmm," murmured Jeremy, looking into it.

Emma started into the dark space. Jeremy halted her, "I know you love an adventure, but we need some preparation first. We don't know to where or to whom this will lead."

She paused, the temptation of the mystery pulling at her. "Do you think…"

"I think we should wait. We need to check with the doctor to confirm what those pills are."

"You're right," she said, absently staring at the space.

He decided to close it, removing the temptation for her.

She turned to him and smiled suddenly. He returned the smile, "Soon."

"I'll hold you to that." She gave him a quick kiss.

He took her hand and headed into the living room. "I know you will. Now, I need to get a book. We'll probably be here a while." He went directly to their room.

Emma looked around and noticed it was empty; the doctor and Patrice were missing.

"Dammit!"

"What is it?" he asked as he returned, reading his book as he walked.

"She left."

That caused him to look up, "But where could they have gone?"

"Check with Tim and Dora. I'll check the hallway. Maybe they're just walking."

She ran down the hallway, checked the elevator, and then used the stairs to run down to the lobby. Quickly, she glanced around the crowded room. There was no sign of Patrice. Pushing at people, she made her way through the crowds. *She isn't here,* she thought, turning in a circle. She saw the door and thought, *Outside!* She went to the door and spoke to the man working there. "Bonjour."

"Bonjour."

"Avez-vous vu une jeune fille? Cheveux bouclés foncés, le long de ses épaules et vêtue d'une robe rose?" *Have you seen a young girl? Dark curly hair, down around her shoulders, and wearing a pink dress?*

"Je suis désolé mais il y a eu trop de gens par moi pour identifier une fille. Si vous voulez bien m'excuser." *I'm sorry but there have been too many people by me to identify one girl. If you will excuse me.* He stepped away to get a carriage for a group of people.

She had disappeared. *What do I do?* Emma felt lost for a moment. *My team, I need my family.* She headed back upstairs.

She pulled the door open and saw Tim, Dora, Jeremy, and surprisingly, the doctor.

They looked at her expectantly. "I couldn't find her," She said, "I checked the stairs, the lobby, and questioned the doorman. She's gone." She turned her wrath and frustration on the doctor. "Where were you? Weren't you supposed to stay with her?"

"Emma!" Dora scolded her.

The doctor replied, not upset at the demand. "No, it's okay. I can explain. I got Patrice settled on the couch and she was resting. Tim came out and asked if I could take a look at Dora."

"Dora! Is something wrong with you?" Emma asked, immediately contrite at her attitude.

"It's just my nerves," said Dora honestly. "Too much has been going on today."

"Yes," Emma agreed, thinking Patrice was on all of their minds, not aware that Tim and Dora's were on Lottie.

"Doctor," said Emma in a calmer tone, "you said she was settled when you went to check on Dora?"

"Yes, and her anxiety was reduced. She had stopped talking and her eyes seemed less dilated."

"That's good," Emma said, somewhat relieved. At least she may have had a clearer mind when she left them.

"What's causing the mania and then the intense sleeping?" asked Jeremy, still wondering about their temporary guest's behavior.

"Could you show me the pills she took?" the doctor requested.

"I have some here," Emma said and unfolded the cloth she had put in her pocket. "Can you identify them?"

The doctor looked at them with a frown and picked up one. He pulled out his knife and scraped at it, putting the edge of it in his mouth for a small taste. Instead of answering her, he asked, "She mentioned someone was giving her a liquid that made her sleep?"

"Yes," Jeremy replied.

"The pills are cocaine," the doctor said.

"That's medication, isn't it?" asked Emma.

"I don't use it for my patients. I find there are features to the drug that can have terrible side effects. I saw those in Patrice's behavior."

"And the other? The liquid?" Jeremy asked.

"That sounds like laudanum," the doctor commented. "She had the normal symptoms for a too-high dosage."

"Does she look like a long-term user of cocaine? There are rumors the drug is addictive," said Emma.

"No, I didn't see any indication of that."

"Someone is trying to keep Patrice off-kilter, both high and low," Emma observed.

"Yes, I think so." He checked his watch and said, "I do need to go now."

"Doctor, I'll walk you out," Emma said. When they reached the door, she put a hand on his arm, and, when he turned toward her, she said, "I want to apologize for my rudeness. I should have waited for you to tell me."

"You were concerned and thought I had been negligent in my duties," he said, looking into her eyes.

She had the grace to blush red. "Again, I apologize."

"Call me if she returns. I'd like to monitor the behavior changes."

"Thank you," she said and closed the door behind him, then leaned on it. She pushed herself off the door and headed back in.

"Where could she have gone?" she asked, exasperated.

Jeremy sank down on the couch, "I don't know, and I'm not sure she wasn't just out of her head."

"Do we look for her?" she asked, sitting next to him and putting her head on his shoulder.

"She knows where we are. If she decides she needs our help, she'll be back."

"Until then?"

"We're in Paris. I think we should go out and see it."

"I agree," she said, though she didn't move away from him.

Tim stepped out of the bedroom and shut the door softly behind him.

"Is Dora okay?" asked Emma.

"Just too much excitement. No sign of Patrice?" he asked as he looked around.

"No," said Emma shortly.

Tim frowned. "She just left?"

"We think so," Jeremy replied.

"What are the plans? Will you go after her?"

"Where would we start?" commented Jeremy. "We don't know her or Paris well enough to find her."

"Yeah," said Tim. "If you aren't going after her, what are your plans?"

"We're going out," said Emma definitively.

"And if she comes back? What do we do?" Tim asked, not wanting another worry. Dora was not handling the stress well.

"She isn't our prisoner. If she wants help, then she can stay," indicated Jeremy.

"Alright," Tim said slowly.

"Tim," said Emma, "Patrice isn't your concern. Don't stay here on the chance she'll return."

He looked conflicted.

"Can you promise me?" she asked.

"Yes, I can," he said, somewhat relieved at being told he didn't need to help out.

They got up from the sofa and retrieved their coat and hats. Emma paused, taking Jeremy by the arm. She turned toward Tim, "Tim, is there something you want to tell me?" Instinct made her ask.

Tim went as still as stone and stuttered out, "What makes you ask that?"

"Nothing," she said slowly. She wanted to push him further, but instead, she sent him a long look and turned back to leave.

"Emma," called Tim.

"Yes," she said, turning back to him.

"I'll let you know if we need anything. I promise," he said. He wanted to tell her more than anything. Dora was right; Emma and Jeremy could help. But he was too scared to take the chance that something they did could affect Lottie negatively.

She nodded and they headed out.

They pulled the door closed behind them and headed to the elevator. Jeremy pushed the call button and leaned on the wall as they waited, "What was that about?"

"I'm not sure. I just thought I'd put the question out there. Dora didn't seem like herself when she came back from the exposition today."

"She may have been tired," he suggested.

"Yes, but I thought it best to say something."

"Is it because they spent the afternoon with Michael and Lenora?"

"Yes," she admitted.

"You think it's something that may have happened today?" he asked.

"Yes."

"So, we have a case of a vanishing girl and…" he said.

"For now, the mysterious couple," she supplied.

"Looks like," he confirmed.

The elevator arrived and they headed downstairs. They got through the crowded lobby to the entrance and stepped outside. The man working the door hailed a cab for them. It pulled up in front and the driver asked, "Où ça?" *Where to?*

Jeremy looked at Emma, "I want to go to the exposition and see that Edison exhibit," she said. "Papa mentioned he'll be in town this weekend."

Jeremy turned to the driver, "Bonjour. La foire s'il vous plait."

The driver nodded and clicked his tongue to get the horses moving through the crowded street. They made good time and arrived at the Eiffel Tower in under twenty minutes. The carriage pulled to a stop and they got out. Emma stood, still awed by the design. *This will change the future design of buildings*, she thought.

She looked around as Jeremy paid the driver. "Au revoir," he said to them and drove away.

"What is that?" asked Jeremy, motioning toward the box-like structure under the tower. He hadn't noticed it previously.

"That's probably the elevator Papa mentioned," she said, studying it.

"Didn't I read something about that? That there was some talk of the safety of the device?" he asked.

"Papa mentioned it. They're Otis Elevators. It moves people up the legs to the first level of the tower," Emma said.

"What was the safety concern?"

"There wasn't one. Several journalists expressed concern. To prove it was safe, the Otis technicians filled one elevator with three thousand kilograms of lead, simulating passengers, and then cut the cable with an axe. The elevator's fall was halted ten feet above the ground by the Otis safety brakes," she explained.

"Do you want to get in line and go up now?" he asked, watching it move people up the tower.

"No, Papa mentioned the best view is at night."

"We haven't stayed for the light shows at night."

"I'd like to see it," she said wistfully. "Maybe tonight?"

"Ellis mentioned it's a combination of electric light around the water and gas lights on the tower, protected by opal glass cases. There's also a three-colored beacon housed in the campanile that sends out blue, white, and red light over Paris."

"That will be a sight to see," she said, her eyes shining.

"We'll come back tonight," he promised.

She turned to him and smiled. "I'd enjoy that."

"Train or walk?"

"Let's walk," she requested. When they didn't move forward, Emma asked curiously. Je. "What are you looking for?"

"Not a what. A who—Julian," he said drolly. "Doesn't he normally turn up at this time? He has been our constant companion since we got to Paris."

"That's true." She frowned and followed his gaze. "It's rather odd that we haven't seen him today. I still haven't talked to Papa about their relationship. I think there's something there."

"And his connection to Michael and Lenora," Jeremy reminded her.

They started their walk, trying to avoid the larger crowds as they watched the flowing water and white statues. "I could stay here for months and not just weeks," Emma commented. Jeremy thought about that as they continued to admire the buildings leading to the main dome.

The crowds thickened as they made their way to it. She commented, "I thought the reason for the exposition was supposed to keep people away."

"Yes, that's true, it was supposed to." As they passed groups of people, the languages varied but the queen's English was prevalent. "Especially the English."

"I guess the spectacle was too hard to miss," observed Emma.

"That's true," said Jeremy.

They made it to the Gallery of Machines pavilion. Looking around, they saw signs for Edison's exhibit and realized that two-thirds of it were his works.

"What do you want to see first?" he asked.

"Edison's phonograph. I understand we will hear both the American and French national anthems playing it."

As they walked through the space, they marveled at the engines, dynamos, and transformers on display.

"Whoever put this together knows quite a lot about how much spacing and power is required for this design," Jeremy said.

"There is an easy explanation for that," said Emma. "The president of France Sadi Carnot, Jr and he had a part in planning the exposition. He had the advantage of being raised by Sadi Carnot, who gave us the second law of thermodynamics—the scientific law that limits how much power a machine will produce. He believes The modern world is being 'forged out of iron and smoke.'"

"Iron and smoke?" commented Jeremy.

"The future is in the room," said Emma. "We'll see the future being built by the men who have created such amazing devices. Besides electricity and the phonograph, Papa mentioned we need to go to the moving pictures exhibit."

"Moving pictures?" he asked. "What's that?"

"Let's find out."

They looked around, trying to locate the area where the demonstration was set up.

"I think it's there," Emma commented, pointing to the huge crowd.

"You're probably right," Jeremy said as they headed toward it.

Large signs were suspended over the displays and, as they got closer, she could read them. "This is the phonograph demonstration. I understand you can buy these now."

Jeremy looked around, "Let's see what they're like."

They got to the long lines waiting to put earphones in their ears. There were multiple stations and the lines moved quickly. They reached the phonograph, and Emma was handed earphones. She eagerly lifted them to her ears and listened to the French and American national anthems. Her face lit up as she listened. She couldn't wait to hand the device to Jeremy.

He took it from her and put the device to his ear. "Wow," he mouthed. She nodded as she watched his reaction.

They passed on the earphones to the next eager person in the line. She said, "We should get one of these when we get back home."

"I agree. It's amazing."

They heard an announcer call out, "In 1888, American inventor and entrepreneur Thomas Alva Edison conceived of a device that would do 'for the Eye what the phonograph does for the Ear.'"

They followed the crowds to the demonstration area; smaller groups were taken inside.

"Who's that on the stage?" asked Jeremy as they got closer.

Emma didn't know and was about to reply when a lady standing in front of them turned and said, "Bonjour, that is Étienne-Jules Marey. He invented the chronophotographic gun instrument capable of capturing images at a rate of twelve frames per second."

"Thank you," Emma said. The woman turned to look forward again. "What's being shown?" asked Emma.

"Monkey shines," Jeremy read on the sign.

They entered the darkened room and the demonstration started. "Tiny photos appear to be used," muttered Emma as the movie started. It was a woman who appeared to be exercising. Emma's head was humming as they left. Jeremy watched as she drummed her fingers on her lips; it told him she was planning something.

"What are you thinking about?" he asked.

"The future. If we had equipment like this, investigations could be improved. I was thinking Jake would love this development. We'll have to get as much information as we can for him." Jake Cooper was a team member and part of their family. He had lived in the boarding house since they met him in 1883. He was a forensic photographer with the Chicago police department and provided his expertise to the team as needed. Currently, he was home; he didn't take to traveling well.

They continued to wander around observing the displays for Telegraphone, General Electric, Westinghouse, and Tesla. They had been there for a few hours, going exhibit to exhibit, when she commented to Jeremy, "Still no Julian."

He looked up from his study of a large transformer in the Westinghouse display. "There's a lot to see here. Maybe he's just busy," he reasoned.

"You're probably right." Her voice drifted off. Julian's continued absences bothered her. The man had been with them almost constantly since coming over on the ship, always showing up when least expected and asking questions that she didn't want to answer. Emma had gotten used to his presence and was disappointed he hadn't shown up yet. *Maybe something happened to him* she thought. Before she could voice her concerns, an announcement was made—that the lights would be turned on at the Edison exhibit. "Would you like to go back and see it?" she asked.

"I would. I heard that the display is supposed to demonstrate color."

They headed to the crowded area, hoping to get close enough to see the lights. They held their breath, waiting for the demonstration. They watched as the lights flashed briefly but did not come on. Emma watched the men in charge of the exhibit. One of them flipped the switch next to him several times and whispered furiously to the man next to him. The man nodded and headed to the side of the exhibit.

"Something's wrong," she murmured to Jeremy pointing to the man moving to the side of the exhibit. They watched, expecting the lights to activate. Instead, that same man ran out and waved frantically, calling, "Police! Police!"

Emma frowned. "Something's happened. Let's go over and see if we can help."

Jeremy nodded and walked over with her. They got close but stayed back to observe. In a short time, the police had arrived and were setting up a boundary to keep the crowds back.

"Pardon, monsieur?" Emma asked the officer assigned to keep the crowds out.

"Oui, Madam?" he asked.

"Est-ce qu'il s'est passé quelque chose ici?" *Has something happened here?*

He looked down at her from his considerable height. "Je ne peux pas répondre à cette question." *I cannot answer that.*

She commented, "J'espérais offrir de l'aide." *I was hoping to offer some help.*

"Ce n'est pas necessaire, Madame," *That is not necessary, Madam,* he answered stiffly

A voice spoke up in English just behind the officer. "Just a moment, officer. Are you Mademoiselle Emma Evans?"

"Yes," Emma said watching as the man stepped from behind the officer.

"You may let her and her companion..." He looked at Jeremy.

"Jeremy Tilden," he supplied.

"Mademoiselle Evans and Monsieur Tilden may step in," he said.

"Emma, please."

"And Jeremy, please."

"Thank you." He reached over to take her hands, "I'm Inspector Levan. I have heard you were in Paris." He looked over at the young officer and said, "She's a detective and her observation skills are well known."

"Jeremy is also a detective," Emma supplied, "he's with the Pinkerton Detective Agency."

Levan nodded; he was aware of the agency. "I'd appreciate your review of the scene."

"We'd like to help," Emma said for them.

"Wonderful, walk this way." The inspector motioned to the officer to lower the barricade so they could enter the controlled area.

They followed the inspector, not knowing what they were being taken to see. The door he opened led into a long utility corridor. The double doors at the end of the hallway stood open. As they entered, they saw a man lying on the floor, face down.

"Do you see anything?" Levan asked as they watched the man being turned over.

"Shot," she mentioned, examining the body first and not the face.

Jeremy touched her arm, "It's Julian."

Emma's eyes moved to the body's face and her eyes widened. She muttered, "Oh my."

"You know this man," the inspector stated as fact.

"Yes, yes we do. He's Julian Barnard," she commented shakily.

Jeremy supplied, "We met him on the steamship on our way from New York."

"Were you close friends?" Levan asked.

"No, just acquaintances," commented Emma.

"Do you know anyone he might have been close to?" he asked.

"I'm not sure close is the right word." She looked over at Jeremy.

He looked at the inspector, "Michael and Lenora Cervantes. We've seen them together a few times."

"Where was this?" the inspector asked.

"They were also on our steamship from New York."

"Were they friends?"

"No, I don't think so." Emma said, "When we saw them together, they were arguing."

"Do you know where they're located now?"

"I believe they have a room at our hotel, the Grand Palais."

"Have you spent time with them?"

"No, we haven't spent any time together. They have been spending time with my sister Dora and her husband Tim."

"Where are your sister and brother-in-law now?"

"They're back at the hotel, resting," she murmured.

"Where were they this morning?"

"I believe they were at the exposition this morning," Jeremy said.

"Do you know which exhibits?" the inspector asked.

"They mentioned the Gallery de Machines and that they were meeting Lenora and Michael," Emma said truthfully.

"We'll want to question them," Levan said.

"Of course, would you like to come by this evening?" Emma asked.

"Yes—I have to conclude things here. You will make sure your sister and her husband are available?"

"Yes, I can do that," Emma said. She looked around, "Isn't this room normally secure? I thought I noticed a guard earlier."

He started to talk and a voice called, "Inspector!"

He went in the direction indicated, then called back over his shoulder, "Emma and Jeremy, could you come here?"

They followed his direction and saw him with a lifeless body, this one in a uniform. He was slumped behind the transformer, against the wall.

"Careful," she called. "Don't touch him; he might be connected to the power. Check all around him and make sure he isn't touching anything."

They did as she asked and called back, "He isn't touching anything."

"Is he alive?" she asked.

"No, it does not appear so."

"Can you move him out?"

The inspector directed his men to carefully remove the man and place him in the middle of the room.

She knelt down and noticed his hands; they appeared to have a black mark.

"There doesn't appear to be an injury," commented the inspector.

"I think he's been in contact with the electricity," she said.

The inspector was not familiar with the new technology. "What makes you say that?" he asked, trying to see what she saw on the body.

"I've read that the circuit will try to be completed through the person if there's contact. Look at his hands and probably his feet also."

"Enlever ses chaussures," he directed his officers.

They removed his shoes and found another black mark. The inspector looked at her, "One electrical accident and one murder in the same area at the same time?"

Emma was frowning at the question. She didn't say anything but thought, *Julian mentioned there were radical people against electricity. He said they could be violent in their beliefs.*

The inspector stroked his beard and commented, "Michael and Lenora are our main lead. The questioning of your sister and her husband is a priority."

"I understand. We'll contact you as soon as we see them."

The manager of the Edison lighting exhibit walked over to them, "May we turn back on the transformer?"

The inspector knew Paris was relying on the exposition being a success, "Yes, we have it under control. You may turn it back on."

The manager looked relived, "Thank you so much." He nodded to the staff and a switch was flipped. They could hear the crowds respond to the lights as they came on.

The inspector watched as his men covered the victims with sheets.

"How will you move them?" Jeremy asked.

"We have several exits that will allow us to be discrete. Now, you must go on your way. We'll see you soon."

"Bonsoir," they called and walked out of the room, barely glancing at the now brightly lit exhibit, the excitement drained by Julian's murder.

Jeremy watched Emma drum her fingers on her lips, "What are you thinking?"

"That it's very coincidental that Julian and Michael and Lenora fight and then he's murdered."

"Do you think they had something to do with it?" he asked, thinking of the times they had seen them together.

"It's possible. I never liked how they avoided us."

"What about Tim and Dora? Do you think they knew about this?"

"I hope not. The injuries and blood lead me to believe this all happened this morning."

"You didn't mention that when you were evaluating the body earlier."

"No, I wanted to make sure I didn't accidentally lock Tim and Dora into a time where they don't have an alibi," she admitted.

"You think they're somehow involved?" he asked, startled.

"It's possible. Think of how Dora looked earlier today. She was as white as a ghost."

"Why don't we stop for some afternoon tea and gather our

thoughts before beginning a long conversation with Dora and Tim?"

They headed out of the exposition grounds. The food there was good but the wait was too long. The further they got from the exposition, the more likely they'd be able to get a table.

They walked a few blocks and across the bridge before finding a free carriage. They requested a restaurant for afternoon tea. The driver took them to the 5th Arrondissement, on the Left Bank of the Seine, the Latin Quarter.

He let them off at a small restaurant with outdoor seating.

"This is nice," Emma said as they sat down.

"You know," he said, "we never checked out that secret staircase in the middle room at the hotel."

"With so much going on, I forgot about it," she admitted as she looked at the menu.

"Secret passages have shown up in your cases before this," he said, referencing a previous case where one had been utilized to move about a murder house.

"It's true—they do seem a popular addition," she said quietly. "Though I think Julian's murder will take priority over that, especially if Tim and Dora are involved."

"It still might be worth checking out when we get back," he murmured.

"If there's time," she agreed. She laid down her menu and glanced at the area around them. "It's so beautiful here."

"Isn't this area named the Latin Quarter because of the Latin being spoken at the school?"

"Exactly, it's also one of the oldest areas."

The waiter came over and they ordered their tea and cakes. They sat enjoying their afternoon, not talking about their current cases. She stood up and went over to him, hugging him close.

"What's this for?" he asked, returning the hug, not that he minded getting free hugs.

"For this," she said, referencing the area around them. "It's wonderful to finally forget what's happening outside of here."

He didn't say it, but he knew as soon as they left the area that their reality would be back in full force. Julian, Michael, and Lenora; Dora and Tim's involvement, and Patrice.

"Why don't we head back to the hotel?" he suggested.

"Okay. I assume Tim and Dora will be there." She checked her timepiece, "The police might be on their way, they didn't give us a time."

They passed a patisserie "Want to take some meat, cheese, bread, and wine back with us?" Jeremy asked.

"I think that would be wonderful."

They stepped into the shop and picked items for their dinner. On their way out, she looked around wistfully, "I'd like to stay here more full time."

"Yes, it's lovely. Maybe one day we'll live here."

"I'd like that," she murmured, looking around again.

They hailed a carriage and went back to the hotel. She continued to watch as the Latin Quarter got smaller behind them. As they entered the lobby, she paused to see if she could locate Patrice. When she didn't see her, she was two parts exasperated, and one part worried. "She's still not back."

"She might turn up. Maybe she's just playing hide and seek," suggested Jeremy with a twinkle in his eye.

"Hide and seek? Why would she do that?" she asked sharply.

"Hey, I was kidding." He held his hands up, "I surrender." He watched as she moved her fingers to her lips and began drumming them. "All right, what are you thinking?"

"I might know where she is," she said, mulling over the "hide and seek" comment.

"Where?"

"Follow me," she directed and headed toward the elevator.

They had a short wait for it. As they got off on their floor, Emma continue to think about everything they knew about

Patrice. She increased her pace and almost ran to the door. Jeremy was close behind with the key. They went in and Emma called out, "Tim! Dora! Are you here?" She knew they had a responsibility to the police to question them.

Jeremy took the food to the small kitchen area as Emma ran quickly to Tim and Dora's room and knocked on their door. When she received no answer, she went into the room. She came out quickly, "They're gone."

"They may have just gone out to dinner or went to see some sites," he suggested, knowing she was worried.

"You're probably right," she said looking at Patrice's door. "We have some time?"

"I think we do," he said and followed her to the middle room. She paused by the table to pick up her knife and her small portable kerosene lamp.

They immediately went to the wall they had opened earlier. She inserted the knife into the seam and pulled it back. As the door opened, she turned to Jeremy, "This time, I plan to go in."

He stopped her with a hand on his shoulder. "Why do you think she's in there?"

"I don't know, but I also didn't think she'd run from us."

"That was my thought. I wondered where she could be. She knows no one but us. And that little ghost."

"Exactly, he has been on my mind," she said as she entered the dark space, her heart beating so hard her chest hurt. She lit the lamp to illuminate the area. There was an opening the size of a closet. She called over her shoulder, "The stairs start right away and only go up."

"I'm behind you," he said. She felt his warm breath on her neck. She moved her skirt and held it so she could negotiate the narrow steps. They had walked for a few minutes when she said, "There's some sort of landing."

He was quiet as they continued up. When they reached the landing, she shined the light onto the floor. A huddled figure was there. She ran over and lifted her face, "Patrice," she said. Jeremy was silent as she checked her pulse. "Alive," she said.

"Good," he said. "Let me carry her back to her room." Emma backed out and allowed Jeremy to reach her. He lifted Patrice, and Emma led them back down and into the room. He moved her to the bed and placed her gently down.

He was frowning heavily as he looked down at the girl, "I'm sorry I said we should investigate the space later. We could have found her earlier."

"I don't think so," Emma said, watching Patrice closely. She used her hand to move Patrice's hair from her head.

"You don't?" he asked.

"She couldn't have been there yet. I don't know why she left the room, but I think she must have come in from where this finally lets out. We won't know until she wakes," she said, looking toward the passageway.

"We'll have to investigate that later," he cautioned when he saw where her eyes strayed.

"I know. I was thinking we should close it in case someone tries to come in again."

"Yeah—we don't want them to know we know it's there," he said.

"She mentioned a ghost before," she said, glancing at the now-closed secret passage.

"Do you think that's how it might have come in?"

"Yes. I should have taken the ghost talk more seriously," she murmured.

"You couldn't have known," he argued, keeping his voice low. "So, who is the ghost, and why are they haunting Patrice? Questions we'll have to ask Patrice."

"Oh, I think the ghost can also answer some questions," she said.

"What are you thinking?"

"We talk to Patrice," she said, thinking.

CHAPTER 14

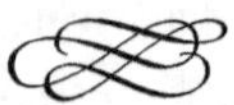

Earlier in the day with Tim and Dora

Meanwhile, as Emma and Jeremy made their way to the exposition, Tim and Dora stared at the closed door. Dora was pensive. "I know they said not to wait for Patrice..."

Tim interrupted firmly, "Lottie's our priority. Jeremy and Emma decided they could leave without finding Patrice. So can we."

"You're right," she said, her thoughts turning to Lottie. They silently gathered their things.

"Should we leave a note?" he asked.

Dora shook her head. "No. They know if we aren't here then we're at the exposition for sightseeing."

"Are you ready?" Tim asked. They had looked at their clothes to determine what could be used to hide their identities at the meeting.

"Yes, I had some netting on my evening dress. I was able to remove it and whip-stitched it to my hat. What about you?"

"I will keep my hat pulled down and keep my scarf wrapped around my face. Do you think they'll be there?"

"I hope so," she said. "They haven't been in contact yet to tell us what our role is in this plot." They were just thinking of the next steps and not focusing on the possible outcomes.

They were quiet as they left the room to get to the elevator. They walked a few blocks and then hailed a cab. He donned his hat and scarf while she pulled the netting down to cover her face.

"If there's enough of a crowd, we should blend in," Tim said.

"If there's not?"

"It won't matter. We'll get some answers," he replied determinedly.

She nodded.

The trip did not take long; the neighborhood was removed from the tourist areas and not crowded. The driver looked over his shoulder, "Êtes-vous sûr de l'adresse?" Clearly, he thought his passengers were lost.

"Oui," Tim said. He paid the driver and they both exited the carriage.

As the carriage rolled away, they saw the location was an old building that appeared to be an apartment.

"She mentioned the basement," Tim said. Dora nodded and followed him. He stopped abruptly, "Wait a moment." He watched a couple walk up and head into the building.

He took her hand and they followed them in. They watched as the other couple took a door to the left of the stairs. They waited a few seconds and followed behind them. The stairs led down to what must have been the basement, gas lamps helping to guide the way. The closer they got to the bottom, they heard voices getting louder. The group seemed to be in the middle of an argument. They tried to get in without being seen and sat in the back.

"We need to come to order," called a young man from the front of the room. Everyone sat down and the two people they were looking for stood with the speaker. "We have to move forward at this time," said the apparent leader.

"What's happened that makes us have to move our plans up?" yelled a man from the audience.

"We had an investigator on our trail."

That caused the room to murmur loudly.

Tim muttered to Dora, "Julian was an investigator?" They didn't know that piece of the puzzle. It would explain the arguments with Michael and Lenora.

Another person from the group asked, "What are the final plans?"

"We're keeping that quiet, but we'll tell you that it will involve electricity and will show everyone that it's too dangerous."

"Are we sure no one will be hurt?" a voice shouted from the group.

"Yes, we'll make sure," they assured everyone.

Tim uncovered his mouth, deepened his voice, and yelled out in French, "What about the investigator and security guard killed today?"

Tim put his scarf back on and moved with Dora back into the shadows.

"What is he talking about?" several people in the group yelled. "You said we wouldn't hurt anyone!"

"How can you be sure, with your plan, and so many people at the exposition?" someone else yelled out.

Lenora and Michael came up from the first row and went to stand on either side of the gentleman running the meeting. They started all talking at once, trying to calm the crowd.

"We're sure. I want to remind everyone why we're doing this," said Michael.

Lenora tried to get them back to their cause. "Electricity is dangerous."

A woman with dark hair stood, "We must protect everyone from these devices. They're putting our families in danger."

"I'll not be part of murder," an older man with gray hair said, standing. Those around him agreed and departed the space.

"Are those of you left committed to our cause?" Lenora asked.

They took a moment to wait for the group to respond. The response was positive and they went on to discuss the main events where they would place the bombs. The meeting ended and the group stood and moved toward the exit. Tim and Dora watched each file out while they kept an eye on Michael and Lenora in the front of the room.

They stood and went over to them, Tim taking off his hat and Dora raising her veil.

"Ah, good. You're here. Now we don't have to find you," Lenora said, the satisfaction clear in her voice.

Michael looked over at Tim, "That was you," he accused. "Shouting out Julian and the guard. Are you trying to destroy our cause?"

Tim didn't care for Michael or Lenora. "We want to see Lottie," he said forcefully. Dora gripped his hand, offering her support.

"Ah ah ah." Lenora stated, "You're in no place to make any demands; we're in charge here."

"That's where you're wrong. You need us. We're not doing anything until we see our daughter. How do we know you haven't hurt her?"

"You don't, but you will get her back after you help us."

Tim lowered his voice, "What do you expect us to do?" Dora was shocked at his response. She hadn't expected him to acquiesce to their demands. She tried to hide her reaction by lowering her head.

Lenora looked happy at the turnaround, "Well! We'll let you know our plans tomorrow."

"Tomorrow?" asked Tim. "Is something happening tomorrow?"

"Yes," they said noncommittally.

He nodded. "Then we'll head out and wait for you to contact us."

"No," said Michael. "I don't think so. I think it was a mistake to have you out of our grasp."

"You can't hold us here," Dora said.

"Oh, I think I can," Lenora said. Tim and Dora saw the woman had a gun pointed at them. "We'll be staying here tonight."

"In a damp basement?" asked Dora wrapping her arms around herself and shivering.

"No, we have an apartment upstairs," said Michael calmly. He seemed the more balanced member of their team.

"We thought you were staying at the hotel," Tim commented.

"Yes, that was more convenient, but someone searched our room today so we had to make a move."

Dora said loudly, "Emma will know something is wrong if we don't come back tonight."

"We can take care of that. You'll write her a note assuring that you're okay; that it got late and you're staying overnight with your new close friends," supplied Lenora.

Emma will never believe that, Dora thought but kept her mouth shut.

Michael led the way as Lenora kept the gun trained on their backs. They made their way up the stairs and into the first-floor hallway. The area was clean but had cracks in the walls and scratches on the floors. They took in all they could as they made their way upstairs to Michael and Lenora's apartment. It was located on the second floor. Michael opened the door and stood back to allow them entry. "It's not the Grand Palais hotel," muttered Tim. They were crowded into the small space that contained a living room and a kitchen. There were pads on the floor where they assumed they were going to be sleeping.

Dora's eyes darted around the room and landed on Lottie's lace band on the table. "Can I have that please?" she asked, a note of pleading in her voice.

Michael looked at Lenora. She shrugged. "Sure, why not."

Tim retrieved it, rubbing it with his fingers before giving it to

Dora. Dora took it and squeezed her eyes shut, trying to stop the emotion from overwhelming her. Tim put his arm on her shoulder and pulled her to him.

"Is there any food?" asked Tim.

"There are some things in the icebox. Not as good as you've eaten since we got here, but it's food," Michael said. He walked over to the icebox to pull out ham, cheese, fruit, and a round loaf of bread.

When Dora didn't make a move to the table for the food, Michael said almost kindly, "It won't do any good to starve yourself."

They sat and ate. Each couple thought that, were this a day ago, the conversation would have flowed between them. Michael broke the silence, "We really did like you, you know." Lenora didn't say anything but kept her head down.

"Then why would you do this? Take our child?" Dora burst out.

"It's just part of the plan," Michael said, looking over at Lenora, who still had her head down.

"Was killing Julian and the guard part of the plan?" asked Tim.

Lenora lifted her head; her eyes glinted. "We'll do whatever it takes to prove electricity is wrong."

"What's so wrong with electricity?" Tim asked, not understanding such passion over a scientific advancement.

"We have our reasons," she commented, trying to shut down the conversation.

"Don't you think we deserve to know what those are?" Tim demanded.

"I think you should tell them," Michael commented. When she glared at him, he continued, "We have involved their family in our troubles. I think it's time."

"Fine. My brother... they're trying to kill him with electricity," Lenora said abruptly.

Tim glanced at Dora and she shrugged. "We don't understand."

Lenora stood and paced the small kitchen. She started to talk. "My brother made a mistake and he went to prison. It should have ended there, but now, the Edison invention has been experimented with and will be used to execute people."

"What did he do that he'd be executed over?"

"He didn't do anything that would warrant this!" she burst out.

"What's his name?" Tim asked.

Michael supplied, "William Kemmler."

Dora jumped. Emma had mentioned him and his case to their team when his case went to trial. William Kemmler had been convicted of murdering his lover Matilda Ziegler—with an axe!

Tim remembered also and reached out to squeeze her hand. "Why do you think this will stop the execution? Wouldn't it just stop the electrocution?" he asked.

"It's not humane; they do not know if it will kill him. It's an experiment. I don't want him to be hurt like that. He's my brother."

Lenora left the room. They looked at Michael.

"Do you think he did it?" Dora asked.

"Yes, I do. But he's her brother and she believes this plan is a just cause."

"Why would Edison be a part of something like this?" Dora asked.

"I don't believe this came from him. From what I have read, electrocution was suggested by Dr. Albert Southwick. He had witnessed an elderly drunkard 'painlessly' killed after touching the terminals of an electrical generator in Buffalo, New York," Michael said.

"If not electrocution, wouldn't he be hung?" Tim asked.

"Yes," he said quietly, staring at the door his wife had exited through.

"Why do you think he'll be first?" asked Dora quietly.

"Earlier this year, New York's Electrical Execution Law, the first of its kind in the world, went into effect, and Edwin R. Davis, the Auburn Prison electrician, was commissioned to design an electric chair. We have been notified he'd be first and that led us to put a plan together," Michael informed them.

"And you think by staging this event you can stop them from doing that?" Tim asked in amazement.

"We do. Once we show them how dangerous electricity is, it will make others question the use of the invention."

Once they had finished eating, Lenora returned and handed Dora a piece of paper and a pencil. "Write out what I tell you."

Dora took the paper and pencil and began writing.

Emma,

We're going to stay with friends tonight. They have an apartment in town. We'll join you at the exposition tomorrow.

Dora

"Will we?" Tim asked as Dora finished the note.

"Of course, you will. Just do as we say and we'll let you go," said Michael.

Lenora didn't comment but just stared at the note in Dora's hand.

"And we'll get Lottie back?" asked Dora softly.

"And, of course, you will have her back," Michael assured her.

Dora completed the note and handed it to Lenora.

Lenora checked it to see if she had added anything.

"When will you let us know our role in this 'event'?" asked Tim.

"Tomorrow," she said briskly, folding the note up not offering any information.

She left and Michael said, "I don't want to have to keep the gun on you, but you're too big for me to wrestle."

"You can lower it," Tim said, "I won't cause any problems."

Dora knew it wasn't the gun keeping Tim from attacking Michael; it was Lottie. They had to see this through.

CHAPTER 15

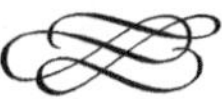

BACK AT THE HOTEL

*P*atrice was finally stirring again. She opened her eyes, and saw Emma, "You found me!"

"How did you end up in that space?" asked Jeremy as they watched her reaction closely.

She turned her eyes to him, "The little ghost. He was at the door. I opened it to confront him and he ran off. I chased after him."

"You followed him… Why?" Emma asked curiously.

"I don't know, to prove he was real. So much of what I told you seems like a dream."

"Where did he lead you?" Jeremy asked.

"He went into the stairway. We climbed so many stairs, they seemed to go forever. I got so tired that I sat down and closed my eyes."

"What happened then?"

"I opened my eyes and he was there. I asked him if he was real."

"What did he say?" asked Emma, fascinated by the story.

"He said 'drink this.' I was so tired that, when he held it to my lips, I drank it."

"Patrice! You really *have* to stop taking things from strangers," Emma said curtly.

"I know," the girl acknowledged unhappily. "I'll try."

"How did you end up back here in that space?" Emma asked, thinking about where they'd found her.

"I don't know. I dreamed that I was being lifted and then I woke here."

"That was probably the laudanum's effects," said Emma, thinking of what the doctor said.

Patrice looked around. She frowned, "Has the furniture been moved around in here?"

Jeremy started to explain about the dresser when they heard a knock on the hotel door.

Emma frowned, "It must be the police officers. Should we mention this?" The case was getting more involved by the minute. They could use some help.

"Please don't!" cried Patrice. "We haven't found Mama yet." The hotel staff had already threatened to lock her up, and she didn't know who to trust outside this room.

"No, you're right. We're in a location where we don't trust who we're working with," Jeremy said.

"And we need to know where that passage goes and just who that little ghost is," Emma said. The more she thought about it, the more she believed they needed more data before bringing the police into it.

Another knock sounded on the door, more demanding this time. "I'll stay here," said Jeremy, "if you want to answer the door."

Emma walked quickly out of the room, closing the door behind her. She took a deep breath and went to answer the loud knocks. As she opened it, she noticed not only the officers from earlier but also a bellhop from the hotel. "Come in, please," she told them.

Levan came in first, "We're here to interview Dora and Tim."

"Just a moment." Emma looked at the bellhop, "Bonjour, como talley vous?"

"A note," he said and handed it to her. She reached into her pocket and handed him several francs. "Merci."

She opened the note and saw it was Dora's handwriting. She looked directly at the police inspector, "Well, I'm sorry to say they're staying with friends tonight."

"Where are they?" asked Levan. This was their second dead end today.

"She doesn't say," she replied lightly, tapping the note on her hand.

"Do you know these friends?" Levan asked, opening up his notebook.

"I'm not sure. She doesn't mention their names." She didn't want to answer questions that might get Tim and Dora in trouble.

"Did they have any other friends here?"

"No, I don't think so." She decided to ask her own questions. "Did you look into Michael and Lenora?"

One officer glanced at the other. The inspector responded to her question. "We did and they're no longer at the hotel."

"They're not?" Jeremy asked as he walked into the room.

"They checked out," he said simply.

"Did they say when?" she asked pulling out her own notebook. Jeremy's mouth quirked as he looked at both of them comparing notebooks.

The inspector glanced down at his notes, "It looks like last night."

"Can we see their room?" she asked.

"No, the hotel has already booked another family."

"That was fast," she muttered.

"The exposition," Levan explained. "Would you mind if we go through Dora and Tim's room here?"

"I don't see why not. It is that far one."

He waved the other officers to the room. A few minutes later, they returned, and the officer stated, "We're finished. Thank you."

"Did you find anything?" Jeremy asked.

Levan looked over, "One thing." He pulled a folded paper out of his pocket and showed them.

It was a cartoon showing the hazards of electricity. Emma frowned, reaching for it. "I haven't seen this before."

"We have trouble in the city with these people. They're meeting and making threats. Have Dora and Tim been talking about these groups?"

"No, they haven't." Not that she was aware of.

"What about Michael and Lenora? Could they be part of this group?" the inspector asked.

"I haven't heard them say anything," she said truthfully. She thought about Julian's warnings but didn't mention them.

"We'll want to see them as soon as they arrive here. Do you understand?" Levan said with a frown.

"Yes, I understand." She'd find them and see what was happening.

The police took the pamphlet back and left the hotel room. She closed the door behind them and leaned on it.

Jeremy stood, "Coming back?"

"Yes," she responded and went to Patrice's doorway. "How is she?"

"Better," he said. "What about Tim and Dora?"

Emma handed him the note, "I'm worried about them, but we have no way of knowing where to look."

"Are they wrapped up in Julian's death?" he asked after reading the note.

"I think they're somehow involved," she said, thinking of Dora's response earlier that day.

She looked over at Patrice and could see the girl was feeling better. She was sitting up and had some color on her face. Her hair was a tumble and she was still in her gown, but her eyes were clear. "It's time for a hard conversation," Emma said.

"Do you think it would be all right to move her into our room?" Jeremy asked, eyeing the secret passageway door.

"Yes, I think so."

They put the question to Patrice. "What do you think?"

"I'd love that. Can I change?" The clothes she was wearing were dirty from the passageway.

Emma had sent out her clothes to be cleaned. "They should have been delivered. Let me check."

"No, please, could you stay with me? I don't want to be here alone," Patrice requested. Things happened when she was alone.

"I'll stay," she promised. "Jeremy, can you check to see if the clothes have arrived?"

"Of course." He went to check and called from the living room. "They're back." He carried them into the room and laid them on the bed. "I'll be out here."

He closed the door and Emma smiled. "He's such a good guy."

Patrice moved to the edge of the bed, "The last few days have been a blur."

"Yes, hopefully, we can hear everything and see how to move forward."

She nodded and stood.

"Careful," Emma said, walking over to the girl with a pitcher of water and a rag. Once she was refreshed, Emma retrieved her skirt and top and helped her dress.

She saw Patrice grimace and asked, "What is it?" Was something else wrong with her?

"My hair is so tangled. Can I borrow a brush?"

Her response represented her age so much that it made Emma laugh out loud. "Yes, I can help with that." She handed her the brush and she pulled it through. When she finished, Emma said, "Let's move to the living room."

She took Patrice's arm and helped her walk to the couch in the living room. Once settled, Emma and Jeremy sat across from her, "Would you like to tell us the whole story now?" Emma asked.

At that moment, Patrice's stomach rumbled. She put a hand on it, "I'm so hungry. Can I eat first?"

"Yes," Emma and Jeremy said together and laughed.

"We haven't eaten either," Emma admitted.

"But," Jeremy said, getting up and walking to the dining area, "we did bring food back with us." He pulled out the rotisserie chicken and containers of vegetables and some round bread. "What would you like to drink?" he asked them.

"A little wine, please," Emma requested.

Emma and Jeremy set up their plates and moved them back to the living room. They ate, letting the silence settle around them. Once they finished, Patrice said, "Okay, I'm ready for your questions."

"Where are you from?" Emma asked. She knew from the accent that Patrice had spent some time in the United Kingdom.

"London," she confirmed. "My mum and I lived there up until this week."

"Why are you in Paris?" Jeremy asked.

"That is a long story."

"I think we need to hear the whole thing to make sense of this," Emma told her.

"Of course. Then I'll start with how my papa met my mum. She was educated by her father. She was part of his household and, after her mum died, he let her stay on and manage his home. When he died and she wanted to find a life for herself. She applied at a hotel for a personnel management position."

Emma was impressed. Women were just entering the work-force and management positions were difficult. She had seen a woman in her own life move into a management position within an engineering company. Hopefully, this would continue to be true.

"Is that where she met your father?" asked Emma.

"Yes, Papa was there to oversee the restructuring of the staff. There had been some theft and he wanted to make sure he had people in positions he could trust. It was on the day Mum went for her interview that she met him."

~

He stood outside the hiring manager's door, concerned about the quality of personnel being hired for his new hotel in England. What he had not expected to hear was an argument. He could hear the woman quite clearly as she stated her case. Her voice was clear and concise regarding how she expected to be treated.

"You have applied for the wrong position," stated Mr. Horace Brooks. "You may apply for the positions listed." He indicated the sheet in her hand.

She looked down at it, "These are for maids. I do not want to apply for a maid position. As you can see from my education, I'd like to work for your management staff."

"I don't see how that would be possible. We do not hire people like you for those types of positions."

"And why not? I'm qualified," the woman said with quiet dignity.

He gave her a long look, "You know why. Why not just take one of the maid positions?"

The office door opened. Mr. Brooks was surprised to see Charles, the owner of the hotel. Horace stood immediately, "Mr. Lanier, we did not expect you this morning."

"I know. I wanted to check in on our hiring process." It was then he got his first look at the applicant. He stood still, taking in her visage; she was a lovely light negroid woman.

She sent him a cool steady gaze, expecting the same response that she had gotten from Mr. Brooks.

Surprising her, he stuck out his hand to her, "I'm Charles Lanier, the owner of this hotel. What position are you here for?"

"Personnel manager," Catherine said, feeling like it would be her way to make positive changes in the workforce.

"Mr. Brooks, let me take over the interview from here," Charles said.

"Yes, sir," Brooks said and stood to leave the room. He looked back and realized he had no say in if she'd be hired that day.

Charles sat at the desk and picked up the paper listing her credentials. "Miss Catherine Belle."

"Yes?" she asked, wondering where this was going.

"I want you to have a fair interview. Can you tell me about your background and why you think you're the right person for this job?"

"I have been educated by tutors at my residence and I'm well-read. I have also managed my father's household since I was sixteen."

"How large was this residence?" he asked, thinking about how many people she'd be responsible for at the hotel.

"We had over twenty-five servants and multiple locations."

He continued to ask detailed questions about the budgets, payments, schedules, hiring, and firing. Each one was followed up with a professional response.

"May I ask, what made you leave your father's home? It sounds like you were happy where you were."

Catherine looked down for a moment and back up to him, directly in the eye. "My father died and the bulk of the estate went to his white family."

He asked gently, "Do you have papers that allow you to work?"

Catherine knew what he was asking; he wanted to know if she was a free woman.

"Yes, I have my papers. My papa made sure I was a free woman as part of his will."

"I'm glad," Charles said, not wishing any hardship on her. He sat back, "I'd like to allow you to run the personnel department, but you must be aware you have chosen the area where the staff may not want a woman directing them. Can you handle that?"

"I can if I have the approval to replace whomever I might need to," she said firmly.

"You do, but you must not leave us understaffed," he warned.

"I understand." She knew if he took a chance on her there would be little room for mistakes.

"There will be pushback, not just the fact that you're a woman but also because you're black. But this is my hotel. You will come to me if things become too much for you."

"I will," she said, hoping she hadn't picked too big of a challenge.

"I'll need to meet with my central management, but plan on starting tomorrow," he said, standing and extending his hand to her. At their touch, her face grew red and his smile broadened.

The next day, Catherine did as Charles asked and entered the hotel, ready to start work. She was dressed in a dark blue skirt, a dark blue jacket, and a white shirt. She kept her hat to a small size. Entering, she felt the employee's eyes on her, but when she looked toward the main desk, she saw Charles waiting for her.

"Welcome to your first day. Let me walk you to your office."

They made their way there; she was so excited, her hands were shaking. She clasped her hands and told herself to calm down. The office was at the end of a long hallway. When it opened, she saw she had windows, a desk, and a table to work at.

"Will this do?" he asked.

"It will," she murmured, running her hand across the desk.

"The position you have taken on will require long hours, especially in the beginning. We're restructuring and you're a big part of that process."

~

"Was she a success?" Emma asked, fascinated by another woman not wanting to take the traditional path in life.

"It wasn't easy," Patrice admitted. "Some people would not change. There were several violent confrontations. Papa had to make sure she had an armed guard with her."

"How long until it was okay for her to go without them?" Jeremy asked.

"Almost two years."

People don't change easily, Emma thought. "When did your parents marry?" she asked.

"That was about the two-year mark. When she started feeling safe."

"You mentioned your mum and you live in the United Kingdom? Does your father live there with you?" asked Jeremy.

"He lived with us when he wasn't in France checking on his other hotels. Like this one," she said, looking around.

"Why isn't he here with you and your mum?" Emma asked.

"He said it was time for us to meet and start acting like a family. He arranged everything and went ahead of us. He was supposed to meet us here."

"Have you never been here before?" asked Emma.

"No, Papa's family didn't approve of his marriage."

"But I thought Parisians were more open about…"

"Interracial marriages?" she supplied. "They are, but some of the older families would prefer it didn't happen to them."

"So, you just didn't meet?"

"Papa said it was easier this way, that his family could be vicious."

"Were you happy?"

"Yes, we were very happy," she said simply.

"Okay, let's go back over when you arrived at the hotel here," said Emma, thinking methodically.

"We arrived three nights ago. Mum and I were standing in a

long line; we got in late and there were delays in getting the rooms."

"Yes, I saw you," Emma said.

"Did you see Mum with me?" Patrice asked excitedly. No one had believed that she and her mother had checked in together.

Emma cautioned, "I saw someone but it was from the back. What was she wearing when you checked in?"

"She had this plumb-colored suit she loves and a matching hat. I've tried to get her to change it for ages."

Emma nodded, "About how tall is she?"

"She's about 5'3, coming to here," Patrice said, holding up her hand to her shoulder.

"That sounds like who I saw, but I didn't see a face."

"Oh," the girl said, looking down, her disappointment apparent.

"What happened next?" Jeremy prodded.

"We got to our rooms and Mum wasn't feeling well, so she didn't leave her room."

"Had she seen anyone or taken anything that day?" Emma asked, thinking of the cocaine and laudanum that kept being fed to Patrice.

"Not that I..." She trailed off. "There was the clerk at the desk; he offered her some water. I had forgotten about that."

"Did she drink all of it?" Emma asked.

"No, I don't think so," Patrice answered, frowning.

"How was she when you got to your rooms?"

"Tired but able to walk."

"She didn't finish the water, so the effects would have been less than the ones you experienced," Jeremy said.

"Did you get the doctor at that time?" asked Emma.

"No, we thought it was the traveling that did it to her. She just wanted to rest."

"What about your father? You were there to meet him. Was he

aware you were at the hotel?" Jeremy asked, thinking if it was him, he'd have been waiting at the ship for them.

"Mum had told the desk manager to let him know we had arrived. We waited for him all through the next day," she said forlornly. "That evening, after dinner, she seemed to get worse, so I went downstairs to get a doctor."

"Did you order that dinner?" Emma asked.

"Mum thought the hotel sent it, because of Papa."

"Did you eat any of it?"

"No, I'm not a good traveler; my stomach was still upset."

"Did your mum eat it?"

"Yes, she was hungry."

"How soon after she ate did she get sick?" asked Emma.

"Soon," she confirmed.

"There was another opportunity to feed her laudanum," commented Jeremy. They knew the rest.

"I also demanded to see my papa."

"Did they call for him?"

"They said he was unavailable. I don't think they believed I was his daughter," she said unhappily.

"We need to follow up on that," Emma said to Jeremy. He nodded.

"And there's still been no word from your papa since you have been here?" questioned Emma.

"No," Patrice said miserably.

Emma glanced over at Jeremy, "I think we have a lot to investigate, but we'll have to do it so that no one can get to Patrice."

"Agreed, but we also need for Patrice," he turned and talked directed to the girl, "to stay here and not be led away. And, not to eat or drink anything that comes from someone you don't know."

"What to do," Emma said and looked at Patrice.

Patrice immediately responded "I can lock myself in your room until you get back. I want to find Mum."

"That's an idea. We don't need to be worrying if you will be here if we go," Jeremy said. "Okay, let's get her organized in our room."

"Yes, we should confirm the walls are all solid in there," Emma replied. They both went and tested all of the walls. "Solid," she said.

They moved Patrice back into their room and gave her several books and some desserts. "I won't budge from here or open the door," she promised.

"Oh, just a second," Emma said and opened a drawer, pulling out pants and a shirt.

Jeremy saw what she was holding, "Were you expecting something to happen on the trip?"

"You never know," she said philosophically.

They closed the door and Jeremy called, "Lock the door!" They waited for the click. Once they heard it, they moved back to Patrice's room.

"First, I'd like to go into the passage," commented Emma, studying the wall.

"Somehow, I knew you'd want to do that first," teased Jeremy.

She dropped her voice, "Should we do this and leave her alone?"

"I don't think we have a lot of options. Whoever is sneaking into her room will have to be caught. We can't do that if we don't know where they're coming from."

She changed quickly and laid her skirt and top on the couch. She pulled on a cloth hat and stuffed her hair into her collar.

"Ready?" he asked.

"Yes," she said as she pulled out her portable kerosene lamp. They headed back into Patrice's room and opened the passage. It was narrow, requiring them to go single file. Emma led the way. She could see footprints on the dusty floor and commented over her shoulder to Jeremy about it.

"I don't guess there has been housekeeping in here," he said reasonably.

They continued up and noticed there were no other openings on the ascending floors. She called back, "Keep going?"

"Why not?"

They continued to ascend and found what must be the final door. She put her ear to it, trying to listen.

Jeremy leaned in, "Anything?"

"I don't think so," she said, shaking her head.

"Want to try it?" he asked as he felt for a way to open the door.

"Yes," she said. She extinguished her lamp and moved to help him push the door open.

They both paused as the door eased open. The room wasn't what they had expected. Dazzled by the décor they moved slowly into the room. It was done in a grand manner and it was full of furniture, rugs, and art. Hints of gold were found around the room and walls that seemed to have no end. "This must take up the entire top floor," Emma said, moving further into the space.

Jeremy followed her and muttered, "I don't want to be arrested for breaking and entering." He listened intently for any steps that might be coming their way.

"You have a point. Let's head back." They passed a gallery wall. "The family that lives here?" she murmured. She studied them closely. Emma paused when one caught her eye. "Well, well," she said.

"What is it?" Jeremy asked, he had moved back to the door they entered.

"Paul!" a voice called from another room. Emma rushed over to the door where he was waiting. "I'll explain downstairs." They hurried back into the passage, down their stairs, and back into Patrice's room.

"Another question to add to our list. Who lives on the top floor of the building?" he asked.

Emma nodded, mulling over who that might be, based on that painting she'd seen. She looked at Jeremy, "We'll need confirmation, but I think it's a relative of Patrice."

He asked curiously, "What did you see that makes you believe Patrice's story about her father?"

"Patrice has very distinctive blue eyes. The painting I saw could have been Patrice in fifty years."

"The likeness was that close?"

"Yes," she said. "Definitely."

"Let's check with Patrice and let her know she can come out." They knocked softly and called to her.

Patrice answered the door quickly, "Did you find anything?"

"Why don't we move back into the living room?" Emma suggested.

They sat and discussed what they'd seen. "Where do we go from here?" Patrice asked.

"The goal would be to have more answers to our many questions," Jeremy said. "I'd like to find out who lives on the top floor of the building."

"Do you think it's my papa's family behind all of this?" she asked, hoping it wasn't true.

"We'll reserve judgment, but they're somehow involved," Emma told her.

Jeremy said, "We'll have to have one person with Patrice."

"I'll stay with her," Emma said, "while you try to get those questions answered."

"I'll do that. You might want to get cleaned up," he suggested.

She looked down and grimaced at the dirt. "Yes, that would be a good idea. You might do that also."

"I'll get my clothes changed and head downstairs." He got organized and headed out, locking the door behind him.

Emma looked over at Patrice, who got the message, "I'll stay here and not answer the door."

She glanced at the middle room and back over at Patrice. "Come help me with this." They went into Patrice's room and Emma stood to one side of the dresser. She motioned Patrice to the other side and they moved it in front of the wall and blocked the door into the passageway. "There, that should keep it closed until I get cleaned up."

Emma washed up quickly, changed, and stepped back out of her room. When she didn't see Patrice right away, she called for her. "Patrice, where are you!" When she still didn't see her, she ran around the large room. She heard a door open and was relieved when she saw Patrice come out.

"I'm sorry." The girl apologized, "I went to get a book from the bedroom."

"That's okay," Emma said relieved. "Why don't you come sit with me and tell me more about your mum and papa? When did they marry? Did they come to Paris for the ceremony?" She was curious if her mum had been here before this.

"No, they married but Mum never came to Paris."

"Why not? Wasn't his business based in Paris?"

"Yes, but his family didn't approve of mum. They didn't want anyone they hadn't picked out. And my mum, they felt she was too common. She works, you see."

*J*eremy took the stairs, contemplating the questions he would ask. The most important of these was trying to locate Patrice's father. *The exposition happening at the same time is complicating things,* he thought, looking at the crowded lobby. *Whose idea was the timing of this move?*

He mulled those questions as he waited in the long line at the desk. He resigned himself to a long wait. When he finally reached the front, the clerk inquired, "Bonjour, vous avez une reservation?"

"Bonjour," Jeremy responded and asked for the manager.

The clerk gave him a long look and then called another clerk over. "If you will step over here," the clerk said, "I'll go get him."

Jeremy stepped out of the line and waited for the manager. The clerk returned with the manager. He stopped when he saw it was Jeremy.

"Bonjour," the manager said, with no welcoming smile this time. "Please follow me." He turned and exited the desk area. Jeremy followed behind into what must be his office.

The room was large and had a desk on the far wall. He sat in his chair and asked, his voice weary, "I thought we had settled this matter. We do not know the girl and she has never been registered at this hotel."

"I have new information that might be of interest to you," Jeremy commented laconically.

"And that is?"

"She's the daughter of Charles Lanier and granddaughter of Sasha Lanier."

The manager looked down at his desk before he asked, "The name is fairly common. How can you be sure?"

"I'm fairly certain," Jeremy said, thinking of that painting Emma had seen.

The manager sat back and looked contemplative. "Monsieur Lanier has not been around for a while now."

"I understand the family owns the hotel."

"Yes, this one and many others," the manager confirmed, wondering where the other man was going with this line of questions.

"Does the family live on the top floor?" Jeremy asked.

The manager's eyes dropped, "Part of the family does occupy that space."

"Can I get a message to them?"

"They will not see you," he said in a firm voice.

Jeremy frowned, "But if I have Monsieur Lanier's daughter, wouldn't they want to know?"

The manager stood and went over to his decanter. He inquired, "Would you like a drink? Scotch?"

Jeremy nodded and walked to where the manager stood. Drinks were poured. Jeremy drank some and enjoyed the smooth scotch.

The manager pulled at his tie, "You know, I have worked for this family for most of my life. I started out moving luggage and then working the desk, and now I'm the manager."

"You must like them if you have stayed this long," Jeremy commented.

"Hmm. I'm not sure about that. I was hired by Charles Lanier's grandfather. I worked with him, the father, and then finally Charles."

"You don't like Charles?"

"I do, but he's not in France as much as I'd like."

"Who do you report to when he's not here?"

"His sister," he said simply.

"Have you seen Charles in the past few weeks?"

"No, he hasn't been here. His sister says he's in England."

"Do you know why he spends so much time there?" Jeremy asked, wondering if this man knew more than he let on.

He looked like he didn't want to answer.

"You know about his wife and daughter!" accused Jeremy.

"I only know of them; they have never been here," the other man said defensively. "I wouldn't be able to identify her."

"But you know she'd be mixed race."

"I do know that," the manager acknowledged, "but there has to be more proof, or Charles' sister will not accept it. There are many mixed-race people living here. This girl could have been anyone."

"Tell me about her. Would she have welcomed her brother's daughter? Or helped her if she were in trouble?"

The other man let out a strangled sound, "Her? No, I think not. The sister runs things. Their father died two months ago and Charles was notified to come home and take over the business."

"What about the other family members? Grandparents? Other siblings?"

"Gone," he said. "The father died and left everything to Charles."

"All of it? Then why is his sister running things now?" Jeremy asked, trying to remember everything.

"Once Charles came back, it was assumed he'd take over and replace his sister."

"But he hasn't returned?"

"No, not that I know of. There are other hotels he could be working at, but I have no information."

"I need to speak with the sister," Jeremy commented.

"Her name is Abella, but you may have a better time speaking to the Madam."

"The Madam?"

"Their mother."

"Then we need to see her. Where is she?"

"That might be a problem. She's in mourning for her husband and has not left her rooms."

"Is she in this hotel?"

"She has her home in one of the older ones in the arrondissement."

"Also owned by the family?"

"One of our finest," he confirmed.

The manager watched as Jeremy set his glass down and asked, "What will you do now?" Before Jeremy could answer, the manager's eyes widened as he said, "Oh no, the girl's mother is actually missing!"

"Well yeah. That's what we've been trying to tell you," Jeremy said, "We still have to find her and we may also have to look for her father. We'll take care of Patrice and make sure nothing else happens to her."

"Is that her name?" the manager asked. He hadn't taken the time before this to find out.

"Yes," Jeremy said, watching the manager's face show regret.

"You might mention that to the Madam," he suggested.

Jeremy raised his eyes brows and asked, "Why?"

"Her name is also Patrice," he explained.

"I'll keep that in mind," he said as he held out his hand for the other man to shake. "I'll be on my way."

"You might try Madam early tomorrow," the manager said as Jeremy walked to the door.

"Why is that?"

"Mademoiselle Abella sleeps in," the manager said helpfully.

Mulling all of the information over, Jeremy headed back upstairs to share what he'd learned. He exited the elevator and saw a boy of about nine in the hallway. Jeremy stopped and said, "Bonjour."

The boy stared at the door and didn't appear to hear. "Are you all right?" Jeremy asked.

The boy looked startled at his appearance and violently shook his head before running off in the opposite direction.

"That was strange," Jeremy muttered. He put the boy out of his mind and used his key to open the door. When he entered, he saw Patrice and Emma were still talking.

Emma called out, "Did you find out anything?"

"Always impatient," he called back. "Let me sit down first." He went in, sat down, and deliberately took his time starting.

"Jeremy!" Emma said loudly.

"Okay, okay, a few things," he said and looked at Patrice. "Your grandmother is in residence at another hotel in the city."

"Then who's on the top floor?" Emma asked, thinking of the painting she'd seen.

"Abella, Patrice's aunt," Jeremy supplied.

That made Patrice frown. Emma was watching her, "What's the matter? That news seemed to bother you."

"Papa mentioned we were to live in this hotel," Patrice said, remembering her papa's description of their new life here.

Hmm, thought Emma, *something to think about. What if Abella didn't want to move?* "Does anyone else lives with her?" Emma asked Jeremy.

"I didn't ask," he admitted.

"We'll have to find out. I expect the 'ghost' lives there," said Emma. "You mentioned a grandmother. What are you thinking?"

"I think we need to go see her. Also, I found out her name is Patrice."

"It is?" she asked, as she glanced over at Patrice.

"I was named after her," the other girl said helpfully.

Emma smiled, "Then we'll have to see her. I think, once she takes a look at you, there'll be a large number of questions answered."

"When will we go?" asked Patrice, ready for this to be over.

"Tomorrow morning?" Jeremy suggested.

"Why not now?" Emma asked.

"Well, I learned that Abella likes to sleep in. So, I'm thinking that'll make it easier to leave without her being notified."

"I like it," Emma confirmed. "We'll need to be refreshed and ready for the meeting,"

Patrice was hopeful for the first time, "Do you think she knows where my mum and papa are?"

"I think that'll be a good start," Jeremy said.

"We should try to get some rest," suggested Emma.

"What about that?" Jeremy used his head to indicate Patrice's room.

"I think we've had enough drama tonight. Patrice can sleep with me in our room," said Emma. "You can sleep in Dora and Tim's room."

"What about Patrice's room? What if someone comes into the suite?" asked Jeremy.

"Patrice and I moved the dresser in front of the door. We can also move something heavy in front of the hallway door. If the 'ghost' tries to come in, he shouldn't be able to move it," said Emma. After they closed the door to the room and moved a bookcase in front of it.

"That's done," said Emma. "Bedtime." She took Patrice's hand and headed toward their room.

Jeremy stopped them, "I learned one more thing. We may have a difficult time getting to Patrice's grandmother."

"Why's that?" asked Emma.

"Her husband," he looked at Patrice with a serious expression, "your grandfather, has passed away. I was told she's in mourning and may not be seeing anyone."

"Grandfather? I never even got to meet him." The small happiness Patrice felt drained out of her.

"We're sorry," Emma said in sympathy.

They headed to get their things to prepare for bed. Jeremy exited their room and Emma followed him. "Hey, I'll miss you," she said softly as she kissed him.

"It's only for the night," he reminded her, tucking her hair that had become loose behind her ear.

"I hope this goes well tomorrow."

"Me, too," he said. He noticed she was staring toward Tim and Dora's room.

"We'll find them tomorrow," he promised.

"Yes, once we get Patrice settled, we can find them," she said determinedly.

CHAPTER 17

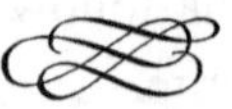

The next morning, Emma, Jeremy, and Patrice entered the Assond Hotel. They paused and Jeremy observed, "I don't think we're going to get anywhere with the desk. Their main job is to keep people from bothering her, especially now."

"I agree," Emma said and they headed to the elevator. It opened as they approached and they stepped in. Emma studied the board and noted the highest floor just under the penthouse. Jeremy frowned and she mouthed, *Later.* She didn't want the elevator operator to know where they were going.

"Floor?" the elevator operator asked in French.

"Nine please." The three were quiet as the elevator made its way to the requested floor. When the elevator stopped, they disembarked and waited until the elevator doors closes before moving.

"Why didn't we go to the top?" asked Jeremy.

"I think we wouldn't have been allowed up there. I bet the elevator opens into the residence," she said.

Emma started down the hallway to an unmarked door. Patrice and Jeremy followed. She reached out and tried the knob. It was locked.

"We'll have the same issue; this time a locked door," Patrice said, looking at it.

"Oh, that's okay, locked doors are not an issue," Emma said as she pulled out her lockpick kit. Jeremy watched with a smile.

After a few minutes, the lock clicked, and the three made their way inside and up the stairs. "I'm hoping this is the service entrance."

They climbed the stairs, each person lost in their own thoughts, not wanting to voice their nerves. The stairs stopped at another locked door.

"Will you open this one?" asked Patrice.

Emma looked thoughtful, "Hmmm. I think I'll just knock on this one." Jeremy grinned at her. "Ready?" she asked her small group.

"Yes," Jeremy and Patrice answered together.

Emma raised her hand and knocked. It was only a few moments before the door swung open, revealing a tall man dressed in a black suit and tie. *Butler,* thought Emma.

"Oui, vous avez une livraison?" he asked, looking at their hands. *Yes, you have a delivery?* He frowned and continued in French, "How did you get up here if you were not accompanied? This is a private residence. I'll have to contact security and report you."

They heard a woman's voice ask in French, "What is happening here?"

"Nothing, madam, these people have made a mistake. I'll have it corrected."

Emma raised her voice to make sure she was heard. "Patrice we can come back later."

"Patrice?" the woman questioned, her voice faint.

Emma answered for her. "Elle s'appelle Patrice Lanier."

"Move aside, William," they heard the other woman say in English. The man moved and, for the first time, they saw the woman they had been speaking with. She was in all-black lace. It was an intricate dress with a high neck and long sleeves. Her dark hair, streaked with grey, was done elaborately on her head. "Patrice, come to me," she said in a commanding voice.

Patrice kept her eyes downward and gripped Emma's hand tightly. Emma looked at the Madam, then back at Patrice, "It's okay, go on," she encouraged

Patrice removed her hand from Emma's and went to where the Madam stood.

"Let me see your eyes," the Madam commanded, using her right hand to lift Patrice's chin gently.

When brilliant blue eyes met an identical set, they both gasped.

"You're Charles' Patrice," the woman said and pulled her into a fierce hug. The Madam looked over Patrice's shoulder at Emma, "You're not Catherine."

"No, I'm Emma Evans and this is Jeremy Tilden," Emma answered.

"Let us move into the sitting room. I think we're offending William's sensibilities."

They observed William and saw he was indeed uncomfortable. Emma answered, "Of course." They moved to follow the Madam.

William rushed ahead of her and held the door open for them. The room they entered was large and similar to the penthouse at their hotel. It was decorated in dark browns and burgundy, with large couches and rugs that covered the space. The dining room was located at the far end of the room.

Patrice wasn't interested in the room; she was staring at her grandmother.

The Madam sat, "Now, sit." She kept Patrice next to her and asked, "Where is your mother? I have wanted to meet her for such a long time."

"You have?" Patrice asked, astonished at her grandmother's statement.

"Yes, *I* have," said the Madam. Her emphasis was noted by Emma.

"Mum is missing," Patrice said loudly. She lowered her voice and continued, "She disappeared from the hotel."

The Madam seemed shocked and looked over at Emma and Jeremy for confirmation. "And what do you know about this?" the Madam asked Emma. It came out as a demand, but Emma could see the worry in her eyes.

"I can tell you what we know," Emma commented. She and Jeremy went into the description of how they met Patrice. They hadn't yet mentioned the ghost or the secret panel.

"You say the hotel claimed you didn't have a room?" Her voice raised at this outrage, that someone from her family would have been treated this way.

"Yes," commented Patrice.

"Why isn't my son with you?"

"Papa told us to meet him at the hotel. Mum thought we'd be seeing him and then visiting you. Did you know we were coming to Paris?" Patrice asked.

"No, I haven't been myself as of late," her grandmother replied, touching the broach at her throat.

"We heard that Grandfather passed. I'm sorry," commented Patrice.

The Madam pulled herself back from her memories, "Yes, thank you." Her gaze moved back to Emma and Jeremy, "Did you speak to the manager of the hotel? Or just a clerk?"

"I did speak to both," commented Jeremy. "I was shown the register and was told neither Patrice nor Catherine ever had a room there. They also mentioned that no one accompanied Patrice."

"Who would have set up the room for them?" Emma asked.

"My son would have done that. You say Catherine was sick?"

"She seemed to be," Patrice said and looked at Emma and Jeremy for support.

"There's another part of the story you're not aware of," commented Emma.

"Well, tell me," the Madam said impatiently.

Instead of answering, Emma said, "We're staying in a suite on the third floor."

The Madam was a little shocked, "How would you have gotten that room?"

"What do you mean?" Jeremy asked.

"That room is normally only for guests we need to have private meetings with."

"So, you do know about the secret panel that leads to the penthouse?" he asked.

"I do, but I don't know who would have assigned it to you." She frowned at them, trying to understand their part in her family drama. "What does this have to do with Patrice's mum being sick?"

"Someone has been drugging Patrice to keep her off balance," Emma answered, "We believe her mum was also drugged before her disappearance."

The Madam looked at her without expression. Instead of responding to that, she asked, "What was your purpose for coming to Paris?"

Emma decided to let the Madam guide the conversation. and she responded, "We were invited by The Art Curator's Society. They said it was because of my work on a case a few years back, that saved art within their community."

Madam studied Emma with renewed interest, "Yes, I read about that, but that name you mentioned, The Art Curator's Society, I have never heard of it."

"Neither had the local gallery owners," Emma informed her. They had received confirmation from the museum manager that the society wasn't real.

"You were brought here under false circumstances," stated the Madam.

"Yes, we believe so."

The Madam asked, "Do you think someone at the hotel might

be involved in this?"

"We're not sure," Emma admitted and looked over at Jeremy.

He started, "The manager that Patrice dealt with was not the same one that's there now."

"Did you inquire about the man?" the Madam asked.

"I was told he left and isn't expected to return."

She frowned but didn't say anything.

Patrice asked, "Grandmeir, you own the hotel, can you inquire about this man?"

"That is rather complicated," the Madam said and glanced away.

"Why is that?" Emma asked.

The older woman sighed, stood, and walked to the mantle. She picked up a small painting and looked at it for a long time. Finally, she turned back to them still clutching the picture tightly. "Abella is running the hotel. I'm not involved in the day-to-day business there. She would not like my interference."

"I thought Papa was running the hotels here in Paris," commented Patrice.

"He does. But that one… I agreed to let my daughter run it."

"What is the concern?" Emma asked.

"It was a trial having her run it, and she wasn't working out. Charles was going to come back and take over. Which is why I was finally going to meet my family. Charles needed to relocate here." The Madam looked thoughtful and asked, "The passageway you mentioned, did you see anyone come through into that room?"

"Yes, a small boy of about nine. He's blond with blue eyes and a slim build." Emma saw Jeremy's surprise at the description and explained, "Patrice remembered more when you were with the manager."

"I saw a boy that met that description in the hallway near our hotel room," Jeremy responded.

"What was he doing?" the Madam asked.

"Watching the door," he commented, wishing he had stopped him and asked who he was.

"You didn't think that odd?" the Madam asked.

"No, not at that time. We've seen kids all over the hotel. I just thought it was another one running around."

"Is this him?" asked the Madam as she held out the portrait to them.

Jeremy took it first and studied it. "Yes, I believe so." He passed it on to Patrice, "Do you recognize him?"

Patrice's face went white, "It's him."

"He's my grandson, Paul," the Madam said tightly.

"Do you think his mother did something to Mum?" Patrice asked tremulously.

"I hope not," her grandmother said as she walked over to take Patrice's hand. She was resolved and asked, "Where do we go from here?"

"I was thinking about that," said Emma. "Patrice, how did you find us? How did you know to come to our suite?"

"The bellman told me," Patrice said.

"The bellman?"

"Yes, I was giving up hope and the hotel had threatened to have me removed, then this man in a uniform came up and whispered to me that Emma could help me."

"What happened next?" Jeremy asked.

"He helped me to your room and left me outside your door."

"Why didn't he stay and how did he know about Emma?"

"I don't know," Patrice answered simply.

"We need to talk to this bellman. Did you know his name? Can you give us a description?" asked Emma.

"I don't think there was a name, but he had a mark on his hand. A black circle."

"Thank you, Patrice, that'll give us something to go on," Emma told the girl, "We'll need to go there next." She glanced over at the Madam, "We need a safe place for Patrice to stay."

"She will stay here," she said firmly. She placed a hand on her hair and asked, "Would you like that?"

"I would!"

"Good, we have a lot to talk about," The Madam said and smiled at her granddaughter warmly.

Patrice smiled back. "I'd like that."

"We'll leave now and investigate this," Emma said softly. "Please, keep her presence here quiet."

"I will," promised the Madam.

"Your staff…" started Emma.

"They can be trusted," the Madam said, her tone brooking no argument.

"Patrice, we'll be back," Emma assured the girl.

"I'll be okay here," she said, her hand still in the Madam's hands.

They stood and turned back toward the kitchen. The Madam called to them, a laugh in her voice. "You may use the front entrance to leave."

"I'll take them, Madam," William said quietly. He had entered the room and heard her last comment.

Emma grinned back and Jeremy laughed as they adjusted their path and followed William to the elevator. "Thank you," Jeremy said.

William nodded and pushed the call button for them. When it appeared, the operator looked surprised at the persons waiting to board. How they had gotten to the penthouse without him seeing. His frown spoke volumes and William spoke up, "You need not concern yourself."

The operator opened and closed his mouth several times but didn't say anything. He finally nodded and waved them into the elevator. He didn't say anything as they rode down and exited into the lobby.

Emma pulled Jeremy to a halt as they strode through the lobby. "This is a beautiful hotel," she observed.

"Expensive," he murmured, taking in his surroundings.

"There's a lot of money at stake here, and only one sibling left to take it all," she said contemplatively.

He nodded. "Let's find that bellboy."

They were able to get a carriage to take them back to their hotel. Once there they found the lobby was full of people. Emma asked, "How do we find him?"

"Let's ask them," Jeremy said, indicating the bellmen grouped across the room.

"Casually, we need to look for that mark," she suggested.

They headed over to them. Jeremy asked in French, "Can I get directions to a local patisserie?"

Two of the men pointed. Emma shook her head; she didn't see the mark. They needed to talk to one of the men alone. She continued her observations and saw a man standing away from the other bellman on the opposite side of the desk. Emma cleared her throat and nodded toward him.

Jeremy and Emma walked over to him, "Sir, can I speak to you for a moment?" she asked.

The bellman had straightened as they approached. "Do you need some help with your bags?"

"No, we have a question about another bellman. He has a circle mark on the back of his hand," Emma said, keeping her voice low.

He glanced around quickly, "Not here." He nodded to the corner and they followed him to a closet where bags were stored when rooms were unavailable.

"His name is Etienne and you won't find him here," he said.

"Where is he?" asked Emma.

"He's gone," he said simply.

"Do you know if he left of his own accord?"

"Definitely not. He supports his family and he's worried about his job. He's in hiding."

"Why?"

"For helping that girl and getting her to you," the bellman said.

"You know about that?"

"Etienne and I are friends," he said simply.

"Do you know his address?" Jeremy asked.

"I do, but he isn't there."

Emma's mouth twisted; her patience was waning. "Do you know where he is?"

"Yes," he answered simply.

"And," Jeremy prompted.

"He's at my place," the man admitted. "It's in the 18 Arrondissement." He wrote it down quickly and handed it to Emma.

A voice called the bellman's name. He was distracted by the call and said, "I have to go. I have to keep this job."

"Go on," Emma said. "We'll be getting back with you."

"Don't let anything happen to Etienne," he pressed.

"We won't," she promised.

They studied the address. Jeremy said, "Should we head over there now?"

She looked conflicted. "Jeremy, I know this is important but I am worried. What if Dora and Tim are with Michael and Lenora?"

"Isn't that what we suspected all along?"

"Yes, but what if they're there against their will? Inspector Levan mentioned they had checked out," she speculated.

"Before we head to the bellboy's apartment, we should probably go check their hotel room," Jeremy suggested. He glanced over at the desk, "I see the manager who talked to me earlier. Let me see if I can get their room number."

She nodded and stayed where she was as he went to the desk.

"Let's go up to the room," he said coming back.

They went two floors up and stood in front of room 2958. Jeremy knocked and they waited, not expecting anyone to answer. However, they were surprised to come face to face with someone they didn't recognize.

"Yes?" the man asked.

"I'm sorry to bother you. We're looking for information about the couple who stayed here. Could you tell me when you checked in?" inquired Jeremy.

"Well," the man admitted. "I was lucky. I showed up without a reservation and the hotel was full. I was told that the room had come available at just that moment."

"When was this?" asked Emma.

"Yesterday evening."

"Thank you," said Jeremy.

The door closed and Emma observed, "That was when we received the note about yesterday. They must have come by to the hotel to leave the note and check out."

The worry about Dora and Tim made its way to the surface. "Two cases," she said, "both involving vanishing people."

"Do you think they're connected?" Jeremy asked.

"I don't think so; these appear to be two separate cases."

"Where to next? Bellman?"

"It's our best bet for finding Patrice's mum," she confirmed.

"And Tim and Dora?" he asked, knowing she was worried. Should that case take precedence over this one?

She shook her head and said, "We should move forward on Patrice's case. We have a definite location for the bellboy. We can re-evaluate after that."

They exited the hotel and walked a few blocks to get a cab. "This would be easier," she muttered, "if it wasn't so crowded."

Jeremy just smiled in response.

The cab took them to an older apartment building. They paid the driver and went into the older building. There they found the door and knocked. A scurrying could be heard inside but the sounds did not approach the door. "Etienne, we're here to ask you questions about Patrice," she called in French.

"You might mention your name," Jeremy suggested.

"Etienne, Etienne, I'm Emma you told Patrice to come to me

for help."

After she made that statement, the lock on the door could be heard unlatching.

A young man appeared. "Etienne?" she asked.

"Oui." This was confirmed when he rubbed his hand across his face and they saw the round mark on his hand.

His eyes went to Jeremy. "He's with me," she said firmly. She saw his hesitance and said, "We want to help Patrice."

He stepped back, "Come in, and you can speak English."

They entered the apartment and he locked the door quickly behind them.

When he noticed the security measures, Jeremy asked, "Is someone threatening you?"

Etienne didn't answer. Instead, he waved them to the small sitting area, "Please, sit." He waited for them to take their seats and took the one across from them. He started to explain his role in Patrice's adventure. "It all started when Monsieur Lanier told me to keep an eye out for his wife and daughter."

"When was this?" asked Emma, pulling out her notebook.

"It was the morning before Patrice and her mother arrived. He said he was being called out of the country on critical business. His father had died and there were concerns he needed to deal with immediately."

"Did it seem like it was planned?" Jeremy asked.

"No, he found out after his family was already traveling. He said he'd leave them a letter."

Emma made note of that; there had been no mention of a letter. "What did he ask you to do?"

"To watch out for them," he said simply.

"Watch out?" Jeremy questioned. "Why?"

"At the time, I thought it was just the request from a worried husband and father."

"And now?" Emma asked.

"I think he knew something might happen while he was gone,"

Etienne admitted.

"What were his exact instructions?" Emma asked. She had to know the connection between Patrice and herself.

"He said if Patrice or her mother needed help for any reason, I should tell them to find you," he explained.

"How would you know where we were located?" asked Jeremy. *What was the tie-in to their suite?*

"Mister Lanier saw your name on the reservation books. He moved you to that suite you're in now. He wanted to make sure his wife and daughter could find you if they needed help."

"So, our being located in that room *is* related to the Vanishing lady case," Emma murmured to Jeremy.

"Did you see Patrice's mother arrive at the hotel?" asked Jeremy

"They arrived late, and I was off duty at that time."

"Did you follow up the next day?" asked Emma.

"No," he said miserably. "My directions were that they'd come to me if they needed anything. I should have checked them that day. I told myself they were resting."

"How did you know they'd checked in?" Jeremy asked as he thought of his conversation with the manager.

"I checked the reservation book," Etienne admitted. It was normally off-limits to personnel other than the clerks assigned to that area.

"Are you sure?" asked Jeremy. "I saw the reservation book; it didn't list either of them."

Etienne nodded his head, "Oh, I'm sure. Their names were both listed."

"There must be a second book. We need to find it," Emma told Jeremy.

And what else did the manager hide from me? Jeremy thought.

"Why are you hiding?" Emma asked.

"I had to. After Patrice's mum disappeared. The managers were making plans to have Patrice taken away. I heard them discussing how troublesome she was becoming. I knew I had to act and get her to you. Then I left."

"Who knew that you did this?"

"Just my friend Howard. He let me stay here. We can trust him."

"No one else?" Emma asked as she took notes on his statements.

"No, no one," he confirmed.

"Why not take her to her family, her aunt lives in the hotel," asked Emma

"Mr. Lanier," Etienne supplied. "When I asked him why I just didn't take her to them, he was clear I was not to do that."

Emma frowned, "Why would he say that?"

He turned red, "I don't like to gossip, but his sister never liked Mister Lanier. They do not get along. I believe she has also said some terrible things about Patrice and her mum."

"How do you know that?"

"That one, she can be loud and doesn't care who's listening."

"We took Patrice to her grandmother. Will she be safe there?"

"If she is with the Madam, then yes. Listen, I'm planning to leave town until I have heard from my friend that it's safe to come back."

"We understand. How do we get in touch with you?"

"Let Howard know; he'll find me."

"Thank you. You probably saved Patrice's life," Emma said.

"I wish I'd done more, but I was so scared," he said, looking down at his hands.

"Maybe next time something like this comes up, you will," she suggested quietly.

He nodded.

They stood and Jeremy said, "Etienne, we wish you well and will try to get word to you soon."

"I hope so, thank you," the other man said gratefully.

Jeremy and Emma stood in the hallway after the door was

closed and locked. Jeremy leaned against the wall, "It looks like Abella is behind all of this."

"Yes, and everyone seems to know," Emma said wonderingly. "How could she do this to her family?"

"Do you think Patrice's mum is still alive?" asked Jeremy, wondering if they were chasing a ghost.

"I do. It makes the most sense. It would be hard to get rid of a body, especially with all of those crowds."

"But then they'd have to house and feed her," he reasoned.

"That's true," she said contemplatively. He noticed she raised her fingers to her lips to drum them.

"What are you thinking?"

"*If* she's alive and Abella is involved, I'd say she's in the penthouse of our hotel."

"Sounds reasonable," he said, always up for an adventure. "When do we go in?"

"Tonight, late. Agreed?"

"Agreed." He could see her face becoming more serious. "What are you thinking of?"

"The same thing that's been on my mind for the last day."

"Tim and Dora," he guessed.

"Yes," she said.

"We can work on their case. Where do you want to start?"

"Michael, Lenora, and Julian seem connected to the Galerie des Machines."

"That's true. Since we've been in Paris, that's where we have seen them together."

"And that's where Julian died," she reminded him. "I'd also like to talk to Papa and find out about the meeting he had with Julian. We need to know if he's aware of what Julian was involved in."

"So, we go to the Galerie des Machines?"

"Yes. We can stop for something to eat on the way and then head to the exposition."

He offered his elbow to her; she took it and they walked

downstairs. "I think I saw a small café nearby."

"Lead the way."

They found it and had a light lunch with a round loaf of bread, cheese, and wine.

They finished quickly and found a cab to the exposition. "This has been an active vacation," Jeremy commented.

"Aren't they all?" Emma teased as she leaned on him.

"It does make things interesting."

"Yes, it does," she murmured, tilting her head back to kiss him. After their kiss, she settled with her head on his shoulder. Emma didn't mind that the ride took some time.

As they arrive, they stepped off the carriage. "It seems more people are here than in the morning," she said. Jeremy nodded, took her hand, and started walking with her through the crowds.

"Want to try the train?" she called.

"If we can get on it," he called back, continuing to go through the crowd that seemed to flow to the long train line. "We haven't made our way to the country exhibits yet," he said, looking toward that area.

"Funny thing about that. Julian wasn't sure we should. He didn't believe it adequately represented the different cultures. Though I'd still like to see them," said Emma.

"We'll get over there before we head home," he promised.

She continued to look around as they made their way to the front of the line. They boarded and took their seats. As it started to move, she glanced to her right and frowned. "Is that? It has to be…Jeremy," she said in a low whisper. "It's them, isn't it?"

"It's them, Lenora and Michael," Jeremy muttered, watching the duo.

Before he could stop her, Emma jumped up and yelled out the window, "Lenora! Michael! Stop!" Her voice must have carried because the two stopped in the crowd and turned toward the moving train. When they saw her, they took off at a run. The train was moving smoothly, but they were faster.

"We need to get off," she muttered as she dropped back into her seat.

Jeremy wanted to as well, but the train was very crowded and would likely not stop for them. She sat back reluctantly in her chair.

"They're headed toward the gallery," he commented, continuing to monitor their movements from the window.

Emma's enjoyment was gone for the train ride; she strained, trying to catch a glimpse of Lenora and Michael. The train came to a stop and they filed out. Emma and Jeremy were seated in the middle and had to wait until the people in front of them moved.

Once they were off, they moved through the crowd quickly, breaking into a run as they got closer to the Gallery de Machines' outer entrance. They pulled open the large glass doors and entered quickly, running through the exhibits. They were no longer fascinating, they were in the way. They continued to run through the maze of machines. Jeremy was a little ahead of her and said over his shoulder, "They've split up. You go after her and I'll go after him."

She nodded and headed in the direction he indicated. She slipped her hand into her skirt pocket and pulled out her knife, palming it as she ran. Lenora was just ahead on a parallel walkway. Emma jumped on a table, crossing quickly, and leaped onto Lenora's back. Emma pulled her hair back and placed the knife under her chin. "Go along with what I say," she growled in a low voice, "and you might live. Do you understand?"

Lenora nodded and they stood up. Instead of going docilely forward, she pivoted and, to Emma's surprise, was wielding her own knife.

Emma had just a moment to respond. She bent backward to escape the slicing motion of the knife. The corset limited her movement, but when she felt the knife go across her ribs, there was a quick burn but not a deep cut. *Corsets? Who knew?*

She pulled herself back up and kicked the other woman in the stomach. It knocked the breath out of Lenora and the knife flew out of her hand. Emma deftly caught it.

"Are you ready to accompany me now?" Emma asked, rubbing the blades together.

"Yes," Lenora mumbled.

A group of people had formed a circle around them.

Emma palmed the knives, "All part of the show folks, we were just having fun, weren't we?" She nudged the other woman to respond.

"Yes, we're friends," Lenora said, standing close to Emma.

"Was that you running across the displays?" asked the owner of the area she had run across.

"I'm sorry. I got carried away with our game," Emma apologized.

"Take it outside," he demanded.

She nodded and turned to Lenora, "Come with me."

The group parted as they left the area. Lenora started to struggle against the firm hold Emma had on her as she was pulled along through the crowd. Lenora continued to slow their progress by dragging her feet, which caused Emma to stop short.

Emma turned back towards her, "Come on. Stop stalling."

Lenora's eyes widened and she opened her mouth. The expected sound didn't come out; instead, blood flowed out and she fell forward into Emma's arms. "What?" Emma stopped when she saw the knife sticking out of Lenora's back. What she heard next was a scream.

Damn. Should I stay or make a run for it? she thought for a brief moment. *Stay,* she decided and lay Lenora's body down. Emma took off her jacket to staunch the flow of blood. Voices penetrated her intense concentration and she realized another crowd had formed around them.

"Get help!" she yelled at them.

Her order seemed to unfreeze them. "Police! Police!" several voices called out.

A policeman ran up and told the crowd to clear. He knelt, feeling for a pulse. "I do not believe that is necessary any longer," he said to Emma, causing her to stop pressing down on the wound.

She nodded and thought, *Who killed Lenora?*

The officer pulled her up and away. More officers arrived and quickly removed the body to a nearby room. The people who had organized the exposition would want to minimize any publicity of the event.

"You will need to come with me to the station," the policeman said brusquely. He was still unsure what her role in the murder had been. "Wait here. Do not leave, I need to tell the detectives I am taking you to the station."

"Of course," Emma said. She knew the procedure would require questioning her. *Though*, she thought, *I don't know how much information she could provide.*

There was a noise coming toward her; a man pushed through the crowd. Jeremy's face came into view. He took in the scene, "Are you okay?" he asked.

Emma looked down and felt where Lenora's knife had made contact with her. "You know, there's something positive about corsets. The whalebone in the garment helped protect me. It was just a glancing blow."

Jeremy put his hand on the torn fabric and said, "Good. Maybe you should wear those back home."

"I'm thinking the same thing."

"So, what happened? Who killed Lenora?"

"I don't know. I was trying to get her out of here to question her and then this happened," she said, waving her hand towards the policemen taking away Lenora's body.

They continued to watch the policemen discuss the scene. Two bodies in two days; there would be questions. An officer walked over to her, "You know this woman? You were with her?"

"I was," Emma answered.

"We understand that you jumped on her and effectively dragged her away." It was a statement, not a question

"I just wanted to speak with her."

"Do you speak to everyone in that manner?" the officer asked as he watched her carefully.

She kept her face blank, "Sometimes."

A familiar voice spoke. "Two scenes in two days," Inspector Levan said in an almost jovial manner.

"Inspector Levan," she said, relieved to see a familiar face.

Jeremy stepped up, "Can we go somewhere to talk?" He didn't want Emma taken into the station.

Levan looked at them and back at the scene. He dismissed the two officers by saying, "Get pictures before you move her." He looked back at them and said, "Come with me."

He seemed to realize where they were. "There is nowhere in the city to be alone anymore," he said, shaking his head. "Over here." He waved them into a workroom that seemed to be for cleaning supplies. He closed the door and turned toward Emma, "Did you kill her?"

"No," she answered without hesitation.

"The weapon used to kill her was a knife," he said with little emotion in his voice. "I understand that the knife is your weapon of choice."

"It is," she commented. A knock on the door interrupted their questioning.

He frowned heavily toward it and said loudly, "Come in." The officer came in and handed him something wrapped in a cloth. "You may leave now." The officer glared at him and stomped out of the room.

Levan revealed what the cloth covered. It was a lethal-looking knife. It was hard for her not to reach for it. She studied it and thought, *It was well-balanced and the artistry is there.* He watched her, "Is this yours?"

"No, it's not."

"I don't think you'd admit to it, even if it was," he said, examining the knife, then back at her.

"I wouldn't," she admitted.

Jeremy stayed silent, letting the scene play out. He didn't think she was in trouble, but the inspector knew there was more to the story.

"You told me that you didn't have a relationship with Lenora and her husband Michael," Levan accused.

"We didn't. They're friends of Dora and Tim."

"The ones we cannot seem to find to interview," he murmured.

"Yes, they're missing and we think Michael and Lenora know where they are," she said boldly.

"That is what I thought. Why not tell us right away so we could help out?"

"I thought we could handle it ourselves."

He let that go, "Tell me what you know."

Jeremy stepped up, "We don't have a lot of information so far."

"Have Tim or Dora shown back up?" asked Levan.

"Not yet," Emma admitted.

"How did you know to come here? How does the Galerie des Machines factor into this? How did you know Lenora would be here?"

"Michael was here also," commented Jeremy. "I chased him but he got away."

Emma answered the inspector's question. "Since arriving in Paris, besides the hotel, this was the only location we've seen them. It seemed like the most likely spot."

Levan looked around, "What is it about this particular exhibit that would be of such interest or a location for intrigue?"

"We think there's going to be some kind of planned event by the anti-electrical people," Emma admitted.

"Oui," Levan murmured, "it all seems to be going that way. But if they are behind this, why would they go after one of their leaders?"

Emma's gaze first went to Jeremy and then back at Levan, "We'd hoped to get information on their plans from Lenora. Someone must have decided she was a weak point." At that moment, the door opened. They saw the body being taken away.

They were silent as they watched it go by. "Our main goal is to find Tim and Dora and make sure they're okay," Jeremy said.

"If that is true, why wait until today to investigate their disappearance?" Levan asked.

Emma said, "We've had another case that needed us."

"Another case?" he murmured. "Maybe it's something I can help with?"

"Possibly. It's stable right now, but we may need your help soon."

"Are things normally this interesting around you?" he asked.

Jeremy answered that with a hearty laugh. "Yeah, this is pretty normal for us."

"I think I can help with Dora and Tim's disappearance," the inspector said thoughtfully.

"How so?" Emma asked eagerly. She was desperate to have something to help move the case forward and get her family home.

"We have a lead on Lenora and Michael," he stated.

"You started to look into them?"

"Yes, there were just too many coincidences, and now this."

"What did you find?" asked Jeremy.

Levan checked his notes, "They're actually from the United States."

"That isn't much of a lead," she commented. "They came over with us."

"Yes, you're right, but we did find out they rent several apartments in the city. We also had several anti-electricity demonstrators picked up who were able to identify them."

"What type of demonstration were they involved in?" asked Jeremy. He wondered about their level of violence. They knew

Lenora and Michael would do what they had to, but what about their other demonstrators? Were they as committed?

"Up until now, they've been just a nuisance. They hate the tower, they hate the changes for the exposition, and they hate anything to do with electricity."

"Electricity," Emma murmured. *It keeps coming up. Could that be it?* she thought, looking at the exhibits showing through the door. But why involve Tim and Dora?

"What are you thinking?" Levan asked.

"Tim and Dora. Why would someone involved with the anti-electricity movement want them?" she asked. "They're no one special. They don't have any connections to any of this. Unless...."

Levan didn't interrupt, waiting for her to explain her thoughts. Jeremy watched Emma formulate ideas and possibilities in her mind, discarding some, and accepting others. He saw her eyes widen.

"Jeremy!" she said, turning to him, "It must be Papa!"

"Ellis? How so?" he asked, trying to keep up with her.

"Come on, I'll show you." Before Jeremy and Levan knew it, she had exited the room. They had to run to keep pace. She stopped abruptly in front of the Edison exhibit. "This is it," she said and whirled around.

When they didn't respond, she held her arms open wide, taking in her surroundings, "Don't you see? They hate electricity; they're here on the world's biggest stage to prove something."

"Prove what and how?" asked Levan.

"That, I'm not sure of," she admitted, "but I think Papa, Tim, Dora, and Mr. Edison are all connected to this. "

"Why?" Jeremy asked.

"Papa's note," she said. "There's something very special happening this evening and I believe it involves Mr. Edison."

"And they want to interfere in that, to prove a point about electricity?" Levan asked.

"Yes, but I think it's more than interference," she said.

Levan protested. "These people are normally not violent; they demonstrate and loudly discuss their concerns and then leave."

"I think Lenora and Michael were pushing for a dramatic demonstration. You know we were sent tickets and brought over by people who haven't revealed themselves yet."

"You think it was them," the inspector asked.

Jeremy spoke up, "I think we were brought here for a reason and this, along with Tim and Dora disappearing, seems to confirm it."

"Where do we go from here?" muttered Emma, looking at the brilliant lighting exhibit.

"Find Tim and Dora," suggested Jeremy.

"I wonder," Emma said, "what about the security for tonight, in case something is planned."

The Inspector was surprised, "Yes, we'll have extra security but we do not expect the crowds to be unruly."

Emma looked around, "Oh, the crowds will be involved, but not in the way you think. I think they want a large group of people here to prove their point…"

"That electricity can be dangerous," Jeremy finished her statement.

The inspector's face went white and he put a hand to his heart. "We can't call off the event." He walked closer to them and lowered his voice. "Edison and Tesla will be here tonight."

"Both of them? Here?" asked Emma, astonished. "I thought they didn't get along."

"That is just a rumor," said Levan. "They're meeting at the Eiffel Tower."

"That must be it," Jeremy said, "That would be quite a splash. Go after the men at the head of the technology."

"No, I don't think so." Emma said slowly. "I read about this. The tower was supposed to be electrically lit, but there were problems and they had to use gas lamps."

"Then where?" Jeremy asked.

"It could be anywhere," she admitted.

"But that installation is very big. We don't have time to find it," Levan said. He was right; the sun was starting to set.

Emma said, "Inspector, can you round up your people and start inspecting the lines?"

"Even if we could, there's no way we'd be able to walk all the lines," the inspector insisted.

"Can we stop the program?" Jeremy asked.

The inspector said, "France's national pride was tied up in this exposition. Anything but that."

"What time is it expected to start?" Emma asked, thinking about what they could do.

"At 10PM."

"We have four hours then."

Levan was resigned, "I can have my men walk the lines, but what are we looking for?"

"A bomb," Emma said with certainty.

"A bomb?" questioned Jeremy. "What makes you think it must be that?"

"It's the electricity. A bomb could be used to complete the circuit. It could be anywhere." She glanced at the inspector, "Do you need a drawing of what types of things to look for?" She could draw out the basics for them.

He shook his head and assured her, "No, we have studied the 1884 and 85 London bombings. We have drawings of the devices, so we're good with the identification."

"Are there drawings of the light exhibit?" she asked, wanting to narrow down the options.

"I'm not sure," Levan admitted.

"Papa said something special was happening tonight; he must have meant Edison and the installation," she murmured.

Jeremy looked at the inspector, "You start the search, and we'll find Ellis."

"I think he's probably at the Eiffel Tower," said Emma.

The trio separated, their tasks clear.

The inspector called to his men and headed toward the outdoor lighting installation.

Emma and Jeremy headed toward the Eiffel Tower. They were jogging, but the crowds prevented them from moving too quickly. She wanted to push. The people seemed to be deliberately getting in their way. Jeremy had her hand and was pulling her through the crowd. They were feeling desperate and she told him, "Keep going. I'll keep up."

He looked at her, "Grab my coat and hang on."

She got a grip and called, "Go!" They forced their way through with complaints all around.

They pushed past a very large man. "Hey!" the man called loudly. He was obviously American. "Where are you going in such a hurry?" he said, grabbing Jeremy by the collar and lifting him off of his feet.

We don't have time for this, thought Emma. The man holding Jeremy didn't seem to notice her. The crowd naturally gave the large man space, not wanting trouble. He had a firm hold on Jeremy but swayed from the alcohol he had imbibed. She glanced around quickly and saw he had a bottle of wine next to him on the fountain basin's edge.

Jeremy hammered his fist at the hands holding his collar, but the man had a stranglehold on his neck. Emma took the opportunity to kick him in the back of the legs. It had a dual effect; he dropped Jeremy and fell to his knees. The man was still on his knees when he turned toward her and yelled out, "You, girl, come here!"

Before the large man could get to his feet, Jeremy grabbed her hand and pulled her into the crowds. They saw a police officer and Jeremy thought fast. "Officer, officer! There's a man back there, he's waving a gun...at a woman." He waved toward the man still barreling in their direction.

The man yelled at them, "There you are. I need to talk with

you!"

The officer saw the man pushing people out of his path. When he shoved a child to the ground, the policeman quickly turned away from Jeremy and called on his men. They could not stop him with one person, so several jumped on his back.

Emma and Jeremy sank back into the crowd and looked toward the elevator. "We don't have time for the line," Jeremy commented.

"No, we don't," Emma said, reviewing the area. "It will have to be the stairs." There was also a line there, but it seemed to be progressing more smoothly.

They headed over, trying to find a way to skip the line. They didn't have to work out a plan as the people moved out of the way to watch the large man fighting with the policeman. She and Jeremy moved quickly up the stairs. He looked back and saw the police had wrestled the man to the ground. Jeremy smiled; the big guy had actually helped them.

They made it to the first level, both breathing heavily, but they didn't delay as they headed to the next set of stairs. They were almost vacant; most people stopped on the first floor for the restaurants and the view. The second level was steeper and harder. Once they exited and headed to the final stairs, Emma doubled over trying to catch her breath. "Ready?" she asked gasping.

"The things I do for you," he muttered, following her up another set of stairs.

"Oh, you love it," she said cheekily as they ran.

They headed to the last stairs, which were a spiral, and realized there were guards. *This part should be easy*, she thought. "Bonjour, Monsieur et Monsieur," she addressed them.

"Personne n'est autorisé à monter."

"What now?" Jeremy muttered.

"I have this," said Emma as she leaned toward him. She looked at the guards and said in French, "Please tell Ellis Evans his daughter is here."

The guard watched her closely and finally observed her nod to the other guard, "Tell him to come down and see her."

"Where's the trust," muttered Jeremy.

She smiled slightly as they waited.

They heard a shout from up above. They looked up and saw Ellis and Abbey waving down at them.

"Papa! Abbey!" she called.

He called down to the guards, "I'll claim her. She's my daughter; she can come up."

The guards separated to let her pass but stepped together again when Jeremy tried to go through.

"Uhm, Ellis!??" Jeremy said.

Abbey whispered into Ellis' ear.

Ellis laughed, "Oh, all right, him also,"

The guards begrudgingly separated to let Jeremy pass.

Emma had gone ahead up the final stairs. When she reached the top, she hugged him. "Papa!"

"Emma, what made you come up here tonight? Jeremy, my boy. It's good to see you," he said, reaching around her to shake Jeremy's hand.

"Ellis," Jeremy commented as he shook the other man's hand. "Had me worried there for a minute."

"Papa, can we talk in private?"

"Well, that will be difficult here," Papa said laconically.

She frowned, "Why is that?"

"Come on up and I'll show you," he directed. They followed him up into a room.

The apartment he had told her about, she thought.

It wasn't the office that Jeremy noticed; it was the people in the room. "Emma." He nudged her.

"What?" she asked, finally looking at the people in the room.

She felt faint as she identified Thomas Edison, Nikola Tesla, and Gustave Eiffel all in the same room.

"Tesla and Edison," commented Emma faintly. "I thought ..."

"That we didn't get along? Yeah, well, that's sometimes true," Edison said and laughed. Tesla started laughing as well.

"They're here for the initial unveiling of my tower," Eiffel said. "Emma, we have heard much about you. Jeremy, it's nice to meet you."

"Thank you," Emma said, forgetting for a moment why she was there. She shook herself out of the daze and said bluntly, "We have a concern. There's a possibility of a bomb being placed by the anti-electrical groups."

Edison was contemplative. "Using the circuitry to set it off. Yes. That would work and, to their minds, prove electricity is indeed dangerous."

"It's something we fight continually. We want to normalize it so that it's in every household," Tesla added.

"We've had a few demonstrations by these anti-electrical people when they found out about the lighting displays. We didn't publicize Thomas' trip to prevent a similar demonstration," Eiffel said.

"Sir," Emma asked Edison, "did anyone know you were coming to Paris, especially to the tower?"

"Well, yes, we did keep it a secret, but household staff, family members, and the people who work with me were aware I was coming over. Also, we have employees here working at the Galerie des Machines to maintain the exhibits."

"That's a large number of people and word could have gotten out."

Jeremy nodded.

"What are you thinking, little girl?" Papa asked.

"I think the two people who traveled over with us are involved with the anti-electric people and are trying to create a big event here. We also think they're behind the tickets that got us here. And then," she said, studying her papa, "then there is Julian."

Papa sat suddenly and Abbey went over to him to hold his hand.

"Who was he, Papa?" she asked, giving him a long steady look.

"Was?" That shook Ellis, "What has happened?" he asked.

She sent Jeremy a wide eye look and then shifted back to her papa. "I thought you knew. Papa, he was murdered, in the Galerie des Machines."

Edison stood up and paced. He turned to her, "Where? What display?"

"It was in one of the rooms that supplied the electricity, with the large cabinets and cables," she responded.

"How did he die?" asked Papa.

"He was shot, but we believe he was meant to be electrocuted. They did electrocute a guard."

Edison paled and sat down. "This isn't good. They are serious this time."

"That's what we believe," Jeremy confirmed.

"Papa, who was he? Who was Julian?" she asked again.

Papa pulled his hands down his face and then turned a pale face toward Emma. "He is—*was*—an old friend. Someone I knew a long time ago."

"Is he some type of police officer or detective?" she guessed.

"I shouldn't be surprised that you worked that out," he said dryly. "Yes, he was with Interpol. I met him while working on a special project in London. He approached me and asked me to work for him as a specialist when needed."

Emma smiled suddenly, "Oh, is that why you thought of using specialists for me?" Papa had introduced Emma to different people with skills to teach her and that she used in her adventures.

"It is. If you wanted a life like Julian's, I wanted to make sure you were ready for that."

"Oh, Papa," she said and went to him. "Now, why was he here?"

"He was trailing Lenora and Michael, investigating them. There were suspicions that they were up to something nefarious at the exposition. He wasn't sure what the actual plan was."

"Did he think Tim and Dora were targeted?"

He looked at her appraisingly. "Yes, we had words about that."

"Was that when you and Julian were arguing at the hotel?"

Papa laughed suddenly, "You don't miss much, little girl." He sobered suddenly and said, "Yes, he wanted to let it play out to determine what their plan was."

"And you?"

"I didn't want my children to be in an unsafe condition. I told him we needed to remove them from this observation. He pushed for a few more days; he felt he was close."

"Then he died."

"Yes," he said, wiping his eyes. The emotion of losing an old friend was overwhelming him. Abbey clasped his hand and pulled it to her.

Emma studied Edison and Tesla, "Where do you think would be the worst place to put something that would interfere and cause a large explosion?"

"That would cause the biggest problem?" Edison asked.

"Yes,"

"The transformer room," Tesla and Edison answered at the same time.

"Tim and Dora took Michael and Lenora there during their tour," said Emma.

"When?" Edison asked. "It's a secure room; no one should have been allowed."

"They used my name, didn't they?" Ellis asked.

"Yes," confirmed Emma.

"When was this?" Edison asked.

"Earlier in the week."

Edison said, "Ellis, we need to get to the transformers."

Emma held up her hands to stop him, "Sir, the last thing I think we should do is put their enemy in the area."

Ellis said, "Tom, she's right. You need to stay here."

"Mr. Edison, what should we be looking for?" Emma asked the scientist

"My engineer will be in the area. He should be able to help. If not, there should be a main panel that completes the circuit. If there is something, it should be there."

"Got it." Emma and Jeremy stood and started to head to the door. Ellis started to join them,

"Ellis, dear, I'd like you to stay with me," Abby told him.

He was conflicted, but knowing he'd slow them down, he agreed, "I'll stay here."

The group watched Emma and Jeremy leave and when the door closed, Ellis followed Edison to the windows.

"What do you think it could be now that we know the location?" Ellis asked him.

"I'm thinking they're correct; it's a bomb. It makes the most sense for a large-scale demonstration and maximizes the death count," Edison commented.

"It'll be hard to watch and not be involved. Will they need help?" Ellis asked, gripping Abbey's hand tightly.

"Jeremy and Emma indicated the policemen were searching the lines. We can have our security tell them to meet them at the transformer," suggested Edison.

Ellis nodded. Edison walked out to call one of the guards up. He walked back over, "Do you think they will stop it?"

"I do. If anyone can, those two can," Ellis said as he pulled out his pipe and tobacco.

Edison looked over the crowd and back at Ellis, "So, this Julian. Is there more to the story?"

"Yes."

"Well, go ahead," Edison prompted.

Ellis told his story.

CHAPTER 18

$\mathcal{E}$mma and Jeremy got through the crowds, trying not to create a scene this time. They could see the building in the distance and made their way to the entrance. When they got there, they started to approach the guards, Emma grabbed his arm and suggested, "Let's look around first."

Jeremy hesitated and looked around. "Okay." They waited for the two guards standing at the door to walk away before they made their way around to find an alternate entrance.

"Over there," said Emma pointing to the door.

Jeremy looked around and said, "It's clear," Emma pulled out her lockpicks and knelt quickly by the door.

It took her moments to get the door opened. She pushed it wide and saw it led to a hallway. Emma held up a finger to her lips; he nodded and reached down to slip off his shoes. She did the same and they crept down the hallway. There were several locked doors. She knelt and used her picks to open it up.

"Just a closet," she muttered and they continued to the next door. Once it was opened, they saw it was an office. "Should we go in?" she asked.

"Why not?"

They went in and closed the door behind them. The room wasn't big; there was a desk and chair on the far wall and what looked to be a small storage area. Jeremy gestured toward it, "I'll check the closet if you check the desk."

She nodded and headed to the chair. She turned it to face her and let out a strangled scream. A man was in the chair, dead, shot in the head.

Jeremy turned toward her in reaction to her scream. "Same thing over here." She hurried over and saw another person lying against the wall, looking like he was asleep except for the bullet hole in his head.

"Where are their clothes?" Emma asked. "It's odd they're undressed. Why do that?"

"I believe these two are the guards."

"The people guarding the building are the anti-electrical people," she deduced.

"It appears that way," he agreed in a low voice.

"Too many people have died already. We have to get to the main room and find the device."

They left the room, taking time to lock it behind them. As they continued down the hall, they heard a buzzing as they moved closer got louder. Jeremy nodded toward it, "That should be it. Do you think anyone is in the room?"

She thought about that, "They may feel safe enough not to worry about that. Though someone will need to come in to connect the circuit."

"Do you think they're aware that the person flipping the switch will probably be blown up with the room?"

"I don't know how committed these people are," she responded. "Would it be a suicide or another sacrifice to the cause?"

With that, they made their way to the door. Emma turned the knob; she pushed, expecting the door to open. When it didn't, she looked around.

"Should you pick the lock?" Jeremy asked.

"No, I think we need an element of surprise." *There had to be another way.*

The other buildings in the exhibit were built out in extreme detail. This being a utility building, it was more basic. There were utility panels in the ceiling. Emma pointed up and Jeremy got the message. He knelt, and she climbed on his shoulders. He stood carefully, and she was able to reach the panel. She pushed on it and dislodged it. "I got it."

"Can you climb up?"

"I can," she said. She put her hands up into the structure and found it was supported with iron and was structurally sound.

Once she was up in the space, he asked, "Can you see into the electrical room?"

"No," she called. She stuck her head out. "I need to move further in. It appears to have a similarly structured ceiling to that of the main Galerie des Machines."

"Okay, be careful," he cautioned.

"I will." She smiled and blew him a kiss.

Emma inched her way forward and searched for an opening into the electrical room. She found the opening and raised it by an inch and looked into the room. It appear to be empty, as she started to remove the panel so she could jump down. With her legs dangling in the opening, a young man eating an apple walked under her. She didn't hesitate and dropped down on him. Taking him by surprise, and he fell on his hands and knees. She twisted his arm behind him and when he yelped, she put her clutch knife to his neck to silence him.

She said, "No. You will stay silent. You be very quiet or you'll find out how sharp my knife is. Can you do that?"

He nodded, taking her threat seriously.

"Okay. I want you to remove that block from the door there."

He frowned, "Why should I?" She tightened her hold on his arm. "I'll do it."

"I'll let you go, but remember, I have a very sharp knife," she reminded him.

He walked to the door to do her bidding, but before he got there, he reached for something in his pocket. He turned suddenly and slashed at her with a knife. Emma reacted instantly, kicking it out of his hands. Next, she kicked him in the stomach to make him move back. She gathered up his knife watching him cough and stay bent over on the floor. "Well, that was stupid," she said as she walked to the door and quickly removed the block to let Jeremy into the room. As Jeremy entered, the boy looked surprised. He wasn't aware there was someone besides her.

Once they tied him up, Jeremy asked "Any problems?"

"Him?" she laughed.

Jeremy pulled the boy to his knees, "Okay, what do you know?"

"About what?" he asked belligerently.

"About the switch, you're supposed to flip," Jeremy said.

He responded without thinking. "How did you know about that?"

"We didn't know for sure," Emma said, "But you just confirmed it. Answer now, what's your part in this? Are you a member of the anti-electrical group?"

"Non, I was given some money and told to flip that switch," the boy said, indicating the panel behind him.

"When?" she asked.

"What time is it?" the boy asked.

Emma checked her timepiece, "It's 9:40."

"About twenty minutes," he answered "They said it needed to be dark."

"What's your name?" Emma asked the boy.

"Jacques."

"Look, Jacques. What do you think will happen when you flip that switch?"

"The lights will come on," Jacques said with a rather blank expression.

"Why would they have YOU do this? Where are the people who run this place?" She knew the answer but wanted to know what part he played.

"I don't know. I was just told to be here."

"Who let you into the building?"

"Monsieur Alaire and Monsieur Garnier."

"Are those the men outside?" Jeremy asked. *They probably killed the men they found.*

"Yes."

"How do you know them?" asked Emma, wondering how this kid got picked to die for their cause.

"My mama goes to the meetings."

"We have some news for you; you weren't meant to make it out of here tonight."

"What are you talking about? I was told to leave as soon as I flipped the switch."

While he was talking, Emma traced the line from the box through the room. "Found it," she called.

Jeremy walked over, dragging the boy with him. They looked at the rather unassuming device, which consisted of a package of dynamite. Connected to it was a rubber tube filled with gunpowder and some detonators. The circuit connection would like off the gunpowder and set off the dynamite. "What is it?" Jacques asked.

"A bomb," said Emma bluntly. "Had you flipped the switch, it would have set it off and the building would have gone with it."

"But what about me?" the boy asked, finally realizing what would have happened to him.

"You'd have been gone with the building."

He turned pasty white at that comment and held a hand to his mouth.

"Hey, don't throw up here," said Emma. "Take deep breaths." She looked at Jeremy. "We need to remove it."

He was studying it, "I think, as long as there's no power, we can remove it."

He started working on the connections and Emma took the device from him once the dynamite was removed. It was a fascinating device.

"I think I can hook everything back up to the main line," said Jeremy, examining the line. It was simply a matter of hooking the disconnected lines back up.

She looked at it consideringly. "Wouldn't it be shocking to them if the lights came on and there was no explosion?" she smiled "Yes, let's hook it back up."

She continued to examine the device. "Are we sure this is the only one?" Jeremy asked as he worked.

"I walked down the entire line here, and this is the only one."

"What if there are different bombs outside the building?"

"I don't think so. They wanted Dora and Tim primarily to access this building. I think anywhere else would have been too obvious."

"I can't believe they were going to leave me here to die. Did my mama know?" Tears were starting to make their way down Jacques' face.

"I don't know," she said quietly.

At that moment, the police rushed into the room. Emma showed them the device was disabled, "Were you able to check the cables?"

"We walked them all down; no extra devices were attached," Levan reassured her

She checked her timepiece," I think it's time to light up the exposition." She walked over to the panel, "Everyone ready?"

Everyone responded in the affirmative. Even with the assurances of safety, they held their breath as Emma flipped the switch. The lights in the room blinked, and then an officer ran in.

"The lights! They're on! Come see!"

They followed him out and saw that the lights had come on and highlighted the fountains and area around them. The area glowed lending a magical air to the night.

Emma pulled on Jeremy's sleeve. "We need to tell them about the guards."

"Yes."

They turned and faced the police, Emma and Jeremy were resolved to the grim task of showing the police the two bodies that had been found earlier. They had already taken the fake guards into custody.

They waited in the hallway as the police. At that moment the outside door opened and Levan walked in with Tim and Dora.

"We were able to locate them at one of their two apartments."

"Are you okay?" Emma asked as she ran over and took Dora's hands swiftly.

"Yes."

She noticed that, even though Dora had been released, she didn't look happy. Her face was red and her nose was running. "What's wrong?"

"Emma, they have Lottie," Dora said and burst into tears.

"What are you talking about?" Emma asked, confused.

Tim answered, wiping tears from his eyes. "They have Lottie and were forcing us to help them get access to this building."

"We used Papa's name and told the guards that we were interested in the exhibit. They let us come in whenever we liked," Dora admitted.

Jeremy and Emma stared at Tim and Dora. "How could they get Lottie?" Emma asked trying to make sense of the conversation, "She's home with Amy. You know she'd never let her out of her sight."

"I thought that, but Lenora gave me this," her sister said as she placed her hand in her pocket and pulled out the lace hairband she had been holding onto for days.

Emma frowned when she saw it, "Yes this is Lottie's—or *was*."

"*Was?*" Dora asked through her tears, feeling hopeful for the first time in days.

"Yes," she said taking it from her and tossing it in the air. The group watched it go up and then come back down to Emma's hand. "Funny thing about this, Lottie gave it to me when I kissed her goodnight. She said she wanted her Aunt Emma to take it to Paris with her."

"Then why did they have it?" Tim asked.

"I left it on the table in the foyer. I didn't realize until we were on the train."

Dora felt faint. "You think she's home and never part of this?"

"I do," Emma confirmed. "I can't imagine that they'd want to care for a baby all of this time. I also think we'd have heard about it."

Dora and Tim embraced, praying Emma was right and Lottie was safe.

Emma watched them, understanding their concerns. She loved that little girl so much. "I know she is home."

Tim felt relief wash over him and took Dora in his arms.

Emma gave them privacy and walked over to where Jeremy stood. "Want to go see the lights?" He nodded.

"Dora, Tim do you want to see the lights."

"There are some unhappy people out there," he said, looking at the crowd. *How many were the anti-electrical people?*

"Yes, do you think they will be apprehended?" she asked Levan.

"We have a good chance with this young man here," the inspector said, referencing Jacques. "He says he's willing to give us names of people who attended those meetings. We'll send word to you to come to the station once we have them in custody."

"I guess them sacrificing him for the cause didn't sit well with him."

They didn't leave the area until adequate security was in place. They started toward the tower, but this time they moved at a slower pace now that they were four instead of two. Jeremy was leading the group and accidentally bumped into someone.

Emma saw who it was, "Oh, no."

Jeremy was resigned, and put up his fists.

The big guy who had inadvertently helped them earlier saw who it was and raised his fists. A friend next to him said, "It's not worth it. Enjoy the lights."

"You're right," the man said. With one last glare, he turned back to them.

The tower was still extremely crowded, but this time Eiffel had left word the foursome was able to come up at any time. They were allowed to bypass the crowds. They ascended at a slower pace than before and stopped at the main deck and strolled to the outer boundary.

The four stood together and, for the first time in days, enjoyed the sites in front of them. "It's so magical," said Dora, watching the shining lights. "Imagine one day having this in our homes."

"Yes, we'll probably always have people fighting against changes like these."

"Why was Lenora so passionate about this? Why this topic and why now? And to make the process so involved with so many people?" asked Emma.

"It was her brother," Dora explained and told Emma and Jeremy all the details of the electric chair.

They went upward, hesitating at each level to see the different vantage points. At the final floor, the guards let them up without question. As they entered the room, introductions were made.

Mr. Edison walked over to Emma and Jeremy, "It appears you were able to remove the device."

"We were, sir," Emma said. They explained what they had found.

"Hmm, they were serious about this. It wasn't just a demonstration this time," Edison observed.

"Yes, a large number of people would have been killed to prove their point."

They watched the lights continue to sparkle below.

"What will happen next?"

Jeremy answered that. "The police are gathering up the demonstrators and will find out more about the movement."

"Let me know the outcome."

"We will," they promised.

They stayed and enjoyed the company. A knock was heard at the door. Eiffel got up to answer it.

"Emma and Jeremy, it's for you."

Emma jumped up and accompanied Jeremy to the door, "I hope this is what I think it is."

It was an officer and he said formally, "Mademoiselle, we have been sent to bring you, Jeremy, Tim, and Dora to the department." Dora and Tim were already up and ready to leave. They wanted to hear from Michael that Emma was right, that their baby was safe at home.

They followed the officer down the many flights of stairs. Reaching the bottom, he said, "We have a carriage, but we'll need to walk a few blocks to reach it. The crowds are making the roads impassable."

They walked briskly. Most people were still arriving to witness the light display. Everyone was quiet during the carriage ride to the station. They arrived and ran up the front steps. As they entered, they saw the police force was being kept busy by the people from the exposition.

Inspector Levan came out of the back, "We're back here." They met him and followed him down to the interview room. He stopped them, "Michael's in this room and he knows his plan has come to naught." He looked at Emma and Jeremy, "Would you like to interview him?"

"What are you charging him with?" she asked.

"We'll start with kidnapping." He nodded to Tim and Dora. "Then conspiracy and terrorism."

"And the two dead men at the station?" she inquired.

"Yes, that will also be included."

She took a deep breath "I'm ready." She held out her hand to Jeremy.

Before they could go, Dora stopped her, "Please ask about Lottie."

"We will," she promised, knowing what her sister was asking her to do. Lottie was on all of their minds.

Tim and Dora stepped back and sat on the nearby benches. The officer opened the door and entered; Emma and Jeremy followed close behind. She had known Michael but didn't expect to see him look so much older than on the steamship. The stress of this had changed him. *Was it the failure of the plan or Lenora's death?*

She sat down and looked at him.

He spoke first. "You never did like us, did you?"

"That's not true," she corrected. "I never got to know you. You and your wife avoided any interaction with us."

"Yeah, well, we couldn't take the chance you'd catch on," he muttered.

There were questions she wanted answered. "Why were Dora and Tim involved?" She didn't mention Lottie.

She didn't have to; he brought her up first. "They were perfect. We could get access to anywhere Ellis Evans could go. We just had to get close to Dora and Tim."

Emma had been thinking about this for a while, "Did you pay for our trip and send us the invitations?"

"We did," he conceded. "Having you along was a chance we had to take. Your investigative skills were a challenge, and we knew we had to stay away as much as possible."

"Did you take Lottie?" Emma asked bluntly.

He knew the child abduction charge could lead to his death.

"No, we just needed something from the house we could say was hers so that we could persuade Tim and Dora to help us. Lenora saw the hairband as soon as she entered your house."

"When was this?" Emma asked, trying to put the timeline together.

"The morning you headed to the train."

"You were in Chicago?" she asked, surprised.

"Yes, we needed to make sure you got on that train. We all needed to arrive at the same time."

She frowned. "Why was there a timing element here; what's driving that?"

He looked down, then suddenly back up and into Emma's eyes. "Lenora's brother."

"Yes, we heard about that. All of your posturing about the general public being harmed by electricity was a lie. You were just trying to keep Lenora's brother from being electrocuted."

"He was her only family," he said simply.

"She had you!" she protested.

"She didn't see it that way, and I'd do anything for her," he said quietly.

"Do you know who killed her?"

He put his head in his hands and mumbled, "Yes. We had a contingent at the Gallery, mapping things out. One of our more fanatic members saw you take Lenora into custody and took it upon herself to remove her."

"Who was this person?" Jeremy asked.

Taking his hands down slowly he said, "Analise Fontaine."

"Well, well," said the inspector from the wall. "That is Jacques' mother."

"Wow," said Jeremy.

Emma continued. "Why did you continue after Lenora died?"

"I wanted to make sure her dream was fulfilled and that her brother was not electrocuted."

"And the people involved in the taking of the station?"

"People I stirred up with my rhetoric. They wanted something to fight for, and I provided the cause."

Emma watched him, "If it had worked, do you think it would have stopped electricity from moving forward? Sir, nothing is going to stop this. Nothing."

"I know that now."

Jeremy asked suddenly, "Who killed the men in the station?"

His eyes dropped to his hands and he mumbled. "I told them to just capture them and tie them up so they wouldn't interfere."

"That sounds good, but the number of explosives would have killed anyone in that building and a fair radius around it. They'd have died anyway," Emma observed.

He had no answer for that and went quiet.

"You know you'll be in a Paris prison for the rest of your life?"

"Yes," he acknowledged.

With that, she sat back and said, "That's all the questions I have."

"You may leave. We have a few details to take care of. This matter is far from over." Inspector Levan stated.

"We'll be outside," Jeremy said.

They exited. Tim and Dora stared but didn't say anything.

"They don't have her," Emma said.

"You're sure?" they asked, not believing what they were hearing.

"Yes," she said firmly. "He knew exactly where the hairband was located. He also has nothing to gain by lying."

"Tim, I want to go home," Dora said into his chest.

"I do as well," he said, hugging her close.

"We can check on tickets back for you both, but I don't think there are any available." The exposition had strained resources and there wouldn't be any available on ships to return home early. "Why not stay?" Emma reasoned. "We're only here about a week longer and we can head home together." She didn't mention the other case was still in the works and needed to be resolved.

Tim said quietly, "Why not stay a little longer? We have parts of Paris we've yet to see."

"Yes, I'd like that. I wish telegraphs could make it across the ocean," Dora said. The transatlantic cables had been laid but were not available yet in France.

Their group moved into the hotel. The clerk at the desk called to Dora. "Mademoiselle, You have mail."

"Mail?" Dora asked, puzzled. They walked over to the desk to see what had arrived. It was a letter from Amy. Dora tore it open and out came a ribbon. *Lottie wanted to send this to you. She and Patrick are doing wonderful and can't wait to hear about Paris.*

"She's home," she said, crushing the letter to her. Tim asked to see it. He grinned ear-to-ear.

Emma understood she needed the reassurance that her baby was safe and back home. "Why don't we go upstairs? I'll order some tea and a tray of sweets to be brought up."

The three went on upstairs and Emma stayed to place the food order. Just as she walked to the elevator and pushed the button, the doors opened unexpectantly. A very stylish woman in a large, somewhat overdone hat walked out, pushing past her. *I must be invisible*, she thought.

Emma watched her and noticed she was trailed by a little boy who looked about nine. *Could it be...* She turned and found a bellboy to ask, "Who is that?"

His mouth twisted and he responded, "That is the owner of the hotel. Madam Lanier."

"And the boy?"

"Her son."

"Oh," she said, watching the other woman carefully. Her appearance was impeccable; the tailoring and detail on her clothes were flawless. She was also a striking woman. The similarities to Patrice were visible. *Did this woman go to extremes to not only get rid of Patrice's mom but also try to get her locked up in an asylum?*

Emma tapped her fingers on her lips, planning. She glanced at the elevator and then back at the bellboy. "Could you also see this note is delivered to my room?" She pulled out her notebook and wrote that she needed to go out for a little while and would be back. *"Don't worry,"* she penned.

She knew her family. They trusted her to take care of herself. Emma hurriedly gave the bellboy the note and a tip. She ran outside quickly when she saw the woman and boy walking out the front door.

Abella Lanier's carriage was waiting for her. She and the boy climbed in. Emma looked and saw a bike parked outside. She ran over quickly and picked the lock. *I'll return it before they need it.* The carriage headed out and Emma followed. They had gone a few blocks when Emma realized where they were. They were at Patrice's grandmother's hotel, exactly where Patrice was. *Oh no! Did we leave her with the wrong person?* She slowed the bike and parked it by the wall of the hotel. The woman and child walked into the hotel with Emma right behind them.

"Please tell my mother I'm in the lobby and would like to come up," Abella said in a demanding voice.

"Yes, Madam." The clerk pulled out a piece of paper. After he finished writing, instead of giving it to a bellboy to transport, he took out a container and slipped it inside. He opened a slot in the wall behind him and put the container in. With the door closed, he flipped a switch. A whooshing sound could be heard as it started its journey.

Pneumatic tubes, thought Emma. She had heard about them but had never seen them in practice. It reduced the number of personnel needed to transport messages. London was said to have twenty-one miles of tubing in place.

Within seconds, the whooshing sound could be heard again, this time with a plopping sound. The manager turned and opened the door. He took out the capsule and removed the paper. He read it silently, "You may go up," he told Abella. She and the boy headed to the elevator.

Emma walked slowly over and waited next to the elevator nonchalantly. The woman looked Emma over and then moved herself and her son some distance away. When the elevator arrived the three boarded. Emma got off on the floor she and Jeremy had used during their last visit and made her way to the kitchen door. She knocked and, when it opened, the same butler answered. He didn't look surprised at the intrusion.

"I saw the Madam's daughter come over to the hotel. I wanted to make sure Patrice is okay."

"Who, me?" asked Patrice. The butler stepped back and revealed Patrice. She appeared to be snacking on chocolate; and from the multiple empty dessert glasses in front of her, she was enjoying it.

The butler waved her in. Emma immediately went to Patrice," Are you okay?"

"Oh, yes, Grandmeir and I are getting along famously," she said with a grin.

"Do you know who's coming in the elevator?" Emma asked.

"Yes—Grandmeir said I'm to stay in here and not make a sound," she replied.

"Good," Emma said, mulling over what to do next.

"Mademoiselle, would you like to hear what is being said?" William asked.

She glanced over and said, "I most definitely would."

The butler moved to the vent; they had a boiler hooked up and the vent would carry steam as well as voices. "The sound can go both ways," he said as he put his fingers to his lips.

Emma and Patrice understood and were quiet as he opened it. Immediately, she could hear the conversation between the Madam and her daughter

"Abella, you've come to see me. Paul, how are you?" The elder Patrice's tone was less warm than Emma had heard in her conversations with her.

Emma leaned in to hear more.

"How is the hotel getting on? The rooms are full?" she asked, her tone brisk.

"Yes, Mama, I have it under control," Abella said, her voice bored.

"Hmm," the Madam murmured. "Shouldn't he be in school?"

"I pulled him out," Abella said defensively. "I need him."

"For what? I'd assume you have enough servants at your beck and call." Her mother's tone was derisive.

"Yes, but I missed him."

"Humph. That would have been the first time," the Madam muttered, her tone not changing.

"How dare you?" Abella said, her voice going shrill.

"Abella, you'd think I don't know you. That boy needs to be in school." There was silence for a few moments and then, "Have you heard from Charles?"

"No. Have you?" she asked.

"No," her mother responded. "Abella, it's time to get to the point."

"What point, Maman?" Abella asked, sounding board again.

"Charles' wife and daughter are in town to meet me."

"Are they? You'd think they'd stay at one of our hotels," Abella said dismissively.

"They were."

"Were?"

"Yes, I have reason to believe Catherine is missing."

"No loss there," her daughter responded.

"Abella, I'll not dignify that with a response!"

"Why should I care about them? Are we even sure he married her?"

Emma glanced over at Patrice; tears streamed down the girl's face. She turned to William and asked him in a low voice, "Can you take Patrice to another room while I listen?"

"I can. Mademoiselle Patrice, would you like to see our small dogs?" William tempted in a low voice.

She was torn she wanted to stay but wanted to escape more. "Yes, please. You'll let me know what happens, Emma?"

Emma nodded and continued to listen as she watched them exit to another part of the house.

The Madam's patience appeared to have waned, "Have you seen them at Charles' hotel?"

"You mean my hotel," her daughter said, the shrill tone returning.

"You know the hotel is only yours until Charles returns," her mother reminded the other woman.

"And if he doesn't?"

"If you have done something to my son…" the Madam started to warn her.

"My son," Abella mocked. "Yes, you're always so protective of him, the golden boy. The heir apparent."

"You know this is what his father wanted."

"Yes, HIS father. Why is it you always say it that way?"

"I don't know what you're talking about," said the Madam. She was sounding defensive now.

"You don't know! Why am I treated differently from Charles? Why is it that? I have a talent for management, yet I'm discarded and my hotel is given to my 'brother'."

"I don't want to talk about this," the Madam said stiffly.

"You will talk about this." There was a sound of breaking glass.

"Do not speak to her that way!" Emma jumped at the new voice.

That voice was the butler! What's going on here? Emma asked herself.

"Why should I listen to you?" Abella asked belligerently.

"You know why," William said with authority in his voice.

The room became quiet and the Madam finally broke the silence, saying in a faint voice, "You know."

Know what? thought Emma.

There was a second sound of glass breaking.

"Just stop this," William's voice sounded again. "You've known for a while."

"When did you find out that he's your father?" asked the Madam.

Wow! thought Emma.

"I was sixteen," Abella said nonchalantly.

"Who told you?"

"That was 'Papa,'" she said lightly.

"François told you? But why? Why would he do that?"

"He was writing out his will and said he refused to leave any part of the business to the butler's daughter. At first, I didn't understand," Abella's voice sounded bitter.

"What happened then?"

"He explained in quite a lot of detail about you and your "relationship" and that he had allowed you to stay after he found out."

"He forgave me," the Madam said, "and I was allowed to keep you. For years after you were born, he seemed to have a genuine affection for you."

"I know what made that change," her daughter said, her voice bitter.

"Charles was born," William said. "I could see it in him. The affection he usually displayed for Abella was now reserved for Charles."

"I didn't notice," the Madam commented faintly.

"No, you didn't, but it was also when I was sent away to school," she snapped.

"All proper young ladies go to boarding school," the Madam said defensively.

"I wasn't allowed to come home for vacations," Abella reminded her mother.

"Your father told me you didn't want to come home, that you were having a good time with friends," the Madam said weakly.

"And you believed him! You never asked me!"

"You never wrote me."

"I did. You never wrote back."

"But I never received them,"

"I intercepted them," William admitted.

"You did?" Abella asked her father.

"Yes. And I came to see you," he commented.

"Yes, you did," she said faintly. "It was the only thing that got me through those terrible days."

"I'm glad I was there."

The room went quiet.

Emma heard the kitchen door opening into the back staircase and glanced toward it. She saw Patrice. Emma reached up and closed the vent before she asked, "Where are you going?"

"Away from these people. They did something to Mum and Papa." With that, she left through the door and down the stairs.

Emma followed and grabbed her arm to stop her. "Patrice, wait. We need more information before we make accusations like that."

"You heard the same thing I did."

"Yes, but what I also heard were people having a hard time with their circumstances."

Patrice stopped struggling, "So, we should give them a chance?"

"Yes."

Patrice stood still a moment longer and said, "Okay, I'll give them a chance." They headed back upstairs.

"What now?" Patrice asked.

"We go in," Emma said determinedly.

Patrice squared her shoulders, "I'm ready."

They headed in and walked to the door that led to the main room. She moved her gaze toward Patrice, who nodded. Emma pushed the door open and they both entered. Paul's eyes opened wide and he moved to hide behind his mother's chair. Of the three, the surprise was most evident in Abella.

Abella sat up from her slumped position in her chair and

stared at Patrice. "That settles it. She could be my twin," she said, her voice resolved. Her eyes moved to Emma for the first time, "And you, weren't you in the elevator with me?"

"Yes, that was me," Emma answered.

"What do you have to do with this? This is a private family issue," Abella said in French.

The Madam said, "Use English."

"Why should I? For them? Bah! This is France. They should speak French!"

"If not for them, for me, please," her mother requested.

Abella's mouth tightened but nodded in agreement.

"Emma is here for me," Patrice said.

Emma took Patrice's hand and asked Abella the hard question. "Did you do something to Patrice's mum or papa?"

She watched Abella for any tells. The first thing she noticed was hesitation.

Patrice pulled on Emma's hand and leaned in to whisper, "The little ghost is here."

"Where?" she whispered back.

"There, behind her chair," the girl said, indicating the chair Abella sat in.

"Is someone behind your chair?" Emma asked.

Again, it appeared that Abella wasn't going to answer.

"Abella answer." The Madam said. When she continued to stay silent, the Madam said, "Paul! Come out from behind there."

A small figure came slowly from the back of the chair. "It's him," whispered Patrice furiously.

"You're sure?" Emma asked.

She nodded frantically. Emma didn't confront the child but chose at that point to say to the Madam, "He was in our suite."

The Madam studied her daughter, "Did you place Emma in the suite?"

"No," Abella said. "I didn't know who she was."

"But you knew when Patrice was with us," Emma said.

"How would she have known that?" William asked defensively, wanting to protect his daughter.

"I know because that little guy there," Emma motioned to Paul, "was entering Patrice's room through a secret passage."

The Madam took a long moment to observe them, and frowned, "Why was he there, Abella?"

Abella hugged her son close but didn't say anything.

"They were giving her drugs," Emma said, "one to make her feel out of control and another that put her to sleep. We believe they were cocaine and laudanum."

The Madam jumped up and glared at Abella accusingly. "Is this true?"

Abella wouldn't talk, but Paul spoke up, "I took the medicine to her through the door."

"Why?" asked the Madam. She didn't want to believe her daughter could be behind this.

"Maman said we had to. She said that girl could take our home from us," the boy explained.

Patrice had heard enough and asked Abella directly, "Did you take my mum?"

The answer was immediate, with no hesitation. "No, I did not."

"Do you know where she is?" Patrice asked, wanting answers from these people.

"I was informed when you and your mother arrived," Abella started.

"By whom?" asked Emma, taking over the questioning.

"The night manager."

The one they have not been able to locate. "So, there was a record of Catherine and Patrice at the hotel?" asked Emma.

"Yes, the managers keep two books in case an important guest needed privacy. That way, the log can't be accessed easily."

"I'll ask Patrice's question again: do you know where her mum is and who might have taken her?"

"I think so," muttered Abella. The desperation was clear in her voice when she said, "I didn't take her."

"But you took advantage of the circumstances and did nothing to help," Emma said.

"I did," she admitted. "I was desperate."

"Tell us everything!" shouted Patrice.

Emma thought about what she had been told "It's the night manager, isn't it? He's behind the abduction?"

Abella was surprised at the observation and agreed, "That's my suspicion."

"Who's the night manager?" asked the Madam. She hadn't been involved in the daily operation of that hotel for a while.

"It's Alfred Remy," Abella said, lowering her head.

The Madam's face went white and she said faintly. "I know that name." She explained to Emma and Patrice, "He was around, always following Abella like a lost puppy."

"He wanted more than I could give, and then I met Paul's father," she explained to Patrice and Emma.

"Were you still friends?" Emma asked.

"Yes, and he's an excellent manager," she said.

"Well, he's gone," stated Emma.

"Gone?" Her face turned white with the news. "I didn't realize."

"Yes, and he was the only person who could confirm that Patrice's mother was actually at the hotel. He disappeared the same night she did."

"Where do you think he has her?" asked William.

"Them," Abella murmured.

"Them?" Emma asked. "A second person was taken?"

"I believe so. I received word a few days ago that Charles never arrived at the hotel in Germany," Abella admitted.

"Charles is missing?" asked the Madam, going white.

William grabbed her hand in his and patted it.

"Where are they? Where are my mum and papa?" asked Patrice.

"I'm not sure, but Alfred has an apartment in the city," said Abella.

"Don't his parents live just outside the city?" asked the Madam.

"Yes. We should also check there," Abella said.

Emma was thinking ahead. "It's time to call in the police. Can we get access to that private sign-in book?" she asked Abella.

"Yes, it's in the safe of the manager's office."

"Can we go there now? I'd also like to notify the police to meet us there," commented Emma.

William stood and said, "I can have them meet you at the hotel."

They confirmed their plans and stood. Abella went over to Patrice and took her hands in hers. "I took advantage of something I shouldn't have. I hope you will forgive my part in this."

Patrice slowly pulled her hands away, "Once we find my parents, we can talk again."

Abella stepped back and gave her some space. "I understand." She stepped away to take her son's hand. They moved to the elevator and Abella, "Maman, you should stay here."

"No, this involves my family. I want to be there."

Abella understood and didn't try to stop her mother. They stood together and waited for the elevator. The doors opened, they went in and rode to the lobby. Once there, they separated; William went to the police and the rest got in a carriage headed to the other hotel. Once they arrived, they made their way to the desk. The crowd recognized the Madam and whispers followed them.

It was only a matter of moments before the manager on duty came up swiftly to them. "Madam, welcome. We were not expecting you this evening."

"Yes, we're here about something important," she said.

Abella spoke up, "We need to talk to you in the office."

He saw Patrice and his eyes widened. It was time for him to face how he had treated this girl.

They headed that way and Emma heard Jeremy call her. She turned toward him and saw him exiting the stairway. She waved him over.

"What is going on?" he asked

"We have some movement on The Vanishing Lady case."

He didn't respond but followed the group into the office.

Abella stopped at the door and turned. She noticed Jeremy, "Can I help you?"

"He's with me," Emma said, her tone firm.

Abella nodded and allowed them into the room. The manager stopped midway, "What is this about?"

Abella answered, "I need to review the registration book from two nights ago."

"The book. I'll need to go back out to the lobby," he said and started that way.

Abella stopped him, "I need the one we keep for special visitors."

He halted suddenly and looked around. His glance landed on Emma and Jeremy. "With them here?"

"Yes. Please retrieve it," Abella said firmly.

He nodded slowly and went over to the picture hanging behind his desk. He took it down and a safe was revealed. He twirled the dial and turned the lever to reveal the inside. The logbook was on top. It was black and red and large. He slid it out and started to hand it to Abella.

"Hand it to me," the Madam said. It wasn't a request.

He didn't hesitate. She had spent her life working in the hotel business, from the smallest beginnings of four rooms to their empire now. She had worked every job and could read the book. She quickly flipped to the page she needed and found Patrice's mom's signature. "That firms it up."

"What are you talking about?" asked the manager.

"This." She showed him.

He felt faint when he saw the name. He focused his gaze on Patrice. "Miss, I'm so sorry I didn't believe you."

Patrice nodded but didn't say anything. The apologies would have to wait until her parents were found.

"Where is Alfred, the night manager?" asked Abella.

"He's out on vacation," the manager responded, wondering why that question was being asked.

"Was it planned?" Emma asked.

"No, we had canceled all vacations because of the exposition."

"Why was it allowed?" asked the Madam.

"Alfred came to me and said that it was personal. I approved it."

A knock sounded on the door. The manager went over to open it and found the police standing there; Inspector Levan was with them. "What is happening here? We understand there's been a kidnapping?"

"Yes, it's my mum and possibly my papa," said Patrice.

The officer with him frowned, "Now, miss, I talked to you a few days ago and the management here assured me you were not accompanied and you did not have a room at this hotel."

He moved his gaze to the manager, who said, "I was wrong when I reported that. You need to listen to them."

Emma filled them in on what had occurred. She left the drugs and the small boy's role out. The family would need to work that out.

"I can send men out to Alfred's apartment and his parents' house. It will take a few hours to check both," Levan said.

As they were separating to investigate, Paul boy walked over to Emma and Jeremy, "There is another hiding place."

"There is?" she asked, bending down to hear him. "Where might that be?"

"The basement is full of rooms," he explained.

Jeremy and Emma said to the group, "Wait, we should check the basement first. Abella, how do we access the basement?"

"This way," she said. They followed a long hallway that led to the staff's quarters. She took out her key and inserted it into a door lock. "We'll need to take the stairs." They followed her down and found another locked door. This time, her keys wouldn't work. "The locks have been changed," Abella muttered. "We'll have to get someone down here to open it."

"No, I can take care of it," Emma said as she knelt and pulled out her tools. She chose two to turn the tumblers and unlock the door.

"You will have to tell me more about yourself when this is over," Abella said in admiration.

Inspector Levan spoke up, "Please, step back." They did so while he rushed in to investigate. He came back out, "This place is a maze. Does anyone know how to navigate it?"

"I do," Paul said.

"Can he help?" asked Abella.

"Yes, he can." He looked down at Paul and said, "I'm going to carry you and, if there's any danger, we'll move you quickly."

Paul nodded and the inspector lifted him onto his shoulder. The boy directed them through the maze of long hallways. "There's a far room at the other end that has running water," he said.

Levan placed Paul to the side and rushed to the far room. It had a lock; this time they didn't need a key. An officer rammed it, shattering the door and entering the room.

Their group followed closely behind. Patrice didn't hesitate, she pushed past the officers and entered the room. The two people that meant the world to her were there and chained to a bed. "Mum, Papa!" She rushed to embrace them. The officers moved quickly to cut their chains off. When they were free, they both put their arms around her and held her tight. "I told them you were with me. Nobody believed me!" she said.

"Where's Alfred?" asked Abella.

"He comes in the evenings, but I think he stays elsewhere," Charles stated.

"We have men at his apartment," Levan said, "If he's there, he'll be found. Let's get you both upstairs." They nodded gratefully, ready to get out of there.

"Maman, Abella, did you help with finding us?" Charles asked.

"That is something we need to discuss privately," said the Madam.

Before they climbed up the stairs, the Madam turned to Charles, "I'd like to formally meet my daughter-in-law, please."

"Of course, Maman," he said and took his wife's hand in his. "Maman, this is Catherine."

"I have waited for so long to meet you. We need to talk soon, but I think we all need some rest tonight," the Madam said warmly.

"Thank you," said Catherine.

They started to walk away, and Charles stopped Emma and Jeremy. "I can only thank you. I'd like to speak to you later."

"We're glad you and your wife are well. We also have some questions, when you're ready," said Emma.

Patrice said something low to her mum and ran over to Emma and Jeremy. She hugged them both quickly and then returned to her parents.

"Tired?" Jeremy asked Emma.

"Not at all." She smiled. "I'm so glad William got the officers here so quickly."

Jeremy shook his head, "He didn't. I called them when I got your note. I figured the final confrontation was happening."

She drummed her fingers on her lips. "If William didn't get the police officers, then where did he go? I'll have to think about that."

He pulled her to him, "Would you like to walk with me while you think?"

"That would be nice," she said. They walked around and enjoyed the night air, then slowly made their way to their room.

CHAPTER 19

hey returned to their room to retire for the evening. A knock sounded at the door. Emma frowned, drew her knife, and accompanied Jeremy to it. "Yes?" she called. Too much had already happened that evening.

"I have a note for you," a voice called.

"Slide it under the door," Jeremy requested.

"Under the door?" the voice questioned.

"Yes, just slide it under," he said again.

There was a moment of hesitation and then the note appeared. Jeremy reached for it and opened it.

Emma reached into her pocket and pulled out a few francs and pushed them under the door.

"Merci!" he called. They could hear him walking away from the door.

"Who is it from?" Emma asked.

"It's from Abella. She wants us to come upstairs."

"This late? I thought we were going to meet in the morning. Hopefully, after they catch the night manager."

"Yes," he said as he continued to study it.

"Can I see it?"

He handed it to her.

She stared at it for a long moment.

"What do you see?" he asked, wondering what he had missed.

"It's in English," she said.

"Oh, I get it. She prefers French," he said, Emma had told him of the conversations with Abella.

"Yes," she said, thinking back to her response to the Madam's request for her to speak English to them. Jeremy asked, "What do you think it means?"

"We haven't heard that they found the night manager yet," she murmured.

"We haven't," he agreed.

"So, I think he's up there with her."

"Why would he want us up there with him? He wants her to himself."

"I don't know, but I think we need to go up there. Tim?" she called, "Could you come out here?"

He did so and closed the door softly behind him.

"How's Dora?" asked Emma.

"I think she truly believes that Lottie is safe and at home, but she just wants to see and hold her." He moved to the side chair and slumped down.

"I know. Should I go into her?" asked Emma, setting aside the note for a moment.

"No." He sighed and put his head back. "She's finally resting."

Jeremy nodded at the note. "Good. Tim, could you go downstairs and tell Inspector Levan we need some of his men sent up to the owner's apartment on the top floor?"

He was surprised, "Is something wrong?" He glanced at their room in a worried manner.

"We're not sure, but better to be safe and have the officers on the way."

"All right, I'll be quick. What do you think is happening?" Tim asked as he gathered his coat.

"We think it's the night manager who took Patrice's parents. He may have Abella," said Emma.

"But I thought they went after him in the countryside." They had told Tim the facts when they got back to their room.

"They did, but we now believe he's upstairs." Emma handed her brother-in-law the note and he headed downstairs. He walked quickly; he didn't want to be away from Dora for long. She glanced toward Jeremy, "I'll go in the elevator."

"I'll go through the passageway," he confirmed.

"I'll meet you up there."

Before he left, he grabbed her and gave her a long kiss. He stepped back, "Be careful."

"I will," she said and patted her leg where her knife was strapped. "You too."

He nodded and headed to the secret passageway.

She went out the door and made sure it was locked securely behind her. She made her way to the elevator, deliberately taking her time. That would give Tim and Jeremy time to get their individual tasks completed.

She called for the elevator and waited. It opened and she stepped in. "Top floor, please." The attendant nodded, having been told she was coming up.

As the door closed, she saw Tim exit the stairs. He gave her a quick okay symbol to let her know he had completed his task. She smiled and nodded and the doors closed. The elevator made its way slowly up to the top floor. The doors opened and William was not there to greet her as expected. The elevator operator broke into her thoughts, "Miss, you're to go in alone and I was told to take the elevator back down."

She nodded, slipped her hand into her pocket, and fingered the handle of her knife. As she made her way across the wide-open room, she called out, "Hello. Abella, I'm here."

She heard something and turned to her left. The sound she heard was a gun being cocked. A man stood there, pointing it at her. "Monsieur Alfred Remy I assume?" she asked, though she already knew the answer. When he didn't respond, she asked, "Where's Abella?"

"Oh, not to worry, she's fine," he said.

"If that's true, why am I here?"

"I asked her to get you to come up," he explained.

"Where's Abella?" she asked again, trying to delay him until Jeremy could get into the space through the secret door. She had expected him before now.

"She and my son," he said proudly, "are in the other room."

Your son, she thought. *Is that real or fantasy?* "Can I see them?" she asked.

"What for? You won't be around long," he said threateningly.

"Won't I?" she murmured and watched him fall to the ground. Jeremy stood behind him holding a mallet from the kitchen.

"About time you showed up. Grab that," she said, indicating the curtain tie.

He got the tie and they bundled the man and dragged him to a closet just off the kitchen. "Any idea what his plan was?" he asked as they closed the door.

"Maybe," she said and glanced around, drumming her fingers on her lips. "I wonder," she said and motioned to him to move into the kitchen. She moved to the vent and opened it. She wanted to know what was being said in other areas of the house.

"Do you think he took care of it?" They heard a man's voice ask.

Jeremy turned to Emma and he mouthed, "Who is that?"

"I guess your dalliance has finally led to something good," the man's voice said again.

"It's William!" Emma whispered. They both continued to listen intently.

"Papa, I didn't know you were involved with Alfred, and I didn't know about Charles and Catherine being taken."

"I did it for you, Chéri. Always for you. Otherwise, the hotels will go to Charles and there would be nothing for you."

"Papa, we need to stop." Abella pleaded. "This is my family."

"I'm your family," he said shortly. "This is all for us."

"But this has to stop. They've been found now. Why not just let them be?"

"Why?" he yelled. "Because all of these hotels should be yours but for that Emma person. We need to get rid of her or we'll lose everything."

"We?" Abella wondered if William meant only himself. Her feelings were never taken into consideration.

"I'll go check on that bungler," he said.

Emma and Jeremy stayed in the kitchen, not making a sound.

A door opened and closed. "Where is he?" William asked.

"Papa, I don't know…"

"We have to find all of them!" he thundered. "Or my plans will be for naught."

Again 'my', not our, thought Abella.

Jeremy cleared his voice and said in a low voice, "Let's get out of here."

"Wait," murmured Emma, listening intently.

"But, Papa, I think we need to stop. This is wrong." Abella pleaded.

"Girl, you will do as I say!" William said, turning his ire on her.

"No, Papa, I don't think I will this time. I'm going to notify the police. This has gone far enough."

"You're in this as deep as I am. You'll be turning yourself in."

"No, Papa, I'm not. You pulled my son into this without my knowledge."

"Yes, but you covered for me and told them it was you," he reminded her.

"I wanted to protect you," she said, miserable, knowing no one would do that for her.

"They will never believe you; they won't support you. You will go to prison and be separated from your son," he said nastily.

"They will believe me if I give them the evidence about you killing the Madam's husband," she said. Her voice had steadied.

"You wouldn't!" William shouted. Shattering glass sounded.

"I would. It's time this game was over," Abella said. The elevator sounded at that moment.

"It's the police," Emma mouthed. "Now, we go in."

The duo burst out of the kitchen as the police flooded into the room from the elevator.

Paul ran in from his room and toward his mama. She pulled him close, away from William.

Emma saw William go for the gun on the table in front of him. She quickly lunged for it and turned it on him. He put his hands in the air and waited. The police quickly took him into custody. The inspector accepted the gun from Emma.

"Can someone else tell me what is happening here?" the inspector asked, glaring at William.

He stared mutinously back without saying a word.

Jeremy and Emma started to step up to explain but were surprised when Abella cut them off. "I think I can provide what you need."

The inspector cocked his brow at her, "Would you come to the station?"

Her hands shook as she realized she could be separated from Paul. "Can we do it here?"

The inspector saw Paul clinging to her, "I think we can work that out."

Emma and Jeremy were listening. The inspector turned his gaze to them, "I'll need you two to stay also. I assume you have more information to share with me?"

"You might want to check the closet," Emma suggested.

The inspector sent her a crooked smile and turned to his officers, "Go check that room."

They went and called back, "There is a man here."

"Alive?"

"Yes."

"Bring him out," muttered the inspector. "Should I check any other rooms?" he asked with a look at Emma.

Jeremy responded in the same tone, "No, that should just about do it."

"Is that Alfred?" the inspector asked incredulously. He had men in the country and the city searching for this man. He wiped a hand down his face and then stared at Emma and Jeremy.

"It is," Emma said.

"I'll need to know what happened here. Don't leave until I speak with you."

They nodded and watched as he moved into another room with Abella to begin questioning her.

The officers woke Alfred and when he came to, he was complaining about his head. They started to remove him, and he blurted out, "No, I belong here. This is my family."

"You can explain downtown," the officer said.

Alfred struggled, but their hold would not be broken.

Once they took him out, Emma smiled over at Jeremy, "There's always the vent in the kitchen." she suggested

He shook his head regretfully, "No, we'll wait here."

She humphed sat in a large chair and watched the door where the inspector and Abella were talking. It was a long time before the door opened. When it did, Abella and the inspector exited, and she appeared to have been crying.

The elevator signaled someone was coming up. They all watched as the doors opened; to everyone's shock, it was the Madam and Charles.

"What is happening here?" demanded the Madam.

The inspector answered, "Your daughter just explained her and her father's role in the kidnapping and drugging of Patrice, her mother, and her father."

"We can offer information to support that her father was forcing her to help him and that she wasn't aware of Paul's involvement until after the fact," said Emma firmly. "We can give you a statement."

Abella started crying again, not expecting any support.

"This is all my fault," the Madam said, "Her father never understood I wanted to be with my husband and not him."

Charles took Abella's hand in his, "Abella wasn't involved. We don't want her charged in this." Abella sank into his arms. Paul ran over to his grandmother.

Her eyes wide and hopeful she asked, "Charles, really?" They had been close until she found out about her real father.

The Madam's voice sounded imperious. "Abella, come here."

Abella would have liked to stay with Charles, but she stepped back and walked over to her mother. "Child, you should have come to me when this started."

"I should have, Maman," she acknowledged. "William said he loved me and wanted us to be his family."

The Madam appearance had changed, her head was no longer held at a regal level. She swayed on her feet, "Mama!" called Charles and Abella. They went over to her and guided her to a chair. The Madam said, "He told me the same. François was away so much when we were first married, and William was so sympathetic to a young bride."

Charles wasn't surprised; he had known about Abella's parentage long ago.

Inspector Levan spoke up, "We'll need to take everyone's statements." The Madam started to object and he said, "We can handle this privately here."

She let out a deep breath, "Thank you."

"Maman, you need to know, William killed Papa," Abella said quietly. "I didn't know."

The Madam and Charles were very quiet. The Madam finally said, "I suspected he might be involved."

Charles reacted first, "Maman!"

She reached over and patted his hand. "I had no proof but felt that William started behaving differently after your father died. He has been taking privileges he was not allowed."

Emma and Jeremy didn't want those details. The night went on with everyone giving statements.

Abella and her son were allowed to go to their bedrooms to rest. Charles and the Madam sat quietly as the police departed.

"Thank you for helping us," The Madam said, "I apologize I couldn't tell you more information on what might be happening."

"Did you know William was involved in Patrice's mother's kidnapping?" Emma asked.

"No," the Madam said honestly.

Jeremy asked Charles, "Did you know your wife and daughter might be in danger?"

"Things were happening quickly. My father had just passed away, and I was called home to take over the business. I notified Catherine to meet me here with Patrice. It was the day they were due to arrive that I was told our German hotel was having problems and I'd need to go there before my family arrived. I was suspicious of the trip and the arrival of my family."

"Who notified you the hotel was having problems?" Jeremy asked.

"I received a telegram."

"Did anyone special deliver it?" Emma asked.

"Alfred," he admitted. "I got organized and made a plan that could be in place in case something happened."

"How were we involved in your plan?" Emma asked.

"You were my backup. I recognized your name on the reservation list and moved you to the suite."

"So, it was a coincidence?" murmured Emma.

"Yes, but I told Etienne that I trusted that, if anything happened, he was to get Patrice and Catherine to you."

"I'm glad we were here to help," she said sincerely.

"We are also," he commented.

Emma thought of Etienne and said, "You might try to notify him that he can come back, the poor boy is in hiding."

"I will take care of it. He will be rewarded for helping us," said Charles.

"What about Abella? What will happen?" Emma asked.

"We have to take responsibility for much of these events occurring," Charles said, looking regretful. "Once I was born, Papa essentially cut her off from his affection."

"Yes," said the Madam. "Before that, they were always together and so similar. It just broke my heart."

"When he sent her away, I never contacted or visited her. We'll have to do better," Charles said.

"How will you do that?" Jeremy asked.

"I think we'll move in with Maman and let her get to know Catherine and Patrice."

"And Abella?" asked Emma.

"She and Paul can stay at the new hotel." He laughed suddenly and said, "She's doing a good job there."

CHAPTER 20

Finally, making their way back to their room, Jeremy studied Emma and said, "You know, this is two vacations we've had weird things have happened. I say next vacation, we don't leave our room."

She smiled, and stepped into his arms, "What? Murder, kidnapping, and mayhem were too much for you?"

As he lowered his head to kiss her, he said, "Well, maybe not."

She smiled and let herself be pulled to him again. They stepped apart and continued to hold hands as they opened their door. For the first time in a week, it was quiet in their suite. It was such a relief to them both. He took the opportunity and pulled her on top of him and onto the couch.

"This is nice," she said as she lowered her head to kiss him. Just then, there was a knock on the door. "Hmm, it was nice while it lasted," she said and rolled off of him. She patted her hair while Jeremy went to the door.

Several men entered carrying trays. "The Madam thought you'd like this," one of the men said. The duo's eyes went wide at the assortment of meats, cheeses, breads, and pastries.

"Set it here." Jeremy directed them to the living room. As they were setting up, Emma went and knocked lightly on Dora and Tim's door. "Would you like to join us?" she asked when Tim answered, waving her arm behind her.

He marveled at all the food laid out, "Yes. Let me check with Dora."

A more subdued Dora came out. Emma went over to her sister and put her arms around her. "She's okay. I know she is," she mumbled into Dora's neck.

Her sister hugged her tighter.

"Will you come eat?" Emma asked.

"Yes," Dora said and held Emma's hand as they made their way to the couch.

The food was eaten, and the wine was drunk. The four sat back on the two couches. "That was good," said Tim, rubbing his belly.

"We have not had a bad meal here," Jeremy said.

"No, but we have had a lot of intrigue," said Emma. "I think we'll all be ready to head home at the end of the week."

"Yes," Jeremy, Tim, and Dora said at once.

"Will we hear what's behind all of this?" asked Tim.

"We can tell you what we know," Emma said. She and Jeremy went into detail about The Vanishing Lady case.

CHAPTER 21

The foursome decided to be tourists the next day and was joined by Papa and Abbey. They made their way to the Latin Quarter to see the church located there and wandered around the area, shopping and sampling the food.

That afternoon, they were resting from their busy morning when the inspector sent them a note asking them to meet at the Madam's that evening. They wondered if new information would be disclosed.

They made their way to the Madam's apartments at the other hotel. Tim and Dora chose to stay at their hotel and have a late dinner in the room. They dressed for the evening. Emma in the dress given to her by Abbey and Jeremy in a black jacket and tie.

They were taken up directly on the elevator and escorted into the Madam's apartment. They were greeted by a cheerful Paul. The child's mood seemed reflective of the overall group feeling.

"It looks like they're more settled," murmured Jeremy.

"And happy," said Emma. She watched Abella enter the room with Catherine; they were laughing. Abella's bitterness seemed to have faded away.

Following them were Charles and the Madam. "We're happy

you accepted our invitation. You have done so much for our family," greeted Charles.

They didn't discuss the case until after dinner. Emma asked, "What happens now?"

"William and Alfred are going to prison," stated Charles.

Emma was curious and asked, "Are you doing well with all of this?"

Abella said, "I'm doing better. Maman thinks it may be better to get some separation between us and William. We'll do that and see what the future holds."

Their evening ended and they promised to keep in touch.

CHAPTER 22

Their days in Paris continued with Dora appearing to become more brittle as they passed. The four were in the lobby talking about their plans for the day. Emma said, "One last stop at the exposition, and we will finally see the cultural areas…" She tapered off, noticing a lady with a scarf wrapped around her face. *Is that the rude lady they had traveled with from New York and then again in the hotel The scarf is very familiar. But was it her? She seems taller than before.*

Two men followed her, carrying the truck that had arrived empty. *It's certainly full of something now,* she thought and watched the men struggle with it. She decided it was time to find out what was in that trunk. She moved close and stuck her foot out, tripping one of the men. He went down with a twisting motion and the trunk went with him. It crashed to the ground, breaking the clasp, with personal contents spilling out. The lady with the scarf began yelling at the men, "Pick it up!"

Before the woman could stop Emma, she pulled the top of the trunk open. There was a woman's body. *It was the wife. Then that must be…* She strode over and pulled the scarf off of 'her' and saw the husband.

"Why can't you mind your own business?" he said and took a swing at Emma. She ducked and didn't see Dora jump on his back.

"Leave my sister alone!" Dora yelled, pounding on him with her fist.

An officer in the area went to remove her. Dora responded instinctively and hit him in the eye with her fist. That act seemed to set off a large fight within the lobby. Jeremy got involved and tried to pull Emma away from the man dressed as a woman.

An army of policemen arrived and wouldn't listen to anyone; they moved everyone out to wagons and then to the station.

"So, is that the whole story?" asked Cole. Amazed at all he had missed. "There was The Case of the Vanishing Lady and The Woman Who Knew Too Much?"

Emma laughed, "A-ha! Finally! We could never decide on a name for Dora's case."

The group laughed in response.

"The lady in the trunk? How did you know she was in there?" Cole asked.

"I didn't," Emma admitted. "I suspected it might be the much-beleaguered husband. When I saw her in the lobby, I thought the height and weight were troubling."

"Yes, he admitted that he thought his wife planned to kill him, so he went after her first."

"Is that likely? The outfit seems planned. He couldn't have fit into her clothes."

"That's what the officers are asking," Cole said humorously.

"Will I need to stay to testify?" Emma asked, knowing her family wanted to head home on time.

He laughed. "No, there were plenty of Parisians who witnessed the body in the trunk." He looked at the much-maligned group and asked, "Anyone want to go to the exposition with me?"

They laughed and said, "Yes."

As they were leaving the police station Cole stopped.

"Oh, Emma. I was asked to deliver this to you." He handed her a letter.

"Who's it from?" Emma opened the letter and read it.

"Dora! It's from Savannah!"

"What does she say?" Dora asked, walking over to her.

"She says Patrick and Lottie are doing fine. And… Ethan proposed to her!"

"How wonderful!" Dora exclaimed.

"Savannah asks if they can have the wedding at the house and if we'll help her with the details."

"Of course, we will. She didn't need to ask. When are they planning the wedding for?"

"They want to have it at Christmas in honor of when they met."

"Oh, how lovely and December wedding, I love the idea of a Christmas wedding…"

Emma and Dora's voices faded out as they walked down the street planning their friend's wedding.

CHAPTER 23

The week ended in Paris, and the foursome boarded the steamboat for their trip home. Cole took them to the train and stood with Emma while the others boarded. "Emma, could you give this to Amy?"

"What is it," she asked curiously.

He mumbled, "Some lace handkerchiefs and some pictures from the exposition. I thought she might like them."

Emma didn't react, she took the package and said casually, "That is nice. I will make sure she gets them."

"Thank you," he said. The train whistle sounded and Emma ran to jump on. She turned and waved to Cole. He would stay in Paris with his close friends Ellis and Abbey. They'd spend another month there together.

She joined the group in the carriage. "What is that?" asked Jeremy.

"A little something for Amy from Cole," said Emma with no inflection in her voice.

"That's nice," said Jeremy as he opened his book to start reading.

Dora raised her eyebrows and Emma shrugged. Tim caught that exchange and wondered what he had missed.

The trip to New York was relaxing, though Dora walked more than she slept. They disembarked and moved to the day train and then the week-long train trip. When their final stop approached, Dora had her handbag and was waiting impatiently to disembark.

They hailed a cab quickly and went to the boarding house. Dora didn't wait for it to stop and bounded down before Tim could stop her. He was close behind as she ran up the stoop. They entered and Dora started running from room to room shouting, "Lottie! Patrick!"

Tim stopped her, "Check the kitchen. I'll run up to the bedroom. Maybe she's taking a nap."

She ran to the kitchen and back to the foyer. Tim walked down the stairs and she asked, her voice strained, "Was she in there?"

He slowly shook his head. She responded by collapsing on the stairs where she stood. "My baby." Tim went to her and pulled her into his arms.

Jeremy and Emma had come in and watched, helpless how to help. She had felt sure Lottie was there.

Bang! Bang! The sound was someone pulling something up the stoop. All four went still as they watched the door open. Amy entered, talking animatedly.

Dora and Tim saw who she carried with her and ran down the remaining stairs. Dora took Lottie in her arms. Tim enveloped them and they stood together.

Amy was confused. "You're back?"

"Why don't we leave them alone?" Emma said and took Amy and Jeremy to the kitchen.

"Why don't you tell her what happened," suggested Jeremy.

Emma explained to Amy what had occurred in Paris.

"Dora should know I'd never let Lottie out of my sight," Amy said, shocked.

"We know," Emma said, "but we had no way to communicate with you." She thought of the package and reached into her bag. "Amy, Cole sent this from Paris for you."

Amy's cheeks went red and she said, "I will open it later."

Everyone came into the kitchen talking at once. Emma's gaze took in her home and her family. She commented softly, "It's so good to be home."

Jeremy reached over and took her hand in his, "Yes, it is."

<h1 style="text-align:center">HISTORICAL NOTES</h1>

Historical Note: The Case of the Woman Who Knew Too Much

Lenora's brother was based loosely on William Kemmler. On August 6, 1890, he became the first person to be sent to the electric chair. After he was strapped in, a charge of approximately 700 volts was delivered for only 17 seconds before the current failed. Witnesses reported smelling burnt clothing and charred flesh, but Kemmler was far from dead, and a second shock was prepared. The second charge was 1,030 volts and was applied for about two minutes. Smoke was observed coming from the head of the deceased Kemmler. An autopsy showed that the electrode attached to his back had burned through to the spine.

Dr. Alfred Southwick, the inventor of the electric chair, applauded Kemmler's execution with the declaration, "We live in a higher civilization from this day on." While American inventor George Westinghouse, an innovator of the use of electricity, remarked, "They'd have done better with an ax."

Historical Note: The Case of the Vanishing Lady

Mostly considered a French urban legend set during the time of the 1889 Paris Exposition. A girl and her mother were traveling together in France. The girl left the room to get medication for her sick mother. When she returned, her mother was gone and the staff said she had never checked in.

Another version of the story was that the mother had died of the plague and the hotel covered it up by calling the girl crazy.

There are different stories -did it happen? Maybe or Maybe not. It made for an interesting story.

Notebook Mysteries

Books
1 - 2 - 3

KIMBERLY
MULLINS